THE BOOK

OF

STRANGE

NEW THINGS

A NOVEL

MICHEL FABER

HOGARTH

LONDON / NEW YORK

Copyright © 2014 by Michel Faber

DEC 1 5 2014

All rights reserved.
Published in the United States by Hogarth, an imprint of the Crown Publishing Group,
a division of Random House LLC, a Penguin Random House Company, New York.
www.crownpublishing.com

HOGARTH is a trademark of the Random House Group Limited,
and the H colophon is a trademark of Random House LLC.

Simultaneously published in Great Britain in 2014 by Canongate Books, Ltd.

Lyrics from "Yah-Ta-Ta, Yah-Ta-Ta" by Jimmy Burke and Jimmy Van Heusen,
© Warner/Chappell Music, Inc., Bourne Co., Spirit Two Music o/b/o My Dad's Songs,
Spirit Two Music o/b/o Reganesque Music, Spirit Two Music o/b/o Limerick Music.
Lyrics from "Walkin' After Midnight" by Alan Block and Don Hecht,
© 1957 Sony/ATV Music Publishing LLC.

Library of Congress Cataloging-in-Publication Data
Faber, Michel.
The book of strange new things : a novel / Michel Faber.
pages cm
1. Man-woman relationships—Fiction. I. Title.
PR6056.A27B66 2014
823'.914—dc23   2014013938

ISBN 978-0-553-41884-2
eBook ISBN 978-0-553-41885-9

Printed in the United States of America

Book design by Lauren Dong
Jacket design by Christopher Brand
Jacket photography © George Baier IV

1 3 5 7 9 10 8 6 4 2

First Edition

For Eva, always.

I

THY WILL

BE DONE

1

FORTY MINUTES LATER

HE WAS UP IN THE SKY.

"I was going to say something," he said.

"So say it," she said.

He was quiet, keeping his eyes on the road. In the darkness of the city's outskirts, there was nothing to see except the tail-lights of other cars in the distance, the endless unfurling roll of tarmac, the giant utilitarian fixtures of the motorway.

"God may be disappointed in me for even thinking it," he said.

"Well," she sighed, "He knows already, so you may as well tell me."

He glanced at her face, to judge what mood she was in as she said this, but the top half of her head, including her eyes, was veiled in a shadow cast by the edge of the windscreen. The bottom half of her face was lunar bright. The sight of her cheek, lips and chin—so intimately familiar to him, so much a part of life as he had known it—made him feel a sharp grief at the thought of losing her.

"The world looks nicer with man-made lights," he said.

They drove on in silence. Neither of them could abide the chatter of radio or the intrusion of pre-recorded music. It was one of the many ways they were compatible.

"Is that it?" she said.

"Yes," he said. "What I mean is . . . Unspoiled nature is supposed to be the ultimate in perfection, isn't it, and all the man-made stuff is supposed to be a shame, just cluttering it up. But we wouldn't enjoy the world half as much if we—man . . . that is, human beings . . ."

(She gave him one of her *get-on-with-it* grunts.)

" . . . if we hadn't put electric lights all over it. Electric lights are actually attractive. They make a night drive like this bearable. Beautiful, even. I mean, just imagine if we had to do this drive in total darkness. Because that's what the natural state of the world is, at night, isn't it? Total darkness. Just imagine. You'd have the stress of not having a clue where you were going, not being able to see more than a few meters in front of you. And if you were heading for a city—well, in a non-technological world there wouldn't *be* cities, I suppose—but if you were heading for a place where other people lived, living there naturally, maybe with a few campfires . . . You wouldn't see them until you actually arrived. There wouldn't be that magical vista when you're a few miles away from a city, and all the lights are twinkling, like stars on the hillside."

"Uh-huh."

"And even inside this car, assuming you could *have* a car, or some sort of vehicle, in this natural world, pulled by horses I suppose . . . It would be pitch black. And very cold, too, on a winter's night. But instead, look what we've got here." He took one hand off the steering wheel (he always drove with both hands laid symmetrically on the wheel) and indicated the dashboard. The usual little lights glowed back at them. Temperature. Time. Water level. Oil. Speed. Fuel consumption.

"Peter . . ."

"Oh, look!" Several hundred meters up ahead, a tiny overburdened figure, standing in a puddle of lamplight. "A hitchhiker. I'll stop, shall I?"

"No, don't."

The tone of her voice made him think better of challenging her, even though they seldom missed an opportunity to show kindness to strangers.

The hitchhiker raised his head in hope. As the headlights enveloped him, his body was—just for an instant—transformed from a vaguely humanoid shape into a recognizably individual person. He was holding a sign that said HETHROW.

"How strange," said Peter, as they zoomed past. "You'd think he'd just take the Tube."

"Last day in the UK," said Beatrice. "Last chance to have a good time.

He probably used up his British money in a pub, thinking he'd keep just enough for the train. Six drinks later he's out in the fresh air, sobering up, and all he's got left is his plane ticket and £1.70."

It sounded plausible. But if it was true, then why leave this lost sheep in the lurch? It wasn't like Bea to leave anybody stranded.

He turned toward her darkened face again, and was alarmed to see teardrops twinkling on her jaw and in the corners of her mouth.

"Peter . . ." she said.

He took one hand off the steering wheel again, this time to squeeze her shoulder. Suspended over the highway up ahead was a sign with a symbol of an aeroplane on it.

"Peter, this is our last chance."

"Last chance?"

"To make love."

The indicator lights flashed gently and went tick, tick, tick, as he eased the car into the airport lane. The words "make love" bumbled against his brain, trying to get in, even though there was no room in there. He almost said, "You're joking." But, even though she had a fine sense of humor and loved to laugh, she never joked about things that mattered.

As he drove on, the sense that they were not on the same page—that they needed different things at this crucial time—entered the car like a discomfiting presence. He'd thought—he'd felt—that yesterday morning had been their proper leavetaking, and that this trip to the airport was just . . . a postscript, almost. Yesterday morning had been so *right*. They'd finally worked their way to the bottom of their "To-Do" list. His bag was already packed. Bea had the day off work, they'd slept like logs, they'd woken up to brilliant sunshine warming the yellow duvet of their bed. Joshua the cat had been lying in a comical pose at their feet; they'd nudged him off and made love, without speaking, slowly and with great tenderness. Afterward, Joshua had jumped back on the bed and tentatively laid one forepaw on Peter's naked shin, as if to say, *Don't go; I will hold you here.* It was a poignant moment, expressing the situation better than language could have, or perhaps it was just that the exotic cuteness of the cat put a protective furry layer over the raw human pain, making it endurable. Whatever. It was perfection. They'd lain there listening to Joshua's throaty purr, enfolded in each other's arms, their sweat evaporating in the sun, their heart-rates gradually reverting to normal.

"One more time," she said to him now, above the engine noise on a dark motorway on the way to the plane that would take him to America and beyond.

He consulted the digital clock on the dashboard. He was supposed to be at the check-in counter in two hours; they were about fifteen minutes from the airport.

"You're wonderful," he said. Perhaps if he pronounced the words in exactly the right way, she might get the message that they shouldn't try to improve on yesterday, that they should just leave it at that.

"I don't want to be wonderful," she said. "I want you inside me."

He drove for a few seconds in silence, adjusting quickly to the circumstances. Prompt adjustment to changed circumstances was another thing they had in common.

"There are lots of those horrible corporate hotels right near the airport," he said. "We could rent a room just for an hour." He regretted the "horrible" bit; it sounded as though he was trying to dissuade her while pretending not to. He only meant that the hotels were the sort they both avoided if they possibly could.

"Just find a quiet lay-by," she said. "We can do it in the car."

"Crisis!" he said, and they both laughed. *Crisis* was the word he'd trained himself to say instead of *Christ*, when he'd first become a Christian. The two words were close enough in sound for him to be able to defuse a blasphemy when it was already half out of his mouth.

"I mean it," she said. "Anywhere will do. Just don't park in a place where another car's likely to run into the back of us."

The highway looked different to him now, as they drove on. In theory it was the same stretch of tarmac, bounded by the same traffic paraphernalia and flimsy metal fences, but it had been transformed by their own intent. It was no longer a straight line to an airport, it was a mysterious hinterland of shadowy detours and hidey-holes. Proof, once again, that reality was not objective, but always waiting to be reshaped and redefined by one's attitude.

Of course, everybody on earth had the power to reshape reality. It was one of the things Peter and Beatrice talked about a lot. The challenge of getting people to grasp that life was only as grim and confining as you perceived it to be. The challenge of getting people to see that the immutable facts of existence were not so immutable after all. The challenge of finding a simpler word for *immutable* than *immutable*.

"How about here?"

Beatrice didn't answer, only put her hand on his thigh. He steered the car smoothly into a truckstop. They would have to trust that getting squashed flat by a 44-ton lorry was not in God's plan.

"I've never done this before," he said, when he'd switched the ignition off.

"You think I have?" she said. "We'll manage. Let's get in the back."

They swung out of their respective doors and were reunited several seconds later on the back seat. They sat like passengers, shoulder to shoulder. The upholstery smelled of other people—friends, neighbors, members of their church, hitchhikers. It made Peter doubt all the more whether he could or should make love here, now. Although . . . there was something exciting about it, too. They reached for each other, aiming for a smooth embrace, but their hands were clumsy in the dark.

"How fast would the cabin light drain the car's battery?" she said.

"I've no idea," he said. "Best not to risk it. Besides, it would make us a sideshow for all the passing traffic."

"I doubt it," she said, turning her face toward the headlights whizzing by. "I read an article once about a little girl who was being abducted. She managed to jump out of the car when it slowed down on the motorway. The kidnapper grabbed her, she put up a good fight, she was screaming for help. A stream of cars went past. Nobody stopped. They interviewed one of those drivers later. He said, 'I was traveling so fast, I didn't believe what I was seeing.'"

He shifted uncomfortably. "What an awful story. And maybe not the best of times to tell it."

"I know, I know, I'm sorry. I'm a bit . . . out of my mind just now." She laughed nervously. "It's just so hard . . . losing you."

"You're not losing me. I'm just going away for a while. I'll be . . ."

"Peter, please. Not now. We've done that part. We've done what we can with that part."

She leaned forward, and he thought she was going to start sobbing. But she was fishing something out from the gap between the two front seats. A small battery-operated torch. She switched it on and balanced it on the headrest of the front passenger seat; it fell off. Then she wedged it in the narrow space between the seat and the door, angled it so that its beam shone on the floor.

"Nice and subdued," she said, her voice steady again. "Just enough light so we can make each other out."

"I'm not sure I can do this," he said.

"Let's just see what happens," she said, and began to unbutton her shirt, exposing her white bra and the swell of her bosom. She allowed the shirt to fall down her arms, wiggled her shoulders and elbows to shake the silky material off her wrists. She removed her skirt, panties and pantyhose all together, hooked in her strong thumbs, and made the motion look graceful and easy.

"Now you."

He unclasped his trousers and she helped him remove them. Then she slid onto her back, contorting her arms to remove her bra, and he tried to reposition himself without squashing her with his knees. His head bumped against the ceiling.

"We're like a couple of clueless teenagers here," he complained. "This is . . ."

She laid her hand on his face, covering his mouth.

"We're you and me," she said. "You and me. Man and wife. Everything's fine."

She was naked now except for the wristwatch on her thin wrist and the pearl necklace around her throat. In the torchlight, the necklace was no longer an elegant wedding anniversary gift but became a primitive erotic adornment. Her breasts shook with the force of her heartbeat.

"Come on," she said. "Do it."

And so they began. Pressed close together, they could no longer see each other; the torchlight's purpose was over. Their mouths were joined, their eyes clasped shut, their bodies could have been anyone's bodies since the world was created.

"Harder," Beatrice gasped after a while. Her voice had a harsh edge to it, a brute tenacity he'd never heard in her before. Their lovemaking had always been decorous, friendly, impeccably considerate. Sometimes serene, sometimes energetic, sometimes athletic, even—but never desperate. "Harder!"

Confined and uncomfortable, with his toes knocking against the window and his knees chafing on the furry viscose of the car seat, he did his best, but the rhythm and angle weren't right and he misjudged how much longer she needed and how long he could last.

"Don't stop! Go on! Go on!"

But it was over.

"It's OK," she finally said, and wriggled from under him, clammy with sweat. "It's OK."

They were at Heathrow in plenty of time. The check-in lady gave Peter's passport the once-over. "Traveling one-way to Orlando, Florida, yes?" she said. "Yes," he said. She asked him if he had any suitcases to check in. He swung a sports bag and a rucksack onto the belt. It came across as dodgy somehow. But the logistics of his journey were too complicated and uncertain for a return booking. He wished Beatrice weren't standing next to him, listening to these confirmations of his imminent departure into thin air; wished she'd been spared hearing the word "one-way."

And then, of course, once he was handed his boarding pass, there was more time to fill before he would actually be allowed on the plane. Side by side, he and Beatrice meandered away from the check-in desks, a little dazzled by the excessive light and monstrous scale of the terminal. Was it the fluorescent glare that made Beatrice's face look drawn and anxious? Peter put his arm around the small of her back. She smiled up at him reassuringly, but he was not reassured. WHY NOT START YOUR HOLIDAY UPSTAIRS? the billboards leered. WITH OUR EVER-EXPANDING SHOPPING OPPORTUNITIES, YOU MAY NOT WANT TO LEAVE!

At this hour of evening, the airport was not too crowded, but there were still plenty of people trundling luggage and browsing in the shops. Peter and Beatrice took their seats near an information screen, to await the number of his departure gate. They joined hands, not looking at each other, looking instead at the dozens of would-be passengers filing past. A gaggle of pretty young girls, dressed like pole dancers at the start of a shift, emerged from a duty-free store burdened with shopping bags. They tottered along in high heels, scarcely able to carry their multiple prizes. Peter leaned toward Beatrice's face and murmured: "Why would anybody want to go on a flight so heavily laden? And then when they get to wherever they're going, they'll buy even more stuff. And look: they can barely walk."

"Uh-huh."

"But maybe that's the whole point. Maybe this is a display put on specially for us. The sheer impracticality of it all—right down to the ridiculous shoes. It lets everyone know these girls are so rich they don't have to worry about the real world. Their wealth makes them like a different creature, an exotic thing that doesn't have to function like a human."

Bea shook her head. "These girls aren't rich," she said. "Rich people don't travel in packs. And rich females don't walk as if they're not used to high heels. These girls are just young and they enjoy shopping. They're having an adventure. They're showing off to each other, not to us. We're invisible to them."

Peter watched the girls stagger toward Starbucks. Their buttocks quivered inside their wrinkled skirts and their voices became raucous, betraying regional accents. Bea was right.

He sighed, squeezed her hand. What was he going to do without her, out in the field? How would he cope, not being able to discuss his perceptions? She was the one who stopped him coming out with claptrap, curbed his tendency to construct grand theories that encompassed everything. She brought him down to earth. Having her by his side on this mission would have been worth a million dollars.

But it was costing a great deal more than a million dollars to send him alone, and USIC was footing the bill.

"Are you hungry? Can I get you anything?"

"We ate at home."

"A chocolate bar or something?"

She smiled but looked tired. "I'm fine. Honestly."

"I feel so bad about letting you down."

"Letting me down?"

"You know . . . In the car. It feels unfair, unfinished, and today of all days . . . I hate to leave you like this."

"It'll be awful," she said. "But not because of that."

"The angle, the unfamiliar angle made me . . ."

"Please, Peter, there's no need for this. I'm not keeping a scorecard or a balance sheet. We made love. That's enough for me."

"I feel I've . . ."

She stopped his mouth with her finger, then kissed him. "You're the best man in the world." She kissed him again, on the forehead. "If you're going to do post-mortems, I'm sure there'll be much better reasons on this mission."

His brow furrowed against her lips. What did she mean by "post-mortems"? Was she just referring to the inevitability of encountering obstacles and setbacks? Or was she convinced that the mission as a whole would end in failure? In death?

He stood up; she stood up with him. They held each other tight. A large party of tourists poured into the hall, fresh from a coach and keen to travel to the sun. Surging toward their appointed gate, the babbling revelers split into two streams, flowing around Peter and Bea. When they'd all gone and the hall was relatively quiet again, a voice through the PA said: "Please keep your belongings with you at all times. Unattended items will be removed and may be destroyed."

"Do you have some sort of . . . instinct my mission will fail?" he asked her.

She shook her head, bumping his jaw with her skull.

"You don't feel God's hand in this?" he persisted.

She nodded.

"Do you think He would send me all the way to—"

"Please, Peter. Don't talk." Her voice was husky. "We've covered all this ground so many times. It's pointless now. We've just got to have faith."

They sat back down, tried to make themselves comfortable in the chairs. She laid her head on his shoulder. He thought about history, the hidden human anxieties behind momentous events. The tiny trivial things that were probably bothering Einstein or Darwin or Newton as they formulated their theories: arguments with the landlady, maybe, or concern over a blocked fireplace. The pilots who bombed Dresden, fretting over a phrase in a letter from back home: What did she *mean* by that? Or what about Columbus, when he was sailing toward the New Land . . . who knows what was on his mind? The last words spoken to him by an old friend, perhaps, a person not even remembered in history books . . .

"Have you decided," said Bea, "what your first words will be?"

"First words?"

"To *them*. When you meet them."

He tried to think. "It'll depend . . ." he said uneasily. "I have no idea what I'm going to find. God will guide me. He'll give me the words I need."

"But when you imagine it . . . the meeting . . . what picture comes to your mind?"

He stared straight ahead. An airport employee dressed in overalls with bright yellow reflective sashes was unlocking a door labeled KEEP LOCKED AT ALL TIMES. "I don't picture it in advance," he said. "You know what I'm like. I can't live through stuff until it happens. And anyway, the way things really turn out is always different from what we might imagine."

She sighed. "I have a picture. A mental picture."

"Tell me."

"Promise you won't make fun of me."

"I promise."

She spoke into his chest. "I see you standing on the shore of a huge lake. It's night and the sky is full of stars. On the water, there's hundreds of small fishing boats, bobbing up and down. Each boat has at least one person in it, some have three or four, but I can't see any of them properly, it's too dark. None of the boats are going anywhere, they've all dropped anchor, because everyone is listening. The air is so calm you don't even have to shout. Your voice just carries over the water."

He stroked her shoulder. "A nice . . ." He was about to say "dream," but it would have sounded dismissive. "Vision."

She made a sound that could have been a croon of assent, or a subdued cry of pain. Her body was heavy against him, but he let her settle and tried not to fidget.

Diagonally opposite Peter and Beatrice's seats was a chocolate and biscuit shop. It was still doing a brisk trade despite the lateness of the hour; five customers stood queued at the checkout, and several others were browsing. Peter watched as a young, well-dressed woman selected an armful of purchases from the display racks. Jumbo-size boxes of pralines, long slim cartons of shortbreads, a Toblerone the size of a truncheon. Hugging them all to her breast, she ambled beyond the pylon supporting the shop's ceiling, as if to check out whether there were more goodies displayed outside. Then she simply walked away, into the swirl of passers-by, toward the ladies' toilets.

"I've just witnessed a crime," Peter murmured into Beatrice's hair. "Have you?"

"Yes."

"I thought you might be dozing off."

"No, I saw her too."

"Should we have nabbed her?"

"Nabbed her? You mean, like, a citizen's arrest?"

"Or at least reported her to the shop staff."

Beatrice pressed her head harder against his shoulder as they watched the woman disappear into the loo. "Would that help anyone?"

"It might remind her that stealing is wrong."

"I doubt it. Getting caught would just make her hate the people catching her."

"So, as Christians, we should just let her get on with stealing?"

"As Christians, we should spread the love of Christ. If we do our job right, we'll create people who don't *want* to do wrong."

" 'Create'?"

"You know what I mean. Inspire. Educate. Show the way." She lifted her head, kissed his brow. "Exactly what you're about to do. On this mission. My brave man."

He blushed, gratefully swallowing the compliment like a thirsty child. He hadn't realized how much he needed it just now. It was so huge inside him he thought his chest would burst.

"I'm going to the prayer room," he said. "Want to come?"

"In a little while. You go ahead."

He stood up and walked without hesitation toward Heathrow's chapel. It was the one place in Heathrow, Gatwick, Edinburgh, Dublin and

Manchester airports that he knew how to find without any bother. It was always the ugliest, dowdiest room in the entire complex, a far cry from the glittery hives of commerce. But there was soul in it.

Having found it again, he perused the timetable posted on the door in case he'd arrived just in time for a rare Communion. But the next one wasn't scheduled till Thursday afternoon at three, by which time he would be an unimaginable distance away from here, and Beatrice would have started her long months of sleeping alone with Joshua.

He pushed the door open gently. The three Muslims kneeling inside didn't acknowledge him as he walked in. They were facing a piece of paper attached to the wall, a computer-printed pictogram of a large arrow, like a traffic sign. It pointed to Mecca. The Muslims bowed, thrusting their rumps in the air, and kissed the fabric of the brightly-colored mats provided. They were immaculately dressed men, with expensive watches and bespoke suits. Their polished patent-leather shoes had been tossed aside. The balls of their stockinged feet squirmed with the enthusiasm of their obeisance.

Peter cast a quick glance behind the curtain that divided the room down the middle. As he'd suspected, there was a woman there, another Muslim, shrouded in gray, performing the same mute ritual. She had a child with her, a miraculously well-behaved boy dressed like Little Lord Fauntleroy. He was sitting near his mother's feet, ignoring her prostrations, reading a comic. Spider-Man.

Peter walked over to the cabinet where the Holy Books and pamphlets were kept. The Bible (a Gideon edition), a separate New Testament and *Psalms*, a Qur'an, a tatty book in Indonesian that was probably another New Testament. Stacked on a lower shelf, next to the *Watchtower* and the Salvation Army newspapers, was an optimistically large pile of leaflets. The logos looked familiar, so he bent down to identify them. They were from a very large American evangelical sect whose London pastor had been interviewed for this same mission. Peter actually met him in the USIC foyer, leaving in a huff. "Bunch of time-wasters," the guy hissed as he headed for the exit. Peter had expected to be unsuccessful too, but instead . . . he had been chosen. Why him and not someone from a church with loads of money and political clout? He still wasn't sure. He opened one of the leaflets, immediately saw the usual stuff about the numerological significance of 666, barcodes and the Whore of Babylon. Maybe that was the problem right there: fanaticism wasn't what USIC was looking for.

The quiet of the room was interrupted by an intercom message, piped through a small speaker attached, limpet-like, to the ceiling.

"Allied Airlines regrets to announce that there has been a further delay to Flight AB31 to Alicante. This is due to technical problems with the aircraft. The next announcement will be made at 22:30. Any remaining passengers who have not yet picked up their meal vouchers are requested to do so. Allied Airlines would like to apologize once again for any inconvenience."

Peter fancied he could hear a collective moan of lamentation start up outside, but it was probably his imagination.

He opened the Visitors Book and leafed through its ledger-size pages, reading the comments scribbled one beneath the other by travelers from all over the world. They didn't disappoint him; they never did. Today's entries alone filled three pages. Some were in Chinese characters, or Arabic script, but most were in English, halting or otherwise. The Lord was here, poured forth in this welter of biro ink and felt-tip pen.

It always struck him, whenever he was in an airport, that the entire, vast, multi-storied complex pretended to be a playground of secular delights, a galaxy of consumerism in which religious faith simply did not exist. Every shop, every billboard, every inch of the building right down to the rivets and the toilet plugholes, radiated the presumption that no one had any need for God here. The crowds that queued for snacks and knick-knacks, the constant stream of passengers recorded by the closed-circuit TVs, were wondrous proof of the sheer variety of human specimens, except that they were presumed to be identically faithless inside, duty-free in every sense of that word. And yet these hordes of bargain-hunters, honeymooners, sunbathers, business executives preoccupied with their deals, fashionistas haggling for their upgrades . . . no one would guess how many of them ducked into this little room and wrote heartfelt messages to the Almighty and to their fellow believers.

Dear God, please take all the bad parts out of the world—Johnathan.
A child, he guessed.

Yuko Oyama, Hyoyo, Japan. I pray for the children of illness and peace of planet. And I pray for finding a good partner.

Where is the CROSS of CHRIST our RISEN LORD? Wake UP!

Charlotte Hogg, Birmingham. Please pray that my beloved daughter and grandson will be able to accept my illness. And pray for everyone in distress.

Marijn Tegelaars, London/Belgium. My dearest friend G, that she may find the courage to be who she is.

Jill, England. Please pray for my late mother's soul to rest peacefully and pray for my family who are not united and hate each other.

Allah is the best! God rules!

The next entry was indecipherably crossed out. A nasty, intolerant rebuttal of the Muslim message above, most likely, deleted by another Muslim or by the caretaker of the Prayer Room.

Coralie Sidebottom, Slough, Berks. Thanks for God's wonderful creation.

Pat & Ray Murchiston, Langton, Kent. For our dear son, Dave, killed in a car crash yesterday. Forever in our hearts.

Thorne, Frederick, Co. Armagh, Ireland. I pray for the healing of the planet and the awakening of ALL peoples on it.

A mother. My heart is broken as my son has not spoken to me since my remarriage 7 years ago. Please pray for reconciliation.

Awful smell of cheap air freshener you can do better than this.

Moira Venger, South Africa. God is in control.

Michael Lupin, Hummock Cottages, Chiswick. Some other smell than antiseptic.

Jamie Shapcott, 27 Pinley Grove, Yeovil, Somerset. Please can my BA plane to Newcastle not crash. Thank you.

Victoria Sams, Tamworth, Staffs. Nice décor but the lights keep going on and off.

Lucy, Lossiemouth. Bring my man back safely.

He closed the book. His hands were trembling. He knew that there was quite a decent chance that he would die in the next thirty days, or that, even if he survived the journey, he would never return. This was his Gethsemane moment. He clenched his eyes shut and prayed to God to tell him what He wanted him to do; whether it would serve His purpose better if he grabbed Beatrice by the hand and ran with her to the exit and out to the car park, and drove straight back home before Joshua had even registered that he was gone.

By way of answer, God let him listen to the hysterical babble of his own inner voice, let it echo in the vault of his skull. Then, behind him, he heard a jingle of loose change as one of the Muslims jumped up to retrieve his shoes. Peter turned around. The Muslim man nodded courteously at him on his way out. The woman behind the curtain was touching up her lipstick, primping her eyelashes with her little finger, tucking stray hairs inside the edges of her hijab. The arrow on the wall fluttered slightly as the man swung open the door.

Peter's hands had ceased trembling. He had been granted perspective. This was not Gethsemane: he wasn't headed for Golgotha, he was embarking on a great adventure. He'd been chosen out of thousands, to pursue the most important missionary calling since the Apostles had ventured forth to conquer Rome with the power of love, and he was going to do his best.

Beatrice wasn't in the seat where he'd left her. For a few seconds he thought she'd lost her nerve and fled the terminal rather than say her last goodbye. He felt a pang of grief. But then he spotted her a few rows further toward the coffee and muffin kiosk. She was on the floor on her hands and knees, her face obscured by loose hair. Hunkered down in front of her, also on its hands and knees, was a child—a fat toddler, whose elasticated trousers bulged with an ill-concealed nappy.

"Look! I've got . . . ten fingers!" she was telling the child. "Have *you* got ten fingers?"

The fat toddler slid his hands forward, almost touching Bea's. She made a show of counting the digits, then said "A hundred! No, ten!" The boy laughed. An older child, a girl, stood shyly back, sucking on her knuckles. She kept looking back at her mother, but the mother was looking neither at her children nor at Beatrice; instead, she was focused on a hand-held gadget.

"Oh, hi," said Beatrice when she saw Peter coming. She brushed her hair off her face, tucked it behind her ears. "This is Jason and Gemma. They're going to Alicante."

"We hope," said the mother wearily. The gadget made a small beeping noise, having analyzed the glucose levels of the woman's blood.

"These people have been here since two p.m.," explained Beatrice. "They're stressed out."

"Never again," muttered the woman as she rummaged in a travel pouch for her insulin injections. "I swear. They take your money and they don't give a shit."

"Joanne, this is my husband, Peter. Peter, this is Joanne."

Joanne nodded in greeting but was too bound up in her misfortune to make small talk. "It all looks dead cheap on the brochure," she remarked bitterly, "but you pay for it in grief."

"Oh, don't be like that, Joanne," counseled Beatrice. "You'll have a lovely time. Nothing bad has actually happened. Just think: if the plane had been scheduled to leave eight hours later, you would've been doing the same thing as you're doing now—waiting, except at home."

"These two should be in bed," grumbled the woman, baring a roll of abdominal flesh and sticking the needle in.

Jason and Gemma, righteously offended by the allegation that they were sleepy rather than maltreated, looked poised for a fresh set of tantrums. Beatrice got on her hands and knees again. "I think I've lost my feet," she said, peering nearsightedly around the floor. "Where have they gone?" "They're here!" cried little Jason, as she turned away from him. "Where?" she said, spinning back.

"Thank God," said Joanne. "Here comes Freddie with the food."

A hassled-looking fellow with no chin and a porridge-colored windcheater lumbered into view, several paper bags clutched in each hand.

"World's biggest rip-off," he announced. "They keep you standing there with your little voucher for two quid or whatever. It's like the dole office. I tell you, in another half an hour, if this lot don't bloody well—"

"Freddie," said Beatrice brightly, "this is my husband, Peter."

The man put down his packages and shook Peter's hand.

"Your wife's a bit of an angel, Pete. Is she always taking pity on waifs and strays?"

"We . . . we both believe in being friendly," said Peter. "It costs nothing and it makes life more interesting."

"When are we gonna see the sea?" said Gemma, and yawned.

"Tomorrow, when you wake up," said the mother.

"Will the nice lady be there?"

"No, she's going to America."

Beatrice motioned the little girl to come and sit against her hip. The toddler had already dropped off to sleep, sprawled against a canvas backpack filled to the bursting point. "Wires slightly crossed," said Beatrice. "It's my husband who's going, not me."

"You stay home with the kids, huh?"

"We don't have any," said Beatrice. "Yet."

"Do yourselves a favor," sighed the man. "Don't. Just skip it."

"Oh, you don't mean that," said Beatrice. And Peter, seeing that the man was about to make an off-hand retort, added: "Not *really*."

And so the conversation went on. Beatrice and Peter got into rhythm, perfectly united in purpose. They'd done this hundreds of times before. Conversation, genuine unforced conversation, but with the potential to become something much more significant if the moment arose when it was right to mention Jesus. Maybe that moment would come; maybe it wouldn't. Maybe they would just say "God bless you" in parting and that would be it. Not every encounter could be transformative. Some conversations were just amiable exchanges of breath.

Coaxed into this exchange, the two strangers relaxed despite themselves. Within minutes they were even laughing. They were from Merton, they had diabetes and depression respectively, they both worked in a hardware superstore, they'd saved up for this holiday for a year. They were none too bright and not very fascinating. The woman had an unattractive snort and the man stank terribly of musk aftershave. They were human beings, and precious in the eyes of God.

"My plane is about to board," said Peter at last.

Beatrice was still on the floor, the head of a stranger's child lolling on her thigh. Her eyes were glassy with tears.

"If I come with you to Security," she said, "and hold you when you're about to go through, I won't be able to cope, I swear. I'll lose it, I'll cause a scene. So kiss me goodbye here."

Peter felt as if his heart were being cleaved in half. What had seemed

like a grand adventure in the prayer room now bereaved him like a sacrifice. He clung to the words of the Apostle: *Do the work of an evangelist,
make full proof of thy ministry. For I am now ready to be offered, and the time
of my departure is at hand.*

He bent down and Beatrice gave him a quick, rough kiss on the lips,
clasping the back of his head with one hand as she did so. He straightened
up, dazed. This whole scenario with the strangers—she'd engineered it to
happen, he could see that now.

"I'll write," he promised.

She nodded, and the motion shook the tears out onto her cheeks.

He walked briskly to Departures. Forty minutes later he was up in
the sky.

2

HE WOULD NEVER SEE OTHER HUMANS THE SAME WAY AGAIN.

The USIC chauffeur emerged from the gas station with a bottle of Tang and a spotless, supernaturally yellow banana. Dazzled by the sun, he scanned the forecourt for his tanked-up limousine and its precious foreign cargo. That cargo was Peter, who was using this fuel stop to stretch his legs and attempt one last call.

"Excuse me," said Peter. "Can you help me with this phone?"

The man seemed flummoxed by this request, jerking his hands around to indicate that they were both full. In his dark blue suit, complete with tie, he was overdressed for the Florida heat, and was still suffering some residual stress from the plane's delayed arrival. It was almost as if he held Peter personally responsible for the turbulent atmospheric conditions over the North Atlantic ocean.

"What's the problem with it?" he said, as he balanced the drink and the banana on the sun-blazed surface of the limousine's roof.

"Probably nothing," said Peter, squinting down at the gadget in his palm. "I probably don't know how to use it properly."

That was true. He wasn't good with gadgets, and used a phone only when circumstances forced him to; the rest of the time it would hibernate in his clothing, eventually becoming obsolete. Every year or so, Beatrice would tell him what his new number was, or what her new number was, because yet another service provider had become too frustrating to deal with or had gone bust. Businesses were going bust with alarming frequency these days; Bea kept up with stuff like that, Peter didn't. All he knew was that memorizing two new telephone numbers every year was not easy for him, despite his ability to memorize long passages of Scripture. And his unease with technology was such that if he pressed the gadget's call symbol and nothing happened—as he'd just done, here in the blinding limbo of Florida—he couldn't imagine what to do next.

The chauffeur was keen to resume the drive: there was still a long way to go. Biting off a mouthful of banana, he took hold of Peter's phone and examined it mistrustfully.

"Has this got the right kinda card in it?" he mumbled as he chewed. "For calling . . . ah . . . England?"

"I think so," said Peter. "I believe so."

The chauffeur handed it back, non-committal. "Looks like a healthy cellphone to me."

Peter stepped under the shade of a metal canopy that overhung the fuel pumps. He tried once more to tap the correct sequence of symbols. This time, he was rewarded with a staccato melody: the international code followed by Bea's number. He held the metal lozenge to his ear and stared out at the unfamiliarly blue sky and the sculpted trees surrounding the truck-stop.

"Hello?"

"It's me," he said.

". . . ello?"

"Can you hear me?" he said.

". . . hear you . . ." said Bea. Her voice was enveloped in a blizzard of static. Random words jumped out of the phone's tiny amplifier like stray sparks.

"I'm in Florida," he said.

". . . middle . . . night," she answered.

"I'm sorry. Did I wake you?"

". . . love you . . . how are . . . know what . . . ?"

"I'm safe and sound," he said. Sweat was making the phone slippery in his fingers. "Sorry to be calling you now but I may not get another chance later. The plane was delayed and we're in a big hurry."

". . . e . . . o . . . in the . . . me . . . guy know anything about . . . ?"

He walked further away from the vehicle, leaving the shade of the metal canopy. "This guy knows nothing about anything," he murmured, trusting that his words were being transmitted more clearly to her than hers were to him. "I'm not even sure if he works for USIC."

". . . haven't ask . . . ?"

"No, I haven't asked yet. I will." He felt a bit sheepish. He'd spent twenty, thirty minutes in the car with this chauffeur already and hadn't even established if he was an actual USIC employee or just a driver for hire. All he'd learned so far was that the photo of the little girl on the dashboard was the driver's daughter, that the driver was newly divorced from the little girl's mother, and that the mother's mom was an attorney who was working hard to make the driver regret the day he was born. "It's all very . . . hectic at the moment. And I didn't sleep on the flight. I'll write to you when I'm . . . you know, when I get to the other end. Then I'll have plenty of time and I'll put you in the picture. It'll be just like we're traveling together."

There was a rush of static and he wasn't sure if she had fallen silent or if her words were being swallowed up. He raised his voice: "How's Joshua?"

". . . first few . . . he just . . . o . . . ink . . . side . . ."

"I'm sorry, you're breaking up. And this guy wants me to stop talking. I have to go. I love you. I wish . . . I love you."

". . . you too . . ."

And she was gone.

"That your wife?" said the driver when Peter had settled back into the vehicle and they were pulling out of the truckstop.

Actually, no, Peter felt like saying, *that was not my wife, that was a bunch of disassembled electronic noises coming out of a small metal device.* "Yes," he said. His almost obsessional preference for face-to-face communication was too difficult to explain to a stranger. Even Beatrice had trouble understanding it sometimes.

"And your kid's called Joshua?" The driver seemed unconcerned by any social taboo against eavesdropping.

"Joshua's our cat," said Peter. "We don't have children."

"Saves a lot of drama," said the driver.

"You're the second person in two days who's told me that. But I'm sure you love your daughter."

"No choice!" The driver waved one hand toward the windscreen, to indicate the whole world of experience, destiny, whatever. "What does your wife do?"

"She's a nurse."

"That's a good job. Better than an attorney anyways. Making people's lives better instead of making them worse."

"Well, I hope being a minister achieves the same thing."

"Sure," said the driver breezily. He didn't sound sure at all.

"And what about you?" said Peter. "Are you a USIC . . . uh . . . staff member, or do they just hire you for taxi jobs?"

"Been a driver for USIC for nine, ten years," said the chauffeur. "Goods, mainly. Academics sometimes. USIC holds a lot of conferences. And then every now and then, there's an astronaut."

Peter nodded. For a second he imagined the driver picking up an astronaut from Orlando Airport, pictured a square-jawed hulk in a bulbous space suit lumbering through the arrivals hall toward the placard-wielding chauffeur. Then he twigged.

"I've never thought of myself as an astronaut," he said.

"It's an old-fashioned word," conceded the chauffeur. "I use it out of respect for tradition, I guess. The world changes too fast. You take your eyes off something that's always been there, and the next minute it's just a memory."

Peter looked out the window. The motorway looked much the same as a motorway in the UK, but there were giant metal signs informing him that splendid attractions like the Econlockhatchee River and the Hal Scott Regional Nature Preserve were somewhere nearby, hidden beyond the windbreaks. Stylized illustrations on billboards evoked the joys of camping and horseback riding.

"One of the good things about USIC," said the driver, "is that they have some respect for tradition. Or maybe they just recognize the value of a brand. They bought Cape Canaveral, you know that? They own the whole place. Must have cost them a fortune, and they could've built their launch site somewhere else, there's so much real estate up for grabs these days. But they wanted Cape Canaveral. I call that class."

Peter made a vague noise of agreement. The classiness—or otherwise—of multinational corporations was not a subject on which he had strong opinions. One of the few things he knew about USIC was that it owned lots of formerly defunct factories in formerly destitute towns in sloughed-off parts of the former Soviet Union. He somehow doubted that "classy" was the right word for what went on there. As for Cape Canaveral, the history of space travel had never been of the slightest interest to him, even as a kid. He'd not even noticed that NASA had ceased to exist. It was the sort of nugget of useless information that Beatrice was liable to unearth while reading the newspapers that would later be put underneath Joshua's food bowls.

He missed Joshua already. Beatrice often left for work at dawn, when Joshua was still fast asleep on the bed. Even if he stirred and meowed, she would hurry off and say, "Daddy will feed you." And sure enough, an hour or two later, Peter would be sitting in the kitchen, munching sweet cereal, while Joshua munched savory cereal on the floor nearby. Then Joshua would jump on the kitchen table and lick the milk dregs from Peter's bowl. Not something he was allowed to do when Mummy was around.

"The training is tough, am I right?" said the chauffeur.

Peter sensed he was expected to tell stories of military-style exercise regimens, Olympic tests of endurance. He had no such tales to tell. "There's a physical," he conceded. "But most of the screening is . . . questions."

"Yeah?" said the driver. A few moments later, he switched on the car radio. ". . . continues in Pakistan," an earnest voice began, "as antigovernment forces . . ." The chauffeur switched to a music station, and the vintage sounds of A Flock of Seagulls warbled out.

Peter leaned back and recalled some of the questions in his screening interviews. These sessions, held in a boardroom on the tenth floor of a swanky London hotel, had gone on for hours at a time. One American woman was a constant presence: an elegant, tiny anorexic, who carried herself like a famous choreographer or retired ballet dancer. Bright-eyed and nasal-voiced, she nursed glass mugs of decaffeinated coffee as she worked, aided by a changeable team of other interrogators. "Interrogators" was the wrong word, perhaps, since everyone was friendly and there was an odd sense that they were rooting for him to succeed.

"How long can you go without your favorite ice cream?"

"I don't have a favorite ice cream."

"What smell reminds you most of your childhood?"

"I don't know. Maybe custard."

"Do you like custard?"

"It's OK. These days I mainly have it on Christmas pudding."

"What do you think of when you think of Christmas?"

"Christ's Mass, a celebration of Jesus's birth, held at the time of the Roman winter solstice. John Chrysostom. Syncretism. Santa Claus. Snow."

"Do you celebrate it yourself?"

"We make a big deal of it in our church. We organize presents for disadvantaged children, put on Christmas dinner at our drop-in center . . . A lot of people feel horribly lost and depressed at that time of year. You have to try to get them through it."

"How well do you sleep in beds that aren't your own?"

He'd had to think about that one. Cast his mind back to the cheap hotels he and Bea had stayed in when they'd participated in evangelist rallies in other cities. The friends' sofas that converted into mattresses of a kind. Or, further back still in his life, the tough choice between keeping your coat on so you'd shiver less, or using it as a pillow to soften the concrete against your skull. "I'm probably . . . average," he said. "As long as it's a bed and I'm horizontal, I think I'm fine."

"Are you irritable before your first coffee of the day?"

"I don't drink coffee."

"Tea?"

"Sometimes."

"Sometimes you're irritable?"

"I don't get annoyed easily." This was true, and these interrogations provided additional proof. He enjoyed the sparring, felt he was being tested rather than judged. The rapid-fire questions were an invigorating change from church services where he was expected to orate for an hour while others sat silent. He wanted the job, wanted it badly, but the outcome was in God's hands, and there was nothing to be gained by getting anxious, giving dishonest answers or straining to please. He would be himself, and hope that that was enough.

"How would you feel about wearing sandals?"

"Why, will I have to?"

"You might." This from a man whose feet were sheathed in expensive black leather shoes so shiny that Peter's face was reflected in them.

"How do you feel if you haven't accessed social media for a day?"

"I don't access social media. At least I don't think so. What do you mean exactly by 'social media'?"

"It's OK." Whenever a question got tangled, they tended to change tack. "Which politician do you hate most?"

"I don't hate anyone. And I don't really follow politics."

"It's nine o'clock at night and the power fails. What do you do?"

"Fix it, if I can."

"But how would you spend the time if you couldn't?"

"Talk to my wife, if she was at home at the time."

"How do you think she'll cope if *you're* away from home for a while?"

"She's a very independent and capable woman."

"Would you say you're an independent and capable man?"

"I hope so."

"When did you last get drunk?"

"About seven, eight years ago."

"Do you feel like a drink now?"

"I wouldn't mind some more of this peach juice."

"With ice?"

"Yes, thank you."

"Imagine this," the woman said. "You visit a foreign city and your hosts invite you out for dinner. The restaurant they take you to is pleasant and lively. There's a large transparent enclosure of cute white ducklings running around behind their mother. Every few minutes, a chef grabs one of the ducklings and tosses it into a vat of boiling oil. When it's fried, it gets served up to the diners and everyone is happy and relaxed. Your hosts order duckling and say you should try it, it's fantastic. What do you do?"

"Is there anything else on the menu?"

"Sure, lots of things."

"Then I'd order something else."

"You could still sit there and eat?"

"It would depend on what I was doing in these people's company in the first place."

"What if you disapproved of them?"

"I'd try to steer the conversation toward the things I disapproved of, and then I'd be honest about what I thought was wrong."

"You don't have a problem specifically with the duckling thing?"

"Humans eat all sorts of animals. They slaughter pigs, who are much more intelligent than birds."

"So if an animal is dumb it's OK to kill it?"

"I'm not a butcher. Or a chef. I've chosen to do something else with my life. That's a choice against killing, if you like."

"But what about the ducklings?"

"What *about* the ducklings?"

"You wouldn't feel compelled to save them? For example, would you consider smashing the glass enclosure, so they could escape?"

"Instinctively, I might. But it probably wouldn't do those ducklings any good. If I was really haunted by what I saw in that restaurant, I suppose I could devote my whole life to reeducating the people in that society so they would kill the ducks more humanely. But I would rather devote my life to something that might persuade human beings to treat *each other* more humanely. Because human beings suffer so much more than ducks."

"You might not think so if you were a duck."

"I don't think I would think much about *anything* if I were a duck. It's higher consciousness that causes all our griefs and tortures, don't you think?"

"Would you step on a cricket?" interjected one of the other questioners.

"No."

"A cockroach?"

"Maybe."

"You're not a Buddhist, then."

"I never claimed to be a Buddhist."

"You wouldn't say that all life is sacred?"

"It's a beautiful concept, but every time I wash, I kill microscopic creatures that were hoping to live on me."

"So where's the dividing line for you?" the woman rejoined. "Dogs? Horses? What if the restaurant was frying live kittens?"

"Let *me* ask *you* a question," he said. "Are you sending me to a place where people are doing terrible, cruel things to other creatures?"

"Of course not."

"Then why ask me these sorts of questions?"

"OK, how about this one: Your cruise ship has sunk, and now you're stuck in a life raft with an extremely irritating man who also happens to be homosexual . . ."

And so it went on. For days and days. So long, in fact, that Bea lost patience and began to wonder if he should tell USIC that his time was too precious to waste on any more of these charades.

"No, they want me," he'd reassured her. "I can tell."

Now, on a balmy morning in Florida, having earned the corporation's stamp of approval, Peter turned to face the driver and posed the question to which, in all these months, he hadn't been given a straight answer.

"What *is* USIC, exactly?"

The driver shrugged. "These days, the bigger the company, the less you can figure out what it does. Time was when a car company made cars, a mining company dug mines. It's not like that anymore. You ask USIC what they specialize in and they tell you things like . . . Logistics. Human resources. Large-scale project development." The driver sucked the last of the Tang through a straw, making an ugly gurgling sound.

"But where does all the money come from?" said Peter. "They're not funded by the government."

The driver frowned, distracted. He needed to make sure his vehicle was in the correct lane. "Investments."

"Investments in what?"

"Lots of things."

Peter shielded his eyes with one hand; the glare was giving him a headache. He recalled that he'd asked the same question of his USIC interrogators, at one of the early interviews when Beatrice was still sitting in.

"We invest in *people*," the elegant female had replied, shaking her artfully clipped gray mane, laying her scrawny, delicate hands on the table.

"All corporations say that," Beatrice remarked, a bit rudely he thought.

"Well, we really mean it," said the older woman. Her gray eyes were sincere and animated by intelligence. "Nothing can be achieved without people. Individuals, unique individuals with very special skills." She turned to Peter. "That's why we're talking to you."

He'd smiled at the cleverness of this phrasing: it could function as flattery—they were talking to him because it was obvious he was one of these special people—or it could be a preamble to rejection—they were talking to him to maintain the high standards that would, in the end, disqualify him. One thing was for sure: the hints that he and Bea dropped about what a fine team they'd make if they could go on this mission together fell like cookie crumbs and disappeared into the carpet.

"One of us needs to stay and look after Joshua, anyway," said Bea when they discussed it afterward. "It would be cruel to leave him for so long. And there's the church. And the house, the expenses; I need to keep working." All valid concerns—although an advance payment from USIC, even a small fraction of the full sum, would have covered an awful lot of cat food, neighborly visits and heating bills. "It just would have been nice to be invited, that's all."

Yes, it would have been nice. But they were not blind to good fortune when it was offered. Peter had been chosen, from among many others who were not.

"So," he said to the driver, "how did *you* first get involved with USIC?"

"Bank foreclosed on our house."

"I'm sorry to hear that."

"Bank foreclosed on just about every damn house in Gary. Repossessed them, couldn't sell them, let them fall apart and rot. But USIC made us a deal. They took on the debt, we got to keep the house, and in exchange we worked for them, for like, grocery money. Some of my old pals called it slavery. I call it . . . humanitarian. And those old pals of mine, they're in trailer parks now. And here's me, driving a limousine."

Peter nodded. He'd already forgotten the name of the place where this guy was from, and he had only the vaguest grasp on the current health of the American economy, but he understood very well what it meant to be thrown a lifeline.

The limousine cruised gently to the right and was cloaked in cooling shade from the pine trees on the verge. A wooden road sign—the sort that normally advertised campsites, roadside grills or log-house holidays—announced an imminent turn-off for USIC.

"You go to any sinking city in the country," continued the driver, "and you'll find lots of people in the same boat. They may tell you they're work-ing for this or that company, but scratch underneath, and they're working for USIC."

"I don't even know what the letters in 'USIC' stand for," said Peter.

"Search me," said the driver. "A lot of companies these days got mean-ingless names. All the meaningful names have been taken. It's a trademark thing."

"I assume the US part means United States."

"I guess. They're multinational, though. Somebody even told me they started up in Africa. All I know is, they're good to work for. Never screwed me around. You'll be in good hands."

Into thy hands I commend my spirit, Peter naturally thought. *Luke 23:46*, fulfilling the prophesy of *Psalms 31:5*. Except that it wasn't clear into whose hands he was about to be delivered.

"This will sting some," said the black woman in the white lab coat. "In fact, it will be real unpleasant. You'll feel like a pint of cold yogurt is traveling up your veins."

"Gee, thanks. I can hardly wait." He settled his head uneasily in the padded polystyrene hollow of his coffin-like crib and tried not to look at the spike that was approaching his tourniquetted arm.

"We wouldn't want you to think there was anything wrong, that's all."

"If I die, please tell my—"

"You won't die. Not with this stuff inside you. Just relax and think nice thoughts."

The cannula was in his vein; the IV drip was activated; the translu-cent substance moved into him. He thought he might vomit from the sheer ghastliness of it. They ought to have given him a sedative or something. He wondered if his three fellow travelers were braver than him. They were nes-tled in identical cribs, elsewhere in the building, but he couldn't see them. He would meet them in a month from now, when he woke up.

The woman who had administered the infusion stood calmly watching over him. Without warning—but how could there be any warning?—her lipsticked mouth started to drift to the left of her face, the lips traveling across the flesh of her cheek like a tiny red canoe. The mouth did not stop until it reached her forehead, where it came to rest above her eyebrows. Then her eyes, complete with eyelids and lashes, moved down toward her jawline, blinking normally as they relocated.

"Don't fight it, just go with it," the mouth on the forehead advised. "It's temporary."

He was too frightened to speak. This was no hallucination. This was what happened to the universe when you were no longer able to hold it together. Atoms in clusters, rays of light, forming ephemeral shapes before moving on. His greatest fear, as he dissolved into the dark, was that he would never see other humans the same way again.

3

THE GRAND ADVENTURE COULD

SURELY WAIT.

"Man, man, *man*." A deep, rueful voice from the formless void. "That shit is one bad, *bad* motherfucker."

"Mind your language, BG. We got a religious person here with us."

"Well, ain't *that* a lick on the dick. Gimme a hand outta this coffin, man."

A third voice: "Me too. Me first."

"You'll regret it, children." (This said with sing-song condescension.) "But OK." And there was a rustling and a grunting and a gasping and a muttering of hard labor.

Peter opened his eyes, but was too nauseous to turn his head toward the voices. The ceiling and walls seemed to be convulsing; the lights yo-yo'd. It was as though the solid framework of the room had turned elastic, walls billowing, ceiling flailing around. He shut his eyes against the delirium, but that was worse: the convulsions continued inside his skull, as though his eyeballs were inflating like balloons, as though the pulpy insides of his face might, any moment, squirt out through his nostrils. He imagined he could feel his brain filling up with—or being drained of—some vile, caustic liquor.

From elsewhere in the cabin, the grunting and scuffling went on, accompanied by deranged laughter.

"You know, it's pretty entertaining," remarked the mocking, sober voice, removed from the other two, "watching you guys flopping around on the floor like a couple of sprayed bugs."

"Hey, no fair! Damn system should wake us all up at the same time. Then we'd see who's most fit."

"Well . . ." (The superior voice again.) "Somebody has to be first, I guess. To make the coffee and check that everything's working."

"So go check, Tuska, and leave me and BG to slug it out for second place."

"Suit yourselves." Footsteps. A door opening. "You think you'll have privacy? Dream on, people. I can watch you squirming around on the surveillance cameras. Smile!"

The door clicked shut.

"Thinks the sun shines out of his ass," muttered a voice from the floor.

"That's 'cause you're always kissin' it, man."

Peter lay still, gathering his strength. Intuitively he understood that his body would settle back to normal in its own good time, and that there was nothing gained in trying to function too soon, unless you were the competitive type. The two men on the floor continued to grunt and giggle and heave themselves about, in defiance of the chemicals that had allowed them to survive the Jump.

"You gonna be the first one standing or am I?"

"I'm up already, bro . . . see?"

"You're so full of shit, man. That ain't standing, that's leaning. Let go the bench."

Sound of a body falling to the floor; more laughter.

"See *you* do better, bro . . ."

"Easy."

Sound of another body falling to the floor; dopey hysterics.

"Forgot how bad it was, man."

"Nothing a half dozen cans of Coke won't fix."

"Fuck that, man. A *line* of coke and you're talkin.'"

"If you want more drugs after this, you must be dumber than I thought."

"Just stronger, bro, just stronger."

And so it went on. The two men sparred with each other, expelling bravado into the atmosphere, biding time, until they were both on their feet. They grunted and panted as they rummaged in plastic bags, mocked each other's taste in clothing, put on shoes, tested their bipedalism by walking around. Peter lay in his crib, breathing shallowly, waiting for the room to stop moving. The ceiling had calmed down, at least.

"Yo, bro."

A large face loomed into his range of view. For a second, Peter couldn't recognize it as human: it seemed to be attached to the neck upside-down, with eyebrows on the chin and a beard at the top. But no: it was human, of course it was human, just very different from his own. Dark brown skin, a shapeless nose, small ears, beautiful brown eyes tinged with red. Neck muscles that could raise and lower an elevator in a twenty-storey shaft. And those eyebrow-like things on the chin? A beard. Not a full, furry beard, but one of those finely-sculpted fashion statements you could buy from a fancy barber. Years ago, it must have looked like a neat line drawn with a black felt-tip marker, but the man was middle-aged now, and the beard was patchy and speckled with gray. Advancing baldness had left him with just a few knobs of frizz on his head.

"Pleased to meet you," croaked Peter. "I'm Peter."

"BG, bro," said the black man, extending a hand. "You want I pull you outta there?"

"I . . . I might prefer to lie here a bit longer."

"Don't wait too long, bro," said BG, with a radiant white grin. "You shit your pants, and it's a small ship."

Peter smiled, unsure of whether BG meant this as a warning of what might happen or as an observation of what had already happened. The viscose swaddling of the crib felt damp and heavy, but it had felt that way even when the woman in the lab coat first wrapped him in it.

Another face swung into view. Sunburnt white, fiftyish, with thinning gray hair cut to a military bristle. Eyes as bloodshot as BG's, but blue and full of painful childhood and messy divorce and violent upheavals in employment.

"Severin," he said.

"I beg your pardon?"

"Artie Severin. We gotta get you out of there, pal. Sooner you start drinking, sooner you'll feel like a human being."

BG and Severin lifted him out of the crib as though they were extracting a newly purchased piece of equipment from its box: not exactly gently, but with sufficient care not to tear or break anything. His feet barely touched the floor as they carried him out of the room, down a short corridor and into a bathroom. There they stripped him of the gauzy loincloth he'd worn for the last month, sprayed him with blue foam from neck to ankles, and wiped him down with paper towels. A large transparent plastic waste bag got filled halfway to the top with blue and brown muck before they were finished.

"Is there a shower?" he asked, when it was over and he still felt sticky. "I mean, with water?"

"Water is *gold*, bro," said BG. "Every drop we got, goes into here." He tapped his throat. "It don't do nobody no good out *there*." And he nodded toward the wall, the outer shell of the ship, the barrier between them and the vast airless emptiness in which they were suspended.

"Sorry," said Peter. "That was naïve of me."

"Naïve's not a problem," said BG. "We all gotta ride the learning curve. I done this trip once before. First time I didn't know shit."

"You'll have all the water you want when we get to Oasis," said Severin. "Right now, you'd better drink some."

Peter was handed a plastic bottle with a resealable nipple. He took a big swig and, ten seconds later, fainted.

His recovery from the Jump took him longer than he would have liked. He would have liked to spring up like a momentarily winded boxer, and impress the other men. But the other men shook off the effects of the Jump rapidly and got busy doing whatever it was that they were doing, while he lolled helpless in a bunk, occasionally managing a sip of water. Before take-off he'd been warned that he would feel as though he'd been disassembled and put back together again, which was not exactly how the Jump worked, scientifically speaking, but was indeed the way it felt.

He spent the afternoon . . . well, no, those words made no sense, did they? There was no such thing as afternoon, morning or night here. In the darkened room where BG and Severin had stowed him after cleaning him up, he woke occasionally from his woozy slumber and looked at his watch. The numbers were only symbols. Real time would not resume until he had ground underfoot, and there was a sun rising and setting.

Once he got to Oasis, there would be facilities for sending a message to

Beatrice. "I'll write to you every day," he'd promised. "Every single day, if God allows me." He tried to imagine what she might be doing at this moment, how she might be dressed, whether she would have her hair pinned up or hanging loose over her shoulders. That was what his watch was for, he realized: not to tell him anything useful about his own situation, but to allow him to imagine Beatrice existing in the same reality as himself.

He looked at his watch again. In England, it was 2:43 in the morning. Beatrice would be asleep, with Joshua stretched opportunistically on his side of the bed, legs spread. Joshua, that is, not Beatrice. She would be on her left side, one arm dangling over the edge, the other thrown up, elbow covering her ear, fingers so close to his pillow that he could kiss them from where he lay. Not now, of course.

Maybe Beatrice was awake. Maybe she was worrying about him. A month had passed without contact between them, and they were used to communicating every day.

"What if my husband dies en route?" she'd asked the USIC people.

"He will not die en route," was the reply.

"But what if he does?"

"We would let you know immediately. In other words, no news is good news."

Good news it was, then. But still . . . Bea had spent these last thirty days conscious of his absence, while he'd been oblivious to hers.

He pictured their bedroom, lit in subdued tones by the bedside lamp; he pictured Bea's pale blue uniform slung over the chair, the jumble of shoes on the floor, the yellow duvet with Joshua's fur all over it. Beatrice sitting up against the headboard, bare-legged but with a sweater on, reading and rereading the uninformative info pack sent by USIC.

"USIC cannot and does not guarantee the safety of any travelers on its craft or domiciled in its facilities or in the pursuit of any activities related to, or not related to, USIC activities. *Safety* is defined as health both physical and mental and includes, but is not restricted to, survival and/or return from Oasis, either within the time period specified by this agreement or beyond that period. USIC undertakes to minimize risk to any persons participating in its projects but signature of this document is deemed to constitute acknowledgment of understanding that USIC's efforts in this regard (i.e., minimizing risk) are subject to circumstances beyond USIC's control. These circumstances, because unforeseen and unprecedented, cannot be detailed in advance of occurrence. They may include, but are not restricted to, disease, accident, mechanical failure, adverse weather, and any other events commonly categorized as Acts of God."

The door of the dormitory cell swung open, silhouetting the massive body of BG.

"Yo, bro."

"Hi." In Peter's experience, it was better to speak in one's own idiom than echo the idioms and accents of others. Rastafarians and cockney Pakistanis did not come to Christ through being patronized by evangelists making clownish attempts to talk like them, so there was no reason to suppose that black Americans might.

"You wanna eat with us, you better get yourself out of bed, bro."

"Sounds fine to me," said Peter, swinging his legs out of the bunk. "I think I'm up for it."

BG's massive arms were poised to lend assistance. "Noodles," he said. "Beef noodles."

"Sounds just fine." Still barefoot, dressed only in underpants and an unbuttoned shirt, Peter waddled out of the room. It was like being six again, when he was spaced out on liquid paracetamol and his mother fetched him out of bed to celebrate his birthday. The prospect of opening presents was not sufficiently adrenalizing to dispel the effects of chickenpox.

BG led him into a corridor whose walls were papered with floor-to-ceiling color photographs of green meadows, the kind of adhesive enlargements he was more accustomed to seeing on the sides of buses. Some thoughtful designer must have decided that a vista of grass, spring flowers and an azure sky was just the thing to combat the claustrophobia of airless space.

"You ain't a vegetarian, are you, bro?"

"Uh . . . no," said Peter.

"Well, I am," declared BG, steering him round a corner, where the verdant if slightly blurry scenery was repeated. "But one thing you learn when you go on a trip like this, man, is you gotta relax your principles sometimes."

* * *

Dinner was served in the control room; that is, the room that contained the piloting and navigation hardware. Contrary to Peter's expectations, he was not met with a breathtaking sight when he stepped inside. There was no giant window facing out onto a vast expanse of space, stars and nebulae. There was no window at all; no central focus of attention, just reinforced plastic walls punctuated by air conditioning vents, light switches, humidity adjustors, and a couple of laminated posters. Peter had seen the imagery before, on the USIC pamphlets when he'd first applied for this vacancy. The posters were glossy corporate productions, depicting a stylized ship, a stylized bird with a stylized twig in its beak, and a small amount of text extolling USIC's high standards of business practice and unlimited potential to benefit mankind.

The ship's controls were also less impressive than Peter had imagined: no giant rig of knobs and dials and meters and flashing lights, just a few compact keyboards, slimline monitors and one freestanding computer cabinet that resembled a snack dispenser or automatic bankteller machine. In all honesty, the control room was less a ship's bridge than an office—a somewhat pokey office, at that. There was nothing here to do justice to the fact that they were floating in a foreign solar system, trillions of miles from home.

Tuska the pilot had swiveled his chair away from the monitors and was staring into a small plastic tub held up near his face. Steam obscured his features. His legs, crossed casually over one another, were bare and hairy, clad only in oversize shorts and tennis shoes without socks.

"Welcome back to the land of the living," he said, lowering the tub to rest against his rotund belly. "Sleep well?"

"I don't know if I was sleeping, really," said Peter. "More just waiting to feel human again."

"Takes a while," conceded Tuska, and raised the noodle tub to his face again. He had a mouse-colored beard, and was obviously well-practiced in the logistics of conveying sloppy food past the hazards of facial hair. He twirled some noodles round his fork and closed his neat red lips over them.

"Here's yours, Pete," said Severin. "I've torn the foil off for you."

"That's very kind," said Peter, taking his seat at a black plastic table, where BG and Severin were tucking into their own noodle tubs with their own plastic forks. Three unopened cans of Coke stood ready. Peter shut his eyes, recited a silent prayer of thanks for what he was about to receive.

"You're a Christian, right?" said BG.

"Right," said Peter. The beef noodle stew had been cooked unevenly in the microwave: some parts were bubbling hot, other parts were still ever-so-slightly crunchy with ice. He stirred them into a warm compromise.

"I used to be Nation of Islam, long time ago," said BG. "Got me through some tough times. But it's high maintenance, man. Can't do this, can't do that." BG opened his considerable mouth and forked a quivering freight of noodles in, chewed three times, swallowed. "Ya gotta hate Jews and white people, too. They say it's not mandatory and all that shit. But you get the message, man. Loud and clear." Another mouthful of noodles. "I make my own decisions who I'm gonna hate, know what I'm saying? Somebody fucks with me, I hate 'em—they can be white, black, aquamareeeen, man; don't make no difference to me."

"I suppose what you're saying, also," said Peter, "is that you make your own decisions about who you'll love."

"Damn right. White pussy, black pussy, it's all good."

Tuska snorted. "You're making a fine impression on our minister, I'm sure." He'd finished his meal and was wiping his face and beard with a towelette.

"I'm not that easy to scandalize," said Peter. "Not with words, anyway. The world has room for lots of different ways of talking."

"We're not in the world now," said Severin with a lugubrious grin. He cracked open a can of Coke and a frothing jet of brown liquid sprayed up toward the ceiling.

"Jee-sus," exclaimed Tuska, falling half off his chair. BG just chuckled.

"I'll take care of it, I'll take care of it," said Severin, snatching a handful of paper towels from a dispenser. Peter helped him mop the sticky liquid from the tabletop.

"I do that every goddamn time," muttered Severin, dabbing at his chest, his forearm, the chairs, the coolbox from which the Cokes had come. He bent down to dab at the floor, whose carpet was fortuitously already brown.

"How many times have you made this trip?" asked Peter.

"Three. Swore I wouldn't go back each time."

"Why?"

"Oasis drives people crazy."

BG grunted. "You're crazy already, bro."

"Mr. Severin and Mr. Graham are both seriously unbalanced individuals, Pete," said Tuska, magistrate-solemn. "I've known 'em for years. Oasis is the most suitable place for guys like them. Keeps 'em off the streets." He tossed his empty noodle tub into a garbage bin. "Also, they're extremely good at what they do. The best. That's why USIC keeps spending the money on 'em."

"What about *you*, bro?" BG asked Peter. "Are you the best?"

"The best what?"

"The best preacher."

"I don't really think of myself as a preacher."

"What do you think of yourself as, bro?"

Peter swallowed hard, stumped. His brain was still residually affected by the same violent forces that had shaken up the cans of Coke. He wished Beatrice was here with him, to parry the questions, change the nature of this all-male atmosphere, deflect the conversation onto more fruitful paths.

"I'm just someone who loves people and wants to help them, whatever shape they're in."

Another big grin spread across BG's massive face, as though he was about to unleash another wisecrack. Then he abruptly turned serious. "You really mean that? No shit?"

Peter stared him straight in the eyes. "No shit."

BG nodded. Peter sensed that in the big man's consideration, he had passed some sort of test. Reclassified. Not exactly "one of the boys," but no longer an exotic animal that might be a major annoyance.

"Hey, Severin!" BG called. "I never asked you: what religion are you, man?"

"Me? I'm nothing," said Severin. "And that's the way it's staying."

Severin had finished the Coca-Cola clean-up and was wiping blue detergent gel off his fingers with paper towels.

"Fingers are still sticky," he complained. "I'm gonna be driven crazy until I get soap and water."

The computer cabinet started beeping gently.

"Looks like your prayer has been answered, Severin," remarked Tuska, turning his attention to one of the monitors. "The system has just figured out where we are."

All four men were silent as Tuska scrolled through the details. It was as though they were giving him the opportunity to check for emails or bid in an internet auction. He was, in fact, ascertaining whether they would live or die. The ship had not yet begun the piloted phase of its journey; it had merely been catapulted through time and space by the physics-defying technology of the Jump. Now they were spinning aimlessly, somewhere in the general vicinity of where they needed to be, a ship in the shape of a swollen tick: big belly of fuel, tiny head. And inside that head, four men were breathing from a limited supply of nitrogen, oxygen and argon. They were breathing faster than necessary. Unspoken, but hanging in the filtered air, was the fear that the Jump might have slung them too far wide of the mark, and that there might be insufficient fuel for the final part of the journey. A margin for error that was almost unmeasurably small at the beginning of the Jump could have grown into a fatal enormity at the other end.

Tuska studied the numbers, tickled the keyboard with nimble stubby fingers, scrolled through geometrical designs that were, in fact, maps of the unmappable.

"Good news, people," he said at last. "Looks like practice makes perfect."

"Meaning?" said Severin.

"Meaning we should send a prayer of thanks to the tech-heads in Florida."

"Meaning what, exactly, for us, here?"

"Meaning that when we divide the fuel over the distance we've got to travel, we've got *lots* of juice. We can use it up like it's beer at a frat party."

"Meaning how many days, Tuska?"

"Days?" Tuska paused for effect. "Twenty-eight hours, tops."

BG leapt to his feet and punched the air. "*Whooo*-hoo!"

From this moment onward, the atmosphere in the control room was triumphal, slightly hysterical. BG paced around restlessly, pumping his arms, doing the locomotion. Severin grinned, revealing teeth discolored by nicotine, and drummed on his knees to a tune only he could hear. To simulate the cymbal-clashes, he flicked his fist periodically into empty air and winced as though buffeted by joyful noise. Tuska went off to change his clothes—maybe because he'd got a noodle stain on his sweater, or maybe because he felt his imminent piloting duties warranted a ceremonial gesture. Freshly decked out in a crisp white shirt and gray trousers, he took his seat at the keyboard on which their trajectory to Oasis would be typed.

"Just do it, Tuska," said Severin. "What do you want, a brass band? Cheerleaders?"

Tuska blew a kiss, then made a decisive keystroke. "Gentlemen and crew sluts," he declared, in a mockingly oratorical tone. "Welcome onboard the USIC shuttle service to Oasis. Please give your full attention to the safety demonstration even if you are a frequent flyer. The seatbelt is fastened and unfastened as shown. No seatbelt on your seat? Hey, live with it."

He jabbed another key. The floor began to vibrate.

"In the event of a loss of cabin pressure, oxygen will be provided. It will be pumped straight into the mouth of the pilot. The rest of you just hold your breath and sit tight." (Laughter from BG and Severin.) "In the event of a collision, low-level lighting will guide you to an exit, where you will be sucked instantly to your death. Please remember that the nearest usable planet may be three billion miles behind you."

He jabbed another key. A graph on the computer screen began to rise and fall like waves. "This craft is equipped with one emergency escape pod: one at the front, none in the middle and none at the rear. There's room for the pilot and five really hot chicks." (Guffaws from BG; snickering from Severin.) "Take your high heels off, girls, before using the escape pod. Hell, take it *all* off. Blow on my tube if it fails to inflate. There is a light and a whistle for attracting attention, but don't worry, I'll get around to all of you in turn. Please consult the instruction card that shows you the position you must adopt if you hear the command 'Suck, suck.' We recommend you keep your head down at all times."

He made one more keystroke, then held a fist up in the air. "We appreciate that you had no choice of airlines today, and so we would like to thank you for choosing USIC."

Severin and BG applauded and whooped. Peter put his hands together shyly, but made no noise with them. He hoped he could stand by unobtrusively, part of the gathering but not subject to scrutiny. It was, he knew, not a very impressive start to his mission to win the hearts and souls of an entire population. But he hoped he could be forgiven. He was far from home, his head ached and buzzed, the beef noodles sat in his stomach like a stone, he kept hallucinating that his body parts had been disassembled and put back together slightly wrong, and all he wanted to do was crawl into bed with Beatrice and Joshua and go to sleep. The grand adventure could surely wait.

4

"HELLO EVERYBODY,"

HE SAID.

Dear Bea,

Finally, a chance to communicate with you properly! Shall we call this my First Epistle to the Joshuans? Oh, I know we both have our misgivings about St. Paul and his slant on things, but the guy sure knew how to write a good letter and I'm going to need all the inspiration I can get, especially in my current state. (Half-delirious with exhaustion.) So, until I can come up with something wonderfully original: "Grace be unto you, and peace, from God our Father, and from the Lord Jesus Christ." I doubt whether Paul had any women in mind when he wrote that greeting, given his problems with females, but maybe if he'd known YOU, he would have!

I would love to put you in the picture, but there's not much to describe yet. No windows in this ship. There are millions of stars out there and possibly other amazing sights, but all I can see is the walls, the ceiling and the floor. It's a good thing I'm not claustrophobic.

I'm writing this with pencil and paper. (I had a bunch of pens but they must have exploded during the Jump—there's ink all over the insides of my bag. No surprise they didn't survive the trip, given how my own head felt . . . !) Anyway, when sophisticated technology fails, primitive technology steps in to do the job. Back to the sharpened stick with the sliver of graphite inside, and the sheets of pressed wood-pulp . . .

Have I gone insane, you're wondering? No, don't worry (yet). I'm not under the delusion I can put this letter in an envelope and stick a stamp on it. I'm still in transit—we've got about 25 hours' journey left to go. As soon as I'm on Oasis and settled in, I'll transcribe these jottings. Someone will plug me into the network and I'll be able to send a message to the thing that USIC installed in our house. And you can forget about calling it a "Zhou-23 Messenger Mainframe" like we were told to. I mentioned that term to the guys here and they just laughed. They refer to it as a Shoot. Typical of Americans to shorten everything to a monosyllable. (It's catchy, though.)

I suppose, instead of waiting a whole day, I could use the Shoot that's here on board, especially since I'm too wound up to sleep and it would be a good way of filling the time until we land. But it wouldn't be private, and I need privacy for what I'm going to say next. The other men on this ship are—how can I put this?—not exactly models of discretion and sensitivity. If I wrote this on their machine, I can just imagine one of them retrieving my message and reading it out loud, to general hilarity.

Bea, forgive me for not being able to let this go, but I'm still upset about what happened in the car. I feel I let you down. I wish I could take you in my arms and make it right. It's a silly thing to obsess about, I know. I suppose it just makes me confront how far away we are from each other now. Have any husband and wife ever been separated by so vast a distance? It seems like only yesterday I could reach out my arm and you'd be right there. On our last morning in bed together, you looked so satisfied and serene. But in the car you looked distraught.

As well as being shaken about that, I can't say I'm feeling confident about my mission. It's probably just physical and temporary, but I wonder if I'm up to it. The other men on the ship, raucous though they are, have been very nice to me, in a condescending sort of way. But I'm sure they're wondering why USIC would pay a fortune to transport me to Oasis, and I must admit I'm confused myself. Each member of the team has a clearly defined role.

Tuska (not sure of his Christian name) is the pilot, and on Oasis he works with computers. Billy Graham, nicknamed BG, is an engineer with huge experience in the oilmining industry. Arthur Severin is another sort of engineer, something to do with hydro-metallurgical processes; it's way above my head. In conversation, these guys come across like construction workers (and I suppose they are!) but they're a lot cleverer than they appear and, unlike me, they are supremely qualified for their assignments.

Well, I think that's enough self-doubt for one day!

The part of this letter that I scribbled on the ship has now come to an end—I didn't manage to achieve much with my pencil and paper, did I? Everything from here on is written (well, typed) on Oasis. Yes, I've arrived, I'm here! And the first thing I'm doing is writing to you.

It was a safe landing—weirdly smooth in fact, not even the shuddery bump you get when an airplane's wheels hit the ground. More like a lift arriving at the correct floor. I would have preferred something more dramatic, or even frightening, to dispel the sense of unreality. Instead, you're told that you've landed, the doors open, and you walk out into one of those tube-tunnel things just like at an airport, and then you're in a big ugly building that looks like any other big ugly building you've ever been in. I expected something more exotic, something architecturally outlandish. But maybe the same people designed this place as designed USIC's facilities in Florida.

Anyway, I'm in my quarters now. I'd assumed that upon arrival I would immediately have to be ferried somewhere else, a journey across some amazing terrain. But the airport—if you can call it that, it's more like a huge car park—has several wings of accommodation facilities attached to it. I've been shunted from one box to another.

Not that my quarters are small. In fact the bedroom is bigger than our bedroom, there's a proper bathroom/shower (which I'm too tired to use yet), a fridge (completely empty except for a plastic ice-cube tray, also empty), a table, two chairs and, of course, the Shoot that I'm typing this on. The ambience is very "hotel chain"; I could be in a conference center in Watford. But I expect I'll be asleep very soon. Severin told me that it's quite common for people to experience insomnia for a couple of days after the Jump, and then to sleep for 24 hours straight. I'm sure he knows what he's talking about.

We parted on slightly awkward terms, Severin and I. The fact that the Jump's aim was more accurate than expected meant that, even with unrestricted use of fuel to get us to Oasis in the fastest possible time, we still had a huge amount left over. So we just jettisoned it all before arrival. Can you imagine? Thousands of liters of fuel squirted out into space, along with our body wastes, dirty tissues, empty noodle containers. I couldn't help saying, Surely there must be a better way. Severin took offense (I think he was sticking up for Tuska, who was technically responsible for the decision—those two have a love/hate thing going). Anyway, Severin asked me if I thought I could land a ship with that much fuel "hanging off its ass." He said it was like tossing a bottle of milk off a skyscraper and hoping it wouldn't come to any harm when it reached the ground. I said that if science could come up with something like the Jump it could surely solve a problem like that. Severin seized hold of that word, "science." Science, he said, is not some mysterious larger-than-life force, it's just the name we give to the bright ideas that individual guys have when they're lying in bed at night, and that if the fuel thing bothered me so much, there was nothing stopping me from having a bright idea to solve it and submitting it to USIC. He said it in an off-hand sort of tone but there was aggression behind it. You know how men can be.

I can't believe I'm talking about a spat I had with an engineer! By the grace of God I've been sent to another world, the first Christian missionary ever to do so, and here I am gossiping about my fellow travelers!

My dear Beatrice, please regard this First Epistle as a prelude, a trial run, a rough turning over of the soil before I plant something beautiful in it. That's partly why I decided to transcribe the penciled scribblings I wrote on the ship, and type them unchanged and unedited into this Shoot message to you. If I changed one sentence I would be tempted to change them all; if I gave myself permission to omit one dull detail I'd probably end up discarding the whole thing. Better that you get these jetlagged, barely coherent ramblings than nothing.

I'm going to go to bed now. It's night. It will be night for the next three days, if you know what I mean. I haven't seen the sky yet, not properly, just a glimpse through the transparent ceiling of the arrivals hall as I was being escorted to my quarters. A very solicitous USIC liaison officer whose name I've forgotten was chattering at me and trying to carry my bag and I just sort of got swept along. My quarters have big windows but they're shuttered with a Venetian blind that's presumably electronic and I'm too tired & disoriented to figure out how it works. I should get some sleep before I start pressing buttons. Except, of course, for the button I will now press to send this message to you.

Shoot through space, little light beams, and bounce off all the right satellites to reach the woman I love! But how can these words, translated into blinks of binary code, travel so impossibly far? I won't quite believe it until I get a reply from you. If I can be granted that one small miracle, all the others will follow, I'm sure.

Love,

Peter

He slept, and awoke to the sound of rain.

For a long time he lay in the dark, too weary to stir, listening. The rain sounded different from rain back home. Its intensity waxed and waned in a rapid cyclical rhythm, three seconds at most between surges. He synchronized the fluctuations with his own breathing, inhaling when the rain fell softer, exhaling when it fell hard. What made the rain do that? Was it natural, or was it caused by the design of the building: a wind-trap, an exhaust fan, a faulty portal opening and closing? Could it be something as mundane as his own window flapping in the breeze? He could see no further than the slats of the Venetian blind.

Eventually his curiosity got the better of his fatigue. He staggered out of bed, fumbled for the bathroom light, was momentarily blinded by halogen overkill. He squinted at his watch, the only item of apparel he'd kept on when he'd gone to bed. He'd slept . . . how long? . . . only seven hours . . . unless he'd slept thirty-one. He checked the date. No, only seven. What had woken him? His erection, perhaps.

The bathroom was in all respects identical to a bathroom one might expect to find in a hotel, except that the toilet, instead of employing a flush mechanism, was the kind that sucked out its contents in a whoosh of compressed air. Peter pissed slowly and with some discomfort, waiting for his penis to unstiffen. His urine was dark orange. Alarmed, he filled a glass with water from the tap. The liquid was pale green. Clean and transparent, but pale green. Stuck to the wall above the sink was a printed notice: COLOR OF WATER IS GREEN. THIS IS NORMAL AND CERTIFIED SAFE. IF IN DOUBT, BOTTLED WATER & SOFT DRINKS ARE AVAILABLE, SUBJECT TO AVAILABILITY, FROM USIC STORE, $50 PER 300ML.

Peter stared at the glass of green liquid, parched but wary. All those stories of British tourists drinking foreign water while on holiday and getting poisoned. Delhi belly and all that. Two reassuring Scripture quotations came to his mind, "Take no thought for what ye shall drink" from *Matthew 6:25* and "To the pure, all things are pure" from *Titus 1:15*, but those were clearly meant for other contexts. He looked again at the placard for the bottled alternative: $50 PER 300ML. Out of the question. He and Bea had already discussed what they would do with the money he earned on this mission. Pay off their mortgage. Rebuild the nursery room of their church so the children had more light and sunshine. Buy a van adapted for wheelchairs. The list went on and on. Every dollar he spent here would cross something worthwhile off it. He lifted the glass and drank.

It tasted good. Divine, in fact. Was that a blasphemous thought? "Oh, give it a rest," Beatrice would no doubt advise him. "There are more important things in the world to fret about." What things might there be to fret about in *this* world? He would find out soon enough. He stood up, flushed the toilet, drank more of the green water. It tasted ever-so-slightly of honeydew melon, or maybe he was imagining that.

Still naked, he walked to the bedroom window. There must be a way of raising the blind, even though there were no switches or buttons in sight.

He felt around the edges of the slats, and his fingers snagged in a cord. He tugged on it and the blind lifted. It occurred to him as he continued pulling on the cord that he might be exposing his nakedness to anyone who happened to be passing by, but it was too late to worry about that now. The window—one large pane of Plexiglass—was wholly revealed.

Outside, darkness still ruled. The area surrounding the USIC airport complex was a wasteland, a dead zone of featureless bitumen, dismal shed-like buildings, and spindly steel lamps. It was like a supermarket car park that went on forever. And yet Peter's heart pumped hard, and he breathed shallowly in his excitement. The rain! The rain wasn't falling in straight lines, it was . . . dancing! Could one say that about rainfall? Water had no intelligence. And yet, this rainfall swept from side to side, hundreds of thousands of silvery lines all describing the same elegant arcs. It was nothing like when rain back home was flung around erratically by gusts of wind. No, the air here seemed calm, and the rain's motion was graceful, a leisurely sweeping from one side of the sky to the other—hence the rhythmic spattering against his window.

He pressed his forehead to the glass. It was blessedly cool. He realized he was running a slight fever, wondered if he was hallucinating the curvature of the rainfall. Peering out into the dark, he made an effort to focus on the hazes of light around the lampposts. Inside these halo-like spheres of illumination, the raindrops were picked out bright as tinfoil confetti. Their sensuous, undulating pattern could not be clearer.

Peter stepped back from the window. His reflection was ghostly, criss-crossed by the unearthly rain. His normally rosy-cheeked, cheerful face had a haunted look, and the tungsten glow of a distant lamppost blazed inside his abdomen. His genitals had the sculptured, alabaster appearance of Greek statuary. He raised his hand, to break the spell, to reorient himself to his own familiar humanity. But it might as well have been a stranger waving back.

My dear Beatrice,
No word from you. I feel as though I'm literally suspended—as though I can't let out my breath until I have proof that we can communicate with each other. I once read a Science Fiction story

in which a young man traveled to an alien planet, leaving his wife behind. He was only away for a few weeks and then he returned to Earth. But the punchline of the story was that Time passed at a different rate for her than it did for him. So when he got back home, he discovered that 75 earth years had sped by, and his wife had died the week before. He arrived just in time to attend the funeral, and all the old folks were wondering who this distraught young man might be. It was a cheesy, run-of-the-mill Sci-Fi tale but I read it when I was at an impressionable age and it really got to me. And of course now I'm scared it will come true. BG, Severin and Tuska have all been to Oasis & back several times over the years and I suppose I should take that as proof that you're not wrinkling up like a prune! (Although I would still love you if you did!)

As you can probably tell from my babbling, I'm still horribly jetlagged. Slept well but nowhere near enough. It's still dark here, smack dab in the middle of the three-day night. I haven't been outside yet, but I've seen the rain. The rain here is amazing. It sways backward and forward, like one of those bead curtains.

There's a well-appointed bathroom here and I've just had a shower. The water is green! Safe to drink, apparently. Wonderful to have a proper wash at last, even though I still smell odd (I'm sure you'd laugh to see me sitting here, sniffing my own armpits with a frown on my face) and my urine is a weird color.

Well, that's not the note I wanted to end on, but I can't think of anything else to say right now. I just need to hear from you. Are you there? Please speak!

Love,

Peter

Having sent this missive, Peter loitered around his quarters, at a loss for what to do next. The USIC representative who'd escorted him off the ship had made all the correct noises about being available for him if he needed anything. But she hadn't specified how this availability would work. Had she even divulged her name? Peter couldn't recall. There certainly wasn't any note left lying on the table, to welcome him, give him a few pointers and tell him how to get in touch. There was a red button on the wall labeled EMERGENCY, but no button labeled BEWILDERMENT. He spent quite a while searching for the key to his quarters, mindful that it might not look like a conventional key but might be a plastic card of the sort issued by hotels. He found nothing that even vaguely resembled a key. Eventually, he opened his door and examined the lock, or rather the place where a lock would be if there'd been one. There was only an old-fashioned swivel handle, as though Peter's quarters were a bedroom within an unusually large home. *In my father's house are many mansions.* USIC evidently wasn't concerned about security or privacy. OK, maybe its personnel had nothing to steal and nothing to hide, but even so . . . Odd. Peter looked up and down the corridor; it was vacant and his was the only door in view.

Back inside, he opened the fridge, verified that the empty ice cube tray was the only thing in it. An apple wouldn't have been too much to expect, would it? Or perhaps it would. He kept forgetting how far from home he was.

It was time to go out and face that.

He got dressed in the clothes he'd worn yesterday—underpants, jeans, flannel shirt, denim jacket, socks, lace-up shoes. He combed his hair, had another drink of greenish water. His empty stomach gurgled and grunted, having processed and eliminated the noodles he'd eaten on the ship. He strode to the door; hesitated, sank to his knees, bowed his head in prayer. He had not yet thanked God for delivering him safe to his destination; he thanked Him now. He thanked Him for some other things, too, but then got the distinct feeling that Jesus was standing at his back, prodding him, good-humoredly accusing him of stalling. So he sprang to his feet and left at once.

The USIC mess hall was humming, not with human activity, but with recorded music. It was a large room, one wall of which consisted almost wholly of glass, and the music hung around it like a fog, piped from vents in the ceiling. Apart from a vague impression of watery glitter on the window, the rain outside was felt rather than seen; it added a sense of cosy, muffled enclosure to the hall.

I stopped to see a weeping willow
Crying on his pillow
Maybe he's crying for me . . .

sang a ghostly female voice, seemingly channeled through miles of subterranean tunnels to emerge at last from an accidental aperture.

And as the skies turn gloomy,
Night blooms whisper to me,
I'm lonesome as I can be . . .

There were four USIC employees in the mess hall, all of them young men unknown to Peter. One, an overweight, crewcut Chinese, dozed in an armchair next to a well-stocked magazine rack, his face slumped on a fist. One was working at the coffee bar, his tall spindly body draped in an over-size T-shirt. He was intently fiddling with a touch-sensitive screen balanced on the counter, poking at it with a metal pencil. He chewed at his swollen lips with large white teeth. His hair was heavy with some sort of gelatinous haircare product. He looked Slavic. The other two men were black. They were seated at one of the tables, studying a book together. It was too large and slim to be a Bible; more likely a technical manual. At their elbows were large mugs of coffee and a couple of dessert plates, bare except for crumbs. Peter could smell no food in the room.

I go out walking after midnight,
Out in the starlight.
Just hoping you may be . . .

The three awake men noted his arrival with a nod of low-key welcome but did not otherwise interrupt what they were doing. The snoozing Asian and the two men with the book were all dressed the same: loose Middle

Eastern–style shirt, loose cotton trousers, no socks, and chunky sports shoes. Islamic basketball players.

"Hi, I'm Peter," said Peter, fronting up to the counter. "I'm new here. I'd love something to eat, if you've got it."

The Slavic-looking young man shook his prognathous face slowly to and fro.

"Too late, bro."

"Too late?"

"Twenty-four-hourly stock appraisal, bro. Began an hour ago."

"I was told by the USIC people that food is provided whenever we need it."

"Correct, bro. You just gotta make sure you don't need it at the wrong time."

Peter digested this. The female voice on the PA system had come to the end of her song. A male announcement followed, sonorous and theatrically intimate.

"You're listening to *Night Blooms*, a documentary chronicle of Patsy Cline's performances of 'Walkin' After Midnight' from 1957 right through to the posthumous duets in 1999. Well, listeners, did you do what I asked? Did you hold in your memory the girlish shyness that radiated from Patsy's voice in the version she performed for her debut on *Arthur Godfrey's Talent Scouts*? What a difference eleven months makes! The second version you've just heard was recorded on December 14, 1957, for the Grand Ole Opry. By then, she clearly had more of an inkling of the song's uncanny power. But the aura of wisdom and unbearable sadness that you'll hear in the *next* version owes something to personal tragedy, too. On June 14, 1961, Patsy was almost killed in a head-on car collision. Incredibly, only a few days after she left hospital, we find her performing 'After Midnight' at the Cimarron Ballroom in Tulsa, Oklahoma. Listen, people, listen closely, and you will hear the pain of that terrible auto accident, the grief she must have felt at the deep scars on her forehead, which never healed . . ."

The ghostly female voice wafted across the ceiling once more.

I go out walking after midnight,
Out in the moonlight just like we used to do.

I'm always walking after midnight,
Searching for you . . .

"When is the next food delivery?" asked Peter.

"Food's already here, bro," said the Slavic man, patting the counter. "Released for consumption in six hours and . . . twenty-seven minutes."

"I'm sorry, I'm new here; I didn't know about this system. And I really am very hungry. Couldn't you . . . uh . . . release something early, and just mark it as having been served in six hours from now?"

The Slav narrowed his eyes.

"That would be . . . committing an untruth, bro."

Peter smiled and hung his head in defeat. Patsy Cline sang *"Well, that's just my way of saying I love you . . ."* as he walked away from the counter and sat down in one of the armchairs near the magazine rack, directly behind the sleeping man.

As soon as his back sank into the upholstery he felt exhausted and he knew that if he didn't get up again, quite soon he would fall asleep. He leaned toward the magazines, taking a quick mental inventory of the selection. *Cosmopolitan, Retro Gamer, Men's Health, Your Dog, Vogue, Vintage Aircraft, Dirty Sperm Whores, House & Garden, Innate Immunity, Autosport, Science Digest, Super Food Ideas* . . . Pretty much the full range. Well-thumbed and only slightly out of date.

"Hey, preacher!"

He turned in his chair. The two black men sharing the table had shut their book, finished with it for the night. One of them was holding aloft a foil-wrapped object the size of a tennis ball, wiggling it demonstratively. As soon as he had Peter's attention, he tossed the object across the room. Peter caught it easily, without even a hint of a fumble. He had always been an excellent catcher. The two black men raised a friendly fist each, congratulating him. He unwrapped the foil, found a hunk of blueberry muffin.

"Thank you!" His voice sounded strange in the acoustics of the mess hall, competing with the DJ, who had resumed his exegesis of Patsy Cline. By this stage of the narrative, Patsy had perished in a plane crash.

". . . personal belongings left behind after the sale of her home. The tape passed from hand to hand, unrecognized for the treasure it was, before finally ending up stored in the closet of a jeweller for several years. Imagine it, friends! Those divine sounds you just heard, dormant inside an unassuming reel of magnetic tape, locked up in a dark closet, perhaps never to see the light of day. But we can be eternally grateful that the jeweller eventually woke up and negotiated a deal with MCA Records . . ."

The blueberry muffin was delicious; among the best things Peter had ever tasted. And how sweet it was, too, to know that he was in not altogether hostile territory.

"Welcome to Heaven, preacher!" called one of his benefactors, and everyone except the sleeping Asian laughed.

Peter turned to face them, beamed them a smile. "Well, things are certainly looking up from what they were a few minutes ago."

"Onwards and upward, preach! That's the USIC motto, more or less."

"So," said Peter, "do you guys like it here?"

The black man who'd thrown the muffin went pensive, considering the question seriously. "It's OK, man. As good as anywhere."

"Cool weather," his companion chipped in.

"He means nice *warm* weather."

"Which is *cool*, man, is what I'm saying."

"You know, I haven't even been outside yet," said Peter.

"Oh, you should go," said the first man, as though acknowledging the possibility that Peter might prefer to spend his entire Oasis sojourn inside his quarters. "Check it out before the light comes up."

Peter stood up. "I'd like that. Where's . . . uh . . . the nearest door?"

The coffee bar attendant pointed a long, bony finger past an illuminated plastic sign that said ENJOY! in large letters and, underneath in smaller print, EAT AND DRINK RESPONSIBLY. REMEMBER THAT BOTTLED WATER, CARBONATED SOFT DRINKS, CAKES, CONFECTIONERY AND YELLOW-STICKERED ITEMS ARE NOT INCLUDED IN THE FOOD AND DRINK ALLOWANCE AND WILL BE DEDUCTED FROM YOUR EARNINGS.

"Thanks for the tip," said Peter, as he was leaving. "And the food!"

"Have a good one, bro."

The last thing he heard was Patsy Cline's voice, this time in a celebrity duet recorded, through the miracle of modern technology, decades after her death.

* * *

Peter stepped through the sliding door into the air of Oasis and, contrary to his apprehensions, he did not instantly die, get sucked into an airless vortex, or shrivel up like a scrap of fat on a griddle. Instead, he was enveloped in a moist, warm breeze, a swirling balm that felt like steam except that it didn't make his throat catch. He strolled into the dark, his way unlit except by several distant lamps. In the dreary environs of the USIC airport, there was nothing much to see anyway, just acres of wet black bitumen, but he'd wanted to walk outside, and so here he was, walking, outside.

The sky was dark, dark aquamarine. Aquamareeeeeen, as BG might say. There were only a few dozen stars visible, far fewer than he was used to, but each one shone brightly, without any flicker, and with a pale green aura. There was no moon.

The rain had stopped now, but the atmosphere still seemed substantially composed of water. If he closed his eyes, he could almost imagine he'd waded into a warm swimming pool. The air lapped against his cheeks, tickled his ears, flowed over his lips and hands. It penetrated his clothing, breathing into the collar of his shirt and down his backbone, making his shoulderblades and chest dewy, making his shirtcuffs adhere to his wrists. The warmth—it was extreme warmth rather than heat—caused his skin to prickle with sweat, making him intimately aware of his armpit hair, the clefts of his groin, the shape of his toes inside their humid footwear.

He was dressed all wrong. Those USIC guys with their loose Arabic duds had it sussed, didn't they? He would have to emulate them as soon as possible.

As he walked, he tried to sort out which unusual phenomena were occurring inside of him and which were external realities. His heart was beating a little faster than usual; he put that down to excitement. His gait was a little wonky, as though skewed by alcohol; he wondered if he was merely suffering the after-effects of the Jump, jetlag, and general exhaustion. His feet seemed to bounce slightly with every step, as though the bitumen was rubberized. He knelt for a moment and rapped on the ground with his knuckles. It was hard, unyielding. Whatever it was made of—presumably some combination of the local earth and imported chemicals—it had an asphalt-like consistency. He stood up, and the action of standing was perhaps easier than it should be. An ever-so-slight trampoline effect. But this was counterbalanced by the watery density of the air. He lifted his hand, pushed his palm forward into space, testing for resistance. There was none, and yet the air swirled around his wrist and up his forearm, tickling him. He didn't know whether he liked it, or found it creepy. Atmosphere, in his experience, had always been an absence. The air here was a presence, a presence so palpable that he was tempted to believe he could let himself fall and the air would simply catch him like a pillow. It wouldn't, of course. But as it nuzzled against his skin, it almost promised that it would.

He took a deep breath, concentrating on the texture of it as it went in. It felt and tasted no different from normal air. He knew from the USIC brochures that the composition was much the same mix of nitrogen and oxygen he'd been breathing all his life, with a bit less carbon dioxide and a bit more ozone and a few trace elements he might not have had before. The brochures hadn't mentioned the water vapor, although Oasis's climate had been described as "tropical," so maybe that covered it.

Something tickled his left ear and, as a reflex, he brushed at it. Something squishy, like a wet cornflake or a rotting leaf, passed across his fingers but fell off before he could hold it up to his eyes and examine it. His fingers were streaked with a sticky fluid. Blood? No, not blood. Or if it was, it wasn't his. It was as green as spinach.

He turned around and looked at the building he'd emerged from. It was monumentally ugly, like all architecture not built by religious devotees or mad eccentrics. Its only redeeming feature was the transparency of the mess hall's window, lit up like a video screen in the dark. Although he'd walked quite a long way, he could still recognize the coffee bar and the magazine rack, and even fancied he could make out the Asian man still slumped on one of the chairs. At this distance, these details looked like a neat assortment of items stored inside a coin-operated dispenser. A luminous little box, surrounded by a great sea of strange air; and above it, a trillion miles of darkness.

He'd experienced moments like this before, on the planet that was supposed to be his home. Sleepless and wandering the streets of shabby British towns at two, three in the morning, he would find himself at a bus shelter in Stockport, a woebegone shopping mall in Reading, or the empty husks of Camden market in the hours before dawn—and it was at those times, in those places, that he was struck by a vision of human insignificance in all its unbearable pathos. People and their dwellings were such a thin dust on the surface of the globe, like invisible specks of bacteria on an orange, and the feeble lights of kebab shops and supermarkets failed utterly to register on the infinities of space above. If it weren't for God, the almighty vacuum would be too crushing to endure, but once God was with you, it was a different story.

Peter turned again and kept walking. His vague hope was that if he walked far enough, the featureless tarmac of the airport environs would finally come to an end, and he would step over into the landscape of Oasis, the real Oasis.

His denim jacket was growing heavy with moisture and his flannel shirt was swollen with perspiration. His jeans made a comical whooping noise as he walked, rough wet cotton rubbing against itself. The waistband was starting to chafe against his hips; a rivulet of sweat ran into the cleft of his arse. He stopped to hitch up his trousers and to wipe his face. He pressed his fingertips to his ears, to clear them of a sibilant undertone he'd been attributing to his sinuses. But the noise was not from within. The atmosphere was full of rustling. Worldless whispering, the sound of agitated leaves, except that there was no vegetation anywhere to be seen. It was as though the air currents, so similar to water currents, could not move silently, but must churn and hiss like ocean waves.

He was sure he'd adjust, in time. It would be like living near a railway line, or, indeed, near the ocean. After a while you wouldn't hear it anymore.

He walked further, resisting an impulse to remove his clothes and toss them on the ground for retrieval on his return. The tarmac showed no sign of ending. What could USIC possibly want with all this blank bitumen? Maybe there were plans to extend the accommodation wings, or build squash courts, or a shopping mall. Oasis was tipped, in "the very near future," to become a "thriving community." By which USIC meant a thriving community of foreign settlers, of course. This world's indigenous inhabitants, thriving or otherwise, were scarcely mentioned in USIC's literature, except for fastidious assurances that nothing was planned or implemented without their full and informed consent. USIC was "in partnership" with the citizens of Oasis—whoever they might be.

Peter was certainly very much looking forward to meeting them. They were, after all, the whole reason he had come.

From one of his jacket pockets, he extracted a compact camera. He'd been warned by the preparatory literature that it was "not practicable" to use a camera on Oasis, but he'd brought one anyway. "Not practicable"—what did that mean? Was it a veiled threat? Might his camera get impounded by authorities of some sort? Well, he would cross that bridge when he came to it. Right now, he wanted to take some pictures. For Bea. When he returned to her, any photo he'd bothered to snap would be worth a thousand words. He raised the gadget and captured the eerie tarmac, the lonely buildings, the glow of light from the cafeteria. He even tried to capture the aquamarine sky, but a quick inspection of the stored image confirmed it was a rectangle of pure black.

He pocketed the camera and walked on. How long had he been walking? His watch was not the illuminated digital kind; it was an old-fashioned one with hands, a gift from his father. He held it close to his face, trying to angle it so that it caught the light from the nearest lamp. But the nearest lamp was at least a hundred meters away.

Something glittered on his forearm, near the wristwatch band. Something alive. A mosquito? No, it was too big for that. A dragonfly, or some creature resembling a dragonfly. A tiny, trembling matchstick body shrouded in translucent wings. Peter wiggled his wrist, and the creature fell off. Or maybe it jumped, or flew, or got sucked into the swirling atmosphere. Whatever: it was gone.

He suddenly became aware that the whispering of the air was supplemented by a new noise, a mechanical whir, behind him. A vehicle cruised into view. It was steely-gray and bullet-shaped, with large wheels and thick vulcanized tires designed for rough terrain. The driver was difficult to make out through the tinted windscreen, but was humanoid in shape. The car slowed and came to a halt right next to him, its metal flank only a few inches from where he stood. Its headlights pierced the darkness he'd been heading for, revealing a wire-mesh perimeter fence that he would have reached in another minute or two of walking.

"Howdy."

A female voice, with an American accent.

"Hi," he replied.

"Let me give you a ride back."

It was the USIC woman who'd met him upon his arrival, the one who'd escorted him to his quarters and told him she was available if he needed anything. She opened the passenger door for him and waited, piano-playing her fingers on the steering wheel.

"I'd been hoping to walk a little farther, actually," said Peter. "Maybe meet some of the local . . . uh . . . people."

"We'll do that after sunrise," the woman said. "The settlement is about fifty miles away. You'll need a vehicle. Do you drive?"

"Yes."

"Good. Have you discussed requisition of a vehicle?"

"I don't think so."

"You don't think so?"

"Uh . . . my wife handled most of the practicalities with USIC. I don't know if they covered that."

There was a pause, then a good-natured laugh. "Please get in, or the air conditioning will get all messed up."

He swung into the car and closed the door. The air was dry and cool, and immediately made him aware that he was drenched to the skin. His feet, relieved of the weight of his body, made a sucking sound inside his socks.

The woman was dressed in a white smock, thin white cotton slacks and a taupe headscarf that hung loose over her chest. Her face was bare of makeup, and she had a puckered scar on her forehead, just under the hairline. Her hair, a lusterless brown, was very short and she might have passed for a young male soldier were it not for her soft dark eyebrows, tiny ears and pretty mouth.

"I'm sorry," said Peter. "I've forgotten your name. I was very tired . . ."

"Grainger," she said.

"Grainger," he said.

"Christian names aren't a big thing among USIC employees, in case you haven't noticed."

"I've noticed."

"It's a bit like the army. Except we don't harm people."

"I should hope not."

She revved the engine and steered the car back toward the airport complex. As she drove, she leaned forward, frowning in concentration, and even though the inside of the cabin was poorly lit, he spotted the tell-tale edges of contact lenses on her eyeballs. Beatrice was a contact lens wearer: that's how he knew.

"Did you come out specially to fetch me?"

"Yes."

"Are you watching my every move? Keeping tabs on my every half-muffin?"

The allusion was lost on her. "I just dropped by the mess hall, and one of the guys said you'd gone out walking."

"Does that worry you?" He kept his tone light and amiable.

"You've just arrived," she said, not taking her eyes off the windscreen. "We wouldn't want you to come to harm on your first foray out of doors."

"What about the disclaimer I signed? The one that emphasizes in twelve different ways that USIC accepts no responsibility for anything that might happen to me?"

She seemed nettled by this. "That was a legalistic document written by paranoid lawyers who've never even been here. I'm a nice person and I'm here and I welcomed you off that ship and I said I would keep an eye out for you. So that's what I'm doing."

"I appreciate that," he said.

"I take an interest in people," she said. "Gets me in trouble sometimes."

"I'll try not to get you in trouble," he said. The eerily-lit cafeteria seemed to be moving toward them in the dark, as if it was another vehicle threatening a head-on collision. He wished he hadn't been fetched back so soon. "I hope you understand that I didn't come here to sit and read magazines in a cafeteria. I want to go and find the people of Oasis, wherever they are. I'll probably live among them, if they'll let me. So it may not be feasible for you to . . . uh . . . keep an eye out for me."

She maneuvered the vehicle into a garage; they'd arrived.

"We'll cross that bridge when we come to it."

"I'm hoping to cross it pretty soon," he said, still maintaining a light tone. "As soon as possible. I don't mean to be pushy, but . . . I'm going to be pushy. When are you available to drive me out of here?"

She switched off the engine, removed her small feet from the pedals. "Give me an hour to get things ready."

"Things?"

"Food, mainly. You'll have noticed that the mess hall isn't serving right now."

He nodded, and a ticklish trickle of sweat ran down his face. "I can't really figure out how the day/night routine is supposed to work, if it's dark for three days straight. I mean, right now, it's officially night, yes?"

"Yes, it's night." She rubbed her eyes, but gingerly, so as not to dislodge the lenses.

"So do you just let the clock decide when the days begin and end?"

"Sure. It's not much different than living in the Arctic Circle, I guess. You adjust your sleep pattern so that you're awake when everybody else is."

"What about those guys in the mess hall right now?"

She shrugged. "Stanko's scheduled to be there because he's on night duty. The other guys . . . well, people get insomnia sometimes. Or they get all slept out."

"What about the people of Oasis—the . . . uh . . . natives? Are they asleep right now? I mean, should we wait until the sun comes up?"

She faced him with an unblinking, defensive stare. "I have no idea when they sleep. Or even *if* they sleep. To be straight with you, I know almost nothing about them, even though I probably know more than anyone here. They're . . . kind of hard to get to know. I'm not sure they *want* to be known."

He grinned. "Nevertheless . . . I'm here to know them."

"OK," she sighed. "It's your call. But you look tired. Are you sure you've had enough rest?"

"I'm fine. What about you?"

"Fine also. Like I said, give me an hour. If, in that time, you change your mind and want to sleep some more, let me know."

"How would I do that?"

"The Shoot. There's a scroll-down menu behind the USIC icon. I'm on it."

"Glad to hear there's one menu that's got something on it." He meant it as a rueful comment on the mess hall, but as soon as the words left his mouth, he worried she might take them the wrong way.

She opened her door, he did the same on his side, and they stepped out into the moist swirling dark.

"Any other advice?" he called over the top of the vehicle.

"Yes," she shot back. "Forget the denim jacket."

The power of suggestion? She'd told him he looked tired and he hadn't felt tired when she said it, but he felt tired now. Befuddled, too. As though the excessive humidity had seeped into his brain and fogged his thoughts. He hoped Grainger would escort him all the way back to his quarters, but she didn't. She led him into the building through a different door from the one he'd used as an exit, and, within half a minute, was bidding him au revoir at a T-junction in the corridors.

He walked off in the opposite direction from her, as she clearly expected him to, but he had no clear idea where he was going. The passage was empty and silent and he couldn't recall having seen it before. The walls were painted a cheerful blue (turned somewhat darker by the subdued lighting) but were otherwise nondescript, with no signs or pointers. Not that there was any reason to expect a sign pointing to his quarters. USIC had made it clear, during one of the interviews, that he would not "in any way, shape or form" be the official pastor of the base and shouldn't be surprised if there wasn't much call for his services. His true responsibility was to the indigenous inhabitants. Indeed, that was his job description in the contract: *Minister (Christian) to Indigenous Population.*

"But you do have a minister for the USIC personnel's needs, surely?" he'd asked.

"Actually, at the moment, no," the interviewer had replied.

"Does that mean the colony is officially atheist?" Bea had asked.

"It's not a colony," another of the USIC interviewers said, with an edge to her voice. "It's a community. We do not use the word colony. And we do not promote any faith or lack of faith. We're looking for the best people, that's all."

"A pastor specifically for the USIC staff is a fine idea, in principle," the first interviewer reassured them. "Especially if he—or she—had other useful skills. We've included such individuals in the team at various times in the past. Right now, it's not a priority."

"But my mission *is* a priority?" Peter had said, still scarcely able to believe it.

"We would classify it 'urgent,'" the interviewer said. "So urgent, in fact, that I must ask you . . ." He leaned forward, looked straight into Peter's eyes. "How soon can you leave?"

Now there was a light glowing around the next bend in the corridor, and a faint harmonious noise which he identified, after a moment, as piped music. He had walked too far, failed to spot his own room, and ended up back at the mess hall.

When he reentered, he found that there had been a few changes. The ghostly croon of Patsy Cline had vanished from the airwaves, replaced by cocktail jazz so bland that it barely existed. The two black guys had left. The Chinese guy had woken up and was leafing through a magazine. A petite middle-aged woman, maybe Korean or Vietnamese, with a dyed streak of orange through her black hair, was staring meditatively at a cup in her lap. The Slavic-looking guy behind the counter was still on duty. He appeared not to notice Peter walking in, mesmerized as he was by a game he was playing with two squeezable plastic bottles—ketchup and mustard. He was trying to balance them against each other, tipped at an angle so that only their nozzles touched. His long fingers hovered above the fragile arrangement, ready to enfold the bottles when they fell.

Peter paused in the doorway, suddenly cold in his sweat-soaked denims and bedraggled hair. How ridiculous he must look! For just a few seconds, the sheer alienness of these people, and his irrelevance to them, threatened to flood his spirit with fear, the paralysis of shyness, the terror that a child feels when faced with a new school filled with strangers. But then God calmed him with an infusion of courage and he stepped forward.

"Hello everybody," he said.

5

JUST AS HE RECOGNIZED THEM
FOR WHAT THEY WERE.

In the eyes of God, all men and women are naked. Clothes are nothing more than a fig leaf. And the bodies beneath are just another layer of clothing, an outfit of flesh with an impractically thin leather exterior, in various shades of pink, yellow and brown. The souls alone are real. Seen in this way, there can never be any such thing as social unease or shyness or embarrassment. All you need do is greet your fellow soul.

At Peter's greeting, Stanko set the bottles to rights, looked up and grinned. The Chinese guy gave a thumbs-up salute. And the woman, who'd been dozing with her eyes open, unfortunately got a fright and jerked her legs, spilling coffee into her lap.

"Oh my . . . !" cried Peter, and rushed over to her. "I'm so sorry!"

She was wide awake now. She had on a loose smock and pants, much like Grainger's but beige. The spilled liquid added a large brown blotch.

"It's OK, it's OK," she said. "It wasn't that hot."

An object flew past Peter's face, landing on the woman's knee. It was a tea towel, tossed by Stanko. Calmly she began to swab and dab. She lifted the hem of her dress, revealing two damp patches on her gauzy cotton slacks.

"Can I help?" said Peter.

She laughed. "I don't think so."

"My wife uses vinegar on coffee stains," he said, keeping his eyes on her face so that she wouldn't think he was ogling her thighs.

"This isn't real coffee," the woman said. "Don't worry about it." She balled up the tea towel and placed it on the table, in an unhurried, methodical motion. Then she settled back into her chair, apparently in no rush to change. The jazz muzak lapsed into silence for a moment, then the cymbals and snare drum were tickled by a pair of brushes, the saxophone exhaled, and the noodling began once more. Stanko busied himself with something tactfully noisy, and the Chinese guy studied his magazine. Bless them, they were trying to give him space.

"Have I blown my chance to introduce myself?" he said. "I'm Peter."

"Moro. Pleased to meet you." The woman extended her right hand. He hesitated before shaking it, having noticed that one of her fingers ended at a knuckle stub and her pinky was missing altogether. He took hold and she squeezed, confidently.

"You know, that's very unusual," he said, sitting down next to her.

"Factory accident," she said. "Happens every day."

"No, I meant the way you offered me that hand. I've met lots of people with fingers missing from their right hand. They always offer the left one for a handshake. Because they don't want to make the other person feel uncomfortable."

She seemed mildly surprised. "Is that a fact?" Then she smiled and shook her head, as if to say, *Some people sure are weird.* Her gaze was direct and yet guarded, examining him for identifiers that could be logged in the as-yet empty file labeled Missionary From England.

"I just went out for a walk," he said, gesturing at the darkness outside. "My first time."

"Not much to see," she said.

"Well, it is night," he said.

"Even in daylight, there's not much to see. But we're working on that." She didn't sound proud or off-hand, just descriptive.

"What's your job here?"

"Engineering technologist."

He allowed himself to look bemused, signaling: *Please explain.* She parried with a look that signaled: *It's late and I'm tired.*

"Also," she said, "I do some work in the kitchens, cooking and baking, every ninety-six hours." She raked her fingers through her hair. There were gray roots under the glossy black and orange. "That's kinda fun, I look forward to that."

"Volunteer work?"

"No, it's all part of my schedule. You'll find a lot of us have more than one function here." She stood up. It wasn't until she extended her hand again that Peter realized their encounter was over.

"I'd better get cleaned up," she explained.

"Nice to have met you, Moro," he said.

"Likewise," she said, and walked out.

"Makes good dim sum parcels," said the Chinese man when she'd gone.

"Excuse me?" said Peter.

"Dim sum pastry is a difficult thing," said the Chinese man. "It's fragile. The dough. But it's gotta be thin or it's not dim sum. Tricky. But she's good at it. We can always tell when she's been on kitchen duty."

Peter moved to a vacant chair next to the Chinese man.

"I'm Peter," he said.

"Werner," said the Chinese man. His hand was five-fingered and pudgy, and exerted a carefully measured firmness in the handshake. "So, you've been exploring."

"Not much yet. I'm still very tired. Just got here."

"Takes a while to adjust. Those molecules in you gotta calm down. When's your first shift?"

"Uh . . . I don't really . . . I'm here as a pastor. I suppose I expect to be on duty all the time."

Werner nodded, but there was a hint of bemusement on his face, as though Peter had just confessed to signing a shonky contract without proper legal advice.

"Doing God's work is a privilege and a joy," said Peter. "I don't need any breaks from it."

Werner nodded again. Peter noted at a glance that the magazine he'd been reading was *Pneumatics & Hydraulics Informatics*, with a full-color cover photo of machine innards and the snappy headline "Making Gear Pumps More Versatile."

"This pastor thing . . ." said Werner. "What are you gonna be doing, exactly? On a day-to-day basis?"

Peter smiled. "I'll have to wait and see."

"See how the land lays," suggested Werner.

"Exactly," said Peter. Tiredness was swamping him again. He felt as if he might pass out right there in his chair, slide onto the floor for Stanko to mop up.

"I gotta admit," said Werner, "I don't know much about religion."

"And I don't know much about pneumatics and hydraulics," said Peter.

"Not my line, either," said Werner, reaching over with some effort to replace the magazine in the racks. "I just picked it up out of curiosity." He faced Peter again. There was something he wanted to clarify. "China didn't even *have* religion for a long time, under, like, one of the dynasties."

"What dynasty was that?" For some reason, the word "Tokugawa" popped into Peter's mind, but then he realized he was confusing Japanese and Chinese history.

"The Mao dynasty," said Werner. "It was bad, man. People getting killed left, right and center. Then things loosened up. People could do what they liked. If you wanted to believe in God, fine. Buddha, too. Shinto. Whatever."

"What about you? Were you ever interested in any faith?"

Werner peered up at the ceiling. "I read this huge book once. Must've been four hundred pages. Scientology. Interesting. Food for thought."

Oh, Bea, thought Peter, *I need you here by my side.*

"You gotta understand," Werner went on, "I've read a lot of books. I learn words from them. Vocabulary building. So if I ever come across a weird word one day, in a situation where it matters, I'm, like, ready for it."

The saxophone hazarded a squawk that might almost have been considered raucous, but immediately resolved itself into sweet melody.

"There are lots of Christians in China nowadays," Peter observed. "Millions."

"Yeah, but out of the total population it's, like, one percent, half of one percent, whatever. Growing up, I hardly ever met one. Exotic."

Peter drew a deep breath, fighting nausea. He hoped he was only imagining the sensation in his head, of his brain shifting position, adjusting its fit against the lubricated shell of his skull. "The Chinese . . . the Chinese are very focused on family, yes?"

Werner looked pensive. "So they say."

"Not you?"

"I was fostered. To a German military couple based in Chengdu. Then when I was fourteen they moved to Singapore." He paused; then, in case there might be doubt, he added: "With me."

"That must be a very unusual story for China."

"I couldn't give you stats. But, yeah. Very unusual, I'm sure. Nice folks, too."

"How do they feel about you being here?"

"They died," said Werner, with no change of expression. "Not long before I was selected."

"I'm sorry to hear that."

Werner nodded, to confirm agreement that his step-parents' demise was, in the final analysis, a regrettable event. "They were good folks. Supportive. A lot of the guys here didn't have that. I had that. Lucky."

"Are you in touch with anyone else back home?"

"There's a lot of folks I'd like to touch base with. Fine people."

"Any one special person?"

Werner shrugged. "I wouldn't rate them one over the other. All unique, you know. Talented. Some of them, I really owe. Like, they helped me. Gave me pointers, introduced me to . . . opportunities." His eyes went glassy as he reconnected, momentarily, with a distant past.

"When do you go back?" said Peter.

"Go back?" Werner took a second or two to decode the question, as though Peter had voiced it in an impenetrably thick accent. "Nothing scheduled for the foreseeable. Some guys, like Severin for instance, have been back and forth, back and forth, every few years. I'm like, why? It takes you three, four years to hit your stride. Acclimatization-wise, expertise-wise, focus-wise. It's a big project. After a while you get to the point where you can see how everything joins up with everything else. How the work of an engineer ties in with the work of a plumber and an electrician and a cook and a . . . a horticulturalist." His pudgy hands cupped an invisible sphere, to indicate some sort of holistic concept.

Suddenly, Werner's hands appeared to swell in size, each finger ballooning to the thickness of a baby's arm. His face changed shape, too, sprouting multiple eyes and mouths that swarmed loose from the flesh and swirled around the room. Then something hit Peter smack on the forehead. It was the floor.

A few seconds or minutes later, strong hands hooked under his shoulders and heaved him onto his back.

"Are you OK?" said Stanko, strangely unfazed by the delirious see-sawing of the walls and ceiling all around him. Werner, whose face and hands were back to normal, was likewise unaware of any problem—except the problem of a sweat-soaked, foolishly overdressed missionary sprawled insensible on the floor. "Are you with us, bro?"

Peter blinked hard. The room turned slower. "I'm with you."

"You need to be in bed," said Stanko.

"I think you're right," said Peter. "But I . . . I don't know where . . ."

"It'll be in the directory," said Stanko, and went off to check.

Within sixty seconds, Peter was being carried out of the mess hall and into the dim blue corridor by Stanko and Werner. Neither man was as strong as BG so they made slow and lurching progress, pausing every few meters to adjust their grip. Stanko's bony fingers dug into Peter's armpits and shoulders, sure to leave bruises, while Werner had the easy job, the ankles.

"I can walk, I can walk," said Peter, but he wasn't sure if that was true and his two Samaritans ignored him anyway. In any case, his quarters weren't far from the mess hall. Before he knew it, he was being laid down—or rather, dumped—on his bed.

"Nice talking with you," said Werner, panting slightly. "Good luck with . . . whatever."

"Just close your eyes and relax, bro," advised Stanko, already halfway to the door. "Sleep it off."

Sleep it off. These were words he'd heard many times before in his life. He had even heard them spoken by men who'd scooped him off a floor and carried him away—although usually to a dumping-place much less pleasant than a bed. On occasion, the guys who'd lugged him out of the nightclubs and other drinking-holes where he'd disgraced himself had given him a few kicks in the ribs before hoisting him up. Once, they'd tossed him into a back street and a delivery van had passed right over him, its tires miraculously missing his head and limbs, just tearing off a hunk of his hair. That was in the days before he was ready to admit there was a higher power keeping him alive.

Uncanny how similar the after-effects of the Jump were to extremes of alcohol abuse. But worse. Like the mother of all hangovers combined with a dose of magic mushrooms. Neither BG nor Severin had mentioned hallucinations, but maybe these guys were simply more robust than him. Or maybe they were both fast asleep right now, quietly recuperating instead of making fools of themselves.

He waited for the room to become a geometric space of fixed angles anchored in gravity, and then he got up. He checked the Shoot for messages. Still no word from Bea. Perhaps he should have asked Grainger to come to his room to check his machine, make sure he was using it correctly. But it was night and she was a woman and he barely knew her. Nor would their relationship have got off to an auspicious start if he'd hallucinated that she was sprouting multiple eyes and mouths and then collapsed at her feet.

Besides, the Shoot was so simple to operate that he couldn't imagine how anyone—even a technophobe like himself—might misunderstand it. The thing sent and received messages: that was all. It didn't play movies, make noises, offer to sell him products, inform him about the plight of mistreated donkeys or the Brazilian rainforest. It didn't offer him the opportunity to check the weather in southern England or the current number of Christians in China or the names and dates of dynasties. It just confirmed that his messages had been sent, and that there was no reply.

Abruptly he glimpsed—not on the matte gray screen of the Shoot, but in his own mind—a picture of tangled wreckage on an English motorway, at night, garishly lit by the headlights of emergency vehicles. Bea, dead, somewhere on the road between Heathrow and home. Loose pearls scattered across the asphalt, black slicks of blood. A month ago already. History. Such things could happen. One person embarks on an outrageously hazardous journey and arrives unscathed; another goes for a short, routine drive and gets killed. "God's sick sense of humor," as one grieving parent (soon to leave the church) had once put it. For a few seconds, the nightmarish vision of Beatrice lying dead on the road was real to Peter, and a nauseous thrill of terror passed through his guts.

But no. He mustn't let himself be deluded by imaginary horrors. God was never cruel. Life could be cruel, but not God. In a universe made dangerous by the gift of free will, God could be relied upon for support no matter what happened, and He appreciated the potentials and limitations of each of His children. Peter knew that if anything awful happened to Bea, there was no way he'd be able to function here. The mission would be over before it began. And if there was one thing that had become clear in all the months of thought and prayer leading up to his journey to Oasis, it was that God really wanted him here. He was safe in God's hands, and so was Bea. She must be.

As for the Shoot, there was one easy way of checking whether he was using it correctly. He located the USIC icon—a stylized green scarab—on the screen, and clicked open the menu behind it. It wasn't much of a menu, just three items: *Maintenance (repairs)*, *Admin* and *Graigner,* obviously set up in haste by Grainger herself. If he wanted a more substantial list of correspondents, it was up to him to organize it.

He opened a fresh message page, and wrote:

Dear Grainger. Then deleted "Dear" and substituted "Hi," then deleted that and just had "Grainger," then reinstated "Dear," then deleted it again. Unwarranted intimacy versus unfriendly brusqueness . . . a flurry of confused gestures before communication could begin. Letter-writing must have been so much easier in the olden days when everyone, even the bank manager or the tax department, was Dear.

> Hi Grainger.
> You were right. I am tired. I should sleep some more. Sorry for any inconvenience.
>> Best wishes,
>> Peter

Laboriously, he undressed. Every item of his clothing was swollen with damp, like he'd been caught in a downpour. His socks peeled away from his wrinkled feet like muddy clumps of foliage. His trousers and jacket clung obstinately to him, resisting his attempts to tug free. Everything he removed weighed heavy and fell to the floor with a dull whump. At first, he thought that fragments of his clothing had actually crumbled off and rolled across the floor, but on closer inspection, the loose bits were dead insects. He picked up one of the bodies and held it between his fingers. The wings had lost their silvery translucence, and were stained red with dye. Legs had been lost. It was an effort, actually, to perceive this mangled husk as an insect at all: it looked and felt like the pulverized remains of a hand-rolled cigarette. Why had these creatures hitched a ride in his clothes? He'd probably killed them just by the friction of walking.

Remembering the camera, he fished it out of his jacket pocket. It was slippery with moisture. He switched it on, intending to review the pictures he'd taken of the USIC perimeter and to snap a few more here, to show Bea his quarters, his sodden clothes, maybe one of the insects. A spark leapt from the mechanism, stinging him, and the light died. He held the camera in his hand, staring down at it as though it were a bird whose tiny heart had burst from fright. He knew the thing was unfixable and yet he half-hoped that if he waited a while, it would hiccup back into life. Just a moment ago, it had been a clever little storehouse of memories for Bea, a trove of images which would come to his aid in a near future he'd already inhabited in his imagination. Him and Bea on the bed, the gadget glowing between them, her pointing, him following the line of her finger, him saying "That? Oh, that was . . ." "And that was . . ." "And that was . . ." Now suddenly none of it was. In his palm lay a small metal shape with no purpose.

As the minutes passed, he became aware that his naked flesh smelled strange. It was that same faint honeydew melon scent he detected in the drinking water. The atmosphere swirling around out there had not been content merely to lick and stroke his skin, it had made him fragrant, as well as provoking copious sweat.

He was too tired to wash, and a slight quaver in the straight line of the skirting board warned him that the whole room might soon start moving again if he didn't shut his eyes and rest. He collapsed on the bed and slept for an eternity which, when he awoke, turned out to have been forty-odd minutes.

He checked the Shoot for messages. Nothing. Not even from Grainger. Maybe he didn't know how to use this machine after all. The message he'd sent Grainger was not a foolproof test, because he'd worded it in such a way that it hadn't strictly required a response. He thought for a minute, then wrote:

Hello again Grainger,
Sorry to bother you, but I haven't noticed any phones or any other method of getting hold of somebody directly. Are there none?
      Best wishes,
      Peter

He showered, toweled himself half-dry and lay on the bed again, still naked. If his messages to Grainger had failed to get through and she turned up a few minutes from now, he would wrap himself in a sheet and talk to her through the door. Unless she walked right in without knocking. She wouldn't do that, would she? Surely the social conventions of the USIC base weren't *that* different from the norm? He looked around the room for a suitable object to wedge against the door, but there was nothing.

Once, years ago, while going through the complicated procedure of locking up the church (deadbolts, padlocks, mortice locks, even a chain), he'd suggested to Beatrice that they should have an open-door policy.

"But we do," she'd said, puzzled.

"No, I mean no locks at all. The doors open to anyone, any time. 'Entertaining angels unawares,' as the Scripture puts it."

She'd stroked his head as if he were a child. "You're sweet."

"I'm serious."

"So are the drug addicts."

"We don't have any drugs here. And nothing that could be sold for drugs." He gestured at the walls decorated with children's drawings, the pews with their comfy old cushions, the wobbly lectern, the stacks of well-worn Bibles, the general absence of silver candelabras, antique sculptures and precious ornaments.

Bea sighed. "Anything can be sold for drugs. Or at least the person can try. If he's desperate enough." And she gave him a *You'd know all about that, wouldn't you?* look.

Indeed, he knew all about that. He just had a tendency to forget.

* * *

Despite his resolution to stay awake until the time Grainger might show up if she hadn't received his message, Peter fell asleep. Two hours passed and, when he woke, the room was stable and the view through the window was unchanged: lonesome expanses of darkness, speckled with eerie lamplight. He shambled out of bed and his foot kicked something flimsy across the floor: one of his socks, dried out and stiff, transformed from cotton into cardboard. He sat at the Shoot and read a fresh response from Grainger that had his own "sorry to bother you" lure hanging off it.

A telephone call would have bothered me a lot more, she wrote, especialy if Id been asleep. No, there are no phones. USIC tried setting them up in the early days but reception ranged from lousy to nonexistant. The atmosphere is wrong, too thick or something. So weve done without. And its been OK. Lets face it, most of what phones get used for is a total waste of time anyway. Weve got red buttons all over the place for emergencies (and never need them!). Our work schedules are on printed rosters so we know where to turn up and what to do. As far as chat goes we talk face to face if were not too busy—and if were too busy we shouldnt be trying to chat. When special announcements need to be made, we pipe them over the PA. We can use the Shoot also but most people wait until they can discuss things face to face. Everybodys an expert here and discussions can get quite technical and then theres the give+take of problem solving in situ. Writing stuff down so as the other person can understand it and then waiting for an answer is a nightmare.
Hope this helps,
    Grainger.

He smiled. In one sentence, she'd flushed thousands of years of written communication briskly down the toilet, having already discarded a century and a half of telephone use in the previous dump. The "hope this helps" chaser was a cute touch, too. Chutzpah of a kind.

* * *

Still smiling, and picturing the boyish face of Grainger in his head, he checked for messages from Beatrice, not really expecting any. A long scroll of text manifested on the screen and, because it appeared instantaneously, without fuss or fanfare, he was slow to recognize it for what it was. The screen was full to overflowing. He looked into the nest of words, and spotted the name Joshua. A cluster of six letters, meaningless to most other people, but it sprang into his soul and made it come alive with vivid images: Joshua's paws, with their comical white tufts between the pink pads; Joshua covered in plaster dust from next door's renovations; Joshua performing his death-defying circus leap from the top of the fridge to the ironing board; Joshua scratching at the kitchen window, his soft cry inaudible over the peak-hour traffic; Joshua asleep in the basket of dried washing; Joshua on the kitchen table, stroking his furry jaw against the earthenware teapot that never got used for any other purpose than this; Joshua in bed with him and Bea. And then he saw Bea: Bea only half-covered by the yellow duvet, reluctant to move because the cat was asleep against her thigh. Bea's ribcage and bosom, poking through the threadbare cotton of her favorite T-shirt which was too old to be worn in public anymore but which was just right for bed. Bea's neck, long and smooth except for two pale creases like seams. Bea's mouth, her lips.

Dear Peter, her letter began.

Oh, the preciousness to him of those words! If there'd been no more to her message than this, he would have been satisfied. He would have read Dear Peter, Dear Peter, Dear Peter over and over, not out of vanity, but because these were words from her to him.

Dear Peter,
I'm crying with relief as I write this. Knowing that you're alive has made me all shaky and woozy, as if I've been holding my breath for a month and I've finally let it out. Praise the Lord that He kept you safe.

What's it like where you are? I don't mean the room, I mean outside, the whole place in general. Please tell me, I'm desperate to know. Have you taken any pictures?

As for me, relax, I haven't aged fifty years or even developed any wrinkles since you last saw me. Just some bags under my eyes from lack of sleep (more about that later).

Seriously, the last four weeks have been hard, not knowing if you would get there in one piece or if you were already dead and nobody told me. I kept loitering around this machine even though I knew that nothing would come through for ages yet.

Then when your message finally did come I wasn't here to receive it. I was trapped at work. I did a morning shift which went OK and I was about to go home but by 2:45 it was clear we would be 3 staff members down—Leah and Owen phoned in sick and Susannah just didn't turn up. No joy from the nursing agency so I was asked to stay on and do a double, which I did. Then at 11 PM, guess what?—half the night staff didn't show up either. So I was pressured to do a triple shift! Highly illegal, but do they care?

Tony from next door popped round to feed Joshua but didn't sound too happy when I phoned him. "We've all got problems," he said. All the more reason to help each other, I almost said. But he sounded stressed out. If this happens again, I may have to ask the students on the other side. I'd probably have to teach them how to use a tin opener.

Speaking of Joshua, he isn't coping well with your absence. He wakes me up at 4 AM, meowing in my ear and then flopping down demonstratively on your side of the bed. Then I lie awake until I have to get ready for work. Oh, the joys of being an abandoned mother.

I've been checking the news on my phone obsessively, in case there was a news report about you. I know that's daft. USIC is not exactly the world's most high-profile organization, is it? We'd never even heard of them before they approached you. But still . . .

Anyway, you're safe now—I'm so indescribably relieved. I've finally stopped trembling and I feel less woozy. I've read and re-read your two messages over and over! And yes, you're right to assume that it's better to write to me when your brain is scrambled than not to write at all. Perfection is not ours to achieve.

Which reminds me: please stop worrying about the last time we made love. I told you it was all right and it was (and is). The orgasm wasn't primarily what I wanted from the experience, trust me.

Also, stop worrying about what these guys (Severin etc) think of you. It's irrelevant. You didn't go to Oasis to impress them. You went to Oasis to witness to souls who have never heard of Jesus. In any case these USIC guys have jobs to do and you'll probably not see much of them.

I can't really picture the Oasis rain from your description but green water sounds a bit alarming. The weather here has been terrible since you left. Heavy downpours every day. I wouldn't say it's like bead curtains, more like getting a bucket of water emptied over your head. There's been flooding in some towns in the Midlands, cars floating down the street, etc. We're OK except that the toilet bowl is slow to drain after a flush, ditto the plughole in the shower cubicle. Not sure what's going on there. Too busy to get it seen to.

Life in our parish continues hectic. The situation with Mirah (?Meerah) and her husband has reached crisis point. She finally told him she's been attending our church and he hit the roof. Or to be more precise, he hit Mirah. Many times. Her face is a swollen mess, she can barely see. She says she wants to leave him and she needs our (my) help with the legalities—housing, employment, benefits, etc. I've been making some preliminary phone calls (ie, a few hours so far) but mainly just providing TLC. Her prospects for independence are not good. She can barely speak English, she's totally unskilled and to be honest I think she's of below average intelligence. I see my role as being there for her emotionally until her face heals a bit and she goes back to her husband. In the meantime I hope our house doesn't become the scene of an Arabic honor killing. I'm sure that would traumatize Joshua no end.

I know I sound flippant, but the bottom line is that I don't think Meerah (?Mirah—I'll have to get the spelling straight if I'm to be filling in application forms for Crisis Loans, etc) is ready to receive the support & strength she would get if she gave her heart to Christ. I think she's attracted to the friendly, tolerant atmosphere of our church and the tantalizing notion of being a free woman. She talks about being a Christian as if it's a gym club membership you can sign up for.

Well, I see that it's about 1:30 AM which is bad news for me because Joshua will no doubt wake me two and a half hours from now, and I'm not even in bed yet. I hear rain again. I love you and miss you. Don't worry about anything. Trust in Jesus. He has made the journey with you. (I only wish I had.) Remember that Jesus is working through you even at those times when you feel you're out of your depth.

As for our old friend Saint Paul, he might not approve of how much I wish I could curl up in bed next to you right now. But yes, let's quote his wise advice on other matters. My darling, we both know that the effects of your travels will eventually pass and you'll be rested and then you'll no longer be able to sit in your cosy quarters writing epistles to me and looking out at the rain. You'll have to open the door and start work. As Paul says, "Walk in wisdom toward them that are without, redeeming the time." And remember I'm thinking of you!

Kisses, hugs, and a headbutt from Joshua,

Beatrice

Peter read this letter eight or nine times at least before he could bear to part with it. Then he fetched his bag, the one that the Virgin check-in girl had doubted was enough for a one-way transatlantic flight, dumped it on the bed and zipped it open. It was time to get dressed for work.

Apart from his Bible, notepads, a second pair of jeans, polished black shoes, trainers, sandals, three T-shirts and three pairs of socks and underpants, the bag contained one item of apparel that had seemed uselessly exotic when he'd packed it, an item he'd figured he was about as likely to wear as a tutu or a tuxedo. The USIC interviewers had advised him that there was no particular dress code on Oasis but that if he intended to spend a significant amount of time outdoors, he might wish to invest in some Arabic-style garments. Indeed, they'd dropped strong hints that he might regret it if he didn't. So, Beatrice had bought him a dishdasha from the local cut-price Muslim outfitters.

"It was the plainest one I could find," she said, showing it to him a couple of nights before his departure. "They had ones with gold brocade, spangles, embroidery . . ."

He'd held it against his body. "It's very long," he said.

"It means you won't need trousers," she said, half-smiling. "You can be naked underneath. If you want."

He thanked her but didn't try it on.

"You don't think it's too girly, do you?" she said. "I think it's very masculine."

"It's fine," he said, packing it away. It wasn't effeminacy that worried him; it was that he couldn't imagine himself swanning about like an actor in an old Bible movie. It seemed vainglorious, and not at all what modern Christianity was about.

One walk in the Oasan atmosphere had changed all that. His denim jacket, still in a crumpled heap on the floor, had dried stiff as tarpaulin. An Arabic smock and pajama-style pants, such as he'd seen several of the USIC staff wearing, was probably the ideal alternative, but his ankle-length dishdasha would do nicely too. He could wear it with sandals. So what if he looked like a fancy-dress party sheikh? This was about practicality. He pulled the dishdasha out of the bag, let it unfurl.

To his dismay, it was spattered and stained with black ink. The ballpoint pens that had exploded during the flight had splurted their contents directly onto the white fabric. To make matters worse, he'd evidently scrunched the garment further down in the bag when he was preparing to leave the ship, causing the ink stains to reproduce themselves in Rorschach fashion.

And yet . . . and yet . . . He shook the garment straight, held it at arm's length. Something astonishing had happened. The ink pattern, created randomly, had turned into a cross, a Christian cross, right in the middle of the chest. If it had been red instead of black, it would almost be the insignia on the tunic of a medieval crusader. Almost. The ink stains were untidy, with globs and stray extra lines marring the perfection of the design. Although . . . although . . . those faint lines ghosting under the crossbar could be interpreted as the skeletally thin arms of the crucified Christ . . . and those spiky smudges higher up could be seen as thorns from Jesus's crown. He shook his head: reading too much into things was a weakness of his. And yet here it was, the cross on his garment where no cross was before. He prodded the ink, to check if it stained his fingers. Apart from a slightly tacky patch in the very center, it was dry. Ready to wear.

He threw the dishdasha over his head and allowed the cool fabric to slide across his skin, sheathing his nakedness. Turning to appraise his reflection in the window, he confirmed that Bea had chosen well. The thing fitted him, as though a tailor in the Middle East had measured his shoulders, cut the cloth and sewn it for him specially.

The window he'd been using as a mirror became a window again, as lights flared up outside. Two glowing points, like the eyes of some monstrous organism approaching. He stepped closer to the glass and peered through, but the vehicle's headlights disappeared just as he recognized them for what they were.

6

HIS WHOLE LIFE HAD BEEN
LEADING UP TO THIS.

A rendezvous between a married man and a female stranger, each of them far from home, in the obscure hours before dawn. If there was anything improper or potentially complicated about that, Peter didn't waste energy worrying over it. He and Grainger both had jobs to do, and God was watching.

Besides, Grainger's reaction to him, when he opened the door to her knock, was hardly encouraging. She did a double-take: a classic cartoon-style double-take. Her head jerked so hard he thought she might teeter backward into the corridor, but she just swayed on her feet and stared. The provocation, of course, was the big inky cross on his chest. Seeing it through her eyes, he was suddenly embarrassed.

"I took your advice," he tried to joke, plucking at the sleeves of the dishdasha. "About the denim jacket."

She didn't smile, just stared some more.

"You could've gone to, like, a T-shirt place," she said at last, "and got that done . . . uh . . . professionally." Her own attire was unchanged since their first meeting: still the white smock, cotton slacks, and headscarf. Not conventional Western dress, by any means, yet somehow, on her, it looked more natural, less affected, than his own get-up.

"The cross was . . . an accident," he explained. "A bunch of ink pens exploded."

"Uh . . . OK," she said. "Well, I guess it gives . . . kind of a homespun impression. Amateur—in a good way."

This condescending gesture of diplomacy made him smile. "You think I look like a ponce."

"A what?"

"A poseur."

She glanced down the corridor, toward the exit. "Not for me to say. You ready?"

Side by side they walked out of the building, into the darkness. The warm air embraced them with balmy enthusiasm and Peter instantly felt less self-conscious about his outfit, as it was perfect for the climate. Transporting his old clothes all the way to Oasis had been pointless, he appreciated that now. He must reinvent himself, and this morning was a good time to begin.

Grainger's vehicle was parked right next to the compound, illuminated by a lamp jutting from the concrete façade. It was a big, military-looking thing, clearly much more powerful than the frugal little runabout Peter and Bea owned.

"I really appreciate you making a car available for me," said Peter. "I imagine you have to ration them. The fuel and so on."

"Best to keep 'em in use," said Grainger. "They go to hell otherwise. Technically speaking. The moisture's a killer. Let me show you something."

She stepped up to the vehicle and flipped open the hatch to show him the engine. Peter dutifully leaned over and looked, although he knew nothing about the inner workings of cars, hadn't even mastered such basics as Bea could manage, like topping up oil, applying anti-freeze or attaching jump leads. Even so, he could tell that there was something unusual here.

"It's . . . disgusting," he said, and laughed at his own tactlessness. But it was true: the whole engine was caked in a greasy gunk that stank like old cat food.

"Sure," said Grainger, "but I hope you understand this isn't damage, this is the cure. The prevention."

"Oh."

She pushed the hatch down with just the right amount of force to make it snap shut. "Takes a full hour to grease up a vehicle like this. Do a few of 'em and you stink for the whole day."

Instinctively, he tried to smell her, or at least retrieve a memory of how she'd smelled before they stepped out into the muggy air. She smelled neutral. Nice, even.

"Is that one of your jobs? Greasing up the cars?"

She motioned him to get in. "We all get grease duty sometimes."

"Very democratic. Nobody complains?"

"This is not the place for complainers," she said, swinging into the driver's seat.

He opened the passenger door and joined her inside. No sooner had his body settled into position than she switched on the ignition and got the motor revving.

"What about the people at the top?" he asked. "Do they get grease duty too?"

"People at the top?"

"The . . . administration. Managers. Whatever you call them here."

Grainger blinked, as though she'd been asked a question about lion tamers or circus clowns. "We don't really have managers," she said, as she steered the vehicle and got into gear. "We all pitch in, take turns. It's pretty obvious what needs to be done. If there's any disagreement, we vote. Mostly we just follow the USIC guidelines."

"Sounds too good to be true."

"Too good to be true?" Grainger shook her head. "No offense, but that's what some people might say about religion. Not about a simple duty roster for keeping your vehicles' engines from corroding."

The rhetoric was neat, but something in Grainger's tone of voice made Peter suspect that she didn't quite believe it. He had a pretty good radar for the doubts that people hid beneath bravado.

"But there must be someone," he insisted, "who takes responsibility for the project as a whole?"

"Sure," she said. The car was picking up speed now and the lights of the compound rapidly receded into the gloom. "But they're a long way away. Can't expect them to hold our hands, can we?"

As they drove through the dark toward the invisible horizon, they munched on raisin bread. Grainger had positioned a big fresh loaf of it in the gap between the front seats, propped up against the gearstick, and they each helped themselves to slice after slice.

"This is good," he said.

"It's made here," she said, with a hint of pride.

"Including the raisins?"

"No, not the raisins. Or the egg. But the flour and the shortening and the sweetener and the sodium bicarbonate are. And the loaves are baked here. We have a bakery."

"Very nice." He munched some more, swallowed. They'd left the base perimeter fifteen minutes ago. Nothing remarkable had happened yet. There was little to be seen in the vehicle's headlight beam, which was the only light for miles around. Not for the first time, Peter thought about how much of our lives we spend sequestered inside small patches of electric brightness, blind to everything beyond the reach of those fragile bulbs.

"When is sunrise?" he asked.

"In about three, four hours," she said. "Or maybe two, I'm not sure, don't quote me. It's a gradual process. Not so dramatic."

They were driving straight over raw, uncultivated ground. There was no road or track or any evidence that anyone had ever driven or walked here before, although Grainger assured him that she made this trip regularly. In the absence of tracks or lights, it was sometimes difficult to believe they were moving, despite the gentle vibration of the vehicle's chassis. The view in every direction was the same. Grainger would occasionally glance at the dashboard's computerized navigation system, which kept her informed when they were about to stray from the correct course.

The landscape—what little Peter could see of it in the dark—was surprisingly bare given the climate. The earth was chocolate-brown, and so densely compacted that the tires traveled smoothly across it with no jolts to the suspension. Here and there, the terrain was spotted with patches of white mushroom, or speckled with a haze of greenish stuff that might be moss. No trees, no bushes, not even any grass. A dark, moist tundra.

He took another slice of raisin bread. It was losing its appeal, but he was hungry.

"I wouldn't have thought," he remarked, "that eggs could survive the Jump intact. I certainly felt a bit scrambled myself, when I went through it."

"Egg powder," said Grainger. "We use egg powder."

"Of course."

Through the side window, he spotted a single swirl of rain in an otherwise vacant sky: a curved glitter of water-drops about the size of a Ferris wheel, making its way across the land. It was traveling at a different tangent from their own, so Grainger would have to detour in order to drive through it. He considered asking her if they could do so, for the fun of it, like children chasing a rotating garden sprinkler. But she was intent on her navigation, staring out at the non-road ahead, both hands clamped on the steering wheel. The shimmering rain-swirl dimmed as the headlight beams passed it by, and then was swept into the darkness of their wake.

"So," said Peter. "Tell me what you know."

"About what?" Her relaxed demeanour was gone in a flash.

"About the people we're going to see."

"They're not people."

"Well . . ." He drew a deep breath. "Here's an idea, Grainger. How about we agree to use the term 'people' in its extended sense of 'inhabitants'? The original Roman etymology isn't clear, so who knows?—maybe it meant 'inhabitants' anyway. Of course, we could use 'creature' instead, but there are problems with that, don't you think? I mean, personally, I'd love to use 'creature,' if we could just take it back to its Latin origins: *creatura*: 'created thing.' Because we're all created things, aren't we? But it's suffered a bit of a decline, that word, through the centuries. To the point where 'creature,' to most people, means 'monster,' or at least 'animal.' Which reminds me: wouldn't it be nice to use 'animal' for all beings that breathe? After all, the Greek word *anima* means 'breath' or 'soul,' which pretty much covers everything we're looking for, doesn't it?"

Silence settled in the cabin. Grainger drove, keeping her eyes straight on the headlight beam just as before. After thirty seconds or so, which seemed quite a long time in the circumstances, she said:

"Well, it's plain to see you're not an uneducated holy roller from Hicksville."

"I never said I was."

She glanced aside at him, caught him smiling, smiled back. "Tell me, Peter. What made you decide to come *here*, and do *this*?"

"I didn't decide," he said. "God did."

"He sent you an email?"

"Sure." He grinned wider. "You wake up in the morning, go to the inbox of your heart, check what's loaded in. Sometimes there's a message."

"That's kind of a corny way of putting it."

He stopped smiling, not because he was offended, but because the discussion was turning serious. "Most true things are kind of corny, don't you think? But we make them more sophisticated out of sheer embarrassment. Simple truths with complicated clothes on. The only purpose of the linguistic dressing-up is so people won't look at the contents of our naked hearts and minds and say 'How naff.'"

She frowned. "'Naff'?"

"It's a British slang term, meaning trite or banal, but with an extra overtone of . . . uh . . . nerdishness. Uncoolness. Dorkishness."

"Wow. Did they teach American slang in your Bible School too?"

Peter took a few swigs from a water-bottle. "I never went to Bible School. I went to the University of Hard Drinking and Drug Abuse. Got my degree in Toilet Bowl Interior Decoration and . . . uh . . . Hospital Casualty Ward Occupancy."

"And then you found God?"

"Then I found a woman called Beatrice. We fell in love."

"Guys don't often put it that way."

"What do you mean?"

"Guys say 'we got together' or 'you can guess the rest' or something like that. Something that doesn't sound quite so . . ."

"Naff?"

"Exactly."

"Well, we fell in love," said Peter. "I quit the booze and drugs to impress her."

"I hope she was impressed."

"Yes." He took a last swig, screwed the top back on the bottle and slid it onto the floor between his feet. "Although she didn't tell me so until years later. Addicts don't handle praise well. The pressure of living up to it drives them back to drink and drugs."

"Yup."

"Have you had some experience of these things in your life?"

"Yup."

"Do you want to talk about it?"

"Not right now." She readjusted her posture in the seat, revved the engine, drove a little faster. The blush on her face made her look more feminine, although it accentuated the white scar under her hairline. She had pulled off her headscarf so that it hung loosely around her neck; her short crop of soft mousy hair fluttered in the air conditioning. "Your girlfriend sounds like a smart cookie."

"She's my wife. And yes, she's smart. Smarter—or at least wiser—than I am, that's for sure."

"Then why was it *you* that got chosen for this mission?"

Peter rested his head against the seat. "I've wondered about that myself. I suppose God must have other plans for Beatrice at home."

Grainger didn't comment. Peter looked out the side window. The sky was a little lighter. Perhaps he was only imagining it. A particularly large clump of mushrooms trembled as they swept by.

"You didn't answer my question," he said.

"I told you I didn't want to talk about it," she said.

"No, I meant my question about the people we're going to see. What do you know about them?"

"They're . . . ah . . ." She struggled for several seconds to find the right words. "They like their privacy."

"I could've guessed that. Not a single photo in any of the brochures and reports USIC gave me. I was expecting at least one smiley picture of your top brass shaking hands with the locals."

She chuckled. "That would be difficult to arrange."

"No hands?"

"Sure they have hands. They just don't like to be touched."

"So: describe them."

"It's difficult," she sighed. "I'm not good at descriptions. We'll see them soon enough."

"Do try." He batted his eyelashes. "I'd appreciate it."

"Well . . . they wear long robes and hoods. Like monks, I guess."

"So they're human in shape?"

"I guess. It's kind of hard to tell."

"But they have two arms, two legs, a torso . . ."

"Sure."

He shook his head. "That surprises me. All along, I've been telling my-self I mustn't assume the human design is some sort of universal standard. So I was trying to imagine . . . uh . . . big spider-like things, or eyes on stalks, or giant hairless possums . . ."

"Giant hairless possums?" She beamed. "I love it. Very sci-fi."

"But why *should* they have human form, Grainger, of all the forms they might conceivably have? Isn't that exactly what you'd expect from sci-fi?"

"Yeah, I guess . . . Or religion, maybe. Didn't God create man in His own image?"

"I wouldn't use the word 'man.' The Hebrew is *ha-adam*, which I would argue encompasses both sexes."

"Pleased to hear it," she said, deadpan.

Again, they drove on for a couple of minutes in silence. On the horizon, Peter was certain he could see the beginnings of a glow. A subtle haze of illumination, turning the junction of sky and earth from dark aquamarine-against-black to green-against-brown. If you stared at it too long, you began to wonder whether it was just an optical illusion, a hallucination, a frus-trated yearning for the end of night.

And inside that hesitant glow, was that . . . ? Yes, there was something else on the horizon. Raised structures of some sort. Mountains? Boulders? Buildings? A town? A city? Grainger had said that the "settlement" was about fifty miles away. They must have traveled half that distance by now, surely.

"Do they have genders?" he said at last.

"Who?" she said.

"The people we're going to see."

Grainger looked exasperated. "Why don't you just come straight out and use the word *aliens*?"

"Because *we're* the aliens here."

She laughed out loud. "I love it! A politically correct missionary! Forgive me for saying so, but it seems a total contradiction in terms."

"I forgive you, Grainger," he winked. "And my attitudes shouldn't strike you as a contradiction. God loves every creature equally."

The smile faded from her face. "Not in my experience," she said.

Silence descended on the cabin once more. Peter deliberated whether to push; decided not to. Not in that direction, anyway. Not yet.

"So," he rejoined lightly, "do they have genders?"

"I have no idea," said Grainger, in a flat, business-like tone. "You'll have to lift up their robes and take a look."

They drove for ten, fifteen minutes without further conversation. The topmost slice of the raisin bread dried out. The haze of light on the horizon became more distinct. The mysterious structures straight ahead were definitely architecture of some kind, although the sky was still too dark for Peter to make out exact shapes or details.

Eventually he said, "I need to have a pee."

"No problem," said Grainger, and slowed the car to a halt. On the dashboard, an electronic gauge estimating the fuel consumption per mile flickered through its numbers and settled on an abstract symbol.

Peter opened the door and, as he stepped out onto the earth, was enveloped at once by the humid, whispering air. He'd grown unaccustomed to it, having spent so long in the air-conditioned bubble of the vehicle. It was enjoyable, this sudden all-out luxury of atmosphere, but also an assault: the way the air immediately ran up the sleeves of his shirt, licked his eyelids and ears, dampened his chest. He hitched the hem of his dishdasha up to his abdomen and pissed straight onto the ground, since the landscape offered no trees or boulders to hide behind. The earth was already moist and dark brown, so the urine made little difference to its color or consistency. It sank in without pause.

He heard Grainger opening and shutting the door on her side of the vehicle. To give her some privacy, he stood for a while and appraised the scenery. The plants that he'd taken for mushrooms were flowers, grayish-white flowers with a tinge of mauve, almost luminous in the gloom. They grew in small, neat clumps. There was no distinction between blossom, leaf and stalk: the whole plant was slightly furry, leathery and yet so thin as to be almost transparent, like the ear of a kitten. Evidently no other plants were viable in this part of the world. Or perhaps he'd simply come at the wrong time of year.

Grainger's door slammed, and he turned to join her. She was crumpling a cardboard box of disposable tissues into the glove compartment as he took his seat.

"OK," she said. "Last few miles coming up."

He shut his door and the air conditioning promptly restored the neutral atmosphere of the cabin. Peter settled back in his seat, and shivered as a trapped wisp of balmy Oasan air slipped between his shoulderblades and out of his collar.

"I must say you built your landing base a respectfully long way out," he said. "The planners of London's airports were never so considerate of local residents."

Grainger unscrewed a water-bottle, drank deep, coughed. A rivulet ran down her chin, and she mopped it up with a handful of her headscarf.

"Actually . . ." She cleared her throat. "Actually, when we first built the base, the . . . ah . . . local residents lived just two miles away. They relocated. Took everything with them. I mean *everything*. A couple of our guys had a look around the old settlement when it was all over. Like, maybe we can learn something from what they left behind. But it was stripped clean. Just the shells of houses. Not even a single mushroom left in the ground." She consulted one of the gauges on the dashboard. "The fifty miles must have taken them forever to walk."

"It sounds like they really do value their privacy. Unless . . ." He hesitated, trying to think of a diplomatic way of asking whether USIC had done something outrageously offensive. Before he could frame the question, Grainger answered it.

"It was out of the blue. They just told us they were moving. We asked if we were doing anything wrong. Like, was there some problem we could fix so they'd reconsider? They said no, no problem."

Grainger revved the engine and they were off again.

"When you say 'we asked,'" said Peter, "do you mean 'we' as in . . . ?"

"I wasn't personally a party to these negotiations, no."

"Do you speak their language?"

"No."

"Not a word?"

"Not a word."

"So . . . uh . . . how good is their English? I mean, I tried to find out about this before I came, but I couldn't get a straight answer."

"There isn't a straight answer. Some of them . . . maybe most of them, don't . . ." Her voice trailed off. She chewed her lip. "Listen, this is gonna sound bad. It's not meant to. The thing is, we don't know how many of them there are. Partly because they keep themselves hidden, and partly because we can't tell the difference between them . . . No disrespect, but we just can't. There's a few individuals we have dealings with. Maybe a dozen. Or maybe it's the same five or six guys in different clothes, we just can't tell. They speak some English. Enough."

"Who taught them?"

"I think they just kind of picked it up, I don't know." She glanced up at the rear-view mirror, as though there might be a traffic snarl he was distracting her from dealing with safely. "You'd have to ask Tartaglione. If he was still with us."

"Sorry?"

"Tartaglione was a linguist. He came here to study the language. He was going to compile a dictionary and so forth. But he . . . ah . . . disappeared."

Peter chewed on that for a couple of seconds. "Right," he said. "You do drop lots of little morsels of info, don't you, if I only wait long enough . . ."

She sighed, annoyed again. "I already *told* you most of this stuff when I first met you, escorting you off the ship."

This was news to him. He strained to recall their walk together, on that first day. The words had evaporated. All he recalled, vaguely, was her presence at his side.

"Forgive me. I was very tired."

"You're forgiven."

They traveled on. A few hundred meters ahead and to the side of them, there was another isolated swirl of rain, cartwheeling along the land.

"Can we drive through that?" Peter asked.

"Sure."

She swerved slightly, and they ploughed through the whirl of brilliant water-drops, which enveloped them momentarily in its fairy-light display.

"Psychedelic, huh," remarked Grainger, deadpan, switching on the windscreen wipers.

"Beautiful," he said.

After another few minutes of driving, the shapes on the horizon had firmed up into the unmistakable contours of buildings. Nothing fancy or monumental. Square blocks, like British tower blocks, cheap utilitarian housing. Not exactly the diamantine spires of a fantastical city.

"What do they call themselves?" asked Peter.

"I've no idea," said Grainger. "Something we couldn't pronounce, I guess."

"So who named this place Oasis?"

"A little girl from Oskaloosa, Iowa."

"You're kidding."

She cast him a bemused glance. "You didn't read about it? It's gotta be the *only* thing the average person knows about this place. There were articles about this little girl in magazines, she was on TV . . ."

"I don't read magazines, and I don't have a TV."

Now it was her turn to say, "You're kidding."

He smiled. "I'm not kidding. One day I got a message from the Lord saying, 'Get rid of the TV, Peter, it's a huge waste of time.' So I did."

She shook her head. "I don't know how to take you."

"Straight," he said. "Always straight. Anyway: this little girl from . . . uh . . ."

"Oskaloosa. She won a competition. 'Name a New World.' I'm *so* amazed you didn't hear about it. There were hundreds of thousands of entries, most of them unbelievably wrong. It was like a nerd jamboree. The USIC staff in the building where I worked kept an internal dossier of the worst names. Every week we'd have new favorites. We ended up using them for a competition we ran ourselves, to name the janitor's supply room. 'Nuvo Opportunus,' that was a great one. 'Zion II.' 'Atlanto.' 'Arnold'—that had real pizzazz, I thought. 'Splendoramus.' Uh . . . 'Einsteinia.' I forget the rest. Oh, yeah: 'Traveler's Rest,' that was another one. 'Newfoundplanet.' 'Cervix.' 'Hendrix.' 'Elvis.' They just kept on coming."

"And the little girl?"

"She got lucky, I guess. There must've been hundreds of other people who came up with 'Oasis.' She won $50,000. The family needed it, too, because the mother had just lost her job, and the father had been diagnosed with some kind of rare disease."

"So how did the story end?"

"Just like you'd expect. The dad died. The mom talked about it on TV and became an alcoholic. Then the media moved on and you never got to know what happened next."

"Can you remember the girl's name? I'd like to pray for her."

Grainger butted her palms against the steering wheel irritably, and rolled her eyes upward. "Puh-*lease*. There were a million Americans praying for her, and it didn't stop her life going down the toilet."

He shut up, faced front. They drove in silence for forty seconds or so.

"Coretta," she said at last.

"Thank you," said Peter. He tried to picture Coretta, so that she wouldn't be just a name to him when he prayed. Any sort of face was better than none at all. He thought of the children he knew, the kids in his congregation back home, but the ones that sprang to mind were too old or too young or the wrong sex. In any case, as a minister, in his own church, he wasn't so involved with the little ones; Bea took them into another room for play activities during his sermons. Not that he was unaware of them while he preached: the walls were so thin that if he paused for effect between sentences, the silence was often filled by laughter or snatches of song or even the galumphing of small feet. But he didn't know any of the kids particularly well.

"This Coretta," he said, pushing his luck with Grainger. "Is she black or white?" One child had popped into his memory: the daughter of that new Somali couple, the cheeky girl who was always dressed like a miniature nineteenth-century Southern belle . . . what was her name?—Lulu. Adorable kid.

"White," said Grainger. "Blond hair. Or maybe a redhead, I forget. It was a long time ago, and there's no way of checking."

"Can't you look her up?"

She blinked. "Look her up?"

"On a computer or something?" Even as he said it, he realized it was a stupid suggestion. Oasis was far beyond the reach of any information superhighways; there were no world wide webs laden with morsels of trivia, no industrious search engines offering up millions of Oskaloosas and Corettas. If what you wanted to know was not to be found in the stuff you'd brought along with you—the books, the magic discs, the memory sticks, the old copies of *Hydraulics* magazine—you could forget it. "Sorry," he said. "Not thinking clearly."

"This atmosphere will do that to you," she said. "I hate the way it *pushes*. Right inside your *ears*, even. Never lets up. Sometimes you just wanna . . ." She didn't pursue the thought, just puffed a mouthful of breath upward, dislodging a damp lock of hair from her forehead. "There's no point talking about it with the guys here. They're used to it, they don't have a problem with it, they don't notice it anymore. Maybe they even enjoy it."

"Maybe they hate it but don't complain."

Her face went stiff. "OK, message received," she said.

Peter groaned inwardly. He should have thought the implications through before opening his mouth. What was wrong with him today? He was usually so tactful. Could it be the atmosphere, as Grainger said? He'd always imagined his brain as a wholly enclosed thing, safe inside a shell of bone, but maybe, in this strange new environment, the seal was more permeable and his brain was being infiltrated by insidious vapors. He wiped sweat off his eyelids and made an effort to be a hundred percent alert, facing front and peering through the dirt-hazed windscreen. The terrain was looser, less stable, the closer they came to their destination. Particles of clammy soil were being thrown up by the tires and enveloping the vehicle in a kind of halo of filth. The outline of the native settlement seemed grim and unwelcoming somehow.

Suddenly, the magnitude of the challenge hit home. Until now, it had been all about *him* and his ability to keep himself in one piece: to survive the journey, to recover from the Jump, to adjust to the strange new air and the shock of separation. But there was so much more to it than that. The scale of the unknown remained just as immense whether he was feeling well or unwell; he was approaching monolithic barriers of foreignness that existed oblivious to him, indifferent to how rested or unrested he was, how bleary-eyed or attentive, how keen or dull.

Psalm 139 came to his mind, as it so often did when he needed reassurance. But today, the reminder of God's omniscience was no comfort; instead, it heightened his own sense of unease. *How precious are thy thoughts unto me, O God! How great is the sum of them! If I should count them, they are more in number than the sand.* Each and every mote of dirt flung up by the vehicle's wheels was like a truth that he needed to learn, a ridiculously large number of truths which he had neither the time nor the wisdom to grasp. He was not God, and maybe only God could do what needed to be done here.

Grainger switched on the windscreen wipers once more. The view went smeary for a while, then the glass cleared and the native settlement was revealed afresh, lit up now by the rising sun. The sun made all the difference.

Yes, the mission was daunting and, yes, he wasn't in the best shape. But here he was, on the threshold of meeting an entirely new kind of people, an encounter chosen for him by God. Whatever was fated to happen, it would surely be precious and amazing. His whole life—he understood that now, as the façades of the unknown city loomed up before him, harboring unimaginable wonders—his whole life had been leading up to this.

7

APPROVED, TRANSMITTED.

"Well," said Grainger, "here we are."

Sometimes a statement of the bloody obvious was the only appropriate way forward. As if to give life ceremonious permission to proceed.

"Are you OK?" she asked.

"Uh . . . yes," he said, swaying in his seat. The dizziness he'd felt back at the base had come over him again. "I'm probably over-excited. It's my first time, after all."

She gave him a look he recognized very well, a look he'd seen on thousands of faces during his years as a pastor, a look that said: *Nothing is worth getting excited about; everything is a disappointment.* He would have to try to do something about that look, if he could, later.

In the meantime, he had to admit that their surroundings were not exactly awesomely impressive. The Oasan settlement wasn't what you'd call a city. More like a suburb, erected in the middle of a wasteland. There were no streets in the formal sense, no pavements, no signs, no vehicles, and— despite the dim light and broad shadows of early dawn—no lamps, or any evidence of electricity or fire. Just a community of buildings resting on bare ground. How many dwellings altogether? Peter couldn't guess. Maybe five hundred. Maybe more. They were spread out in unruly clusters, ranging in scale from single-story to three-floor blocks, all flat-roofed. The buildings were brick, obviously made of the same clay as the earth, but baked marble-smooth and caramel-colored. There was not a soul to be seen. All the doors and windows were shut. Well, that wasn't quite true: the doors weren't made of wood nor the windows of glass; they were merely holes in the buildings, shrouded with bead curtains. The beads were crystalline, like extravagant strings of jewelry. They swayed gently in the breeze. But there was nobody parting those curtains to peek out, nobody walking through the doorways.

Grainger parked the vehicle right in front of a building which looked like all the others except that it was marked by a painted white star, the bottom point of which had trickled slightly and dried that way. Peter and Grainger stepped out and submitted to the atmosphere's embrace. Grainger wrapped her scarf around her face, covering her mouth and nose, as though she considered the air impure. From a pocket of her slacks she removed a metal gadget which Peter assumed was a weapon. She pointed it at the vehicle and pressed the trigger twice. The engine switched off and a hatch in the back flipped open.

In the absence of motor noise, the sounds of the Oasan settlement ventured onto the airwaves like opportunistic wildlife. The burble of running water, from an invisible source. The occasional muffled clank or clunk, suggesting routine struggles with domestic objects. Distant squeaks and chortles that might be birds or children or machinery. And, closer by, the unintelligible murmur of voices, subtle and diffuse, emanating from the buildings like a hum. This place, despite outward appearances, was no ghost town.

"So, do we just yell hello?" said Peter.

"They know we're here," said Grainger. "That's why they're hiding." Her voice, muffled slightly by the scarf, sounded tense. She had her arms folded, and he could see a tongue of dark sweat in the armpit of her smock.

"How many times have you been here?" he asked.

"Dozens. I bring them their drug supply."

"You're kidding."

"I'm a pharmacist."

"I didn't know that."

She sighed. "Looks like I totally wasted my breath when we first met. You didn't absorb a word I said, did you? My big speech of welcome, my detailed explanation of the procedure for getting stuff from the pharmacy if you need it."

"Sorry, my brains must have been scrambled."

"The Jump does that to some people."

"The wimpy ones, huh?"

"I didn't say that." Grainger hugged herself tightly, squeezing her upper arms in stress. "Come *on*, let's get this over with." This last was not addressed to him; she was staring at the building with the star painted on it.

"Are we in any danger?"

"None that I know of."

Peter leaned against the crash-bar of the vehicle and made a more careful study of what he could see of the settlement. The buildings, although rectangular, had no hard edges: each brick was a well-buffed lozenge, a glassy loaf of amber. The mortar had no grit to it; it was like plastic sealant. There wasn't a hard angle anywhere, nothing sharp or corrugated. It was as though the architect's aesthetics had been formed in homage to children's play centers. Not that these buildings were in any way infantile or crass: they had their own uniform dignity, and they were obviously rock-solid, and the warm colors were . . . well . . . warm. But Peter couldn't say he found the overall effect attractive. If God blessed him with the opportunity to build a church here, it would have to strike a different note, stand out against the squatness all around. At the very least it would need to have . . . Yes, that's it: he'd worked out what was so dispiriting about this place. There was no attempt to reach up into the heavens. No tower, no turret, no flagpole, not even a modest triangular roof. Oh, for a spire!

Peter's vision of a church steeple shone in his mind just long enough for him to be oblivious to a movement in the bead curtain of the nearest doorway. By the time he blinked and focused, the figure had already stepped out and was confronting Grainger. The event had occurred too suddenly, he felt; it lacked the drama appropriate to his first sighting of an Oasan native. It ought to have happened with ceremonial slowness, in an amphitheater, or at the summit of a long staircase. Instead, the encounter was already under way, and Peter had missed its beginning.

The creature—the person—stood upright, but not tall. Five foot three, maybe five foot four. (Funny how those imperial measurements—inches, miles—stubbornly refused to be left behind.) Anyway, he, or she, was delicate. Small-boned, narrow-shouldered, an unassuming presence—not at all the fearsome figure Peter had prepared himself to confront. As foretold, a hood and monkish robes—made of a pastel-blue fabric disconcertingly like bathtowel—covered almost all of the body, its hems brushing the toes of soft leather boots. There was no swell of bosom, so Peter—aware that this was flimsy evidence on which to base a judgment, but unwilling to clutter his brain with unwieldy repetitions of "he or she"—decided to think of the creature as male.

"Hi," said Grainger, extending her hand.

The Oasan extended his hand in return, but did not grasp Grainger's; rather he touched her gently on the wrist with his fingertips. He was gloved. The gloves had five digits.

"You, here, now . . ." he said. "A ꞇurpriꞇe." His voice was soft, reedy, asthmatic-sounding. Where the "s"s should have been, there was a noise like a ripe fruit being thumbed into two halves.

"Not a bad surprise, I hope," said Grainger.

"I hope ꞇogether with you."

The Oasan turned to look at Peter, tilted his head slightly so that the shadows from the hood slid back. Peter, having been lulled by the Oasan's familiar shape and five-fingered hands into expecting a more-or-less human face, flinched.

Here was a face that was nothing like a face. Instead, it was a massive whitish-pink walnut kernel. Or no: even more, it resembled a placenta with two fetuses—maybe three-month-old twins, hairless and blind—nestled head to head, knee to knee. Their swollen heads constituted the Oasan's clefted forehead, so to speak; their puny ribbed backs formed his cheeks, their spindly arms and webbed feet merged in a tangle of translucent flesh that might contain—in some form unrecognizable to him—a mouth, nose, eyes.

Of course, there were no fetuses there, not really: the face was what it was, the face of an Oasan, nothing else. But try as he might, Peter couldn't decode it on its own terms; he could only compare it to something he knew. He *had* to see it as a grotesque pair of fetuses perched on someone's shoulders, half-shrouded in a cowl. Because if he didn't allow it to resemble that, he would probably always have to stare at it dumbfounded, reliving the initial shock, dizzy with the vertigo of unsupported falling, in that gut-wrenching instant before a solid comparison is found to clasp onto.

"You and I," said the Oasan. "Never before now." The vertical cleft in the middle of his face squirmed slightly as he formed the words. The fetuses rubbed knees, so to speak. Peter smiled but could not summon a response.

"He means he hasn't met you before," said Grainger. "In other words, he's saying hello."

"Hello," said Peter. "I'm Peter."

The Oasan nodded. "You are Peⴟer. I will remember." He turned back to Grainger. "You bring mediⵤine?"

"A little."

"How liⴟle?"

"I'll show you," said Grainger, walking around to the back of the vehicle and lifting the hatch. She rummaged in the jumbled contents—bottles of water, toilet paper, canvas bags, tools, tarps—and extracted a plastic tub no bigger than a schoolchild's lunch-box. The Oasan followed every movement, although Peter was still unable to work out which parts of the face were its eyes. *His* eyes, sorry.

"This is all I could get from our pharmacy," said Grainger. "Today is not one of the official supply days, you understand? We're here for a different reason. But I didn't want to come with nothing. So this"—she handed him the tub—"is extra. A gift."

"We are diⵤappoinⴟful," said the Oasan. "And in the ⵤame breath we are graⴟeful."

There was a pause. The Oasan stood holding his plastic tub; Grainger and Peter stood watching him hold it. A ray of sunlight found its way to the roof of the vehicle, making it glow.

"So . . . uh . . . How are you?" said Grainger. Sweat twinkled in her eyebrows and on her cheeks.

"I alone?" inquired the Oasan. "Or I and we ⴟogether?" He gestured vaguely at the settlement behind him.

"All of you."

The Oasan appeared to give this a great deal of thought. At last he said: "Good."

There was another pause.

"Is anyone else coming out today?" asked Grainger. "To see us, I mean?"

Again, the Oasan mulled over the question as though it were immensely complex.

"No," he concluded. "I ᛉoday am only one." He gestured solemnly at both Grainger and Peter, in acknowledgment, perhaps, of his regret for the 2:1 imbalance between number of visitors and welcoming party.

"Peter here is a special guest of USIC," said Grainger. "He's a . . . he's a Christian missionary. He wants to . . . uh . . . live with you." She glanced at Peter for uneasy confirmation. "If I've got that right."

"Yes," said Peter, brightly. There was a glistening, champignon-like thing roughly halfway down the central cleft of the Oasan's face that he'd decided was his eye, and he looked straight at that, doing his best to radiate friendliness. "I have good news to tell you. The best news you've ever heard."

The Oasan cocked his head to one side. The two fetuses—no, not fetuses, his brow and cheeks, please!—blushed, revealing a spidery network of capillaries just beneath the skin. His voice, when it came, was even more asthmatic-sounding than before. "The Goᛋpel?"

The words hung in the whispering air for a second before Peter was able to take them in. He couldn't believe he'd heard correctly. Then he noticed that the Oasan's gloved hands had been pressed together in a steeple shape.

"Yes!" Peter cried, dizzy with elation. "Praise Jesus!"

The Oasan turned to Grainger again. His gloved hands were trembling against the tub he held. "We have waiᛉed long for the man Peᛉer," he said. "Thank you, Grainger." And without further explanation he hurried through the doorway, leaving the crystalline beads swinging in his wake.

"Well I'll be damned," said Grainger, yanking her scarf loose and wiping her face with it. "He never called me by name before."

They stood waiting for twenty minutes or so. The sun continued to rise, a sliver of brilliant burning orange, like a great bubble of lava on the horizon. The walls of the buildings glowed as if each brick had a light inside.

At last, the Oasan returned, still clutching the plastic tub, which was now empty. He handed it back to Grainger, very slowly and carefully, only letting it go when her grip on it was secure.

"Medi☾ine have all gone," he said. "Gone in☾ide the gra☲eful."

"I'm sorry there wasn't more," said Grainger. "There'll be more next time."

The Oasan nodded. "We abide."

Grainger, stiff with unease, walked to the rear of the vehicle to stow the tub back in the trunk. As soon as her back was turned, the Oasan sidled up to Peter, bringing them face to face.

"Have you the book?"

"The book?"

"The Book of ☲☲range New Thing☾."

Peter blinked and tried to breathe normally. Up close, the Oasan's flesh smelled sweet: not the sweet of rot, but sweet like fresh fruit.

"You mean the Bible," he said.

"We ☾peak never the name. Power of the book forbid. Flame give warmth . . ." With outstretched hands, he mimed the action of warming oneself on a fire, getting too close, and being burned.

"But you mean the Word of God," said Peter. "The Gospel."

"The Go☾pel. The ☲echnique of Je☾u☾."

Peter nodded, but it took him a few seconds to decode the last word from its impeded passage through the Oasan's head cleft.

"Jesus," he echoed in wonder.

The Oasan reached out one hand, and, with an unmistakably tender motion, stroked Peter's cheek with the tip of a glove. "We pray Je☾u☾ for your coming," he said.

Grainger's failure to rejoin them was, by now, obvious. Peter glanced round and saw her leaning on the back of the vehicle, pretending to study the gadget with which she'd unlocked the trunk. In that fraction of a second before he turned back to the Oasan, he felt the full intensity of her embarrassment.

"The book? You have the book?" the Oasan repeated.

"Uh . . . not on me right now," said Peter, chastising himself for leaving his Bible back at the base. "But yes, of course. Of course!"

The Oasan clapped his hands in a gesture of delight, or prayer, or both. "Comfor☲ and joy. Glad day. Come back ☾oon, Pe☲er, oh very ☾oon, ☾ooner than you can. Read for u☾ the Book of ☲☲range New Thing☾, read and read and read until we understand. In reward we give you . . . give you . . ." The Oasan trembled with the effort of finding adequate words, then threw his hands wide, as if to indicate everything under the sun.

"Yes," said Peter, laying a reassuring hand on the Oasan's shoulder. "Soon."

The Oasan's brow—the heads of the fetuses, so to speak—swelled slightly. Peter decided that this, in these miraculous new people, was a smile.

> Dear Peter, wrote Beatrice.
> I love you and hope you are well but I must start this letter with
> some very bad news.

It was like running toward an open doorway in a state of high enthusiasm and colliding with a pane of glass. He had spent the entire journey back to the base almost levitating with excitement; it was a wonder he hadn't floated straight through the roof of Grainger's vehicle. Dear Bea . . . God be praised . . . We ask for a small break and God gives us a miracle . . . these were some of the ways he'd thought of beginning his message to Beatrice upon returning to his room. His fingers were poised to type at delirious speed, to shoot his delight through space, mistakes and all.

> There has been a terrible tragedy in the Maldives. A tidal wave.
> It was the height of the tourist season. The place was teeming with
> visitors and it's got a population of about a third of a million. Had.
> You know how when disasters happen, usually the media talks about
> how many people are estimated to have died? In this one, they're
> talking about how many people may be LEFT ALIVE. It's one vast
> swamp of bodies. You see it on the news footage but you can't take
> it in. All those people with individual quirks and family secrets and
> special ways of wearing their hair, etc, reduced to what looks like a
> huge bog of meat that goes on for miles.
> The Maldives has (HAD . . .) lots of islands, most of them at risk
> of flooding, so the government had been pushing for years to get
> the population to relocate to the biggest, best-fortified atoll. By

coincidence, there was a TV documentary crew making a film about a few islanders on one of the smaller atolls who were protesting at being rehoused. The cameras were rolling when the tsunami hit. I've seen clips on my phone. You cannot believe what you are seeing. One second, an American anchorperson voice is saying something about papaya groves, and the next second, a zillion tons of seawater smashes across the screen. Rescue crews saved some of the Americans, a few tourists, a few of the locals. And the cameras, of course. That sounds cynical. I think they did what they could.

Our church is considering what we can do to help. Sending people over there isn't an option. There's nothing we can achieve. Most of the islands are wiped off, there is nothing left except humps in the ocean. Even the biggest islands are probably never going to recover. All the fresh water has been fouled. There is not one fully intact, usable building. There is nowhere safe to land, nowhere to set up a hospital, no way of burying the dead. Helicopters are buzzing around like seagulls over an oilspill full of dead fish. At this stage, all we can do is pray for the relatives of Maldivans everywhere. And maybe, in time, there'll be refugees.

I'm sorry to start this way. You can imagine my head and heart are full of it. It doesn't mean I haven't been thinking of you.

Peter leaned back in his chair, lifted his face to the ceiling. The electric light was still on, superfluous now that the sunshine was beaming in, almost too bright to bear. He shivered, feeling the dampness in his clothes turning chilly in the air conditioning. He felt grief for the people of the Maldives, but, to his shame, the grief was mingled with a purely selfish pang: the sense that he and Beatrice, for the first time since the beginning of their relationship, were not going through the same things together. In the past, whatever happened would happen to them both, like a power blackout or a late-night visit from a distressed friend or a rattling window-frame while they were trying to sleep. Or like sex.

I miss you, wrote Beatrice. This Maldives thing wouldn't have upset me so much if you'd been here. Tell me more about your mission. Is it horrendously difficult? Remember that unexpected breakthroughs often come directly after everything has seemed impossible. The ones who insist they don't want or need God are the ones who want and need Him most.

Joshua is still playing his tricks. I'm seriously considering slipping him a Mickey Finn in his evening milk. Or hitting him on the head with a mallet when he wakes me up yet again at 4 AM. Alternatively, maybe I should make a life-size dummy of you to lie next to me in the bed. That might fool him. Sadly, it wouldn't fool me.

The Mirah situation is under control now. I got together with a Muslim social worker, Khadija, who liaises with the imam at Mirah's local mosque. Basically we're trying to sell it to the imam as a human decency issue (the husband's violence/lack of respect) rather than a religion vs religion issue. It's hardcore diplomacy, as you can imagine, like brokering a peace deal between Syria and the USA. But Khadija is brilliant.

I got a message from USIC saying you're fine. How would they know? I suppose they mean they can verify you didn't get vaporized. The message was sent by Alex Grainger. Have you met him? Tell him he can't spell "liaise." Or maybe there's a simplified American way of spelling it now? Bitch, bitch, bitch. But I've been tolerant all day, honest! (Very difficult new patient on the ward. Supposedly transferred down from Psych for medical reasons but I think they were just desperate to get rid of her.) Anyway, I feel like being outrageously unfair to someone for just three minutes, to let it rip. I won't, of course. I'll be very nice, even to Joshua when he wakes me up AGAIN in the small hours.

Seriously, I'm missing you terribly. Wish I could spend just a few minutes in your arms. (OK, maybe an hour.) Weather is better, lovely sunshine today, but it's not cheering me up. Went to the supermarket for some comfort food (chocolate mousse, tiramisu, you know the sort of thing). Turns out lots of other people had the same idea. Everything I wanted was out of stock, a blank space on the shelf. Settled for one of those rollette things with the fake cream inside.

Head full of Maldives tragedy, stomach full of dessert. What fortunate people we are in our Western playground . . . We watch the footage of foreign dead on video clips and then mosey out to the supermarket in search of our favorite treats. Of course when I say "we," I can't speak for you right now. You are far from all of this. Far from me.

Ignore this self-pitying prattle, I'll be fine by tomorrow. Let me know how you're going. I'm so proud of you.

Kisses, hugs (I wish!)

Beatrice

PS: Want a cat?

My dear Bea, he wrote back.

I hardly know what to say. How dreadful about the Maldives. The scale of such a tragedy is, as you say, almost impossible to imagine. I'll pray for them.

Those sentences, short as they were, took him a long while to write. A full three to five minutes for each. He racked his brains for an additional sentence that would make a dignified transition from the disaster to his own glad tidings. Nothing came.

I have had my first meeting with an Oasan native, he went on, trusting that Bea would understand. Contrary to my wildest hopes they are hungry for Christ. They know of the Bible. I didn't have mine with me at the time—that'll teach me never to go anywhere without it! I don't know why I left it behind. I suppose I assumed that the first visit would be basically reconnaissance, and that the response would be negative. But as Jesus says in John 4, "Say not ye, There are yet four months before the harvest; behold, I say unto you, Lift up your eyes and look upon the fields, for they are ripe already!"

The settlement is not at all what I expected. There is no evidence of industrialization, it could be the Middle East in the middle ages (with different architecture, of course). No electricity, apparently! It's also in the middle of nowhere, a long, long way from the USIC base. I don't think it will be feasible for me to live here and travel there on a regular basis. I will have to go and live with the Oasans. And as soon as possible. I haven't discussed any of the practicalities. (Yes, yes, I know . . . I really need you with me. But God is well aware that I'm clueless in that area.) I'll have to trust that everything will fall into place. There seems plenty of reason to hope that it will!

The Oasans—assuming the one I met was typical—are average height and look remarkably like us, except for their faces which are a gruesome sort of jumble, impossible to describe really, like fetuses. You don't know what to look at when you're talking to them. They speak English with a strong accent. Well, the one I met did. Maybe he's the only one who speaks any English, and my original assumption—that I would spend several months learning the language before I made any headway—will still be borne out. But I have a feeling that God has been at work here already, more than I dared imagine.

Anyway, I'm going straight back there as soon as I can. I was going to say "tomorrow," but with the periods of daylight being several "days" long here, the word "tomorrow" is a problem. I must find out what the USIC personnel do to get round that one. I'm sure they have a solution. I'll ask Grainger during the drive, if I remember. My mind's a bit over-excited, as you can imagine! I'm just raring to go back to that settlement, take my place amongst these extraordinary people and satisfy their thirst for the Gospel.

What a privilege to

He stopped typing, midway through "What a privilege to serve the Lord." He had remembered the Maldives, or, more to the point, he'd become aware that he'd forgotten all about them in his enthusiasm. Bea's uneasy, almost anxious mood—so unlike her!—was at odds with his exuberance, like a funeral dirge interrupted by the cheery hootings of a passing carnival. Rereading the opening line of his letter, he could see that his acknowledgment of her distress was pretty cursory. In normal circumstances, he would have embraced her; the pressure of his arms against her back and the nudge of his cheek against her hair would have said it all. But now, the written word was all he had.

He considered elaborating on how he felt about the Maldives. But he didn't feel much, at least not about the Maldives themselves. His feelings were largely regret—disappointment, even—that the tragedy had affected Beatrice so badly, just when he wanted her to be happy and all right and getting on with things as usual and receptive to his wonderful news about the Oasans.

His stomach gurgled loudly. He hadn't eaten since the drive back from the settlement, when he and Grainger had nibbled at the dried-out remainder of the raisin bread. ("Five bucks a slice," she'd remarked ruefully. He hadn't asked who was footing the bill.) As if by mutual agreement, they had not discussed the Oasan's extraordinary response to Peter. Instead, Grainger explained various routine procedures relating to laundry, electric appliances, availability of vehicles, canteen etiquette. She was irritable, insisting that she'd briefed him on these things before, when she first escorted him off the ship. The forgiveness joke didn't work a third time.

Peter stood up and walked to the window. The sun—egg-yellow and hazy-edged at this time of day—was clearly visible from his quarters, right in the middle of the sky. It was four or five times bigger than the sun he'd grown up with, and it cast a rim of golden light along the contours of the airport compound's drab buildings. Puddles of rainwater, left by last night's deluge, had been evaporating steadily since then. The vapors twirled and danced as they flew off the ground and past the rooftops into oblivion, as if the puddles were blowing sophisticated smoke rings.

The air conditioning in his room was unnecessarily cool. He found that if he stepped closer to the window, almost pressing his body against it, the warmth from outside radiated through the glass and permeated his clothing. He would have to ask Grainger about adjusting the air-con; it was one of the points they hadn't covered.

Back at the message screen, he finished typing serve the Lord and started a fresh paragraph.

> Even in my joy at this wonderful opportunity that God has laid before me, I feel an ache of grief that I can't hold you and comfort you. I only realized today that this is the first time you & I have been apart for longer than a couple of nights. Couldn't I have gone on a mini-mission to Manchester or Cardiff first, as a practice exercise, before coming all the way here?
>
> I think you would find Oasis as beautiful as I do. The sun is huge and yellow. The air swirls around constantly and slips in and out of your clothes. That may sound unpleasant, I know, but you get used to it. The water is green and my urine comes out orange. I'm doing a great job of selling the place to you, aren't I? I should have taken a course in novel-writing before I volunteered for this. I should have insisted to USIC that we went together or I didn't go at all.
>
> Maybe, if we'd bent their arm on that one, we could then have insisted that Joshua came along too. Not sure how he would have fared in the Jump, though. Probably would have been transformed into a furry tea cosy.
>
> Feeble cat jokes. My equivalent of your chocolate rollettes, I suppose.
>
> Darling, I love you. Keep well. Take the wise advice that you've given me so often: don't be hard on yourself, and don't let the bad blind you to the good. I'll join you in prayer for the relatives of the dead in the Maldives. Join me in prayer for the people here, who are thrilled at the prospect of a new life in Christ. Oh, and also: there is a girl in Oskaloosa called Coretta whose father has recently died and whose mother has hit the booze. Pray for her too, if you remember.
>
> Love,
> Peter

He read the text of his message over, but didn't tinker with it any further, feeling suddenly faint with hunger and fatigue. He pressed a button. For several minutes, his 793 inadequate words hung there, trembling slightly, as if unsure what to do. That was normal for the Shoot, he'd found. The process kept you in suspense each time, tempting you to fear that it would fail. Then his words vanished and the screen went blank, except for the automated logo that said: APPROVED, TRANSMITTED.

8

TAKE A DEEP BREATH AND
COUNT TO A MILLION.

Everything looked different in daylight. The USIC mess hall, which had seemed so lonesome and eerie during the long hours of darkness, was a hive of cheerful activity now. A happy congregation. The glass wall on the eastern side of the building, although tinted, let in so much light and warmth that Peter had to shield his face from it. A glow was cast over the entire room, transforming coffee machines into jeweled sculptures, aluminium chairs into precious metal, magazine racks into ziggurats, bald heads into lamps. Thirty or forty people were gathered together, eating, chatting, fetching refills from the coffee bar, lolling around in the armchairs, gesticulating over the tables, raising their voices to compete with the raised voices of the others. Most were dressed in white, just like Peter, although *sans* the big inky crucifix on the chest. There were quite a few black faces, including BG's. BG didn't look up when Peter arrived; he was involved in an animated discussion with a rather butch-looking white woman. There was no sign of Grainger.

Peter stepped into the throng. Piped music was still issuing from the PA system but it was barely audible above the clamor of conversation; Peter couldn't tell whether it was the same Patsy Cline documentary or an electronic disco song or a piece of classical music. Just another voice in the hubbub.

"Hey, preacher!"

It was the black man who'd tossed him the blueberry muffin. He was seated at the same table as last night, but with a different pal, a fat white guy. In fact, both of them were fat: exactly the same weight, and with similar features. Coincidences like that served as a reminder that, variations in pigment aside, humans were all part of the same species.

"Hi there," said Peter, pulling up a seat and joining them. They each glanced at his chest to check out the ink-stained design there, but, having satisfied themselves that it was a crucifix rather than something they might wish to comment on, pulled their heads back again.

"How's things, man?" The black guy extended his hand for a handshake. Mathematical formulae were jotted on the sleeve of his shirt, right up to the elbow.

"Very good," said Peter. It had never occurred to him before that dark-skinned people didn't have the option of jotting numbers on their skin. You learned something new about human diversity every day.

"You got yourself fed yet?" The black man had just polished off a plate of something brown and saucy. He nursed a jumbo plastic mug of coffee. His friend nodded a greeting to Peter, and unwrapped a soggy napkin from around a large sandwich.

"No, I'm still functioning on half a muffin," said Peter, blinking dazedly in the light. "Actually, that's not quite true: I've had some raisin bread since then."

"Lay off that raisin bread, man. It's NRC."

"NRC?" Peter consulted his mental database of acronyms. "Not recommended for children?"

"Not Real Coke."

"I don't follow you."

"It's our cute way of saying that it was made here, not back home. Probably contains monocycloparaffins or cyclohexyldodecanoic acid or some shit like that." The black man was half-smiling, but his eyes were serious. The polysyllabic chemical terms had rolled off his tongue with the ease of obscenities. Again, Peter was reminded that each and every member of this personnel must possess skills that amply justified the cost of his or her passage to Oasis. Every member except him.

The black man took a loud slurp of coffee.

Peter asked: "Do you never eat anything that's been made here?"

"My body is my temple, preacher, and you gotta keep it holy. The Bible says that."

"The Bible says a lot of things, Mooney," his pal remarked, and took a big bite out of his sandwich, which dripped gray sauce. Peter glanced across the room at BG. The butch-looking white woman was laughing, almost doubled up. She had one hand on BG's knee, for balance. The piped music poked through a gap in the noise, revealing the chorus of a Broadway song from the mid-twentieth century, the sort of stuff Peter had always associated with provincial charity shops or the record collections of lonely old men.

"How's your sandwich?" he inquired. "Looks pretty good."

"Mmf," nodded the fat white guy. "It *is* good."

"What's in it?"

"Whiteflower."

"Apart from the bread . . ."

"Whiteflower, preacher. Not white *flour*. *White*flower. Roast whiteflower."

Mooney came to the rescue. "My friend Roussos is talking about a flower." He made an elegant hand gesture, unfurling his plump fingers in imitation of an opening blossom. "A flower that grows here. Just about the *only* thing that grows here . . ."

"Tastes like the best pastrami you ever had in your life," said Roussos.

"It's very adaptable," Mooney conceded. "Depending on the flavors you put in, it can be made to taste like just about any damn thing. Chicken. Fudge. Beefsteak. Banana. Sweetcorn. Mushroom. Add water and it's soup. Boil it down and it's jelly. Grind and bake it and it's bread. The universal food."

"You're doing a very good job of selling it," said Peter, "for someone who refuses to eat it."

"Sure he eats it," said Roussos. "He loves the banana fritters!"

"They're OK," sniffed Mooney. "I don't make a habit of it. Mainly I insist on the real deal."

"But isn't it expensive," asked Peter, "if you only eat and drink . . . uh . . . imported stuff?"

"You bet, preacher. At the rate I'm drinking real Coke, I estimate I owe USIC maybe in the region of . . . fifty thousand bucks."

"Easy," confirmed Roussos. "That, and the Twinkies."

"Hell yeah! The prices these sharks charge for a Twinkie! Or a Hershey bar. I tell ya, if I wasn't the easy-going type . . ."

Mooney slid his empty plate toward Peter.

"If I hadn't eaten it all, I could show ya something else," he said. "Vanilla ice cream and chocolate sauce. The vanilla essence and the chocolate is imported, the sauce has maybe some whiteflower in it, but the ice cream . . . the ice cream is pure entomophagy, know what I'm saying?"

Peter reflected a moment. "No, Mooney, I don't know what you're saying."

"Bugs, man. Grubs. *You scream, I scream, we all scream for* . . . whipped bugs!"

"Very funny," mumbled Roussos, and continued chewing his mouthful with less enthusiasm than before.

"And they do a delicious rice dessert that uses—can you *believe* this?—it uses maggots."

Roussos put down his sandwich. "Mooney, you're my pal, I love you a lot, but . . ."

"Not dirty maggots, you understand," Mooney explained. "Clean, fresh, specially bred ones."

Roussos had had enough. "Mooney, put a goddamn sock in it. There are some things it's better for a person not to know."

As if alerted by the sounds of dispute, BG abruptly hove into view.

"Hey, Peter! How's tricks, bro?" The white woman was no longer at his side.

"Excellent, BG. And you?"

"On top of it, man, on top of it. We got the solar panels putting out two hundred and fifty percent of our electric power now. We're ready to pump the surplus into some seriously smart systems." He nodded toward an invisible location somewhere beyond the mess hall, on the opposite side from where Peter had explored. "You seen that new building out there?"

"They all look new to me, BG."

"Yeah, well, this one is *real* new." BG's face was serene with pride. "You go out there and look at it sometime, when you get the oppor*toon*ity. It's a beautiful piece of engineering. Our new rain-collecting centrifuge."

"Otherwise known as the Big Brassiere," interjected Roussos, mopping up the sauce with a fragment of bread-crust.

"Hey, we ain't looking to win no architecture prizes," grinned BG. "Just figuring out how to catch that water."

"Actually," said Peter, "now that you mention it, it's just occurred to me: despite all the rain . . . I haven't seen any rivers or lakes. Not even a pond."

"The ground is like a sponge. Anything that goes in, you don't get back. But most of the rain evaporates in, like, five minutes. You can't see it happening, it's constant. Invisible steam. That's a oxymoron, right?"

"I suppose so," said Peter.

"Anyway, we got to grab that rain before it disappears. That's what me and the team been designing. Vacuum nets. Flow concentrators. Big, big toys. And what about you, bro? You got yourself a church yet?"

The question was asked lightly, as if churches were tools or other necessary supplies that could be requisitioned—which, on reflection, they were.

"Not the physical building, BG," said Peter. "But that's never been what a church is about. A church is made of hearts and minds."

"Low-budget construction," quipped Roussos.

"Show some respect, asshole," said Mooney.

"Actually, BG," said Peter, "I'm kind of in a state of shock—or happy astonishment would be a better word. Last night . . . uh . . . this morning . . . earlier today, Grainger took me to the Oasan settlement . . ."

"The what, bro?"

"The Oasan settlement."

The three men laughed. "You mean Freaktown," said Roussos.

"C-2," corrected BG, abruptly serious. "We call it C-2."

"Anyway," Peter continued, "I got the most *amazing* welcome. These people are desperate to learn about God!"

"Well, ain't that a lick on the dick," said BG.

"They already know about the Bible!"

"This calls for celebration, bro. Lemme buy you a drink."

"I don't drink, BG."

BG raised one eyebrow. "I meant a coffee, bro. If you want alcohol, you're gonna need to set up your church *real* fast."

"Sorry . . . ?"

"Donations, bro. Lotsa donations. One beer will set you back a loooong way."

BG lumbered toward the coffee bar. Peter was left alone with the two fat guys, who took synchronized sips from their plastic mugs.

"It's extraordinary the way you can be driven through a landscape for hours and yet not notice the most striking thing about it," reflected Peter. "All that rain, and none of it collected in lakes or reservoirs . . . I wonder how the Oasans cope."

"No problem," said Roussos. "It rains every day. They get what they need when they need it. It's like, on tap." He held up his plastic mug to an imagined sky.

"In fact," added Mooney, "it would be a problem if the ground *didn't* soak it up. Imagine the floods, man."

"Oh!" said Peter, suddenly remembering. "Have you heard about the Maldives?"

"The Maldives?" Roussos looked wary, as though suspecting that Peter was about to launch into an evangelistic parable.

"The Maldives. A bunch of islands in the Indian Ocean," said Peter. "They got wiped out by tidal waves. Almost everyone who lived there is dead."

"I didn't know that," said Mooney, impassive, as though Peter had just imparted a fragment of knowledge from a branch of science outside his own.

"Wiped out?" said Roussos. "That's bad."

BG returned to the table with a steaming mug of coffee in each fist.

"Thanks," said Peter, taking hold of his. There was a jokey message printed on it: YOU DON'T NEED TO BE HUMAN TO WORK HERE, BUT IT HELPS. BG's said something different. "Hey, I've just realized," said Peter. "These mugs are real plastic. I mean, er . . . *thick* plastic. I mean, not Styrofoam, not disposable . . ."

"We got better things to transport halfway across the universe than disposable cups, bro," said BG.

"Yeah, like Hershey bars," said Mooney.

"Like Christian ministers," said BG, without a hint of mockery.

My dear Bea, wrote Peter an hour later.

No reply from you yet, and maybe it's a bit soon for me to be writing you another letter. But I couldn't wait to tell you—I've just had a MOST eye-opening conversation with some of the USIC guys. It turns out I'm not the first Christian missionary that's been sent here. Before me, there was a man called Marty Kurtzberg. A Baptist apparently, despite the Jewish name. His ministry was welcomed by the natives, but then he disappeared. That was a year ago. No one knows what became of him. Of course the men joke that the Oasans probably ate him, like in those old cartoons of missionaries tied up & getting boiled in a pot by hungry savages. They shouldn't talk like that, it's racist, but anyway I know in my heart that these people—the Oasans, that is—aren't dangerous. Not to me, anyway. Maybe that's a rash assessment, since I've only met one so far. But I'm sure you recall the times when you & I were witnessing for the Lord in some unfamiliar place/context, and we suddenly sensed that we should beat a hasty retreat if we wanted to stay alive! Well, I don't get that feeling here.

Despite the cannibalism jokes, USIC and the Oasans have what appears to be quite a decent trading relationship. It's not the colonial model of exploitation that you'd expect. There's a regular exchange of goods, formal and low-key. The Oasans provide us with basic foodstuffs. As I understand it, the main thing we've been giving the Oasans is medicines. There's not a great variety of plants growing here, which is surprising given the amount of rain. But since most medicines are made from plants I suspect that the scope for discovering/making analgesics, antibiotics, etc, here has been limited. Or maybe this is USIC's evil plan to get the locals hooked on drugs? I won't be able to make authoritative statements about that until I know these people better.

Anyway, are you sitting down?—because I have some amazing news that may knock you flat. The Oasans want only one thing (besides medicines)—the word of God. They've been asking USIC to supply them with another pastor. Asking?– Demanding! According to the men I just spoke to, they (Oasans) have let it be known, politely, that their continued co-operation with USIC's activities depends on it! And here's you and me thinking that USIC was being fantastically generous in offering me this opportunity to come here . . . Well, far from me being here under sufferance, it turns out the whole project may depend on me! If I'd known this before, I would have INSISTED that you came too. But then maybe USIC would have passed me over in favor of someone else, someone less troublesome. There must have been hundreds of applicants. (I still don't understand Why Me. But perhaps the right question is Why Not?)

Anyway, it's clear that I'll be given whatever assistance I require in the setting up of my church. A vehicle, building materials, even laborers. The way things are shaping up, it looks like my yoke is going to be easier than that of just about any missionary since the beginning of Christian evangelism. When you think of Saint Paul, getting beaten up, stoned, shipwrecked, starved, imprisoned . . . I'm almost looking forward to my first setback! (ALMOST)

He paused. That was all he wanted to say, but he felt he should make some reference to the Maldives. And then felt guilty for feeling he should, rather than wanting to.

Love,
Peter

After he vomited up the coffee, he felt better. He wasn't much of a coffee drinker at the best of times—it was a stimulant, after all, and he'd weaned himself off artificial stimulants years ago—but the stuff BG had presented him with tasted foul. Maybe it was made of Oasan flowers, or maybe the combination of imported coffee and Oasan water was bad news. Either way, he felt better rid of it. In fact, he felt almost normal. The effects of the Jump were leaving his system at last. He took a long swig of water straight from the tap. Delicious. He would drink only water from now on.

Energy returned to his body, as though each cell was a microscopic sponge that swelled in gratitude for being fed. Maybe it was. He strapped on his sandals and left his quarters, ostensibly to get the hang of his surroundings but also to celebrate feeling vigorous again. He'd been cooped up too long. Free at last!

Well, free to walk the labyrinth of the USIC base. A welcome change from his room, but not exactly the wide open prairie. Just empty corridors, brightly-lit tunnels of wall, ceiling and floor. And every few meters, a door.

Each door had a name tag on it—surname and initial only—with the person's job description in larger letters. Thus, W. HEK, CHEF; S. MORTELLARO, DENTAL SURGEON; D. ROSEN, SURVEYOR; L. MORO, ENGINEERING TECHNOLOGIST; B. GRAHAM, CENTRIFUGE ENGINEER; J. MOONEY, ELECTRICAL ENGINEER, and so on. The word "engineer" came up often, as did professions ending in "-ist."

No sound came through those doors, and the corridors were likewise silent. Evidently, the USIC staff were either at work or hanging out in the cafeteria. There was nothing sinister in their absence, no reason to feel spooked, yet Peter felt spooked. His initial relief at being able to reconnoiter alone, unwatched, gave way to a hankering for signs of life. He walked with increasing pace, turned corners with increasing resolution, and was met each time with the same rectangular passageways and rows of identical doors. In a place like this, you couldn't even be sure if you were lost.

Just as he was starting to sweat, needled with memories of being trapped in juvenile corrective institutions, the spell was broken—turning another corner, he almost collided, chest-to-chest, with Werner.

"Whoa! Where's the fire?" Werner said, patting his fat torso as if checking that the surprise hadn't done him any harm.

"Sorry," said Peter.

"You OK?"

"Yes, thank you."

"That's good," nodded Werner, cordial but in no mood to chat. "Stay with it, man." A catchphrase or a caution? Hard to tell.

Within seconds, Peter was alone once more. His moment of panic had passed. He could see now that there was a difference between wandering around in an unfamiliar building and being trapped in a prison. Werner was right: he needed to get a grip.

* * *

Back in his own quarters, Peter prayed. Prayed for guidance. No answer came to him, at least not immediately.

The alien—the Oasan—had begged him to return to the settlement as soon as he could. So . . . should he go right away? The claustrophobia that had threatened him in the corridors suggested that he still wasn't fully back to normal—he wasn't a panicker, usually. And it wasn't long since he'd been fainting, vomiting and hallucinating. Perhaps he should continue resting up until he was a hundred percent sure he was himself again. But the Oasan had begged him to return, and USIC hadn't brought him all this way for him to lie in bed staring at his toes. He should go. He should go.

The thing was, it would mean being out of contact with Bea for a number of days. That would be hard on both of them. Yet, in the circumstances, there was no avoiding it; the best he could do was delay his departure just a little while longer, so that they had more time to write to each other first.

He checked the Shoot. Nothing.

Come back ***soon****, Pe****ɤ****er, oh very* ***soon****,* ***soon****er than you can. Read for u****ɤ*** *the Book of* ***ɤ****range New Thing****ɤ****.* He could still hear the Oasan's voice, wheezy and strained as though each word was well-nigh impossible to produce, a bleat from a musical instrument made of preposterously ill-suited materials. A trombone carved out of a watermelon, held together with rubber bands.

But never mind the physicalities: here were souls hungry for Christ, waiting for him to return as he had promised.

But had he promised, in so many words? He couldn't recall.

God's answer resounded in his head. *Don't make everything so complicated. Do what you came here for.*

Yes, Lord, he responded in turn, *but is it OK if I wait for just one more letter from Bea?*

Frazzled from waiting, he went out into the corridors again. They were silent as before, still empty, and smelled of nothing, not even floor cleaner, although they were very clean. Not showroom-pristine or shiny, but free of noticeable dirt or dust. Sensibly clean.

He'd been wrong to feel claustrophobic. Only a few of the passageways were enclosed; others had windows, big ones with sunshine beaming in. How could he have missed this before? How had he managed to choose only the windowless passageways? That was the sort of thing crazy people did—instinctively choosing the experiences that confirmed their own negative attitudes. He was a past master of stuff like that; God had shown him a better way. God and Bea.

He walked along, rereading the names on the doors, trying to commit them to memory in case he ever needed to know where to find someone. He was struck anew by how odd it was that none of the doors was fitted with a lock, just a simple handle which any stranger could open.

"You planning to steal my toothpaste?" Roussos had teased when Peter remarked on this earlier on.

"No, but you might have possessions that are very individual to you."

"You planning to steal my shoes?"

Peter *had* stolen someone's shoes once, and considered mentioning it, but Mooney interrupted:

"He wants your muffins, man! Watch your muffins!"

By coincidence, Peter noted the nameplate of F. ROUSSOS, OPERATING ENGINEER on one of the doors, and walked on. Seconds later, he noted another name in passing and then almost lost his balance when it registered on his consciousness: M. KURTZBERG, PASTOR.

Why was he so surprised? Kurtzberg was missing in action, but no one had said he was dead. Until his fate was established, there was no reason to reallocate his quarters or remove his name. He might return anytime.

On impulse, Peter knocked at the door. There was no answer. He knocked again, louder. Again, no answer. He should, of course, move on. But he did not. Within moments, he was standing inside the room. It was a room identical to his own, in design and décor at least. The window blind was shut.

"Hello?" he called quietly, to verify that he was alone. He tried to convince himself that Kurtzberg, if he *had* been here, would have urged him to come in, and although this was probably true, it didn't alter the fact that it was wrong to enter a stranger's home uninvited.

But this isn't a home, is it? he thought to himself. *The USIC base isn't a home for anybody. It's just one big workplace.* Self-justifying sophistry? Perhaps. But no, it was an instinct that went deeper than that. Bea would have sensed it too. There was something weird about the USIC personnel, something Bea could have helped him articulate. These people had been living here for years; they obviously enjoyed a degree of camaraderie; and yet . . . and yet.

He stepped deeper into Kurtzberg's apartment. There was no evidence of any other illicit visits before this one. The atmosphere was stale, and a film of dust covered the flat surfaces. There was no Shoot on the table, just a bottle of filtered water (half-empty and pure-looking) and a plastic mug. The bed was unmade, with one pillow hanging off the edge, poised to fall, placidly established in that poise, set to hang there forever. Spread out on the bed was one of Kurtzberg's shirts, its sleeves upflung as if in surrender. The armpits were discolored with mildew.

Disappointingly, there were no documents anywhere to be seen: no diaries or notebooks. There was a Bible—a neat paperback Revised Standard Version—lying on a chair. Peter opened it, riffled through the pages. Kurtzberg, he soon realized, was not the sort of person who underlined verses that struck him as particularly significant or who scribbled annotations in the margins. There was nothing here but pristine Scripture. Peter, in his own sermons, would occasionally tell a joke or an aphorism to drive home a point, and one of the dictums he enjoyed quoting, whenever he sensed that people in the congregation were staring at his grubby, decrepit, dog-eared New Testament, was "Clean Bible—dirty Christian. Dirty Bible—clean Christian." Marty Kurtzberg obviously did not subscribe to this view.

Peter opened the wardrobe. A formal suit jacket, in powder-blue linen, hung there, next to a pair of white slacks with faint gray stains on the knees. Kurtzberg was a compact man, no taller than five foot six, and his shoulders were narrow. Two more coat-hangers were cloaked in shirts of the same kind as the one on the bed, replete with classy silk ties slung loosely around the collars. On the bottom of the wardrobe lay a pair of leather shoes, polished to a gleam, and a wadded-up pair of cream socks that were furry with mold.

I'm not going to learn anything here, thought Peter, and turned to leave. As he turned, though, he noticed something lying under the window, a litter of what looked like flower petals. On closer inspection, it proved to be torn fragments of adhesive bandage. Dozens of them. As if Kurtzberg had stood at the window, staring out at goodness knows what, and ripped up an entire packet of Band-Aids one by one, into shreds as small as possible, letting them fall at his feet.

After his visit to Kurtzberg's quarters, Peter lost all motivation to explore the USIC compound any further. A pity, because this was his chance to make up for forgetting all the orienteering info Grainger had told him on arrival. Walking around was good exercise, too; no doubt his muscles needed it, but . . . well, to be truthful, this place made him depressed.

He wasn't sure why. The compound was spacious, clean, cheerfully painted, and there were plenty of windows. OK, a few of the corridors were a bit tunnel-like, but they couldn't *all* face onto the sky, could they? And OK, a few potted plants here and there might have been nice, but USIC could hardly be blamed if the soil of Oasis didn't support ferns and rhododendrons. And it wasn't as if no attempt had been made to finesse the décor. At regular intervals in the corridors hung nicely framed posters that were intended, presumably, to raise a smile. Peter noted perennial favorites like the photo of the worried-looking kitten hanging upside-down from a twig, captioned OH, SHIT . . . , the dog sharing his basket with two ducks, Laurel and Hardy cluelessly attempting to build a house, the elephant balancing on a ball, the convoy of forward-striding cartoon men in Robert Crumb's "Keep On Truckin," and—at impressive size, from chest-height to just under the ceiling—Charles Ebbets' famous monochrome of construction workers eating lunch on an iron girder suspended vertiginously above the streets of Manhattan. A little further on, Peter wondered whether the 1940s propaganda painting titled *We Can Do It!*, showing "Rosie the Riveter" flexing her well-muscled forearm, was intended sincerely to inspire the personnel, or if it had been fixed there with a wink of irony. In any case, some sly graffitist had added, in felt-tip, NO THANKS ROSIE.

Not all the pictures alluded to construction projects and tough challenges; there was a quotient of art-for-art's-sake as well. Peter noted several classic screenprints by Mucha and Toulouse-Lautrec, a collage by Braque or someone of that ilk, and a giant photograph labeled "Andreas Gursky: Rhine II" that was almost abstract in its simple stripes of green field and blue river. There were also facsimiles of old movie posters featuring matinee idols from the far distant past: Bing Crosby, Bob Hope, Marlene Dietrich, even Rudolph Valentino. Something for everybody. The range couldn't be faulted, really, although there was a curious absence of any image that evoked a specific, currently existing spot on Earth, or a passionate emotion.

Craving fresh air, Peter headed for the nearest door that led outside.

Whether the ocean of humid air that rushed to greet him when he emerged into the sunshine could be called "fresh" was, of course, debatable. It certainly wasn't stagnant. Wisps of it lifted locks of his hair to caress his scalp, while other currents slipped into his clothing and sought out the flesh he'd tried to keep covered. But it was better this time. His dishdasha was a single layer between him and the atmosphere, and once it became damp—which happened within seconds—it hung off him loosely, a bit heavy on the shoulders but comfortable everywhere else. The fabric, though thin enough not to be stifling, was tightly woven enough to conceal the fact that he wore nothing else underneath, and stiff enough not to cling. The atmosphere got on well with it.

He walked briskly along the tarmac, along the outer wall of the USIC building, taking advantage of the shade cast by the concrete monstrosity. The sandals allowed his feet to breathe; the sweat between his toes evaporated as soon as it formed. The air tickled his shins and ankles, which ought to have been unpleasant but was really quite delightful. His mood was much improved, the unease he'd felt indoors already forgotten.

Turning a corner, he found himself passing alongside the windowed exterior of the mess hall. The sun blazed on the glass, making it difficult for him to see through, but he got a vague impression of the tables and chairs and the people gathered in there. He waved blindly into the haze, in case anyone had spotted him and might be waving to him. He wouldn't want them to think he was snubbing them.

Averting his eyes from the glare, he caught sight of something unexpected: a large gazebo, situated a couple of hundred meters from the main building. Its canopy was bright yellow, made of canvas or sailcloth, slackly stretched over the support struts. Peter had once conducted a wedding under such a structure; he'd also seen them at the seaside and in public gardens. They provided shelter from sun and rain and could be easily dismantled, although this one looked more permanent. There was movement inside its shade, so he ambled over to investigate.

Four—no, five—people were under the gazebo, dancing. Not in pairs but alone. Actually, no, maybe they weren't dancing: maybe it was a Tai Chi session.

Approaching nearer still, Peter saw that they were in fact exercising. This place was a sort of outdoor gym, furnished not with high-tech electric treadmills and ergometers but with simple wooden and metal structures that resembled children's playground equipment. Moro was there, pumping her legs on the padded sidebars of a weighted wheel. BG was there, lifting sandbags on a pulley. The other three were unknown to Peter. Wet with sweat, all five applied themselves to their brightly-painted mechanisms, stretching, pacing, twisting, bowing.

"Yay, Peter!" called BG, without interrupting the rhythm of his workout. His arms, as he flexed them to raise and lower the bags, were as thick as Peter's legs, and the knots of muscle bulged as though inflated by a puffer. He wore baggy shorts that reached down to his calves and a skimpy cotton singlet through which his nipples poked like rivets.

"That looks like hard work, BG," said Peter.

"Work, play, it's all the same to me," BG replied.

Moro didn't acknowledge Peter's arrival, but then the position she was in—flat on her back with her legs in the air, pedaling—might have made that problematic. She wore a white shalwar whose waistband had slipped under her hip-bones, and a sleeveless T-shirt that left her midriff bare. Sweat had saturated the fabric, rendering it semi-transparent; she breathed loudly and rhythmically. BG had an unimpeded view.

"On top of it, man, on top of it," he exclaimed.

At first, Peter took this to be a bawdy pun. It would fit in with the sexualized banter on the ship and BG's generally bullish air. But as he looked into

BG's face, he realized that the man was abstracted, gazing at no particular object, focused on his own exercise. Moro might or might not be registering on his consciousness as a blur of movement, but as a woman she was invisible to him.

There was another female here, too, a tall, sinewy Caucasian with sparse red hair pulled into a ponytail. Her legs dangled inches off the ground as she supported herself between two parallel bars. She smiled at Peter but it was a smile that said "Let's be properly introduced someday when I'm not so busy." The two unknown men were similarly preoccupied. One stood on a low pedestal with a swivel base, his eyes fixed on his own feet as he gyrated his hips. The other sat on a spider-like structure with many rungs, and was touching his cheeks to his knees. His hands were interlocked behind his head, as tightly as the metal rungs in which he'd hooked his feet. He was a closed circuit of exertion. He heaved himself forward, and one of his knotty vertebrae seemed to pop out of his skin and fly into the air. Actually, it was an insect. The gazebo was a harbor for grasshopper-like bugs which settled calmly on the humans here and there, but mostly just crawled on the canvas, green against the yellow.

The gazebo area contained enough equipment for a dozen people. Peter wondered if it was bad form not to join in. Maybe he should pick a gadget and do a small workout, just a few minutes—enough to be able to walk away without seeming to have come here solely to spectate. But he'd never been a formal-exercise kind of guy and he would feel foolish pretending. Anyway, he was a newbie and surely people could understand that he needed to check the place out.

"Nice day," remarked Moro. She'd stopped pedaling and was taking a breather.

"More than nice. Beautiful," said Peter.

"Sure is," said Moro, and swigged some water from a bottle. One of the green insects had attached itself to her top, between the breasts, like a brooch. She paid it no mind.

"Did the coffee come out?" said Peter.

She looked at him uncomprehendingly. "Coffee?"

"The coffee I made you spill."

"Oh, that." Her expression implied she'd engaged with a dozen challenges and activities since then, and could hardly be expected to remember an event so trivial. "It wasn't coffee."

"Whiteflower?"

"Chicory and rye extract. And yeah, just a bit of whiteflower. To give it body."

"I must try it sometime."

"It's worth trying. Don't expect the most wonderful thing on earth and you won't be disappointed."

"A sound philosophy as a general rule," he said.

Again she looked at him as if he was talking gibberish. He smiled, waved and walked away. There were some people you would never click with, no matter how many times you tried, no matter how many shared experiences came your way, and maybe Moro was one of those. But it didn't matter. As the USIC interviewers had reminded him at every opportunity, he wasn't here for her.

Reluctant to go back inside just yet, Peter strayed further and further from the USIC base. He would be in trouble, he supposed, if he got suddenly tired or unwell, but it was a risk he was willing to take. His health and endurance would be tested to the limit soon enough anyway, when he delivered himself to the Oasan settlement with no supplies apart from a Bible and the clothes he stood up in.

Stark against the horizon towered two silos or chimneys, he wasn't sure which. Obviously not the Big Brassiere, judging from the shape, but what it was he couldn't guess. No smoke coming out, so maybe they were silos after all. Might this be one of the many things that Grainger had explained to him, as she escorted him off the ship? The conversation they were supposed to have had, which he had so embarrassingly forgotten, threatened to grow to mythical proportions: a grand tour of everything, with scripted commentary answering all conceivable questions. He should bear in mind that there was a limit to how much she could have passed on to him at first sight.

He walked toward the silos for ten, twenty minutes, but they didn't get any closer. A trick of perspective. In cities, the buildings and streets gave you a more accurate sense of how far or near the horizon was. In natural, unspoiled landscapes, you didn't have a clue. What looked like a mile or two might be several days' journey.

He should conserve his energy. He should turn around and make his way back to the base. Just as he'd made this decision, however, a vehicle drove into view, coming from the direction of the silos. It was a jeep identical to Grainger's, but as it came closer he could see it wasn't Grainger at the wheel. It was the big, butch-looking woman who'd been talking to BG in the mess hall earlier on. She smoothed the car to a standstill right nearby and wound down the window.

"Running away from home?"

He smiled. "Just exploring."

She gave him the once-over.

"You done?"

He laughed. "Yes."

She tipped her head in a *get-in* gesture and he complied. The interior of the vehicle was messy—there wouldn't have been room for him in the back—and humid, without air conditioning. Unlike Grainger, this woman evidently didn't feel the need to exclude the Oasan atmosphere. Her skin was shiny with sweat and the spiky tips of her bleached hair drooped with moisture.

"Time for lunch," she said.

"Seems we just *had* lunch," he said. "Or was that breakfast?"

"I'm a growing girl," she said. Her tone tipped him off that she was aware she was hefty but couldn't care less. Her arms were well-muscled and her bosom, encased in a bra whose underwiring pushed against the fabric of her white T-shirt, was matronly.

"I was wondering what those are," said Peter, indicating the silos.

She glanced up at the rear-view mirror as they got under way. "Them? They're oil."

"Petroleum?"

"Not exactly. Something like it."

"But you can convert it into fuel?"

She sighed ruefully. "Well now, that's a question that's got other questions hanging off of it. I mean, which way do you go? Design new engines to work with the new fuel or monkey around with the fuel so it works with the old engines? We've had some . . . *discussions* about that, over the years." The way she pronounced the word "discussions" suggested a personal stake in the matter, and a degree of exasperation.

"And who won?"

She rolled her eyes. "The chemistry guys. They figured out how to adapt the fuel. It's like . . . changing the design of the butt so the butt fits the chair. But hey, who am I to argue."

They drove past the yellow gazebo. Moro had left, but the other four were still hard at it.

"Do you ever exercise there?" Peter asked. The woman still hadn't volunteered her name and it felt awkward to ask it now.

"Sometimes," she said. "But my job is more physical than some other people's, so . . ."

"You're a friend of BG's?" said Peter. They would be back at the base within seconds and that would be it, conversation over.

"He's a fun guy," the woman said. "They should have called him BS. You never know what will come out of his mouth. Keeps things interesting."

"Where did he stand on the fuel question?"

She snorted. "No opinion. That's BG! It takes a lot of muscle to be that weak." She slowed the vehicle down and parked it neatly in the shade of the main building. "But he's a great guy," she added. "We get along great. Everybody gets along great. It's a great team."

"Except when you disagree."

She reached forward to pull the key from the ignition. Her upper arm, just below the shoulder, sported a tattoo. "Sported" was probably the wrong word, since the tattoo involved the vestiges of a name, rendered illegible under a later design of a snake crushing a rodent.

"Best not to think about winning and losing here, Mr. Preacher Man," she said, swinging the door open and heaving her body out. "Take a deep breath and count to a million."

9

THE CHOIR RESUMED.

Peter did not wish to count to a million. He was ready now. Pacing his quarters, itching for his rendezvous. His rucksack was packed and he'd already tested its weight on his shoulders. As soon as Grainger was ready to take him, he would go.

His Bible, much annotated, dog-eared and interleaved with paper place-markers, was stashed in the rucksack along with his socks, notebooks and so on. He didn't need to consult it just now: the relevant verses were deeply engraved in his memory. *Psalms* was the obvious resource, the first port of call if you needed courage in the face of a huge, possibly dangerous challenge. The valley of the shadow of death. Somehow, he doubted that he was about to be taken there.

But then, he had a very poor instinct for danger. That time in Tottenham when he almost got knifed—he would have just kept talking to that street gang as they grew in number and pressed more closely and aggressively around him, if it hadn't been for Beatrice whisking him into a minicab.

"You are completely insane," she'd said to him as the doors slammed shut and obscenities ricocheted off the car's surface.

"But look, some of them are waving to us," he'd protested, as they accelerated away from the mob. She looked, and it was true.

Dear Peter, she wrote.
What thrilling news, that the Oasans have already heard of Jesus.
It doesn't surprise me, though. Remember when I asked USIC what

contact there'd been with Christians so far? They were cagey, keen
to maintain their "USIC is non-religious" stance. But there must
have been quite a few Christians among the personnel over the years
and we both know that if you put a real Christian anywhere, things
happen! Even the smallest seed can grow.

And now you're there, my darling, and you can plant more. Many
more!

Peter noted that she wasn't mentioning Kurtzberg. Evidently, when she
wrote this, she hadn't yet received his most recent message. Maybe she was
reading it right now, at exactly the same moment as he was reading hers.
Unlikely, but the thought of such synchronous intimacy was too seductive
to resist.

Don't agonize about the fact that I'm not there with you. If God
had meant us to go on this mission together, He would have fixed it
so we did. I have my own little "missions" here, not as groundbreaking
or exotic as yours, but worthwhile all the same. Wherever we are, life
throws lost souls into our path. Angry, frightened souls who ignore
the light of Christ while cursing the darkness.

Mind you, Christians are capable of ignoring the light of Christ,
too. There's been a ridiculous fuss in our church since you went
away—a storm in a teacup but it has caused me some grief. A few of
our congregation—the older members, mostly—have been grumbling
that we've got "no business" preaching the word of God to "aliens."
The argument goes that Jesus died for humans only. In fact if you
pressed Mrs. Shankland on the issue, she'd probably tell you that
Jesus died for white middle-class English people from the Home
Counties! Geoff has been doing a reasonable job as pastor overall
but he's acutely conscious of being a "stand-in" and he wants to be
popular. His sermons are sincere but safe, he never lays anything on
the line like you do. So . . . the grumblings go on. "Why not China?
There's millions needing it there, dear." Thanks, Mrs. Shanks, for
those words of wisdom.

Well, my darling, I really must go now and have a shower

(assuming the plumbing hasn't gone bung again) and rustle up something to eat. Supplies of my favorite comfort foods continue to be conspicuously absent from the supermarket shelves (even the horrid but serviceable "lo-fat" rollettes have been out of stock for days!) so I've been forced into the arms of another dessert, a sort of chocolate and raisin éclair made by the local baker. Probably just as well: I should be supporting local businesses anyway.

On which edifying note, much love from your excited and admiring wife!

Bea

Peter tried to picture Mrs. Shankland. He had obviously met and talked to her; he'd met and talked to everyone in the congregation. His mind was a blank, though. Maybe he knew her as something other than Mrs. Shankland. Edith, Millicent, Doris. She sounded like a Doris.

Dear Bea, he wrote,

Let's groom Mrs. Shankland for a mission to China. She could convert a thousand people per hour with a few well-aimed words.

Seriously, things have begun moving quickly now, and I may not have another opportunity to write to you for some time. A couple of weeks, even. (A couple of weeks for you—a few days for me, if you know what I mean.) It's a scary prospect but I feel I'm in the Lord's hands—ironically at the same time as I've got the feeling that I'm being used by USIC for some purpose that has yet to be revealed.

Sorry to sound so mysterious. It's USIC's secrecy about Kurtzberg and their caginess about the indigenous people in general that's made me feel this way.

To my great relief, I'm finally over my jetlag or whatever it should be called in the circumstances. I'm sure I would benefit from some more sleep and I'm not sure how I'm going to manage that with 72 hours of sunshine coming up, but at least the sense of disorientation is gone. My urine is still bright orange but I don't think it's dehydration, I think it's something to do with the water. I feel quite well. Rested, if a bit restless. Actually, I'm buzzing with energy. The first thing I'm going to do (once I finish this letter to you) is pack a bag and get myself driven back to the settlement (officially called C-2, although some of the men call it "Freaktown"—charming, eh?) and just be left there. Dumped, if you like. It's no good being ferried about in some sort of protective bubble, venturing out for a quick meet & greet while a USIC chauffeur is parked nearby with the motor running. And if I have my own vehicle, that still seems to say, I'm paying a visit, and I'll leave when I've had enough. Bad message! If God has a plan for me here, among these people, then I must deliver myself into their hands.

OK, that might not have been the wisest course of action for Paul among the Corinthians and Ephesians, but I can hardly claim to be in hostile territory, can I? The most hostility I've had to endure so far is Severin being in a bit of a snit with me on the way over. (Haven't seen him since, by the way.)

In my excitement about what's to come, I must try to remember what I have & haven't described to you so far. How I wish you were here with me, seeing it with your own eyes. Not because it would save me the trouble of trying to describe it (although I must admit my lack of skill in that department is becoming ever more obvious!) but because I miss you. I miss living through the visible moments of life with you. Without you at my side, I feel as though my eyes are just a camera, like a closed-circuit camera without film in it, registering what's out there, second by second, letting it all vanish instantly to be replaced by more images, none of them properly appreciated.

If only I could send you a photo or a movie! How quickly we adjust to what's provided for us and want MORE . . . The technology that allows me to send these words to you, across unimaginable distances, is truly miraculous (—a blasphemous assertion??) yet as soon as I've used it a few times, I think: Why can't I send pictures as well?

Peter stared at the screen. It was pearlescent gray, and his text hung suspended in the plasma, but if he adjusted his focus he could see his ghostly visage: his unruly blond hair, his big bright eyes, his strong cheekbones. His face, strange and familiar.

He seldom looked in mirrors. In his daily routine at home, he acted on the assumption that after he'd showered, shaved and pulled a comb through his hair (straight back across the scalp, no styling), there was no way a mirror could help improve his appearance further. During the years when he was permanently wasted on booze and drugs, he'd begun many mornings examining his reflection, assessing the damage from the night before: cuts, bruises, bloodshot eyeballs, jaundice, purple lips. Since he'd straightened out, there was no need; he could trust that nothing drastic had happened to him since he'd last checked. He would notice the length of his hair only when it started to fall in his eyes, whereupon he would ask Bea to cut it for him; he was only reminded of the deep scar between his eyebrows when she'd stroke it tenderly with her fingers after lovemaking, frowning in concern as though she'd noticed for the first time that he was injured. The shape of his chin only became real to him when he was nestling it in the soft hollow of her shoulder. His neck materialized inside her palm.

He missed her. God, how he missed her.

> The weather is dry just now, he typed. I'm told it will be dry for the next ten hours, then it will rain for several hours, then be dry again for ten hours, then rain, etc. All very reliable. The sun is very warm, but not scorching. There are some insects but they don't bite. I've just had a proper meal. Lentil stew and pita bread. Very filling, if a bit on the stodgy side. The pita bread was made from local flowers. The lentils were imported, I think. Then I had a chocolate pudding that wasn't really chocolate. I wonder if it would have passed muster with you, given your highly developed tastes in that area! It tasted fine to me. Maybe the chocolate was real but the pudding was made of something else—yes, that's it.

He stood up from the table and walked over to the window, allowing the warm light to blaze on his skin. He was aware that the tinted-glass rectangle, big as it was, showed only a tiny fraction of the sky out there, yet even this circumscribed portion was too big to take in at once and suffused with an indescribable variety of subtle colors. Bea, receiving his missives, would be gazing at a glassy rectangle too. She would see nothing of what he saw, not even his ghostly reflection. Only his words. With each inadequate message, her view of him got fainter and foggier. She had no choice but to imagine him in a void, with odd details floating around him like space debris: a plastic ice-cube tray, a glass of green water, a bowl of lentil stew.

My dear Bea, I want you. I wish you were standing here with me, with the light and warmth of the sun on your naked skin, and my arm around your waist, my fingers cradling your ribcage. I'm ready for you. I wish you could verify how ready! If I close my eyes, I can almost feel my chest settling against your breastbone, your legs wrapping themselves around me, welcoming me home.

There is so little said in the New Testament about sexual love, and most of it consists of Paul heaving a deep sigh and tolerating it like a weakness. But I feel certain Jesus didn't see it that way. It was He who talked of two lovers becoming one flesh. It was He who showed compassion to prostitutes and adulterers. If He could feel that way toward people who misused sexual desire, why would He be disappointed if they were happily married instead? It's significant that the only miracle He ever performed for "non-emergency" reasons, but just because He wanted to cheer people up, was at a wedding. We even know He had no problem with being caressed by a female, or He wouldn't have allowed the woman in Luke 7 to kiss His feet and wipe them with her hair. (That's as sexy as anything in Song of Solomon!) How did His face look, I wonder, while she was doing it? An old-fashioned religious painting would no doubt depict Him staring stonily ahead, ignoring her as if nothing was going on. But Jesus didn't ignore people. He was tender and solicitous toward them. He wouldn't have made her feel like a fool.

I know John says, "Love not the world, nor the things of the world. For all that is in the world, the lust of the flesh, and the lust of the eyes, and the pride of life, is not of the Father, but of the world. And the world passeth away, and the lust thereof: but he that doeth the will of God abideth forever." But that's a different point, a point about ALL the mundane stuff we concern ourselves with, all the baggage of being physical beings. And I think John is being too harsh on people. He assumed the Second Coming would happen in his own lifetime—it might come any day, maybe tomorrow afternoon, certainly not centuries in the future. All the early Christians thought that, and it made them intolerant of any activity that wasn't urgently focused on Heaven. But Jesus understood—God understands—that people have a whole life to live before they die. They have friends and family and jobs, and children to give birth to and raise, and lovers to cherish.

My dear, sexy, wonderful wife, I know you are with me in spirit, but I'm feeling sad that your body is so far away. I hope that when you read this, it will be after a long, refreshing night's sleep full of good dreams (and undisturbed by Joshua!). In a few hours or days from now, my desire to hold you will still be unfulfilled, but I hope to be the bearer of some glad tidings on another front.

Love,

Peter

Grainger emerged from her vehicle blinking, ready for their rendezvous. She hadn't changed her clothes—still the same cotton top and slacks, a bit crumpled by now. Her headscarf was inelegantly slung around her neck, speckled with water-drops from her hair, which stuck up from her scalp like the fur of a rain-drenched cat. He wondered if an alarm clock had jolted her from a deep sleep and she'd only had time to splash a few handfuls of water on her face. Maybe it was insensitive to oblige her to drive him again so soon. But when they'd parted, she'd emphasized that she was at his disposal.

"I'm sorry if this is inconvenient," he said. He was standing in the shade of USIC's accommodation wing, just outside the exit door nearest his own quarters. His rucksack hung on his back, already slippery with sweat.

"It's not inconvenient," she said. Her damp hair, exposed to the attentive air, began to emit faint, spidery plumes of steam. "And I'm sorry I was grouchy on the way back this morning. The sight of religious passion always freaks me out."

"I'll try not to be too passionate this time."

"I meant the alien," she said, pronouncing the word without any sign of having taken Peter's little lecture to heart.

"He didn't mean to unnerve you, obviously."

She shrugged. "They give me the creeps. Always. Even when they keep real quiet and don't get too close."

He ventured out of the shade and she stepped aside, away from the vehicle, allowing him access to the trunk, which she'd swung open for him. The engine was purring in readiness.

"You think they mean you harm?" he said.

"No, it's just the sight of them," she said, turning her head toward the horizon. "You try and look at their face and it's like staring into a pile of entrails."

"I thought of fetuses myself."

She shuddered. "Puh-*lease*."

"Well," he said cheerily, stepping up to the vehicle, "that's us off on the wrong foot again."

Out of the corner of his eye, he observed Grainger sizing up his rucksack as he unhitched it from his shoulders. She did a slight double-take as she registered that it was his only luggage.

"You look as if you're going hill-walking. Your little knapsack on your back."

He grinned as he tossed the bag into the trunk.

"*Val-de-reee!*" he sang in a mock-operatic baritone. "*Val-de-raa! Val-de-reee! Val-de-ra-ha-ha-ha-ha . . .*"

"Now you're making fun of one of my idols," she said, placing her fists on her hips.

"Sorry?"

"Bing Crosby."

Peter looked at her in bemusement. The sun was still quite near the horizon, and Grainger was silhouetted in front of it, the crooks of her arms framing triangles of rosy light. "Uh . . ." he said. "Did Bing Crosby sing 'The Happy Wanderer' too?"

"I thought it was his song," she said.

"It's an ancient German folk tune," he said.

"I didn't know that," she said. "I thought it was a Bing number. It was all over the airwaves last year."

He scratched the back of his head, taking pleasure in the bizarreness of everything today: the endless sky with its outsize sun, the playground under the gazebo, his strange new parishioners waiting for another taste of the Gospel, and this dispute over the authorship of "The Happy Wanderer." The air took advantage of his raised arm to find different entry points into his clothing. Tendrils of atmosphere licked him between his sweaty shoulderblades, twirled around his nipples, counted his ribs.

"I didn't know Bing Crosby was back in fashion," he said.

"Those artists are beyond fashion," declared Grainger, with undisguised fervor. "Nobody wants mindless dance music anymore, or cheap, sleazy rock." She imitated an arrogant rock star striking a chord on his phallic guitar. Disdainful though the gesture was, Peter found it attractive: her thin arm, slamming against the invisible guitar strings, pushed her bosom out, reminding him how soft and malleable the flesh of a woman's breast was. "People have had enough of all that," she said. "They want something with class, something that's stood the test of time."

"I'm all for that," he said.

Once they were safely sealed inside the vehicle and driving into the wilderness, Peter raised the issue of communication again.

"You wrote to my wife," he said.

"Yes, I sent her a courtesy message. To let her know you'd arrived safely."

"Thank you. I've been writing to her myself, whenever I can."

"That's sweet," she said. Her eyes were on the featureless brown horizon.

"You're sure there's no possibility of organizing a Shoot for me in the Oasan settlement?"

"I told you, they don't have electricity."

"Couldn't a Shoot run on batteries?"

"Sure it could. You can write on it anywhere. You can write a whole book if you want. But to actually send a message, you need more than a machine that lights up when you switch it on. You need a connection to the USIC system."

"Isn't there a . . . I'm not sure what to call it . . . a relay? A signal tower?" Even as he uttered the words they sounded foolish. The territory stretching into the distance ahead was stark and empty.

"Nope," she replied. "We never needed anything like that. You've got to remember that the original settlement was right near the base."

Peter sighed, leaned his head hard against the seat. "I'm going to miss communicating with Bea," he said, half to himself.

"Nobody's insisting you go and live with these . . . people," Grainger reminded him. "That's your choice."

He kept silent, but his unspoken objection might as well have written itself on the windscreen in front of them in big red letters: GOD DECIDES THESE THINGS.

"I *enjoy* driving," added Grainger after a minute or two. "It relaxes me. I could've driven you there and back every twelve hours, easy."

He nodded.

"You could've had daily contact with your wife," she carried on. "You could've had a shower, a meal . . ."

"I'm sure these people won't let me starve or get filthy," he said. "The one who came out to meet us looked clean enough to me."

"Suit yourself," she said, and revved the accelerator. They jumped forward with a gentle whiplash effect, and a quantity of damp earth was thrown up behind them.

"I'm not suiting myself," he said. "Suiting myself would mean taking you up on your generous offer. I have to consider what's best for these people."

"God knows," she muttered, then, realizing what she'd just said, graced him with a big self-conscious smile.

The landscape was no more colorful or varied now that the sun had fully risen, but it had its own sober beauty, in common with all endless vistas of the same substance, whether it be sea, sky or desert. There were no mountains or hills, but the topography had gentle gradients, patterned with ripples similar to those in wind-swept deserts. The mushroom-like blossoms—whiteflower, he supposed—glowed brilliant.

"It's a lovely day," he said.

"Uh-huh," said Grainger, matter-of-fact.

The sky's color was elusive; the gradations were too subtle for the eye to discern. There were no clouds, although occasionally a patch of air would shimmer and become slightly blurry for a few seconds, before shivering back into transparency. The first few times Peter observed this phenomenon, he stared intently, straining to understand it, or perhaps appreciate it. But it just made him feel as though his eyes were defective, and he quickly learned to shift his gaze elsewhere whenever the blurring began to occur. The roadless earth, dark and moist and sprinkled with pale blooms, was the most restful sight. Your eyes could just relax on it.

Overall, though, he had to admit that the scenery here was less beautiful than he'd seen in, well, quite a few other places. He had expected mind-boggling landscapes, canyons shrouded in swirling mists, tropical swamps teeming with exotic new wildlife. It suddenly occurred to him that this world might be quite a dowdy one compared to his own. And the poignancy of that thought made him feel a rush of love for the people who lived here and knew no better.

"Hey, I've just realized!" he said to Grainger. "I haven't seen any animals. Just a few bugs."

"Yeah, it's kind of . . . low diversity here," she said. "Not much scope for a zoo."

"It's a big world. Maybe we're just on a sparse little bit of it."

She nodded. "Whenever I go to C-2, I could swear there's more bugs there than at the base. Also, there's supposed to be some birds. I've never seen them myself. But Tartaglione used to hang around C-2 all the time, and he told me he saw birds once. Maybe it was a hallucination. Living in the wilderness can do scary things to the brain."

"I'll try to keep my brain in reasonable condition," he promised. "But seriously, what do you think really happened to him? And to Kurtzberg?"

"No idea," she said. "Both of them just went AWOL."

"How do you know they're not dead?"

She shrugged. "They didn't vanish overnight. It was kinda gradual. They would come back to the base less and less often. They became . . . distant. Didn't want to stick around. Tartaglione used to be a real gregarious guy. Blabbermouth maybe, but I liked him. Kurtzberg was friendly too. An army chaplain. He used to reminisce to me about his wife; he was one of those sentimental old widowers who never remarry. Forty years ago was only yesterday for him, it was like she'd never died. Like she was just slow getting dressed, she'd be along any minute. Kind of sad, but so romantic."

Observing a wistful glow transfiguring her face, Peter felt a pang of jealousy. Childish as it might be, he wanted Grainger to admire him as much as she'd admired Kurtzberg. Or more.

"How did you find him as a pastor?" he asked.

"Find him?"

"What was he like? As a minister?"

"I wouldn't know. He was here from the beginning, before my time. He . . . counseled the personnel who were having problems adjusting. In the early days, there were people who didn't really belong here. I guess Kurtzberg tried to talk them through it. But it was no use, they bailed out anyway. So USIC tightened up the screening process. Cut the wastage." The wistful glow was gone; her face was neutral again.

"He must have felt like a failure," suggested Peter.

"He didn't come across that way. He was the chirpy type. And he got a boost when Tartaglione came. The two of them really got along, they were a team. They were a hit with the aliens, the natives, whatever you want to call them. Making big progress. The natives were learning English, Tartaglione was learning . . . whatever." A couple of insects flew against the windscreen, their bodies disintegrating on impact. Brown juice scrawled across the glass. "And then something came over them."

"Maybe they caught some sort of disease?"

"I don't know. I'm a pharmacist, not a doctor."

"Speaking of which . . ." said Peter. "Have you got some more drugs to give the Oasans?"

She frowned. "No, I didn't have time to raid the pharmacy. You need clearance for stuff like that."

"Stuff like morphine?"

She drew a deep breath. "It's not what you think."

"I haven't told you what I think."

"You think we're handing out narcotics here. It's not like that. The drugs we give them are medicines. Antibiotics, anti-inflammatories, simple analgesics. I'm confident they're being used for the correct purpose."

"I wasn't accusing you of anything," he said. "I'm just trying to get a handle on what these people have and don't have. They don't have hospitals, then?"

"I guess not. Technology isn't their forte." She pronounced it "for-*tay*," with almost mocking exaggeration, the way Americans tended to when quoting French.

"So they're primitives, would you say?"

She shrugged. "I guess."

He leaned his head back again and reviewed what he knew about his flock so far. He had only met one of them, which was a small sample by any standards. That person had worn a robe and cowl which looked as though it was probably handmade. His gloves and boots . . . ? Again, probably handmade, albeit to a sophisticated standard. You'd need a machine to sew leather so neatly, surely? Or perhaps just very strong fingers.

He recalled the architecture of the settlement. Complexity-wise, it was in a class above mud huts or dolmens, but it was hardly high-tech manufacture. He could imagine each stone being fashioned by hand, baked in rudimentary ovens, hauled into place by sheer human—or inhuman—effort. Maybe, inside the buildings, undiscovered by the likes of Grainger, there were all sorts of mechanical marvels. Or maybe not. But one thing was certain: there was no electricity, and there would be nowhere to plug in a Shoot.

He wondered how God would feel about him announcing, right here in the car, that he really, desperately needed to know whether Bea had written to him, and that Grainger must therefore turn the vehicle around and drive all the way back to the base. To Grainger, it would look like a failure of nerve. Or maybe she'd be touched by the ardency of his love. And then again, maybe what seemed like a backward step would in fact be God pushing him forward, God using the delay to put him in exactly the right place at exactly the right time. Or was he just straining to find a theological justification for his own lack of courage? He was being tested, that much was obvious, but what was the nature of the test? Whether he had the humility to appear weak in the eyes of Grainger, or whether he had the strength to push on?

Oh Lord, he prayed. *I know it's impossible, but I wish I could know whether Bea has written back to me yet. I wish I could just close my eyes and see her words before me, right here in the car.*

"OK, Peter, this is your last chance," said Grainger.

"Last chance?"

"To check for a message from your wife."

"I don't understand."

"There's a Shoot in this vehicle. We're still in range of USIC reception. Another five, ten minutes of driving, and we'll lose it."

He could feel himself blushing, with a big daft smile so broad it made his cheeks ache. He felt like hugging her.

"Yes, please!"

Grainger stopped the vehicle but did not switch off the motor. She flipped open a hatch in the dashboard and pulled out a slim contraption of plastic and steel, which unfolded to reveal a monitor and miniature keyboard. He made the inarticulate noise of surprise and admiration that was called for in the circumstances. There was momentary confusion as to which of them would take responsibility for switching the thing on, and their fingers met on the back of the console.

"Take your time," said Grainger, settling back in her seat and turning her face toward the window, in a display of respect for his privacy.

For nearly a minute—sixty agonizing seconds—nothing manifested on the Shoot except a computerized promise that a search was under way. Then the screen filled up from top to bottom with unfamiliar words: Bea's words. God bless her, she'd responded.

Dear Peter, she wrote.

I'm upstairs in our study. It's six o'clock in the evening, still full daylight, indeed nicer than it's been all day. The sun is at a low angle now, mild and buttery yellow, streaming through the window straight onto the wall-hanging/collage that Rachel & Billy & Keiko made for me. Those kids must be teenagers by now, but their wonderful depiction of the ark and its animals is still as cute and eccentric as when it was first done. The way Rachel used bits of orange wool for the lion's mane never ceases to charm me, especially when it's lit up by the evening sun as it is now. One of the giraffes' necks is dangling down, though; I'll have to stick it back into place.

I only just arrived home from work—bliss to be sitting down at last. Too tired to have a shower yet. Your message was waiting for me when I rushed upstairs to check.

I can understand that you would be eager to go and live with the Oasans ASAP. Of course God is with you and you shouldn't delay unnecessarily. Try not to sacrifice common sense, though! Remember when that crazy Swedish guy at our Bible study dedicated himself to Jesus? He said his faith in the Lord was so strong that he could just ignore the council's eviction notice, and God would organize a miraculous last-minute reprieve! Two days later he's on our doorstep with his bin-bag of possessions . . . I'm not implying you're a nutcase like him, just reminding you that practicalities are not your strong suit and that bad things can happen to ill-prepared Christians just as they can happen to anyone else. We need to strike a balance between trusting in our Lord to provide, and showing due respect for the gift of life and this body we've been lent.

Which means: when you do go to live with your new flock, please make sure you've got (1) some way of calling for help if you're in trouble, (2) an emergency supply of food and water, (3) DIARRHEA MEDICATION, (4) the compass co-ordinates of the USIC base and the Oasan settlement, (5) a compass, obviously.

Peter glanced up at Grainger, just in case she was reading over his shoulder. But she was still gazing out the window, feigning deep interest in the landscape. Her hands were loosely clasped in the lap of her gown. Small hands, well formed, with pale, stubby-nailed fingers.

He was embarrassed that, apart from a bottle of green water filled from the tap, he'd taken none of the precautions Bea was urging him to. Not even the diarrhea pills she'd bought for him specially. They would hardly have weighed down his rucksack, those pills, and yet he'd removed them. Why had he removed them? Was he being as foolish as the crazy Swede? Maybe he was indulging a stubborn pride in his minimal baggage, his statement of single-minded intent: two Bibles (King James and New Living Translation, 4th edition), half a dozen indelible marker pens, notebook, towel, scissors, roll of adhesive tape, comb, flashlight, plastic wallet of photographs, T-shirt, underpants. He closed his eyes and prayed: *Am I drunk on my own mission?*

The answer came, as it so often did, in the form of a sensation of well-being, as if a benign substance in his bloodstream was suddenly taking effect.

"Have you fallen asleep?" asked Grainger.

"No, no, I was just . . . thinking," he said.

"Uh-huh," she said.

He returned to Bea's message, and Grainger returned to her study of the empty scrubland.

Joshua is helping me type, as usual: lying between the keyboard and the monitor, his back legs and tail obscuring the top row of keys. People think I'm being pedantic when I write numbers out as words, or type "pounds" instead of "£," but the fact is that I have to lift up a comatose cat every time I want to use those symbol keys. I did it just now and Joshua made that "njurp" sound that he makes. Last night, he slept right through, didn't utter a peep (purred a bit). Maybe he's adjusting to your absence at last. I wish I could! But don't worry, I'm getting on with things.

The Maldives tragedy has dropped out of the media. There are still small articles on the inner pages of some newspapers, and a few ads placed by charities for donations, but the front pages and the prime-time coverage (as far as I can tell from the clips on my phone) have moved on to other things. An American congressman has just been arrested for shooting his wife. Point-blank range, with a shotgun, in the head, while she was swimming in their private pool with her lover. The newspaper journalists must be so relieved—with the Maldives thing they had to evoke gruesomeness without appearing prurient, whereas with this they can be as gross as they like. The woman's head was blown off from the jaw up, and her brains (juicy detail!) were floating around in the water. The lover was shot too, in the abdomen ("possibly aiming for the groin"). Lots of supplementary articles about the congressman, his life history, achievements, college graduation photo, etc. The wife looked (when she still had a head) exactly as you'd expect: glamorous, not quite real.

Mirah and her husband are getting along much better. I met her at the bus stop and she was giggly, almost flirtatious. She didn't raise the issue of converting to Christianity again, just talked about the weather (it's been bucketing down again). She only got serious when she talked about the Maldives. Most of the islanders were Sunni Muslims; Mirah's theory is that they must have displeased Allah by "doing bad things with tourists." A very confused young lady, but I'm glad she's no longer in crisis and I'll continue to pray for her. (I'll pray for your Coretta too.)

Speaking of Muslims, I know they consider it a terrible sin to throw away old or damaged copies of the Qur'an. Well, I'm about to commit a similar sin. You know the big cardboard box of New Testaments we had sitting in the front room? It looks like they'll have to be dumped. I can imagine this might upset you to hear, given your news about the Oasans being so hungry for the Gospel. But we've had some flooding. The rain was ridiculous, it didn't let up for five hours, full pelt. There were torrents flowing along the footpaths; the drains just aren't designed to take that kind of volume. It's all right now, in fact the weather is lovely, but half the houses in our street have suffered damage. In our case, it's just some patches of sopping-wet carpet, but unfortunately the books were right on one of those patches and it was a while before I realized they'd been soaking up the water. I tried drying them out in front of the heater. Big mistake! Yesterday they were New Testaments, today they're blocks of wood pulp.

Anyway, not your problem. Hope this reaches you before you set off!

Bea

Peter drew a deep breath, past the lump in his throat. "Do I have time to write her a reply?" he asked.

Grainger smiled. "Maybe I should've brought a book."

"I'll be quick," he promised.

Dear Bea, he wrote, then got stuck. His heart was beating hard, Grainger was waiting, the engine was running. It was impossible.

No time for a proper "epistle"—think of this as a postcard. I'm on my way!

Love,

Peter

"OK, that's it," he said, after he pressed the button. His words hung on the screen more briefly than usual; the transmission was almost instant. Maybe the open air was conducive to the Shoot's function, or maybe it had something to do with the small amount of text.

"Really?" said Grainger. "You're done?"

"Yes, I'm done."

She leaned across him and replaced the Shoot in its slot. He could smell the fresh sweat inside her clothing.

"OK," she said. "Let's hit the road."

They spoke little on the remainder of the drive. They'd discussed the essentials—or agreed not to discuss them further—and neither of them wanted to part on bad terms.

The Oasan settlement was visible a long time before they reached it.

In full daylight, it glowed amber in the light of the sun. Not exactly magnificent, but not without beauty either. A church spire would make all the difference.

"Are you sure you'll be OK?" said Grainger, when they had a mile or so to go.

"Yes, I'm sure."

"You might get sick."

"Yes, I might. But I'd be surprised if I died."

"What if you really need to come back?"

"Then the Lord will make it possible for me to come back somehow."

She chewed on that for a few seconds, as if it were a dry mouthful of bread.

"The next official USIC visit—our regular trading exchange—is in five days," she said, in an efficient, professionally neutral voice. "That's five *real* days, not days according to your watch. Five cycles of sunrise and sunset. Three hundred . . ." (she consulted the clock on the dashboard) ". . . three hundred and sixty-odd hours from now."

"Thanks," he said. It seemed impolite not to make a note of it, if only on his palm, but he knew perfectly well that he was unable to calculate three hundred and sixty hours into the future, when he'd be sleeping and waking up at various points along the way. He would have to take everything as it came.

At the final approach, C-2 appeared deserted. Their vehicle pulled up at the outermost of the settlement's buildings, the same place as before, marked with the white star. Except that the building was now marked with something else as well: a large message, freshly painted in white letters three feet tall.

WEL COME

"Wow," said Grainger. "Didn't know they had it in them."

She stopped the car and flipped open the hatch. Peter got out and fetched his rucksack from the boot, strapping it onto his shoulders so that his arms were free. He wondered what the correct way of taking his leave of Grainger might be: a handshake, a courteous nod, a casual wave, or what.

The crystalline curtain that veiled the nearest doorway sparkled as its trails of beads were brushed aside to allow someone through—a hooded figure, small and solemn. Peter couldn't tell if it was the same person he'd met before. He remembered the Oasan's robe as being blue, whereas this one's was pastel yellow. No sooner had the person stepped out into the light than another person followed him, parting the beads with his delicate gloves. This one's robe was pale green.

One by one, the Oasans emerged from the building. They were all hooded and gloved, all daintily built, all wearing the same soft leather boots. Their robes were all the same design, but there was scarcely a color repeated. Pink, mauve, orange, yellow, chestnut, faun, lilac, terra-cotta, salmon, watermelon, olive, copper, moss, lavender, peach, powder blue . . .

On and on they came, making room for each new arrival, but standing as close together as a family. Within a few minutes, a crowd of seventy or eighty souls had gathered, including smaller creatures who were evidently children. Their faces were mostly obscured, but here and there a whitish-pink swell of flesh peeped out.

Peter gaped back at them, light-headed with exhilaration.

The frontmost of the Oasans turned to face his people, raised his arms high and gave a signal.

"*Amaaaaaaaaaaaaaaaaaaaa* . . ." they sang, sweet and high and pure. The vowel floated for five, ten seconds without pause, a grand communal ex-halation, sustained so long that Peter interpreted it as an abstract sound, un-related to language or melody. But then it incorporated a consonant—albeit an unidentifiable one—and shifted in pitch: ". . . *ꙅiiiiiiing graaaaaaaaꙅe! How ꙅweeeeeeeꙅ a ꙅouuuuuund thaꙅ ꙅaaaaaaaaaaaaaved a wreeeeꙅꙨ liiiiike meeeeeeeeeee!*"

In synchronized obedience to an energetic hand gesture from the front-most Oasan, they all stopped at once. There was a huge intake of breath, a seventy-strong sigh. Peter fell to his knees, having only just recognized the hymn: the anthem of fuddy-duddy evangelism, the archetype of Salvation Army naffness, the epitome of everything he had despised when he'd been a young punk snorting lines of speed off piss-stained toilet lids, of everything he dismissed as stupid when he was liable to wake in a pool of congealed vomit, of everything he considered contemptible when he was stealing money from prostitutes' handbags, of everything he laughed off as worthless when he himself was a toxic waste of space. *I once was lost, and now I'm found.*

The conductor gestured again. The choir resumed.

II

ON EARTH

10

THE HAPPIEST DAY OF MY LIFE.

Peter hung suspended between ground and sky, in a net, his body covered with dark blue insects. They weren't feeding on him, they were just using him as a place to be. Every time he stretched or coughed, the bugs would hover up from his skin or hop elsewhere, then settle back. He didn't mind. Their legs didn't tickle. They were quiet.

He'd been awake for hours, resting his cheek on his upflung arm so that his eyes were in line with the horizon. The sun was rising. It was the end of the long night, his fifth night spent among the Oasans.

Not that he was among the Oasans now, strictly speaking. He was alone on his improvised hammock, strung aloft between two pillars of his church. His church-in-progress. Four walls, four internal pillars, no roof. No contents except for a few tools and coils of rope and vats of mortar and braziers of oil. The braziers of oil were cold now, glimmering in the dawn light. Far from serving any religious purpose, they had a purely practical function— throughout the long dark spell, for the duration of each working "day," they were ignited to throw light on the proceedings, and extinguished again when the last of the Oasans had gone home and "Father Peรer" was ready to retire.

His congregation were laboring as fast as they could to build this place, but they weren't here with him today; not yet. They were still asleep, he supposed, in their own houses. Oasans slept a lot; they got tired easily. They'd work for an hour or two, and then, whether the task had been arduous or not, they would go home and rest in bed for a while.

Peter stretched in his hammock, recalling what those beds looked like, glad he wasn't in one now. They resembled old-fashioned bathtubs, sculpted out of a sort of tough, dense moss, as lightweight as balsa wood. The tubs were lined with many layers of a cotton-like material, swaddling the sleeper in a loose, fluffy cocoon.

Three hundred hours ago, when he first succumbed to tiredness after the great exhilarations of his first day, Peter had been offered such a bed. He'd accepted it, in deference to his hosts' hospitality, and there had been much ceremonial well-wishing for a good long rest. But he hadn't been able to sleep.

For one thing, it was daytime, and the Oasans felt no need to darken their bedchambers, positioning their cots right under the brightest sunbeams. He'd climbed in anyway, squinting against the glare, hoping he might lose consciousness through sheer exhaustion. Unfortunately, the bed itself was an obstacle to sleep; the bed, in fact, was insufferable. The fluffy blankets were soon drenched with sweat and vapor, they exuded a sickly coconutty smell, and the tub was slightly too small, even though it was larger than the standard model. He suspected it had been carved specially for him, which made him all the more determined to adjust to it if he could.

But it was no good. As well as the absurd bed and the excessive light, there was also a noise problem. On that first day, there were four Oasans sleeping near him—the four who called themselves Jeſuſ Lover One, Jeſuſ Lover Fifſy-Four, Jeſuſ Lover Sevenſy-Eighſ and Jeſuſ Lover Sevenſy-Nine—and all four of them breathed very loudly, creating an obnoxious symphony of sucking and gurgling. Their cots were in another room, but Oasan houses had no closeable doors, and he could hear the sleepers' every breath, every snuffle, every glutinous swallow. In his bed back home, he was used to the barely audible breathing of Bea and an occasional sigh from Joshua the cat, not this kind of racket. Lying in the house of the Oasans, he reconnected with a long-forgotten episode from his past life: the memory of being lured off the street by a charity worker and put in a hostel for rough sleepers, most of them alcoholics and addicts like himself. The memory, too, of sneaking out of there in the middle of the night, back onto the bitter streets, to look for his own quiet space to doss down in.

So: here he was in a hammock, suspended in his half-built church, in the open air, in the absolute desert stillness of the Oasan dawn.

He had slept well and deeply. He'd always been able to sleep outdoors: a legacy of his homeless years, perhaps, when he'd lain comatose in public parks and doorways, lain so still that people would mistake him for a dead body. Without alcohol, it was a bit more difficult to drift off, but not much. The intrusiveness of the vaporous Oasan atmosphere was easier to deal with, he felt, if he surrendered himself to it. Being indoors and yet not truly enclosed was the worst of both worlds. The Oasans' houses weren't sealed and air-conditioned like the USIC base; they were ventilated by open windows through which the insidious atmosphere swirled freely. There was something disconcerting about lying tucked up in a bed and imagining every minute that the surrounding air was lifting the blankets with invisible fingers and slipping in beside you. Much better to lie exposed, wearing nothing but a single cotton garment. After a while, if you were sleepy enough, you felt as though you were reclining in a shallow stream, with the water flowing gently over you.

On waking today, he'd noted that the exposed flesh of his arms was intricately patterned with diamond-shaped welts, the after-impression of the net. It gave him a crocodilian appearance. For a minute or two, until the marks faded, he enjoyed the fantasy of having turned into a lizard-man.

His hosts had taken his rejection of their bed very well. On that first day, several hours after the formal commencement of communal sleep, when Peter had already been sitting upright for a long while, praying, thinking, fidgeting, taking sips from his plastic bottle of water, filling in the time before he dared to offend everyone by escaping outside, he sensed a presence enter his room. It was Jesus Lover One, the Oasan who'd first welcomed him to the settlement. Peter considered pretending to have been jolted out of a deep sleep, but decided that such childish dissembling would fool no one. He smiled and waved hello.

Jesus Lover One walked to the foot of Peter's cot and stood there, head bowed. He was fully dressed in his blue robe, complete with hood, boots and gloves, his hands clasped in front of his abdomen. The lowered head and the cowl obscured his grisly visage, allowing Peter to imagine human features in that shadowy occlusion.

Lover One's voice, when it came, was hushed so as not to wake the others. A soft, suppressed sound, eerie as the creak of a door in a distant building.

"You are praying," he said.

"Yes," whispered Peter.

"I al𝐬o am praying," said Lover One. "Praying in hope for the hearing of God."

The two of them were silent for a while. In the adjacent room, the other Oasans snorted on. Eventually, Lover One added:

"I fear all my praying go a𝐬𝐬ray."

Peter replayed the half-dissolved word in his mind several times. "Astray?" he echoed.

"A𝐬𝐬ray," confirmed Lover One, unclasping his hands. With one he pointed upward. "God abide there." With the other he pointed downward. "Prayer go here."

"Prayers don't travel in space, Lover One," said Peter. "Prayers don't *go* anywhere; they just *are*. God is here with us."

"You hear God? Now?" The Oasan raised his head in rapt attention; the cleft in his face quivered.

Peter stretched his cramped limbs, aware suddenly of a full bladder.

"Right now, I only hear my body telling me I need to pass water."

The Oasan nodded, and motioned for them to go. Peter clambered out of the cot and found his sandals. There were no toilets in Oasan dwellings, as far as he'd been able to tell during the first twenty-odd hours of his visit. Wastes were disposed of out-of-doors.

Together, Peter and Jesus Lover One left the bedchamber. In the adjacent room, they passed the other sleepers, who lay swaddled in their cocoons, immobile as corpses apart from their raucous respirations. Peter tip-toed; Lover One walked normally, the velvety skin of his boots making no noise on the floor. Side by side they passed through a vaulted corridor, and emerged through a curtain of beads into the open air (if the air on Oasis could ever truly be called open). The sun shone into Peter's swollen eyes, and he was even more aware of how sweaty and itchy the bedding had made him.

Glancing back at the building he'd emerged from, he noticed that, in the hours since his arrival, the Oasan atmosphere had been applying its energies to the

WEL COME

on the outer wall, loosening the paint's purchase, transforming it into a perspirous froth that now trickled toward the ground, the letters blurred into Cyrillic patterns.

Jesus Lover One saw him looking at the remains of the message. "Word on wall ѕoon gone," he said. "Word, in memory, abide." And he touched his chest, as if to indicate where memory abided for his kind, or maybe he was signaling heartfelt emotion. Peter nodded.

Then Jesus Lover One led him through the streets (could unpaved paths be called streets, if they were wide enough?), further into the settlement. There was no one else about, no sign of life, although Peter knew that the throng of people he'd met earlier in the day must be in there somewhere. The buildings all looked the same. Oblong, oblong, oblong; amber, amber, amber. If this settlement and the USIC base constituted the only architecture on Oasis, then this was a world where aesthetic niceties weren't wanted and utilitarianism ruled. It shouldn't bother him, but it did. All along, he'd assumed that the church he would build here should be simple and unpretentious, to give the message that its outward form didn't matter, only the souls inside; but now he was inclined to make it a thing of beauty.

With every step, he grew more desperate to piss and wondered if Lover One was going to unnecessary lengths to find him a private place to do it. Oasans themselves had no such concern for privacy, at least not when it came to toilet matters. Peter had seen them expelling their wastes freely in the streets, unheedful of the loss. They'd be walking along, solemnly focused on where they were going, and then, out of the bottom of their robes, a trail of turdlets would patter onto the earth: gray-green pellets that didn't smell and, if accidentally stepped on by other people, disintegrated into a powdery pulp, like meringue. Nor did the feces linger long on the ground. Either the wind blew it away, or it got swallowed up by the earth. Peter had not seen any Oasan expelling liquid waste. Perhaps they didn't need to.

Peter most certainly needed to. He was just about to tell Lover One that they must stop right now, *anywhere*, when the Oasan came to a halt in front of a circular structure, the architectural equivalent of a biscuit tin, but the size of a warehouse. Its low roof was festooned with chimneys . . . no, funnels—large, ceramic-looking funnels, like kiln-fired vases—all pointing up at the sky. Lover One motioned Peter to enter through the beaded doorway. Peter obeyed. Inside, he was faced with a jumbled array of vats and canisters and kegs, each different and handmade, each fed from tubes that snaked up to the ceiling. The containers were arranged around the sides of the room, leaving the center free. An artificial pond, the size of a backyard swimming pool in the wealthier parts of Los Angeles, glimmered with pale emerald water.

"Waᵭer," said Lover One.

"Very . . . clever," Peter complimented him, having rejected the word "resourceful" as too difficult. The sight of the full pond and the dozens of tubes fogged with moisture made him only more convinced that he was about to wet himself.

"Enough?" inquired Lover One, as they turned to leave.

"Uh . . ." hesitated Peter, nonplussed.

"Enough waᵭer? We paᵴ now?"

At last, Peter understood the misunderstanding. "Pass water"—of course! Such collisions between the literal and the colloquial—he'd read about them so often in accounts of other missionary expeditions, and had promised himself he would avoid ambiguity at all times. But Lover One's acquiescence to his request had been so low-key, so smooth, that there was no hint of a communication glitch.

"Excuse me," said Peter, and strode ahead of Lover One, to the middle of the street, where he hitched up his dishdasha and allowed the urine to squirt free. After what seemed like several minutes of pissing he was ready to turn and face Jesus Lover One again. And as soon as he did, Jesus Lover One released a solitary ball of feces onto the ground. A gesture of respect for an unfathomable ritual, like kissing a European the correct number of times on the correct sides of the face.

"Now, again, you ᵴleep?" The Oasan pointed back the way they'd come: back toward the sweat-drenched coconut-stinky tub in the house of snorers.

Peter smiled non-committally. "First, take me to where our church will be. I want to see it again."

And so the two of them had walked out of the settlement, across the scrubland, to the chosen site. Nothing had been built yet. The site was marked with four gouges in the soil, to demarcate the four corners of the future structure. And, inside those demarcations, Peter had scratched the basic design of the interior, explaining to the seventy-seven souls gathered around him what the lines represented. Now that he saw his drawing again, on the deserted patch of earth, after a gap of many hours and through eyes bleary with exhaustion, he saw it as the Oasans might have seen it: crude, mysterious gouges in the dirt. He felt unequal to the task ahead of him: grossly so. Bea would no doubt counsel him that this meant he was confusing objective reality with the amount of sleep he'd had, and of course she'd be right.

The site contained a few other traces of the Jesus Lovers' assembly. The small posset of vomit that one of the infant Oasans had disgorged during Peter's opening speech. A pair of boots, specially made as a gift for Peter, but several inches too small for him (a mistake which appeared to cause neither embarrassment nor amusement: just mute acceptance). A semi-transparent amber water jug, almost empty. A metallic blister foil (medicine courtesy of USIC) from which the last tablet had been expressed. Two scattered cushions, on which a couple of the younger children had snoozed when the grown-ups' discussion strayed too far into invisible realms.

Peter hesitated for a few seconds, then fetched the cushions and arranged them one near the other. Then he lowered himself to the ground, pillowing his head and his hip. His weariness immediately began to drain out of his flesh, as if seeping into the soil. He wished he was alone.

"You were un✺a✺i✺fied in our bed," Jesus Lover One remarked.

The sibilant cluster in the third word rendered it unintelligible to Peter. "Sorry, I didn't quite hear what you just . . . ?"

"You were . . . unglad," said Lover One, clenching his gloves with the effort of finding a pronounceable word. "In our bed. ✺leep came never."

"Yes, that's true," conceded Peter, with a grin. "Sleep came never." Honesty was the best policy, he felt. There would be misunderstandings enough without creating more with diplomacy.

"Here, ᴄsleep will come for you," Lover One observed, indicating, with a wave of his gloved hand, the open space around them.

"Yes, here sleep will come for me."

"Good," concluded the Oasan. "Then all will be well."

Would all be well? There seemed reason to hope that it would. Peter had a good feeling about his ministry here. Already, inexplicably felicitous things had happened—small things, true, not strictly miraculous, but enough to indicate that God was taking a special interest in the way things were panning out. For example, when he'd told the story of Noah and the Flood (at the Oasans' request) and, at the instant that the heavens opened in the Scripture, it started raining for real. And then there was that amazing occasion, after they'd all stopped work for the night and the braziers had been extinguished and they'd been sitting there in the dark, when he'd recited the opening verses of Genesis (again at their request) and, at the exact instant that God said "Let there be light," one of the braziers had sputtered back into life, bathing them all in a golden glow. Coincidences, no doubt. Peter was not a superstitious person. Much closer to genuine miracles, in his opinion, were the sincere declarations of faith and fellowship from these people so incredibly different from himself.

Then again, there had been a few disappointments. Or not exactly disappointments, just failures to communicate. And he couldn't even figure out why these encounters had fallen flat; he didn't understand what it was he hadn't understood.

For example, the photographs. If he'd learned one thing over the years, it was that the best—and quickest—way of forging intimacy with strangers was to show them photos of your wife, your home, yourself when younger and decked out in the fashions and haircuts of a bygone decade, your parents, your brothers and sisters, your pets, your children. (Well, he didn't have children, but that in itself was a talking point. "Children?" people would always say, as if they hoped he was saving the best photos for last.)

Perhaps what had gone wrong with his show-and-tell with the Oasans was that the group was too large. Seventy-odd people examining his photos and handing them on, almost all of those people contemplating an image that was unrelated to the commentary he was giving at that point. Although, to be honest, the responses of the Jesus Lovers who'd been sitting right nearby, who had the opportunity to make the connection between the image and his explanation of it, were just as hard to fathom.

"This is my wife," he'd said, extracting the topmost of the photographs from the plastic wallet and handing it to Jesus Lover One. "Beatrice."

"Bea𝛾ri𝒸," repeated Jesus Lover One, his shoulders contorting with effort.

"Bea for short," said Peter.

"Bea𝛾ri𝒸," said Jesus Lover One. He held the photograph gently in his gloved fingers, at a strict horizontal angle, as if the miniature Beatrice posing in her mulberry-colored jeans and imitation cashmere sweater was in danger of sliding off the paper. Peter wondered if these people could even *see* in the conventional sense, since there was nothing on their faces he could identify as an eye. They weren't blind, that was obvious, but . . . maybe they couldn't decode two-dimensional images?

"Your wife," said Jesus Lover One. "Hair very long."

"It was, then," said Peter. "It's shorter now." He wondered if long hair was attractive or repulsive to those who had none at all.

"Your wife love Je𝒸u𝒸?"

"She certainly does."

"Good," said Jesus Lover One, handing the photograph to the person next to him, who accepted it as though it were a sacrament.

"This next one," said Peter, "is the house where we live. It's in a satellite . . . uh . . . a town not far from London, in England. As you can see, our house is much the same as the houses all around it. But inside, it's different. Just like a person can look the same as those all around him, but inside, because of his faith in the Lord, he's very different." Peter looked up to assess how this simile was going over. Dozens of Oasans were kneeling in concentric circles around him, waiting solemnly for a rectangle of card to be conveyed toward them. Apart from the colors of their robes and some slight variations in height, they all looked the same. There were no fat ones, no musclebound ones, no lanky lunks, no bent-backed crones. No women, no men. Only rows of compact, standardized beings squatting in the same pose, dressed in garments of identical design. And, inside each of their hoods, a coagulated stew of meat that he could not, could not, simply could not translate into a face.

"Needle," said the creature called Jesus Lover Fifty-Four, shuddering. "Row of needle. Row of . . . knife."

Peter had no idea what he was talking about. The photograph, which showed nothing more than a drab ex–council house and a flimsy metal fence, was handed on.

"And this one," he said, "is our cat, Joshua."

Jesus Lover One contemplated the photo for fifteen or twenty seconds.

"Jeſuſ Lover?" he asked at last.

Peter laughed. "He can't love Jesus," he said. "He's a cat." This information was greeted with silence. "He's not . . . He's an animal. He can't think . . ." The word "self-consciously" came to his mind, but he rejected it. Too many sibilants, for a start. "His brain is very small. He can't think about right and wrong, or why he's alive. He can only eat and sleep." It felt like a disloyal thing to say. Joshua could do a lot more than that. But it was true he was an amoral creature, and had never worried about why he'd been put on the earth.

"We love him, though," Peter added.

Jesus Lover One nodded.

"We alſo love thoſe who have no love for Jeſuſ. However, they will die."

Peter doled out another picture. "This one," he said, "is my church back home." He almost repeated BG's wisecrack about not winning any architecture prizes, but managed to swallow the words. Transparency and simplicity were what was called for here, at least until he figured out how these people ticked.

"Needle, ſo many needle," said one of the Oasans whose Jesus Lover number Peter hadn't yet learned.

Peter leaned forward to look at the picture upside-down. There were no needles anywhere to be seen. Just the ugly blockish exterior of the church, lent a modicum of style by a faux-Gothic arch in the metal gate surrounding the building. Then he noticed the spikes on the tops of the railings.

"We need to keep the thieves out," he explained.

"Thief will die," agreed one of the Oasans.

Next in the pile was another photo of Joshua, curled up on the duvet with one paw shielding his eyes. Peter shuffled the picture to the back of the pile and selected another.

"This is the back yard of the church. It used to be a car park. Just concrete. We got the concrete ripped up and replaced with soil. We figured people could walk to church or maybe find parking in the street . . ." Even as he spoke, he knew that half of what he was saying—maybe all of it—must be incomprehensible to these people. Yet he couldn't stop. "It was a risk. But it paid . . . it was . . . it led to success. It led to a good thing. Grass grew. We planted shrubs and flowers, even some trees. Now the children play out there, when the weather is warm. Not that the weather is often very warm where I come from . . ." He was babbling. *Get a grip.*

"Where you?"

"Sorry?"

The Oasan held up the photograph. "Where you?"

"I'm not in this one," said Peter.

The Oasan nodded, handed the picture to his neighbor.

Peter extracted the next photo from the plastic wallet. Even if the Oasan air had not been so humid, he would have been sweating by now.

"This is me as a child," he said. "It was taken by an auntie, I think. The sister of my mother."

Jesus Lover One examined the snapshot of Peter at age three. In it, Peter was dwarfed by his surroundings but still conspicuous in a bright yellow parka and orange mittens, waving at the camera. It was one of the few family photos found in Peter's mother's house when she died. Peter hoped the Oasans didn't ask to see a photograph of his dad, because his mother had destroyed them all.

"Very high building," commented Jesus Lover Fifty-Four. He meant the tower block in the background of the picture.

"It was a horrible place," said Peter. "Depressing. And dangerous, too."

"Very high," confirmed Jesus Lover Fifty-Four, passing the square of card on to the next in line.

"We moved to somewhere better not long after that," he said. "Somewhere safer, anyway."

The Oasans hummed approvingly. Moving to somewhere better and safer was a concept they could understand.

The already handed-out photos, meanwhile, were making their way among the crowd. One of the Oasans had a question about the photo of Peter's church. In the picture, a few members of the congregation were gathered outside the building, queuing to enter the blue door. One of them was Ian Dewar, the Afghanistan veteran who got around on crutches, having refused the MoD's offer of an artificial leg because he valued any opportunity to talk about the war.

"Man have no leg," observed the Oasan.

"That's right," said Peter. "There was a war. His leg was badly injured and the doctors had to cut it off."

"Man dead now?"

"No, he's fine, he's perfectly fine."

There was a communal murmur of wonder, and several utterances of "Praiꞇe the Lord."

"And this," said Peter, "is my wedding day. Me and my wife Beatrice, on the day we got married. Do *you* have marriage?"

"We have marriage," said Jesus Lover One. A mildly amused retort? Exasperated? Weary? Simply informative? Peter couldn't tell from the tone. There *was* no tone, as far as he could hear. Only the straining of exotic flesh to imitate the action of vocal cords.

"She introduced me to Christ," added Peter. "She brought me to God."

This provoked a more excited reaction than the photos.

"Your wife find the Book," said Jesus Lover Seventy-something. "Read, read, read, read before you. Learn the ꞇechnique of Jeꞇouꞇ. Then your wife come for you and ꞇay, I have found the Book of ꞇꞇrange New Thingꞇ. Read now, you. We ꞇhall noꞇ periꞇh, buꞇ have eꞇernal life."

Summarized like that, it sounded more like the serpent's overtures to Eve in the Garden of Eden than Bea's matter-of-fact allusions to Christianity in the hospital ward where she first met him. But it was interesting that the Oasan went to such strenuous effort to quote from *John 3:16* verbatim. Kurtzberg must have taught them that.

"Did Kurtzberg teach you that?"

The Jesus Lover who'd spoken did not reply.

"Whosoever believes in Him shall not perish, but have everlasting life," said Peter.

"Amen," said Jesus Lover One, and the whole congregation murmured likewise. The word "amen" seemed mercifully tailored to their mouths, or whatever part of their bodies they used to speak with. "Amen, amen, amen."

The wedding photo reached an Oasan in an olive-green robe. He—or she?—recoiled.

"Knife," the Oasan said. "Knife."

It was true: in the picture, Peter and Bea were both clutching the hilt of an outsized knife, ready to cut the ceremonial slice from their wedding cake.

"It's a custom," said Peter. "A ritual. It was a very happy day."

"Happy day," echoed the Oasan, in a voice like wet bracken being crushed underfoot.

Peter shifted in his hammock, turned away from the rising sun. The molten orange light was getting a little intense. He lay on his back, staring up into the sky, and watched the purple retinal after-images dancing in the cloudless expanse. Soon the after-images vanished and the sky was a uniform gold. Were the sunrises back home ever gold like this? He couldn't recall. He could remember golden light on the bed, lighting up Joshua's fur and the exposed curves of Bea's legs if it was a warm morning and she'd kicked the sheets off. But that wasn't the same as the whole sky being gold; the sky outside their bedroom would be blue, surely? He was annoyed with himself for forgetting.

There was so much to tell Bea, and he'd written too little of it down. When the next opportunity came for him to transmit a letter, he would no doubt manage, with the help of the notes he'd scribbled in his notebooks, to list the most significant things that had happened in the last three hundred and sixty hours. But he would miss the nuances. He would forget the quiet, unspoken moments of intimacy between him and his new friends, the unexpected glimmers of understanding in areas of communication that he'd assumed would be hopelessly dark. He might even forget to mention the gold sky.

His notebooks were in his rucksack, somewhere below. Perhaps he should've kept them up here in the hammock, so that he could jot down his thoughts and reflections whenever they came to him. But then he might stab himself in his sleep with the pencil, or the pencil might fall through the net onto the hard floor below. A pencil could land in such a way that the internal sliver of graphite got shattered in a dozen places, rendering it unsharpenable. Peter's pencils were precious to him. Properly taken care of, they would continue to be of service when all the ballpoint pens had leaked and all the felt-tips had dried up and all the machines had malfunctioned.

Besides, he enjoyed the hours he spent in his hammock, free of anything to do. While he was on the ground, working with his flock, his brain was buzzing constantly, alive to challenges and opportunities. Every encounter might prove crucial in his ministry. Nothing could be taken for granted. The Oasans believed themselves to be Christians, but their grasp of Christ's teachings was remarkably weak. Their hearts were full of amorphous faith, but their minds lacked understanding—and they knew it. Their pastor needed to concentrate hard every minute, listening to them, watching their reactions, searching for a glimpse of a light going on.

And, more mundanely, he also needed to concentrate on the physical jobs at hand: the carrying of stones, the spreading of mortar, the digging of holes. When the day's work was over, and the Oasans had gone home, it was bliss to climb into his hammock, and know that he could do nothing more. As though the net had scooped him out of the stream of responsibility and suspended him in limbo. Not the Catholic idea of Limbo, of course. A benign limbo between today's work and tomorrow's. A chance to be a lazy animal, owning nothing but its skin, stretched out in the dark, or dozing in the sun.

The net from which his hammock had been fashioned was just one of several on the site. Nets were what the Oasans used for carrying bricks. They carried the bricks from . . . from where? From wherever the bricks came from. Then across the scrubland to the church. Four Oasans, each with a corner of the net knotted around his (or her?) shoulder, would march solemnly, like pallbearers, carrying a pile of bricks slung in between them. Even though the church site was not far from the main cluster of buildings— just far enough away to give it the necessary status of a place outside the common run of things—it was still quite a long walk, Peter imagined, if you were carrying bricks. There seemed to be no wheeled transport available.

Peter found this a little hard to believe. The wheel was a self-evidently nifty invention, wasn't it? You'd think that the Oasans, even if they'd never conceived of it before, would have adopted the wheel as soon as they'd seen it being used by the USIC workforce. Pre-technological lifestyle was all very dignified, he wasn't putting it down, but surely nobody, if they had a choice, would lug bricks around in a fishing net.

Fishing net? He called it that because that's what it looked like, but it must have been designed for some other purpose—maybe even specifically for carrying bricks. There was nothing else to use nets for, here. There were no oceans on Oasis, no large bodies of water, and presumably no fish.

No fish. He wondered whether this would cause comprehension problems when it came to certain crucial fish-related Bible stories. There were so many of those: Jonah and the whale, the miracle of the loaves and the fishes, the Galilean disciples being fishermen, the whole "fishers of men" analogy . . . The bit in *Matthew 13* about the kingdom of Heaven being like a net cast into the sea, gathering fish of every kind . . . Even in the opening chapter of *Genesis*, the first animals God made were sea creatures. How much of the Bible would he have to give up as untranslatable?

But no, he mustn't get too downhearted about this. His problems were far from unique; they were par for the course. Missionaries in Papua New Guinea in the twentieth century had been forced to find a way around the fact that the native people didn't know what sheep were, and that the local equivalent—pigs—didn't work so well in the context of the Christian parables, because Papuans regarded their pigs as prey to be slaughtered. Here on Oasis, he would be faced with similar challenges and he would simply have to find the best compromises he could.

All things considered, he and the Oasans were communicating very well so far.

He rolled onto his belly and looked through the netting at the ground below. His sandals were positioned neatly, side by side, directly underneath him, on the smooth cement floor. Oasan cement barely needed troweling; it spread out almost by itself and dried with a satiny finish, feeling less like concrete to the touch than unvarnished wood. It had just enough traction for the soft leather boots of the Oasans not to slip on it.

Next to his sandals lay one of the few tools on the site: a large spoon, the size of a . . . how would he describe it to Bea? The size of a small spade? Bicycle pump? Police baton? Anyway, it wasn't made of wood or metal, but of a kind of glass, as strong as steel. Its function was to stir the mortar in the mortar vat, preventing it from drying too quickly. Last night—that is to say, five or six hours ago—before he'd climbed into his hammock to sleep, he'd spent a good twenty minutes cleaning mortar off this spoon, scraping at it with his fingers. The debris lay scattered all around. He had done a thorough job, despite his tiredness. The spoon was ready for another day's stirring. Father Peter was the one who did that job, since he was the strongest.

He smiled at the thought of it. He had never been a particularly strong man before. In a past life, he'd been beaten up by other alcoholics, and tossed casually into the lock-up by police. Once, he had done his back in attempting to carry Bea to bed. ("I'm too fat! I'm too fat!" she'd cried, thus compounding the embarrassment all around when he was forced to let her fall.) Here, among the Oasans, he was a mighty creature. Here, he stood at the mortar vat and churned its contents with a giant spoon, admired by the weaker beings around him. It was ridiculous, he knew that, but there was something very morale-boosting about it, nonetheless.

The whole process of constructing a house was absurdly simple here, yet effective. The mortar-vat, primitive as a cauldron and stirred by hand, was typical of the level of sophistication. In the church walls as they took shape, there was no skeletal infrastructure: no metal stanchions, no wooden framework. The lozenge-shaped bricks were simply glued to the foundations and then fastened one to the other, layer upon layer. It seemed a dangerously simpleminded way to construct a building.

"What if there's a storm?" he'd asked Jesus Lover One.

"ᴧᴕorm?" The upper parts of the cleft in Lover One's face—the foreheads of the babies, so to speak—contorted gently.

"What if a very great wind comes? Will it blow the church to the ground?" Peter puffed hard and loud through his lips, waved his hands, and mimed the collapse of a building.

Lover One's grotesque face contorted a little further, into a shape that might signal amusement, or bemusement, or perhaps meant nothing. "Bond break never," he said. "Bond ⳬ⳨rong, oh very ⳬ⳨rong. Wind like . . ." He reached out and stroked Peter's hair, barely ruffling it, to show how ineffectual the wind was.

The reassurance was no less childlike than the construction method, but Peter decided to trust that the Oasans knew what they were doing. Their settlement, while not exactly impressive architecturally, seemed stable enough. And he had to admit that the mortar which bound the bricks was amazingly strong. When freshly spread, it looked like maple syrup, but within an hour it was hard as amber, and the join was unbreakable.

There was no scaffolding employed in the construction of this church, no ladders, nothing made of wood or metal. Instead, access to the higher reaches of the walls was provided by a method that was at once grossly cumbersome and beautifully practical. Large carved blocks of hardened moss—the same material as was used for the Oasans' beds—were assembled into staircases, stacked against the outside of the building. Each staircase was about two meters wide and as high as it needed to be; additional steps could be affixed as the level of the bricklaying moved higher off the ground. Over the last few days, the staircases had grown in scale until they were twice Peter's height, but despite their bulk they were obviously temporary, a building tool that was no more a part of the final conception than a ladder would have been. They were even portable—just. They could be shifted sideways if everyone pitched in. Peter had helped to shift a staircase several times, and although he couldn't confidently estimate how much it weighed because of the communal musclepower pushing against it, he didn't think it was heavier than, say, a refrigerator.

The utter simplicity of the technology charmed him. Granted, it wouldn't be adequate to the task of building a skyscraper or a cathedral, unless the surrounding area could accommodate a staircase the size of a football stadium. But for building a modest little church, it was blindingly sensible. The Oasans would simply walk up the steps, each carrying a single brick. They would pause at the summit of their makeshift staircase and cast their eyes (or eye, or viewing cleft, or whatever) over the wall's top layer, surveying it as a concert pianist might contemplate his keyboard. Then they would glue the next brick in its correct spot, and walk down the steps again.

By any standards, the work method was labor-intensive. There were perhaps forty Oasans on site at the busiest time of day, and Peter had the impression that there would have been even more were it not for the risk of getting in each other's way. The work was conducted in an orderly fashion, unhurriedly, but without pause—until each Oasan reached what was evidently his (or her?) limit, and went home for a while. They worked in silence mostly, conferring only when there was some new challenge to master, some risk of getting something wrong. He could not tell if they were happy. It was his fervent intention to get to know them well enough to know if they were happy.

Were they happy when they sang? You would think that if singing was torture for them, they wouldn't do it. As their pastor, he certainly hadn't expected them to greet him with a massed chorus of "Amazing Grace," and they could easily have arranged some other gesture of welcome. Maybe they needed a channel for their joy.

Happiness was such an elusive thing to spot: it was like a camouflaged moth that might or might not be hidden in the forest in front of you, or might have flown away. A young woman, newly in Christ, had said to him once, "If you could've seen me a year ago, going out on the piss with my mates, we was so happy, we was laughing our heads off, we never stopped laughing, people was turning their heads to see what's so funny, wishing they could be having as good a time as us, we was flying, I was on top of the world, and all the time underneath I was thinking, God help me, I am so fucking lonely, I am so fucking sad, I wish I was dead, I cannot stand this life one minute longer, you know what I mean?" And then there was Ian Dewar, ranting about his time in the military, complaining about the cheapskates and the beancounters who'd robbed the troops of essential supplies, "buy your own binoculars, mate, here's one flak jacket for every two guys, and if you get your foot blown off take two of these wee tablets 'cause we've not got any morphine for you." Fifteen minutes into one of these rants, mindful that there were other people patiently waiting to speak to him, Peter had interrupted: "Ian, forgive me, but you don't need to keep revisiting this stuff. God was there. He was there with you. He saw it happen. He saw everything." And Ian had broken down and sobbed and said he knew that, he knew that, and that's why underneath it all, underneath the complaining and the anger, he was happy, truly happy.

And then there was Beatrice, on the day when he proposed to her, a day on which every conceivable thing had gone wrong. He'd proposed at 10:30 in the morning, in sweltering heat, as they stood at an automatic teller machine in the high street, preparing to do some grocery shopping at the supermarket. Maybe he should have gone down on one knee, because her "Yes, let's" had sounded hesitant and unromantic, as though she regarded his proposal as nothing more than a pragmatic solution to the inconvenience of high rents. Then the teller machine had swallowed her debit card and she'd had to go into the bank to sort it out, which involved a meeting with the manager and a lamentable episode in which she was grilled for half an hour as if she was an imposter trying to defraud another Beatrice whose card she had stolen. This humiliation ended with Bea canceling her relationship with the bank in a righteous fury. They'd gone shopping then, but were able to afford barely half the things on their list, and, when they emerged into the car park, they found that a vandal had scratched a crude swastika into the paintwork of their car. If it had been anything other than a swastika—a cartoon penis, a swear word, *anything*—they would probably have just lived with it, but *this* they had no choice but to get fixed, and it would cost them a fortune.

And so the day went on: Bea's phone ran out of battery and died, the first garage they drove to was shut, the second garage was booked up solid and not interested, a banana they tried to eat for lunch was rotten inside, a perished strap on Bea's shoe snapped, forcing her to limp, the car's engine started making a mysterious noise, a third garage gave them the bad news about what a new coat of enamel would cost, as well as pointing out that their exhaust was corroded. In the end it took them so long to get back to Bea's flat that the expensive lamb chops they'd bought had discolored badly in the heat. That, for Peter, was the final straw. Rage sped through his nervous system; he seized the tray and was about to throw it into the rubbish bin, throw it with wildly excessive force, to punish the meat for being so vulnerable to decay. But it wasn't him who'd paid for it and he managed—

just—to control himself. He put the groceries away in the fridge, splashed some water on his face and went in search of Bea.

He found her on the balcony, gazing down at the brick wall that surrounded her block of flats, a wall crowned with barbed wire and spikes of broken glass. Her cheeks were wet.

"I'm sorry," he said.

She fumbled for his hand, and their fingers interlocked.

"I'm crying because I'm happy," she explained, as the sun allowed itself to be veiled in clouds, the air grew milder and a gentle breeze stroked their hair. "This is the happiest day of my life."

11

HE REALIZED FOR THE FIRST TIME
THAT SHE WAS BEAUTIFUL, TOO.

"God bless our reunion, Father Peter," a voice called to him.

Dazzled by the light, he turned clumsily, almost falling out of the hammock. The approaching Oasan was a silhouette against the rising sun. All Peter knew was that the voice was not Jesus Lover Fifty-Four's, the only voice he could put a name to without additional clues.

"Good morning," he responded. The "God bless our reunion" had meant no more than that. Oasans invoked the blessing of God for everything, which either meant they understood the notion of blessedness better than most Christians, or not at all.

"I come to build our church again."

Two weeks in these people's midst had sharpened Peter's ear; he immediately understood that "church" was "church." He mulled over the voice, matched it with the canary-yellow robe.

"Jesus Lover Five?"

"Yes."

"Thank you for coming."

"For God I will do whatever he wishes, any thing, any time."

Even as he was listening to Lover Five speak, Peter wondered what it was that made this voice different from, say, Lover Fifty-Four's. Not the *sound* of it, that was for sure. The marvelous variety of voices he was accustomed to back home—or even at the USIC base—was non-existent among the Oasans. There were no sonorous baritones here, no squeaky sopranos, husky altos, nervous tenors. No shades of brightness or dullness, shyness or aggression, sangfroid or seductiveness, arrogance or humility, breeziness or sorrow. Maybe, in his clueless foreignness, he was missing the nuances, but he was pretty sure he wasn't. It was like expecting one seagull or blackbird or pigeon to squawk differently from the others of its kind. They just weren't designed to.

What the Oasans *could* do was deploy language in distinctive ways. Jesus Lover Fifty-Four, for example, was ingenious in avoiding words he couldn't pronounce, always managing to come up with a sibilant-free alternative. These evasions ("lay-a-bed" for "sleep," "give knowledge" for "teach," and so forth) made his speech eccentric but fluent, promoting the illusion that he was at ease with the alien tongue. By contrast, Jesus Lover Five didn't bother with avoidance; she just tried to speak conventional English and if there were lots of "t"s and "s"s in the words she needed, well, too bad. Then again, she made less effort to speak clearly than some of the other Oasans—her shoulders didn't contort as much when she was coughing up a consonant—and this made her more difficult to understand, sometimes.

Her, her, her. Why did he think of her as female? Was it just the canary-yellow robe? Or did he actually sense something, on a level too instinctive to analyze?

"There's not much we can do until the others arrive," he said, lowering himself out of the hammock. "You could have slept longer."

"I wake in fear. Fear you will be gone."

"Gone?"

"U⳽IC will come ⳾oday," she reminded him. "⳾ake you home."

"The USIC base is not my home," he said, fastening his sandals. Squatting to do so, he was almost head-to-head with Jesus Lover Five. She was small for an adult. If she was an adult. Maybe she was a child—no, she couldn't be. Maybe she was incredibly old. He just didn't know. He knew that she was forthright, even by the standards of Oasans; that she could only work for twenty or thirty minutes at a time before wandering off; and that she was related to someone who was not a Jesus Lover, which caused her sadness, or something he interpreted as sadness. Actually, he couldn't even swear that this non-believer was a blood relative of hers; maybe it was a friend. And the sadness thing was kind of a hunch on his part; Oasans didn't weep or sigh or cover their faces with their hands, so she must have said something to make him come to that conclusion.

He tried to recall other things about Jesus Lover Five, but couldn't. The human brain was like that, unfortunately: it sifted intimacies and perceptions, allowed them to trickle through the sieve of memory, until only a token few remained, perhaps not even the most significant ones.

He really must write more things down, next time.

"U૨IC will ૪ake you," Jesus Lover Five repeated. "I fear you will no૪ re૪urn."

He walked to a gap in the wall that would eventually be a door, passed through it, and stood in the shade of his church, to relieve himself on the ground. His pee was a darker orange than before, making him wonder if he was drinking too little. The Oasans drank sparingly and he'd learned to do the same. One long swig of his plastic bottle first thing upon waking, a few swigs at measured intervals throughout the working day, and that was it. The Oasans refilled his bottle without fuss whenever it ran low, walking all the way back to the settlement with it and back again, but he didn't want to cause them undue bother.

They'd taken superb care of him, really. An intensely private people, who spent the bulk of their time quietly conversing with close friends and family inside their homes, they had nevertheless welcomed him with open arms. Metaphorically speaking. They were not what you'd call touchy-feely. But their goodwill toward him was unmistakable. At intervals throughout each day, as he worked on the church site, he would glimpse someone walking across the scrubland, bearing a gift. A plate of fried globs resembling samosas, a tumbler of lukewarm savory gloop, a hunk of something crumbly and sweet. His fellow workers seldom ate on site, preferring to take formal meals at home; occasionally someone might pick a few blossoms of whiteflower straight off the ground, if they were newly-sprouted and juicy. But the cooked treats, the little offerings, were for him alone. He accepted them with unfeigned gratitude, because he was hungry all the time.

Less so now. Loath to earn a reputation as a glutton, he'd grown accustomed, over the last three hundred and sixty-odd hours, to a sharply reduced calorie intake, and relearned something that he'd known well during his wasted years: that a man could survive, and even keep active, on very little fuel. If he was forced to. Or too drunk to care. Or—as was currently the case—happily preoccupied.

When he rejoined Jesus Lover Five, she was seated on the floor, her back propped against a wall. Her posture rucked up her robe so that her thin thighs and the space between them were carelessly exposed. Glimpsing Lover Five's nakedness, Peter thought he could detect an anus, but nothing that resembled genitals.

"Tell me more from the Book of Strange New Things," she said.

Male and female created he them, was the phrase that came to his mind.

"Do you know the story of Adam and Eve?" he asked.

"God bless all stories from the Book. They are all of them good."

"Yes, but do you know it? Have you heard it before?"

"Long before," she conceded. "Now again."

"Did you hear it from Kurtzberg?"

"Yes."

"Why isn't Kurtzberg here to tell you the story again himself?" Peter had posed this same question in half a dozen different ways since arriving at the settlement. He hadn't got a satisfactory answer yet.

"Father Kurtzberg go away. Leave us in lack of him. Like you will leave." Her clefted face, usually a healthy pink, was whitish pale in its complicated contours.

"I'm only going for a little while. I'll be back soon."

"Yes, keep your prophecy, please." She said it neither playfully nor imploringly, as far as he could tell. She was matter-of-fact and, although she spoke no louder than other Oasans, emphatic. Or maybe he was just imagining that. Maybe he was imagining everything, perceiving differences that weren't there, in his keenness to get a grip on these people. He and Bea had read an article once, in some magazine or other, which explained that cats were not really individuals, despite what their owners liked to think. All the distinctive noises and eccentric behaviors that your cat exhibited were merely standard-issue genetic features built into that particular sub-breed. A horrible article, written by a smug little journalist with a receding hairline. Bea had been thoroughly shaken by it. And it took a lot to shake Bea.

"Tell me, Jesus Lover Five," said Peter. "The person you love who makes you sad, the one who doesn't believe in Jesus. Is he your son?"

"My . . . brother."

"And have you other brothers and sisters?"

"One alive. One in the earth."

"And your mother and father?"

"In the earth."

"Do you have children of your own?"

"God plea☙e no."

Peter nodded, as if he understood. He knew he was not much the wiser, and that he still had no proof of Lover Five's gender.

"Please forgive my stupidity, Jesus Lover Five, but are you male or female?"

She didn't reply, only cocked her head to one side. Her facial cleft did not contort, he'd noticed, when she was confused: not like Jesus Lover One's. He wondered if this meant that she was smarter, or just more guarded.

"You just referred . . . You just told me of your brother. You called him your brother, not your sister. What makes him your brother and not your sister?"

She considered this for a few seconds. "God."

He tried again. "Are you your brother's brother or your brother's sister?"

Again she pondered. "For you, I will name me with the word brother," she said. "Becau☙e the word ☙i☙❧er i☙ very hard ❧o ☙peak."

"But if you could say 'sister' more easily, is that what you would say?"

She shifted her posture, so that the robe again covered her groin. "I would ☙ay nothing."

"In the story of Adam and Eve," he pressed on, "God created man and woman. Male and female. Two different kinds of people. Are there two different kinds here too?"

"We are all differen❧," she said.

Peter smiled and looked away. He knew when he was beaten. Through a hole in the wall, which in the very near future would be a beautiful stained-glass window, he spied, in the distance, a procession of Oasans carrying nets full of bricks.

A thought occurred to him, and, along with that thought, the realization that he hadn't asked anyone at USIC to show him the Oasans' old settlement, the one they'd mysteriously abandoned. It was one of those oversights that Bea, if she'd been here, would never have been guilty of. The mere mention of a place called C-2 would have made her curious about C-1. Honestly, what was wrong with him? Beatrice, on the rare occasions she became exasperated with these sorts of lapses, would accuse him of having one of his "Korsakoff moments." That was a joke, of course. They both knew that alcohol had nothing to do with it.

"Lover Five?" he said.

She didn't respond. Oasans didn't waste words. You could take it for granted that they were listening, waiting for you to get around to the part of your question they could answer.

"When Kurtzberg was with you," he continued, "in the previous . . . in the settlement where you lived before, the one near the USIC base, did you build a church there?"

"No," she replied.

"Why not?"

She thought about it for a minute. "No," she said.

"Where did you worship?"

"Father Kurༀ๖berg came ๖o uໄ in our houໄe," she said. "The whole day, he go from one houໄe ๖o another houໄe ๖o another houໄe. We waiༀ for him. We waiༀ a long ๖ime. Then he come, read from the Book, we pray, then he go."

"That's one way of doing it," said Peter diplomatically. "A very good way. Jesus himself said, 'Where two or three are gathered together in my name, there am I in the midst of them.'"

"We ໄaw never Jeໄouໄ," said Jesus Lover Five. "ௌurௌ iໄ be๖er."

Peter smiled, unable to suppress a surge of pride. He sincerely hoped that a physical church would, indeed, be better.

"But where did Kurtzberg live?" he pushed on. "I mean, where did he sleep, while he was here with you?" He imagined Kurtzberg swaddled in a bathtub-shaped cocoon, sweating all night into fancy pajamas. As a short man, the pastor would at least have been the right size to fit into an Oasan bed.

"Father Kur𝕩𝖘berg have car," said Jesus Lover Five.

"Car?"

"Big car." With her hands, she sketched a shape in the air: a crude rect-angle that did not suggest any particular kind of vehicle.

"You mean he would just drive off to spend the night . . . uh . . . to sleep at the USIC base?"

"No. Car have bed. Car have food. Car have everything."

Peter nodded. *Of course.* It was the obvious way to tackle the challenge. And no doubt such a vehicle—maybe even the same vehicle Kurtzberg had used—would have been made available for him, too, if he'd requested it. But he'd deliberately decided not to go down that route, and he didn't regret it. There was, he sensed, a distance between Kurtzberg and his flock, a barrier which no amount of mutual respect and fellowship had been able to remove. The Oasans regarded their first pastor as an alien, and not just in the literal sense. Camping out in his car, Kurtzberg signaled that he was perpetually ready to switch on the ignition, press the accelerator and drive away.

"Where do you think Kurtzberg is now?"

Lover Five was silent for a while. The other Jesus Lovers were very near now, the tread of their soft boots making only a slight noise on the soil. The bricks were no doubt heavy but the Oasans bore them without grunting or flinching.

"Here," said Lover Five at last, waving her hand in front of her. She seemed to be indicating the world in general.

"You think he's alive?"

"I believe. God willing."

"When he . . . uh . . ." Peter paused to compose a question that was spe-cific enough for her to answer. "Did he say goodbye? I mean, when you saw him last. When he was leaving, did he say, 'I'm going away and not coming back,' or did he say 'I'll see you next week' or . . . what did he say?"

Again she was silent. Then: "No goodbye."

"God ble𝖘 our reunion, Father Pe𝕩er," a voice called to him.

And so the Oasans came to build their church, or, as they put it, their 𝖆ur𝖆. Peter hoped one day to wean them off that word in favor of another.

Here these folk were, constructing a church brick by brick, and yet they couldn't pronounce the name of what they were laboring so devotedly to make. There was something unfair about that.

Lately, as often as possible without overselling the idea, Peter used the phrase "our haven" instead of "church." "We build our haven," he'd say (no sibilants at all!), or he would link the two words together in the same sentence. And, mindful to nip any misunderstandings in the bud, he took care to explain that "haven" was different from "Heaven." Both places offered a safe, welcoming home for those who'd accepted Jesus into their heart, but one was a physical locale and the other was a state of eternal spiritual union with God.

A few of the Oasans had started using the word; not many. Most preferred to say "ᴓurᴓ" even though it convulsed their bodies. And the ones who did say "haven" pronounced it no differently from "Heaven," despite reassuring him that they understood the difference.

"Heaven there," Jesus Lover Fifteen said, pointing up into the sky. Then, pointing at the half-built church: "Heaven here."

Peter had smiled. In his own belief, Heaven was not located up in the sky; it had no astronomical coordinates; it co-existed with all things everywhere. But perhaps it was too soon to engage the Oasans in such metaphysics. They could distinguish between the place they were building and the God they wanted to be part of: that was good.

"Good," he said.

"Praiᴓe Jeᴓuᴓ," Jesus Lover Fifteen replied, sounding, as he spoke, like a foot pulled out of sucking mud.

"Praise Jesus," agreed Peter, a little sadly. It was a pity, in a way that Jesus had been christened "Jesus." It was a fine name, a lovely name, but "Daniel" or "David" or even "Nehemiah" would have been easier here. As for "C-2," or "Oasis," or the little girl from Oskaloosa who'd named it, they were best not even mentioned.

"What do *you* call this place?" he'd asked several people several times.

"Here," they said.

"This whole world," he specified. "Not just your homes, but all the land around your homes, as far as you can see, and the places even further that you can't see, beyond the horizon where the sun goes down."

"Life," they said.

"God," they said.

"What about in your own language?" he'd insisted.

"You could noⴥ ᴤpeak the word," Jesus Lover One said.

"I could try."

"You could noⴥ ᴤpeak the word." It was impossible to tell if this repetition signaled testiness, obstinacy, an immovable force, or if Lover One was calmly making the same assessment twice in a row.

"Could Kurtzberg speak the word?"

"No."

"Did Kurtzberg . . . When he was with you, did Kurtzberg learn any words of your language?"

"No."

"Did *you* speak any words of *our* language, when you first met Kurtzberg?"

"Few."

"That must have made things very difficult."

"God help uᴤ."

Peter couldn't tell whether this was a rueful, good-humored exclamation—a sort of upward roll of the eyes, if there had been eyes to roll—or whether the Oasan was literally stating that God had helped.

"You speak my language so well," he complimented them. "Who taught you? Kurtzberg? Tartaglione?"

"Frank."

"Frank?"

"Frank." Presumably this was Tartaglione's Christian name. Speaking of which . . .

"Was Frank a Christian? A Jesus Lover?"

"No. Frank a . . . language lover."

"Did Kurtzberg teach you too?"

"Language, no. He ⴥeaⴂ only the word of God. He read from the Book of ᴤⴥrange New Thingᴤ. In the beginning, we underᴤⴥand nothing. Then, with help of Frank, and with help of God, word upon word we underᴤⴥand."

"And Tart . . . Frank. Where is he now?"

"Noঽ with uৎ," said a voice from inside the hood of an olive-green robe.

"He go away," said the voice from inside the hood of the canary-yellow robe. "Leave uৎ in lack of him."

Peter tried to imagine what questions Bea might ask if she were here—what bigger picture she would see. She had a knack for noticing not just what was present, but what was absent. Peter cast his eyes over the congregation, dozens of small people clothed in pastel colors, weird-faced inside their hoods, slightly soiled on the soles of their booties. They gazed at him as if he were an exotic obelisk, transmitting messages from afar. Behind them, blurred in the humid mist, the blockish structures of their city glowed amber. There was room in there for many more than were seated here before him.

"Did Frank teach only Jesus Lovers?" he asked. "Or did he teach anybody who wanted to learn?"

"Thoৎe who have no love for Jeৎuৎ alৎo have no wiৎh for learning. They ৎay, 'Why ৎhould we ৎpeak a language made for other bodieৎ?'"

"Are they . . . The ones who don't wish to learn English, are they angry that USIC came here?"

But it was no use asking the Oasans about feelings. Especially the feelings of others.

"Is it difficult," he asked, trying a different tack, "to produce the food that you give to USIC?"

"We provide."

"But the quantity . . . Is it . . . Are you struggling to come up with that much food? Is it too much?"

"We provide."

"But is it . . . If USIC wasn't here, would your lives be easier?"

"UৎIC bring you to uৎ. We are graঽeful."

"But . . . uh . . ." He was determined to winkle out some insight into how those Oasans who weren't Jesus Lovers regarded USIC's presence. "Every one of you works to produce the food, is that right? The Jesus Lovers, and the . . . uh . . . others. You all work together."

"Many hand make brief work."

"OK. Sure. But is there anyone among you who says, 'Why should we do this? Let the USIC people grow their own food'?"

"All know the need for mediςine."

Peter chewed on this for a moment. "Does that mean you're all . . . uh . . . Are all of you taking medicine?"

"No. Only few. Few of few. All Jeςuς Lover here ᴤoday need no mediςine, praiςe Jeςuς."

"And what about the ones who don't love Jesus? Are they more likely to be sick?"

This provoked some disagreement—a rare thing among Oasans. Some voices seemed to be saying yes, the non-Lovers were more susceptible to illness. Others seemed to be saying no, it was the same regardless of belief. The last word was given to Jesus Lover One, whose take was that everyone was missing the main point.

"They will die," he said. "With mediςine or with no mediςine, they will die forever."

And then, all too soon, his time was over. Grainger arrived pretty much when she'd promised she would: three hundred and sixty-eight hours from when they'd last spoken. At least, he assumed it was Grainger.

She'd warned him that she would be driving a bigger vehicle next time, a proper supply truck rather than the jeep. Sure enough, a truck was what came into view, approaching C-2 from the shimmering obscurity of the horizon, camouflaged by the morning glare. Peter supposed that the settlement must strike Grainger as a ghost town, because, as usual, there was no outward sign of the sociable life that hummed within. To the Oasan mind, streets were nothing more than conduits from one house to another, not public spaces to be frequented.

The truck came to a halt outside the building with the star on it. Truck? It was more what you'd call a van, a vehicle of the kind that might scoot around a British town delivering milk or bread. The USIC logo on its side was small and discreet, a tattoo rather than a vainglorious trademark. USIC the florists. USIC the fishmongers. Hardly a display of megacorporate might.

Peter was working on the church grounds, stirring the mortar, when the vehicle came. He observed its arrival from a distance of several hundred meters. The Oasans, whose concentration on appointed tasks was unswervingly intense, whose vision was short-sighted, and whose hearing was difficult to gauge, failed to notice it. He wondered what would happen if he pretended he hadn't noticed either, and simply carried on here with his congregation. Would Grainger eventually get out of the truck and walk over to meet them? Or drive the truck to the church grounds? Or lose patience and drive away?

He knew it was ungracious, even childish, of him to keep her waiting, but he wished she would come out of her metal shell and make proper contact with these people whom she refused to call "people," these people who gave her "the creeps." There was really nothing scary or distasteful about them at all. If you stared into their faces long enough, their physiognomy ceased to appear grisly, and the eyeless cleft was no different from a human nose or brow. He wished Grainger could understand that.

Just as he was about to announce to his co-workers that he must take his leave of them for a little while, he spotted a flash of movement in the doorway of the building marked with the star. An Oasan had emerged. It was no one he had met, as far as he knew. The Oasan's robe was mouse-gray. The door of Grainger's vehicle swung open and she stepped out, a vision in white.

Peter turned to make his announcement. But there was no need: his co-workers had noticed the arrival, and stopped working. Everyone put down whatever he or she was holding, carefully and quietly. Jesus Lover Fifty-Two—a female, in Peter's arbitrary estimation—was halfway up the staircase, a brick in her hands. She paused, looked down at the brick, and up at the wall where the syrupy mortar would soon dry out. The choice between continuing and not continuing was plainly a difficult one for her, but after hesitating a few seconds more, she began to descend the staircase. It was as though she'd decided the gluing of the brick was too important a task to be attempted when there were such sensational distractions.

The other Oasans were talking amongst themselves, in their own language. The only word Peter could understand—the only word that evidently did not exist in their vocabulary—was "medi⹁ine." Jesus Lover One approached Peter hesitantly.

"Plea⹁e, Pe⹁er," he said. "If God will be no⹁ di⹁appoin⹁ful ... If Je⹁u⹁ and Holy ⹁piri⹁ will be no⹁ di⹁appoin⹁ful ... I will leave now the building of our ⹁ur⹁, and help delivery of medi⹁ine."

"Of course," said Peter. "Let's go together."

There was a palpable relief of tension, passing through the assembled Oasans like a communal shiver. Peter wondered if Kurtzberg had instilled fear of God's displeasure into them, or if they were merely over-eager to please their new pastor. He made a mental note to speak to them at the earliest opportunity about God's compassion and indulgence: *My yoke is easy and my burden is light* and all that sort of thing. Except he might have to find an alternative to the animal husbandry metaphor.

Peter and Jesus Lover One set off across the scrubland. The other Oasans stayed on site, as though not to alarm the USIC representative with their massed advance, or perhaps in deference to Jesus Lover One as their official go-between.

The gray-robed Oasan who'd come out of the settlement to meet Grainger hadn't moved from his position near the vehicle. A white cardboard box had been handed over to him, and he held it with all the solemnity of a priest holding a sacrament, even though the box resembled a jumbo pizza carton. He seemed in no hurry to carry it away. If he and Grainger had exchanged any words, the conversation was dormant now, as he stared at Jesus Lover One and Peter traversing the distance between the construction site and the settlement.

Grainger watched too. She was dressed, as before, in her white smock and cotton slacks, with a headscarf loosely draped around her hair and neck. Boyishly proportioned though she was, she appeared bulky next to the Oasan.

"Who's that?" Peter said to Lover One as they drew near.

"⹁⹁⹁⹁⹁⹁⹁⹁," replied Lover One.

"Not a Jesus Lover?"

"No."

Peter wondered if there was any hope for him to learn the Oasan language. Without any English to bind it together, it sounded like a field of brittle reeds and rain-sodden lettuces being cleared by a machete.

"Have you missed your chance to get a share of the medicine?"

"Medicine for all," said Lover One. Peter couldn't tell if the tone of voice was serenely confident, plaintively indignant or grimly resolute.

The four of them rendezvoused in the shade of the building with the star. The

WEL COME

had blurred into illegibility now. It could have been the remains of a paint bomb tossed against the wall.

Jesus Lover One bowed to Grainger. "I am regretful for your lingering long here," he said.

"I'll try to leave pronto," she responded. Despite the wisecrack, she was obviously tense. The engine of her vehicle was still running, in defiance of a USIC sticker on the side window that said CONSERVE GAS, IT'S A LONG WAY TO VENEZUELA.

"Hello, Grainger," said Peter.

"Hi, how ya doin'?"

Her voice sounded more American than he remembered, like a caricature of Yankeeness. All at once, he missed Bea with an ache that was like a shove in the stomach. It was as though, having endured all this time without her company, he'd promised himself that she would be there to meet him afterward. The USIC truck should have been a plum-colored Vauxhall, with Bea standing next to it, waving to him in that unguarded childlike way she had, greeting him in her lovely Yorkshire-inflected voice.

"Been sleeping under the sky?" said Grainger.

"Is it that obvious?"

Her eyes narrowed as she gave him the once-over. "Some people tan. Some people just burn."

"I don't feel burnt."

"Looked in a mirror lately?"

"Forgot to bring one."

She nodded, as if to say *That figures.* "We'll get some cream onto you in a minute. A bit late for first-aid, I guess, but hey . . ." She glanced at Jesus Lover One and the other Oasan. "Speaking of which, I've still gotta do this medicine handover. Uh . . . who am I dealing with here? Which of you do I give the run-down to?"

"I under☖☖and more than the other one here," said Jesus Lover One. "E☖plain me the medi☖ine of ☖oday." Then, to his compatriot: "☖☖☖☖☖☖☖☖☖☖, ☖☖☖☖ ☖☖☖☖☖☖☖☖☖."

The other Oasan stepped closer, lifted the lid of the box and angled it so that Grainger and Jesus Lover One had access to the contents. Peter kept his distance, but glimpsed lots of plastic bottles and little cardboard packets, a few of them colorfully commercial, the majority identified with machine-printed pharmacy labels.

"OK," said Grainger, pointing to each of the items in turn. "We have aspirin and acetaminophen, as usual. These ones here are generics."

"Name from where all other name come," said Jesus Lover One.

"Exactly," said Grainger. "Then there's ten packets of branded acetaminophen: Tylenol. You've had it before. And these blue and yellow packets, Soothers, they're like candies, but they've got some dextromethorphan and phenylephrine—a cough suppressant and nasal decongestant. I mean, I don't know if you . . . uh . . ." She coughed. It was unclear whether she was imitating a cough for the Oasan's benefit, or whether she genuinely had something stuck in her throat. "And this one here is diclofenac. It's an analgesic too, and an anti-inflammatory, good for arthritis—pain in the muscles and joints." She wiggled her elbow and gyrated one of her shoulders, to mime the discomfort of arthritis. "Also good for migraines and . . . uh . . . menstrual cramps." Grainger's voice was tainted with despondency. Clearly, she had little faith that her words made any sense to the recipients. She spoke faster and less distinctly as she went on, almost gabbling. Peter had witnessed that sort of behavior before, in inexperienced or ineffectual evangelists who were trying to win over a hostile audience and sensed they were losing the battle. Mumbled invitations to come along to church sometime, spoken as if to satisfy a watchful God that the invitations had been made, rather than with any real hope that anyone would come.

"Also, cortisone creams, the ones you like, in the blue and white tubes,"

Grainger went on. "And a bunch of antibiotics. Gentamicin. Neomycin. Flucloxacillin. A broad range of uses, as I've explained to you before. Depends on the individual. If you ever . . . uh . . . if you're ever ready to give me some feedback on your experience with a particular antibiotic, I may be able to advise you better."

"Anξibioξic welcome," said Jesus Lover One. "But painkiller welcome more. You have other aξpirin and paraξeξamol, in other color and name?"

"No, what I've told you is what there is. But remember there's the diclofenac also. It's highly effective, and well tolerated too, in most . . . uh . . . people. Maybe some gastro-intestinal side-effects, same as with other analgesics." She rubbed her abdomen perfunctorily. Peter could tell she was in distress, and not from gastro-intestinal causes.

"Also," she continued, "we've got something totally different this time, nothing to do with pain. You won't have seen this one before. I don't know if it's any use to you. I mean, not you personally, but . . . uh . . . anyone here."

"The name?"

"The name on the packet is GlucoRapid. That's the brand name. Insulin is what it is. It's for diabetes. Is diabetes something you know about? When the body can't regulate its glucose levels properly?"

The Oasans did not speak nor make any gesture of response, but kept their faces attentively pointed at Grainger's.

"Glucose is like, uh, sugar," she said, voice faltering. She pressed her fingers hard against her perspiring brow, as if she could use a couple of painkillers herself. "I'm sorry, this is probably making no sense whatsoever. But the insulin is spare, so . . ."

"We are graξeful," said Jesus Lover One. "We are graξeful." And he put Grainger out of her misery by signaling for his compatriot to close the box.

Things moved swiftly after that. The gray-robed Oasan and Jesus Lover One conveyed the medicine box into the building with the star. Minutes later, they returned, each of them carrying a bulbous sack, cradled against their chests like a baby. They stashed the sacks in the back of the van, then went to fetch more. After a few such trips, other Oasans, none of them familiar to Peter, joined in to help. As well as the sacks—containing whiteflower in various dried or powdered forms—there were large plastic tubs for the cleverly processed concoctions whose destiny, when USIC's chefs added water, was to become soups and spreads and desserts and goodness knows what else. Smaller tubs and bags contained condiments and spices. Every sack and bag and tub was labeled in crude block-letters with marker pen. Whether by USIC personnel or by some small gloved Oasan hand, impossible to tell.

Peter and Grainger sat inside the vehicle, at Grainger's request. She complained that the humidity was getting to her, but Peter could tell from her face that she didn't expect him to believe her and that the handover of the medicines had wiped her out, psychologically and physically. The air-conditioned cabin—sealed off from the back section where the food was being stockpiled—was a haven where she could recover. She kept her eyes averted from the robed figures filing past the windows. Every few minutes, the chassis was subtly jogged by the deposit of another sack or tub in its rear. Evidently, long-term experience had confirmed that the Oasans could be trusted one hundred percent to fulfill their part of the exchange. Or maybe Grainger was supposed to check, but couldn't bring herself to do so.

"You're gonna give yourself cancer if you're not careful," she said, uncapping a tube of ointment.

"I feel fine," Peter protested, as she dabbed the goo onto his nose and brow with her middle finger. The touch of a woman's hand—not Bea's—gave him a melancholy frisson.

"Your wife won't be very happy if she finds out your face has been fried." Grainger reached up for the rear-view mirror and twisted it sideways so he could see his reflection. The sheen of ointment was unsightly but, as far as he could tell, the underlying damage to his face was minimal: a few blotches, a bit of peeling.

"I'll survive," he said. "But thank you."

"Anything else you need," she said, wiping her fingers clean on a paper tissue, "just let me know when we get back to civilization."

"The Oasans are pretty civilized, I've found. But it must be tough for you as a pharmacist not to have a clue what's going on with them health-wise."

"Peter . . ." She let her head fall back against the seat and sighed. "Let's not go there."

"That's what people always say about places where they already are."

She readjusted the mirror so that her own face was reflected in it. With a corner of the paper tissue she traced a line underneath her left eye, to neaten up the blurred mascara there. She did the same to her right eye. Peter was pretty sure she hadn't worn mascara the last time they'd met.

Outside, a mishap. One of the Oasans, attempting to carry a tub in each hand, dropped one on the ground. A cloud of reddish-brown powder sprang up, covering his boots, shins and the lower parts of his pale blue robe. Another Oasan stopped to survey the damage and said, "ᴄinnamon."

"ᴄinnamon," he confirmed.

The two of them stood still for a few seconds, contemplating. The moist, swirling breeze carried off the loose whiteflower cinnamon, absorbing it into the atmosphere in general. The powder on the robe darkened into a glistening stain. Then, without further comment, the two Oasans resumed their labors.

Peter rolled down the window, to check if the air smelled cinnamon-spiced. It didn't. But the artificial cool of the car's interior was immediately spoiled by a big balmy influx.

"*Please*," Grainger complained.

He rolled the window back up and let the air conditioning resume its campaign. The trapped currents of humid vapor flew around the cabin, as if sensing themselves pursued. In their search for escape or absorption they passed across his face, his knees, the back of his neck. Grainger felt it too, and shuddered.

"Did you see them spill the cinnamon?" Peter said.

"Uh-huh."

"It's so nice the way they didn't make a big drama out of it. The one who dropped the tub didn't put on a show of guilt or frustration. And his friend didn't criticize him or make a fuss. They just noted what had happened and moved on."

"Yeah, it's real inspiring. I could sit here and watch them drop our food on the ground all day."

"Although I must say," Peter remarked, "that the USIC personnel seem quite sensible and relaxed, too." Even as he said it, he had to concede that Grainger could be an exception.

"Yeah," she said. "Drama is a no-no."

"You mean . . . there's an actual rule? Like, a regulation?"

She laughed. "No. We're free to be our sweet little selves. Within reason." The air was growing cooler again, and she wrapped her shawl around her throat.

The Oasans were still carrying supplies to the back of the van. The sacks were all stowed now, but the plastic tubs kept coming, all filled with ingenious whiteflower creations. An awful lot of work had gone into this food, both agricultural and culinary; it seemed like an excessive amount of labor and material to exchange for a few packets of medicine. Well, quite a few packets, but still . . .

"How come USIC has so many drugs to spare?" he said.

"We don't," she said. "We get extra supplies sent specially for this purpose. Every ship has a fresh lot on board: a bunch for us, a bunch for them."

"Sounds like quite an operation," he said.

"Not really. Expenditure-wise, logistics-wise, it's no problem at all. Drugs don't take up much room and they weigh very little. Compared to magazines or . . . uh . . . raisins . . . or Pepsi. Or human beings, of course."

It looked as though the last item had been deposited in the rear. Peter peered through the tinted window to find Jesus Lover One. He couldn't see him anymore. "I'll do my best to justify my freight costs," he said.

"Nobody's complaining," said Grainger. "These . . . people—the Oasans, as you call them—wanted you, and they got you. So everybody's happy, right?"

But Grainger did not look happy. She adjusted the rear-view mirror to its correct position, which took a bit of fiddling, and her sleeve slipped off her wrist as far as her elbow. Peter noticed scars on her forearm: old self-harm, long-healed, but indelible. History written on the flesh. He'd known so many self-harmers. They were always beautiful. Seeing Grainger's scars, he realized for the first time that she was beautiful, too.

12

LOOKING BACK, ALMOST CERTAINLY, THAT WAS WHEN IT HAPPENED.

The engine purred as it bore him back toward what Grainger called civilization. Inside the cabin, the atmosphere was cool and filtered. Outside, the landscape had been abruptly transformed. For hundreds of hours, it had been the ground beneath his feet, a changeless environment for his daily routine, rock-solid under slowly evolving skies, familiar in every detail. Now it was insubstantial: a display of images flickering past tinted glass. The sun had slipped out of sight, hidden by the roof. Peter leaned his face near to the window and tried to look back, to catch a glimpse of the settlement. It was already gone.

Grainger drove with her usual careless competence, but seemed preoccupied, irritable. As well as keeping the steering wheel steady, she tapped keys on the dashboard and made numbers and symbols dance on an emerald-green screen. She rubbed at her eyes, blinked hard and, evidently deciding that there was too much air blowing onto her contact lenses, adjusted the air-con settings.

How strange it was to be inside a machine again! All his life he'd been inside machines, whether he realized it or not. Modern houses were machines. Shopping centers were machines. Schools. Cars. Trains. Cities. They were all sophisticated technological constructs, wired up with lights and motors. You switched them on, and didn't spare them a thought while they pampered you with unnatural services.

"Looks like you're the King of Freaktown," Grainger remarked breezily.

Then, before he could take her to task for boorish disrespect: ". . . as some of my USIC colleagues would no doubt put it."

"We're working together," said Peter. "The Oasans and I."

"Sounds cosy. But they're doing exactly what you want, right?"

He looked across at her. She had her eyes fixed on the terrain ahead. He half-expected her to be chewing gum. It would have matched her tone.

"They want to learn more about God," he said. "So we're building a church. Of course it's not essential to have a physical place; you can worship God anywhere. But a church provides a focus."

"A signal that you mean business, huh?"

Again he looked across at her, this time staring hard until she acknowledged him with a sideways glance.

"Grainger," he said, "why do I get the feeling our roles are reversed here? In this conversation, I mean? *You're* the employee of a giant corporation, establishing a colony here. *I'm* the leftie pastor, the one who's supposed to be concerned about whether the little guys are being exploited."

"OK, I'll try to be more stereotypical," she said lightly. "Maybe a coffee will do it."

She fetched a Thermos up from the floor and balanced it next to her thigh. With her left hand on the steering wheel, she attempted, with her right hand, to unscrew the firmly-sealed cap. Her wrist trembled.

"Let me do that for you."

She handed it over. He unscrewed the cup and poured her a coffee. The oily brown liquid was no longer hot enough to give off steam.

"Here."

"Thanks," she said, and took a sip. "This tastes like shit."

He laughed. Grainger's face looked odd to him when he saw it up close. Beautiful yet unreal, like a plastic doll's head mold. Her lips were too perfect, her skin too pale. But maybe it was the golden sunrise thing all over again: maybe he had already, in the last three hundred and sixty-eight hours, adjusted to the way Oasans looked, and begun to accept their faces as the norm. Grainger didn't fit.

"Hey, I just thought of something," he said. "The drugs you give the Oasans are requisitioned especially for them, right?"

"Right."

"But, from what you were saying back there, when you were talking to Jesus Lover One . . ."

"Jesus *what?*"

"Jesus Lover One. That's his name."

"The name you've given him?"

"No, the name he's given himself."

"Oh. OK."

Her face was impassive, with perhaps just the hint of a smirk. He couldn't tell if she disapproved of him deeply, or thought the whole thing was just ridiculous.

"Anyway," he pressed on, "when you were talking about diabetes, I got the impression the Oasans don't even know what diabetes *is.* So why offer them insulin?"

Grainger finished her coffee and screwed the cup back onto the thermos. "I guess I didn't want it to go to waste," she said. "The insulin wasn't meant for them; it was our own supply. But we don't need it anymore." She paused for a couple of beats. "Severin died."

"Severin? The guy I traveled with?"

"Yup."

"He's a diabetic?"

"Was."

Peter tried to recall the journey he'd shared with Severin. It felt like something that had happened in another phase of his life, much longer ago than a few weeks.

"When did he die?"

"Last night. That phrase doesn't mean much here, I know. Toward the end of the night." She consulted her watch. "About eighteen hours ago." Another couple of beats' pause. "You're conducting the funeral service. If you're willing, that is."

Again, Peter tried to cast his mind back to the time he'd shared with Severin. He recalled BG asking Severin what religion he was, and Severin replying, *I'm nothing, and that's the way it's staying.*

"Severin might not have wanted a funeral service. He didn't have a religion."

"A lot of people here don't have a religion. But the thing is, we cannot throw a dead person into an incinerator without giving him some kind of a send-off."

Peter pondered this a moment.

"Can you . . . er . . . give me a rough idea what sort of send-off the majority of the personnel might consider . . ."

"Totally up to you. We've got some Catholics, we've got some Baptists, we've got some Buddhists . . . You name it, we've got some. I wouldn't sweat about that. You were chosen because . . . Well, let's just say that if you were a strict Pentecostal or a strict *anything*, you wouldn't be here. Somebody studied your résumé and made a judgment that you can handle it."

"Handle funerals?"

"Handle . . . whatever." She clenched her fists on the steering wheel, drew a deep breath. "Whatever."

Peter sat in silence for a while. The landscape continued to flicker by. A rich, fragrant smell of whiteflower in various forms began to suffuse the cabin, seeping in from the back.

Dear Peter, wrote Bea. We are in big trouble.

He was sitting in his quarters, still unwashed, and naked. Goose pimples prickled on his flesh: *big trouble.*

His wife's words had been sent a fortnight ago, or twelve days to be precise. She had kept silent for the first forty-eight hours of his stay among the Oasans, evidently counseling herself that anything she wrote would go unread until his return. But after two days she'd written regardless. And written again the next day, and the next. She'd written eleven more messages, all of them now stored in glowing capsules at the bottom of his screen. Each capsule bore a number: the date of transmission. To his wife, these messages were already History. To him, they were a frozen Present, yet to be experienced. His head buzzed with the urgent need to open them all, to crack open those capsules with eleven rapid-fire jabs of his finger—and buzzed also with the knowledge that he could only take them in one at a time.

He could've started reading them an hour earlier, in the vehicle on the way back from the settlement. But Grainger's odd mood during the drive had discouraged him from asking her to tell him when they were close enough to the USIC base for the Shoot to work. Although he wasn't usually secretive or prone to embarrassment, he'd felt self-conscious at the prospect of reading his wife's personal communications right next to Grainger. What if Bea made some unguardedly intimate reference? A gesture of sexual affection? No, it was better to restrain his eagerness and wait until he had privacy.

On entering his USIC apartment, he'd stripped off his clothes, determined to shower before he tackled anything else. These last couple of weeks, working with the Oasans and sleeping out in the open, he'd become inured to sweat and dust, but his journey back to base in the air conditioned vehicle had awakened his awareness of the muck that clung to him. It was a feeling he remembered well from his homeless years: being invited into somebody's immaculate home and perching on the edge of their pale velour sofa, self-conscious about tainting it with his grimy arse. So, as soon as he stepped into his apartment, he decided that while the Shoot was warming up, doing its routine checks of its electronic innards, he could have a quick wash. Unexpectedly, however, Beatrice's messages loaded in at once. Their sudden arrival was a potent presence in the room, forcing him to sit down, dirty as he was.

We are in big trouble, Bea said. I don't want to worry you when you're so far away and there's nothing you can do. But things are falling apart fast. I don't mean you and me of course darling. I mean things in general, the whole country (probably). In our local supermarket there are apology stickers on most of the shelves, empty spaces everywhere. Yesterday there was no fresh milk and no fresh bread. Today, all the UHT milk, flavored milk, condensed milk, even coffee whitener has gone, likewise all the muffins, bagels, scones, chapattis, etc etc. I overheard two people in the checkout queue having a testy discussion about how many cartons of custard one person should be allowed to buy. The term "moral responsibility" was used.

The news says that the supply problems are due to chaos on the motorways because of the earthquake in Bedworth a few days back.

That makes a kind of sense, judging by the footage. (You know the way the top of a cake bursts open when it's risen dramatically in the oven?—well, a long stretch of the M6 looks like that.) Of course the other roads are jammed solid now, trying to accommodate the diverted traffic.

But on the other hand, you would think there must be lots of bakeries and dairies located south of the quake site. I mean, surely we're not dependent on a truck coming down the M6 all the way from Birmingham to bring us a loaf of bread! I suspect what we're seeing here is sheer inflexibility in the way supermarkets operate; I bet they just aren't equipped to negotiate with a different bunch of suppliers at such short notice. If the market was allowed to respond more organically (no pun intended) to an event like this, I'm sure that bakeries and dairies in Southampton or wherever would be delighted to step into the breach.

Anyway, the Bedworth quake is not the full story, regardless of what the news says. Food supplies have been erratic for ages. And the weather just gets weirder and weirder. We've had sunshine and mild conditions here (the carpets have finally dried out, thank goodness) but there have been freak hailstorms in other places, so bad that a couple of people have been killed. Killed by hailstones!

It's been a good week for the news networks, I must say. The footage of the quake, the hailstorms and—stand by, folks!—a spectacular riot in central London. It started as a peaceful protest against the military action in China, and ended with cars being set alight, mass brawling, baton charges, the whole shebang. Even the cleaning up afterward made for good pictures: there was fake blood (red paint) dripping off the stone lions in Trafalgar Square and real blood splattered on the ground. The cameramen must have been peeing themselves with delight. Sorry to sound cynical but the media gets so energized by this sort of thing. Nobody ever seems sad about it, there's no moral dimension, it's just the latest action-packed event. And while these photogenic calamities are flashed past, ordinary people get on with their lives, just doing their best to come to terms with everyday unhappiness.

Anyway, I shouldn't try so hard to understand the Big Picture. Only God understands that, and He's in control. I have my life to lead, work to go to. It's early morning here, beautiful light, chilly, with Joshua perched on top of the filing cabinet snoozing in a sunbeam. My shift doesn't start till 2:30, so I'm going to do some chores and cook tonight's dinner so that when I come home from work I can just tuck in, instead of eating peanut butter on toast like I usually do. I should eat some breakfast now to boost my energy but there's nothing in the house I fancy. The plight of a cereal addict in withdrawal! I'm sipping stale jasmine tea (left over from when we had Ludmila staying with us) because normal tea without milk tastes wrong to me. Too much compromise!

OK, back again. (I just went to the front door to pick up the mail.) Nice postcard from some people in Hastings thanking us for our kindness—Can't think what kindness they're referring to, but they invite us to visit them. Could be difficult for you right now! Also a letter from Sheila Frame. Remember her? She's the mother of Rachel and Billy, the kids who made our Noah's Ark wall-hanging/collage. Rachel is 12 now and "doing OK" says Sheila (whatever "OK" means) and Billy is 14 and seriously depressed. That's why Sheila is writing to us. Her letter doesn't make much sense, she must have written it when she was stressed out. She keeps mentioning "the snow leopard," assuming we must know all about "the snow leopard." I've tried to phone but she's at work, and by the time I get home tonight it'll be 11:30 at least. I might try to phone from the ward during my meal break.

Enough about my routine & uneventful life without my dear husband. Please tell me what's been happening with you. I wish I could see your face. I don't understand why the technology that allows us to communicate with each other like this can't stretch to sending a few pictures as well! But I suppose that's being greedy. It's miraculous enough that we can read each other's words at such a mind-boggling distance. Assuming you can still read them, of course . . . Please write soon to let me know you're all right.

I feel I ought to have more specific questions & comments about your mission, but to be frank you haven't told me very much about it. You're more of a speaker than a writer, I know that. There have been times I've sat in the congregation when you've preached, and I see you glancing down at your notes—the same notes I've seen you scribbling the night before—and I'm aware that on that little scrap of paper there's just a few disjointed phrases, and yet this wonderful, eloquent, coherent speech comes out, a beautifully formed story that keeps everyone spellbound for an hour. I admire you so much at those times, my darling. I wish I could hear what you're saying to your new flock. I don't suppose you're writing any of it down afterward? Or keeping a record of what they're saying to you? I don't feel I KNOW these people at all; it's frustrating. Are you learning a new language? I suppose you must be.

Love,

Bea

Peter rubbed his face, and the sweaty, oily dirt accumulated into dark, seed-like particles in the palms of his hands. Reading his wife's letter had made him agitated and confused. He hadn't felt that way until now. For the duration of his stay with the Oasans, he'd been calm and emotionally stable, just getting on with the job. If he'd been occasionally bewildered, it was a happy sort of bewilderment. Now he felt out of his depth. There was a tightness squeezing his chest.

He moved the Shoot's cursor to the next capsule in chronological sequence, and opened a message that Beatrice had sent him a mere twenty hours after the last. It must have been the middle of her night.

I miss you, she wrote. Oh, how I miss you. I didn't know it would feel like this. I thought the time would fly and you would be back. If I could just hold you once, just hug you tight for a few minutes, I could cope with your absence again. Even ten seconds would do it. Ten seconds with my arms around you. Then I could sleep.

And, next day:

Horrible, ghastly things in the news; I can't bear to read, can't bear
to look. Almost took the day off work today. Sat weeping in the
toilets at break time. You are so far away, so incredibly far away,
further away than any man has ever been from his woman, the sheer
distance makes me ill. I don't know what's wrong with me. Forgive
me for spilling my guts like this, I know it can't be helping you do
whatever you're doing. Oh, how I wish you could be in touch now.
Touching me. Holding me. Kissing me.

The words hit him hard. They were the sort of thing he'd wanted to receive from her but now that he'd received them, they caused him distress. A
fortnight ago, he had missed her sexually and craved confirmation that she
felt the same. She'd assured him that she missed him, that she wanted to
hold him, sure, but the overall tone of her letters was sensible, preoccupied,
as though his presence was a luxury rather than a necessity. She'd seemed
so self-reliant, he'd wondered if he was indulging in testosterone-fueled self-
pity—or if that's how she saw it.

Once he'd taken his place among the Oasans, this insecurity had evaporated. He didn't have time for it. And, trusting in the easy mutuality that
he and Bea had always enjoyed, he'd assumed—if he thought about it at
all—that Bea was in the same state of mind, that she was simply getting on
with the daily business of life, that her love for him was like the color of her
eyes: constantly there, but not in any way an impediment to useful activity.

Instead, while he'd been laying the stones of his church and dozing
happy in his hammock, she was in pain.

His fingers hung suspended over the keyboard, poised to respond to
her. But how could he, when she'd written nine more messages to him,
in hours and days that were already gone from her, but of which he knew
nothing?

He opened another capsule.

Dear Peter,
Please don't worry about me. I've got a grip now. I don't know why
I went off the deep end like that. Too little sleep? The atmosphere
has been oppressive these last few weeks. Yes, I know I said it was

beautiful weather here and that's true, in the sense that it's warm and sunny. But at nights it's close and rather hard to breathe.

A large chunk of North Korea was wiped out a few days ago. Not by a nuclear strike, or even a nuclear accident, but by a cyclone called Toraji. It came off the Sea of Japan and swept inland "like a ceremonial sword" (I didn't make that simile up, obviously). Tens of thousands dead, probably more than a million homeless. The government denied the severity of the damage at first, so all we had were satellite pictures. It was surreal. Here's this woman in a tailored yellow outfit, with immaculate hair and manicured nails, standing in front of this giant projected image, pointing at the various smudges and blobs, interpreting what they mean. You got the message that there were lots of wrecked houses and dead bodies in there somewhere, but all you could see was these beautifully buffed hands gesturing over what looked like an abstract painting.

Then the government let some South Korean and Chinese aid workers in, and the proper video footage started coming through. Peter, I've seen things I wish I hadn't seen. Maybe that's why I got so frantic about missing you. Of course I love you and miss you and need you. But I also needed to see these things WITH you, or else be spared from seeing them at all.

I saw a huge concrete enclosure, like a giant pig kennel, or whatever you call the enclosures where they farm pigs, the roof of it just peeping out of a huge lake of slimy water. A team of men were hacking at the roof with pick-axes, not achieving much. Then they blew a hole in it with explosives. A weird mixture of soupy stuff gurgled out of the hole. It was people. People and water. Half-blended, like . . . I don't want to describe it. I will never forget it. Why do we get shown these things? Why, when we can't help? Later I saw villagers using dead bodies as sandbags. Rescue workers with candles strapped to their heads, the candle-fat running down their cheeks. How can such things be possible in the 21st century? I'm watching a high-resolution video clip that was recorded with a micro-camera hidden in somebody's hat-brim or whatever, and yet the technology of life-saving is straight from the Stone Age!

I want to write more, even though I don't want to remember. I wish I could send you the images, even though I also wish I could erase them from my mind. Is it the lowest form of selfishness to want to share the burden like this? And what IS my burden, exactly, sitting on my sofa in England, eating liquorice allsorts, watching foreign corpses swirling around in muddy whirlpools, foreign children queuing for a scrap of tarpaulin?

Someone at work said to me this morning, "Where is God in all this?" I didn't rise to the bait. I can never understand why people ask that question. The real question for the bystanders of tragedy is "Where are WE in all this?" I've always tried to come up with answers to that challenge. I don't know if I can at the moment. Pray for me.

Love,

Bea.

Peter clasped his hands. They were tacky with grime: new sweat on old sweat. He stood up and walked to the shower cubicle. His erection nodded comically with each step. He positioned himself under the metal nozzle and switched on the water, letting it douse his upturned face first. His scalp stung as the stream penetrated his matted hair, finding little scratches and scabs he hadn't realized were there. Stone-cold at first, the water warmed up fast, dissolving the dirt off him, enfolding him in a cloud. He kept his eyes closed and let his face be bathed, almost scalded, under the pressurized spray. He cupped his testicles in his hands, and, with his wrists, pressed his penis hard against his belly until the semen came. Then he soaped himself up from head to toes, and washed thoroughly. The water that swilled around the plughole was gray for longer than he would have thought possible.

When he was clean, he continued to stand under the hot stream, and might have remained there for half an hour or more, if the water hadn't suddenly sputtered to a trickle. An LED display inside the shower dial flashed 0:00. He hadn't twigged the significance of the gauge until now. Of course! It made perfect sense that duration of water use should be limited by a built-in timer. It's just that USIC was an American corporation and the idea of a frugal, resource-conscious American corporation almost defied belief.

As soon as the drain stopped gurgling, he was able to discern that a noise he'd been aware of for a while, which he'd attributed to the pipes, was in fact someone knocking at the door.

"Hi," said Grainger when he opened it. Her eyes barely flickered at the sight of him standing there wet, clad only in a bath towel knotted around his waist. She had a dossier clutched to her bosom.

"Sorry, I couldn't hear you," he said.

"I knocked real loud," she said.

"I suppose I expected there to be a doorbell, or a buzzer or an intercom or something."

"USIC isn't big on unnecessary technology."

"Yes, I've noticed that. It's one of the unexpectedly admirable things about you."

"Gee, thanks," said Grainger. "You say the sweetest things."

Behind him, the Shoot emitted a soft noise, like an electronic sigh: the sound it made when its screen went dark to conserve power. He remembered North Korea.

"Have you heard about North Korea?" he said.

"It's a country in . . . uh . . . Asia," she said.

"There's been a terrible cyclone there. Tens of thousands of people are dead."

Grainger blinked hard; flinched, almost. But a moment later, she'd regained her composure. "That's tragic," she said. "Nothing we can do about it, though." She held the dossier out to him. "Everything you always wanted to know about Arthur Severin but were afraid to ask."

He took the file. "Thank you."

"The funeral is in three hours."

"Right. How long is that in . . . uh . . ." He gestured vaguely, hoping that a wave of his hand might convey the difference between time as he'd always known it and time here and now.

She smiled, patient with his stupidity. "Three hours," she repeated, and raised her wrist to display her watch. "Three hours means three hours."

"I wasn't expecting quite so little notice," he said.

"Relax. Nobody's expecting you to write fifty pages of rhyming poetry in his honor. Just say a few words. Everyone understands you didn't know him too well. That kind of helps."

"The impersonal touch?"

"It's what the great religions offer, isn't it?" And she lifted her wristwatch again. "I'll come and collect you at 13:30."

She left without another word and shut the door behind her, at exactly the instant that his towel fell off.

"We are gathered here," said Peter to the hushed and solemn assembly, "to honor a man who, only one sunrise ago, was a living, breathing person just like us."

He cast a glance toward the coffin that sat on a rack of metal rollers in front of an incinerator. Instinctively, everyone else in the room looked at it, too. The coffin was made of recycled cardboard, with a lustrous gloss of vegetable glaze to give it that solid-wood effect. The rack was just like the ones attached to x-ray machines at airports.

"A person who drew air into his lungs," Peter continued, "lungs that were a bit the worse for wear, perhaps, but still working fine, delivering oxygen to his blood, the same blood that's pumping in all of us as we stand here today." His voice was loud and clear without amplification, but lacked the reverb resonance it was granted in churches and assembly halls. The funeral room, while large, was acoustically cramped, and the furnace inside the incinerator generated a noise like a distant jet plane passing by.

"Listen to your heart beat," said Peter. "Feel the ever-so-slight tremor inside your chest as your body miraculously keeps functioning. It's such a gentle tremor, such a quiet sound, that we don't appreciate how much it matters. We may not have been always aware of it, we may scarcely have given it a thought from day to day, but we were sharing the world with Art Severin, and he was sharing it with us. Now the sun has come up on a new day, and Art Severin has changed. We are here today to face up to that change."

The mourners numbered fifty-two. Peter wasn't sure how big a proportion of the total USIC staff this was. There were only six women, including

Grainger; the rest were males, making Peter wonder if Severin had failed to win the respect of his female colleagues, or whether this simply reflected the gender distribution of the base. Everyone was dressed in the clothes they might usually wear at work. Nobody wore black.

BG and Tuska stood in the forefront of the crowd. Tuska, clad in a loose green shirt, military camouflage trousers and his trademark tennis shoes, was nevertheless almost unrecognizable, having shaved off his beard. BG was unmistakable as ever, the biggest body in the room, his facial hair maintained with scalpel-fine precision. A white T-shirt clung to his musculature like paint. A wrinkled white sirwal hung off his hips, its cuffs puddling over incongruous polished shoes. His arms were folded across his chest, his face composed and imperiously tolerant. A few people in the ranks behind him were looking more quizzical, nudged off-balance by the eulogy's opening salvo.

"Arthur Laurence Severin died young," said Peter, "but he lived many lives. He was born in Bend, Oregon, forty-eight years ago, to parents he never knew, and was adopted by Jim and Peggy Severin. They gave him a happy and active childhood, mostly in the open air. Jim repaired and maintained campsites, hunting lodges and military outposts. Art could drive a tractor by the time he was ten, operate a chainsaw, shoot deer, all that dangerous stuff that kids shouldn't be allowed to do. He was all set to take over the family business. Then his adoptive parents divorced and Art started getting into trouble. His teenage years were spent in and out of juvenile corrective institutions and rehabilitation programs. By the time he was old enough to go to jail, he already had a long record of crack cocaine abuse and DUI offences."

The mourners were not so blank-faced now. A thrill of unease was passing through them, a thrill of interest and anxiety. Heads tilted, brows knitted, lower lips folding under top ones. Faster breathing. Children drawn in by a story.

"Art Severin got time off for good behavior and was soon back on the streets of Oregon. But not for long. Frustrated at lack of employment opportunities in the US for young ex-crims, he relocated to Sabah, Malaysia, where he started a tool supply business with some drug dealing on the side. It was in Sabah that he met Kamelia, a local entrepreneur who supplied female companionship to the timber industry. They fell in love, married, and, although Kamelia was already in her forties, produced two daughters, Nora and Pao-Pei, always known as May. When Kamelia's brothel was shut down by the authorities and Art's business was squeezed by competition, he found work in the timber trade, and it was only then that he first discovered his lifelong fascination with the mechanics and chemistry of soil erosion."

With measured assurance, Peter began to walk toward the coffin. The hand in which he had been holding his Bible swung at his side, and everyone could see that his thumb was pressed against a small scrap of hand-scribbled paper inside the Scripture.

"Art Severin's next life was in Australia," he said, gazing down at the casket's lustrous surface. "Sponsored by a company that recognized his potential, he studied geotechnics and soil mechanics at the University of Sydney. He graduated in record time—this young man who'd dropped out of high school only nine years before—and was soon being headhunted by engineering firms because of his deep understanding of soil behavior, and also because of his custom-made equipment. He could've made a fortune in patents, but he never saw himself as an inventor, merely as a worker who, as he put it, 'got mad at crappy tools.'"

There was a murmur of recognition in the crowd. Peter laid his free hand on the coffin lid, gently but firmly, as if laying it on Art Severin's shoulder. "Whenever he found that the available apparatus couldn't deliver the quality of data he demanded, he simply designed and built technology that would. Among his inventions was . . ." (and here he consulted the scrap of paper inside his Bible) ". . . a new sampling tool for use in cohesion-less sands below groundwater level. Among his academic papers—again, written by this man whose high school teachers considered him a hope-less delinquent—were 'Undrained triaxial tests on saturated sands and their significance to a comprehensive theory of shear strength,' 'Achieving constant pressure control for the triaxial compression test,' 'Stability gain due to pore pressure dissipation in a soft clay foundation,' 'Overhauling Terzaghi's principle of effective stress: some suggested solutions to anomalies at low hydraulic gradients,' and dozens more."

Peter closed his Bible and hugged it to his abdomen, directly under the crucifix-shaped stain. His dishdasha had been laundered and pressed, but fresh sweat was already spreading in patches all over it. The assembled mourners were perspiring too.

"Now, I'm not going to pretend I have much of a clue what those titles mean," said Peter with a faint grin. "Some of you will. Others won't. The important thing is that Art Severin turned himself into a world-renowned expert on something more useful than taking drugs. Although . . . he didn't let his old skills lapse entirely. Before he worked for USIC, he used to smoke fifty cigarettes a day." A ripple of chuckles passed through the crowd. There had been a solitary, suppressed snort earlier on when he'd referred to the female companionship supplied by Kamelia's business, but this laughter now was unashamed, relaxed.

"But we're getting ahead of the story," he cautioned. "We're leaving out some of his lives. Because Art Severin's *next* life was as a consultant on major dam-building projects in a dozen countries from Zaire to New Zealand. His time in Malaysia had taught him the value of staying out of the limelight, so he rarely took the credit for his achievements, preferring to let politicians and corporate heads bask in the glory. But glorious indeed were the dams he nurtured to completion. He was especially proud of the Aziz Dam in Pakistan, which, if you'll forgive an unintended pun, was truly groundbreaking: a rock-filled earth dam with an impervious clay core. The entire project required a high degree of attention to detail, since it was in an earthquake fault zone. It still stands today." Peter raised his chin, looked out of the nearest window at the alien emptiness beyond. His congregation looked likewise. Whatever was out there symbolized achievement, hard-won achievement within a vast environment that did not change unless dedicated professionals made it happen. A few eyes glinted with moisture.

"Art Severin's next life was not a happy one," said Peter, on the move again, as though inspired by Severin's own restlessness. "Kamelia left him, for reasons he never understood. Both his daughters were badly affected by the breakup: Nora turned against him, and May was diagnosed schizophrenic. A few months after a grueling and expensive divorce settlement, Art was investigated by tax authorities and billed for money he didn't have. Within a year, he was drinking heavily, on welfare, living in a motor home with May, watching her get worse, and getting sicker and sicker himself, with undiagnosed diabetes.

"But here's where the story takes an unexpected direction," he said, turning abruptly, making eye-contact with as many of his listeners as he could. "May went off her medication, committed suicide, and everybody who'd been watching Art Severin's decline assumed he would completely hit the skids and be found dead one day in his trailer. Instead, he sorted out his health, tracked down his real father, borrowed some money, shipped himself back to Oregon, and found work as a tour guide. He did it for ten years, refusing offers of promotion, refusing opportunities to get back into the geotechnics industry—until finally USIC came along. USIC made him an offer he couldn't refuse: the chance to test out, on a grand scale, his theories on the use of soils and soft rocks as engineering materials.

"That grand-scale testing ground," declared Peter, "is here. It's what we are standing on today. Art Severin's skills helped to take this fantastically ambitious experiment as far as it has reached, and, because of Art's generous sharing of his expertise, his skills will live on in his colleagues, you who knew him. I've talked mostly about Art's past, a past many of you may have been scarcely aware of, because Art seldom spoke of it. He was, as I'm sure some of you would agree, a hard man to get to know. I won't pretend to have known him myself. He showed kindness to me on my journey here, but by the time we arrived, we'd exchanged some tense words. I was looking forward to catching up with him later, after I'd settled in to my own work here; I was looking forward to smoothing things over between us. But that's the way it goes with the dead and those they leave behind. Each of you will have your last memory of Art Severin, the last thing you said to him, the final thing he said to you. Maybe it's the smile you shared over some detail of your work together, a smile that will mean something more to you now: a symbol of a relationship that was in pretty good order, pretty much ready to be severed clean. Or maybe you'll remember a look he gave you, one of those what-the-hell-did-he-mean-by-that moments, something that makes you wonder whether there was anything you could or should have done, to make his absence now seem more natural. But either way, we're struggling to make sense of his unreachability, the fact that he's in a different dimension from us now, he's no longer breathing the same air, no longer the same sort of creature. We know there was more to him than the body that's stored in this casket, just as we know that there's more to us than our kidneys and our intestines and our earwax. But we don't have accurate terminology for what that extra thing is. Some of us call it the soul, but what *is* that, really? Is there a research paper on it that we can read, that will explain the properties of Art Severin's soul, and tell us how it differs from the Art Severin we knew, the guy with the discolored teeth and prickly temperament, the guy who found it difficult to trust women, the guy who had a habit of drumming on his knees to rock music that played in his head?"

Peter had been walking forward slowly, getting closer to his congregation, until he stood within arm's-reach of the front row. BG's forehead was contorted with wrinkles, his eyes shone with tears. The woman next to him was weeping. Tuska's jaw was set, his lopsided grin trembling slightly. Grainger, somewhere in the back row, was bone-pale, her expression softened by pain.

"People, you know I'm a Christian. For me, that all-important research paper is the Bible. For me, that vital missing data is Jesus Christ. But I know that some of you are of different faiths. And I know that Art Severin professed to have none. BG asked him what religion he was, and he said 'I'm nothing.' I never got a chance to discuss with him what he really meant by that. And now, I'll never get that chance. But it's not because Art Severin is lying here, dead. No. It's because this body here isn't Art Severin: we all know that, instinctively. Art Severin isn't here anymore; he's somewhere else, somewhere where we can't be. We're standing here, breathing air into those funny spongy bladders we call lungs, our torsos shaking slightly from the pump action of that muscle we call a heart, our legs getting uncomfortable from balancing on our foot bones too long. We are souls shut inside a cage of bones; souls squeezed into a parcel of flesh. We get to hang around in there for a certain number of years, and then we go where souls go. I believe that's into the bosom of God. You may believe it's somewhere different. But one thing's for sure: it's somewhere, and it's not here."

Peter walked back to the coffin, laid his hand on it once again.

"I can't say for sure if Art Severin really, truly believed he was nothing more than the contents of this coffin. If so, he was wrong. Maybe I shouldn't get into another argument with him now; maybe it's in bad taste. But Art: forgive me, forgive us, we've got to tell you: you weren't nothing. It wasn't true that you were going nowhere. You were traveling on the great human journey, and yesterday you broke through the final checkpoint, and you've reached the destination. You were a brave man who lived many lives, and each life required more courage than the last, and now you're in the next life, where your body won't let you down anymore, and you don't need insulin and you don't crave nicotine, and nobody betrays your trust, and every mystery you racked your brains about is clear as day now, and every hurt you ever suffered is OK now, and you're feeling pity for us down here, still dragging our heavy bodies around." There was a grunt of surprise from the audience: BG had lifted his massive arm to wipe his eyes, and his elbow had accidentally bumped against someone's skull.

"Art Severin," proclaimed Peter—and, despite the muffled acoustics of the room, there seemed somehow to be a churchy reverb after all—"we are here today to dispose of your old cage of bones, your parcel of flesh. You don't need that stuff anymore. They are crappy tools. But if it's all right with you, please let us keep a few little souvenirs: our memories. We want to keep you with us, even as we let you go. We want you to live on in our minds, even though you're living somewhere bigger and better than that. One day, we too will go where souls go, where you have traveled before us. Until then: Goodbye, Arthur Laurence Severin. Goodbye."

Back in his own quarters, after he'd spent some time with a few of the mourners who hadn't wanted to leave even after the coffin had been consumed, Peter seated himself once more in front of the Shoot. His clothing was sodden with sweat. He wondered how long the interval was between full water supplies to the shower. His head buzzed with the intimacies and confidences that USIC employees had just shared with him, facts about their lives that he must store in his memory, names he must make sure not to forget. His wife's unopened capsules hung suspended on the screen. Nine more messages he hadn't had time to read until now.

> Dear Peter,
> Excuse what will probably be a short, garbled message. I'm tired
> out. Sheila Frame and the two kids—Rachel and Billy—were here all

afternoon and most of the evening. For them it was the weekend, but I'd worked an early shift, after a late shift the day before. Rachel is a handful. Still kind of sweet but full of borderline obsessive-compulsive habits, quite exhausting to watch. Hormones, I suppose. You wouldn't recognize her, physically. Looks like a porn starlet/ pop star/heiress party girl—the usual mix for pubescent females these days. Billy is painfully polite and shy. Small for his age, and a bit chubby with it. Barely spoke the whole time he was here, and obviously undergoing agonies of embarrassment the more chatty/ nervy his mother became. Sheila smelled a little boozy, or maybe it was just very strong cologne, I don't know. She's buzzing with stress, the whole house is still full of it even though they left an hour ago. How I wished that you and I could have tackled them together—one of us calming Sheila down, the other relating to the kids, maybe taking it in turns. I don't know why they stayed so long; I can't imagine I was much use to them. Billy's one and only moment of candor was when I parked him in front of my computer to play a game. He took one look at the Noah's Ark display and his whole face flinched like someone had hit him. He told me that the snow leopard is extinct. The last surviving specimen died in a zoo a few weeks back. "The snow leopard was my favorite," he said. Then he sat down at the computer and within about 30 seconds he was lost in a realistic prison interior, shooting the guards' heads off, blowing doors open, getting killed.

Must go to bed immediately. Up at 5:30 tomorrow morning. I drank some of the wine that Sheila brought, so she wouldn't be self-conscious about drinking alone. I will regret it when that alarm clock goes off!

Please tell me a little more about how your mission is going. I want to talk specifics with you. It feels so strange not to. Peter, it HURTS not to. I feel like I'm your sister or something, sending you a long screed of complaint, chattering about things that you can't possibly care about. I'm still the same person you've known, the one you can always rely on to give you perspective and confirmation. I just need to have a clearer sense of what you're seeing and doing and experiencing, my darling. Give me some names, some particulars. I know you can't right now, because you're at the settlement and there's no way to read this message. But when you get back. Please. Take some time out to reflect. Let me be there for you.

MUST go to bed now.

Love,

Bea.

Peter rocked on the chair, overloaded with adrenaline, but also tired. He wasn't sure if he should, or even could, read Beatrice's other eight messages without answering this one. It felt cruel, perverse, not to respond. As though Bea were calling out to him, over and over, and he was ignoring her cries.

Dear Bea, he wrote on a fresh page.

Today I conducted a funeral. Art Severin. I didn't know he was a diabetic; he died suddenly while I was away at the settlement. I was given a comprehensive file on his life and about three hours to prepare something. I did my best. Everyone seemed to appreciate it.

Love,

Peter

He stared at the words on the screen, aware that they needed expansion. Details, details. A woman called Maneely had confessed to him that she hadn't given a thought to Christianity since she was a small child, but that she'd felt the presence of God today. He considered telling Bea that. His heart was thumping strangely. He left his message in draft form, unsent, and opened another capsule.

Dear Peter,

Are you sitting down? I hope so.

Darling, I'm pregnant. I know you'll think that's not possible. But I stopped taking the Pill a month before you left.

Please don't be angry with me. I know we agreed to wait another couple of years. But please understand that I was scared you'd never come back. I was scared there'd be an explosion at the launch and your mission would be over before it began. Or that you'd disappear somewhere along the way, just disappear into space, and I would never even know what became of you. So, as the departure date got closer and closer, I got more and more desperate for some part of you to be here with me, no matter what.

I prayed and prayed about it but just didn't feel I'd got an answer. In the end I left it in God's hands whether I would be fertile so soon after coming off the Pill. Of course it was still my decision, I'm not denying that. I wish the decision had been ours together. Maybe it was—or could have been. Maybe if we'd discussed it, you would have said it was exactly what you'd been wanting to suggest yourself. But I was terrified you'd say no. Would you have? Just tell me straight, don't spare me.

Whatever you feel, I hope it makes some difference to you that I'm proud and thrilled to be carrying your baby. Our baby. By the time you come back, I'll be 26 weeks along the way and getting pretty enormous. That's assuming I don't have a miscarriage. I hope I don't. It wouldn't be the end of the world, and we could try again, but it would be a different child. This one I'm carrying feels so precious—already! You know what I was thinking when you made love to me on the way to the airport? I was thinking, I'm ready, this is the moment, this is exactly the right moment, all it needs now is one tiny seed. And I bet that was when it happened. Looking back, almost certainly, that was when it happened.

13

THE ENGINE KINDLED

INTO LIFE.

"And this is where it all started," said the woman solemnly. "This is what it looked like in the beginning."

Peter nodded. He kept his jaw rigid and didn't dare try to make the appropriate interested noises, for fear of breaking into a grin or even laughing out loud. The official opening of this facility was a momentous occasion for everyone gathered here today.

"We put an extra-thick layer of epoxy on the top of the downstream surface," the woman continued, pointing to the relevant parts of the scale model, "to control the migration of water through the foundation. These tubes on the downstream side were connected to pressure transducers."

If she'd been breezy or casual, it wouldn't be so bad, but she was deadly earnest and that made it funnier, and everybody but him seemed to understand what she was talking about, which made it funnier still. Then there was the inherent comicality of an architectural scale model (so dignified, so full of symbolic importance, and yet so . . . *dinky*, like something from a children's playground). And, added to *that*, the shape of the model itself: two inverted cups joined together, fully justifying the "Big Brassiere" nickname.

The real buildings, from a distance, hadn't struck him as particularly comical. He'd seen them, along with everyone else, looming on the horizon earlier in the afternoon as USIC's convoy of vehicles drove across the scrubland, each vehicle ferrying half a dozen employees. The sheer size of the structures, and the fact that one partially obscured the other on approach, made them appear like nothing less than what they were: mighty works of architecture. When the convoy finally cruised to a standstill in front of the foremost structure, the vehicles parked in an area of shade so large that its contours were difficult to tell. Only once Peter and the other USIC personnel were gathered together in the entrance hall, contemplating a replica barely a meter high, was the design of this place revealed in all its bulbous symmetry. The officiating woman, Hayes, an engineer who'd worked closely with Severin, waved her hand in the air over the twin structures, oblivious to the fact that she appeared to be miming a caress of a sofa-size bosom.

". . . the desired g-level . . . self-weight displacements . . . overtopping simulation . . ." Hayes droned on. ". . . uplift pressures with five transducers . . . proximity probe . . ."

Peter's urge to laugh had passed. Now, he could scarcely keep awake. The entrance hall was stiflingly warm and poorly ventilated; it felt rather like being enclosed inside an engine—which was basically what it was, of course. He swayed slightly on his feet, took a deep breath, and made an effort to stand straighter. Bubbles of trapped sweat squelched in his sandals; his eyes stung and Hayes became blurry.

". . . recorded in real time . . ."

He blinked. Hayes muddled back into focus. She was a tiny woman with a military-style masculine haircut and the sort of dress sense that made anything she wore look like a uniform even when it wasn't. He'd made her acquaintance several days ago in the mess hall when she was shoveling her way through a plate of whiteflour mash and gravy. They'd conversed for ten, fifteen minutes and she'd been perfectly pleasant in a dull sort of way. She was from Alaska, used to like dogs and sledding but was content nowadays to read about them in magazines, and didn't believe in any religion, although she kept "kind of an open mind about poltergeists," having had a weird experience in an uncle's house when she was twelve. Her low-pitched monotone was, he'd thought, mildly attractive, reminding him slightly of Bea's melodious croon. But when delivering a lecture on thermodynamics and dam design, it wasn't so scintillating.

Even so, the fact that he was having trouble staying awake annoyed him. Boring experiences didn't normally affect him like this. Usually, he had exceptional tolerance for tedium; homelessness had taught him that. But living in the USIC base was worse than homelessness somehow. He'd been back a week, and his sunburned face had peeled and healed, but his brain wasn't recovering so well. He was wired and wakeful when he should be sleeping, and dopey when he should be alert. And here he was, nodding off, when he should be admiring the engineering genius of USIC's brand new Centrifuge & Power Facility.

". . . mutually exclusive functions . . . couldn't be done . . . Severin . . . vacuum net . . . the vision to let go of photovoltaics . . ."

It *was* impressive, what had been wrought here: a feat of engineering that stretched the limits of what was thought possible. Under normal conditions—that is to say, the conditions everyone was used to back home—rain fell over a large area and accumulated in great pools, or flowed into rivers which moved across the landscape gathering speed. Either way, a substance which, to a person standing under a rainshower, was perceived as individual droplets falling through the air, was transformed by time and volume and momentum into a vast force that could power a hundred thousand engines. These principles did not apply on Oasis. The raindrops manifested, dropped onto the sponge-like terrain, and were gone. If you happened to be outdoors while it was raining and held out a cup, it would be filled, or you could quench your thirst more simply than that, by leaning back with your mouth wide open. But when it was over, it was over, until the next rainfall.

The Big Brassiere's grand bipartite structure defied these limitations. One part of it was designed to suck the rain from the sky, gather the diffuse droplets into a cyclonic whirl, tug the condensed water into a gigantic centrifuge. But that was only half of the project's audacious ingenuity. The amount of electricity required to power this centrifuge was, of course, colossal—far beyond the yield of USIC's existing solar panels. So, the harvested water was not merely flung into a reservoir; it was first put to work in a giant boiler, where fearsome volumes of trapped steam set turbines spinning.

Each of the two buildings fed into each other, providing the energy to catch the water, providing the water to generate the energy. It wasn't exactly a perpetual motion machine—two hundred solar panels stationed in the scrubland all around the facility kept the sun's rays beaming in—but it was mind-bogglingly efficient. Oh, if only a few of these Big Brassieres could be installed in famine-ravaged countries like Angola and Sudan! What a difference they would make! Surely USIC, having just achieved this technological marvel and proved what could be done, must be negotiating such projects? He would have to ask someone about that.

But now was not the time.

"And in conclusion . . ." Hayes was saying. "One last practicality. We're cognizant of the fact that there's been some reluctance to use the official title of this facility, the Centrifuge & Power Facility. We're further cognizant of the fact that there's a nickname currently being usaged that is not what we want to hear. Some people may think it's funny but it's not exactly dignified and I think we owe it to Severin, who worked so hard on this project along with the rest of us, to give it a name that we can all live with. So, in recognition of the fact that a lot of people prefer names that are short and snappy, here's the deal. Officially, we are here today to celebrate the opening of the USIC Centrifuge & Power Facility. Unofficially, we suggest you call it . . . the Mother."

"Because it's one big motherfucker!" someone called out.

"Because necessity is the mother of invention," Hayes explained patiently.

With that, the opening ceremony speech more or less came to an end. The remainder of the visit was, or pretended to be, a guided tour of the facility, to demonstrate how the principles established by the scale model were put into full-size practice. However, so many of the facility's important features and mechanisms were encased in concrete or submerged in water or accessible only by vertiginous steel ladders that there was nothing much to see.

Only when they were driving away, back to the USIC base, in their little convoy, did Peter finally feel the surge of inspiration he hadn't been able to muster during Hayes's speech. Squashed between two strangers on the back seat of a steamy vehicle, he sensed the world darkening a little. He craned round and wiped the condensation off the rear window with his sleeve. The great power utility was already receding in the distance, shimmering slightly in the haze of spent fuel coming out of the jeep's exhaust. But what could be seen more clearly now was the multitude of solar panels—heliostats—that were arranged in a far-flung semi-circle on the landscape all around the Mother. Each of them was meant to catch the sunlight and redirect it straight to the power station. But by coincidence the sun was partially obscured by passing clouds. The heliostats swiveled on their podiums, adjusting the angle of their mirrored surfaces, adjusting, adjusting, adjusting again. They were only rectangular slabs of steel and glass, not in the least human-looking, but still Peter was moved by their insensate confusion. Like all creatures in the universe, they were only waiting for the elusive light that would grant them purpose.

Back in his quarters, Peter checked for messages on the Shoot. He felt guilty checking for fresh communications from Bea when he'd let so much time lapse since writing one himself. In his last letter, he'd reassured her that he was delighted to hear she was pregnant and that, no, of course he wasn't angry with her. The rest of the letter was padded out with mission-related stuff he couldn't recall. The entire letter had been maybe fifteen lines long, twenty at most, and had taken him several hours of sweat to produce.

It was true he felt no anger, but he felt disturbingly little of anything else either, aside from stress at his inability to respond. It was difficult, in his current circumstances, to grab hold of feelings and brand them with a name. If he tried his hardest, he could just about make sense of what was happening on Oasis, but that was because he and the events he was grappling with were in the same space. His mind and heart were trapped in his body, and his body was here.

The news of Bea's pregnancy was like news of some momentous event in Britain's current affairs: he knew it was important but he had no idea what he could or should do about it. He assumed that any other man would be imagining the intimate realities of being a father: the baby in his arms, the corporeal son or daughter bouncing on his knee, the kid's high school graduation or whatever. He could imagine such scenes only in the most contrived and generic way, as if they were two-dimensional panels in a comic book written and drawn by shameless hacks. Trying to visualize Bea with a baby inside her was impossible: there was no baby, yet, and if he tried to conjure up a vision of her belly, his mind's eye played him old footage of her slim abdomen inside the T-shirt she wore to bed. Or, if he tried harder, an x-ray of a pelvis that could have been anyone's, speckled with cryptic lucencies that could be a grub-like embryo, could be gas, could be cancer.

You must be extra careful now to take care of yourself, he'd written. His use of "care" twice in one short sentence was not ideal, but it had taken him long enough to come up with the words and he meant them so he'd sent them. Sincere as the sentiment was, though, he had to admit it was the sort of thing an auntie or a brother might say.

And since then, he'd not yet managed to write her another letter, despite receiving several from her. More than once, he'd forced himself to sit down and begin, but had got stuck after **Dear Bea** and taken it no further. Today, he tried to convince himself to type a few words about his visit to the Big Brassiere, but he doubted that his wife was hanging out for information on this topic.

There was nothing new from her today, which was unusual. He hoped nothing bad had happened. To Beatrice, that is. Bad things were happening to the world in general all the time, it seemed.

Of course, the world had always been crowded with mishaps and disasters, just as it had also been graced with fine achievements and beautiful endeavors which the media tended to ignore—if only because honor and contentment were hard to capture on film. But, even allowing for all that, Peter felt that the dispatches he was getting from Beatrice were alarmingly crammed with bad news. More bad news than he knew what to do with. There was only so much calamitous change you could hear about, events that rewrote what you thought was general knowledge, before your brain stopped digesting and you clung on to older realities. He accepted that Mirah had gone back to her husband and that an American politician's wife had been shot dead in her swimming pool. He remembered that there was a little girl in Oskaloosa called Coretta who'd lost her father. He accepted, with some difficulty, that the Maldives had been wiped out by a tidal wave. But when he thought of North Korea, he pictured a calm cityscape of totalitarian architecture, with legions of bicycle-riding citizens going about their normal business. There was no room in the picture for a catastrophic cyclone.

No fresh disasters today, though. No news is good news, as some people might say. Uncomforted, he retrieved one of Bea's older letters and re-read it.

Dear Peter,

I got your message last night. I'm so relieved you're not angry with me, unless the shortness of what you wrote indicates that you ARE angry but just keeping it under control. But I don't think so. You must be unbelievably preoccupied with your mission, learning the language and tackling all sorts of challenges that no one has ever faced before. (Please tell me a little more about those, when you have a minute.)

From what you HAVE said, it sounds like you're adjusting to the weather, at least. That's not really possible here because it's gone haywire again. More torrential rainfall, with the occasional gale force wind as a bonus. The house smells of damp. Mildew on the furniture and walls. Opening the windows lets in fresh air but also rain, it's hard to know what to do. I know it's very wet where you are too, but from the little you've told me about how the Oasans live, the place seems "designed" for it. Here in England, everything is set up on the basis that the weather will stay mostly dry and moderate. We're just not very good at planning for emergencies. Denial, I suppose.

Heard from Sheila again. Billy is clinically depressed, she says. Not good in a 14-year-old boy. I arranged to take him out somewhere on the day that the family is scheduled to move house. (Did I mention that Sheila and Mark split up? Neither one of them could meet the mortgage repayments alone so they've decided to sell up and move into flats. Actually, Mark is going to Romania.) I'm not convinced it's wise to move house without letting your kids be part of the process, but Sheila says Billy genuinely doesn't want to know and it's better if he just gets delivered to the flat when it's a fait accompli. She's given me money to take him to a movie but I'm actually going to take him to a Cat Show which happens to be on at the Sports & Leisure Center on that day. It's risky because (A) he may be the sort of kid who gets freaked out at animals being kept in small cages and (B) it will remind him of the snow leopard, but I hope that seeing all those different cats gathered together in one place will reassure him somehow.

Whew! If you could have heard the crash that just reverberated through the house! It almost gave me a heart attack. The window of the bathroom is shattered, hundreds of glass shards in the bathtub and on the floor. I thought it was vandalism at first, but it was the wind. A big gust ripped an apple off the tree in the backyard and flung it against our window. But fear not! Someone from the church is coming to fix it ASAP, within two hours, he said. Graeme Stone. Remember him? His wife died of cirrhosis.

I went to the supermarket yesterday, it was closed. No explanation, just a sellotaped piece of paper saying it wouldn't open until further notice. Quite a lot of people outside, would-be customers peering through the glass. Inside, the lights were on, everything looked as normal, the shelves stocked up. A couple of security guys stationed near the doors. A few staff(?) walking around the aisles talking calmly, as though nobody could see them, as though they were in their own living room instead of on public display in the high street. Weird. I stood there for about five minutes, I don't know why. Eventually a cheeky young West Indian man called through the glass to one of the security guys, saying "Can I have a packet of 20 Benson & Hedges, mate?" No response, so he adds, "It's for me mum, mate!" A ripple of laughter went through the crowd. It was one of those communal things, when something small and funny happens that everyone "gets," and for just an instant everyone's united. I love those moments. Anyway it was obviously downhill from there so I walked to the 24-hour convenience store and tried to score some milk there but no joy.

What are you eating, my darling? Anything I would fancy a bite of?

* * *

The USIC mess hall was bathed in orange light. It was afternoon. It would be afternoon for ages yet.

He ordered cream of chicken soup and a bread roll from the food counter. A woman was working there today, a Greek-looking beauty he hadn't yet got to know. He'd made conversation with most of the USIC personnel, to gauge whether he could be of use to anyone on a spiritual level, and had found them to be an uncommonly phlegmatic, self-contained bunch. This Greek woman was a new one on him, though, and there was a look in her eyes that offered hope that there might be a God-shaped hole in her life. He wondered if he should pursue the opportunity. But he was hungry and besides, his mind was full of the Oasans. His next departure was less than an hour away.

The soup was tasty, despite containing neither cream nor pieces of chicken. It had a rich chicken stock flavor, no doubt transported here in powder form. The whiteflower roll was crisp on the outside and spongy on the inside, still slightly warm—exactly as a bread roll should be. He ate and gave thanks to God for every mouthful.

The sound filtering through the PA was some sort of Dixieland jazz he couldn't identify. Ancient music wasn't his specialty. Every few minutes, a recorded announcement recited a list of trombonists and trumpeters and pianists and so on.

He finished his meal and returned the bowl to the counter.

"Thank you," he said.

"You're welcome," the woman said. Her wrist, as she picked up the bowl, was knobbly yet delicate, like Bea's. He wished he could link fingers with Bea just for three seconds and feel the bone of her wrist against his own flesh. The need of it struck him as he stood there, his eyes misted over; then he pulled himself together.

He returned to his seat, to allow the food to settle in his stomach. Stroking his palm down the front of his tunic, he was stung by a spark of static electricity, a phenomenon he'd noticed often before when he was too full of anticipation. He closed his eyes and sent a prayer to God for calm. A measure of calm was granted.

On the public address system, the Dixieland jazz had given way to something less hectic. He started to leaf through magazines from the racks near his armchair, spending a couple of minutes on each one before neatly replacing it.

His initial impression had been that USIC offered a comprehensive selection of what might be on sale in a newsagent's back home. Now that he examined the magazines more carefully, he wasn't so sure. *House & Garden, Hot Goss, Aquarium Fish, Men's Health, Lesbian Action, The Chemical Engineer, Classic Jazz, Vogue* . . . Yes, they were fairly recent, having arrived on the same ship that brought him to Oasis. And yes, they covered a broad range of interests, but . . . there was no hard news in any of them. He scanned the buzzwords and the teasers emblazoned on the covers. They were the same buzzwords and teasers that had appeared on these sorts of publications for decades. Absent from the racks was any magazine that reported on what was happening on the front lines, so to speak. You could read about jazz or how to harden your abdominal muscles or what to feed your fish, but where were the political crises, the earthquakes, the wars, the demises of major corporations? He picked up *Hot Goss*, a showbiz tattle mag, and flipped through it. Article after article was about celebrities he'd never heard of. Two pages came loose in his hand, alerting him to the fact that another two pages further on had been torn out. He found the relevant place. Sure enough, the numbering jumped from 32 to 37. He flipped back to the contents page and consulted the blurbs for a clue to the missing material. *"Umber Rosaria Goes To Africa! Our fave party girl swaps rehab for refugee camp."*

"Hey, preacher!"

He looked up. A sardonic-looking man with several days' growth of stubble was standing over him.

"Hi, Tuska," said Peter. "Good to see you. Growing the beard back?"

Tuska shrugged. "No big deal. Different display panel, same machine." He sat down in the nearest armchair and nodded toward the *Hot Goss* in Peter's hands. "That crap will turn your brain to jelly."

"I'm just checking out what's available here," said Peter. "And I noticed a couple of pages have been torn out."

Tuska leaned back, crossed one leg over the other. "Only a couple? Jeez, you should check out *Lesbian Action*. A third of it is gone, easy." He winked. "We'd probably need to break into Hayes's quarters to get it back."

Peter maintained eye contact with Tuska but did not allow his face to express approval or disapproval. This often acted as a moral mirror, he'd found, reflecting back at a person what they'd just said.

"No disrespect meant, you understand," added Tuska. "She's a damn good engineer. Keeps herself to herself. Like all of us here, I guess."

Peter replaced *Hot Goss* on the racks. "Are you married, Tuska?"

Tuska raised one bushy brow. "A long time ago in a galaxy far, far away," he intoned theatrically, wiggling his fingers in the air to emphasize the antiquated pop-culture reference. Then, in his normal voice, "Haven't heard from her in twenty years. More."

"Is there a special person in your life right now?"

Tuska narrowed his eyes pensively, play-acted a thorough scrutiny of the available data. "Nope," he said after four or five seconds. "Can't say that there is."

Peter smiled to signal that he understood the joke, but somewhere in his eyes there must have been a stray glint of pity, because Tuska felt provoked to explain further.

"You know, Peter, I'm surprised you got through the USIC screening process. Real surprised, as a matter of fact." For several beats, he kept Peter waiting for elaboration. "If you look at the guys and gals working here, you'll find that pretty much all of us are . . . ah . . . free agents. No wives or husbands back home. No steady girlfriends, no dependent children, no moms checking the mailbox. No strings."

"Because of the high risk of us dying on the way here?"

"Dying? Who's dying? We've had one accident in all these years and it had nothing to do with the Jump, it was a freak thing that could've happened to a commercial jet plane on its way to LA. The kinda thing insurance companies call an Act of God." He winked, then got back to the point. "Nah, the screening process . . . it's about conditions here. Life here. What can I say? 'Isolated' would be a fair word for it. The big risk, for anybody, is going crazy. Not psycho-killer, axe-murderer crazy, just . . . crazy. So-o-o . . ." He drew a deep, indulgent breath. "So it's best if you've got a team of individuals that understand what it's like to be in permanent . . . limbo. To have no other plans . . . nowhere else to go . . . nobody in the picture who particularly gives a damn. Know what I'm saying? People who can deal with that."

"A team of loners? Sounds like a contradiction in terms."

"It's the Légion Étrangère is what it is."

"Sorry?"

Tuska leaned forward, in storyteller mode now. "The French Foreign Legion," he said. "An elite army corps. They fought in lots of wars back in the day. A great team. You didn't have to be French to join. You could come from anywhere. You didn't have to tell them your real name, your past, your criminal record, nothing. So, as you can imagine, a lot of those guys were trouble with a capital T. They didn't fit in anywhere. Not even in the regular army. It didn't matter. They were *Legionnaires*."

Peter considered this for a few seconds. "Are you saying everybody here is trouble with a capital T?"

Tuska laughed. "Ah, we're pussycats," he schmoozed. "Fine and upstanding citizens one and all."

"In my interviews with USIC," reflected Peter, "I didn't get the impression I could've lied about anything. They'd done their research. I had to get medical checks, certificates, testimonials . . ."

"Sure, sure," said Tuska. "We're all hand-picked here. My analogy with the Legion is not that there's no questions asked. Far from it. My analogy is that we can deal with *being here*, period. *Legio Patria Nostra*, that was the motto of the Legionnaires. The Legion Is Our Homeland."

"Yet you've been back," observed Peter.

"Well, I'm the pilot."

"And BG and Severin; they went back a couple of times too."

"Yeah, but they spent years here in between trips. *Years*. You've seen Severin's files. You know how much time he spent in this place, doing his job every day, drinking green water, pissing orange piss, moseying on down to the mess hall every evening and eating adapted fungus or whatever the hell it is, maybe leafing through some year-old magazines like you'd find in a dentist's waiting room, going to bed at night and staring at the ceiling. That's what we do here. And we deal with it. You know how long the first USIC workers here lasted? The first couple batches of personnel, in the very early days? Three weeks, on average. We're talking about ultra-fit, highly trained, well-adjusted people from loving families blah blah blah. Six weeks, max. Sometimes six *days*. Then they would go out of their skulls, weeping, begging, crawling up the walls, and USIC would have to send them back. Back *ho-ome*." While uttering this last word, he made a grandiloquent sweep of his arms, to add a sarcastic halo of importance to the concept. "OK, I know USIC has a lot of money. But not *that* much money."

"What about Kurtzberg?" said Peter quietly. "And Tartaglione? They didn't go home, did they?"

"No," conceded Tuska. "They went native."

"Isn't that just a different way of adapting?"

"You tell me," said Tuska with a hint of mischief. "You just came back from Freaktown and now you're going again. What's your hurry? Don't you love us anymore?"

"Yes, I love you," said Peter, aiming for a light, good-humored tone that might simultaneously convey that he really did love everyone here. "But I wasn't brought here . . . uh . . . USIC made it clear I shouldn't expect . . ." He faltered, dismayed. His tone was neither bantering nor sincere; it was defensive.

"We're not your job," summarized Tuska. "I know that."

Out of the corner of his eye, Peter noticed that Grainger had entered the mess hall, ready to drive him to the settlement. "I do care," he said, suppressing the urge to bring up Severin's funeral, to remind Tuska how hard he'd tried to come up with something decent at short notice. "If you . . . if anyone actually . . . reached out to me, I'd be there for them."

"Sure you would," the pilot shrugged. Leaning back in his seat again, he noticed Grainger edging nearer, and gave her a casual salute.

"Your chariot awaits," announced Grainger.

Rather than taking the cafeteria exit and walking round the building to where the vehicle was parked, Grainger escorted Peter through a maze of internal corridors, postponing when they'd have to wade into the muggy air. This route through the base took them past the USIC pharmacy, Grainger's domain. It was shut and Peter would have walked right by without noticing it, if not for the bright green plastic cross mounted on its otherwise nonde-script door. He paused for a proper look, and Grainger paused with him.

"The serpent of Epidaurus," he murmured, surprised that whoever had made this cross had bothered to embellish it, in silver metallic inlay, with the ancient symbol of the snake encircling the staff.

"Yeah?" she said.

"It symbolizes wisdom. Immortality. Healing."

"And 'Pharmacy,' " she added.

He wondered if the door was unlocked. "What if someone shows up while we're gone, wanting you?"

"Unlikely," she said.

"USIC doesn't keep you that busy?"

"I do lots of other things besides the drugs. I analyze all the food, to check we're not poisoning ourselves. I do research. I pitch in."

He hadn't meant to make her justify her wage; he was only curious about that door. Having burgled quite a few pharmacies in his time, he struggled to believe that a storehouse of pharmaceutical goodies wouldn't be a temptation for even one of the people here. "Is it locked?"

"Of course it's locked."

"The only door in the whole place that's locked?"

She shot him a suspicious glance. He felt she'd peered straight into his conscience, eavesdropping on his guilty memory of trespassing in Kurtz-berg's quarters. What had possessed him to do that?

"It's not that I think anybody would steal anything," she said. "It's just . . . procedure. Can we go now?"

They walked to the corridor's end, where Grainger took a deep breath and opened the door to the outside. The cool, neutral air of the interior was sucked from behind them into the atmosphere beyond, exerting a tug on their bodies as they stepped out of the building. Then the flood of gaseous moisture enveloped them, a shock as always, until you got used to it.

"I overheard you tell Tuska you love him," said Grainger as they ap-proached the vehicle.

"He was bantering," said Peter, "and I was . . . uh . . . bantering back." The air currents ruffled his hair, ran under his clothing, blurred his vision. Distracted, he almost blundered against Grainger, having followed her to the driver's side before he remembered that he should be heading for the passenger's side. "But on a deeper level," he said, as he backtracked, "yes, it's true. I'm a Christian. I try to love everybody."

They took their seats in the front of the van and slammed the doors shut, sealing themselves into the air conditioned cabin. The short time they'd spent in the open air had been enough to dampen their skin all over, so that they both shivered at the same instant, a coincidence which made them smile.

"Tuska isn't very lovable," Grainger remarked.

"He means well," said Peter.

"Yeah?" she said tartly. "I guess he's more fun if you're a guy." She dabbed her face dry with a hunk of her shawl and, peering up into a mirror, brushed her hair. "All that sex talk. You should hear him sometimes. Real locker room stuff. So much hot air."

"You wouldn't want it to be more than hot air, would you?"

"God forbid," she scoffed. "I can imagine why his wife left him."

"Maybe he left her," said Peter, wondering why she was drawing him into this peculiar conversation, and why they weren't moving yet. "Or maybe it was a mutual decision."

"The end of a marriage is never a mutual decision," she said.

He nodded, as if deferring to her greater wisdom on this point. Still she made no move to start the vehicle. "Are there any married couples here?" he asked.

She shook her head. "Uh-*uh*. We've got work to do, we've all got to get along."

"I get along with my wife," he said. "We've always worked together. I wish she was here."

"You think she'd enjoy it here?"

He almost said, *That wouldn't matter, she'd be with me*, then realized how incredibly arrogant that would sound. "I hope so."

"My guess is she wouldn't be a happy bunny," said Grainger. "This is not the place for a real woman."

You're a real woman, he wanted to say, but his professional intuition warned him against it. "Well, there are a lot of women working here," he said. "They seem real enough to me."

"Yeah? Maybe you need to look at them a bit closer."

He looked at her a bit closer. A pimple had flared up on her temple, on the tender skin stretched tight just above her right eyebrow. It looked sore. He wondered if she was pre-menstrual. Bea got flare-ups of acne at certain times of the month, and was liable to start strange conversations full of non sequiturs, criticize work colleagues—and talk about sex.

"When I first started working here," Grainger went on, "I didn't even notice that nobody hooked up with anybody else. I figured it was probably going on behind my back. The way BG talks, and Tuska . . . But then time goes by, years go by, and you know what?—it never happens. Nobody holds hands. Nobody kisses. Nobody skips work for an hour and comes back with their hair all mussed up and their skirt inside their pants."

"Do you want them to?" The decorous reserve of the Oasans had made him less impressed than ever with the reckless ruttings of humans.

She sighed, exasperated. "I'd just like to see some signs of life sometimes."

He stopped short of telling her that she was being too harsh. He only said: "People don't have to be sexually active to be alive."

She looked at him askance. "Hey, you're not . . . uh . . . I forgot the word . . . when priests take, like, a vow . . . ?"

"Celibate?" He smiled. "No. No, of course not. You *know* I'm married."

"Yeah, but I didn't know what the deal was. I mean, there are all kinds of deals between a man and a woman."

Peter shut his eyes, tried to transport himself back to the bed with the yellow duvet, where his wife lay naked and waiting for him. He couldn't picture her. Couldn't even picture the yellow duvet, couldn't even recall the precise hue. Instead, he saw the yellow of Jesus Lover Five's robe, a distinct canary-yellow he'd trained himself to be able to distinguish from other yellows worn by other Jesus Lovers, because she was his favorite.

"Ours is . . . the full thing," he assured Grainger.

"That's nice," she said. "I'm glad." Whereupon, with a touch of her hand, the engine kindled into life.

14

LOST IN THE MIGHTY

UNISON.

His body jerked erect. "I'm sorry, I didn't mean to fall asleep on you," he said.

"It's OK," she said.

"Was I out for long?"

She consulted the dashboard. "Maybe twenty minutes. A catnap. At first, I figured you were deep in thought."

He checked the view through the side window, then faced front. The landscape looked exactly the same as when he'd nodded off.

"Not much to look at, I know," said Grainger.

"It's beautiful," he said. "I just haven't been sleeping well."

"Happy to help, go right ahead."

He examined her face, trying to judge whether she was annoyed with him, but she'd put on dark glasses at some point during the drive, and her whole head was ablaze with sunlight.

"Your lips," she said, "are too dry. You're not drinking enough." Keeping one hand on the wheel, she used the other to fetch up a water bottle from the floor between her legs. She handed it over to him, only momentarily taking her eyes off her driving, and fetched up another bottle for herself. Hers was already opened; his was still sealed.

"Remember to keep drinking," she said. "Dehydration is a killer. And be careful in the sun. Don't get burned like last time."

"You're talking like my wife," he said.

"Well, maybe between the two of us, we can keep you alive."

He uncapped the bottle and drank deep. The colorless liquid was chilled and it tasted harsh—so harsh that he almost coughed. As discreetly as he could, he glanced at the label, which read, simply, WATER: $50 PER 300ML. She was giving him an expensive imported gift.

"Thank you," he said, trying to sound chuffed, while actually thinking how strange it was that someone who'd lived on Oasis longer than him could fail to appreciate the superiority of the local water. When his mission was over and he had to return home, he would certainly miss the taste of honeydew.

Near the end of the long drive, Peter decided that the Oasan settlement deserved a better name than C-2 or Freaktown. He'd tried to find out what the Oasans themselves called it, so he could refer to it by that name, but they appeared not to understand the question, and kept identifying their settlement, in English, as "here." At first he assumed this was because its real name was unpronounceable, but no, there *was* no real name. Such marvelous humility! The human race would have been spared a great deal of grief and bloodshed if people hadn't been so attached to names like Stalingrad, Fallujah and Rome, and simply been content to live "here," whatever and wherever "here" might be.

Even so, "Freaktown" was a problem, and needed fixing.

"Tell me," he said, when the settlement was within sight. "If you had to give this place a new name, what would you call it?"

She turned toward him, still wearing her dark shades. "What's wrong with C-2?"

"It sounds like something you'd see on a canister of poison gas."

"Sounds neutral to me."

"Well, maybe something less neutral would be an improvement."

"Like . . . let me guess . . . New Jerusalem?"

"That would be disrespectful to the ones who aren't Christians," he said. "And anyway, they have a lot of trouble pronouncing 's' sounds."

Grainger thought for a minute. "Maybe this is a job for Coretta. You know, the girl from Oskaloosa . . ."

"I remember her. She's in my prayers." Anticipating that Grainger might have trouble with this, he immediately lightened his tone. "Although, maybe this *isn't* a job for Coretta. I mean, look at 'Oasis'—it has two 's's in it. Maybe she's really hooked on 's's. Maybe she'd suggest 'Oskaloosa.'"

The joke fell flat and Grainger remained silent. It seemed his mention of prayer had been a mistake.

Abruptly the wilderness ended and they were driving into the town's perimeter. Grainger steered the vehicle toward the same building as before. The word WELCOME, in man-size letters, had been painted afresh on the wall, although this time it read

WEL   WEL   COME

as if to add emphasis.

"Just drive straight to the church," said Peter.

"The church?"

He doubted she could have failed to notice the construction site last time she picked him up, but, OK, fine, she needed to play this game and he would indulge her. He pointed toward the horizon, where the large, vaguely Gothic structure, still lacking a roof or a spire, was silhouetted against the afternoon sky. "That building there," he said. "It's not finished, but I'll be camping out in it."

"OK," she said. "But I still have to do my drug delivery." And she jerked her head toward the paint-daubed building they'd just left behind.

Glancing backward, he noted all the vacant space in the rear of the vehicle, and the box of medicines in the middle of it. "Sorry, I forgot. Would you like some moral support?"

"No, thank you."

"I really don't mind staying with you for as long as it takes. I should have remembered."

"Not your job."

She was already steering the car across the scrubland toward the church. There was no point trying to persuade her to turn back and get her drug delivery over with first, even though he was convinced she'd be less stressed if she had company, less spooked if someone of her own kind was at her side. But he couldn't push. Grainger was a touchy character—and getting touchier the longer he knew her.

They slowed to a standstill, alongside the western wall of the church. Even without the roof on, the building was big enough to cast shade all over and around them.

"OK, then," said Grainger, removing her sunglasses. "Have a good time."

"I'm sure it will be interesting," said Peter. "Thanks again for driving me here."

"All the way to . . . Peterville," she quipped, as he unsealed the car door.

He laughed. "Out of the question. They have trouble pronouncing 't' sounds too."

The humid atmosphere, kept at bay for so long, swirled gleefully into the cabin, licking their faces, clouding the window, slipping into their sleeves, stirring the locks of their hair. Grainger's face, small and pale inside her swaddle of headscarf, was balmed over with perspiration within a couple of seconds. She frowned irritably, and sweat twinkled in the lush brown hairs where her eyebrows almost met.

"Are you really praying for her?" she said abruptly, just as he was about to climb out of his seat.

"You mean Coretta?"

"Yes."

"Every day."

"But you don't know her at all."

"God knows her."

She winced. "Can you pray for one more person?"

"Of course. Who?"

"Charlie." She hesitated. "Charlie Grainger."

"Your father?" It was a guess, an intuition. Brother was a possibility; son he didn't think was likely.

"Yes," she said, her cheeks blossoming red.

"What's the main concern in his life?"

"He's going to die soon."

"Are you close?"

"No. Not at all. But . . ." She pulled her scarf down off her head, shook her bared head like an animal. "I don't want him to suffer."

"Understood," said Peter. "Thanks. See you next week." And he left her in peace, and walked through the door of his church.

* * *

The Oasans had made him a pulpit. God bless them, they'd made him a pulpit, carved and molded from the same amber material as the bricks. It stood proudly inside the four walls as if it had sprung up from the soil, a tree in the shape of a pulpit, growing in the open air. Just before his departure, Peter had hinted that the roof should be put on as soon as possible, but there was no roof. Nor had any progress been made on the windows, which were still just holes in the walls.

Standing here reminded him of childhood visits to medieval ruins, where tourists would potter around the remains of a once-thriving abbey abandoned to the elements. Except that this church wasn't a ruin, and there was no need to worry about the effects of exposure. The roof and windows, when they finally came, would be a grand gesture of completion but, in truth, this church had been ready for use since the moment it was conceived. It was never going to be a hermetically sealed bunker like the USIC base. The roof would serve to keep a downpour out, but the air inside would be the same as the air outside, and the floor would still be trampled earth. The church would contain no perishable bric-a-brac or fragile fabrics that could be ruined by weather; the Oasans regarded this place purely as a gathering-point for bodies and souls—which boded well for their growth in Christ.

And yet, they'd made him a pulpit. And they had finished the entrance. The two halves of the door which, when he was here last, had lain flat on the ground, fresh from the kiln, had been lifted into place and affixed. Peter swung them open and closed, open and closed, admiring the smooth motion and the perfectly straight line where the two halves met. No metal hinges or screws had been used; instead, the joints were cleverly dovetailed: finger-like appendages on the inner edges of the doors nestled snugly in matching holes in the jambs. He was pretty sure that if he were to seize hold of these doors and lift them, they would come away from the jambs as easily as a foot from a shoe—and could be replaced just as readily. Was it foolhardy to construct a building in such a way that a mischievous vandal could pull its doors off? Even if there were no vandals here to cause such mischief? And did building a church on this spongy earth qualify as "building a house on sand," as warned against in *Matthew 7:24–26*? He doubted it. Matthew was speaking metaphorically, making a point not about architecture but about faith in action.

The Oasans were slow workers, pathologically careful, but they never gave less than their best. The door had been decorated with intricate carvings. When first carried here across the scrubland, the two halves were smooth as glass. Now they were scored with dozens of tiny crosses, executed in such a variety of styles that Peter suspected each individual Jesus Lover had added one of his or her own. Near the tapered pinnacle of the door were three outsized human eyes, arranged in a pyramid. They had a blind look to them, pictorially elegant but produced without any understanding of what makes an eye an eye. There were also some gouges which might be mistaken for abstract curlicues but which he knew were meant to be shepherds' staffs—or "ㄣﾞaffㄣ," as the Oasans had struggled to identify them when they'd discussed it.

He had offered to learn their language, but they were reluctant to teach him and, deep down, he conceded it might be a waste of time. In order to imitate the sounds they produced, he'd probably need to rip his own head off and gargle through the stump. Whereas the Oasans, thanks to the pioneering efforts of Tartaglione and Kurtzberg, and to the zeal of their own faith, had made extraordinary progress in English—a language they were as unsuited to learn as a lamb was unsuited to climb a ladder. Yet they climbed, and Peter felt keenly the pathos of their strivings. He could tell, from the Bible verses they'd managed to memorize, that Kurtzberg had made no concessions to their physical handicaps: whatever was printed in Scripture was what they must voice.

Peter was determined to show more sensitivity than that. During his sleepless week back at the USIC base, he'd done a lot of work translating Bible terms into equivalents that his flock would find easier to pronounce. "Pastures," for example, would be "green land." "Righteousness" would simply be "Good." "Shepherd" would be "he who care for me" (niceties of grammar were less important than the meaning, and anyway, the phrase had quite a poetical ring to it). "Staff" would be "care wand." He'd sweated over that one. The hint of hocus pocus was regrettable, and "care wand" lacked the straightforward vigor of "staff," but it was better than "crook" (too much potential for confusion with the concept of crookedness), it was merciful on the Oasan throat, and it incorporated the right elements of pastoral concern and divine potency.

The fruits of these labors were in his rucksack. He swung it off his shoulder and dumped it next to the pulpit, then sat down next to it. A feeling of tranquility descended, like a warm infusion of alcohol spreading through his system. The awkward drive with Grainger faded from his mind; the earlier conversation with Tuska already seemed long ago; he had difficulty retrieving anything from Bea's most recent letter except that she intended to take Billy Frame to a cat show. Oddly enough, the Noah's Ark wall-hanging that Billy and Rachel had made was vivid in his memory, as though it had come on the journey with him and was hanging somewhere nearby.

He was so looking forward to living with the Oasans again. It truly was a privilege. Ministering to his congregation in England was a privilege, too, but it was also difficult sometimes, what with the perverse, immature behavior that various individuals were liable to spring on you. That Asian woman, Mirah, and her violent husband . . . She giggly and gossipy, he fat and peevish, poncing about like an overfed sultan . . . they were precious souls, sure, but not exactly restful company. The Oasans were a tonic for the spirit.

He sat for a while, in a state of prayer without forming any words, just allowing the membrane between himself and Heaven to become permeable. A small red insect, like a ladybird but with longer legs, settled on his hand. He aligned his fingertips in a triangle and let the creature walk up the incline of one finger and down the slope of another. He let the creature nibble the surplus cells from the surface of his skin. It wasn't greedy; he barely felt it and then it flew away.

Ah, the power of silence. He'd first experienced it as a small boy, parked next to his mother at her Quaker meetings. A room full of people who were content to be quiet, who didn't need to defend the boundaries of their egos. There was so much positive energy in that room that he would not have been surprised if the chairs had started to lift off the floor, levitating the whole circle of worshippers to the ceiling. That was how it felt with the Oasans, too.

Maybe he should have been a Quaker. But they had no ministers, and no God—not in any real, fatherly sense. Sure, it was peaceful to sit in a community of companions, watching the play of sunlight on the pullover worn by the old man opposite, allowing yourself to be mesmerized by glowing wool-fibers as the sunlight moved slowly from one person to another. A similar state of peacefulness could sometimes be granted when you were homeless: a time in the afternoon when you'd found a comfortable spot, and you'd managed to get warm at last, and there was nothing to do but watch the sunlight's incremental shift from one paving-stone to the next. Meditation, some might call it. But in the end, he preferred something less passive.

He took up his position at the pulpit, and rested his fingertips on the burnished toffee-colored surface where he might spread out his notes. The pulpit was slightly too low, as though the Oasans had made it for as tall a creature as they could imagine but, in his absence, had still underestimated his height. Its design was modeled on the spectacular carved pulpits of ancient European cathedrals, where a massive leatherbound Bible might lie on the spread wingspan of an oaken eagle.

As a matter of fact, the Oasans had a photograph of just such a pulpit, given them by Kurtzberg, torn from an old magazine article. They'd shown it to Peter with pride. He'd tried to reassure them that worship was an intimate communication between the individual and God, nothing grandiose about it, and that any props should reflect the local culture of the worshippers, but this was not an easy concept to get across when you had a crowd of fetus-like heads jostling around you, murmuring their admiration for a fragment of a Sunday supplement as though it was a holy relic.

In any event, his pulpit did not much resemble the intricately feathered eagle in the photo. Its streamlined surface, inscribed with randomly chosen letters from the alphabet, might just as easily be an airplane's wings.

"I🝕 i🝕 good?" A soft voice, which he recognized at once. Jesus Lover Five. He'd left the door of the church open and she'd walked in, dressed in her canary-yellow robe as usual.

"It's beautiful," he said. "A lovely welcome."

"God ble🝕 our reunion, Father Pe🝕er."

He looked past her small form, through the doorway behind her. Several dozen Oasans were making their way across the scrubland, but they were far away still; Lover Five had hurried ahead. Hurrying was unusual among her people. She appeared none the worse for it.

"I'm happy to see you," said Peter. "As soon as I left, I wanted to come back."

"God bleʂ our reunion, Father Peʒer." Slung on her shoulder was a net haversack, with a furry, yellow lump stashed in it—the same intense hue as her robe. He thought it might be a shawl, but she pulled it out and held it up for him to examine. It was a pair of boots.

"For you," she said.

Smiling shyly, he plucked them from her gloved hands. Unlike the petite booties he'd been given on his first visit, these looked as though they might actually be his size. He removed his sandals—whose inner soles were misshapen and almost black from constant wear—and slipped the boots onto his feet instead. They fitted perfectly.

He laughed. Bright yellow boots and an Islamic gown that resembled a dress: if he'd had any ambition to be a macho man, this combo would have spelled the end of it. He lifted one foot and then the other, displaying to Lover Five how excellent her handiwork was. Having witnessed the Oasans making clothes on a previous visit, he knew how much labor this project must have cost her—and how much obsessive concentration. Oasans handled sewing-needles with the same care and respect that humans might handle chainsaws or blowtorches. Each stitch was such a ponderous ritual that he couldn't bear to watch.

"They're excellent," he said. "Thank you very much."

"For you," she said again.

They stood together by the open door, watching the rest of the Jesus Lovers make progress toward them.

"How's your brother, Jesus Lover Five?" asked Peter.

"In the ground."

"I mean the other one," said Peter. "The one who's causing you sorrow because he doesn't love Jesus."

"In the ground," she repeated. Then, helpfully, she added: "Alʂo."

"He died? In the last week?"

"The laʂʒ week," she said. "Yeʂ."

Peter stared into the shadowed cleft of her hooded head, wishing he could guess what emotion lay behind her impeded speech. His experience so far had made him suspect that Oasans' emotions were expressed in the rustlings and burbles and squimphs they uttered when not straining to imitate an alien language.

"What did he die of? What happened?"

Lover Five stroked herself perfunctorily over her arms, chest and midriff, to indicate the entire body. "Inﬅide him, many thingﬅ gone the wrong way. Clean thingﬅ became foul. ﬅ￐rong thingﬅ became weak. Full thingﬅ became emp￐y. Cloﬅed thingﬅ became open. Open thingﬅ became cloﬅed. Dry thingﬅ became filled with wa￐er. Many other thingﬅ alﬅo. I have no wordﬅ for all the thingﬅ."

"I'm very sorry to hear this."

She bowed her head, a gesture of shared regret perhaps. "For a long ￐ime already, my brother waﬅ ﬅick. Life remained in him, but with a plan ￐o leave. I go every day ￐o my brother, and hiﬅ life ﬅpoke ￐o me when he fall aﬅleep, ﬅaying, I am here another day, but I will no￐ remain here another day more, I am no￐ welcome in thiﬅ body. While life remained in my brother, grief remained in me. Now he iﬅ in the ground, my grief iﬅ in the ground. God bleﬅ our reunion, Father Pe￐er. ￐oday will be ﬅunday."

Peter nodded, although in truth he didn't know if it was a Sunday. He'd lost track of his accustomed measures of time. But it didn't matter. He and the Oasans were about to worship. That was no doubt what Lover Five meant by "Sunday." And she was right.

"I have something for you, too," said Peter, striding over to where he'd left his rucksack. Her head moved down and up, following the motion of his hands as he fetched out the booklets he'd prepared.

"Bibles," he said. "Or the beginnings of Bibles, anyway. For you to keep." He'd managed to produce twenty pages of Scripture rendered in an English that the Oasans could speak with a minimum of trouble, printed in King James–style columns on ten sheets of paper folded double and stapled in the middle. Not the handsomest display of bookbinding since Gutenberg, but the best he could come up with using the tools available at the USIC base. On the front cover of each booklet, he'd hand-drawn a cross, and colored it gold with a highlight marker.

"The Book of ﬅ￐range New Thingﬅ," confirmed Jesus Lover Five, as her fellow converts began to file into the church. Treading slowly in their padded boots, they made almost no sound on the soft earth, but Lover Five heard them come in, and turned to greet them. "The Book of ﭏrange New Thingﭏ," she repeated, pointing at the booklets that Peter was piling up on his pulpit. "For uﭏ to keep."

There was a murmuring and sighing among the new arrivals. To his shame, Peter recognized individuals only by the color of their robes. He hoped their color-coding hadn't changed since last week. He'd trained himself to tell the difference between brown, bronze, auburn and copper, crimson, burgundy and coral, at least in his mind. Each shade reconnected him with conversations—however brief and stumbling—he had had with that person.

"Friends," he announced, when everyone was in. "I'm very happy to see you. I have brought you these gifts. Small gifts from me, containing much bigger gifts from our Savior."

There were, he estimated, about ninety souls gathered within the four walls, a dazzling flock of different hues. As a minister, he was well-practiced in casting a quick eye over a congregation to do an approximate head count. If his estimate was correct, it suggested the number of Christians had swollen by ten or twenty during his time away.

"As I explained to some of you before," he said, "the Bible that you've seen me carry—and Kurtzberg carry—is a very thick book. Too thick for most people to read. But it was never meant to be read all at once. The Bible is a storehouse of messages, which grew for hundreds of years, as our Lord shared more and more of his thoughts and intentions with whoever was ready to listen." As he spoke, he handed booklets to Lover Five, and she distributed them to her fellow worshippers. Each recipient took the computer-printed pamphlet into his or her gloved hands as though it were a fragile egg.

"When Jesus walked the earth," Peter continued, "people wrote down what He said and did, and after that, they wrote down the things that happened to His followers. But the Bible was begun in the time before Jesus came, the more ancient time when God seemed much further away and more mysterious, and it was harder to know for sure what He wanted. In those days, people told stories about God, and those stories are in the Bible too. Some of these stories require a lot of knowledge of the customs and places that existed before Jesus. Even among my own people, many don't have that knowledge."

He noticed, as he spoke, that every tenth person, rather than taking a booklet from Lover Five, elected to share one with his neighbor. Peter had brought eighty booklets, having judged his congregation to be slightly under that number, not expecting it to grow in his absence. Evidently, the Oasans had counted, at a glance, the number of booklets and—without any consultation or awkwardness—adjusted the logistics of distribution to ensure that the last few people in line weren't left with nothing.

"You have told me," he said, and gestured toward a robe of saffron and a robe of pale lavender, "—you, Jesus Lover Twelve and Jesus Lover Eighteen—that Kurtzberg once told you the story of Nebuchadnezzar, and the story of Balaam and the angel, and of the destruction of Jerusalem, and other stories that you struggled hard to understand and could not understand. Please take heart, my friends. There will be time to understand those stories later, when you have grown in Christ. But for now, Nebuchadnezzar can wait. When God decided to become Jesus, He did it because He wanted to spread His word among strangers, among those who'd never heard of Him, among those who didn't care for religion or understand it. The stories He told were simple. I've tried to put some of the best, most useful ones in your Bibles." He picked up one of the booklets and opened it. "Your books are small and thin, not because I doubt your hunger for Scripture, nor your power to think, but because I've tried to use only words that you and I can speak together in this church, and that you can speak amongst yourselves, with ease. I've worked as fast as I can, yet, as you can see from the smallness of the books, I've been slow. I promise that in future, I'll be faster. As you grow in Christ, your Bibles will grow. But we must begin somewhere. And on this wonderful Sunday, as I stand here filled with happiness to see you all here with me, we will begin with . . . *this*."

And, from the first page, he read Psalm 23. "The Lord be He who care for me. I will need no more . . ." and so on, until he reached "I will dwell in the home of the Lord forever."

Then he read it again.

And again.

Each time he read it, more of the Oasans read it aloud with him. Were they reading or reciting? It didn't matter. Their communal voice was swelling, and it sounded melodious and clear, almost entirely free of vocal impairments. "He bid me lie in green land down. He lead me by river where no one can drown. He make my ꞇoul like new again. He lead me in the path of Good. He do all thiꞇ, for He be God."

By the fifth repetition, his own voice was lost in the mighty unison.

15

HERO OF THE MOMENT,

KING OF THE DAY.

A wise man once asked Peter: "Do you know what you are?"

"What I am?"

"Yes."

It was a question that could mean so many things, depending on who was posing it. It had, for example, been uttered to him on several occasions by angry thugs who'd supplied the answer themselves—"A stupid cunt," or some similar insult—and then beat him up. It had been asked of him by officials and bureaucrats who regarded him, for one reason or other, as a thorn in their side. It had been said affectionately and admiringly too, by people who went on to tell him he was "a total sweetie," "a treasure," or even "my rock." Big things to live up to.

"I try not to think about myself too much. I hope I'm just a man who loves God."

"You're a *people person*," the wise man said, nodding decisively. "That will take you a very long way." The wise man was the pastor of a church that Peter would soon inherit. He was an elderly soul, and had that special mixture of benign tolerance and stoic disappointment typical of a minister who'd been in the job too long. He was intricately familiar with all the ways his parishioners were resistant to change, all the ways they could be a pain in the arse—though he would never use such language, of course.

"You like people. That's actually quite rare," the old pastor went on.

"Isn't it basic human nature to be sociable?"

"I'm not talking about that," said the old man. "I don't think you're necessarily that sociable. A bit of a loner, even. What I mean is, you're not disgusted or irritated by the human animal. You just take them as they come. Some people never get fed up with dogs; they're dog people. Doesn't matter what sort of dog it is, big or small, placid or yappy, well-behaved or naughty—they're all lovable in their own way, because they're dogs and dogs are *a good thing*. A pastor should feel that way about human beings. But you know what?—not many do. Not many at all. You'll go far, Peter."

It had felt odd to be told this, with such certitude, by a sage old-timer who wasn't easily fooled. Peter's co-existence with his fellow humans had not always been a happy one, after all. Could someone who'd behaved as badly as he did when he was in his teens and twenties—lying and breaking promises and stealing from any altruistic fool who gave him the benefit of the doubt—truly be said to love people? And yet the old pastor was well aware of his history. There were no secrets between shepherds.

Now, Peter was sitting cross-legged, dazzled by the light, half-delirious. Right in front of him, also cross-legged, sat a small boy—himself when eight or nine years old. He was a Cub Scout. He was proud and happy to be a Cub Scout, possessor of a green shirt and sewn-on badges and arcane knowledge about knots and tent pitching and the proper way to light a fire. He was looking forward to becoming a fully-fledged Scout soon, not just a Cub, so that he could learn archery and go hiking in the mountains and save the lives of strangers who had been buried under avalanches or bitten by snakes. As it turned out, he would never get to be a Scout—his family circumstances would soon become too awkward, and the Cubs membership would be canceled and his uniform would sit neatly folded in the cupboard until finally the silverfish ruined it—but at eight he didn't know that yet, and he was sitting cross-legged in his shorts and neckerchief, almost levitating with pleasure to be here amongst his wolf pack.

Sweat trickled from his brow into his eyes. He blinked and the blurry world sharpened into view. The child sitting before him was not himself at the age of eight. It was not even a child. It was Jesus Lover Seventeen, a creature unlike him in almost every imaginable way, except that she, or he, or it could sit cross-legged and clasp hands in prayer. Her robe was spinach-green, and so were her soft boots, albeit speckled with brown dirt. The sun, almost directly overhead, cast a shadow under her hood, swallowing her face in blackness.

"What are you thinking, Jesus Lover Seventeen?" he asked.

There was, as always, a pause. The Oasans were unaccustomed to thinking about thinking, or maybe they just found it difficult to translate their thoughts into English.

"Before you came," said Jesus Lover Seventeen, "we were all alone and weak. Now, ᶘogether, we are ᶘᶘrong."

There was something poignant about the fact that her tongue, or vocal cords, or whatever it was she spoke with, could manage the words "alone" and "weak" without much trouble, but that the words "together" and "strong" were almost impossible for her to utter. Her petite form made her look all the more vulnerable, but then everyone sitting round about her was petite and vulnerable-looking too, with their thin arms and narrow shoulders and grubby mittens and booties. He might be ministering to a tribe of children and shrunken old people, a tribe that had lost all its full-size men and women.

That wasn't a fair view of them, of course; it was a failure to perceive their bodies as the norm, and his own as the aberration. He tried as hard as he could to adjust his vision, until the hundred-odd beings squatting before him grew to a mature scale, and he became a hulking monster.

"The Book," suggested Jesus Lover One, from his preferred spot near the middle of the congregation. "Give word from the Book."

"The Book," several other voices agreed, relieved, perhaps, to be voicing two words that did not humiliate them.

Peter nodded, to signal he would comply. His Bible was always close to hand, shrouded in plastic wrapping inside his rucksack to keep the moisture out, and the Oasans would make noises of appreciation whenever he brought it to light. But oftentimes he didn't even need to fetch it, because he had such an exceptional memory for Scripture. He looked inside his head now, and almost instantly found something appropriate, from Paul's letter to the Ephesians. His brain was a weird organ, that's for sure; sometimes he visualized it as a grubby cauliflower covered with scars and scorch-marks from the life he'd led, but at other times it seemed more like a spacious storehouse in which whatever verses he needed at any given moment were on display, already underlined.

"*Now therefore ye are no more strangers and foreigners,*" he quoted, "*but fellow citizens with the saints, and of the household of God; and are built upon the foundation of the apostles and prophets, Jesus Christ himself being the chief corner stone; in whom all the building fitly framed together groweth unto a holy temple in the Lord; in whom ye also are builded together for a habitation of God.*"

A murmur of approval—satisfaction, even—emanated from the brightly dressed creatures sitting before him. The Bible verses were like a particularly mellow alcoholic drink that had been passed around. This was King James liquor—the real stuff. Oh, sure, the Oasans were grateful for the paraphrased booklets Peter had prepared for them. The pages were already much-thumbed, rippled with damp, and the words had been sung and recited often in these long, balmy days that he and his flock had spent together. And yet, Peter could tell that the booklets were not quite the solution he'd hoped they would be. They were referred to as "our Word-in-Hand," a phrase which delighted him at first, until he realized that it served to differentiate the booklets from the genuine Book of Strange New Things. The handmade pamphlets were seen as a local homebrew, a moonshine compromise, whereas the big King James, with its machine-tooled faux-leather cover and gold-embossed spine, was considered pure and definitive—the True Source.

Now, drinking in the verses from *Ephesians*, the Oasans were truly contented. Their hooded heads hung lower, casting all their faces into even deeper shadow. Their clasped hands moved gently in their laps, as though re-tracing, re-savoring, the rhythm of the rhetoric. Such subtle movements were their equivalent of a Southern Baptist congregation hollering "Hallelujah!"

Fond as he was of the King James, Peter was uneasy about the awe it inspired among his flock. It was just a translation, after all, with no greater claim to authenticity than many other translations. Jesus hadn't expressed himself in Jacobean English, nor had Paul or the Old Testament prophets. Did the Oasans understand that? He doubted it. Which was a shame, because once it dawned on you that everyone who wasn't a native speaker of Canaanite Hebrew, Koine Greek or Galilean Aramaic was at an equal disadvantage, you could relax and feel that Scripture in your own tongue was as good as Scripture in anyone else's. Yet he thought he detected, in the Oasans, a sense of inferiority, which troubled him. He didn't want to be like some old-fashioned imperialist missionary, poncing about like Moses in a safari suit, capitalizing on a misconception that he was from the same tribe as Jesus and that God was an Englishman.

He'd considered gently disabusing the Oasans of their veneration of "the Book," with an informative talk on the various languages that lay behind the seventeenth-century text, but decided that such a lecture would only make things more complicated, especially since the Oasans were very attached to key scriptures they'd learned in Kurtzberg's time, and Kurtzberg had evidently been a King James fan. And no wonder. Any Christian preacher who loved language was bound to love the King James: you just couldn't beat those cadences. So maybe, when dealing with these people, 100-percent-proof Jacobean followed by a chaser in plain English was the way to go.

"What Saint Paul is saying to his new friends," Peter explained, "is that once you've heard the word of God, it doesn't matter how foreign you are, how far away you live. You become part of the community of Christians, all the Christians who've ever existed, including the ones who were alive when Jesus walked the earth. Then Paul goes on to compare us to a house. A house is built from many bricks or stones fitted together to make a big structure, and all of us are stones in the house that God is building."

Dozens of hooded heads nodded. "All are ᴧᵹoneᴧ."

"We built our church together," said Peter, "and it's a beautiful thing." Almost in choreographed formation, the Oasans turned their heads to look at the church, a building they considered so sacred that they set foot in it only for formal services, despite Peter's urging that they should treat it as their home. "But you—all of you, gathered together here today, just sitting in the sun—are the real Church that God has built."

Jesus Lover Five, in the front row as always, swayed to and fro in disagreement.

"ᴧurᴧ iᴧ ᴧurᴧ," she stated. "We are we. God iᴧ God."

"When we are filled with the Holy Spirit," said Peter, "we can be *more* than ourselves: we can be God in action."

Jesus Lover Five was unconvinced. "God never die," she said. "We die."

"Our bodies die," said Peter. "Our souls live forever."

Jesus Lover Five pointed a gloved finger straight at Peter's torso. "Your body no𝕩 die," she said.

"Of course it will die," said Peter. "I'm just flesh and blood like anyone else." He certainly felt his flesh-and-bloodness now. The sun was giving him a headache, his buttocks were going numb, and he needed to pee. After some hesitation, he relaxed his bladder and allowed the urine to flow out onto the soil. That was the way it was done here; no point being precious about it.

Jesus Lover Five had fallen silent. Peter couldn't tell if she was persuaded, reassured, sulking or what. What had she meant, anyway? Was Kurtzberg one of those Lutheran-flavored fundamentalists who believed that dead Christians would one day be resurrected into their old bodies—magically freshened up and incorruptible, with no capacity to feel pain, hunger or pleasure—and go on to use those bodies for the rest of eternity? Peter had no time for that doctrine himself. Death was death, decay was decay, only the spirit endured.

"Tell me," he said to those assembled. "What have you heard about life after death?"

Jesus Lover One, in his self-appointed role as custodian of the Oasans' history in the faith, spoke up.

"Corinthian."

It took Peter a while to recognize the word—intimately familiar to him, and yet so unexpected here and now. "Corinthians, yes," he said.

There was a pause.

"Corinthian," Jesus Lover One said again. "Give word from the Book."

Peter consulted the Bible in his head, located *Corinthians 15:54*, but it wasn't a passage he'd ever felt moved to quote in his sermons, so the exact wording was indistinct—*something corruptible something-something incorruption. . . .* The next verse was memorable enough, one of those Bible nuggets that everybody knew even if they ascribed it to Shakespeare, but he figured Jesus Lover One wanted more than a one-liner.

With a grunt of effort, he got to his feet. A hum of anticipation went through the crowd as he walked to his rucksack and extracted the Book from its plastic sheath. The gold-embossed lettering flashed in the sun. He remained standing, to give his muscles a change of tension, as he flicked the pages.

"*So when this corruptible shall have put on incorruption,*" he recited, "*and this mortal shall have put on immortality, then shall be brought to pass the saying that is written, Death is swallowed up in victory. O death, where is thy sting? O grave, where is thy victory?*"

Reading the words aloud, Peter reconnected with why he hadn't ever used them in his sermons. The sentiments were sound enough but the rhetoric was a bit more bombastic than he felt comfortable with. To do those words justice, you'd need a highly dramatic delivery, a touch of thespian pomp, and he just wasn't that kind of orator. Low-key sincerity was more his style.

"What Paul is saying here," he explained, "is that when we give our souls to Christ, the part of us that dies and decays—the body—is clothed with something that cannot die or decay—the eternal spirit. So we have nothing to fear from death."

"Nothing," echoed several of the Oasans. "Fear."

Peter's second sojourn in the place USIC called Freaktown was as bewildering and exciting as the first. He got to know the Oasans better—that was to be expected—but he also saw changes in himself, changes he couldn't articulate but that felt profound and important. Just as the atmosphere penetrated his clothes and seemed to pass through his skin, something unfamiliar was permeating his head, soaking into his mind. It wasn't in the least sinister. It was as benign as benign could be.

Not all of it was enjoyable, though. Halfway into his stay, Peter went through a strange phase which, looking back on it afterward, he could only call the Crying Jag. It happened during one of the long, long nights and he woke up somewhere in the middle of it with tears in his eyes, not knowing what he had dreamt to make him weep. Then, for hours and hours, he continued to cry. Upsurges of sorrow just kept pumping through his bloodstream, as if administered at medically supervised intervals by a gadget inside his body. He cried about the weirdest things, things he had long forgotten, things he would not have imagined could rank very high in his roll-call of griefs.

He cried for the tadpoles he'd kept in a jar when he was a kid, the ones that might have grown into frogs if he'd left them safe in their pond instead of watching them turn to gray sludge. He cried for Cleo the cat, stiff on the kitchen floor, her matted chin stuck to dried gravy on the rim of her plate. He cried for lunch money he'd lost on the way to school; he cried for a stolen bicycle, recalling the exact feel of its rubbery handles in his palms. He cried for the bullied classmate who killed herself after her tormenters squirted ketchup in her hair; he cried for the swallow that flew against his bedroom window and fell lifeless to the concrete far below; he cried for the magazines that kept arriving for his father each month, shrinkwrapped, long after his father had left home; he cried for Mr. Ali's corner newsagency and off-license that went out of business; he cried for the hapless anti-war marchers pushing on through the bucketing rain, their placards drooping, their children sullen.

He cried about the "Quilts for Peace" that his mother sewed for charity auctions. Even when her fellow Quakers took pity and put in a few bids, those quilts never fetched much because they were gaudy patchworks that clashed with every décor known to civilized man. He cried for the quilts that had gone unsold and he cried for the quilts that had found a home and he cried for the way his mother had explained, with such lonely enthusiasm, that all the colors symbolized national flags and the blue and white could be Israel or Argentina and the red polka dots were Japan and the green, yellow and red stripes with the stars in the middle could be Ethiopia, Senegal, Ghana or Cameroon depending on which way you were sleeping.

He cried about his Cubs uniform, eaten by silverfish. Oh, how he cried about that. Each vanished thread of fiber, each pathetic little hole in the useless garments, caused a swelling in his chest and stung his eyes anew. He cried about not having known that the final time he attended the Scout hall was the final time. Someone should have told him.

He cried about stuff that had happened to Bea, too. The family photograph of her when she was six, with a livid rectangular rash across her mouth and cheeks, caused by the adhesive tape. How could someone do that to a kid? He cried about her doing her homework in the toilet while the kitchen was full of strangers and her bedroom was out of bounds. He cried about other incidents from Bea's childhood as well; all of them from before he met her. It was as though different vintages of sadness were stored in different parts of his mind, stacked chronologically, and his tear ducts were on the end of electrical wires that didn't touch any recent decades— just went straight to the distant past. The Bea he wept for was a pretty little ghost conjured up from his wife's stash of photos and anecdotes, but no less pitiable for that.

Toward the end of his weeping fit, he cried about the coin collection his father had given him. It was shop-bought but serious, a handsomely packaged starter set that included a French franc, an Italian lira, a 10-drachma bit, a German 50-pfennig with a woman planting a seedling on it, and other commonplace treasures which, to a clueless boy, seemed like relics from an ancient epoch, the prehistoric empire of numismatics. Ah, happy innocence . . . but not long afterward a schoolfriend murmured in his ear, serpent-like, that this prissy little collection was *not valuable at all*, and persuaded him to swap the lot for a single coin that had been minted, he said, in 333 AD. It was misshapen and corroded but it had a helmeted warrior engraved on it and Peter fell under its spell. His father was furious, when he found out. He kept saying *"If genuine . . . If genuine . . ."* in a fastidiously dubious tone, and lecturing Peter about the extreme commonness of Constantine copper coins, and how damaged this one was, and how the whole damn business of collecting was infested with fakery. Peter kept protesting, hotly, *"You* weren't there!," referring not just to the reign of Constantine but also to the moment when a small, impressionable boy was defeated by a bigger, cleverer one. For years, that poisonous repetition of *"If genuine . . ."* festered in his mind, proof of everything that was creepy and cold about his father. By the time Peter was ready to understand that the quarrel was bluster and that his dad had simply been hurt, the old man was in his grave.

About all these things and more, Peter wept. Then he felt better, as if purged. His raw eyelids, which would have needed careful pampering if he'd been anywhere but here, were soothed by the oily moistness of the warm air. His head, which had started to pound toward the end of his crying jag, felt light and pleasantly anesthetized.

"A very long ʂong," said Jesus Lover Five, sitting with her back against the lectern. He hadn't noticed her arrive. This wasn't the first time she'd come to the church to visit him, at an hour when most others of her kind were sleeping.

"Why aren't you in bed?" he asked, heaving himself up on one elbow. He could barely see her; the entire church was lit with nothing more powerful than a couple of oil flames floating in ceramic soup bowls: toy braziers.

"Awake," she said, as if that explained everything. Perhaps it did.

He replayed her comment in his head. *A very long song.* Evidently, to her, his weeping sounded no different from singing. The distress in his voice was lost in translation; she heard only the horn-like music of whimpering, the rhythm of sobs. Maybe she would have liked to join in, but couldn't make out any words.

"I was remembering things from long ago," he explained.

"Long ago," she echoed. Then: "Long ago, the Lord ᴕaid ᴑo Iᴕrael, I have loved you, my people."

The quote from *Jeremiah* surprised him, not because she had managed to memorize it, but because it was from a more modern translation than the King James—the New Living, if he wasn't mistaken. Did Kurtzberg pick and choose between different Bibles? In the King James, "long ago" was "of old," while the original Hebrew meant something more like "from afar."

Long ago and far away . . . maybe they were the same thing after all. Rousing himself from his scholarly fog, he opened his mouth to ask Jesus Lover Five why she had quoted that bit of Scripture, what it meant to her.

But Lover Five's head was slumped onto her chest. Whatever the reason for her insomnia at home in her own bed, she had found sleep here, with him.

It was during his second sojourn with the Oasans, also, that Peter experienced his first death. His first dead Oasan, that is.

He still had no clear idea of the size of the settlement's population, but was inclined to think that it might be a few thousand, and that the Jesus Lovers represented only a tiny minority of the souls living in this great hive of dwellings. Birth and death must surely be going on as normal inside those amber walls, the same as in any other big town, but he had no access to it—until, one day, Jesus Lover One came and told him that his mother had died.

"My mother," he announced. "Dead."

"Oh! I'm so sorry!" said Peter, instinctively putting his arms around Lover One. He could tell at once that it was the wrong thing to do, like embracing a woman who absolutely doesn't want to be touched by anyone other than her husband. Lover One's shoulders cringed, his body stiffened, his arms trembled, his face turned away lest it brush against Peter's chest. Peter released him and stepped back in embarrassment.

"Your mother," he blurted. "What an awful loss."

Lover One gave this notion some deliberation before responding.

"Mother made me," he said at last. "If mother never be, I never be al𝘴o. Mother therefore very impor𝘵an𝘵 man."

"Woman."

"Woman, ye𝘴."

A few more seconds passed. "When did she die?" asked Peter.

Again there was a pause. Oasans had difficulty choosing the linguistic boxes into which they felt obliged, by others, to put their conceptions of time. "Before you came."

"Before I came to . . . Oasis?"

"Before you came with Word-in-Hand."

Last few days, then. Maybe even yesterday. "Is she . . . Has there been a funeral?"

"Few . . . ?"

"Have you put her in the ground?"

"𝘴oon," said Jesus Lover One, with a pacifying motion of the glove, as if giving his solemn promise that the procedure would be attended to as soon as it was feasible. "Af𝘵er the harve𝘴𝘵."

"After the . . . ?"

Lover One searched his vocabulary for a pronounceable alternative. "The reaping."

Peter nodded, although he didn't really understand. He guessed that this reaping must be the harvest of one of the Oasans' food crops, a job so time-sensitive and labor-intensive that the community simply couldn't fit a funeral into their schedule. The old lady would have to wait. He imagined a wizened, slightly smaller version of Lover One nestled motionless in her bed, one of those cots that already so closely resembled a coffin. He imagined the fluffy wisps of bedding being wrapped around her like a cocoon, in preparation for her burial.

As it turned out, there was no need to guess or imagine. Lover One, speaking in the same tone he might have used to invite a guest to see a notable monument or tree (if this place had had such things as monuments and trees), invited him to come and see the body of his mother.

Peter tried and failed to think of a suitable reply. "Good idea," "Thank you," and "I'd like that" all felt wrong somehow. Instead, in silence, he put on his yellow boots. It was a brilliant morning, and the shade inside his church ill-prepared him for the dazzling sunshine.

He accompanied Jesus Lover One across the scrubland to the compound, taking two steps for every three or four of the Oasan's. He was learning many things on this visit, and how to amble was one of them. There was an art to walking slower than your instinct told you to, keeping pace with a much smaller person, yet not appearing exasperated or clumsy. The trick was to pretend you were wading through waist-deep water, watched by a judge who would award you points for poise.

Side by side, they reached Jesus Lover One's house. It looked identical to all the others, and had not been adorned with any flags, accoutrements or painted messages proclaiming an inhabitant's death. A few people were walking around nearby, no more than normal, and they were getting on with business as usual, as far as Peter could tell. Lover One led him around the back of the building, to the patch of ground where clothing was washed and hung, and where children often played with ᴧ᎐Ꮟ᎐, the Oasan equivalent of *boules*, soft dark balls made of compacted moss.

Today, there were no children or ᴧ᎐Ꮟ᎐, and the washing line strung between two houses was bare. The yard was given over to Jesus Lover One's mother.

Peter gazed at the small body lying uncushioned and uncovered on the ground. It had been stripped of its robe. This alone would have made Peter unable to tell whether he'd known this person or not, as he was still dependent, to a shameful degree, on fabric color. But even if he'd managed to remember some distinctive aspect of this creature's physiognomy—some variation in skin texture or the shape of facial bulges—it wouldn't have helped now, as the body was obscured under a shimmering, shivering layer of insects.

He looked aside at Jesus Lover One, to gauge how alarmed he should be at this nightmarish spectacle. Maybe when Lover One had set off earlier this morning, the corpse had been free of parasites and they'd all seized their opportunity in his absence. If so, Lover One didn't seem perturbed by the swarm. He contemplated the insects as calmly as if they were flowers on a shrub. Admittedly, these bugs were every bit as beautiful as flowers: they had iridescent wings, glossy carapaces of lavender and yellow. Their buzz was musical. They covered almost every inch of flesh, giving the corpse the appearance of a twitching, breathing effigy.

"Your mother . . ." Peter began, lost for further words.

"My mother gone," said Jesus Lover One. "Only her body remain."

Peter nodded, striving to hide the queasy fascination provoked in him by the insect horde. Lover One's philosophical attitude to the situation was perfectly sound—it was what Peter himself would have tried to persuade him to feel, had Lover One been terribly distraught. But the fact that Lover One *wasn't* terribly distraught, or didn't appear to be, confused Peter. It was one thing to deliver a funeral address to a bunch of unbelieving USIC workers, urging them to regard the body merely as a vehicle for the immortal soul; it was quite another thing to be standing next to someone who'd taken that principle so deeply to heart that they could watch their own mother's body being overrun with insects. Peter's eyes were drawn to one of the woman's feet: the bugs, in their restless fidgeting, had exposed the toes. There were eight of them, very small and narrow. He'd assumed, because the Oasans were five-fingered, that they'd be five-toed, too. The mistakenness of that assumption made him realize how far he had to go before he truly understood these people.

"Forgive me for not remembering, Lover One," said Peter, "but did I ever meet your mother? Before today?"

"Never," Lover One replied. "Walk from here ᑐo our ᑕurᑕ . . . ᑐoo far."

Peter wondered whether this was an ironic comment, implying that she'd never summoned up sufficient motivation to visit, or whether it literally meant she'd been too weak or ill to walk the distance. Most likely it was literal.

"My mother begin—only begin—ᴛo know Jeᴛuᴛ," Lover One explained. He made a gesture in the air, gently rotating his hand to indicate slow, stumbling progress. "Every day, we carry your wordᴛ away from ᴅurᴅ in our handᴛ, and we bring them ᴛo her. Every day, wordᴛ go in her like food. Every day, ᴛhe come more near ᴛo the Lord." And he turned his face in the direction of Peter's church, as if watching his mother walk there after all.

In the days that followed, Peter learned what was really meant by "the harvest." He realized that Jesus Lover One's reason for fetching him to see the corpse had nothing to do with emotions. It was educative.

The alighting of the bugs on the flesh was just the first step in an industrious husbandry managed by the Oasans in every detail. The body, Peter learned, had been painted with a poison which intoxicated the bugs so that when they'd finished laying eggs, they were semi-conscious, unable to fly. The Oasans then collected them and, with great care, pulled them to bits. The legs and wings, when ground up and dried, made a fearsomely potent seasoning: one pinch could flavor a vat of food. The bodies yielded a rich nectar which was mixed with water and whiteflower to make honey, or processed into a vivid yellow dye. And, while various members of the Oasan community were busy transforming the insects' remains into useful materials, the insects' eggs were busy hatching. Peter was fetched at regular intervals to witness how things were getting on.

Like most people he'd ever known, except for one frankly barmy biology teacher at school, Peter was not very keen on maggots. Wise and practical though it might be to accept the naturalness of death and decay, the sight of those opportunistic little larvae always disgusted him. But the maggots on the body of Jesus Lover One's mother were like nothing he'd ever seen before. They were calm and fat, rice-white, each the size of a large fruit pip. There were many thousands of them, densely packed and pearlescent, and if you stared at them long enough they didn't look like maggots at all, but like a cornucopia of albino raspberries.

These, too, the Oasans harvested.

* * *

When, at last, the body of Jesus Lover One's mother had yielded all the bounty it was going to yield, she lay exhausted on the ground, in the shade of a couple of gently swaying garments that hung on the washing line nearby. Since she was the only Oasan Peter had seen completely naked, he had no way of telling how much of the grotesquery he saw before him was due to decay and how much of it was what he would have found under the clothing of any healthy, living Oasan. Her flesh, which smelled fermented but not foul, had turned gray as clay, and was pitted with pocks and cavities. She had no breasts or anything else suggesting human femaleness—or maleness. The paradigm he had in his head, based on photographs of human corpses in famines and concentration camps, was of flesh shrunk down to a thin parchment of skin to hold the bones together. That wasn't what confronted him here. Lover One's mother apparently had no ribs, no skeleton, just solid flesh that was liquefying. The holes eaten into her arms and legs exposed a ribbed black substance like liquorice.

Monster was the word that came to his mind as he suppressed a shudder. But then *Creatura: created thing*, he reminded himself.

"Now we puȝ her in the ground," said Lover One on the third day. There was no urgency or ceremonial portent in his voice, nor was it clear what he meant by "now." As far as Peter was aware, no grave had been dug and there was no evidence of the community preparing for a solemn ritual.

"Would you like me to . . . say something?" suggested Peter. "At the funeral?"

"Funeral?"

"It's the custom of our . . ." he began. Then, "When Christians . . ." he began again. Then, "Where I come from, when a person dies and is being buried, someone usually makes a speech before the body is put into the ground. They talk about the person who's died, and they try to remind his friends and family about what made that person special."

Lover One bowed his head in courtesy. "You never know my mother," he pointed out, with stonkingly obvious good sense.

"That's true," Peter conceded. "But you could tell me some things about her, and I could turn those things into a . . . speech." Even as he made the offer, it seemed absurd.

"Word can make no ᘓange in my mother now," said Lover One.

"Words can comfort the friends and family left behind," said Peter. "Would you like me to read from the Book?"˙

Jesus Lover One smoothed his hands over an invisible molehill in the air, signaling that this would not be necessary. "Kur𐌗ᖙberg give uᖙ word from the Book, long before." And he recited them for Peter's approval.

A trickle of lisping nonsense entered Peter's ears. It took him a few seconds to re-play the meaningless syllables and translate them into a Bible verse, a verse which in fact was not from the Bible but from the Book of Common Prayer:

"Aᖙheᖙ 𐌗o aᖙheᖙ, duᖙ𐌗 𐌗o duᖙ𐌗."

For several dozen hours after this incident, Peter lived in fear that some generous soul would bring him, as a special treat, a dish made from maggots. The Oasans were always bringing him snacks and—who knows?— they might think he was getting fed up with whiteflower. *Surprise dessert for Father Peter!*

He knew his revulsion was irrational, as the food would no doubt be delicious and probably very good for him too. Moreover he was aware that every country had its culinary challenges which provoked disgust in squeamish foreigners—the Japanese with their giant fish eyeballs and cod semen and still-squirming octopus, the Africans with their goat heads, the Chinese with their bird's nest soup that was really saliva, and so on. If he'd been ministering in any of these places, chances were he'd be honored with one of these specialties. Wasn't there even an Italian cheese that was rotten and maggot-infested? *Casu marzu*, it was called. (Amazing how he could retrieve that term, which he probably read just once in a magazine years ago, when only yesterday he'd blanked on the name of the street where he lived.)

Of course, he'd never had to eat any of these outlandish substances. All of his ministries, until now, had been in England. The most exotic thing he'd ever been served, at an outreach convention in Bradford, had been caviar, and his problem hadn't been the fish eggs themselves, but the money that the organizers had channeled into the catering when they were supposed to be raising funds for the city's homeless.

Anyway: this wasn't about maggots per se. It was about the vivid memory of Jesus Lover One's mother, and the unerasable, emotionally charged connection between her and the maggots that had fed on her. His mind boggled at how her own son could bear to eat a foodstuff that had been produced in this way.

To this question, as with so many others, God organized a very specific and enlightening answer. Jesus Lover One showed up at the church one evening, carrying a hamper of food. Wordlessly he unpacked it in front of Peter as they sat down together on the bed behind the pulpit. The food smelled wholesome and was still warm. It was whiteflower soup in its mushroom guise, and several hunks of whiteflower bread with brown crusts and pale insides, fresh from the oven.

"I'm glad it's whiteflower," Peter said, deciding to be totally frank. "I was worried you would bring me something made from . . . the creatures you harvested from your mother's body. I don't think I could eat that."

Lover One nodded. "I alᴤo. Other can. Noᴤ I."

Peter absorbed the words, but couldn't interpret their meaning. Maybe Lover One was informing him of the etiquette governing this particular ritual. Or was it an openhearted disclosure? *Tell me more,* he thought, but he knew from experience that keeping silent in the hope that an Oasan would fill the silence didn't work.

"It's a very good and . . . admirable idea," he said, "to . . . do what you people do. With someone who's just died." He wasn't sure how to go on. The bottom line was that no amount of admiration could prevent him being disgusted. If he put that into words, he'd be lecturing Lover One on the irreconcilable differences between their species.

Again Lover One nodded. "We do all thing ᴤo make food. Make food for many." A bowl of soup sat balanced in the lap of his tunic. He had eaten none of it yet.

"I've been dreaming of your mother," Peter confessed. "I didn't know her as a person, I'm not saying . . ." He took a deep breath. "The sight of her covered in insects, and then in maggots, and everyone just . . ." He looked down at Lover One's boots, even though there was no possibility of eye-to-eye confrontation anyway. "I'm not used to it. It upset me."

Lover One sat unmoving. One gloved hand rested on his abdomen, the other held a piece of bread. "I al𝕬o," he said.

"I thought . . . I got the impression you . . . all of you . . . were afraid of death," continued Peter. "And yet . . ."

"We fear death," Lover One affirmed. "However. Fear canno𝕩 hold life in a body when life i𝕬 over. Nothing can hold life in a body. Only the Lord God."

Peter stared straight into the unreadable face of his friend. "There can be moments in a person's life," he suggested, "when grief over the loss of a loved one is stronger than faith."

Lover One waited a long time before responding. He ate a few spoonfuls of the soup, which was now cold, thick and congealed. He ate some bread, tearing off small pieces and inserting them gently into the lipless, toothless hole in his head.

"My mother very impor𝕩an𝕩 woman," he said at last. "For me."

In this second sojourn among the Oasans, God took care to keep Peter's experiences in balance. His first death was followed, not too long afterward, by his first birth. A woman called 𝕬𝕮𝕫𝕭—not a Jesus Lover, evidently—was having a baby and Peter was invited to the delivery. Jesus Lover One, his escort, implied that this was a great honor; it was certainly a surprise, because he'd never been formally acknowledged by the settlement's un-believers. But this was an event so joyous that the usual reticence was put aside and the entire Oasan community was united in hospitality.

The contrast between the death and the birth was striking. Whereas the body of Lover One's mother had lain unattended in a back yard, mourned by no one except her son, left in solitude to attract insects, then treated as if it was nothing more than a vegetable patch, the woman who was about to give birth was the focus of an enormous amount of fuss. The streets leading to the house were remarkably busy, and everyone seemed to be heading for

the same place. When Peter first saw the house, he thought it had caught
fire, but the vapor wafting out of the windows was incense.

Inside, the expectant mother was not lying in a bed surrounded by
medical equipment, or suffering the trials of labor under the supervision
of a midwife, but walking around freely, socializing. Dressed in a snow-
white variant of the Oasans' usual attire—looser, thinner, more like a
nightgown—she held court, accepting visitors' congratulations one by one.
Peter couldn't tell if she was happy or anxious, but she was obviously not in
pain, nor could he detect any swelling in her trim little body. Her gestures
were elegant and formalized, like a medieval dance, with a whole host of
partners. This was ⏸⟨⟩⏸⟩'s Big Day.

Peter knew that the Oasans didn't celebrate marriages. Their sexual
pairings were private arrangements, so discreet as to be seldom alluded to.
But the day of childbirth was a flagrantly public highlight in a woman's life,
a ritual exhibition every bit as extravagant as a wedding party. ⏸⟨⟩⏸⟩'s
house was heaving with well-wishers, dozens of bustling bodies dressed in
bright colors. *All the pencils in the Aquarelle set,* thought Peter, as he strove
to discern the difference between one robe and another. Vermillion, coral,
apricot, copper, cerise, salmon—those were just some of the pinks he could
put a name to; others were beyond his vocabulary. Across the room, weav-
ing through the crowd, a person clad in pale violet was reunited with an old
acquaintance clad in unripe plum, and only when they touched each other,
glove to arm, did Peter see that two robes which he would otherwise have
perceived as identical in color were, in fact, unique. And so it went on, all
over the house—people greeting each other, waving at each other, needing
no more than a glance to know and be known. In the midst of this easily
intimate hubbub, Peter appreciated he would need to develop a whole new
relationship with color if he was ever to recognize more than a couple of
dozen individuals among this city's multitudes.

It was a *lovely party,* Peter might have said, if he'd been asked to describe it
for someone who wasn't there. The only problem was, he felt surplus to re-
quirements. Jesus Lover One had ushered him in, but kept meeting up with

friends who drew him into conversations which, to Peter's ears, were just gargles and wheezes. Asking for translations seemed rude and, in any case, there was no reason to suppose that a stranger would understand much of what was being discussed.

For a while he felt oafishly out of place, towering over everyone here, literally casting a shadow over them, and yet . . . irrelevant. But then he relaxed and began to enjoy himself. This gathering wasn't about *him*: that was actually the beauty of it. He was privileged to observe, but he wasn't on duty, nothing was expected of him; he was, for the first time since coming to Oasis, a tourist. So, he sat on his haunches in a corner of the room, allowed the blueish fog of incense to go to his head, and watched the expectant mother being garlanded with affection.

After what felt like hours of meeting and greeting, ⋒ᘓ⋏Ɔᑲ abruptly signaled that she'd had enough. Exhaustion had apparently overcome her, and she sat on the floor, surrounded by a puddle of her gown's white cloth. Her friends backed away as she pulled the hood off her head, revealing livid flesh sheened with sweat. She bent her head between her knees, as though she was about to faint or vomit.

Then the fontanelle in her head yawned open, and a large pink mass bulged out, glistening with frothy white lather. Peter jerked back in shock, convinced he was witnessing a violent death. One more convulsion and it was over. The baby was disgorged in a slithery spasm, sliding into the mother's waiting arms. ⋒ᘓ⋏Ɔᑲ raised her head high, her fontanelle puckering shut, the fleshy kernels of her face still livid. The whole room erupted in a whuffle of applause and a mass of voices joined forces to make an eerie cooing sound, as loud as a chord pumped out of a cathedral organ.

The baby was alive and well, already squirming to be released from its mother's grasp. It had no umbilical cord and looked amazingly unlike a fetus: instead, it was a perfect miniature person, its arms, legs and head all in adult proportion. And, like a newborn horse or calf, it immediately tried to stand on its legs, figuring out the knack of balance even while its feet were still slippery with placental goo. The crowd applauded and cheered some more. ⋒ᘓ⋏Ɔᑲ ceremoniously acknowledged the ovation, then set about cleaning the gunge off her child's flesh with a damp cloth.

"ᘓᘓ⋏Ɔᑲᘔ," she announced. Another great cheer went up.

"What did she say?" Peter asked Lover One.

"ᴧᴧᴧᴗᴚ," said Lover One.

"Is that the baby's name?"

"Name, yeᴗ," said Lover One.

"Does that name have a meaning, or is it just a name?"

"Name have a meaning," Lover One replied. Then, after a few seconds: "Hope."

The child now stood firmly balanced on the floor, its arms stretched out like unfledged wings. ᴘᴄᴧᴗ sponged the last of the muck off its skin, whereupon someone emerged from the crowd with an armful of soft offerings. A robe, booties, gloves, all in dusky mauve, all tailored exactly to size. Together, ᴘᴄᴧᴗ and the gift-bearer, who might have been a grandmother or aunt, began to dress the infant, who tottered and swayed but did not resist. When the job was done, the child was exquisitely smart and adorable, serenely content to be on display. A male, Peter decided. Unbelievable, the craftsmanship that had gone into those minuscule gloves, each finger snug and velvety! Extraordinary, how the child accepted this second skin!

By this time, Peter was no longer squatting; his legs had begun to ache and he'd stood up to stretch them. The baby, wondrously alert, took the measure of all the creatures in the room, an array of virtual replicas of himself. There was only one creature that didn't fit the picture, only one creature that made no sense in his freshly configured view of the universe. Head tilting back, the child stood arrested, mesmerized by the alien.

ᴘᴄᴧᴗ, noticing her son's quandary, likewise turned her attention to Peter. "ᴘᴧᴧᴘᴚ ᴧᴄᴧᴗᴚ," she called across the room.

"What did she say?" Peter asked Lover One.

"Word," said Lover One. "Word from you."

"You mean . . . a speech?"

Lover One inclined his head diplomatically. "Few word, many word, any word. Any word you can."

"But she's not . . . she's not a Jesus Lover, is she?"

"No," conceded Lover One, while ᴘᴄᴧᴗ made an urgent gesture to speed up Peter's compliance. "On thiᴗ day, all word are good." And he touched Peter's elbow, which, by Lover One's standards, was tantamount to a shove.

So there it was: he was an accessory. A bonus performance to enhance the mother's Big Day. OK, nothing wrong with that. Christianity was used for such purposes all the time. And who knows?—maybe it wasn't even his status as a pastor that this woman wanted to exploit, but his status as a visitor. He stepped forward. Phrases and themes tumbled around in his brain, but one thing was clear: he wanted this speech to be for the benefit of Lover One, so dignified in his bereavement, as much as for the mother and child. Often in his past ministries, he'd had a sudden insight into a staunch member of his congregation, a member who was constantly declaring the joy of knowing Christ, the bountiful blessings of faith, but who was—Peter would realize in a flash—achingly, inconsolably sad. Jesus Lover One might well be one of those souls.

"I've been asked to speak," he said. "To a few of you, what I say will have meaning. To most of you, maybe not. One day, I hope to speak your language. But wait—did you hear it?—I just spoke that wonderful word: *hope*. The name of a feeling, and also the name of this child who has come to live with us today."

The baby lifted first one boot, then the other, and toppled backward. His mother caught him smoothly and eased him to the floor, where he sat in apparent thought.

"Hope is a fragile thing," Peter continued, "as fragile as a flower. Its fragility makes it easy to sneer at, by people who see life as a dark and difficult ordeal, people who get angry when something they can't believe in themselves gives comfort to others. They prefer to crush the flower underfoot, as if to say: *See how weak this thing is, see how easily it can be destroyed.* But, in truth, hope is one of the strongest things in the universe. Empires fall, civilizations vanish into dust, but hope always comes back, pushing up through the ashes, growing from seeds that are invisible and invincible."

The congregation—if he could be so bold as to call it that—was hushed, as if considering the import of each word, although they must surely be quite lost. He knew he should regard his speech as a kind of music, a brief burst of melody from a foreign guest invited to demonstrate an exotic instrument.

"The most cherished of hopes, as we all know," he said, "is a new child. The Bible—the book that some of you love as much as I do—contains many fine stories about the birth of children, including the birth of Jesus, our Lord. But this is not the time and place for me to tell Bible stories. All I will say is that the ancient words of *Ecclesiastes* have helped me make sense of what I've seen in the last few days. *Ecclesiastes* says: To everything there is a season. There is a time to be born, and a time to die; a time to weep, and a time to laugh; a time to plant seeds, and a time to reap. An old person—the mother of Jesus Lover One—has died. That was a very sad thing. A new person—ᴀᴀ,ʌꝛꞗ—has been born today. That is a very happy thing. Let us honor the equal importance of each: in celebrating a new life we remember losing those who've left us, and then in the midst of sadness our spirits are lifted as we welcome new life. So, to little ᴀᴀ,ʌꝛꞗ, most beautiful and precious gift to our community, I say: welcome!"

He hoped he'd invested the last word with sufficient resonance to signal that this was the end of his speech. Evidently he had: the audience emitted a mass murmur, applauded and waved. Even the baby, catching the prevailing mood, extended his tiny gloves. The room, so hushed in the preceding minutes, was once again filled with cooing and conversation; the people who'd briefly been transformed into an audience turned back into a crowd. Peter bowed and retreated to his former spot against the wall.

For one instant, in the midst of the renewed celebrations that followed, his mind was tickled by a thought of his own baby, growing inside the body of his wife far away. But it was just a thought, and not even a properly formed thought—a half-glimpsed reflection of a thought, which couldn't compete with all the commotion right in front of him: the brightly-dressed crowd, the excited gestures, the unearthly cries, the watchful newborn with its spindly limbs, hero of the moment, king of the day.

16

TOPPLING OFF AN AXIS,

FALLING THROUGH SPACE.

On the fifth day, a day of rain and almost unbearable beauty, it slipped Peter's mind that Grainger was coming for him.

It wasn't that he didn't want her to come, and it wasn't that she'd ceased to be real to him. Every now and then, during the three hundred and sixty–odd hours leading up to their scheduled rendezvous, she had been in his thoughts. He wondered, for example, if she would let him help her with her next drug delivery; he recalled the scars on her forearms and speculated about what anguish might have led her younger self to inflict them; and sometimes, at nights before drifting off, he replayed a fleeting vision of her pale, troubled face. However, his life here among the Oasans was very full, and there were so many things he must try to hold in his head. *Observe the opportunity*, as *Ecclesiastes* urged him. *Be not ignorant of anything great or small.*

Oh, he didn't forget to pray for Charlie Grainger and Coretta, and he thought of Grainger each time he did so. But when he woke up on the morning of the fifth day, the long night was finished, the sun had risen, and the rains were drawing near—and that was that. His appointment with USIC's moody pharmacist was erased from his brain.

Keeping track of schedules had never been his strong suit anyhow. The longer he spent among the Oasans, the less point he could see in cling-ing to ways of telling time that were, frankly, irrelevant. A day for him had ceased to feel like twenty-four hours and it certainly didn't consist of 1,440 minutes. A day was a span of daylight, divided from the next by a spell of darkness. While the sun shone, he would stay awake for twenty, maybe twenty-five hours at a stretch. He didn't know exactly how long, because his father's watch had stopped working, ruined by damp. Sad, but there was no point grieving.

Anyway, life wasn't about measurement, it was about getting the most out of each God-given minute. There was so much to do, so much to digest, so many people to commune with . . . When darkness fell, Peter would slip into comatose sleep, his consciousness sinking fast and irretrievable like a car dumped in a lake. After an age spent down on the bottom, he would float up into shallower fathoms where he would doze and dream, get up to pee, then doze and dream some more. It was as though he'd discovered the secret of Joshua—Joshua the cat, that is. The secret of snoozing for hours and days on end without boredom, storing up energy for a future occasion.

And then when he'd slept as much as he possibly could, he would lie awake, staring up at the sky, familiarizing himself with the eighty-seven stars, giving them each a name: Zimran, Jokshan, Medan, Midian, Ishbak, Shuah, Sheba and so on. All those genealogies in *Genesis* and *Exodus* had come in useful after all. They had begat a new constellation.

Mostly, by the light of slow-burning resin candles, he would sit up in bed, working on his paraphrases of Scripture. The King James Bible spread open on his lap, a notepad cradled on his forearm, a pillow for his head whenever he needed to mull over the alternatives. *Unto every province according to the writing thereof, and unto every people after their language*—Mordecai's publishing manifesto, sometime during the Israelites' Babylonian exile. If the Oasans couldn't have the Gospel in their own words, they deserved the next-best thing: a version they could speak and sing.

More than once, he'd walked out from his church into the darkness, knelt in the area of scrubland where he buried his feces, and asked God to tell him honestly if he was falling prey to the sin of Pride. These translations he was spending so much energy on—were they really needed? The Oasans had never asked to be delivered from consonants. They seemed resigned to their humiliation. Kurtzberg had taught them to sing "Amazing Grace," and how sweet the sound had been—yet how excruciating, too. And wasn't that the point? There was grace in their strenuous approximation. More grace, for sure, than you'd find in some complacent congregation in a British village, singing facile hymns while their minds were half-preoccupied with football or soap operas. The Oasans wanted their Book of Strange New Things; maybe he shouldn't dilute its strangeness.

He prayed for guidance. God did not caution him. In the stillness of the balmy Oasan night, with the stars shining greenish in the azure heavens, the overwhelming message he felt in the atmosphere around him was: *All shall be well. Goodwill and compassion can never be wrong. Continue as you began.* Nothing could tarnish the memory of the day when the Oasans sang "Amazing Grace" for him—it was Kurtzberg's gift to them, which they'd passed on to their next pastor. But he, Peter, would give them different gifts. He would give them Scripture that flowed forth from them as easily as breath itself.

Close to a hundred and twenty Jesus Lovers were in the fold now, and Peter was determined to know them all as individuals, which took a lot more effort than simply keeping a mental record of robe colors and Jesus Lover numbers. He was making headway (so to speak) with telling the difference between the faces. The trick was to quit waiting for the features to resolve themselves into a nose, lips, ears, eyes and so on. That wasn't going to happen. Instead, you had to decode a face as you'd decode a tree or a rock formation: abstract, unique, but (after you'd lived with it for a while) familiar.

Even so, to *recognize* was not the same as to *know.* You could train yourself to identify a certain pattern of bulge and color, and realize: this is Jesus Lover Thirteen. But who, really, was Jesus Lover Thirteen? Peter had to admit he was finding it difficult to know the Oasans in any deeper sense. He loved them. For the time being, that would have to do.

Sometimes, he wondered if it would have to do forever. It was hard to remember individuals if they didn't behave like humans, with their circus displays of ego, their compulsive efforts to brand themselves on your mind. Oasans didn't work that way. No one engaged in behaviors that screamed *Look at me!* or *Why won't the world let me be myself?* No one, as far as he could tell, was anxiously pondering the question *Who am I?* They just got on with life. At first, he'd found that impossible to believe, and assumed this equanimity must be a front, and any day now he would discover that the Oasans were as screwed up as anyone else. But no. They were as they appeared to be.

In one way, it was really kind of . . . *restful*, to be spared the melodramas that made things so complicated when you dealt with other humans. But it meant that his tried-and-true method of gaining intimacy with new acquaintances was totally useless here. He and Bea had pulled it off so many times, in all the places where they'd ministered, from opulent hotel lobbies to needle exchanges, always the same message to open people up: *Don't worry, I can see that you're not like everybody else. Don't worry, I can see that you're special.*

The Oasans didn't need Peter to tell them who they were. They bore their individuality with modest self-confidence, neither celebrating nor defending the eccentricities and flaws that distinguished them from others of their kind. They were like the most Buddhist-y Buddhists imaginable—which made their hunger for the Christian religion all the more miraculous.

"You're aware, aren't you," he'd said to Jesus Lover One a while back, "that some of my people believe in different religions from the Christian one?"

"We have heard," Lover One replied.

"Would you like me to tell you something about those religions?"

It seemed the decent thing to offer. Lover One did the fidgety thing with the sleeves of his robe that he always did when he wanted a conversation to go no further.

"We will have no other God than God our ßavior. In Him alone we have hope of Life."

It was what any Christian pastor might yearn to hear from a new convert, yet hearing it stated so baldly, so calmly, was a bit unsettling. Ministering to the Oasans was a joy, but Peter couldn't help thinking that it was too easy.

Or was it? Why *shouldn't* it be easy? When the window of the soul was clear, not smeared and tarnished with the accumulated muck of deviousness and egomania and self-loathing, there was nothing to stop the light from shining straight in. Yes, maybe that was it. Or maybe the Oasans were just too naïve, too impressionable, and it was his responsibility to give their faith some intellectual rigour. He hadn't worked it out yet. He was still praying on it.

Then there were the ones who weren't Jesus Lovers, the ones whose names he couldn't even pronounce. What was he to do about them? They were no less precious in the eyes of God, and no doubt had needs and sorrows every bit as serious as anyone else's. He should be reaching out to them, but they ignored him. Not aggressively; they just behaved as if he wasn't there. No, that wasn't quite right; they acknowledged his presence as one might respect a fragile obstacle—a plant that mustn't be stepped on, a chair that mustn't be knocked over—but they had nothing to say to him. Because, of course, they *literally* had nothing to say to him, nor he to them.

Determined to do more than just preach to the converted, Peter strove to get to know these strangers, noting the nuances of their gestures, the way they related to each other, the roles they seemed to play in the community. Which, in a community as egalitarian as the Oasans', was not easy. There were days when he felt that the best he'd ever achieve with them was a sort of animal tolerance: the kind of relationship that an occasional visitor develops with a cat which, after a while, no longer hisses and hides.

Altogether there were about a dozen non-Christians he recognized on sight and whose mannerisms he felt he was getting a grip on. As for the Jesus Lovers, he knew them all. He kept notes on them, indecipherable notes scrawled sometimes in the dark, smudged with sweat and humidity, qualified with question marks in the margins. It didn't matter. The real, practical knowledge was intuitive, stored in what he liked to think of as the Oasan side of his brain.

He still had no clear idea how many people lived in C-2. The houses had many rooms, like beehives, and he couldn't guess how many of them were inhabited. Which meant he also couldn't estimate how tiny, or not so tiny, the proportion of Christians was. Maybe one percent. Maybe a hundredth of one percent. He just didn't know.

Still, even a hundred Christians was an amazing achievement in a place like this, more than enough to accomplish great things. The church was coming ahead. The building, that is. It had a roof now, sensibly sloped, watertight and utilitarian. His polite requests for a spire had been deflected ("we do all other thing, pleaße, before"); he sensed that they would deflect it forever.

As a compensation, the Oasans had promised to decorate the ceiling. Kurtzberg had once shown them a photograph of a place they called, almost unintelligibly, the ßißßine ßapel. Inspired by the handiwork of Michelangelo, the Oasans were keen to create something similar, except they suggested that all the incidents should be from the life of Jesus rather than from the Old Testament. Peter was all for it. Apart from giving the church some much-needed color, it would give him an insight into the unique nature of these people's perception.

Lover Five, as always, was quickest off the mark, showing him her sketch of the scene she proposed to paint. It was the one outside Jesus's tomb, where Salome and the two Marys find the stone rolled away. Evidently, this story was already familiar to her. Peter couldn't guess which of the four gospel accounts Kurtzberg had used, whether it was Luke's "two men in dazzling raiment" story, Matthew's angel descending from Heaven with earthquake accompaniment, Mark's lone young man sitting on a rock, or John's pair of angels inside the tomb. Whichever it was, Lover Five had rejected these characters and replaced them with the risen Christ. Her mourners, daintily proportioned and clad in hooded robes like herself, confronted a scarecrow-thin figure wearing a loincloth. This Jesus stood erect with arms spread wide, an eye-shaped hole in each palm of His starfish-shaped hands. Above His neck, where His head should be, Lover Five had left a blank space surrounded by a porcupine profusion of lines, to indicate radiance from an incandescent light source. On the ground between Him and the women lay a bagel-like object which Peter realized after a minute must be the discarded crown of thorns.

"No longer dead," Lover Five explained, or maybe that was the title of her drawing.

Lover Five may have been first with her sketch, but she was not the first to get a painting mounted on the church ceiling. That distinction belonged to Jesus Lover Sixty-Three, an extremely shy individual who communicated mainly in gestures, even among his (her?) own people. The Oasans were scrupulous in their respect for others, and gossip was not their style, but Peter gradually got the message that Lover Sixty-Three was disfigured or malformed in some way. Nothing specific was said, only a general sense that Lover Sixty-Three was a pathetic character, soldiering on as though he was normal when everyone could see he wasn't. Peter tried his best, without staring, to see what the problem might be. He noted that the flesh of Lover Sixty-Three's face appeared less raw, less glistening, than other people's. It looked as if it had been dusted with talc, or briefly cooked, like fresh chicken whose pinkness fades to white after a few seconds in boiling water. In Peter's eyes, this made him, if anything, a little easier to behold. But to his neighbors, it was evidence of a pitiable disability.

Whatever Lover Sixty-Three's handicap was, it didn't affect his artistic skill. His painted panel, already affixed to the church ceiling directly above the pulpit, was the sole finished contribution so far, and any subsequent offerings would have to be impressive indeed to equal its quality. It glowed like a stained-glass skylight, and had an uncanny ability to remain visible even when the sun was on the wane and the church's interior grew dim, as though the pigments were luminescent in their own right. It combined bold Expressionist colors with the intricate, exquisitely balanced composition of a medieval altarpiece. The figures were approximately half life-size, crowded onto a rectangle of velvety cloth that was bigger than Jesus Lover Sixty-Three.

His choice of Biblical scene was Thomas the Doubter's meeting with his fellow disciples when they tell him they've seen Jesus. A most unusual subject to tackle: Peter was almost certain that no Christian painter had ever attempted it before. Compared to the more sensational finger-in-the-wound encounter with the resurrected Christ, this earlier episode was devoid of visual drama: an ordinary man in an ordinary room voices his scepticism about what a bunch of other ordinary men have just told him. But in Lover Sixty-Three's conception, it was spectacular. The disciples' robes—all in different colors, of course—were scorched with tiny black crucifixes, as though a barrage of laser beams from the radiant Christ had sizzled brands onto their clothing. Speech bubbles issued from their slitty mouths, like trails of vapor. Inside each bubble was a pair of disembodied hands, in the same starfish design as Lover Five had used. And in the center of each starfish, the eye-shaped hole, adorned with an impasto glob of pure crimson which could either be a pupil or a drop of blood. Thomas's robe was monochrome, unmarked, and his speech bubble was a sober brown. It contained no hands, no images of any kind, only a screed of calligraphy, incomprehensible but elegant, like Arabic.

"This is very beautiful," Peter had said to Jesus Lover Sixty-Three when the painting was formally delivered.

Lover Sixty-Three lowered his head. Assent, embarrassment, acknowledgment, pensiveness, pleasure, pain, who knew?

"It also reminds us of a very important truth about our faith," said Peter. "A truth that's especially important in a place like this, situated so very far away from where Christianity began."

Lover Sixty-Three stooped lower still. Perhaps his head weighed too heavy on his neck.

"Jesus allowed Thomas to put his finger into His wounds," said Peter, "because He understood that some people cannot believe without proof. It's a natural human response." Peter hesitated, wondering if the word "human" needed qualification, then decided it must be obvious by now that he regarded the Oasans as no less human than himself. "But Jesus was aware that it would not be possible for everyone, everywhere, forever afterward, to see and touch Him the way Thomas did. So He said, 'Blessed are they that have not seen, and yet have believed.' And that's us, my friend." He laid a hand gingerly on Lover Sixty-Three's shoulder. "You and me, and all of us here."

"Yeṡ," said Lover Sixty-Three. For him, that constituted fulsome conversation. A group of other Jesus Lovers, who'd accompanied him to the church for the delivery of the painting, made trembling motions with their shoulders. Peter realized that this was probably their equivalent of laughter. Laughter! So they did have a sense of humor after all! He was constantly learning important things of this kind, things which made him feel that the gulf between him and these people was growing shorter with every sunrise.

Lover Sixty-Three's painting was solemnly raised and affixed to the ceiling, inaugurating the church's devotional display. The next day, it was joined by Jesus Lover Twenty's interpretation of Mary Magdalene being purged of her seven devils. The devils—ectoplasmic vapors with vaguely feline shapes—exploded from her torso like fireworks, ignited by Jesus, who stood behind Mary in a spread-armed pose. It was a cruder piece of work than Lover Sixty-Three's, but no less strong, and it, too, glowed with an unfeasible luminescence.

The next day, no one brought a painting, but they did bring Peter a bed, to replace the bundle of rags and nets he'd been sleeping on since his hammock had come down. The Oasans had accepted his hammock unquestioningly, and would have been quite prepared to worship with it dangling in their midst, but Peter had cut it down when he judged the church was so close to finished now that the hammock marred its dignity. The Oasans, noting that their pastor did not necessarily require to hang suspended in order to be comfortable, had quietly constructed a bed for him, according to their usual bathtub/coffin template, albeit larger, shallower and less crammed with swaddly cotton. It was carried across the scrubland to the church, ushered through the door and installed right behind the pulpit, without any pretense that it was anything other than a bed. During the first prayer meeting after its arrival, Peter joked that if he got too tired while speaking, he could always just fall backward and have a sleep. His congregation nodded indulgently. To them, it was a sensible idea.

On the morning that Grainger came to fetch him, Peter awoke to anticipation. Anticipation of the rain. For the natives, this was not unusual; rain occurred at predictable intervals, and they'd had a lifetime to accustom themselves to its rhythms. But Peter was not so attuned, and the rains always caught him by surprise. Until now. He stirred in his bed, slippery with sweat, thick-headed, squinting from the window-shaped rectangle of light that warmed his chest. Yet, dazed as he was, he knew at once that he must lose no time coming to the surface or trying to recall his dreams or continuing to rack his brains for a pronounceable alternative to "Baptist," but that he should get up and go outside.

The rains were about a quarter of a mile away, gaining ground fast. They truly were *rains*, plural. Three colossal networks of water were advancing independently, separated by substantial spaces of clear air. Each network had its own internal logic, replicating and reassembling its glittering patterns over and over, shifting slow and graceful like one of those complex computer graphics that purport to show a city or a spider-web in three dimensions from all angles. Except that here, the screen was the sky, and the display was an awe-inspiring vista on a par with an Aurora Borealis or a nuclear mushroom cloud.

If only Bea could see this, he thought. Every day, provoked by some event or other, he regretted her absence. It wasn't a physical yearning—*that* came and went, and it was at an ebb just now—but rather an uneasy awareness that a huge, complicated phase of his life was passing by, crowded with significant and deeply emotional experiences, none of which Bea was seeing, none of which she was remotely involved in. And again now: these three great shimmering veils of rain, swirling majestically across the plains toward him: they were indescribable, and he would not describe them, but seeing them would leave a mark on him, a mark that would not be left on her.

The rains covered what was left of the distance in minutes. By the time the settlement was gently engulfed, Peter could no longer perceive them as three separate entities. The air all around him was ecstatic with water, bursting with it. Silvery lariats of droplets lashed against the ground, lashed against him. He remembered how, when he was a kid, he would play with the girl at the end of the street and she'd spray him with the garden hose and he'd jump to avoid it but get caught anyway, which was the whole point and pleasure of it. Knowing that it would get you, but that you wouldn't come to harm and you'd love it really.

Soon he was dripping wet and slightly dizzy from watching the patterns swirl before him. So, to give his eyes a rest, he did what the Oasans did: he stood with his head craned back, mouth open, and let the rain fall straight in. Drink the downpour direct from source. It was a sensation which, back home, every child attempts to indulge in once or twice before learning that there's no point standing there gaping like an idiot, straining to catch raindrops which are too far apart and too small. But here, the undulating arcs of the rainfall meant that you would get nothing for a moment or two and then a generous sprinkle, a splash on the tongue. Moreover, the taste of melon was stronger when it came straight out of the sky. Or maybe he only imagined this.

He stood for a long while, getting drenched, drinking the rain. Water filled his ears, and the auditory world inside his head became muted. Rarely had he felt such mindless satisfaction.

But rain, on the Oasan settlement, was not a selfish experience. It was communal and it prompted communal action. Just as the chants of the muezzin called Muslims to prayer, the rains called the Oasans to work. Hard work. Now that Peter knew just how hard, he insisted on laboring in the field alongside the Oasans, putting his muscle into helping them.

Whiteflower was not the only crop the Oasans cultivated. There was also a cotton-like substance called ⸬⸬⸬, which erupted from the soil in sticky white froth that quickly hardened into a fibrous weed. It was from this weed that the Oasans' nets, shoes and clothing were derived. Then there was ⸬⸬⸬, a kind of moss which grew at an amazing rate, completing its metamorphosis from specks of mold to verdant fluff in a single afternoon. What was it for? He had no idea, but he learned how to harvest it.

As for whiteflower, there was, he learned, a catch to its wondrous versatility: each plant had to be individually and frequently assessed to ascertain what stage of its growth cycle it had reached, because different things could be made with it depending on when it was pulled from the ground. On a given day, a plant's roots might be good for "mushroom" soup, its fiber good for "liquorice," its flowers good for bread, its nectar good for "honey," whereas on another day, its roots might be good for "chicken," its fiber good for rope, its flowers good for "custard," its dried sap good for "cinnamon," and so on. Timing was most crucial straight after rainfall, because that's when the oldest plants yielded their best. Morbidly porous, they swelled with water, lost what little stiffness they had left, slumped to the earth, and would swiftly begin to rot if they were not plucked out. Found in time, they were the most useful agricultural product of all, for they provided yeast.

Aware that the Oasans would already be on their way to the field, Peter stopped guzzling the rain and walked back into the church. Water ran down his legs as he crossed the floor, and each step left a paddle-shaped puddle. He strapped on his sandals (the yellow boots were too precious for filthy labor), combed his hair flat against his scalp, took a few bites of a dark-brown pumpernickel-like substance the Jesus Lovers called Our-Daily-Bread, and set off.

The rain dwindled as he walked. The watery swirls still made distinctive shapes in the air but some of the arcs softened into vapor, and there was less force, less impact on the skin. He knew the downpour would last only a few more minutes, and then the sky would clear for a good while—if "clear" was the right word for a sky that was always saturated with moisture. After that, the rains would return once more, then lay off for twenty hours or so, then return twice more again. Yes, he was getting the hang of it now. He was almost a local.

Three hours later, if he'd been counting hours, which he most definitely hadn't, Peter returned from the whiteflower fields. His hands and forearms were stained whitish-gray with the powdery slough of the harvested plant. The front of his dishdasha, from chest to stomach, was so filthy from the armfuls of whiteflower he'd been loading onto the carry-hammocks that the inky crucifix could scarcely be seen. Further down, where his knees had made contact with the ground, the fabric was slimy with sap and soil. Specks of pollen fell from him as he walked.

Emerging from the outskirts of the settlement, he began to cross the stretch of prairie between the town and the church. More conscious of his ridiculously grubby state with every step, he peered up into the sky, looking for signs of the next burst of rain, which was due very soon. The rain would rinse him clean. All he need do was stand naked under the deluge and rub his hands over his flesh, maybe with the aid of the bar of soap he'd brought from home. He would stand just outside his church and the rain would wash him and when he was clean he would hold up his clothes and the rain would wash them too. After that there would be a long sunny spell, excellent drying weather.

As he strode across the wasteland his eyes were focused squarely on the silhouetted church building, and, in anticipation of reaching it, he yanked off his garment and flapped it a couple of times to shake off the excess dirt.

"Whoa!" called a voice.

He swung round. About twenty meters to his left, parked alongside the wall whose welcoming graffiti had long vanished, stood the USIC van. And, leaning against the vehicle's gray metal hull, with a large water-bottle clutched to her breast, stood Grainger.

"Excuse me for interrupting you," she remarked. Her eyes were leveled at his face.

He draped his clothing in front of his genitals. "I . . . I've been working," he said, moving toward her with slightly clumsy steps. "In the fields."

"That's what it looks like," she said, and took another swig from her bottle. It was almost empty.

"Uh . . . Bear with me," he said, gesturing, with his free hand, at the church. "I just need to have a wash; do a few things. I can be getting on with that while you're busy handing over the medicines."

"The drugs handover is done," she said. "Two hours ago."

"And the food?"

"Also done. Two hours ago."

She downed the last of the water, tipping the bottle almost vertical against her lips. Her white throat pulsed as she swallowed. Sweat twinkled on her eyelids.

"Oh, my . . . gosh," he said, as the implications sank in. "I'm so sorry!"

"My fault for not bringing a magazine, I guess," she said.

"I just lost . . ." He would have spread his arms helplessly, had one of them not been covering his nakedness.

"Track of time," she confirmed, as though it might still be worth saving a few precious seconds by finishing his sentence for him.

On the drive back to USIC, Grainger was less peeved than Peter expected. Perhaps she had passed through all the stages—irritation, impatience, rage, worry, boredom, indifference—in the two hours she'd hung around waiting, and she was beyond it all now. Whatever the reason, she was in reasonable humor. Maybe the fact that she'd found him in such an unsavory state, and had caught a glimpse of his shrunken penis clinging to his pubic hair like an albino garden slug, was contributing to her mood of benign condescension.

"You've lost weight," she remarked, as they sped across the flat, feature-less terrain. "Has anybody been feeding you?"

He opened his mouth to reassure her he'd been eating like a king, but realized it wouldn't be true. "I haven't been eating a lot, I admit," he said, laying one palm on his stomach just under the ribs. "Just . . . snacks, I sup-pose you'd call them."

"Very good for your cheekbones," she said.

As a reflex, he appraised Grainger's facial features. Her cheekbones weren't particularly good. She had the sort of face that was beautiful only if she watched her diet and didn't get much older than she was now. As soon as age or over-indulgence filled out her cheeks and thickened her neck, even a little, she would cross a line from elfin allure into mannish homeli-ness. He felt sad for her, sad about the ease with which her physical destiny could be read by anyone who cared to cast a glance over her, sad about the matter-of-factness with which her genes stated the limits of what they were willing to do for her in the years to come, sad in the knowledge that she was at her peak now and still not fulfilled. He thought of Beatrice, whose cheek-bones were worthy of a French chanteuse. At least, that's what he'd told her sometimes; he couldn't actually picture Bea's cheekbones now. A vaguer, more impressionistic vision of his wife's face flickered in his brain, half-obliterated by the sunlight beaming through the vehicle's windscreen and the swirl of recent memories of various Jesus Lovers. Troubled, he strained to envisage her in sharper focus. A string of pearls in the dimness of another time and place, a white bra with familiar flesh inside. Jesus Lover Nine asking to be baptised. The stranger in the fields who'd handed him a scrap of fabric inscribed with the word ᔕᕊᎪᏞᔢᑲᕊ, patted her (her?) chest and said: "My name." "Say it for me again," he'd replied, and, when she did so, he'd contorted his mouth, his tongue, his jaw, every muscle in his face and said "ᔕᕊᎪᏞᔢᑲᕊᎪ," or something sufficiently similar for her to clap her gloved hands in approval. ᔕᕊᎪᏞᔢᑲᕊᎪ. ᔕᕊᎪᏞᔢᑲᕊᎪ. She would assume that he'd forget as soon as she was out of his sight. He must prove her wrong. ᔕᕊᎪᏞᔢᑲᕊᎪ.

"Hello? Are you with us?" Grainger's voice.

"Sorry," he said. A delicious smell was wafting up his nostrils. Raisin bread. Grainger had unsealed a packet of it and was eating a slice.

"Help yourself."

He took some, self-conscious about his soil-grimed fingernails touching the food. The bread was sliced thick—three times as thick as any Oasan would have it—and felt luxuriously spongy, as though it had come out of the oven fifteen minutes ago. He stuffed it into his mouth, suddenly ravenous.

She chuckled. "Couldn't you have put in a request for some loaves and fishes?"

"The Oasans took good care of me," he protested, swallowing hard. "But they're not big eaters themselves and I just sort of . . . fell in with their routine." He extracted another slice of raisin bread. "And I've been busy."

"I'm sure."

Up ahead, two bodies of rain were coming into view. By chance, the sun was perfectly positioned in the clear space between. The peripheries of each body of rain shimmered with subtle rainbow colors, like an inexhaustible launch of noiseless fireworks.

"Are you aware," asked Grainger, "that the tops of your ears are burnt to a crisp?"

"My ears?" He felt them with his fingertips. The texture of the outer lobes was rough. Like fried bacon, toughened on a forgotten plate overnight.

"There's gonna be scars," prophesied Grainger. "I can't *believe* that didn't hurt like hell when it was happening."

"Maybe it did," he said.

The two bodies of rain had moved much nearer now, their approach given the illusion of greater acceleration by the car's speedy progress toward them. A slight turn of the steering wheel, dictated by the navigation computer, meant that the sun had slipped behind a watery veil.

"Are you OK?"

"Yes, yes," he said. He wished she wouldn't interrupt the wonder of nature so often; it buzzed his nerves. Then, in an effort to communicate with her sincerely, he mused: "I don't actually think about whether I'm OK or not. I just . . . am."

"Well, that's just dandy," she said. "But I recommend you take some sunscreen next time. And look in the mirror occasionally. You know, just to check that all your bits are still intact."

"Maybe I should leave that up to you." Neither of them meant this exchange as a bawdy pun, but once it was spoken it hung in the air, and they both smiled.

"I didn't think they'd have you doing heavy labor," said Grainger. "I thought they wanted you for, like, Bible study and stuff like that."

"It wasn't their idea for me to work in the fields. It was mine."

"Well, I guess you'll get a tan. Once the sunburn settles down."

"The thing was," he persisted, "I realized that the food that gets loaded onto this truck each week doesn't come out of nowhere—even though it might seem that way to USIC."

"As a matter of fact, I grew up on a farm," said Grainger. "So if you've got me tagged as one of those people who think corn is made in the nachos factory, you've got it wrong. But tell me: these fields you were working in: where *are* they? I've never seen them."

"They're right in the center."

"The center?"

"Of the settlement. That's why you haven't seen them. They're hidden by the buildings."

She shook her head. "Well, I'll be damned."

"The town is built in a circle around the arable land," he explained. "Which means that whenever there's work to be done, the people come from all directions and converge in the middle, and they've all got a more or less equal distance to walk. It's a beautifully logical idea, don't you think? I can't imagine why it never occurred to all the generations of humanity."

She shot him a *come-off-it* glance. "You really can't imagine? It's because farming is tough, boring work and most people would rather somebody else did it for them. Preferably someplace far away. Because in the city, they need the space for a shopping mall."

"Is that what USIC has planned here?"

It was the sort of comment that might have offended her before, but she seemed unconcerned. "No," she sighed. "Not for the foreseeable future. Our brief is to build a sustainable environment first. Clean water. Renewable power. A team that gets along. A native population that doesn't hate our guts."

"Noble aims," he said, leaning back in his seat, hit by a wave of weariness. "Funny no one thought of them before."

They drove into the rain. The windscreen was dry one second, inundated the next. Elaborate raindrop patterns criss-crossed the glass until swept aside by the wipers. He was inside a metal and glass shell, in an artificially maintained atmosphere of cool air, divided off from the rain that could wash him clean. He should be out there, standing naked under it, letting it flow across his scalp, letting it blur his vision, letting it pelt the bony surfaces of his feet.

"Are you really OK?"

"Yes, I'm fine," he said, with effort. "It just feels a bit . . . strange . . . being enclosed in such a small space."

She nodded, unconvinced. He could tell she was worried about him. He regretted not having insisted that she wait a little longer back at the settlement, so that he could prepare a little better for this return to the base. He would have been in much better shape if he could have had even ten, fifteen minutes to himself before stepping into the vehicle.

"We're within Shoot range now," she said, after a long silence.

He looked at her uncomprehendingly, as if she'd just told him that they were liable to be killed by snipers.

"The Shoot. The messaging system," she said. "You could check if there's anything from your wife."

Not yet, he thought. *Not yet.*

He considered saying, "Thanks, but I'd prefer to wait until I've had a shower, changed my clothes, unwound a bit . . ." It would be the truth. But this truth would make him appear, in Grainger's eyes, less than eager to know how his wife was getting on. He didn't want her to doubt his love for Bea. And besides, here was Grainger showing sensitivity to his needs, or what she guessed his needs might be. She should be rewarded for that.

"Yes, please," he said. The windscreen wipers were squeaking against the glass: the sky was clear above them. Peter twisted in his seat to look at the vista receding behind the vehicle. The rains were on their way to C-2. Soon they would unleash their sweet sussurus on the roof of his church.

"OK, we're connected," said Grainger. Keeping one hand on the steering wheel, she used the other to swivel the Shoot screen over his lap, ready for him to use.

He typed in his password, followed the instructions as usual. There were at least a dozen messages from Bea, maybe even twenty. They were electronically dated, but the dates made no sense to him. He opened the oldest. A large quantity of print swarmed onto the screen. His wife was telling him she loved him. **Peter, I love you**, she said. He re-read her greetings several times, not to savor them, but to wait until the words were something more than pixels configured on a plastic screen, until he could hear her voice.

Just found out why the supermarket was closed. It's gone bust! Incredible. This is Tesco we're talking about, one of the biggest corporations in the world! They had huge fortunes to play with— which was what brought them down, apparently. There was a full report on one of the news sites, a sort of post-mortem, which made me realize it was bound to happen—totally inevitable. It's just that the inevitable can still come as a surprise, can't it? A vast amount of Tesco's money was tied up with ExxonMobil, who've been in trouble ever since the Chinese grabbed the oilfields in Iraq, Iran and Kazakstan (sp?). They also had big interests in shipping companies, which have been hammered by the upsurge in piracy, also a lot of their empire was based in Thailand until the military coup. Plus they were hit hard when Barclays went down the plughole a few years back and took Tesco Stakeholder and Tesco Swipe down with it. Those are the bits I remember from the program, there was a lot more to it. The corporation had its fingers in a hundred pies, all sorts of businesses you wouldn't think of when you're walking down the pet food aisle looking for Joshua's niblets, and suddenly a critical number of those businesses went pear-shaped and hey presto, no more Tesco. "The end of an era," as a news presenter put it—rather pompously, I thought.

Have you ever noticed the way news presenters always round off their reports with a resonant phrase? They even modulate their voices when they're reading the last couple of lines of the script. It's a special kind of vocal music that signals "The End."

Sorry, I'm rambling. Usually I'm the one who teases you about ruminations like this, and here I am indulging in it myself. Maybe I'm trying to fill the silence with my own imitation of your voice! Or maybe it's true what they say, that married people end up blurring their identities, finishing each other's sentences.

Today was the day that the Frame family moved house. Sheila dropped Billy off with me, as agreed. I took him to the cat show. It was a hoot and he seemed to enjoy it immensely despite whispering to me how stupid it all was and how ridiculous the handlers looked. But as I'd hoped, the charm of the animals won him over! And I must admit I was gawping happily at all those different moggies too. God must have had such terrific fun designing all those distinct varieties of furry mammal. (Although maybe I'm showing my own prejudices there. Maybe he had even more fun with the fish and the insects and so on.)

Anyway, Billy and I kept the conversation light most of the day, but just before his mum came to fetch him, he opened up. I asked him how he felt about his father going to another country. He said, "My dad says there aren't any countries anymore. They don't exist. England and Romania are just different parts of the same thing." For a moment I thought, how nice, Mark is reassuring his kid that we're all one world-wide community. But no. Billy said Mark asked him to visualize the world map as a huge thick sheet of plastic floating on the sea, like a raft, with crowds of people balancing on it. And sometimes too many people stand together on one bit and it starts to sink. You just run to another bit where it's better, he said. Then when THAT bit starts to sink, you move again. There's always places where things aren't so bad: cheaper accommodation, cheaper food, cheaper fuel. You go there and it's OK for a while. Then it stops being OK and you get the hell out. It's what animals do, he said. "Animals don't live in countries, they just inhabit territory. What do animals care if a place has a name? Names don't mean shit." That's the word Billy used, so I presume that's word his father used. Quite a heavy lecture in geopolitics for a little boy to swallow! And of course the bit that Mark left out of his analysis was the bit about going off with a 27-year-old concert promoter called Nicole. Who happens to be Romanian. But enough of that.

I've got a blanket over my knees as I type this. You're probably expiring from the heat but it's cold here and I've been without gas for a week now. Not because of any accident or failure in the supply, just because of sheer bureaucratic insanity. The gas company we're with—used to be with, I should say—was being paid by direct debit out of our Barclays bank account. But when Barclays went under and we changed over to Bank of Scotland, something went wrong with the debit arrangement. A computer glitch. And suddenly I got this final demand. I tried to pay it, but here's where it gets insane—they wouldn't talk to me, because I'm not the "account holder." I kept offering to pay them, and they kept saying "Sorry madam, we need to speak to the account holder," ie, you, Peter. I must have spent hours on the phone about this. I considered getting the next door neighbor to pop round and talk into the phone in a deep voice, which would have been morally wrong, of course, but they probably would have asked him your mother's maiden name. In the end, I had to concede that it just wasn't possible to fix. I'll wait until they take us to court and hope it gets sorted out then. In the meantime, I've signed with a different gas supplier but it will be a few days before they can come and connect it. They say that the freak weather in various parts of England has been causing havoc with utilities and (to quote the engineer I spoke to) "there's engineers dashing about all over the place like chickens with their heads cut off." Give that man a job in PR!

Do you remember Archie Hartley? I bumped into him in the cafeteria of the hospital the other day and he

Again he rested his head back against the seat, breathed deeply. Despite the dry cool of the air conditioning, he was sweating. Droplets tickled his forehead and ran into his eyebrows.

"Finished already?" said Grainger.

"Uh . . . just a minute . . ." He felt as though he might be in danger of passing out.

"Bad news?"

"No, I . . . I wouldn't say that. It's just . . . You know, there's a lot to catch up on . . ."

"Peter, listen to me," said Grainger, enunciating each word with earnest emphasis. "This happens. This happens to all of us."

"What do you mean?"

"You're here. She's there. It's natural."

"Natural?"

"The rift," she said. "It grows and grows, and finally . . . there's too much of it to cross. It's like . . ."

Words failed her, and she resorted to a gesture instead. Releasing her grip on the steering wheel for a few moments—a safe enough risk, given that the ground was flat and there was nothing visible in any direction to collide with—she held up her hands, palms parallel, separated by a few inches, as though about to press them together in medieval prayer. But instead, she parted them wider, letting the fingers splay limply, as though each hand was toppling off an axis, falling through space.

17

STILL BLINKING UNDER THE WORD "HERE."

Without Peter inside it, the dishdasha hung like a ghost from the ceiling. Its frayed lower parts swelled gradually with water and began to release drips from the sleeves and hem, slow as melancholy teardrops, even though Peter had wrung the fabric as hard as he could. Never mind: it would dry quickly. He'd adjusted the air conditioning of his quarters, allowing the temperature to rise to the level of the air outside. That was the way he wanted it, even if he hadn't had wet washing to dry. He felt disoriented enough, back in the USIC environment, without the additionally confusing sensation of being trapped in an artificial bubble of chilled oxygen.

His dishdasha—clean now, apart from the ink stain which had faded to a blurry lilac—was suspended from an indoor clothesline operated by a simple mechanical pulley. Once again, Peter was struck by USIC's apparent preference for low-tech solutions. He would've expected an electric clothes dryer with a menu of computerized choices; a million megawatts of energy on tap just to rinse the sweat out of a pair of socks. Even the washing machine—which he hadn't used yet—had a placard stuck to the top saying CONSERVE WATER—COULD THIS LOAD BE HAND-WASHED? To which a previous occupant of the room had added, in felt-tip: ARE YOU OFFERING, LADY?

Who wrote this? One of the nameless employees who hadn't lasted more than a couple of weeks before going insane? Mind you, the way Grainger had looked at him when she picked him up, it was clear she wondered if he was going insane too. Or if he was about to disappear over the same horizon as Tartaglione and Kurtzberg.

Still naked after his shower, Peter stood in front of the mirror and examined the changes that his sojourn among the Oasans had wrought. It was true that the tips of his ears were burnt. There were also ridges of crusted sunburn along the furrows of his brows. Nothing spectacular. Overall, his skin was tanned and healthy-looking. He'd lost weight, and his ribs were showing. He'd just shaved off his beard, and noted that the slight swell of fat under his chin had gone, giving him a sharper facial appearance, a less mild-mannered look. That look had always been deceptive, anyway. In his homeless years, he'd exploited his soft features, radiating an air of bourgeois decency to make people think it was safe to leave him alone in their kitchen or in the back seat of their car for ten minutes. During which he would steal their cameras, their cellphones, their jewelry, whatever was in easy reach. And an hour later he would be selling it, and half an hour after *that* he would be snorting or swallowing the proceeds.

All have sinned, and come short of the glory of God. That was one of the main verses that had saved him, in the end: one of those Bible soundbites that everybody knows but nobody really understands until they're going down for the last time, choking to death on their own filth.

He sprinkled talcum powder in the clefts of his groin, which were a little sore. His scrotum had a few small scabs on the tender flesh—from scratching, obviously, although he couldn't remember breaking the skin. The scabs were dark and clean. Within a day or two, they would vanish. The tops of his ears and the furrows of his brow would shed feathery shreds of white epidermis, revealing hard fresh pink underneath. His concave stomach would fill out, if he ate a few hearty meals. The fungal growth between his toes would clear up after a few applications of the lotion Grainger had given him. The pads of edema in his knees and ankles would shrink away.

If Bea saw him right now, she might be alarmed at the state he was in. She hated to see his skin broken; she would fuss over the merest scratch on his hand, insist on putting Band-Aids on cuts that would be half-healed by the evening. One of her favorite places to kiss him was on his fingertips, whenever he'd bitten a nail to the quick. She'd have plenty to kiss at the moment.

He had not yet written to her. There were at least twenty-five messages banked up. Three or four had arrived in the last few hours, since Bea had calculated he must be back. He was not ready to face her, not even through the veil of the written word. He needed to reacclimatize to life outside the Oasan settlement. He needed to adjust to the complicated trivia of human intercourse.

"So, how were the folks in Freaktown?"

Tuska was smiling broadly, to show he meant no offense. His beard was quite thick by now, mostly gray, which made him look older, and his neck was red from scratching where the wiry hairs tickled his skin. Peter could tell at a glance that the beard's days were numbered: Tuska would shave it off very soon. Why did humans have this compulsion to change their outward appearance, only to revert to what suited them? What on earth was the point?

"Uh . . . they were fine," he replied, a few seconds too late. "They're good people."

"Yeah?" said Tuska. "How can you tell?"

They were sitting at a table in the USIC mess hall. Tuska was tucking into spaghetti Bolognese (whiteflower spaghetti, whiteflower "mince," imported tomato sauce, imported herbs) and Peter was eating a pancake (100 percent local). The air was full of noises: the sound of rain pelting rhythmically against the windows, the mingled conversations of other employees, the clattering of meal trays, the scraping of chairs, the opening and shutting of doors, and Frank Sinatra crooning "My Funny Valentine." It all seemed a grossly excessive amount of bustle and chatter to Peter, but he knew the problem was his perception, and he must try to get in the swing of it. The metaphorical swing, that is: no amount of effort could reconcile him to Frank Sinatra.

A pair of fingers clicked near his face. "Peter, are you with us?" said Tuska.

"Sorry. I really dislike this kind of music."

It was an evasive answer, but also true. Sinatra's self-congratulatory gargle, amplified to be audible over the din, was nudging him across a threshold of tolerance, like repeated pokes in the ribs from a prankster.

"I can live with it," shrugged Tuska. "It's just ripples in the airwaves, Peter. Molecules getting excited for a few seconds and then settling down again. Nothing to get riled about."

"*Each day is Valentine's day,*" smarmed Sinatra, as Tuska assembled another forkload of spaghetti.

"Somebody dissing Ol' Blue Eyes?" A woman who'd been seated at a nearby table sidled over, carrying her dessert bowl. She was a colleague of BG's: they had a similar physique, although this woman was white and blonde. She leveled a mock-censorious stare at Peter. "Did I hear you blaspheming against the godlike Frank?"

"I'm sorry," he said. "I should know better."

"The consummate American songbook," she informed him, deadpan. "Never equaled. One of the great achievements of humankind."

Peter nodded humbly. "Maybe I'm the wrong age to appreciate it."

"How old are you?"

"Thirty-three."

"I'm thirty-two!"

"Well, I'm English, that's another thing . . ."

"Al Bowlly, Noël Coward, Shirley Bassey?" She spoke the names as though any British-born person would swell with pride to hear them.

"Oh dear," sighed Peter. "I'm . . . uh . . . out of my depth here."

There was a pause, during which Frank Sinatra launched into a ditty about a little old ant and a rubber tree plant. "It's OK," said the woman, indulgently. "It's OK. Not everyone likes the same things. It's allowed."

He remembered her name now: Iris. Iris Berns. She came from a Pentecostal family and was an atheist. She liked to play card games, she once had a sister who drowned in a back-yard swimming pool, she had a running joke with BG about centrifugal force, and she was heterosexual despite her butch appearance. None of these bits of information quite fitted into any sensible remark Peter could think of making at this point. Even calling her Iris might come across as an attempt to show off something he'd recalled too late, and anyway, she might want him to call her Berns like everybody else.

Why was even the shallowest human conversation so fraught with pitfalls and tricky calibrations? Why couldn't people just keep silent until they had something essential to say, like the Oasans?

"Give him a break," said Tuska. "He's just come back from a long spell in Freaktown."

"Yeah?" said Berns, plonking down her dessert and taking a seat at the table. "You should take some suntan lotion next time."

"I'll do that," said Peter. He was aware that he was more red-faced than he needed to be, because he'd foolishly worn a sweater over his T-shirt. It had seemed a good idea at the time: a signal that he was a regular urban guy, not some freaky desert-dweller.

"I'm surprised you got so much sun," said Berns, stirring a dollop of dark red syrup through the yogurt-like substance in her bowl until the white turned pink. "They're not exactly outdoors types, are they?"

Peter pulled the neck of his sweater down, to let air in. "They work outside almost every day," he said.

"Yeah?"

"Yes."

"Doing what?"

"Growing and harvesting food for us."

Berns ate a few spoonfuls of dessert. "You know, I've driven all the way round that settlement, and I never saw a plantation, greenhouses, nothing."

"That's because they're right in the center."

"The center?"

"Of the settlement." Peter took a deep breath. His forehead stung with perspiration. "Haven't we been through this already?"

"Must've been with a different woman, honey."

"Don't call him 'honey,'" said Tuska. "He's a preacher."

"The fields are inside the settlement," Peter explained. "The buildings are built in a circle around them."

"It figures," said Berns.

"Figures? Why?"

"They're real secretive."

Peter wiped his brow with his sleeve. "It's not because . . ." His voice was too soft. A flotilla of children had come along to assist Sinatra on the chorus of "High Hopes." Peter's motivation to explain the Oasans' relationship with agriculture faltered under their assault.

Berns stood up and called across the room: "Hey, Stanko! Can we have something instrumental? Our pastor here is having difficulty!"

"No, really," protested Peter, as the eyes of everyone in the mess hall turned on him. "You shouldn't . . ." But he was relieved when the voices of Frank and the school choir disappeared in mid-syllable and were replaced by the tinkling of a piano and some languorously shaken maracas.

Berns sat back down and polished off her dessert. Tuska ate the rest of his Bolognese. Peter had consumed only a few mouthfuls of his pancake but felt stuffed. He leaned back in his chair, and the amiable conversation of several dozen people rustled past his ears, a gentle hubbub of engineering jargon, small talk about food, polite disagreements about solving practical challenges, and the Jabberwocky mishmash of half-heard words and phrases, all interwoven with a Brazilian samba.

"What music *do* you like, Peter?" said Berns.

"Uh . . ." His mind went blank. The names he might usually have rattled off were gone. "To be honest," he said, after taking a deep breath, "I'm not that keen on recorded music. I like music best when it's performed live and I'm actually there when it's happening. That way, it's less like being expected to admire a *thing*, and more a celebration of the moment, of people doing something together in public. Something that *could* go horribly wrong, but through a combination of talent and trust and enthusiasm, it comes out sublime."

"Well, you should join our Glee Club," said Berns.

"Glee club?"

"Our singing group. A bunch of us meet up every hundred and eighty hours and sing together. It's real informal. You'd love it. You a tenor?"

"I . . . I think so."

"BG is the bassiest bass you ever heard. You gotta hear him in action."

"I'd like that."

"We don't do any Sinatra."

"That's reassuring."

"Well, I hope it is." Her tone was sincere. He realized all of a sudden that she was trying to prevent him from drifting away from the bosom of their community, to stop him going native.

"How big is the group?" he asked.

"Depends on our workload. Never less than six. Sometimes up to ten. Anyone's welcome, Peter. It's good for the soul. If you don't mind me saying so."

"Does Tuska sing with you?"

Tuska guffawed. "No chance. Voice like an extractor fan. A *malfunctioning* extractor fan."

"Every person can sing," insisted Berns. "It just takes practice. And confidence."

"Oh, I got loads of confidence," said Tuska. "And a voice like an extractor fan."

Berns looked at him pityingly. "You got sauce on your beard, honey."

"Holy shit—pardon my French." Tuska patted at his facial growth with his fingers. "That does it: this beard has got to go."

"Clean-shaven suits you, Tuska," said Berns, wiping her lips with a table napkin. (A linen napkin: USIC didn't go in for disposable paper.) Then, to Peter: "*Your* beard looked OK, though. I saw you when Grainger brought you back in. Kinda stylish."

"Thank you, but . . . I just didn't have an opportunity to shave while I was away. I use an electric razor, you see, and there wasn't . . . uh . . ." *What garbage I'm talking*, he thought. *Is this the best we can come up with?*

"So," said Berns, "conditions in C-2 really are as primitive as they say?"

"Who says they're primitive?"

"Everybody who's been there."

"Who's been there?"

"Grainger . . ."

"Grainger doesn't venture further in than the perimeter." Even as he spoke the words, he was alarmed at his inability to keep the judgmental overtone out of his voice. "I don't think she's ever set foot inside an Oasan's house."

Berns raised an eyebrow at the word "Oasan," but she caught on instantly. "So what *is* it like? How *do* they live?"

"Well, their living spaces are kind of . . . minimalist. I wouldn't use the word primitive. I think that's how they prefer it."

"So no electricity."

"They don't need it."

"What do they do all day?"

It took all his focus to hide from Berns how exasperated this question made him. "Work. Sleep. Eat. Talk to each other. Same as us."

"What do they talk to each other *about*?"

He opened his mouth to reply, but found that the part of his brain where he went to fetch the answers was filled with incomprehensible babble, abstract whispers in a foreign language. How strange! When he was with the Oasans and overheard them conversing, he was so used to the sound of their voices, and so familiar with their body language, that he almost thought he understood what they were saying.

"I don't know."

"Can you say 'Hello, pleased to meet you' in their language?"

"Sorry, no."

"Tartaglione used to try that one out on us all the time . . ."

Tuska snorted. "That's what he *thought* it meant. He was just repeating what those guys said to him when they met, right? Hell, it could've been 'Step right up, dude, it's a long time since we've eaten Italian!' "

"Jeez, Tuska," said Berns, "can you quit it with the cannibal jokes? These guys are totally harmless."

Tuska leaned across the table, fixing his gaze on Peter. "Which reminds me: you didn't answer my question. You know, before Frank Sinatra so rudely interrupted us."

"Uh . . . can you refresh my memory . . . ?"

"How can you tell that these guys are 'good people'? I mean, what do they do that's so good?"

Peter gave this some thought. Trickles of sweat were tickling the back of his neck. "It's more that they don't do anything bad."

"Yeah? So what's your role?"

"My role?"

"Yeah. A minister is there to connect people to God, right? Or to Christ, Jesus, whatever. Because people commit sins and they need to be forgiven, right? So . . . what sins are these guys committing?"

"None that I can see."

"So . . . don't get me wrong, Peter, but . . . what exactly is the deal here?"

Peter wiped his brow again. "Christianity isn't just about being forgiven. It's about living a fulfilled and joyous life. The thing is, being a Christian is an enormous buzz: that's what a lot of people don't understand. It's deep satisfaction. It's waking up in the morning filled with excitement about every minute that's ahead of you."

"Yeah," said Tuska, deadpan. "You can just see that radiating off of the folks in Freaktown."

Berns, worried that the two men were about to have a serious dispute, touched Peter's forearm and directed his attention to his dinner plate. "Your flapjack's getting cold."

He looked down at the rolled-up pancake. It had dried out somewhat, and resembled a rubber dog bone.

"I think I'll have to leave the rest of this," he said. He got to his feet, realizing as he did so that he was unbearably sleepy, and that he'd been mistaken to think he was in any state for socializing. It took all his effort to move smoothly, rather than lurch like a drunk. "I think I need to lie down for a bit," he said. "Please excuse me."

"Decompression," said Tuska, and winked.

"Get yourself rested," said Berns. And, as he shambled toward the exit: "Don't be a stranger, now."

Back in his quarters, he collapsed on the bed and slept for half an hour or so, then woke with an urgent need to vomit. He spewed the undigested pancake into the toilet bowl, drank some water, and felt better. He wished he had a stalk of 𝕴𝕮𝕴𝕴𝕮𝕴𝕴 to chew on, to keep his mouth fresh without needing to drink. In the settlement, he'd grown accustomed to drinking very little, probably less than a liter a day, despite the heat. Taking in any more just felt excessive, like trying to pour a bucket of water into a small bottle. Your body wasn't big enough to hold it all; your system was pushed to find a way of getting rid of it.

The dishdasha was still damp but drying fast. In anticipation of being able to put it on again, he stripped down to his underpants. Then, a few minutes later, he took those off too. They irritated him.

> Peter, why aren't you writing to me? wrote Bea in the most recent of her messages, freshly arrived. I know you must be very busy but things are difficult here and I'm having trouble coping without your support. I'm just not used to spending day after day without any contact. I won't deny that being pregnant is probably making me feel extra vulnerable and I don't want to come across like a needy, hormonal female but on the other hand the silence from you is deafening.

He felt the blood flush into his face, right to the tips of his ears. He was failing his wife, he was failing his wife. He had promised he would write every day. He'd been busy and bewildered and Bea understood that, but . . . he'd broken his promise and was still breaking it, over and over. And now, under pressure of the anguish he'd caused, she was telling him straight.

If only she'd sent him just that first paragraph—a eight-line message— maybe he could have shot a eight-line response back, instantly. A quick shot of reassurance. But there was more. So much more.

> I'm off work, she went on. My right hand is bandaged up and apart from the hygiene issue I can't nurse one-handed. It's not serious, but it will take a while to heal. It was my own stupid fault. The bathroom window is broken, as you know, and Graeme Stone said he would come and fix it but when days went by and he didn't show up I phoned him and he was very embarrassed—he's moved away. To Birmingham. "That's sudden," I said. Turns out his mum's house was ransacked last week by a gang of thugs and she was left for dead. So he's moved in with his mum. He'll take care of her and fix up the place at the same time, he says. Anyway, I phoned up a window

repair company next but they said there's a huge backlog because of all the storms and vandalism recently, and it could be a long wait. Our bathroom is a mess, muck everywhere, it's too cold to wash in there, I've been washing at the kitchen sink, and the wind keeps slamming doors all through the house. Plus it's not safe, anyone could climb in. So I thought I'd replace the broken pane with a sheet of plastic and some duct tape, and before I knew it I had a gash in my hand. Lots of blood, five stitches. This morning I washed myself left-handed at the kitchen sink while the wind howled through the house and the surviving windows rattled and the toilet door slammed constantly. I had a bit of a cry, I must admit. But then I reminded myself of the extreme suffering and misfortune all over the world.

You won't have heard, but a volcanic eruption has destroyed one of the most densely populated cities in Guatemala, I'm not going to attempt to spell the name of the place but it sounds like an Aztec deity. Anyway, a volcano called Santa Maria blew its stack and spewed ash and lava for hundreds of miles around. The people had 24 hours warning, which only made it worse. There were zillions of vehicles jammed onto the roads, everybody was trying to escape with as many of their possessions as they could carry. Roof racks with half a house teetering on top, bicycles with baby cots balanced on them, crazy stuff like that. Cars were trying to take shortcuts through shops, cars were trying to drive on top of other cars, trapped motorists were smashing through their own windscreens to climb out because they couldn't open the doors, the army wanted to demolish some buildings to widen the bottlenecks but there were too many people in the way. There was nowhere for planes to land or take off, the entire region just became one vast mass grave. People with only seconds to live were filming the lava with their phones and sending the footage to their relatives overseas. And get this: THERE IS NO RESCUE EFFORT. Can you imagine that? There's nothing and nobody to rescue. The city has ceased to exist, it's just part of the volcano now, it's a geological feature. All those people had so many reasons to live and now what are they? Just chemical traces.

The ash cloud is colossal and has stopped planes flying, not just over central America but all over the world. Flights had only just resumed after the bombing of Lahore Airport and now they're grounded again. The airline that took you to the USA has gone out of business. I felt such a surge of distress when I heard that, a lurch in my gut. I remembered standing at Heathrow watching the planes take off and wondering which one was yours and looking forward to you coming back. The airline going bust seems symbolic. It's like a sign that you won't be able to come home.

Everywhere, things are breaking down. Institutions that have been around forever are going to the wall. We've seen this happening for years, I know, but it's accelerating suddenly. And for once, it's not just the underdogs that suffer while the elites carry on as usual. The elites are being hit just as hard. And I'm not only talking about bankruptcy. Some of the wealthiest people in America were murdered last week, dragged out of their homes and beaten to death. Nobody knows exactly why, but it happened during a power blackout in Seattle that lasted four days. All the systems that keep the city functioning ground to a halt. No paychecks, no automatic teller machines, no cash registers, no electronic security locks, no TV, no traffic control, no petrol (I didn't know petrol pumps need electricity to work, but apparently they do). Within 48 hours there was widespread looting and then people started killing each other.

The situation here in the UK is not so stable either. It's got rapidly worse since you left. Sometimes I feel as though your leaving caused things to fall apart!

And there was more. And, in the backlog of previous messages, more still. An inventory of things that were going wrong in the house. Complaints about farcically difficult communications with utilities companies. The sudden impossibility of obtaining fresh eggs. Riots in Madagascar. Joshua pissing on the bed; the washing machine being too small for a queen-size duvet; the local laundromat having closed down. The cancelation of the church's Saturday morning crèche service. Martial law in Georgia. (Georgia in the Russian Federation or Georgia in the USA? He couldn't remember whether Bea had made this clear, and he didn't feel like trawling through the screeds again to check.) Mirah and her husband emigrating to Iran, leaving Mirah's £300 debt to Bea unpaid. A power surge that blew all the lightbulbs in the house. Government-employed "nutrition experts" defending steep rises in the price of full-cream milk. Smashed windows and "For Sale" signs at the Indian restaurant across the road. Bea's morning sickness and what she was taking to suppress it. The sacking of a prominent UK government minister who, in a newspaper interview, had described Britain as "completely fucked." Bea's unrequited cravings for toffee cheesecake and for intimacy with her man. Updates on mutual acquaintances whose faces Peter could not call to mind.

But, through it all, the uncomprehending hurt that he wasn't writing to her.

> This morning, I was so frantic about you, I was sure you must have died. I'd been counting the hours until you were due back from the settlement and as soon as I figured you were back, I checked for messages every two minutes. But . . . nothing. I had visions of you dying of an exotic disease from eating something poisonous, or being murdered by the people you're ministering to. That's how most missionaries die, isn't it? I couldn't think of any other reason why you would leave me in the dark for so long. Finally I cracked and wrote to that USIC guy, Alex Grainger—and got a reply almost immediately. He says you're fine, says you have a beard now. Can you imagine how I felt, begging a stranger for hints of how my own husband is doing? I've eaten many slices of humble pie in my life but that one was hard to swallow. Are you sure you're not angry with me, deep down, for getting pregnant? It was bad of me to stop taking the Pill without telling you, I know that. Please, please forgive me. I did it out of love for you and out of fear that you would die and there'd be nothing of you left. It wasn't a selfish thing, you must believe me. I prayed and prayed about it, trying to figure out if I was just a female hankering for offspring. But in my heart, I can't see it. All I see is love for you and for the baby that will carry some of you into the future. OK, I broke our agreement that we would wait, and

that was wrong, but remember we also had an agreement that you would never drink again and then you went AWOL from the Salford Pentecost Powerhouse and I had to pick up the pieces. I understand why you went off the rails and we got over it and it's in the past, and I'm tremendously proud of you, but the point is that you made me a solemn promise and you broke it, and life went on and so it should. And although I hate to appear as though I'm jockeying for higher moral ground, your going on a bender in Salford wasn't done out of love, whereas my getting pregnant was.

Anyway, enough of that. My hand is throbbing from typing this and your head is probably throbbing from having to read it. I'm sorry. I should lighten up. A workman from the window company is thumping about downstairs, fixing the bathroom. I'd given up hope; I'm ashamed to say I'd even given up praying for it. After all, I'd been told that the waiting list stretched ahead for weeks. But lo and behold: bright and early this morning, the guy showed up and said his boss had told him to shift his schedule around and do our place first. God forgets nothing!

My darling Peter, please write. It doesn't have to be the definitive statement on everything. A few lines would make me so happy. One line even. Just say hello.

Your loving wife,

Bea

He felt feverish and dehydrated. He walked to the fridge and had a swig of water, then stood for a minute with his hot forehead pressed against the cool shell of the machine.

He sat on the edge of the bed. At his feet lay the loose pages of a Bible chapter he was adapting for his flock. *Luke 3*. John the Baptist announcing that there was someone coming soon, "the latchet of whose shoes I am not worthy to unloose." Oh, that awkward word "latchet." And its even more awkward alternatives, "strap" and "shoelace." He'd considered "leather band," but there was the additional problem that Oasans' footwear had no straps or laces and the entire concept might require explanation, which might be more trouble than it was worth, theologically speaking. If only he could think of an equivalent detail to replace the shoe stuff with . . . "whose (something) I am not worthy to (something)" . . . Obviously, to mess around with the metaphors and similes of Jesus was unacceptable, but this was John, a mere mortal, no more divine than any other missionary, his utterances no more sacred than Peter's own. Or were they? The Oasans had made it clear that they preferred their Scripture as literal as possible, and his misguided attempt to translate "manna" as "whiteflower" had caused murmurs of—

"WHAT THE FUCK ARE YOU DOING?"

He flinched. The voice—low-pitched, male and loud—had spoken right near his ear. He wheeled round. No one had entered the room. And God, surely, did not resort to four-letter words.

Dear Bea, he wrote,

I'm so sorry for my silence. I've been busy, true, but that's not the reason I haven't been writing. The real reason is hard to explain but it certainly isn't that I'm angry with you and CERTAINLY not because I don't love you.

This mission has turned out very different from what I anticipated. The things I expected to have a lot of trouble with have gone astonishingly smoothly but I feel out of my depth in other ways I never imagined. I assumed that I would be fighting an uphill battle to minister to the Oasans and that it would take me weeks, maybe even months, to construct even the flimsiest, most provisional bridge between these very foreign minds/hearts and the love of God awaiting them on the other side. But what has actually tested me beyond my abilities is the gulf that has opened up between you and me. I don't mean an emotional gulf, in that my feelings for you have changed in any way. I mean a barrier that circumstances has pushed between us. Of course, physically, we are a huge distance apart. That doesn't help. But the main thing I'm having to confront is that our relationship, until now, has totally depended on us being together. We've always seen and done things as a team and discussed everything as it's come up, day by day, minute by minute—even second by second. Suddenly we're on different paths. And your path has veered off in a frighteningly strange direction.

All these disasters that are befalling the world—the tsunamis and earthquakes and financial meltdowns or whatever—are just so alien to my life here. They don't feel real. I'm ashamed to admit this because obviously to the people suffering through them they're very real indeed but I have enormous trouble getting my head around them. And I very quickly reach a point where I think "If she tells me about one more disaster my brain will seize up." Of course I'm horrified by this failure of compassion, but the more I strain to overcome it the worse it becomes.

Another problem is that I find it almost impossible to talk about the Oasans to anyone who doesn't know them. Not just to you, to the USIC guys as well. My communion with my new brothers and sisters in Christ seems to happen on a different plane, as though I'm speaking their language even though I'm not. Trying to describe it afterward is like trying to explain what a smell looks like or what a sound tastes like.

But I must try.

The basics: The church is built. We worship in it regularly. I've taught the Oasans adapted versions of hymns that they can sing without too much difficulty. (The insides of their faces aren't like ours; they have throats but I'm not convinced they have tongues.) I read to them from the Bible, which they insist on calling The Book of Strange New Things. They have a marked preference for the New Testament over the Old. Thrilling OT adventure stories like Daniel in the lions' den, Samson & Delilah, David & Goliath, etc, don't connect with them. They ask comprehension-type questions but you can tell that even on an "action" level they don't really get it. What floats their boat is Jesus and forgiveness. An evangelist's dream.

They are gentle, kind, humble, hardworking people. It's a privilege to live amongst them. They call themselves Jesus Lover One, Jesus Lover Two, etc. Jesus Lover One was the very first convert, dating back to the early days of Kurtzberg's ministry. I wish I could show you pictures as I'm hopeless at describing them. Their

behavior is not that distinctive compared to ours, eg, I wouldn't
call some of them extrovert & others introvert, some good-humored
& others bad-tempered, some well-balanced & others crazy, etc.
They're all pretty low-key and the differences between them are
quite subtle. It would take a novelist's skill to capture those nuances
in words and, as I've discovered to my embarrassment, I totally lack
that skill. Also, they look physically very similar. Pure, unadulterated
genetic stock. I never thought about this before coming here, but
when we need to tell the difference between people, we get a lot
of help from all the cross-breeding and migration that's gone on
in human history. It's given us such a smorgasbord of different
physical types—caricatures almost. By "we" and "us' I mean people
in the cosmopolitan West, of course. If we were rural Chinese, and
somebody asked us to describe someone else, we wouldn't say, "She's
got straight black hair, dark brown eyes, she's about five foot three"
and so on. We'd have to get more into the nuances. Whereas in the
West there's so much diversity we can say "He's six foot two with
blonde frizzy hair and pale blue eyes," and that immediately sets
him apart from the crowd. Bea, I'm rambling here but the point is
that the Jesus Lovers would all look the same to you except for the
colors of their robes. "By their fruits ye shall know them," I guess. In
a future letter I'll tell you about the contributions that some of the
individual Jesus Lovers have made to the church.

He paused; recognized that Bea might have reason to doubt he would
keep his promise. He racked his brains.

For example, he went on, Jesus Lover Five finally delivered her
painting to be hung on the ceiling with the others. (Oh how I wish
you could see them.) Her painting shows Salome and the two Marys
outside Christ's tomb, with the risen Jesus manifesting to them. He
has His arms spread and He looks as though he's made of light. It's
dazzling, I don't know how she managed to achieve this with just
pigment and cloth; it hits your eyeballs like car headlights on a dark
night. You look up to the ceiling when you're singing or preaching

and you see this crucifix-shaped creature up there, blazing out of the dimness. So that's Jesus Lover Five. A very talented lady (or maybe gentleman—I'm still not 100% sure).

What else should I tell you? I'm struggling to think, which is incredible because so many significant, precious things have happened on this mission and I see so much evidence of God's grace during each hour that I spend in these people's company. So many moments when, if you could only have been by my side, I'm certain we would have exchanged a glance that said: "Yes! God is at work here."

He broke off and stretched. He was coated with sweat, from his greasy brow to the tips of his fingers. His naked buttocks squelched on the vinyl seat. Maybe it had been a mistake to turn off the air conditioning and let this stagnancy take hold. He got to his feet and walked to the window. Another tumbleweed of rain was on its way, swirling across the scrublands toward the base. In five minutes it would be here, streaming down the windows. He looked forward to that. Although there was something sad about enjoying rain on the other side of a glass barrier. He should be out there.

Tired, he threw himself on the bed for a minute. The dishdasha hung between him and the window, silhouetted against the brilliance of daylight. He shielded his eyes with his hands, shuttering his peripheral vision so that he could see the dishdasha without the glare on either side; the garment changed color from dark gray to white. Optical illusions. The subjectivity of reality.

He thought of Bea's wedding dress. She'd insisted on getting married in white, in a church, and on him wearing a white suit. An odd decision for two people who usually avoided ostentation and formality. Plus, there would be alcohol at the reception. He'd wondered if it mightn't be better all round if they just ducked into a registry office in their casuals. No way, said Bea. A registry office wedding would be giving in to shame about their past. As if to say: a guy who used to crawl around in shit-smeared public urinals has no right to repackage himself in a spotless suit; a woman with Bea's family history should forget all about standing up in a church dressed in white. Jesus died on the cross precisely to wipe out that sort of shame. It was like the angel in *Zechariah* 3:2–4 taking off the priest's filthy clothes. *Behold, I have caused thine iniquity to pass from thee, and I will clothe thee with change of raiment.* A clean slate. And there was no bolder celebration of a clean slate than the wedding of Peter and Beatrice.

And in the end, quite a few of the guests got sloshed but Peter didn't touch a drop. And everyone read their speeches from pre-prepared scripts and he hadn't written a thing but when the time came God gave him inspiration and he spoke about his love for Beatrice in elegant, flowing sentences that made people weep.

Then he and his wife went home and Beatrice lay on their bed with her white gown still on, and he thought she was having a rest before getting changed but it soon became obvious that she was inviting him to join her. "We might get it dirty," he said, "and it was so expensive." "All the more reason," she said, "not to shove it into a box with a bunch of mothballs after one day. It's actually a very nice dress. It feels good to touch." And she guided his hand.

She must have worn that dress twenty, thirty times after that. Always indoors, always without any ceremonial flourish or spoken allusion to its symbolic significance: merely as though she'd decided, on a mundane whim, to wear a white dress that evening rather than a green one; an embroidered bodice rather than a V-necked jumper. He never wore his wedding suit again, though.

The rain hit the window at last. Peter lay on his bed as the semen cooled on his midriff. Then he got up, showered again, and returned to the Shoot. The cursor on the screen was still blinking under the word here.

18

I NEED TO TALK TO YOU,

SHE SAID.

The news that Dr. Matthew Everett had died meant nothing to Peter. He'd never met the man. He visited doctors as seldom as possible and, before the obligatory tests that gave him a clean bill of health for the Oasis mission, it had been ages since he'd set foot in any sort of clinic. A doctor had once threatened him that if he continued drinking he would be dead within three months. He'd continued drinking for years. Another doctor, affiliated in some way with the police, had branded him psychopathic and was keen to get him locked up in an institution. Then there was the registrar at Bea's hospital who'd made trouble for her when she "developed an unprofessional attachment to a patient with a history of substance abuse and manipulative behavior."

No, doctors and Peter had never got on. Not even in the years since he'd become a Christian. When medical practitioners heard about your faith, they didn't respond like most people—with bemusement or combative scorn, ready to get into an argument about why-does-God-allow-suffering. Rather, they kept their faces blank and their conversation non-committal, and you felt they were making a mental note in some sort of file on your health issues: *Irrational religious beliefs,* right under *Blepharitis* and *Rosacea.*

"You should go see Doc Everett," several USIC people had told him since his arrival. They meant: to check that you're back in shape after the Jump, or, to get treatment for that sunburn. He'd made polite noises and carried on regardless. And now Doctor Everett was dead.

The fatality had come out of the blue and reduced the USIC medical team from six to five: two paramedics, a nurse called Flores, an MD and surgeon called Austin, and Grainger.

"It's very bad this has happened," said Grainger when Peter met up with her outside the pharmacy. "Very bad." She wasn't wearing her shawl this morning, and her hair was slick with water, newly washed. It sharpened her features, accentuated the scar on her forehead. He imagined a younger Alexandra Grainger, dead drunk, pitching forward, her head splitting open against a metal tap, blood in the sink, blood on the floor, so much blood to be mopped up when she was hauled away. *You've been there*, he thought. *I've been there too.* Beatrice, much as he loved her, had never been there.

"Were you close?" he said.

"He was a nice guy." Her frown and preoccupied tone suggested that her personal relationship with Everett was irrelevant to how bad a thing his death was. Without any further conversation she escorted Peter from the pharmacy into a passageway that led to the medical center.

The medical center was surprisingly big for the number of personnel it served. It was built on two levels and had many rooms, some of which were only half-furnished and waiting to be kitted out with equipment. Two of the three operating tables in the surgical theater were shrouded in plastic wrapping. One particularly large space that Peter peeked into as he passed was painted a cheerful yellow and almost blindingly inundated with daylight from bay windows. It was empty apart from some stacked boxes neatly labeled NEO-NATAL.

The morgue had the same seldom-visited, overly spacious feel as most of the center, even though it was possibly busier than it had ever been: three of the five remaining medical staff were gathered there once Grainger walked in, and Peter was politely introduced—firm handshakes, head nods—to Dr. Austin and Nurse Flores. "Glad to meet you," said the chimpanzee-like Flores, not sounding glad at all, and sat straight back down in her chair, arms folded over her dowdy uniform. Peter wondered what nationality she was. She was four foot ten, tops, and her head looked shrunken. Whatever genetic code had produced her was very different from the one that had produced him. She was almost as alien-looking as the Oasans.

"I'm from England," he said to her, not caring how gauche he sounded. "Where are you from?"

She hesitated. "El Salvador."

"Isn't that in Guatemala?"

"No, but we're . . . neighbors, you could say."

"I heard about the volcano in Guatemala." His mind went into overdrive as he attempted to recall enough details from Bea's letter to support a conversation with Flores. But she held up one wizened hand and said:

"Spare me."

"It's just so awful to think—" he began.

"No, really: spare me," she said, and that was the end of that.

For a few seconds, the mortuary lapsed into silence, apart from a rhythmic groaning sound that was not human in origin. Dr. Austin explained that this noise was coming from the freezers, due to their having been only recently switched on.

"It just didn't make sense to keep a room full of freezers running with nothing in them, year after year," he elaborated. "Especially before we got our energy usage properly sorted out." Austin was Australian, by the sound of him, or perhaps a New Zealander; athletic, muscular, with movie-star good looks apart from an untidy scar gouged into his jawline. He and Flores had been absent from Severin's funeral service, as far as Peter could recall.

"You've done very well, lasting all this time," said Peter.

"Lasting?"

"Not needing to switch the freezers on. Until now."

Austin shrugged. "In the future, as this community grows, we'll need a morgue for sure. In the future, we'll probably have murders, poisonings, all the thrills and spills you get when your population passes a certain point. But these are early days. Or were."

The freezers groaned on.

"Anyway . . ." sighed Austin, and unlatched the drawer containing the deceased, as though Peter had finally requested to see Dr. Everett and shouldn't be kept waiting. Austin pulled at the handles and the plastic crib slid out, exposing the naked body as far as the navel. Matthew Everett's head was nestled on a wipe-clean pillow and his arms lay supported on banana-shaped cushions. He was a presentable middle-aged man with salt-and-pepper hair, a permanent vertical frown creasing his brow, and dimpled cheeks. His eyes were almost but not quite closed, and his mouth hung open. There was a pale dusting of frost on his tongue, and subtle ice-twinkles on his pale flesh. Other than this, he looked well.

"Of course we've had a few deaths over the years," conceded Austin. "Not many; well below average for a community this size, but . . . it happens. People have diabetes, heart conditions . . . Their pre-existing pathology catches up with them. But Matt was healthy as a horse."

"My horse died," said Grainger.

"Beg pardon?" said Austin.

"I used to have a horse, when I was a kid," said Grainger. "He was wonderful. He died."

There was nothing to say to that, so Austin pushed the drawer shut again and fastened the latches. Once again, Peter was struck by the simplicity of the technology: no computerized locking system to be placated with a keypad or a coded swipe-card, just a drawer with a couple of handles. He realized all of a sudden that this simplified design was not the result of cheapskate make-do, a weird mismatch between USIC's colossal wealth and a penchant for outmoded discards. No, these freezers were new. And not just new, but custom made. Some obstinate designer had paid extra for nineteenth-century practicality, had bribed a manufacturer to leave out the computerized sensors, microchipped programs, flashing lights and smart options that an up-to-date mortuary freezer would contain.

Dr. Austin washed his hands in a sink, using a cake of astringent-smelling soap. He dried himself with an ordinary clean towel, then unwrapped a stick of chewing gum and popped it in his mouth. He held the packet out to Peter, a generous gesture since gum was an imported item.

"No thanks," said Peter.

"God knows why I eat it myself," mused Austin. "Zero nutritional value, a ten-second hit of sugar, and your salivary glands give your stomach the message that there's food on the way—which there isn't. Complete waste of time. And bloody expensive here. But I'm addicted."

"You should try ⲁⲋⲟⲩⳅⲥⲟⲩ," said Peter, recalling the pleasant sensation of this plant between his fingers, the burst of sweet juice on his tongue as his teeth first pierced its tough hide, the delicious pulp that yielded hints of fresh flavor even after half an hour of chewing. "You'd never want gum again."

"Beg pardon?"

"ܪܘܚܕܝܘܢ."

Austin nodded tolerantly. Probably adding *Speech impediment* to his mental file of the pastor's health issues.

Silence fell, or what passed for silence in the USIC morgue. Peter thought that the freezers were groaning a bit less noisily than before, but maybe he was just acclimatizing to the sound.

"Did Dr. Everett have family?" he asked.

"I couldn't tell you," said Austin. "He didn't talk about it."

"He had a daughter," said Grainger quietly, almost to herself.

"I didn't know that," said Austin.

"They were estranged," said Grainger.

"It happens," said Austin.

Peter wondered why—given that this meeting wasn't exactly abuzz with convivial chatter—somebody didn't just hand over a dossier on Everett and set a deadline for the funeral address.

"So," he said, "I imagine I'll be doing a funeral service?"

Austin blinked. The concept had caught him by surprise. "Uh . . . Maybe," he said. "Not for a while, though. We're keeping him at negative temp. Frozen, in other words. Until another pathologist arrives." He glanced over to the mortuary drawers, then out the window. "The big concern, of course, is whether there's anything in this environment that might cause people to become ill. That's been a concern from the start. We're breathing air we've never breathed before, eating food that's totally new to our digestive systems. So far, all the evidence suggests it's not a problem. But only time will tell. Lots of time. And it could be very bad news that we've now got a man who had no health problems whatsoever, no reason for him to die, and he's dead."

Peter began to shiver. He'd worn as much clothing as he could tolerate nowadays, even within the USIC base—his dishdasha, a loose sweater, jogging pants, tennis shoes—but it wasn't enough to withstand the chill of the mortuary. He wished he could fling open the window, let the comforting balmy atmosphere swirl in.

"Have you done a . . . uh . . ." The word had slipped out of his vocabulary. Without even intending to, he sliced at the air with an invisible scalpel.

"Autopsy?" Austin shook his head ruefully. "Matt was the one who had the skills in that area. That's why we've got to wait. I mean, *I* can do autopsies if they're straightforward. I could've determined a cause of death for Severin; that was no mystery. But if you've got no clues, you're better off with an expert. And our expert was Matt."

No one spoke for a minute. Austin seemed lost in thought. Grainger stared down at her shoes, which tapped restlessly in the air. Flores, who hadn't uttered a peep since introducing herself, gazed out the window. Maybe she was dumbstruck with grief.

"Well . . ." said Peter. "Is there anything I can do to help?"

"Can't think of anything off-hand," said Austin. "We were actually wondering if there's anything *we* can do to help *you*."

"Help me?"

"Not with your . . . ah . . . evangelizing, obviously," the doctor smiled. "But medically."

Peter's fingers flew up to his brow, touching the flaking skin there. "I'll be more careful next time, I promise," he said. "Grainger's given me some excellent suntan lotion."

"Sunscreen," Grainger corrected him irritably. "SPF 50."

Austin said: "I actually meant the natives. The Oasans, as you call them. We've been supplying them with basic medicines virtually since we first got here. It's the only thing they seem to want from us." He smirked in deference to Peter's mission. "Well, just *about* the only thing. But you know, not one of them has ever shown up here for treatment. Not one! Which means not one of them has ever been checked out or diagnosed properly. We would love to know what's up with them."

"Up?" echoed Peter.

"What ails them," said Austin. "What they're dying of."

Peter had a vivid mental image of his congregation in all their colors, singing hymns and swaying shoulder to shoulder.

"The ones I've been dealing with seem quite healthy to me," he said.

"Do you know what drugs they're taking?" persisted Austin.

The question annoyed Peter and he tried not to show it. "I'm not aware of them taking any. One of my Jesus Lovers—one of my congregation—had a close relative who died not long ago. I never met him. Another one has a brother—or maybe a sister—who's in constant pain, apparently. I imagine that's where some of the painkillers are going."

"Yes, I imagine so." Austin's tone was neutral—breezy, even. There wasn't a milligram of sarcasm detectable in it. But once again, Peter felt that his fellowship with the Oasans was being assessed with a jaundiced eye. The intimacy he shared with the Jesus Lovers was profound, built on a foundation of a thousand solved problems, disentangled misunderstandings, shared history. But as far as the USIC staff could see, his intimacy with the inhabitants of Freaktown hadn't even got off the ground. The quaint Christian had nothing to show for his labors that a rational person could respect. People like Austin had a list of questions which they assumed needed answers before the word "progress" could be uttered.

But that was what the Godless were always so good at, wasn't it? Asking the wrong questions, looking for progress in the wrong places.

"I appreciate why you're curious," said Peter. "It's just that the Oasans I see every day aren't ill. And the ones who are ill don't come to our church."

"Don't you . . . uh . . ." Austin waved one hand vaguely around, to indicate door-to-door evangelism.

"Normally I would," said Peter. "I mean, when I first arrived, I assumed I'd be visiting homes, looking for ways to make contact. But they've been coming to me. A hundred and six of them, last time we met. It's a big congregation for just one pastor with no backup, and it's growing. I'm giving them all my attention, all my energy, and still there's more I could do if I had time—and that's before I even *think* of knocking on the doors of the ones who've been keeping away. Not that they *have* doors . . ."

"Well," said Austin, "if you do find a sick one who'd be willing to come here and, you know, let us check him over . . . Or her . . ."

"Or whatever," said Flores.

"I'll do my best," said Peter. "The thing is, I don't have any medical knowledge. I'm not even sure I could recognize a specific disease in one of *us*, let alone in an Oasan. The signs and symptoms, I mean."

"No, of course not," Austin sighed.

Nurse Flores spoke up again, her simian face unexpectedly illuminated with sharp intelligence. "So, the ones you're dealing with could be sick and you wouldn't know it. Every last one of them could be sick."

"I don't think so," said Peter. "We've built up a lot of trust. They tell me what's on their mind. And I work beside them, I see how they move. They're slow and careful, but that's their way. I think I'd be able to tell if something was badly wrong."

Flores nodded, unconvinced.

"My wife's a nurse," said Peter. "I wish she were here with me."

Austin raised an eyebrow. "You've got a wife?"

"Yes," said Peter. "Beatrice." The mention of her name felt desperate somehow, an attempt to lend her an individual status she could never truly have for these strangers.

"And she's . . ." Austin hesitated. "She's in the picture?"

Peter thought for a moment; remembered his conversation with Tuska: *Is there a special person in your life right now? Nope, can't say that there is.* "Yes."

Austin cocked his head, intrigued. "It's not often we get someone here who's got . . . you know . . . a partner waiting for them back home. I mean, a partner who's . . ."

"In the picture."

"Yeah."

"She would've loved to come too," said Peter. For the first time in ages, his mind retrieved a vividly complete recent memory of Beatrice, sitting beside him at the USIC office, still dressed in her nurse's uniform, her face flinching in distaste at the horribly strong tea she'd been handed. Within a microsecond, she adjusted her expression to imply that the tea was merely too hot, and she turned back toward the USIC examiners with a smile. "It would've made such a difference," Peter went on. "To me and to the whole project. USIC didn't agree."

"Well, she must have failed the suitability tests," said Austin, with an air of commiseration.

"She wasn't given any tests. USIC interviewed us together a couple of times, and then they made it clear that the rest of the interviews were for me alone."

"Take it from me," said Austin. "She failed her ESST. Was Ella Reinman there at the interviews? Small, thin woman with very short gray hair?"

"Yes."

"She does the ESSTs. That's what her questions are all about. Your wife got analyzed on the spot and disqualified, take it from me. The amazing thing is that you didn't. You must've given very different responses."

Peter felt himself blush. His clothing was suddenly plenty warm enough. "Bea and I do everything together. Everything. We're a team."

"I'm sorry to hear that," said Austin. "I mean, I'm sorry she didn't get to come with you." He stood up. Flores and Grainger stood up, too. It was time to leave the mortuary.

After that, there was nowhere to go but his quarters, and his quarters depressed him. He was not, by nature, a depressive person. Self-destructive, yes; he'd been that at times. But not gloomy. There was something about his room in the USIC base that sapped his energy and made him feel boxed in. Maybe it was simple claustrophobia, although he'd never been claustrophobic before, and had once even bedded down inside an industrial garbage skip with the lid closed over him—and was grateful to have the shelter. He could still remember his sense of wonder when, at some point during the night, the mound of garbage on which he lay started heating up, enveloping his half-frozen body with warmth. This unlikely, unexpected generosity from a non-human agency was an early foretaste of how he would feel in the bosom of Christ.

But his quarters at USIC gave him no such feeling. The room might be spacious and clean, yet it seemed to him dismal and tawdry—even when the shutters were lifted and the sunlight made the walls and furnishings almost too bright to behold. How was it possible for a place to be sunlit and yet dismal?

He couldn't get the temperature right, either. He'd killed the air conditioning, as it literally gave him the shivers, but ever since then, he'd been too warm. It was no good having the heat of Oasis without the compensatory caress of the air currents. The Lord knew what He was doing when He made this world, just as surely as He knew what He was doing when He made all the others. The climate was an exquisitely clever system, perfect and self-adjusting. Fighting it was foolish. More than once, Peter had stood at the window of his quarters, his palms pressed against the glass, fantasizing about pushing so hard that the glass shattered and a wave of sweet, balmy air poured in through the hole.

The window-blind allowed him to simulate a few hours of night-time whenever he needed it, which was not possible in the settlement, where the sun shone in on him for seventy-odd hours straight. In theory, this should mean he slept better at USIC base, but no, he slept worse. On waking, he would have a hangover-style headache and feel irritable for an hour or more. Pushing back the doldrums, he would work on his Scripture translations and assemble booklets for the Jesus Lovers, but found that he had less stamina than when he was in the settlement. There, he could push through the exhaustion barrier and remain productive for eighteen, nineteen, even twenty hours, but in his room at USIC he was ready to drop after twelve or thirteen. Nor did he find it easy to fall asleep. He would lie on his firm, well-sprung mattress and stare up at the featureless gray ceiling above him, counting the pock-marks, and each time he began to drift into unconsciousness he would be nudged back into wakefulness by a flash of confusion: Why was the ceiling blank? Where had the beautiful paintings gone?

The only thing the USIC base was essential for was the opportunity to read Bea's messages. Even if he wasn't answering them as often as he should, he still wanted to receive them. As for his laxness, well, that was partly down to how depressed he felt in his quarters. It was obvious he should be writing to Bea in the field, where the action was. How many times had he wished he could send her a quick message immediately after some significant experience with the Oasans, when it was fresh in his thoughts? Dozens! Maybe hundreds! And yet, he had a suspicion that USIC had deliberately fixed things so he couldn't make contact with her anywhere but here. But why? There must be a way to install some sort of electrical generator or relay apparatus in the Oasan settlement! These people could build rain centrifuges, for goodness' sake—they should be able to solve a modest challenge like this. He'd have to discuss the practicalities with Grainger. She kept saying she was there to help. Well, she should help.

If he could communicate with Bea in the field, he'd have the best of both worlds. Out in the field, his mind was clearer, he was more relaxed. Plus, on a practical level, he'd be making better use of the available time. On his mission, there were regular intervals when he must concede that his day was over (regardless of how brilliantly the sun was shining) and he must sit in his bed behind the pulpit, reviewing recent progress and preparing for sleep. Sometimes he'd sit idle for hours, when his mind refused to shut down but his body was weary and the Oasans had all gone home. Those would be the ideal times for writing to Bea. If he could have a Shoot installed in his church, next to his bed, he could write to her at length, each day—each twenty-four hour period, that is. Or even more often. Their communion would be more like conversation and less like . . . like whatever it threatened to become.

Dear Peter,

It was such an enormous relief and pleasure to receive your letter. I've been missing you so much. Even more so because I'm realizing how incredibly rare it is—yet how incredibly NECESSARY—to be in touch with at least one person in this life who we can love and trust. Oh sure, we discuss stuff with colleagues at work and we do things for people in need and we have conversations with strangers and shopkeepers and 'friends' we've known for years but don't feel close to at all. It's all fine as far as it goes but sometimes I feel as if half my soul is missing.

Please don't obsess about what you SHOULD write—just WRITE. Don't hold back! Every time you decide against mentioning an incident, it stays invisible and I'm kept in the dark. Every little detail you describe lights up a precious glimpse of you.

It all sounds fascinating and exciting. And puzzling. Can the Oasans really be as benign as you suggest? No dark side at all? I would imagine they're keen to make a good impression on you, but who knows what will emerge when they relax and "let it all hang out." I'm sure you'll find that they're more individual and eccentric than they appear. Every creature is. Even cats who are from the same breed and look totally identical reveal all sorts of quirks when you get to know them.

Speaking of which . . . Joshua is becoming VERY neurotic. The period when the bathroom window was broken and all the doors were slamming in the wind really didn't do him any good. He jerks at any unfamiliar noise and has taken to sleeping under the bed. I hear him snoring, rustling about amongst the shoes and tissues and defunct alarm clocks and whatever else is under there. I've tried to drag him out but he just crawls straight back. He's jumpy when he eats, too, glancing behind him every few mouthfuls. I've got him on my lap as I type this and I really need to pee but I don't want to dislodge him in case he disappears for the rest of the night. Yesterday I was in the kitchen and I sat down to read an incomprehensible letter from the gas people, and Joshua jumped on my lap. I stayed put for ages with nothing to do and my feet turning to ice. Then an ambulance passed by the house with siren wailing and he jumped off. Should I take him to a cat psychiatrist, I wonder? Right now he's purring. I wish you could hear him. I wish HE could hear YOU and understand that you haven't left forever.

More about your letter . . . I will try not to talk so much about the awful things that are going on in the world right now. I understand that you're in a very different headspace up there, and it must be hard to absorb all the details and implications of what's happening here. As long as you realize that it's not easy for me to absorb this stuff either. It's equally overwhelming and mind-boggling for me. And terrifying.

But today is a good day. My hand is feeling better, healing up nicely. I'm hoping to be back at work next week. The house has just about dried out and the bathroom is back to normal. And I got a letter from the insurance company which, if I interpret the arcane language correctly, suggests that they will cover the damage. Which is a big surprise, I must admit—thank the Lord! The tabloids have been running a campaign of "naming and shaming" the insurance companies that are reneging on claims—lots of picture stories about decent, obese working-class people paying premiums all their lives and being badly let down when their house gets trashed by vandals or whatever. EPIDEMIC OF BETRAYAL, it says here. Such big words for a Daily Express headline! I wonder if this is the first time they've had a headline with two trisyllabic words in it. What's the world coming to! (Sorry, I promised I'd go easy on that topic, didn't I?)

As you know, I don't usually read the tabloids but the Daily Express promised a free Bounty bar for every reader and it's too long since I've had one of those. Chocolate (or the lack of it) looms large in my life right now and I've become an expert in where to get my fix. Biscuit-based bars like Twix and Kit Kats are relatively easy to procure, and there are plenty of Snickers knock-offs that have Arabic writing all over them. But there's something about the insides of a Bounty bar—that almost camphorous aftertaste that goes right up your sinuses—that nothing else can supply. At least not if you're pregnant. But it turned out that the "for every reader" offer was a bit of a scam. It was a voucher that you had to redeem at particular shops that don't exist around here.

But, Bounty bars aside, I'm pretty happy with the food situation today. I've just had a gluttonous fry-up of eggs, tinned mushrooms and bacon. The eggs and bacon came from a street stall, a sort of farmers market that was set up in the car park of where the Tesco used to be. The eggs aren't stamped or dated or anything, they're different sizes with feathers and chicken crap stuck to them. They're fresh and delicious and I doubt very much if these farmers are legally allowed to sell them direct to the public. And the bacon was just wrapped in paper and sliced quite crudely—sliced by the farmer's very own hand, with a knife! Again, probably against regulations. The market was doing brisk business even though it wasn't advertised. The farmers were restocking their trestle tables from out of the backs of their vans, and there wasn't much left in there. Good luck to them, I say. Maybe the collapse of big corporations won't be as disastrous as everybody's been saying. Maybe ordinary people will just trade and sell things locally—the way we SHOULD have been doing all along. I always thought that buying bacon that's been transported all the way from Denmark was crazy anyway.

I shouldn't be eating bacon at all, I suppose. Billy gave me a lecture about meat-eating when we were on our way to the cat show. He's a vegetarian. So was Rachel, but she relapsed. That was the word Billy used. He and his sister are quarreling a lot—maybe that's one of the reasons Billy is so depressed. Sheila says he lives on baked beans, toast and bananas, because he's not actually that keen on vegetables. A very English vegetarian, then! But he's right about the suffering of factory-farmed animals.

It's so complicated, isn't it? Animals suffer, but Jesus ate meat, and he hung around with fishermen. I've been craving fish lately—I must need the vitamin D—and I don't feel any guilt when I squash a bunch of sardines onto a piece of toast, even if I can see their little eyes staring up at me. They're feeding our baby, that's how I rationalize it.

You haven't talked much about the personnel at USIC. Are you still ministering to them as well, or are you focusing solely on the Oasans? Remember that the unwilling and uninterested are just as precious as those who've already given their hearts to Christ. I imagine there must be serious problems among the USIC community, working so far from home in what I suppose are very challenging conditions. Is there a lot of alcohol abuse? Drug abuse? Gambling? Sexual harassment? I imagine there must be.

I phoned up Rebecca to discuss when I'll be going back to work, and she mentioned she's mostly been in A&E and there's been a shocking increase in alcohol-related violence and injury. Sorry, does that count as me telling you about calamities befalling the world? It's hardly on the scale of earthquakes or large corporations going bust. But it's very noticeable on the streets of our town when I go out for a walk in the mornings. I'm certain there never used to be vomit on EVERY corner. I wish children and old people didn't have to see that. I've seriously considered hauling a bucket and mop all around the neighborhood myself. Yesterday I even filled a bucket with soapy water, but when I tried to lift it, I realized it was a bad idea. So I just mopped the vomit off our front porch. Every man must bear his own burdens before bearing another's, as Galatians says, or something to that effect. You would know the verbatim verse, no doubt.

* * *

He sat at the Shoot and flexed his fingers. He'd switched on the air conditioning again and the room was cool. He was dressed in his dishdasha, socks and a pullover, feeling reasonably comfortable if somewhat ridiculous. He had prayed. God had confirmed that there was nothing more urgent or important right now than making contact with his wife. The mission was going well; it could go better still if he devoted himself to it every minute of every day, but God did not expect such superhuman dedication. In another place, far away from this one, God had joined together a man and a woman, and the man had allowed himself to neglect his wife. It was time to make amends.

Dear Bea, he wrote.

I've written too little and too late. I'm sorry. I love you very much. I wish you were here with me. Today I found out that Ella Reinman— that skinny woman at the USIC meetings who looked like a meerkat— was some sort of psychologist who was assessing you, and that she disqualified you from coming here. This news upset me enormously. I felt so outraged on your behalf. Who is she to judge your suitability for a mission like this on the basis of a few snatches of conversation? She only saw you a couple of times and you'd come straight from work and your head was still full of that. You'd had no time to unwind. I can still see that Reinman woman so clearly—her weird head sticking out of her cashmere polo-neck. Judging you.

The sun is going down here. Finally. It's a lovely time of day and lasts for many hours.

I will try harder to paint you a picture. It's been a shock to me how bad I am at describing things in letters. It's a shortcoming we never had to face before, being together every day of our lives. It's made me read the Epistles in a different light. Paul, James, Peter and John didn't say much about their context, did they? Scholars have to dig between the lines to get even the faintest clue about where the apostles might have lived at the time. If only Paul could have spent a few words on describing his prison . . .

Speaking of which, my quarters here are driving me

He paused, then deleted the incomplete sentence. To complain about his living conditions to Bea, who had recently suffered so much discomfort and inconvenience, would be in bad taste.

> Speaking of Paul, he tried again, the verse you alluded to is a bit different in its verbatim form and I'm not sure I agree that "bearing one's own burdens first" is what Galatians 6:5 is really getting at. It's a tricky chapter and the focus changes from verse to verse but overall I think Paul is talking about striking a balance between dissuading others from sin and keeping in mind that we are sinners ourselves. It's not the most crystal-clear passage he ever wrote (and this one was hand-written, too, not dictated like some of the other epistles!) and I must admit that if I were trying to paraphrase it for the Oasans I'd have my job cut out for me. Fortunately, there are plenty of other Bible passages whose meaning is much more transparent and which I'm confident will be vivid and meaningful for my new friends in Christ.

Again he paused. Pictures. Bea needed pictures. Where were the pictures?

> I'm sitting at the shoot wearing my dishdasha and the olive-green pullover and black socks. I look like a complete berk, I imagine. My hair is growing longer all the time. I've considered hacking it shorter with some scissors or even establishing a relationship with the USIC hairdresser, but I've decided to let it go until I'm back with you again. You cut my hair better than anyone. Plus, it's like a symbol of what we do for each other. I don't want to lose those little rituals.

He thought some more.

> I'm so glad to hear that your hand is healing up. You need that hand, and not just for work! I wish I could feel it pressed against the

small of my back. Your hand is warm and always so dry. I don't mean that in a negative way. It's just that it's never clammy, it's always soft and dry, like the finest leather. Like an incredibly expensive glove without any seams. Oh boy, that sounds terrible. I don't have any future as a metaphysical love poet, do I?

Sorry to hear about Joshua. Poor thing, what a state he's in. All I can say to give us hope is that although cats are creatures of habit, the habits don't necessarily stay the same forever. Remember how Joshua went through a phase of attacking/chewing your nursing shoes and then he suddenly moved on to something else? And remember how when we had poor old Titus, we thought we'd have to take him back to the animal shelter, because he went through a phase of howling all night and we were completely exhausted? And then one day he just stopped doing it. So let's not despair about Joshua. The broken window and the wind have obviously spooked him but now that the house is warm and quiet again, I'm sure he'll calm down. I think you're wise not to pull him out from under the bed. He'll come out himself when he's ready. I also don't think there's any need for you to sit in a state of nervous tension when he's on your lap, afraid to move in case he jumps off. He will sense that you're anxious and it may reinforce his own anxiety. My advice is, make a gentle fuss of him when he first jumps on your lap. Enjoy him being there. Then, when you need to go to the toilet or fetch something from another room, tell him affectionately that you've got to get up now, and lift him smoothly and swiftly down onto the floor. Stroke his head once or twice and then walk away. Train him to understand that these interruptions are temporary and no big deal.

My pastoral role here in the USIC base has been pretty limited, I must admit. I've done one funeral service, as you know, and afterward I had a good discussion with a few of the mourners who stayed behind, particularly a woman called Maneely who said she'd felt the presence of God and seemed keen to take it further. But I haven't seen her since except for once in the corridor coming out of the mess hall where she said "Hi" in a nice-to-see-you-but-don't-stop-me-I'm-busy sort of tone. Everyone is busy here. Not in a frantic way, just getting on with what they do. They're not as low-key as the Oasans, but there's definitely less stress than you'd expect.

In fact, I'd have to say that the USIC personnel are an amazingly well-behaved and tolerant lot. They don't quarrel much at all. Just a bit of teasing and low-level bickering sometimes, as you'd expect in any context where a bunch of very different people are trying to get along. As far as I'm aware—and I've only just realized this, talking to you now—there's no police force here. And the strange thing is, it doesn't seem strange, if you know what I mean. All my life, when I've walked around the streets or been in workplaces or at school, I've immediately sensed how instinctively, how INTENSELY people resent other people. Everyone's continually at the limit of their patience, on the brink of losing their cool. You sense the potential for violence. And so the concept of a police force seems logical and necessary. But in a context where everyone's a grown-up and they're just getting on with their appointed tasks, who needs a bunch of guys in uniform circling around? It seems absurd.

Of course, part of the credit has to go to the booze-free environment. In theory, alcohol is available here—it costs a preposterous amount, a substantial chunk of the USIC staff's weekly wage—but nobody buys it. They occasionally make jokes about intending to buy it, they josh each other about procuring booze the way people josh about having sex with people they'd never truly have sex with. But when it comes down to it, they don't seem to need it. Some of the men make references to taking drugs, too. I've learned that this is just male bravado, or maybe an affirmation of who they used to be, once upon a time. I can sniff drugs a mile off (so to speak) and I'm willing to bet there aren't any here. It's not that the USIC staff are fitness freaks or health nuts—they're quite a mixed bag of physical specimens, with some borderline obese ones, some runty ones, and quite a few who look like they used to inflict a lot of punishment on themselves. But they're in another phase now. (Like Joshua soon will be, God willing!)

What else did you raise? Oh yes, gambling, I've seen no evidence of that, either. I've asked plenty of people how they fill their time. "We work," they say. And when I specify "But what do you do in your leisure hours?," they cite harmless activities—they read books about their area of expertise, they flip through old magazines, they go to the gym, they swim, they play cards (not for money), they wash their clothes, they knit fancy covers for pillows, they hang out in the mess hall and talk about work with their colleagues. I've listened in on the most extraordinary discussions. A pitch-black Nigerian and a pale, blond Swede will be sitting shoulder to shoulder, drinking coffee and swapping ideas about thermodynamics non-stop for an hour, in vocabulary of which I understand about three words in every ten. (Mostly "and," "if" and "so"!) At the end of the hour, the Swede will say, "So, my idea's dead in the water, eh?" and the other guy will just shrug and flash him a big grin. That's normal for a Tuesday evening here! (I use 'Tuesday' as a figure of speech, of course. I haven't the foggiest notion what day it is anymore.)

Oh, and another leisure activity. A bunch of them also sing in a choir—a glee club, they call it. Easy, popular old songs. (No Frank Sinatra, I've been assured by a lady who urged me to join, but nothing gloomy or difficult either.) I haven't seen any evidence that any of them write stories or paint or sculpt. They're average people, not in the least arty. Well, when I say average, I don't mean of average intellect, because they're obviously highly skilled and smart. I mean they're interested only in practicalities.

As for sexual harassment

There was a knock on the door. He saved what he'd written as a draft and went to meet the visitor. It was Grainger. Her eyes were bloodshot and swollen from weeping, and the sight of him standing there in a gown, pullover and socks was not sufficiently comical to bring a smile to her lips. She looked in desperate need of a hug.

"I need to talk to you," she said.

19

HE WOULD LEARN IT

IF IT KILLED HIM.

On Peter's bed lay a pile of things Grainger could not quite identify. Or at least, she was obviously having trouble imagining what the hell they were doing there.

"Let me help you out," said Peter with a smile. "They're balls of wool."

She didn't comment or even say "Uh-huh," just stood motionless, staring at the bed. There were only three possible places for a visitor to sit in Peter's quarters—two chairs and the bed. One chair was positioned in front of the Shoot, whose screen displayed his private correspondence with his wife, the other chair was occupied by a large stack of papers, and the bed was covered with a mound of multicolored balls of wool. Purple, yellow, white, baby blue, scarlet, gray, lime green, and many more. Each had a large sewing needle stuck in it, trailing furry thread.

"I'm making booklets," he explained, motioning to the stack of papers. He fetched up a finished one and splayed it open against his chest, showing her the woollen binding sewn through the folded middle.

She blinked in bemusement. "We could have given you a stapler," she said.

"I tried that," he said. "And discovered that the Oasans are worried about pricking themselves on staples. 'Needle-needle hiding from finger,' as they put it."

"Glue?"

"Glue would just dissolve in the watery atmosphere."

She continued to stare. He guessed she was thinking there were too many colors, too much wool, for the purpose.

"This way, each Jesus Lover can have their own personal copy of Scripture," he said. "The different colored thread makes each one unique. That, and my . . . er . . . haphazard sewing technique."

Grainger raked a hand through her hair, in a *this-is-all-too-weird* gesture.

Peter tossed the booklet onto the wool-pile, and hastened to remove the stack of Scripture printouts from the chair. He motioned to Grainger to sit. She sat. She rested her elbows on her knees, clasped her hands, stared at the floor. Thirty seconds of silence followed, which, in the circumstances, felt quite long. When she finally spoke, it was in a dull, uninflected tone, as if she were musing to herself.

"I'm sorry Austin showed you that dead body. I didn't know he was going to do that."

"I've seen bodies before," he said gently.

"It's horrible the way they still look like the person but the person is gone."

"The person is never gone," he said. "But yes, it's sad."

Grainger raised a hand to her mouth and, with abrupt vehemence, like a cat, chewed at the nail of her pinkie. Just as abruptly, she desisted. "Where did you get the wool from?"

"One of the USIC personnel gave it to me."

"Springer?"

"Of course."

"Gay as pink ink, that guy."

"That's not a problem here, surely?"

Grainger sighed and let her head sag low. "Nothing is a problem here. Haven't you noticed?"

He gave her another half a minute, but it was as though she was mesmerized by the carpet. Her bosom rose and fell. She was wearing a white cotton top with sleeves not quite long enough to cover the scars on her forearms. Each time she breathed in, her breasts swelled against the thin fabric of her top.

"You've been crying," he said.

"I haven't."

"You've been crying."

She raised her head and looked him in the eyes. "OK," she said.

"What's causing you this pain?"

She managed a smirk. "You tell *me*, doctor."

He knelt at her feet and got himself comfortable. "Grainger, I'm no good at this cat and mouse stuff. You came here to talk to me. I'm ready. Your heart is grieving. Please tell me why."

"I guess it's what you'd call . . . family problems." She fiddled with her fingertips. He realized she'd once been a smoker and was hankering for the comfort of a cigarette—which made him realize, furthermore, how strange it was that none of the other USIC personnel exhibited those mannerisms, despite the high likelihood that some of them had been heavy smokers in their earlier lives.

"People keep telling me that nobody here has any family to speak of," he said. "La Légion Étrangère, as Tuska puts it. But yes, I haven't forgotten. I pray for Charlie Grainger every day. How is he?"

Grainger snorted and, because she'd just been crying, sprayed some snot onto her lips. With a grunt of irritation, she wiped her face on her sleeve. "God doesn't tell you?"

"Tell me what?"

"Tell you if the people you're praying for are OK."

"God isn't . . . my employee," said Peter. "He's not obliged to send me progress reports. Also, He's well aware that I don't actually *know* your dad. Let's be honest: Charlie Grainger is just a name to me, until you tell me more."

"Are you saying God needs more data before he can . . . ?"

"No, no, I mean that God doesn't need *me* to tell *Him* who Charlie Grainger is. God knows and understands your father, right down to . . . to the molecules in his eyelashes. The purpose of my prayer is not to bring your dad to His attention. It's to express . . ." Peter groped for the right word, even though he'd had this same conversation, more or less, with many people in the past. Each time felt unique. "It's to convey to God my love for another person. It's my opportunity to solemnly voice my concern for the people I care about."

"But you just said my dad is just a name to you."

"I meant *you*. I care about *you*."

Grainger sat rigid, jaw clenched and eyes unblinking. Tears welled up, glimmered, and fell. For a few seconds it looked as if she might start sobbing outright, then she pulled herself together—and got annoyed. Annoyance, Peter realized, was her defense mechanism, a prickliness that protected her soft underbelly like porcupine spines.

"If prayer is just a way of *voicing concern*," she said, "what's the point of it? It's like politicians expressing their *concern* about wars and human rights abuses and all that other bad stuff they're gonna sit back and let happen anyway. It's just empty words, it doesn't change a damn thing."

Peter shook his head. It felt like years since he'd been challenged like this. In his ministry back home, it was an almost daily encounter.

"I understand how you feel," he said. "But God isn't a politician. Or a policeman. He's the creator of the universe. He's an unimaginably huge force, a trillion times bigger than the solar system. And of course, when things go wrong in our lives, it's natural to be angry, and to want to hold someone responsible. Someone who isn't us. But blaming God . . . It's like blaming the laws of physics for allowing suffering, or blaming the principle of gravity for a war."

"I never used the word 'blame,'" she said. "And you're distorting the issue. I wouldn't get down on my knees and pray to the laws of physics, 'cause the laws of physics can't hear me. God is supposed to be on the case."

"You make Him sound—"

"I just wish," she said, "that this magnificent, stupendous *God* of yours could give a *fuck*." And, with a strangled gasp of pain, she broke down and started weeping aloud. Peter leaned forward, still kneeling, and put his arm round her back as she convulsed. They were awkwardly matched, but she leaned forward in the chair and pressed her small head into his shoulder. Her hair tickled his cheek, arousing and confusing him with its intimate softness and alien smell. He missed Bea with a rush of distress.

"I didn't say He didn't care," he murmured. "He cares about us very much. So much that He became one of us. He took human form. Can you imagine that? The creator of everything, the shaper of galaxies, got Himself born as a human baby, and grew up in a lower-class family in a small village in the Middle East."

Still sobbing, she laughed into his pullover, possibly snotting on it. "You don't really believe that."

"Believe me, I do."

She laughed again. "You are such a nutcase."

"No more than anyone else here, surely."

They kept still for a minute, not speaking. Grainger had relaxed now that her anger was purged. Peter drew comfort from her warm body—more comfort than he'd expected when he reached out to her. No one, since BG and Severin had hauled him out of his crib on the flight, had made contact with his flesh other than to shake his hand in greeting. The Oasans were not touchy-feely people, not even with each other. They occasionally stroked each other on the shoulder with gloved hands, but that was about it, and they possessed no lips to kiss with. It had been a long time—too long—since he'd had this contact with a fellow creature.

But his back was getting sore from the unfamiliar position; muscles he seldom used were under strain. If he didn't break the embrace soon, he would lose his balance. The arm that was now laid supportively around her midriff would suddenly bear down on her with his body's weight.

"Tell me a bit about your dad," he said.

She shifted back in the chair, allowing him to move away without appearing to have done so deliberately, just as he'd hoped. A glance confirmed that the weeping hadn't done her any good—her face was blotched, puffy and unfeminine, and she knew it. He looked gallantly askance while she dabbed at her eyes with her sleeve, pecked at her hair with her fingers, and generally tried to compose herself.

"I don't know much about my dad," she said. "I haven't seen him since my mom died. That was twenty-five years ago. I was fifteen."

Peter did the maths. It wasn't the right time for a compliment, but Grainger looked much younger than forty. Even after a bout of crying.

"But you know he's sick?" he prompted. "You told me he was going to die soon."

"I guess. He's an old man now. I shouldn't care. He's had his time." She fidgeted with a phantom pack of cigarettes again. "But he's my dad."

"If you haven't had contact for so long, isn't it possible he's passed away already? Or maybe he's living in retirement somewhere, enjoying a healthy, happy old age."

"No."

"No?"

"No." She shot him a mistrustful look, then softened, as though willing to give him another chance. "Do you ever get intuitions?"

"Intuitions?"

"When you get a feeling about something, something you're sure is happening right at that instant, and there's no way you can technically know it, but you just *know* it. And then a little while later, you find out . . . you get absolute proof, from somebody else maybe, some eyewitness, that what you thought was happening really *did* happen, exactly when you thought of it, in exactly the way you pictured it. Like it was being beamed straight into your brain."

He held her gaze, resisting the reflex urge to nod. There seemed no acceptable response to her question except to agree and start swapping anecdotes about uncanny hunches that had been proved true. The thing was, he'd never had much interest in psychic phenomena, and he and Bea had often noted that the sort of people who were most deeply enthralled by the science of the supernatural were also least able to spot the glaringly obvious reasons why their own lives were in chaos. He couldn't say that to Grainger, of course. He was just about to say something diplomatic about how faith was a bit like an intuition that didn't depend on rare coincidences, when she pressed on:

"Anyway, a few months ago I got this intuition about my dad. I *saw* him in my mind. He was being wheeled down the corridor of a hospital, on a trolley, real fast, by a bunch of medics who were like, '*Gangway!*' It was so clear, it was like I was running along behind. He was conscious but confused, his arm was attached to an IV drip but he was fumbling around for the pocket of his pants, looking for his wallet. 'I can pay, I can pay!' He knew he was in deep shit and he was terrified he'd be refused treatment. His face . . . it wasn't like I remembered, it was unrecognizable, he looked like an old bum that they just scooped off the street. But I knew he was my dad."

"And have you had any other . . . intuitions about him since then?"

She closed her eyes, tired out by revisiting her clairvoyance, or by her intimacy with him. "I think he's hanging in there." She didn't sound at all sure.

"Well," said Peter, "I'm praying for him."

"Even though it makes no difference to the shaper of galaxies, huh?"

"Grainger . . ." he began, but the formality of the surname suddenly exasperated him. "Can't I call you Alex? Or Alexandra, if that's what it's short for?"

She froze as if he had just put his hand between her legs. "How did you . . . ?"

"You wrote to my wife. Remember?"

She considered it for a moment. "Stick to Grainger," she said, but not coldly. And then, when he looked perplexed, she elaborated: "Surnames just work better here. I guess it reminds us that we've all got jobs to do."

He sensed she was finished with the encounter. She had got from it, or failed to get from it, whatever she'd come for. He only wished he'd had the chance to explain more fully how prayer worked. That it wasn't a matter of asking for things and being accepted or rejected, it was a matter of adding one's energy—insignificant in itself—to the vastly greater energy that was God's love. In fact, it was an affirmation of being *part* of God, an aspect of His spirit temporarily housed inside a body. A miracle similar, in principle, to the one that had given human form to Jesus.

"Spoken like a trouper," he said. "But tell me, Grainger: what do you think *my* job is?" He was thinking that maybe the conversation could still be steered back into the waters of faith.

"Keeping the Oasans happy," she said, "so they keep helping us set up this place. Or at least so they don't get in the way."

"That and nothing else?"

She shrugged. "Making Springer's day by taking an interest in his gross collection of knitted cushion covers."

"Hey, he's a lovely guy," protested Peter. "So friendly."

Grainger stood up to leave. "Of course he is, of course he is. Friendly-friendlyfriendly. We're all friendly, aren't we? Pussycats, as Tuska says." She paused for effect, then, in a clear, serenely dismissive voice that chilled him to his soul: "Fucked-up pussycats. With their balls cut off."

A few minutes later, alone and ill-at-ease, Peter resumed his letter to Bea.

> As for sexual harassment, there doesn't seem to be any of that either.

He stared at the screen for a while, trying to decide where to go from here. He felt compassion for Grainger, certainly, and wanted to help her, but he had to admit that wrestling with her troubled spirit had drained him. Strange, because in his ministry back home he was exposed to troubled spirits every day, and it never tired him at all: indeed, he'd always be energized by the thought that this encounter he was having with an angrily defensive soul might lead to a breakthrough. It could happen anytime. You could never predict the moment when a person would finally be able to see that they'd been rejecting their own Creator, fighting against Love itself. For years they blundered and stumbled through life wearing cumbersome armor that was supposed to protect them, and then one day they saw it for the chafing, imprisoning, useless baggage it was, and cast it off, allowing Jesus to enter them. Those moments made everything worthwhile.

> I've just spent some time with Grainger, he wrote, figuring he should share the experience with Bea while it was still fresh. Who, contrary to what you assumed in one of your messages, is a woman. She won't let me call her by her first name, though. Nobody here does. Even the ones who are very friendly prefer to stick to surnames.
>
> Anyway, Grainger is by far the most vulnerable person I've met at the USIC base. She can be in a fine mood one second and then suddenly it's as if you've pressed the wrong button and she changes in a flash. Not nasty, just irritable or withdrawn. But she opened up more today than she has on previous occasions. She's harboring some deep, unresolved hurts, and it would take a very long time to get to the bottom of them, no doubt about that. It's a wonder she was selected for this team, actually. She must have come across more grounded and easy-going during the interviews than she does now.

Or maybe she really WAS more grounded at the time. There are times
of our lives when we feel indestructible even though quite a lot of
things are going wrong, and other times when everything is going
well yet we feel anxious and fragile from the moment we wake up.
Not even the most steadfast Christian is immune to the mysteries of
equilibrium. Anyway, Grainger's main source of grief seems to be a
difficult relationship with her father, who she hasn't seen in 25 years.
I'm sure you can relate to that! In fact, I'm sure you would be the
ideal person to discuss these things with her, if only you were here.

Speaking of which, I found out the real reason why you are NOT
here. A few hours ago I met

In the pause while he searched his brain for Dr. Austin's name, he recalled that he'd already written about this at the beginning of the message,
before Grainger interrupted him. He deleted the redundant words, feeling
more tired every second.

I'm going to say goodbye and send this letter now. It was
hanging around unfinished all the time that Grainger was here and
I'm ashamed that I've kept you waiting so long between responses.
You are right to chide me for my perfectionism. I'm going to do
better from now on! (Joke) Speed up my responses. Send this one
flying toward you while I'm working on the next one.
Love,
Peter.

True to his word, he sent the message, then opened up another of Bea's
letters and refamiliarized himself with its contents. This time, he let go the
idea that he must dutifully address each and every point she raised. She
didn't need that. What she needed was two simple things: an acknowledgment that he'd read her letter, and some sort of message from him in return.
His eyes lit upon the part where she described the almost-healed wound on
her hand: "pale and pink and a bit waxy from the swaddling, but looking good!"
Immediately he began to compose a letter of his own.

Dear Bea,

I'm so happy to hear that your hand is healing so well. I was
horrified to hear you'd hurt yourself and this is a great relief. Please
don't be in a hurry to go back to work. You need to be fully well
in order to take care of others. Plus there are lots of bugs lurking
around in the hospital, as you know—and I'm not just referring to

He pondered for a minute or two, to recall another name that eluded
him, but it wasn't retrievable, despite the fact that he and Bea had mentioned this person every day, probably, for the last two years.

your paranoid colleague with the curly hair.

Despite making good progress here, I'm missing you and wishing
you were with me. Upset that you were disqualified. For my own
selfish sake, of course, but also considering the bigger picture.
Whatever USIC's criteria were, they made a big mistake. Someone
like you is exactly what's missing here. The whole set-up feels . . .
how can I put this? Quite overwhelmingly (overweeningly?) male. I
mean, there are plenty of women around, but they don't make much
difference to the prevailing atmosphere, the esprit de corps, if you
like. It's a kind of camaraderie that you associate with the armed
forces or maybe a major construction project (which I suppose it is).
The women don't rock the boat, they don't try to feminize the place,
they just adjust their natures to fit in.

Maybe that's an unfair generalization. After all, women
shouldn't have to conform to preconceptions of femaleness I have
in my head. But even so, I must admit that this base is not an
environment I feel comfortable in, and I can't help thinking that it
would be hugely improved if there could be a few women like you
added to the mix.

That's not to suggest that there are lots of women like you in the
world! Of course there is only one.

As for gender politics amongst the Oasans, that's a tricky
proposition. I still haven't got to the bottom of their sexes, yet—
they don't understand my questions on that score and I don't

understand their answers! From what I've observed, they don't
have genitals where you'd expect. They do have children—not
very frequently, I gather, but it does happen, so some of my Jesus
Lovers are mothers. I wouldn't say that the ones that are mothers
behave more maternally than the ones who aren't. They're ALL quite
nurturing and connected. In their own way. I've grown very fond of
them. I think you would, too, if you could have shared this adventure
with me.

Another thing I should say about them is that they're very kind.
Very caring. It's not evident at first, and then it dawns on you.
During our most recent gathering in the church, we were all singing,
and suddenly one of the paintings fell off the ceiling (not fastened
securely enough—it's difficult when you're not allowed to use nails,
screws or other sharp objects!). The painting fell right onto Jesus
Lover Five's hand. We all got a big fright. Fortunately the painting
wasn't very heavy and Lover Five was OK—nothing broken, just a
bruise. But the way the others rallied round her was extraordinary.
They each took turns to embrace and stroke her with the utmost
tenderness. I have never seen such an outpouring of communal love
and concern. She went very shy—and she's usually quite verbal! She's
my favorite.

Again he paused. This praising of other females—human or otherwise—
was perhaps not so diplomatic, if his own wife was feeling insecure. He and
Bea had always had the sort of relationship where either of them could
feel free to comment on the admirable points of anyone, regardless of gender, confident that their own relationship was rock-solid and inviolable. But
even so . . . He deleted "my favorite" and wrote:

the one I communicate with best.

There was still something not quite right there.

But of course none of this matters as much to me as our rare and
precious relationship, he wrote. I had such a vivid memory of our

wedding not long ago. And your wedding dress, and how you wore it
in the years since.

Please write again soon. I know you've written a lot already and
I've been very lax in responding, but it doesn't mean I don't value
the contact from you. I do miss you terribly. And I'm sorry I gave you
the impression that certain topics are out of bounds. Write about
anything you like, darling. I'm your husband. We have to be there for
each other.

Love,

Peter

The words were sincere but felt a little forced. That is, he would have spoken them spontaneously if Bea had been cradled in his arms, her head nestled under his shoulder, but . . . typing them onto a screen and sending them into space was a different thing. It changed the color and tone of the sentiments, the way a cheaply photocopied photograph loses warmth and detail. His love for his wife was being cartoonized and he lacked what it took to display it as the vividly figurative painting it should be.

He opened a third letter of Bea's, intending to fire off a third reply, but even as he read "Dear Peter" and anticipated typing "Dear Bea," he worried that she might think he was trying to earn Brownie points. Worried, too, that it might be true. He scanned her message, a long one. There was something in the second paragraph about a bunch of mail that had arrived recently, including a letter from the council urging him to reregister on the electoral roll. A form to be filled in because "your situation has changed." How did they know? Bea couldn't figure out if this was just a more aggressive kind of routine canvassing or a real threat that might have actual consequences. But what was he supposed to do about it? And what did it matter? Did she think he was anxious not to lose the right to vote in the next elections? In case the wrong faceless bureaucrat got in? Why was she telling him this?

Write about anything you like, darling, he'd just told her. He might as well have added: Except the stuff I don't want to deal with.

He swung off his chair, knelt on the floor, clasped his hands between his knees and prayed.

"Lord, please help me. I'm tired and confused, and the challenges I'm facing feel beyond my powers just now. Give me strength and clarity of purpose and . . . poise. My wonderful Bea is lonely and hassled: grant her energy and focus too. Thank You, Lord, for healing her hand. Thank You, also, for revealing Yourself to Jesus Lover Fourteen in her hour of need. She'll be all right now, I hope. I pray for Jesus Lover Thirty-Seven, whose brother still rejects him for his faith in You. Give him comfort. I pray that in the fullness of time, his brother may come to us too. Please sharpen my thoughts and perceptions when I'm next dealing with Jesus Lover Eight. There's something he wants from me that he's too shy to say and I'm too stupid to guess. I pray for Sheila, Rachel and Billy Frame—especially Billy as he continues to struggle with his parents' divorce. I pray for Ray Sherwood as his Parkinson's gets worse."

He faltered. Maybe Ray was dead by now. It had been a long time since he'd had any news. Ray and his Parkinson's had been a recurring feature in his prayers for years, for no better reason than it seemed callous to cease praying for him just because they'd lost touch. Besides, Peter still cared. Ray's face, smiling but tinged with fear at the grim future he and his treacherous body were heading into, manifested clearly in his memory.

"I pray for Charlie Grainger," he went on. "I pray he may see his daughter again one day. I pray for Grainger. I sense she's in danger of being poisoned by bitterness. And Tuska: a lifetime of disillusionment has given him a hard skin. Soften his skin, Lord, if it be your will. I pray for Maneely. I pray that the moment when she glimpsed her need for You may prove to be more than just a fleeting impulse. Please may it strengthen into a serious search for Christ. I pray for Coretta, who named this place and had such hopes that her life would get better rather than worse. Make her life better, Lord."

His stomach was rumbling. But he knew that he'd not yet given God the naked sincerity He deserved. If he left his prayer at this point, there would be something practiced, even slightly glib about it. "I pray for the people of the Maldives and North Korea and . . . uh . . . Guatemala. They're not real to me as individuals, and I'm so ashamed of that. But they're real to You. Forgive me, Lord, for the smallness and selfishness of my mind. Amen."

Unsatisfied still, he reached for his Bible and opened it at random, allowing God to decide which page would come under his eye. He'd done this thousands of times, probably wearing out the spines of several Bibles. Today, the page chosen by the Almighty was 1267, and the first words Peter saw were: "*Do the work of an evangelist, make full proof of thy ministry.*" It was Paul's exhortation to Timothy in 68 AD, but it was also God's advice to Peter right now. Full proof of his ministry? What was full proof? Wasn't he already doing as much as he could? Evidently not, or God wouldn't have directed his gaze to these verses. But what else should or could he do? He scanned the rest of the page for clues. The word "learn" recurred several times. He glanced across at page 1266. Another verse leapt out at him: "*Study to shew thyself approved unto God.*" Study? Study the Bible? He'd devoted endless hours to that. So . . . what was God telling him to study?

He walked over to his window and peered through the glass. The sun had risen but was still quite low in the sky, half-blinding him with its glare. He cupped a hand against his brow. Out on the deserted tarmac, he saw an optical illusion of a legion of human bodies edging forward from behind a far wing of the base. He blinked to make the illusion vanish. It didn't.

A few minutes later, he joined the throng of USIC personnel outside. It seemed the entire population of the base had left the building and was walking en masse toward the scrubland beyond the tarmac. Peter's first thought was that this must be a fire drill, or that there'd been some sort of accident that had filled the base with toxic fumes. But everyone appeared relaxed and in good spirits. Some still carried mugs of coffee. A black man smiled at him and nodded; he was the guy who'd tossed Peter a muffin on the first day but whose name (Rude? Rooney?) Peter couldn't quite retrieve. Two females he'd never been introduced to waved at him as well. An animated babbled rippled through the crowd. It was like a queue for a funfair or a concert.

Peter drew abreast with the nearest person he knew by name, which happened to be Hayes, the literal-minded engineer who'd delivered the speech at the official opening of the Centrifuge & Power Facility. He'd made conversation with her several times since then, and had grown to enjoy how boring she was. Her boringness was so perfect that it had transcended itself to become a kind of eccentricity, and her own unawareness of it was funny and sort of touching. Other USIC personnel felt the same way about her, he'd noticed. There was a twinkle in their eye when she droned on.

"What have we come out here for?" he asked her.

"I don't know why *you've* come," she replied. "I can only speak for why *we've* come." In anyone else, this would be testiness or sarcasm. In her, it was earnest determination to stay within the limits of the subject matter on which she could speak with authority.

"OK," he said, falling into step beside her. "Why have you come out here?"

"We got a call from the team at the Mother," she said.

"Oh yes?" It took him a couple of seconds to figure out she meant the Big Brassiere. Nobody but her called it the Mother, but still she would repeat the term at every opportunity, hoping it would catch on.

"They told us there were animals headed this way. A horde. Or maybe they said a herd." Her brow wrinkled at the ambiguity. "A large number, anyway."

"Animals? What sort of animals?"

She took further cognizance of the parameters of her knowledge. "Native animals," she said.

"I thought there weren't any!"

Hayes mistook his excitement for scepticism. "I'm sure our colleagues at the Mother are reliable eyewitnesses," she said. "I don't believe they would play a practical joke on us. We've discussed practical jokes in USIC briefings, and agreed that they're counterproductive and potentially hazardous."

Peter nodded, his attention wandering to the terrain ahead. Visibility was poor, not only because of the intense glare but because copious amounts of mist were swirling along the ground, spread wide over hundreds of meters like a swarm of spectral tumbleweeds. The eye played tricks: some obscure thing would appear to be moving forward, emerging from the fog, only to be revealed a moment later as a clump of vegetation, demurely rooted in the soil.

The troop of humans reached the end of the tarmac, and the ground underfoot was soft. Peter surveyed the front ranks of the USIC personnel and noted who was walking foremost. It was Stanko, the guy from the mess hall. His gangly frame was graceful in motion; his long arms swung loosely and casually. It suddenly occurred to Peter how odd it was, in the circumstances, that Stanko wasn't carrying a weapon. In fact . . . no one was. In fact . . . in fact, had he seen a gun at all since coming to Oasis? Could this really be a community without weapons? Could there be such a thing? How astonishing, if it were so . . . But on the other hand, wasn't it foolhardy to be so indifferent to danger? Weren't there times when it was crazy to set out without a rifle in hand? Who had authorized this communal foray, armed with nothing but curiosity? Were they all walking to their deaths, doomed to be crushed or torn to pieces by savage animals?

The answer wasn't long in coming. A breeze pushed the mist backward and a large swathe of scrubland was swept clear, abruptly revealing the herd, or horde, of advancing creatures—perhaps eighty or a hundred of them. The USIC personnel gasped, whooped and muttered, each according to their nature. Then, inevitably, there was laughter. The animals were the size of chickens. Small chickens.

"Well, will ya look at that," drawled Stanko, beaming.

The creatures seemed to be half-bird, half-mammal. Featherless, their hide was pink and leathery, mottled with gray. Duck-like heads bobbed with the rhythm of their waddling walk. Puny, vestigial wings hung against their flanks, gently jogged by the motion of the march but otherwise flaccid, like the rumpled lining of pulled-out trouser pockets. Their torsos were remarkably fat—rotund as teapots. Their gait was solemn and hilarious.

"I cannot be-*leeeeve* this!" BG's voice. Peter looked for him in the crowd but there were a dozen people in the way and it would be impolite to cut across them.

By unspoken mutual assent, they stopped moving forward, so as not to spook the animals. The horde was waddling ever closer, apparently unperturbed by the alien onlookers. Their fat bodies kept up the pace, making slow but inexorable progress. At a distance, it had been unclear how many limbs each creature had under its belly, two or four. Closer up, it turned out to be four: squat little legs, unbirdlike in their muscular stockiness. Downy, paddle-like paws of a much darker gray than the rest of the body gave them the appearance of wearing shoes.

"Cute to the power of ten," somebody said.

"Cute to the power of a hundred," somebody else said.

Seen at close range, the animals' heads were not quite so duck-like. Their bills were fleshier, drooping slightly like dog snouts. Their minuscule, expressionless eyes were very close together, conveying an impression of utter stupidity. They didn't look up, around or at each other, only straight ahead. They were on course to pass right by the USIC base, on their way elsewhere. They made no sound apart from the faint, rhythmic *thwuh-thwuh-thwuh-thwuh* of their feet on the soil.

"What are we gonna call these critters?" somebody asked.

"Chickadees."

"Duckaboos."

"How about fatsos?"

"Woglets."

"Xenomammals."

"Flabbits."

"Lunch!"

There was a flurry of laughter but someone immediately hollered: "Forget it, Powell."

"Couldn't we try just one?" protested Powell.

"They may be highly intelligent."

"You're kidding me."

"They may be considered sacred. By the natives."

"Who says they're edible?" called a woman's voice. "They could be poisonous as hell."

"They're headed in the direction of Freaktown," Stanko pointed out. "If they're edible and if it's OK to eat them, we'll probably get some eventually. Like, given to us. And it'll be kosher."

"What do you mean, kosher?"

"I didn't mean . . . I meant, nothing sneaky about it. Just part of the regular deal."

"You're all being disgusting," another woman's voice remarked. "How could anyone even think of eating these? They're so adorable."

"Adorable as a vegetable. Look at those eyes. Three brain cells, max."

"Maybe they bite."

And so they stood there bantering, happy as children, while the exotic procession shuffled past.

"Hey, Peter! How's tricks, bro?" It was BG. He was in a jovial mood, if somewhat in need of a washcloth. This outing had evidently interrupted him in the middle of eating or drinking something white and frothy, judging from the creamy mustache haloing his upper lip.

"I'm fine, BG," said Peter. "A bit tired. And you?"

"On top of it, man, on top of it. Ain't these guys great?" He indicated the horde of animals, whose hundred hefty backsides swayed in formation as they shuffled by.

"A real thrill to see," Peter agreed. "I'm glad I didn't miss them. Nobody told me."

"It was on the PA system, bro. Loud and clear."

"Not in my room."

"Ah, they must've switched it off for you, man. Out of respect. You got your private spiritual stuff to concentrate on. You don't want somebody naggin' in your ear fifty times a day, 'Could So-and-So come to Room 25, please,' 'Could all available personnel report to the loading bay,' 'Haircuts available in one hour in Room 9,' 'Hey everybody, get your asses out of the East Wing entrance, 'cause there's a huge posse of funny-lookin' little motherfuckers headed this way!'"

Peter smiled, but the news of his exclusion from the public address system bothered him. He was disconnected enough from the lives of the USIC personnel as it was. "Well," he sighed, "I would hate to have missed this."

"But you didn't, bro," beamed BG. "You didn't." He wiggled his eyebrows upward at the heavens. "You must've got a tip-off, am I right?"

"Maybe I did." Peter was exhausted all of a sudden, weighed down by his sweat-sodden clothing and his undischarged sense of inadequacy. God's enigmatic instruction about the need for further study and making full proof of his ministry rematerialized in his mind.

BG got down to business: the reason he'd pushed through his colleagues to reach Peter. "So, what would *you* call 'em?"

"Call them?"

"Our cute little pals there," said BG, waving his hand at the retreating army.

Peter thought for a moment. "The Oasans must have a word for them."

"No use to us, bro." BG contorted his face and flapped his tongue idiotically in and out of his lips, emitting a blubbering sound. A second later, with the aplomb of a professional comedian, he composed his features into a mask of dignity. "With Tartaglione gone," he said, "there ain't nobody here can understand the noises those guys make. You heard the old story of the kangaroo, Peter?"

"No, BG: tell me the old story of the kangaroo."

The animal horde was fully past now, making incremental headway toward their destination. Some of the USIC staff stood peering at the dwindling swarm of bodies, but most started ambling back toward the base. BG laid an arm around Peter's shoulder, indicating that they should walk together. "There was this explorer guy," he said, "way back in the day, called Captain Cook. His specialty was landing on brand new pieces of real estate across the ocean, and swiping them off of the black folks that lived there. Anyway, he went all the way down to Australia. You know where that is?"

Peter nodded.

"A lot of folks here get kinda hazy on geography," said BG. "Specially if they never been there. Anyway, Captain Cook landed in Australia and he saw these *amaaazing* animals jumpin' around. Big furry motherfuckers with gigantic rabbit legs and a pouch on their stomach and standin' upright and shit. And he asked the black folks, 'What do you guys call this creature?' and the black folks said 'Kangaroo.'"

"Uh-huh," said Peter, sensing that some sort of punchline was coming.

"Years later, some dude studied the black folks' language, and guess what? 'Kangaroo' meant 'What you sayin', bro?'"

BG bellowed with laughter, his massive body quaking with mirth as he escorted the pastor back to civilization. Peter laughed too, but even as his mouth made the correct shape and his throat produced the appropriate sounds, he knew what God wanted him to do. He would learn the Oasans' language. He would learn it if it killed him.

20

EVERYTHING WOULD BE ALL RIGHT IF SHE ONLY COULD.

And so they began. Pressed close together, Peter and Beatrice could no longer see each other. Their mouths were joined, their eyes clasped shut, their bodies could have been anyone's bodies since the world was created.

A few minutes later, he was wide awake. Bea was a billion miles removed from him, and he was shuffling to the washing machine, holding his soiled bedsheets bundled in his arms. Outside the window, it was the same sunny afternoon as it had been when he'd fallen asleep. The room was bathed in golden light just as before, as though time itself had been baked by the sun, while somewhere far away, his wife's days and nights were flickering unseen.

Peter fed the bedsheets into the metallic drum. The CONSERVE WATER—COULD THIS LOAD BE HAND-WASHED? placard teased at his conscience, but he couldn't recall his semen ever smelling so pungent and he was worried that if he tried to hand-wash the sheets, the odor might permeate his quarters and be instantly noticeable if a visitor walked in. Grainger, for instance.

He scooped some soap flakes into the washing machine from the plastic tub provided. The flakes were waxy, as if shaved from a block of real old-fashioned soap. They certainly weren't any kind of chemical detergent. Might they be whiteflower in one of its myriad forms? He lowered his nose to the tub and sniffed, but the smell of his own body was distracting. He shut the machine and set it going.

Funny, when he was among the Oasans, he never masturbated or had wet dreams. It was as though his sexual nature went into hibernation. He was male, and male equipment hung from his pelvis, but it was just *there*, irrelevant as an earlobe. Only when he returned to the USIC base did his sexuality revive. Likewise, it was only when he was in the USIC base that he felt the full weight of loneliness.

He stood naked next to the Shoot. Its screen was cold and dark, though he couldn't recall switching it off. It must have switched itself off some-time during his sleep, to conserve energy. He hoped he'd managed, before exhaustion overtook him, to send whatever messages he'd been writing to Bea. It was all a bit of a blur. What he'd said; what she'd said. He vaguely remembered something about the carpets in the living room having to be removed and thrown away. Or maybe it was the curtains. And rats. Some-thing about rats. Oh yes: Bea had walked to the curbside to add a garbage bag to the already overflowing wheelie bin there (collections were irregular these days) and she'd got the shock of her life when a rat leapt out, narrowly missing her face.

The rat was probably as frightened as you, he'd reassured her. Or words to that effect.

Locked in the shower cubicle, he lathered himself clean, while his bed-clothes churned nearby. Scalded seeds of his DNA gurgled gently into the drainage pipes.

Sitting at the Shoot, toweled and fresh, he was reaching forward to check for more messages from Bea when he noticed a droplet of blood trickling down his upper arm. He'd washed his hair and, while massaging his scalp, had dislodged a scab from the top of one of his ears. His burns were healing well but the flesh of his ears was rich in blood vessels and needed to be left undisturbed while the epidermal cells did their work. He looked around for toilet paper; remembered that USIC didn't supply any. He had some Band-Aids somewhere, but a fresh droplet tickled his shoulder and he didn't fancy searching through his bag. Instead he picked up a pair of underpants and fitted them on his head so that the fabric nestled against his bleeding ear.

Lord, please don't let Grainger walk in unexpectedly now . . .

Once more he seated himself at the Shoot. A new message had loaded in. He opened it, already visualizing the word "dear" before it manifested on the screen.

Peter,

I am so so angry wiuth you. You're my husband and I love you but I'm hurt and furious.

In all the time we've been apart you have mnentioned NOT ONE WORD about our baby. Are you trying to teach me a lesson or do you just not care? I have dropped a few hints reminding you htat I'm pregnant but I haven't pushed too hard because it's really up to you to decide if you'll engage with it or not.

In the past whenever we discussed having kids you always found reasons why we shouldn't—"not yet." You always assured me you would LOVE to do it one day and that it was only a matter of timing. Well, I'm sorry if I got the timing wrong but I was terrified you would never come back amd you are the only man I want to have childrenb with. Yes I know I sound confused but I don't think I'm as confused as you are. I see now that you've been avoiuding avoiding avoiding fatherhood all these years. It's a scary step, everyone knows that but people take that leap imto the dark and that's how the human race goes on. But your missions were always m,ore compelling weren't they? So many challenges. Another day amnother challenge. Challenges which are really not too hard at all. Because we can try our best to help strangers but utimately those strangers are responsible for their own fate aren't they? If we can't help them it's sad but we just move on and help somepne else. But a child isn't like that. Not when it's your own child. Your own child's fate matters more than anything. You can't AFFORD to fail even thoiugh you probably will and that's what's so scary. But you know what?—for millions of years people have been stupidf enough or brave enough to try anyway. I'm feeling that pressure right now carrying our baby inside me.

And you're clearly not interested.

Peter I'm sorry if it looks like I'm not being sympthaetic to the difficulties that you're no doubt facinfg in your mission. But

you haven't really told me anything about those difficylties. So I
can only imagine. Or more to the point NOT imagine. All I can see,
from the few morsels you've shared with me is that you're having a
big adventure up there. You've been given the cushiest treatment
any Christian missionary has ever had in the entire history of
evangelism. Other missionaries have been thrown into prison, spat
on, speared, pelted wiuth stones, threatened wiht knives and guns,
hacked to death by machetes, crucified upside down. At the very
least they've been given the cold shoukder and frustrated in every
conceivable way. As far as I can tell you arrived to a hero's welcome.
USIC drives you to the Oasans and picks you up again when you're
ready for a rest. Your congregation all love Jesus already and think
you're the bee's knees and want nothing from you but Bible study.
You supervise building works while getting a suntan and every
now and then somebody brings you a painting to hang up on the
ceiling. It sounds like you're compiling your very own Sistine Chapel
up there! And the latest news I get from you is that you just saw a
parade of cute littlw animals.

Peter I know you don't want to hear this but I'M IN TROUBLE.
Things are falling apart at a terrifying rate. Some of it I've told you
about and a lot of it I haven't. Any other husband, once he got wind
ofg what's been going on here would have offered to come home by
now. Or at least made noises about it.

I#m writing this at 5 AM after a sleepless night and I'm almost
hallucinating wioth stress and I will probably regret sending you this
when I#ve finally had some sleep. But you've alwayts been on my
side in the past and now you're hurting me and I don't know where
to turn. Have you given ANY THOUGHT AT ALL to how it might make
me feel when you inform me that Grainger, the person who seems to
be closest to you up there, is a female and that you've "just spent
some time with her" and that she's very "vulnerable" but you're
happy to report that she "opened up" more today than she's done
for you before? I'm sure it will be a wonderful breakthriough for you
both when she lets you call her by her first name and you finally
"get to the bottom" of why she's hurting (maybe it will coincide with

the happy day when this other woman you've been ministering to, Maneater or whatever she;s called, is ready to "take it further")— but Peter has it occurred to you that I might be just a teensy bit "vulnerable" too!

I know you lovbe me and I#m sure you are not doing anything bad withj Grainger but I wish you thought a bit more cvarefully about the language tyou use when talking about her and you. You devote so much time andf energy to pondering exactly the right words to choose in your Bible paraphrases for the Jesus Lovers but when it comes to communicating with me your inbfinite attention to nuance deserts you.

It's nice that you are having such vivid memoeries of our wedding but it would be a lot better for me if you had some vivid memories of the woman you left behibnd a few months ago and what she might need right now.

In tears,

Bea

There was another message, sent a mere two minutes later. He opened it, hoping it might be some sort of retraction or softening of the blow—not an apology exactly, but a step back, a second thought, maybe an admission that she was drunk. Instead, she didn't even call him by name.

As for the rat, PLEASE let's not pretend—it was NOT as frighjtened as me. I'm sure it was having a simply marvelous time being a rat and it's overjoyed that our neighboirhood is choking on its own waste. I just don't know what to do. Lots of people are driving tyheir garbage to other parts of town and dumping it anywhere they think noeone will catch them doing it. I wou;ldn't be surprised if a lot iof the filth that's scattered over our street comes from drive-by dumpings. The police seem powerless to stop it. They seem powerless to stop anything. Tbey just drive arounfd in their squad cars, talking into their handsets. What use is that? What are we paying them for? They're just watching us go under.

* * *

The washing machine gurgled loudly as it sluiced one load of water away to make room for another. Dense white suds clung to the inside of the glass-fronted door. Too much soap. His fault.

He got up from his chair and wandered aimlessly around the room. His heart was beating hard and his intestines felt heavy as clay in his midriff. A stack of Bible booklets lay ready next to the bed, their spines neatly sewn in colorful thread, a labor of many hours during which he had been blissfully unaware of any bad thing.

Dear Bea, he wrote,

I was devastated to get your letter and I'm sorry I've made you feel so hurt. I hope for your own sake—for both our sakes—that the extremity of your distress when you wrote to me was partly due to the state you were in at that moment. All those typos (very unlike you) made me wonder if you'd been drinking. Which is not to suggest that your grief isn't valid, only that I hope you're not feeling this much hurt and anger all the time.

But of course the fault is mine. I can't explain or excuse the way I've been treating you. The closest I can come is to say that this journey—the first time we've been apart for more than a few days at a time—has revealed a frightening lack in me. I don't mean a bad attitude (although that's obviously how you see it), I mean a problem with the way my brain works. I find it almost impossible to keep a grip on things that aren't in my immediate orbit. We've always faced life together and I suppose our togetherness masked this deficiency. When you first met me I was bombarding my system with every toxic substance I could throw at it, and once I cleaned up I blithely assumed that the alcohol and the drugs hadn't inflicted any permanent damage, but I'm now forced to consider that maybe they have. Or maybe I've always been like this. Maybe it's what sent me off the rails in the first place. I don't know.

How can I reassure you about our baby? It's true I've been worried in the past about whether I'm cut out for parenthood. It's true that the responsibility is daunting. But it's not true that I never intended or wanted to have children with you. I want to very much. By the time I get back home, I suppose you'll be heavily pregnant and I hope you'll consent to take time off work. You shouldn't be doing heavy lifting and going through all the stress of the hospital when you're growing a child. How about going on maternity leave as soon as I return? We could relax and prepare things properly.

One thing neither of us has mentioned for a while is money. It's not the factor that we focused on when this mission came up—we were both excited about the project for its own sake. But on the other hand, I will be paid a great deal—more than either of us has ever earned for anything. In the past, once our living expenses were covered, we always ploughed any extra income into the Lord's work. We've funded a lot of worthwhile things. But our child is a worthwhile thing too and I'm sure God will understand if we give the other projects a rest. What I'm suggesting is this: Let's use the money from this mission to move house. Judging from what you've been telling me, it's becoming very unpleasant, even dangerous, to stay in the city. So let's move to the country. It would be a much better environment for our child to spend his/her formative years in. As for our church, by the time I get back they'll have managed for six months without me and I'm sure Geoff will be delighted to carry on as pastor, and if he isn't, someone else will step forward. Churches shouldn't get too fixated on a particular shepherd.

As I write this, it's all becoming clearer in my mind. I was thinking at first that you should go on maternity leave, but as I think about it more, it would make much better sense if you actually quit. A decision which is probably long overdue. The people who run that hospital have caused you so much heartache over the years and it never improves. You can fight them to the last of your energy and they'll just carry on regardless. Well, let's leave them to it. Let's both devote ourselves to being parents, and start a fresh phase of our lives.

All my love,

Peter

* * *

"Hi," said Maneely. "Your ear looks sore."

"It's OK," he said. "It's crusted over now."

She had joined him in the mess hall, where he was sipping tea and trying to persuade himself to order some food. He smiled in welcome, but knew that his nausea and distress must be evident on his face. She, by contrast, looked upbeat and relaxed. She'd had a haircut that suited her. Maybe she'd even had it dyed, because he remembered her as mousy and she was honey-blonde now. Then again, the light in the mess hall had a honeyish tinge. His tea glowed bright orange like a well-brewed beer.

"I've been kind of avoiding you," Maneely said. "Sorry."

"I just assumed you were busy," he said diplomatically. Was this going to be the day when she accepted Jesus into her heart? He didn't feel up to it.

She drank some strawberry soymilk through a straw before getting stuck into a large serving of imitation sausage and mashed potato.

"Your hair suits you," he said.

"Thank you," she said. "You're not eating?"

"I'm . . . taking things slowly today."

She nodded understandingly, as though tolerating a man with a hangover. Several generous slices of sausage disappeared into her mouth and she chased them down with another slurp of soy. "I've been thinking about our conversation after Severin's funeral."

Here it comes, he thought. *Lord, please give me grace.* "Well, you know I'm here for you."

She smirked. "Except when you're in Freaktown getting your ears fried."

"It's not so bad," he said. "I just have to be more careful."

She stared him straight in the eyes, serious again. "Look, I'm sorry about what I said."

"Sorry?"

"I think I got you all excited."

"Excited?"

"Severin was kind of a pal of mine. Not in a romantic way, but we . . . solved a lot of problems together. On various projects. When he died, it hit me hard. Put me into a real vulnerable state. At the funeral, you gave a great speech, and I kind of got half-convinced about . . . you know . . . all this God and Jesus stuff. But it's not me. I've thought it over, and it's just not me. I'm sorry."

"There's no need to apologize. It's like apologizing to gravity or light. God is just *there*, whether we acknowledge him or not."

She shook her head and ate some more. "For a second there I thought you were comparing yourself to the forces of gravity or light."

He winced. "Sometimes I don't express myself very well. I'm just . . . I'm going through . . ." The awareness of Bea's anger coursed through his system like an infection. He thought he might faint from it. "I have problems like anyone else."

"I hope they get resolved," said Maneely. "You're a good guy."

"I don't feel so good right now."

She blessed him with a sisterly smile. "Hey, you'll feel better soon. It's all perceptual. Chemical, even. Feeling down, feeling up, it's a cycle. You wake up one morning and the whole thing looks different. Trust me."

"I appreciate your encouragement," said Peter. "But addressing problems that need to be addressed isn't a matter of . . . you can't be that passive. We have responsibilities. We've got to try to make things better."

Maneely slurped the last of her soy and shoved the glass to one side. "This is about home, right?"

"Home?" Peter swallowed hard.

"When I get stressed about stuff that's out of my control," Maneely counseled him, "I often remember an ancient poem. It's, like, thousands of years old. It goes: *Grant me the serenity to accept the things I cannot change, the courage to change the things I can, and the wisdom to know the difference.*"

"Written by a guy called Reinhold Niebuhr," Peter said. "Except that he actually wrote '*God* grant.'"

"Well, maybe, but it works just as well without." Her gaze was level, seeing right through his pedantry. "Don't beat yourself up about home, Peter. *This* is home now."

"I'm going back soon," he protested.

She shrugged. "Whatever."

* * *

He spent the next couple of hours walking outside, circling the compound. He considered walking all the way to the Oasan settlement. How long would that take him? Weeks, probably. It was a mad idea, mad. He needed to be here to receive Bea's next message. She would be asleep now. She would be asleep for hours yet. They should be sleeping together. Being apart was wrong. Simply lying side by side did more for a relationship than words. A warm bed, a nest of animal intimacy. Words could be misunderstood, whereas loving companionship bred trust.

He returned to his quarters, worked on Bible paraphrases, and moped. Waves of hunger plagued him, interspersed with the urge to vomit. More hours passed. Finally, after having checked the Shoot in vain at least a hundred times, he was put out of his misery:

> Dear Peter,
> No time to write a long letter as I'm about to go to a funeral but
> I am still very distraught and exasperated with you. Am making a
> special effort however to check my spelling so that you don't accuse
> me of being drunk. Actually I'd just about recovered from that
> one when hey presto, you suggest I become an unemployed rural
> housewife!
> Sorry, I know sarcasm is unhelpful.
> I'll write again when I'm back from the funeral. Although I may
> have to spend some time with Sheila first. She's going through hell.
> I do love you, insane as you are,
> Bea

At once he responded:

> Dear Bea,
> It lifted my spirits so much to hear (read) you say that you love
> me. I've barely been able to function all day for grief at the trouble
> between us. You are so much more important to me than my
> mission.
> Although you don't say so in so many words, it's obvious from

your message that Billy Frame committed suicide after all, despite the concern we all felt for him and your recent efforts to offer him support. I can still picture him the way he was when he was a little kid and he was beaming with pride at the wall hanging he and the other children made for us. How awful for Sheila. I can only imagine how stressed you must be by all of this. The fact that you used the word "Hell" to denote something other than eternal separation from God speaks volumes.

I'm sorry you interpreted my suggestions about moving to the country as a plot to turn you into an unemployed rural housewife. I'm sure there will be jobs out there—probably even nursing jobs, less horrible ones (probably) than what you have now. Nor am I suggesting that I'll spend all day chopping wood or growing vegetables (even though I've become quite a happy fieldworker out here). There may be a church that needs a pastor. But whatever work opportunities there are (or aren't), we should leave it in the hands of the Lord.

I'm deeply sorry about the thoughtless way I have spoken about Grainger and Maneely. Yes, they are females but my role in their lives is strictly pastoral—or would be if they were open to the Lord's grace, which they don't seem to be. Maneely has just told me in no uncertain terms that she is not interested.

Words are my profession but I don't always use them wisely, nor are they always the best way of getting things across. I wish I could just hold you and reassure you. I've let you down in the past, in worse ways than I'm doing now, and we got through it together because we love each other. That love is based on communication but it's also based on something that's almost impossible to describe, a sense of rightness when we're in each other's company, a sense we only connect with when we're with other people who aren't right for us. I am missing you so much, darling.

All my love,

Peter

* * *

"What you want won't be easy to arrange," Grainger told him shortly afterward.

"But possible?"

The simplemindedness of the question irked her. "Everything's possible if you throw enough labor and resources at it."

"I don't want to cause havoc for USIC," he said, "but this is very important to me."

"Why not just come back to base at shorter intervals? You might be in better shape if you did."

"It wouldn't work. The Oasans live at their own pace. I need to be among them, share in their routines. I can't just drop in and then get whisked away all the time. But if I had a Shoot out there . . ."

" . . . we might never see you again."

"Please. My wife needs my support. I'm missing her. And maybe whatever you'd have to build to make the Shoot work would come in useful for some other purpose. Once it was there."

She narrowed her eyes. He realized belatedly that he hadn't asked her how she was or made any pleasantries before hitting her with this demand.

"I'll see what we can do," she said.

Dear Peter, he read as soon as he got back.

I wish you had offered to come home instead of reminding me how much money we stand to make if you stay. Yes, I know that it was tremendously laborious and expensive for USIC to invite you. If you'd offered to leave now I probably would have argued you out of it. But it would have been nice to think that you felt enough concern to consider it as a possibility, which you plainly didn't. It's clear you are 100% determined to serve out your time. I understand: it's a once-in-a-lifetime chance.

Your urgings for us to move to the countryside have stirred up my emotions because it's only natural for someone in my position to wish desperately that we could just escape all the fiascos and start afresh in idyllic surroundings. But then my common sense kicks in and I'm exasperated with you. Do you have any idea what the countryside is really like? Do you ever read newspapers?

(Rhetorical question—I know I'm the one with that sordid habit.)
The countryside is a wasteland of decaying factories, bankrupt
farms, long-term unemployed, ugly supermarkets and charity
shops. (Hey, I wonder if the supermarkets have unsold reserves
of chocolate desserts? Now there's an incentive . . .) The money
you'll be paid for your USIC appointment is substantial but it's not
a fortune and a fortune is what we'd need to set ourselves up. There
are still picturesque, safe, middle-class bits of rural Britain where
I'm sure our child would have a nicer start than here in the city but
they come at a very steep price. If our child was dumped in some
godforsaken town where half the population is alcoholic or on drugs,
and the schools are full of low achievers and social work cases,
we'll be no better off. You say, leave it in the hands of the Lord, but
whose decision would it be to move in the first place? Yours.

In any case, grieved as I am about the way things are done at my
hospital, I still have an ongoing commitment to the place and I feel
there's still things I can do to help. I'm also scared that if I quit this
job I won't be able to get another one, because unemployment levels
are soaring as the economy implodes.

Speaking of which: It's only a few days before I'm due to go
back to work and hey presto, I got a letter from Goodman. Once
again, I must say that nobody in the history of the world ever had
a less appropriate name and it's criminal that a person like this
is in charge of deciding how our hospital allocates its resources.
Anyway, the letter is basically a threat. He alludes to some of my
more conspicuous episodes of patient advocacy and hints that in
the "current circumstances," our hospital cannot afford to devote
"disproportionate" staff energies & funds to "clients who are least
likely to respond optimally to our care." Which is Goodmanspeak for:
we shouldn't waste our time on anyone who's mentally ill, bolshie,
ancient or too badly injured/cancer-ridden to ever shake the doctor's
hand and say Ta Ta & Thanks For Everything. What Goodman wants
is more cleft palate repairs, more robust blokes with fractures, kids
with 2nd degree burns, youngish women getting lumps excised,
etc. And he wants my promise that I won't cause trouble. And he

hints that if I don't guarantee better behavior, he may "re-evaluate" whether I'm allowed back at all!

Peter, I'm glad I lifted your spirits by saying I love you, but you're acting like a little boy who feels the whole universe has collapsed when his mother is angry with him but who then feels everything is all right again when she says she loves him. Of course I love you—we've both poured years of commitment and intimacy into our relationship and that's totally integral to our minds and hearts. Our love can't be erased by a bit of unhappiness. But that doesn't mean our love can cure unhappiness, either. It comes down to this—there are frightening, dispiriting things going on in my life right now which I am dealing with on my own, partly because you're not physically here with me but partly also because you are unable or unwilling to offer me emotional support. I hear what you're saying about drug abuse, brain damage, etc, and maybe you're right—in which case it has implications for our relationship that don't exactly cheer me up—but another possibility is that it's a convenient excuse for you, isn't it? You'd like to show an interest in what's going on in my life—or in the world at large, for that matter—but you can't because your brain is damaged. So that's all right then.

I'm sorry if I sound bitter. I'm just very, very overwhelmed. How about we both blame physical factors—you claim brain damage and I claim hormone overload? Ever since I've been pregnant, I've felt more vulnerable. But of course there are plenty of shocking things happening that have nothing to do with my hormones.

Which brings me to the funeral I just went to. The conclusion you jumped to as "obvious"—that Billy committed suicide—was wrong, but understandable. I concluded the same thing when Sheila phoned me. But the truth is worse. It was Rachel. The child who was supposedly OK. There was no clear warning sign, or if there was, Sheila missed it. Maybe she was too preoccupied with Billy's depression to notice. Of course, now, she's tearing herself inside-out about it, trying to remember every tiny thing Rachel did and said. But as far as I can tell, Rachel was behaving pretty much as normal for a teenage girl—going to school, bickering with her brother, listening to bad pop music, fussing over her hair, going on fad diets, declaring she's vegan one day and scoffing roast chicken the next. Of course Sheila now regards all of these things as distress signals but given how difficult 12-year-old girls can be, I think she's being too hard on herself. What was really going through Rachel's head, we'll never know. All we know is that one morning she just took herself to a car scrap yard near her home, crawled through a gap in the wire mesh (the place was abandoned) and hid inside a big stack of car tires. She took a lot of pills—her mum's sleeping pills, painkillers, just household stuff but dozens of them. And she washed them down with flavored milk and huddled inside those tires and died and wasn't found for three days. She left no note.

Billy's coping well, I think. Taking care of Sheila, sort of.

I could write about what's been happening in Pakistan but it's a huge topic and I very much doubt you'd want to hear about it anyway.

Joshua's cowering under the table as if he thinks I'm going to kick him. I wish he would just curl up in his basket and go to sleep. I mean, let's be honest, life really isn't so bad for a cat. Instead he just skulks around. And he doesn't sleep with me anymore, so I don't even have the comfort of his physical presence.

I must have a rest. Big day today. Will write again tomorrow. Will you?

Love,

Bea

•

Peter vomited, then prayed. His head cleared, his guts were soothed with a fuzzy numbness, his fever—which only now he recognized as a fever—ebbed away. God was with him. What Bea was facing now, they had faced together many times in the past. Not the precise circumstances, but the feeling that life had become unbearably complicated, a tangled network of insoluble problems, each requiring all the others to be solved before any progress could be made. It was in the nature of a troubled soul to regard this as objective reality, a hard look at the grim facts that were revealed once the rose-colored glasses were off. But this was a distortion, a tragic misconception. It was the frenzy of the moth butting against the lightbulb when there was an open window nearby. God was that open window.

The things that were worrying Bea were genuine and awful, but they were not beyond the power of God. In their lives together, Peter and Bea had been confronted with police harassment, financial ruin, eviction, a hate campaign by Bea's father, the concerted opposition of local councils, malicious lawsuits, escalating vandalism, threats from knife-wielding gangsters, the theft of their car (twice) and a burglary so bad they were left with little more than their books and a stripped bed. In each case, they had appealed to the mercy of God. In each case, He had untangled the barbed wire of trouble with a firm, invisible hand. The police had suddenly apologized, an anonymous donor saved them from bankruptcy, the landlord had a change of heart, Bea's father died, a Christian lawyer took on the council on their behalf and won, the threatened lawsuits melted away, the vandals were caught red-handed by Peter and ended up joining the church, the gangsters got jailed for rape, one stolen car was found undamaged and the other was replaced by a parishioner, and, when the burglars cleaned them out, the congregation showed such kindness and generosity that Peter and Bea's faith in human goodness was boosted to ecstatic heights.

Dear Bea, he wrote.
Please don't use the word "Godforsaken." I know you're upset and rightly so but we must honor with our mouths the fact that no one is truly forsaken by God. In all your distress, I get the feeling you're not leaning on Him as trustingly as you might. Remember all the hundreds of times we've been at our wits' end and He's come through. Turn to Him now. He will provide. Philippians 4:6 reassures us: "Be careful for nothing (ie, don't be anxious about anything), but in every thing by prayer and supplication with thanksgiving let your requests be made known unto God."

I'm sorry I didn't offer to come home early. I did think of it and was very strongly tempted by the idea but instead of airing it with you I struggled with it inside my own mind before I wrote. Apart from anything else I didn't want to raise false hopes in case USIC told me it wasn't possible. There is already a ship on the way, I gather, containing (no doubt among other things) another doctor to replace one that died.

I'm not as attached to staying here as you think. While it's true that this mission is an extraordinary opportunity, the spread of God's word has its own momentum and its own timescale, and I'm sure the Oasans could do marvelous things on their own, with the input I've had so far. The reality is that I will have to leave them in a few months anyway, and there'll still be a lot to do. The Christian life is a journey, not a self-contained project. I am giving these people my all, but when I have to go, I'll go, and my sights will then be set on our life back home.

Please try to reconnect with the love and protection that God has shown us in the past and which is waiting there to shield you now. Pray to Him. You won't have to wait long for evidence of His hand. And if, in a few days, you still feel distraught, I will do my best to arrange to come home to you, even if it means forfeiting some of my payment. Whatever happens, I'm confident that I'll be treated fairly. These are benign, well-intentioned people. My instincts about them are good.

As for the countryside, yes, I admit ignorance. But as Christians—and, again, with God's help—we have the power to affect what sort of ethos a place has. I'm not saying there won't be problems but we've had big problems in the city too and you're currently having a horrendous time so could it really be worse? I've been spending most of my time outdoors here and there is something so calming about it. I would love to go walking with you in the sunshine and fresh air. And think how Joshua would adore it!

It will be your morning by the time you read this. I hope you slept well.

Love,

Peter

* * *

Having sent this message, Peter was clammy with sweat. And ravenous. He showered and dressed in clean trousers and T-shirt. Then he went to the mess hall and ordered himself the sausages and mash.

When he returned, he resumed work on the Bible booklets. Several of the Jesus Lovers had asked him about the parable of the Good Shepherd, the Hireling and the Sheep. He'd gently urged them to tackle a different episode, because this one involved sheep and wolves, two creatures they'd never seen, and besides, it was full of sibilant letters. But they insisted, as if worried that their natural limitations might prevent them from comprehending something utterly crucial. So, he was tinkering with it. For sheep, he could substitute whiteflower. God could be the Good Farmer, making sure that the crops were tended properly and picked at the correct times; the Hireling could be . . . what could the Hireling be? The Oasans knew nothing about money and recognized no difference between vocation and employment. And what about the conclusion of the story, where the Shepherd lays down his life for his sheep? A farmer couldn't lay down his life for his crops. The whole parable was untranslatable. Yet the Jesus Lovers would not be fobbed off. He would have to teach them about sheep, wolves, shepherds, hirelings. It was an absurd challenge, although it might be worthwhile if it allowed the Oasans access to the concept of the Lamb of God. .

On a sheet of paper, he experimented with drawing a sheep. Art was not one of his strong points. The animal he scrawled had a credibly sheep-like body but its head looked more like a cat's. He struggled to recall ever having seen a sheep in the flesh, or even in photographs. Beyond a vague impression of woolly rotundity, he couldn't summon forth any details about ears, snout, eyes and so on. Was the lower jaw visible? Perhaps there would be something in the USIC library. Granted, many of the books had pages torn out, but he imagined that if there were any pictures of sheep, they'd be intact.

Absentmindedly, out of habit, he checked for new messages on the Shoot. Immediately, one from Bea loaded in. She hadn't gone to bed after all.

Peter, PLEASE PLEASE STOP HARPING ON ABOUT THIS COUNTRYSIDE FANTASY, it's just making me feel worse. You just don't seem to appreciate how fast and how frighteningly and how MUCH things have changed. The housing market has COLLAPSED. Like just about everything eslse in this country IT IS KAPUT. Couldn't you guess that? Wouldn't that be obvious from all the things I've been telling you? Do you really think some nice young coiuple is goimng to be isnepcting our house with a checkbook in their hands? All those nice young couples all over the UK are frozen with TERROR. Everyonbe is just sitting tight, hoping agaimst hope that things will improve. I am sitting tighjt myself, hoping that at last some big truck will finally come and pick up the stinking piles of garbage in front of our home.

As for using the word godforsaken, I'm sure God can forgive me but the question is, can you?

The vehemence of the blow took him by surprise. In the minutes that followed, his brain swirled with hurt, indignation, shame and fear. She was wrong, he was misunderstood, she was wrong, he was misunderstood, she was in trouble, he couldn't help, she was in trouble, he couldn't help, she was deaf to his assurances of love and support, she spoke in a tone he couldn't recognize. Was this what pregnancy had done to her mind? Or had she been harboring these resentments and frustrations for years? Half-formed sentences suggested themselves, drafts of defenses and analyses, ways to demonstrate to her that she was not helping anyone by behaving like this, ways to allude to the deranging effects of hormones and pregnancy without making her angrier still.

As he thought more, however, his urge to argue dwindled and all that was left was love. It didn't matter, for the moment, that she misjudged him. She was overwhelmed, she was in distress, she needed help. Rightness or wrongness was not the point. Giving her strength was the point. He must let go of his grief at how alienated she was from him. The greater problem was that she seemed alienated from God. A barrage of suffering borne in unaccustomed loneliness had weakened her faith. Her mind and heart were closed like the fist of a child in pain. Rhetoric and arguments were useless and, in the circumstances, cruel. He must remember that when he'd been at his own lowest ebb, a single Bible verse had pulled him back from the abyss. God didn't waste words.

> Bea, I love you. Please pray. What is happening all around you is terrifying, I know. But please pray and God will help. Psalm 91: I will say of the Lord, He is my refuge and my fortress. He shall cover thee with His feathers, and under His wings shalt thou trust.

There, it was sent. He clasped his hands and prayed she would pray. Everything would be all right if she only could.

III

AS IT IS

THERE IS NO GOD,

SHE WROTE.

"SⱯↄଫଧtଫⱭ," he said.

"ⱭⱯↄଫଧଖⱭ" she corrected him.

"SⱯↄଫଧtଫⱭ" he tried again.

"ⱭⱯↄଫଧଖⱭ," she corrected him again.

"ⱭⱯↄଫଧଖⱭ," he said.

All round him rose a noise like a flock of birds flapping their wings. It was not birds. It was the sound of applause from dozens of gloved hands. The Oasans—no longer Oasans to him but ⱭↄⰭ—were letting him know he was making excellent progress in their language.

It was a perfect afternoon, just perfect. The air was less clammy than ever before, or perhaps he'd grown accustomed to the humidity at last. His body felt free and unencumbered, almost a part of the atmosphere, with no division between his skin and the surrounding sky. (Funny how he'd always been encouraged to conceive of the sky as something that started at some point far above him, whereas the ⱭↄⰭ word for it—ↄ—recognized that it extended right down to the ground.)

He and the ⱭↄⰭ were sitting outside the church, as was their custom when they were engaged in matters not strictly related to faith. The church was for singing, for sermons (although Peter didn't refer to his Bible talks as such) and for contemplating the pictures his friends had dedicated to the glory of God. Outside, they could speak of other things. Outside, they could be his teachers.

Today, they numbered thirty. Not because the Jesus Lovers had dwindled in total, but because only certain members of the congregation felt confident to give their pastor instruction. Some of the people he was fondest of weren't here, and he was forging a new intimacy with others who'd been a closed book to him before. For example, Jesus Lover Sixty-Three—so shy and awkward in most contexts—displayed a flair for linguistic problem-solving, keeping silent for long periods and then, when everyone was stuck, uttering the word they were searching for. By contrast, Lover One—the original convert to Christ and thus a person of some eminence among the believers—had declined Peter's invitation to take part in the lessons. Declined? "Dismissed" or "rejected" was closer to the mark; Lover One was opposed to Peter attempting anything that might dilute the strangeness of the Book of Strange New Things.

"Forget the Book for a second . . ." Peter had said, but Lover One was so wound up that, for the first time, he interrupted.

"Never forge𐍈 the Book. Never, never. The Book our rock, our hope, our redeemer."

The words were Peter's own, specially selected to be easy for these people to say, but the more often he heard the ⅏⌒ᗩᔕ uttering words like "redeemer," the more he wondered what they really thought they meant.

"I didn't mean . . . I wasn't saying . . ." Peter floundered. Then: "I just want to know *you* better."

"You know enough," Lover One said. "We are they who need more knowing, more word of Je⅏u⅏. Word of Je⅏u⅏ good. Our word no good." And no amount of reassurance could convince him otherwise.

So here they were, a congregation within a congregation, engaged in an activity that had a slightly contentious status—which made it feel more important, of course. They sat on a patch of earth which had been shrouded in shade when they first settled in it, but not anymore. How many hours had they been sitting here? He didn't know. Enough for the sun to move a significant distance across the sky. The sun's name, he'd learned, was ᗩᶫ. Back at the USIC base, stowed in a drawer in Peter's quarters, lay a printout prepared for him by some well-meaning boffin, charting the rising and setting of the sun within the seventy-two-hour diurnal cycle. The heavens were reduced to a geometric grid with USIC at its center; the times of day were represented as incomprehensible multi-digit numbers, and the sun was not dignified with a name. Typical.

Now, under that sun, he sat with his brethren on the mildest, most beautiful day yet. He imagined the scene from above—not very high above, but as if from a beach lifeguard's observation tower. A tanned, lanky, blond-haired man in white, squatting on brown earth, encircled by small robed figures in all the colors of the rainbow. Everyone leaning slightly forward, attentive, occasionally passing a flask of water from hand to hand. Communion of the simplest kind.

He hadn't felt like this since he was six and his parents took him to the dunes in Snowdonia. That summer had been the happiest time of his life, as he'd luxuriated not just in the balmy weather but also in his parents' reconciliation, all coos and hugs and soft words. Even the name "Snowdonia" seemed magical, like an enchanted kingdom rather than a national park in Wales. He'd sat for hour upon hour in the dunes, soaking up the warmth and his parents' togetherness, listening to their benignly meaningless chatter and the lapping of the waves, gazing out at the sea from under his oversized straw hat. Unhappiness was a test that you had to pass, and he'd passed it, and everything would be all right from now on. Or so he'd thought, until his parents' divorce.

The language of the ⅃ᑕᐁᐊᔅ was murder to pronounce but simple to learn. He had a hunch that there were probably only a few thousand words in the vocabulary—certainly far fewer than the quarter million in English. The grammar was logical and transparent. No eccentricities, no traps. There were no cases, no distinctions between singular and plural, no genders, and only three tenses: past, present and future. Even to call them tenses was a stretch: the ⅃ᑕᐁᐊᔅ didn't think that way. They classified a thing according to whether it was gone, or it was here, or it was expected to come.

"Why did you leave the original settlement?" he asked, at one point. "The place where you were living when USIC first came. You left it. Did something go wrong between you and USIC?"

"We are here now," they replied. "Here good."

"But was there a problem?"

"No problem. We are here now."

"It must have been very difficult to build everything again, from nothing."

"Building no problem. Every day a **ᔖᕈ**mall work more. **ᔖᕈ**mall work upon **ᔖᕈ**mall work, day upon day, then the work done."

He tried a different tack. "If USIC had never come, would you still be living in the original settlement?"

"Here good."

Evasiveness? He wasn't sure. The **ᔖᕈᐊᐤ** language didn't appear to contain any conditionals. There was no if.

The home of my Father have room upon room upon room, read one of his Bible paraphrases, carefully refashioned to avoid troublesome words like "house" and "mansions." As for John's next bit, "if it were not so, I would have told you," he'd ditched it and moved straight on to *I will prepare a room for you*—which in retrospect was a wiser decision than he'd known at the time, because the **ᔖᕈᐊᐤ** wouldn't have understood what John's "if it were not so" assurance was supposed to mean. One of the most direct, straight-talking asides in the whole Bible was arcane nonsense here.

And yet, however many problems the **ᔖᕈᐊᐤ** might have with English, it was agreed that Peter would continue to speak of God and Jesus in his own tongue. His flock would have it no other way. The Book of Strange New Things was not translatable, they knew that. In foreign phrases, exotic power lurked.

But there was more to life than God and Jesus, and Peter wanted to share these people's mundane reality. Just a few days after he started to learn the language, he overheard two Jesus Lovers talking, and was delighted to pick up, amongst the meaningless sussurus, a reference to a child refusing breakfast, or maybe not refusing, but doing something with or at breakfast that the grown-ups disapproved of. It was a trivial detail, and his understanding of it made no difference to anything, yet it made a huge difference to how he felt. In that modest moment of comprehension, he was a little less an alien.

"Breakfast" was "**ᗩᒪᔖᑊ ᕐᒐ ᐊᐤᐟ**"—literally, "first food after sleep." A great many **ᔖᕈᐊᐤ** words were composites of other words. Or maybe they were phrases, it was hard to tell. The **ᔖᕈᐊᐤ** made no distinction. Did that mean they were vague? Well, yes and no. He got the impression there was a word for every thing—but just one. Poets would have a hard time here. And a single word might refer to an activity, a concept and a location all in one, as in ⳩⳩⳩, which referred to the whiteflower fields, whiteflower in general, and the farming of the crop. Pronouns didn't exist; you just repeated the noun. You repeated a lot of things.

"⳩⳩⳩ ⳩⳩?" he asked Jesus Lover Twenty-Eight one day, proud that he could manage "Your child?" in the ⳩⳩⳩ language. A small person, clearly not yet mature, was dawdling near the church, waiting for her to finish her worship and return home.

"⳩⳩," she confirmed.

Observing the child, he felt sad that there were no children in his congregation. The Jesus Lovers were all grown-ups.

"Why don't you keep him by your side?" he asked. "He's welcome to join us."

Ten, twenty, thirty seconds went by while they stood there, watching the child watch them. A breeze fluttered the boy's cowl, and he raised his tiny hands to adjust it.

"He no love Je⳩u⳩," Jesus Lover Twenty-Eight said.

"He doesn't have to," said Peter. "He could just sit with you, listen to the singing. Or sleep."

More time passed. The boy stared down at his boots, shifting his weight from one foot to the other.

"He no love Je⳩u⳩," Jesus Lover Twenty-Eight said.

"Maybe in the future."

"Maybe," she said. "I hope." And she walked out of the church into the shimmering heat. Mother and son fell into step without a word. They didn't hold hands, but then ⳩⳩⳩ seldom did.

How much did her child's lack of Christian fellowship grieve her? How contemptuous or tolerant was this boy of his mother's faith? Peter couldn't tell. And asking Lover Twenty-Eight about it probably wouldn't yield much insight. The lack of self-absorption he'd noted in these people from the outset went deep into the language itself: there were no words for most of the emotions that humans devoted endless energy to describing. The sort of intimate confab that longtime girlfriends indulged in, analyzing whether a feeling was True Love or merely lust, affection, infatuation, habit, dysfunction, blah blah blah, was inconceivable here. He couldn't even be sure if there was a word for anger, or if "ᔕ◺ᑕᐊ" merely denoted disappointment, or a neutral recognition that life wasn't turning out as planned. As for "ᑢ◖ᑕᐊ," the word for faith . . . its meaning was not what you'd call precise. Faith, hope, intention, objective, desire, plan, wish, the future, the road ahead . . . these were all the same thing, apparently.

Learning the language, Peter understood better how his new friends' souls functioned. They lived almost wholly in the present, focusing on the tasks at hand. There was no word for yesterday except "yeᔕᔕerday." This didn't mean the ᔕᑫᐁᔋ had a poor memory; they just lived with memory differently. If someone dropped a dish and broke it, they would remember next day that the dish was broken, but rather than reliving the incident when the dish fell, they would be preoccupied with the need to make a new dish. Locating a past event in measured time was something they could do with great effort, as a special favor, but Peter could tell they didn't see the point. Why should it matter exactly how many days, weeks, months or years ago a relative had died? A person was either living amongst them or in the ground.

"Do you miss your brother?" he asked Jesus Lover Five.

"Brother here."

"I mean the one that died. The one that's . . . in the ground."

She remained utterly still. If she'd had eyes he could recognize, he suspected she would be staring at him blankly.

"Do you feel pain that he is in the ground?"

"He feel no pain in the ground," she said. "Before he go in the ground, he feel pain. Big, very big pain."

"But you? Do you feel pain? Not in your body, but in your spirit? Thinking of him, being dead?"

She shuddered gently. "I feel pain," she conceded after half a minute or so. "I feel pain."

It was like a guilty triumph, extracting this confession from her. He knew that the ᔕᑫᐁᔋ felt deep emotions, including grief; he sensed it. They weren't solely practical organisms. They couldn't be, or they wouldn't have such an intense need for Christ.

"Have you ever wished you were dead, Jesus Lover Five?" He knew her real name now, and could even make a fair stab at pronouncing it, but she'd let him know that she preferred him to call her by her Christian honorific. "I have," he went on, hoping for a breakthrough in rapport. "At various bad times in my life. Sometimes the pain is so great, we feel it would be better not to be alive."

She was silent for a long while. "BeⱤer be alive," she said at last, staring down at one of her gloved hands as if it contained a profound secret. "Dead no good. Alive good."

Getting to grips with the language brought him no closer to understanding the origins of ⱭꙨⱭ civilization. The ⱭꙨⱭ never alluded to what had happened in their collective past and appeared to have no concept of ancient history—their own or anyone else's. For example, they either didn't grasp, or considered irrelevant, the fact that Jesus walked the earth several thousand years ago; it might as well have been last week.

In this, they were, of course, excellent Christians.

"Tell me about Kurtzberg," he asked them.

"KurⱤⱭberg gone."

"Some of the workers at USIC say cruel things about that. I think they're not serious, but I can't be sure. They say you killed him."

"Kill him?"

"Made him dead. Like the Romans made Jesus dead."

"JeⱭuⱭ no dead. JeⱭuⱭ alive."

"Yes, but he was killed. The Romans beat him and nailed him to the cross and he died."

"God iⱭ miracle. JeⱭuⱭ no longer dead."

"Yes," agreed Peter. "God is miracle. Jesus no longer dead. But what happened to Kurtzberg? Is he alive too?"

"KurⱤⱭberg alive." A dainty gloved hand gestured at the empty landscape. "Walking. Walking, walking, walking."

Another voice said: "He leave uⱭ in need of him."

Another voice said: "You no leave u‌ඦ."

"I will have to go home eventually," he said. "You understand that."

"Home here."

"My wife is waiting for me," he said.

"Your wife Bea."

"Yes," he said.

"Your wife Bea: one. We are many."

"A very John Stuart Mill observation." At this, they twitched their shoulders in fretful incomprehension. He should have known better than to say it. The ‌ඦඐඣ did not "do" witticism or irony. So why had he bothered?

Maybe he was saying it to Bea, as if she were here to hear.

Solemn truth: If Bea hadn't been OK, he wouldn't have come. He would have postponed his visit, stayed at the base. The disappointment his flock would have felt was a far less serious thing than the distress of the woman he loved. But, to his enormous relief, she had listened to his pleas and prayed.

And, of course, God had come through.

> I went to bed frightened and angry and lonely, I must confess,
> she'd written to him. I was expecting to wake up in a state of
> suppressed panic, as usual, my arms folded around my face to ward
> off whatever nasty surprise the day had in store for me. But next
> morning, the whole world was different.

Yes, that's what God could do. Bea had always known that, but she'd forgotten it, and now she knew it again.

> I may have mentioned (but probably not), her morning-after-
> prayer letter went on, that the central heating has been gurgling/
> thumping/stuttering all day & night for weeks, and suddenly the
> house was quiet. I figured the boiler must have given up the ghost,
> but no, it was fine. Everything working smoothly. As if God just laid
> a finger on it and said "Behave yourself." Joshua seemed more at
> ease, stroking himself against my shins the way he used to. I made a

cup of tea and realized I had no morning sickness. Then there was a knock on the door. I thought it was the postman, until I remembered that deliveries have been coming in the afternoon if they've come at all. But it was four fresh-faced young men, maybe mid-20s, very macho. For a moment I was scared they might rape me and rob me. A lot of that's been going on lately. But guess what? They wanted to remove the piles of stinking garbage! They had a four-wheel drive and a trailer. Their accents were Eastern European, I think. They've been driving all over the area doing this.

"The system is gone to hell!" one of them said, big grin on his face. "We are the new system!"

I asked them how much they're charging. I expected them to say 200 quid or something.

"Give us 20 pounds!"

"And a bottle of some kind of nice drink!"

I told them I didn't have any alcohol in the house.

"Then give us . . . 30 pounds!"

"And think in your mind that we are good strong amazing guys!"

They cleared the lot in two minutes flat. They were showing off, tossing heavy bags into the trailer with one hand, doing leapfrog on the wheelie bins, stuff like that. It was bitter weather, I was shivering in a parka, and these guys were in thin sweatshirts, skintight so that their muscles were well displayed.

"We come to your rescue, yeah?"

"Every day you think, When is somebody gonna come, and today . . . we come!"

"Don't trust the government, it is bullshit. They say, You want the mess cleaned up but it's too much problem. Bullshit! It's not problem! Five minutes work! Good strong guys! Finished!" He was beaming, sweating, he seemed perfectly warm.

I gave them a 50 pound note. They gave me 20 change, then drove off with the garbage, waving bye-bye. The street looked and smelled civilized for the first time in weeks.

I wanted to tell someone what had just happened, so I phoned Claire. I almost didn't—I've hardly used the phone for ages, there's been this hideous crackling on the line, you can barely hear the other person. But this time it was totally noise-free. Again, I thought it must be dead, but it was just working as it should. Claire was not surprised by my news; she's heard about these guys. They make a fortune, she says, because they visit maybe forty homes every day at £20 a pop. Funny how a service you're accustomed to paying a few pence for (in tax) suddenly seems cheap at a hundred times the price.

Anyway, the story gets better. Claire said she'd had a strong mental picture of me ever since she went to bed last night—"as if someone beamed it into my head," she said. She and Keith are moving to Scotland (they got a third of what they originally paid for their house and feel lucky to have sold it) to a much smaller, scummier (Claire's word) place because at least they have a support network there. Anyway, they packed up their possessions and Claire decided she no longer needs half the clothes she's accumulated over the years. So, rather than putting them into a charity bin, which is risky nowadays because people use them for garbage, she brought over three huge bin-bags full. "Take what you want for yourself, Bee Bee; the rest can go to the church," she said. When I opened the bags I almost cried. Claire is exactly the same size as me, if you recall (you probably don't) and I've always loved her taste in clothes. I'm not a covetous person but there were things in those bags that I used to lust after when I'd see Claire wearing them. Well, I'm wearing one of them right now!—a lilac cashmere pullover that's so soft you keep touching it to make sure it's real. It must have cost 10 x more than anything I've ever had on my body apart from my wedding dress. And there are fancy leggings as well—beautifully embroidered, works of art. If you were here I would give you a little fashion parade. Can you even remember what I look like? No, don't answer that.

I start back at work tomorrow. Rebecca tells me that Goodman has gone on holiday! Is that good news or what! And my hand has healed up very nicely. There was still some tingling in the nerves before but that's completely gone now.

I went out to the supermarket today and there was more stock
on the shelves than there's been for ages. I remarked on it to the
manager and he gave me such a smile. "We aim to please," he said.
I suddenly realized what a nightmare he's been living through; it's
only a lousy supermarket but it's his baby. Speaking of which—did
I already mention No Morning Sickness? Just cravings, cravings,
cravings. But in the supermarket, I scored—wait for it (I certainly
have!)—a chocolate dessert! I suppose it's kind of trivial to claim
that God delivers chocolate when you really, really want it. But
maybe he does.

Chocolate and cashmere pullovers. Weirdly exotic things they seemed to
him, under the vast sky of Oasis, observing the incremental progress of ⲁⳑ
from horizon to horizon. And of course he'd been reminded of *Matthew*
6:25 when he'd read Bea's letter. But he knew she was touchy lately and
might not appreciate being reminded of Jesus's cautions against getting too
concerned with food and clothes. The main thing was that she felt encouraged and restored. She'd been in danger of slipping adrift from God's protection and now she was back in it. *Thank you, thank you, thank you, Lord,*
he prayed. He trusted she was doing the same.

USIC had promised him that they would build a transmitter for Shoot
access right near his church very soon, maybe even before his next visit
to C-2. So this was the last time he would be out in the field without the
chance to share his day-to-day impressions with Bea. Once the Shoot was
in place, neither of them would be unreachable anymore.

Bea's mention of Claire and Keith troubled him slightly. He couldn't
remember ever having met them. Were they members of the church, or
acquaintances from somewhere else? People from Bea's hospital? She spoke
as though their identity didn't need explaining. Claire, apparently, had a
body almost identical to Bea's. He strained to recall seeing his wife standing
next to another female who looked very similar. A woman in a lilac cashmere pullover. Nothing came.

Jesus Lover Nine padded over to him, cradling a small pot of whiteflower
sweetmeats. She angled the pot forward, to indicate: *have some.* He took

one. It was delicious but marinaded in a saucy paste that left dark brown marks on the fingers. Lover Nine's gloves were filthy; they would need washing when she got home. Her robe was grubby, too. Quite a few of the ᴄᴧᴅᴧᴄ were a bit soiled today, because before the language lesson they'd been digging a hole for the transmitter.

Even Solomon in all his glory was not arrayed like one of these, he thought.

The communion came to an end, and the ᴄᴧᴅᴧᴄ went back to their homes, and Peter went into his church and slept for a spell. How long? A while, a while. He'd lost touch with whether it was technically day or night or "2200 plus" or whatever stupid formula the USIC people expected him to use, but he was attuned to the rhythms of the ᴄᴧᴅᴧᴄ by now and when he awoke he had a sense that it must be very early morning and it probably was.

A shaft of light illuminated his lower body, emphasizing the sharp contours of his pelvis and the concave valley under his ribcage. He was all bone and sinew, like a dancer or an inmate of a concentration camp. The taut flesh pulsed with his heartbeat. He wasn't hungry, though. Just thirsty. The light was flickering on his abdomen. Why was it flickering? Rain must be on the way. He decided to leave the water bottle untouched by his pillow and to wait for the heavens to open instead.

Outside, naked, he stood watching, his hair flapping with the force of what was approaching. It would be a particularly heavy downpour, he could tell. Four gigantic bodies of water, stacked in a vast pyramidal formation, rolled forward, constantly threatening to merge into one but somehow remaining discrete. Three of them swirled in slow, stately fashion and the fourth spun with centrifugal frenzy. Best to hold tight to something. He braced himself against the wall.

When the deluge hit, it was exhilarating but also scary. The wind rushed past him through the church and he heard the thump and clatter of loose objects being thrown about. One gust almost lifted him off his feet. But the rain was cool and clean and luxurious. He opened his mouth and let it pour in. He felt as though he was diving and swimming—and surfacing, always surfacing—without having to move a muscle.

When it was over, he was dazed and numb and unsteady on his feet. A cursory inspection of the church interior showed no serious damage. Jesus Lover Seventeen's painting, a recent arrival he hadn't yet had time to attach to the ceiling, had been hurled across the floor and the edges of its cloth were frayed, but the picture was unharmed. An Expressionist still-life of a flower, he'd thought at first, but no: what he'd perceived as flower-petals was a circle of robed figures bent backward in astonishment, and what he'd perceived as the stamen was a man growing from the ground: Lazarus.

He stowed the painting back behind the pulpit, ready for hanging. The rainburst had left him pleasantly sated, and his natural inclination was to lie down and allow his skin to tingle for a while. But he knew there was work to be done. Not the Lord's work, but manual labor. The whiteflower fields would be sodden, and within a couple of hours many of the plants would have swelled to maturity, while others would be in danger of collapsing into sludge. The time to act was now.

"God ble🜁 our reunion, Father Pe🜔er."

He waved, but wasted no time saying hello to everyone he knew. Many of the 🜁🜔🜍 gathered here for the harvest were not Jesus Lovers, and they had yet to accept him fully in their midst. It was diplomatic to save the conversation for later. He got down on his knees, and within seconds his hands were caked to the elbows with muck.

The plantation had turned into one big bog, like a pig farm. The soil was more retentive of moisture here than in the open scrublands, and there was also a lot of decaying whiteflower scattered about, from the remnants of plants that had been uprooted last time. A fine, almost imperceptible fog began to rise from the ground, rendering everything less than fully distinct. It didn't matter. The plant in front of you: that was all you needed to see.

Peter enjoyed working in the fields. It took him back to his younger days of strawberry-picking for cash-in-hand, except that this was honest toil and he wasn't doing it because he was on the run from drug buddies he'd robbed. It wasn't mindless drudgery, either, because you had to evaluate each plant to decide whether to leave it alone, tear bits off it, squeeze it, or pull it out.

The ᏣᎳᏏ harvested patiently and with quiet deliberation, more like gardeners than slave-driven serfs. They wore their gloves as usual. Whenever these became too muddy, they would stop for a while to wipe them free of excess dirt or adjust the fit. Sometimes they just sat back and rested for a few minutes. When they'd accumulated a basketful of plants, they would carry it to the edge of the field, where half a dozen nets were spread out. Onto these nets they would distribute the different parts of the plants, each part according to its destiny. It had taken Peter quite a while to get the hang of which bits went on which pile, but he believed he had it sorted now. He was no longer a liability; he was a fellow worker. And he worked harder and faster than any of them.

After an hour or two, despite the fact that there were probably still lots of moribund plants hiding in amongst the resilient ones, the harvesters—mindful of their limited energy—moved on to the next phase. This was the part Peter liked best, because it really did require vigor and stamina—two qualities the ᏣᎳᏏ were not overly endowed with. They were all right at carrying the produce from the fields back into the settlement, for each net could be carried as slowly, and as haltingly, and by as many people, as the weight of its contents demanded. But there was a task which allowed no slack: the making of meat. Beefsteak, lamb, bacon, veal: cunning simulacra of these were favorites among the largely carnivorous USIC personnel, but they weren't easy to create. They required violent effort—not the killing of an animal, but the relentless pounding of whiteflower plants that were on the brink of death. Only the most swollen, senile specimens were chosen. When the water-gorged flesh was pummeled with a stone, the weakened capillaries of the plant diffused a characteristic flavor through the pulpy mess. With each pound, the mess became more elastic and homogenous, until it could be left to solidify into dense lumps which, when carved and seasoned, looked and tasted uncannily like meat. The ᏣᎳᏏ pummeled gingerly, one or two blows at a time. Peter pummeled like a machine.

So absorbed were Peter and the ᏣᎳᏏ in their work that they didn't notice, until it was too late, the arrival of the swarm.

* * *

One of the ⚬⚭⚮ shouted something Peter half-understood, because it contained the same root word for "foreign/alien/unexpected/strange" that was in "The Book of Strange New Things." Smiling in pleasure at this further proof of his progress in the language, he looked to where the person was pointing. At the perimeter of the plantation, barely discernible as anything more than a low mist of pinky-gray, was the horde of bird-like creatures Peter had seen marching past the USIC base.

His first impulse was to whoop with delight and urge his friends to enjoy the spectacle. But the ⚬⚭⚮ were obviously alarmed—and with good reason. The creatures waddled silently into the whiteflower and within seconds a large swathe of the field was obscured by their quivering bodies. Peter ran through the fields to get a closer look, but he knew, he already knew. These animals, these adorable critters, these chicadees, duckaboos, woglets or whatever other cute names they might be given, were rapacious vermin, and they were here to eat the crop.

Mindless as maggots, they hunkered into the juicy whiteflower, making no distinction between old plants and young plants, hard buds and flaccid leaves, flower or stalk. In their downy gray heads, muscles pulsed as they chewed and chomped. Their spherical bodies shivered and swelled and were not satisfied.

Instinctively, he reached down and seized the nearest of them and yanked it free of its feast. At once, his forearm got an electric shock. Or that's how it felt, as the frantic creature lunged round and clamped its fangs into his flesh. He hurled it away in an arc of his own blood. He tried kicking at the creatures, but he was bare-legged apart from his sandals, and a vicious bite on one of his calves sent him reeling backward. There were too many of them, anyway. If he'd had a cudgel, or a gun . . . a machine gun, or a fucking flamethrower! Adrenaline connected him with a younger, angrier Peter, a pre-Christian Peter who was capable of punching a man's nose until it splintered, capable of smashing the windscreen of a car, capable of sweeping a long row of fragile knick-knacks off a mantelpiece in a convulsive gesture of hatred, except that he was capable of nothing now, and his adrenaline was useless, because all he could do was fall back and watch this horde consume the fruits of his people's labor.

Those of the ᗯᑫᕂ who weren't Jesus Lovers had better things to do than stand and watch. The fate of their plantation was obvious. They hurried to the piles of harvested whiteflower and shouldered the nets, heaving them off the ground. They knew that the pests would eat systematically from one end of the field to the other, so there was still time to carry away what was already in the bag, so to speak. The Jesus Lovers swayed anxiously back and forth, torn between their need to salvage the crop and their concern for Peter. He approached them, intending to help them carry the load, but they cringed and swayed all the more. A weird, disturbing sound issued from their heads, a sound he hadn't heard before. Intuition told him it was the sound of lamentation.

His arm, stretched out toward them, dripped blood into the soil. The bite was not just a puncture, but had lifted a flap of skin. His leg, too, was grisly.

"You will die, you will die!" moaned Jesus Lover Five.

"Why? Are those things poisonous?"

"You will die, you will die!" "You will die, you will die!" "You will die, you will die!" Several of the Jesus Lovers had joined in the moaning. Their raised voices, jumbled together, so different from their usual gentle utterances never spoken out of turn, unnerved him.

"Poison?" he asked loud and clear, pointing at the swarm of vermin. He wished he knew the ᗯᑫᕂ word for "poison." "Bad medicine?"

But they did not reply. Instead they hurried away. Only Lover Five hesitated. She'd been in a strange state all through the harvest, hardly working, mostly watching, occasionally lending just one hand—her left—to a simple task. Now she came to him, walking as if drunk or in a daze. She laid her hands—one glove grubby, the other clean—on his hips, then pressed her face hard into his lap. There was nothing sexual in her intent; he doubted if she even knew where or what his genitals were. He guessed she was saying goodbye. And then she was hurrying after the others.

Within minutes, he stood alone in the whiteflower fields, his injured arm and leg itching and burning, his ears filled with the hideous noise of hundreds of rodent mouths gnashing on slimy pulp that, only a few minutes before, had been destined for transformation into bread, lamb, beancurd, ravioli, onion, muᴙhroom, peanuᙏ buᙏer, chocolaᙏe, ᴙoup, ᴙardine, ᴙinnamon and a host of other things.

When Peter limped back to his church, he found a pickup truck parked outside and a USIC employee called Conway sipping from a $50 bottle of pop. A short, bald man in immaculate lime-green overalls and polished black boots, he cut a remarkable contrast to Peter's filthy, blood-spattered appearance.

"Are you OK?" said Conway, then laughed at the absurdity of the question.

"I got bitten," said Peter.

"By what?"

"Uh . . . I don't know what word you guys finally decided on. Flabbits? Chicadees? Whatever."

Conway raked a hand through his non-existent hair. He was an electrical engineer, not a medic. He pointed behind the church, at a brand-new structure that resembled a washing machine with a miniature Eiffel Tower stuck on top. "Your Shoot relay," he explained. In normal circumstances, copious expressions of thanks and admiration would have been in order, and Peter could see that Conway was having trouble letting go of his moment of well-deserved praise.

"I think I'd better get some treatment for this," said Peter, holding up his gory forearm.

"I think maybe you better," agreed Conway.

By the time they reached the USIC base hours later, the bleeding had stopped but the flesh around his wounds was turning dark blue. Necrosis? Probably just bruising. The vermin's jaws had punched him with the force of a power tool. During the drive, he'd had ample opportunity to examine his arm and he couldn't see any bone peeping out, so he supposed the injury could be classified as superficial. He'd tucked the loose flap of skin back into place but he guessed it would need stitches to stay there.

"We got us a new doctor," said Conway. "Just arrived."

"Oh yes?" said Peter. He was losing sensation in his mangled leg.

"Nice guy. And good at his job, too." It seemed a fatuous remark to make: everyone chosen by USIC was nice and good at their job.

"Glad to hear it."

"So," pursued Conway, "let's go see him. Now."

But Peter refused to go straight to the infirmary, insisting that he must first stop off in his quarters. Conway wasn't keen.

"It won't make any difference to the doctor how you're dressed," he pointed out. "And they'll clean you up with disinfectant and stuff."

"I know," said Peter. "I want to check for messages from my wife."

Conway blinked in bemusement. "Can't it wait?" he said.

"No, it can't wait," said Peter.

"OK," said Conway, and nudged the steering wheel. Unlike Peter, who couldn't distinguish one concrete façade from another, he knew exactly where to go.

As soon as Peter walked into the USIC building, he was overcome with a fit of shivering. His teeth chattered as Conway led him to his quarters.

"You're not gonna keel over, are you?"

"I'm fine." The atmosphere inside the complex was glacial, a vacuum laced with chilled, sterile oxygen lacking any of the other natural ingredients that would have made it air. Each breath hurt his lungs. The light seemed bunker-dim, ghastly. But didn't he always feel this way, whenever he'd been in the field for a while? He always needed to acclimatize.

By the time they got to his room, Conway was very agitated indeed. "I'll be right outside," he said. "Try to make it quick. I don't want a dead preacher on my hands."

"I'll do my best," said Peter, and shut him away from view. Fever, or some other disorder, was swelling the vessels in his head, and his teeth were still chattering so hard that his cheeks and jaw ached. Dizziness and lethargy came in waves, trying to knock him off his feet.

As he switched on the Shoot, he wondered if he was wasting precious seconds in which his life could be saved. But he doubted it. If the bite had poisoned him, USIC's medical clinic was unlikely to have an antidote. The poison would do whatever the poison was going to do, and it would either happen with a bunch of concerned faces hanging over him or it would happen in the privacy of his own space. Maybe he had only hours to live. Maybe he would be the new pathologist's first challenge, a corpse full of alien venom.

If so, he wanted, before he lost consciousness, to read just once more that Bea loved him and that she was OK. The Shoot glowed to life and a small green light near the bottom of the screen winked on and off, indicating that an invisible net was sweeping through the universe to find any words that might be from his wife.

Her message, when it came, was brief.

There is no God, she wrote.

2 2

ALONE WITH YOU

BY MY SIDE.

"Carpenter," said a voice floating above him.

"Mm?" he responded.

"When I was a kid, people assumed I'd be a carpenter. I had a talent for it. But then . . . this is all a con, you know."

"A con?"

"This air of sophistication medicine gets wrapped in. The doctor magician, the great master surgeon. Baloney. Fixing the human body doesn't require that much finesse. The skills you need . . . I tell ya, it's just carpentry, plumbing, sewing."

Dr. Adkins was proving his point by pushing a sewing-needle through Peter's flesh to add another loop of fine black thread to the row. He was almost done. The stitches formed an elegant design, like a tattoo of a swallow in flight. Peter felt nothing. He was generously dosed with analgesics on top of having been injected with two whacks of local anesthetic, and this, combined with his exhaustion, put him beyond the reach of pain.

"Do you think I've been poisoned?" he asked. The operating theater seemed to be expanding and contracting slightly, in rhythm with his pulse.

"Nothing in your blood to suggest you have," said Adkins, tying the final knot.

"And what about . . . uh . . . I forgot his name. The doctor you came here to . . . uh . . . the one who died . . ."

"Everett."

"Everett. Have you established what killed him?"

"Yup." Adkins tossed the needle onto the suture tray, which was immediately removed by Nurse Flores. "Death."

Peter laid his embroidered arm across the white linen napkin covering his chest. He wanted to sleep now.

"But the cause?"

Dr. Adkins pursed his lips. "A cardiovascular accident—with the emphasis on 'accident.' His grandfather died the same way, apparently. These things happen. You can eat healthy foods, keep fit, take vitamins . . . But sometimes, you just die. It's your time." He raised one eyebrow. "I guess *you*'d call it an appointment with God."

Peter flexed his fingers, appraised his tattoo of stitches again.

"I thought it was *my* time for a while there."

Adkins chuckled. "You'll live to preach another day. And when you go back, just in case you cross paths with those nasties again, here's my advice." He clamped his hands together, mimed a violent swing. "Take a golf club."

Peter was too drugged to walk, so someone trundled him out of the surgery in a wheelchair. Two pale hands appeared from behind him and spread a cotton blanket over his knees, tucked it around his hips, deposited a transparent plastic bag containing his sandals in his lap.

"Thank you, whoever you are," he said.

"You're welcome, I'm sure," said Grainger.

"Oh, gosh, I'm sorry," said Peter. "I didn't see you in the surgery."

She wheeled him, straight and steady, along the sunlit corridor toward the big double doors. "I was in the waiting room. I don't like the gory stuff."

Peter lifted his arm, displayed the pure white bandage. "All fixed up," he said.

Even before she replied, he could sense she was not impressed. Her wrists, gripping the handles of the wheelchair, were tense—tenser than they needed to be.

"You don't take care of yourself when you're out there," she said. "For Christ's sake, you're skin and bone. And yeah, I know I'm blaspheming. But look at you."

He stared down at his wrists, which had always been bony, he thought.

Well, maybe not *that* bony. The thick bandage made his arm look more emaciated somehow. How angry was Grainger? Just a bit exasperated? Furious? The distance between the medical center and his quarters would take several minutes to cover, which was a long time when you were in the hands of someone who was upset with you. Weakened by the analgesics and the shock of Bea's message—which returned to his mind over and over like a wave of nausea—he was suddenly overcome by a belief that other men had often described to him when he'd given them pastoral counseling—a deep, despondent conviction that no matter what they did, no matter how good their intentions, they were doomed to bitterly disappoint women.

"Hey, I made an effort not to let my ears get so burnt this time," he said. "Give me some points for trying."

"Don't patronize me."

Grainger pushed him through the double doors, veered him sharply to the right.

"Kurtzberg was the same," she remarked. "And Tartaglione. They looked like skeletons in the end."

He sighed. "We all look like skeletons in the end."

Grainger grunted irritably. She wasn't finished chastising him yet. "What goes wrong out there in Freaktown? Is it you or them? They don't feed you, is that it? Or they just don't eat, period?"

"They're very generous," Peter protested. "They've never . . . I've never felt that I'm being starved. It's just that they don't eat a lot themselves. I think most of what they grow and . . . uh . . . process . . . gets put aside to feed the USIC personnel."

"Oh, great! So we're exploiting them now?" Grainger veered him round another corner. "I tell you, we've bent over backward to do the right thing here. Bent over backward. There's too much riding on this to fuck it up with an imperialist fiasco."

Peter wished they'd had this conversation a lot earlier, or that they could have saved it for later—any time but now. "Uh . . . what's riding on this?" he said, struggling to stay upright in the chair.

"Oh, for Christ's sake. Isn't it obvious? Are you *that* much of a babe in the woods?"

I just do God's work; my wife asks the penetrating questions, he was about to say. It was true. Bea was always the one who needed to know *why,* who scratched under the veneer of what she was told, who refused to fall into step with the game everyone else was playing. She was the one who read the fine print in contracts, she was the one who would explain to him why an apparently wonderful opportunity was full of pitfalls, she was the one who could see through a scam even if it came disguised in Christian wrapping. Grainger was right: he was a babe in the woods.

He hadn't been born one, that's for sure. He'd turned himself into one, by force of will. There were many ways of becoming a Christian but the way that had worked for him was to switch off his capacity for cynicism, switch it off like a light. No, that was the wrong comparison . . . he'd . . . he'd switched *on* the light of trust. After so many years of playing games, exploiting everyone he met, stealing and lying and worse, he'd remade himself into an innocent. God had wiped the slate clean. The man who'd once littered his conversation with casual expletives like "Jesus fucking Christ" became the man who said "gosh." There was no other way. You were either a raging alcoholic or you didn't touch drink. Same with cynicism. Bea could handle it—in moderation. He couldn't.

But then: There is no God. From Bea. Please, Lord, no. Not from Bea.

Bea, too, had trundled him in a wheelchair once, in the hospital where they first met. Exactly like Grainger was wheeling him now. He'd broken both his ankles jumping out of a warehouse window and had spent several days in Bea's ward with his legs strung up in the air. Then one afternoon she unshackled him, got him into a wheelchair and pushed him to the x-ray department for a post-op assessment.

"Can you just whizz me through one of these side exits for a minute so I can have a cigarette?" he'd said.

"You don't need nicotine, handsome," she'd replied, from a sweet-smelling spot behind and above him. "You need your life to change."

"Well, here you are," said Grainger. "Your home away from home." They'd reached the door that was labeled P. LEIGH, PASTOR.

As Grainger was helping him to his feet, one of the USIC electricians, Springer, happened to be passing by.

"Welcome back, preach!" he called. "You want any more wool, you know where to find me!" And he sauntered on down the hall.

Grainger's lips were close to Peter's ear as she said softly, "God, I hate this place. And everybody who works here."

But please don't hate me, thought Peter as he pushed open the door and they walked in together. The atmosphere that greeted them was stale and slightly sour from two weeks' lack of air conditioning. Motes of dust, disturbed by the intrusion, swirled in a beam of light. The door fell shut.

Grainger, who'd had one arm on his back in case he lost his balance, threw the other one around him too. In his confusion, he was slow to realize she was embracing him. And not only that: it was a different embrace from the one they'd had before. There was passion and female need in it.

"I care about you," she said, digging her forehead into his shoulder. "Don't die."

He stroked her awkwardly. "I don't intend to."

"You'll die, you'll die, I'll lose you. You'll go weird and distant and then one day you'll just disappear." She was weeping now.

"I won't. I promise."

"You bastard," she cried softly, holding him tighter still. "You scumbag, you lying . . ."

She broke the embrace. The pale fabric of her clothing was marked with dirt from the harvest fields of the ᓴᕝᐊᔅ.

"I won't drive you to see those freaks again," she said. "Someone else can do it."

"I'm sorry," he said. "Whatever you want." But she was already gone.

There was no further message from Bea. At his command, a network of ingenious technology searched the cosmos for her thoughts and found nothing. Only that same cry of desolation, still glowing on the screen, just those four awful words, hanging in a contextless gray void. No name attached— neither hers nor his. Just the raw sentence.

He sat at the Shoot and prayed for strength. He knew that if he didn't

reply now, and keep it short, he was liable to pitch forward and go unconscious right there.

His clumsy fingers were poised to type the words of Psalm 14:1: *The fool
has said in his heart, there is no God.* But then God entered Peter's heart
and cautioned him that this would be stupid. Whatever had happened to
Bea, she didn't need criticism.

Maybe there had been another natural disaster? Some horrific event in
a foreign country that had swamped Bea's head with the pain of useless empathy? Or maybe it had happened closer to home, in Britain? A catastrophe
that had left thousands of people homeless, devastated, bereaved?

Psalms to the rescue again: *Thou shalt not be afraid for the terror by
night; nor for the arrow that flieth by day; Nor for the pestilence that walketh
in darkness; nor for the destruction that wasteth at noonday. A thousand
shall fall at thy side, and ten thousand at thy right hand; but it shall not come
nigh thee.*

But what if . . . what if it *had* come nigh to Bea? What if she'd been
hit by an earthquake or a flood? What if, right at this moment, she was
stranded and dazed, camped in the ruins of their house? But no, no, be
logical, their house must be intact, or else she wouldn't be able to write to
him. USIC had given them a Shoot and it was set up in the study upstairs,
connected to a mainframe the size of a filing cabinet. The existence of
Bea's message proved she was safe. Except that a person alienated from God
could never be safe.

As dihydromorphine, chloroprocaine and exhaustion dragged him
more and more insistently toward sleep, he began to panic. He must write,
and yet he couldn't. He must say something, break the silence, and yet if he
chose the wrong words he would regret it forever.

Finally, he let go of any notion of quoting Bible verses or giving advice.
He was her husband, she was his wife: that was the only thing he could be
sure of.

> Bea, I don't know what's brought you to this point but I love you and
> I want to help you if I can. Please tell me what's wrong and please
> forgive me if it's something I should have already known. I've just

come out of surgery. A few stitches, nothing serious. I got bitten
in the field. Explain later. Will crash for a bit now but please, I'm
worried about you, I love you, I know this sounds absurd but I'm
there for you, I really am.

He sent this flying and collapsed into bed.

A little while later, without speaking, Grainger came and lay next to him.
She rested her head on his naked chest, and her shoulder was in such a
position that it would have been unnatural not to cup it in his hand. So
he cupped it in his hand. She moved closer against him, let him feel the
warmth of her flesh. Her small fingers stroked his abdomen, her palm
traced the hollow where the ribs began. Then she took hold of his penis,
which was already erect. Before he could speak, Bea was there with them,
reassuring him with her eyes that it was all right. Grainger lifted her tunic.
Her pale breasts were freckled. He kissed one while Bea finished undress-
ing and crawled onto the bed. Grainger held his penis upright, allowing
Bea to lower herself onto it. He ejaculated the instant he was inside.

As soon as he awoke, he smelled the odor of betrayal. He had committed adultery in his heart, and—worse—dragged his wife into his disloyal
fantasy, making her an accomplice. He and Bea had always been faithful to
each other; he never took advantage of the vulnerable females who passed
through his ministry. He was a one-woman man and Bea was his woman.
Wasn't she?

He lay still for a while, shielding his eyes from the sunlight with his good
arm. A hangover-style headache throbbed in his temples. His tongue and
lips had dried out. His injured arm felt OK—well, numb—but his shin hurt
like a burn. He had no idea how long he'd slept: fifteen minutes or fifteen
hours. A memory of the dream lingered, tempting him with its phantasm
of love, its enchanted mirage in which all grief and hurt and estrangement
was smoothed over by desire.

Thirst pushed him to his feet. He drank greedily straight from the tap,
noisy as a dog, until his stomach sloshed. The doctor had told him to go
ahead and take showers, get soap and water on his wounds, but not scratch

at the stitches if they got itchy; they would dissolve by themselves when their work was done. Peter unfastened and unrolled the bandages, unveiling the mended flesh. The soft white cotton was hardly stained at all, the injuries neat. He showered, toweled himself dry, carefully reapplied the bandages. He put on jeans and a faded orange T-shirt emblazoned OUTREACH TASKFORCE BASILDON. Both garments felt too big. He rummaged inside his knapsack for some socks, pulled out a small plastic bag with squishy, semi-liquid contents he couldn't identify at first. It was the remains of a meal he'd been given by the ᴌᴖᴀᴤ a long time ago, before he'd grown accustomed to their food: a slab of suety stuff that tasted of vinegar. Loath to offend them, he'd claimed he wasn't hungry and would eat it later. The bag was a clammy weight in his palm, like an animal organ removed from a carcass. He looked around for somewhere conspicuous to put it so that he wouldn't forget it again.

On the table next to the fridge, he spotted something unfamiliar. A plastic medication bottle and a handwritten note.

Take 2 every 4 hours if needed. G.

Had Grainger been here while he slept? Or had she brought these with her when she wheeled him back from the surgery? He couldn't remember her doing anything in his room besides embracing him. But maybe she'd already dropped off the medication earlier, while he was being seen by Doctor Adkins. Forward thinking.

He picked up the bottle, read the contents. These pills were stronger than any you could get over the counter in an English pharmacy. But the pain he felt was not in his flesh.

He checked for new messages from Bea. There were none.

The ghost of Bing Crosby was talking when Peter walked into the mess hall. Mucous membranes in a larynx that had once nestled in a human throat, long since dispersed into the soil of Holy Cross Cemetery in Los Angeles, had made some sounds that were captured on magnetic tape in 1945, and that tape, digitized and lovingly reconfigured, was being broadcast through the cafeteria's public address system. The dozen or so USIC personnel scattered around the armchairs and tables were oblivious, carrying on their conversations or simply focusing on their food and drink. The disembodied voice of Judy Garland—smaller mucous membranes, vibrating more excitedly—joined Crosby's in a rehearsed off-the-cuff routine about trying on hats, intended to epitomize the gulf between men and women. Stanko, behind the coffee bar, switched on the smoothie machine, drowning out the ancient voices under a whirr of crushed coffee-flavored ice.

"What's good today, Stanko?" asked Peter when his turn came.

"Pancakes."

Bing Crosby, having interrupted the flow of Garland's prattle, had started singing: "When I've got my arm around you and we're going for a walk, must you yah-ta-ta, yah-ta-ta, yah-ta-ta, yah-ta-ta, talk, talk, talk . . ."

"Anything savory?"

Stanko lifted the lid on a metal vat, releasing a hearty smell. "Beef Stroganoff."

"I'll have that. And a mug of tea."

"Aristotle, mathematics, economics, antique chairs," warbled Bing. "The classics, the comics, darling, who cares?"

Stanko handed Peter a plastic plate of richly hued, steaming food, a plastic beaker of hot water, a paper sachet of dairy powder and a tea bag with a minuscule picture of Buckingham Palace on the tag.

"Thank you," said Peter.

"Enjoy, bro."

"Looks good."

"Best Stroganoff you can get," affirmed Stanko, deadpan. Sardonic humor? Maybe he was on the level. Right now, Peter doubted his own ability to judge.

He walked to a free table—there was just one left—and sat down with his meal. While Bing Crosby pretended to annoy Judy Garland with chatter about golf, Peter began to eat the beef, which he knew was whiteflower that had been pounded with a stone and then dried and fried. The sauce tasted wrong—too sweet, too cloying. Fragments of young whiteflower stalk had been dyed bright orange to resemble carrot and there were blanched slivers of half-mature whiteflower leaf that were supposed to be onions. He wished

USIC would ditch these faked concoctions and just eat whiteflower the way the ⌂∩⌐⌐ ate it. There were so many good, wholesome recipes going un-used here.

"*When there's music softly playing,*" crooned Judy Garland, "*and I'm sit-ting on your lap, must you yah-ta-ta, yah-ta-ta, yah-ta-ta, yah-ta-ta, yap, yap, yap . . .*"

"Mind if I sit here?" A real, living female voice in competition with a dead, long-ago one.

He looked up. It was Hayes. He motioned her to go ahead, apprehensive that she would ask him how he was, a question he wasn't sure he could answer without breaking down and telling the whole story. But as soon as Hayes took her seat, it became clear that she was only interested in the surface of the table, to rest a thick book on. Glancing at the pages as he ate his food, Peter identified the patterns of Sudoku, Kakuro, Hitori, Fillomino and other mathematical puzzles, neatly completed in pencil. Hayes bent over the book with an eraser clutched between her thumb and forefinger. With fastidious care, she began to rub out the pencil marks.

"*It's so nice to close your lips with mine,*" cooed Bing and Judy in perfect harmony.

Five minutes later, Peter's plate was empty and Hayes's iced coffee was untouched, forgotten. She was hunched over, absorbed in her task. Her mouth was slightly open, her downcast eyes had soft, luxurious lashes; she impressed Peter as prettier and more soulful than he'd previously thought. He was touched, deeply touched, deeply *moved* all of a sudden, by her al-truistic labor.

"That's very considerate of you," he heard himself say.

"Excuse me?"

"Very community-minded."

She stared at him, uncomprehending.

"Rubbing out the pencil marks," he explained, wishing he hadn't spo-ken. "It gives other people a chance to do the puzzles."

She wrinkled her brow. "I'm not doing it for other people. I'm gonna do these puzzles again myself." And she returned to the work at hand.

Peter sat back and drank his tea. Hayes's serene focus no longer struck him as attractive. Instead there was something creepy about it. OK, he wasn't a puzzle man himself, so the appeal of filling in those squares was already mysterious to him, but he appreciated that it presented a pleasant challenge for other minds. But doing the same puzzle over and over . . .

A burst of laughter from the other side of the room failed to disturb Hayes's concentration. It came from Tuska, Maneely and the guy who'd escorted Peter back from the settlement, what was his name—Conway. They appeared to be playing a game of rudimentary magic with three plastic cups and a rivet. "How'd you *do* that? How'd you *do* that?" Conway kept saying, to Tuska's delight. Elsewhere, USIC personnel reclined in armchairs, flipping through *Fly Fishing*, *Classic Cartoons*, *Vogue* and *The Chemical Engineer*. Peter remembered Tuska's "Légion Étrangère" lecture: *It's best if you've got a team of individuals who can deal with being in permanent limbo. People who won't go crazy.* Maybe Hayes was a prime example of a person who wouldn't go crazy. Someone who did her job, caused no trouble beyond a few pages torn out of a lesbian porn magazine, and, when she retired to her quarters, could while away the hours and days and months on perpetually erased puzzles.

". . . of Crosby's fabled modesty that he was able to describe such a sublime work of art as 'fluffy' and 'a novelty,'" the DJ was intoning. "We'll now hear an unissued alternate take. Listen out for Bing stumbling on the word 'annuity' and other evidences of inadequate rehearsal. Worth it, though, for the slightly closer proximity of Garland to the microphone, allowing us to fantasize that she's right in the room with us . . ."

"Sorry to interrupt you again," said Peter.

"No problem," said Hayes, rubbing out just one more numeral before looking up.

"I was wondering about these music broadcasts. Are they old?"

She blinked, then opened her ears to register the sound. "Very old," she said. "Those singers, I don't think they're even alive anymore."

"No, I meant, are these shows, with the announcements and everything, put together by someone here at USIC, or did they already exist?"

Hayes cast an eye around the mess hall. "Rosen does them," she said. "He's not here right now. He's a surveyor and draftsman. You've probably seen his drawings of the Centrifuge & Power Facility displayed in the Projects Hall. Awesomely accurate work. I still stand and look at it sometimes."

She shrugged. "His music I can take or leave. It's background noise to me. I'm glad he likes it so much. Everybody's got to like something, I guess." She didn't sound convinced.

A fresh flush of pain went through Peter—the memory of Bea's message again. "The Mother," he said, trying to get a grip.

"Excuse me?"

"The nickname you suggested for the Centrifuge & Power Utility."

"Facility," she corrected him with a smile. She closed her puzzle book and slipped the eraser into a pocket of her shirt. "Nobody calls it the Mother. I know that. They still call it the Big Brassiere. Or actually the BB." Preparing to leave, she hugged her book to her bosom. "No sense getting upset. As my mom used to say, Don't sweat the small stuff."

When in distress, don't self-obsess, reach out. Bea's motto. Their motto as a couple, actually.

"Do you miss your mom?"

Hayes hugged her book tighter, reflective. "I guess. She died a long time ago. She would've been proud of me, I'm sure, being chosen for this mission. But I had a good job already when she died, so she was proud already. It's not like I was a deadbeat."

"I was a deadbeat once," said Peter, maintaining eye contact. "Alcoholic. Drug addict." Hayes was the wrong person to share such intimacy with, he knew that, but he couldn't help himself. He was, he belatedly realized, in no state to be here at all, among these people. He needed to be unconscious, or among the ⳬⲁⲋ.

"It's not a crime," said Hayes in her unemphatic monotone. "I don't judge anybody."

"I committed crimes," said Peter. "Petty crimes."

"Some people go through that, before they straighten out. Doesn't make them bad people."

"My father was terribly disappointed in me," Peter pushed on. "He died a broken man."

Hayes nodded. "It happens. You work here for a while, you find out that lots of your colleagues have got real sad case histories. And some haven't. No two stories alike. It doesn't matter. We all get to the same point."

"And what point is that?"

She raised her fist in a gesture of triumph, if *triumph* was the right word for a fist so loosely clasped, so amiably raised, so unlikely to be noticed in the context of this convivial cafeteria. "Working toward the future."

Dear Peter, wrote Bea at last, after he had spent what felt like an eternity in prayer and worry.

I'm sorry I didn't respond for so long. I don't want to talk about what's happened but I owe you an explanation. Thanks for reaching out to me. It doesn't change the way things are, and I don't think you can understand where I'm at now, but I do appreciate it.

A lot of things led up to this. Our church has hit a setback, to put it mildly. Geoff has absconded with all funds. He and the treasurer were having an affair and they've flown the coop together, no one knows where. But the accounts are cleared out. They even took the collection bags. Remember how we prayed for God's guidance to choose a pastor to replace you? Well, Geoff was the one. Make of that what you will.

Opinion is divided on what to do next. Some people want to sort out the mess and try to keep it going and some feel we should just start afresh with a new church. They even asked me if I would be pastor! Brilliant timing.

Two days before this fiasco, I started back at work. I thought it would be bliss with Goodman gone. But the place has changed. It's filthy, to begin with. The floors, the walls, the toilets. No cleaning staff and no prospect of getting any. I pulled out a mop and got busy on one of the bathrooms and Moira almost bit my head off. "We're nurses, we're not here to scrub floors" she said. I said "What about staph? What about open wounds?" She just stared me down. And maybe she's right—the workload is bad enough as it is. A&E is pandemonium. People running around unsupervised, shouting, scuffling with the orderlies, trying to wheel their sick mums and dads and kids up to the wards before we've had a chance to triage them.

All the patients are poor now. Not a single well-educated middle-class specimen among them. Moira says that anyone with money has abandoned the NHS completely. The rich ones defect to France or Qatar, the average folks find themselves a nice walk-in pay-per-service clinic (there's loads of them springing up everywhere—whole new communities are forming around them). And our hospital gets the dregs. That's Moira's word for them, but to be honest that's what they are. Stupid, boorish, loud, ugly and very, very frightened. Forget about caritas—it's a struggle to even keep your cool when you've got a drunken lout with blurry tattoos yelling straight into your face and jabbing you in the shoulder with his nicotine-stained finger. It's an endless parade of bloodshot eyes, acne, smashed noses, slashed cheeks, cracked ribs, scalded babies, botched suicides. I know I used to complain that Goodman was trying to fill our hospital with easy cases but there is a difference between offering all levels of society access to medical care and letting an entire hospital be overrun by a pig-ignorant mob.

Time has run out on me, it's 6:30, I have to go to work now. I haven't even told you what happened to make me finally snap but it's hard for me to face it myself and writing takes so long and I didn't know I would write this much about other things. I thought I would just come straight out with it, but it will cause you so much pain and I wish so much I could spare you that pain forever. I must go now.

Love,

Bea.

At once, he responded:

Dear Bea,

I am so worried about you, but relieved to hear your "voice." It's true that we all misunderstand each other—only God has perfect understanding—but we shouldn't let the grief of that frustration stop us trying. My work with the Oasans confirms this over and over.

The news about Geoff and our church is deplorable but the church does not consist of Geoff or the treasurer or a particular building. This setback may prove to be a blessing in disguise. If we owe money we can repay it and even if we can't, it's only money. What goes on in the hearts and souls of human beings is the important thing. It's encouraging that our congregation wants to start afresh with a new church. Ordinarily, people are terrified of change so this is an amazing example of courage and positivity. Why not start a simple fellowship in someone's front room? Just like the early Christians. Complicated infrastructure is a luxury, the real essentials are love and prayer. And it's great that they want you to be pastor. Don't be angry, I think you would do a superb job.

Your comments about the changes at the hospital are only natural given the increased stress but they confirm my sense that maybe now is not the time for you to be working. You have a baby growing inside you. Or at least I hope you do—have you had a miscarriage? Is that what's shaken your faith in God? I'm worried sick. Please tell me.

Whatever it is, it has taken you to a very bad place spiritually. Those "pig-ignorant" people who are crowding into your hospital are all precious souls. God doesn't care whether someone has acne or bad teeth or a bad education. Please remember that when you met me I was an alcoholic waste of space. A deadbeat. If you had treated me with the contempt I deserved I would never have been rescued, I would have just got worse and been "proof" that types like me are beyond redemption. And who knows, some of the women you're seeing on the wards may have family traumas not a million miles away from what happened to you. So please, no matter how hard it is, try to hang on to your compassion. God can make miracles occur in that hospital of yours. You say yourself that these people are frightened. Deep down, they know they desperately need something that medicine can't give them.

Write as soon as you can, I love you,

Peter

Δ was finally going down, turning the horizon golden caramel. There would be a drawn-out dusk of almost wearisome beauty and then it would be night for a long, long time. Peter stowed the putrefying Oasan food in his bag and left the compound.

He walked for a mile or so, in the hope that the USIC base would disappear from his view—or, more to the point, that he would disappear from the view of anyone at USIC who might have seen him leave. But the flat, featureless terrain meant that the buildings remained obstinately in sight, and a trick of perspective made them seem less far-off than they were. Rationally, he knew it was highly improbable he was being watched, but instinctively he felt under constant surveillance. He walked on.

The direction he'd chosen was westward into the wilderness—that is, not toward the Oasan settlement and not toward the Big Brassiere. He'd fantasized that if he walked far enough he would eventually reach mountains, streams, or at least some rocky knoll or marshy bog that would let him know he was elsewhere. But the tundra went on forever. Level brown earth, occasionally enlivened by a clump of whiteflower luminescing in the sunset, and, whenever he turned to look back, the eerie concrete mirage of the USIC base. Tired, he sat down and waited for ᴧ𝐮 to sink below the land.

How long he waited, he couldn't tell. Maybe two hours. Maybe six hours. His consciousness detached itself from his body, hovered above it, somewhere in the ᴌ𝐨. He forgot the purpose of his coming out here. Had he decided he couldn't spend the night in his quarters, and opted to sleep in the open air? His knapsack could serve as a pillow.

When it was almost dark, he sensed he was no longer alone. He squinted into the gloom and spotted a small, pale creature about five meters away. It was one of the bird-like vermin that had consumed the whiteflower harvest and bitten him. Just one, separated from the rest of its kind. It waddled cautiously in a wide circle around Peter, nodding its head. After a while, Peter realized it was not nodding but sniffing: its snout smelled food.

Peter recalled the moment when the flesh of his arm sprayed blood, recalled the nauseating pain of the bite to his leg. A convulsion of anger disturbed the numbness of his grief. He considered killing this vicious creature, stamping on its body, grinding its sharp-fanged little skull under his heel—not in revenge but self-defense, or so he could pretend. But no. The thing was pathetic and comical, hesitant in the dark, vulnerable in its aloneness. And the food it smelled was not Peter's flesh.

Slowly and smoothly, Peter extracted the prize from his knapsack. The creature stopped in its tracks. Peter laid the plastic bag on the ground and shuffled backward. The creature moved in and punctured the bag with its teeth, releasing a sweetish stench. Then it gobbled up the entire pile, plastic shreds and all. Peter wondered if, as a result, the creature would end up dying a more horrible death than if he'd stomped on its head. Maybe this was what the Hindus meant by karma.

After the satisfied animal had left him, Peter sat and stared at the distant lights of the base, his "home away from home," as Grainger had called it. He stared until the lights turned abstract in his brain, until he could imagine the sun rising in England, and Bea hurrying through the car park of her hospital toward the bus stop. Then he imagined Bea getting into that bus and taking a seat amongst a heterogeneous variety of humans, some chocolate brown, some yellowish, some beige or pasty pink. He imagined the bus traveling along a road crowded with vehicles, until it pulled up in front of a store that sold household knick-knacks, cheap toys and other bargains for 99 pence, round the corner from a street with a laundromat on the corner, a hundred and fifty meters from a semi-detached house with no curtains in the front windows, and an internal staircase carpeted in threadbare maroon, leading up to a room in which stood a machine on which Bea could, when she was ready, type the words **"Dear Peter."** He raised himself to his feet and started walking back.

> Dear Peter,
> No I have not had a miscarriage and please don't lecture me about compassion. You just don't understand how impossible everything has become. It's all about the scale of a problem and the available energy to deal with it. When someone gets their leg blown off by a bomb, you rush them into surgery, mend the stump, fit them with a prosthetic, give them physiotherapy, counseling, whatever it takes, and a year later, they may be running a marathon. If a bomb blows off their arms, legs, genitals, intestines, bladder, liver and kidneys, IT IS DIFFERENT. We need a certain proportion of things to be OK in order to be able to cope with other things going wrong. Whether it's

a human body or Christian endeavor or life in general, we can't keep
it going if too much of what we need is taken away from us.

I won't tell you about the other things that were freaking me out
in the last week or two. It's current affairs stories that will only bore
you. New wars in Africa, systematic slaughter of women and children,
mass starvation in rural China, crackdown on protesters in Germany,
the ECB scandal, my pension being wiped out, stuff like that. None
of it will seem real to you up there. You are spooning Bible verses
into the hungry mouths of Oasans, I appreciate that.

Anyway, what you need to know is that last week, for various
reasons, I was stressed out and, as usual when I'm stressed out,
Joshua picks up on my vibes. He was cowering under the furniture,
dashing from room to room, crying, circling round and round my
shins but not letting me pick him up or stroke him. It was the last
thing I needed and it was driving me crazy. I just tried to ignore
him, get on with some chores. I ironed my uniform. The ironing
board was at an awkward angle and the cord didn't have enough
slack and I was too tired and hassled to set it up any other way so I
just coped. At one point, I set the iron down and it fell off the edge
of the board. Instinctively I jumped backward. My heel came down
hard on something, there was a sickening cracking snapping noise
and Joshua screamed, I swear he screamed. Then he was gone.

I found him under the bed, trembling and hyperventilating. Eyes
wide in pain and terror. I'd broken his back leg. I could see that.
There was not one iota of trust in his eyes, he flinched when I spoke.
I was the enemy. I fetched the gardening gloves so that he wouldn't
scratch or bite me and I took hold of his tail and pulled him out. It
was the only way. I got him into the kitchen, put him on the table
and attached the lead to his collar. He was calmer. I thought he was
in shock, maybe in too much pain to do anything except sit there
panting. I picked up the phone to call the vet. The kitchen window
was open as usual. Joshua shot out as if someone fired him from a
cannon.

I looked for him for hours. I covered the same ground over and

over until I just couldn't walk anymore and it was pitch dark. Then
I had to go to work (night shift). It was hell. Don't say anything,
it was hell. At 4 am I was wearing two hospital gowns because my
uniform was covered in feces. An obese insane guy had been tossing
it out of his bed, smearing it on the bedrails, bellowing the place
down. The orderlies were off-duty, it was just me, little Oyama and
a new girl who was sweet but kept disappearing. The feces-tossing
guy's mother was camping out in the visitors' room through the
night—nobody had been able to throw her out. She's in there with a
six-pack of Pepsi and some half-eaten takeaway (this is supposed to
be a hospital!) and every so often she pops her head in and checks
that we're taking good care of her boy. "You a bitch!" she yells at
me. "You cruel! I call police! You not a real nurse! Where the real
nurses?" On and on and on and on.

In the morning, I go home, still wearing the two gowns with a
cardigan over them. Must have looked like an escapee from a loony
bin. I get out of the bus two stops early so I can cut through the
park in case I find Joshua there. It's a long shot and I don't really
have any hope that I'll see him. But I do.

He's strung up by the tail from a tree. Alive. Two kids of maybe
twelve are hoisting him up and down on a rope, making him spin,
jerking him so he twitches. A red haze falls over my eyes. I don't
know what happened next, what I did to these kids, my memory is
a blank. I only know I didn't kill them because they weren't there
anymore when I came to. There's blood on my fists, under my nails.
I wish I'd killed them. Yeah, yeah, yeah, I know—underprivileged
kids, rotten upbringing, in dire need of love and forbearance, why
not come to our Outreach program blah blah blah—THESE EVIL
SCUMBAGS WERE TORTURING JOSHUA!

I pick him up. He's still breathing, but shallowly. The base of his
tail is shredded and one eye looks gouged out but he's alive and I
think he recognizes me. Ten minutes later I'm at the vet's. It's before
opening hours but I must have kicked and screamed because they
open up for me. He lifts Joshua from my arms and gives him an
injection.

"OK, it's done," he says. "Do you want to take him home or leave him here?"

"What do you mean, take him home?" I say. "Aren't you going to do anything for him?"

"I just did," he says.

Afterward, he tells me he had no way of guessing I was willing to pay any amount of money for surgery. "Nobody's bothering with that sort of thing nowadays," he says. "I can go for five, six hours without anyone coming in, and then when someone finally walks through the door with a sick pet, all they want is for it to be put to sleep." He puts Joshua into a plastic bag for me. "I won't charge you," he tells me.

Peter, I'm only going to say this once. This experience is not educational. It is not instructive. It is not God moving in mysterious ways, it is not God figuring out exactly what sublime ultimate purpose can be served by me stepping on Joshua's leg and everything after. The Savior I believed in took an interest in what I did and how I behaved. The Savior I believed in made things happen and stopped things happening. I was deluding myself. I am alone and frightened and married to a missionary who's going to tell me that the fool has said in his heart there is no God, and if you don't say it it will just be because you're being diplomatic, because in your heart you're convinced I made this happen through my faltering of faith, and that makes me feel even more alone. Because you're not coming back to me, are you? You like it up there. Because you're on Planet God. So even if you did come back to me, we still wouldn't be together. Because in your heart you'd still be on Planet God, and I'd be a trillion miles away from you, alone with you by my side.

IV

IN HEAVEN

23

A DRINK WITH YOU.

The bites were poisonous after all. He was sure of it. Underneath the bandages, the wounds looked clean, but the damage was done. The network of veins and arteries inside his flesh was industriously polluting all his organs with infected blood, feeding his brain with venom. It was only a matter of time. First he would become delirious—he felt that coming on already—and then his system would shut down, kidneys, liver, heart, guts, lungs, all those mysteriously interdependent globs of meat which needed poison-free fuel to keep functioning. His body would evict his soul.

Still seated at the Shoot, he lifted his face to the ceiling. He'd been staring at Bea's words so long that they'd burned into his retinas and now reappeared above him, illegible as mildew. The lightbulb hanging above his head was one of those energy-saving ones, more a coil than a bulb, like a segment of radioactive intestine suspended from a wire. Above that, a thin lid of ceiling and roof, and above that . . . what? Where in the universe was Bea? Was she above him, below him, to his right or to his left? If he could fly, if he could launch himself through space faster than the speed of light, what good would it do him? He had no idea where to go.

He mustn't die in this room. No, no, not in this sterile cubicle, sealed inside a glorified warehouse of concrete and glass. Anywhere but this. He would go . . . out there. To the ᓚᕭᔅ. Maybe they had a cure. Some sort of folk remedy. Probably not, given how loudly they'd lamented when they saw him get bitten. But he should die in their company, not here. And he mustn't see Grainger; he must avoid her at all costs. She would waste what little time he had left, trying to keep him at the base, trying to drag him to the infirmary where he would die under pointless observation and then be reduced to a storage problem, rammed into a shelf of a mortuary refrigerator.

How long have I got, Lord? he prayed. *Minutes? Hours? Days?* But there were some questions that one must not ask of God. There were some uncertainties one must face alone.

"Hi," he said to the porky woman with the snake tattoo, the gatekeeper to his escape. "I don't think you ever told me your name. But it's Craig, isn't it? 'B. Craig,' as the nameplate on your door has it. Nice to see you again, B."

She looked at him as though he was covered in hideous sores. "Are you OK?"

"Just a bit . . . underslept," he said, eyeing the vehicles parked behind her in the bay. There were half a dozen, including the one Grainger used for her drug deliveries. He hoped Grainger was fast asleep in bed, drooling into her pillow, keeping those pretty, scarred arms safe under the sheets. He wouldn't want her to feel responsible for what he was about to do. Better to put pressure on Craig, who, like everyone else here, would be indifferent to his death. "What's the 'B' stand for?" he said.

The woman frowned. "Can I help you?"

"I would like to . . . uh . . . requisition a vehicle." Inside his head, banked up on his tongue, he had a barrage of speech ready to push her objections aside, to steamroller her reluctance. *Do what I want. Do what I want. You were told from the beginning I would require a vehicle; now it's happening just as you were warned it would, so don't be difficult, don't resist me, just say yes.* "Just for an hour or two," he added, as the sweat prickled his eyebrows. "Please."

"Sure." She gestured toward a black station wagon that reminded Peter of a hearse. "How about this one? Kurtzberg used it all the time."

He swayed on his feet. The victory was too easy; there must be a catch. "Fine with me."

She opened the door and let him slide in. The key was already in the ignition. He'd expected to have to sign papers, produce a driving license, or at least exert some serious psychological pressure. Maybe God was cutting through the obstacles for him. Or maybe this was just the way things worked here.

"If you're underslept," said Craig, "maybe you shouldn't drive."

Peter glanced over his shoulder. Kurtzberg's bed—actually a small mattress with a floral coverlet and matching pillow—was right there in the back.

"I'll get all the sleep I want, soon," he assured her.

He drove into the wilderness, toward . . . Freaktown. Its official name escaped him for the moment. Peterville. New Zion. Oskaloosa. Please rescue Coretta from trouble, Lord. May your presence be felt in the Maldives.

His brain felt swollen, bulging out against his eyeballs. He shut his eyelids tight, to keep his eyeballs in. It was OK to do that while driving. There was nothing to collide with, no road to veer off or stay on. Only the general direction was important. And he wasn't actually sure if he was going the right way. This vehicle had the same navigation system as Grainger's, but he had no idea how to use it, no idea what buttons to push. Bea would be able to figure it out, if she were given a—

He pressed his foot on the accelerator. Let's see how fast this thing could go. There was a time for taking things easy and a time for really moving.

Was he really moving? It was hard to tell in the dark. The headlights illuminated only an abstract swathe of the terrain and there were no landmarks. He might be traveling at dangerous speed or he might be marooned in the soil, tires churning endlessly, getting nowhere. But no: he could see clumps of whiteflower whizzing past like reflective strips on a highway. He was making progress. Progress away from the USIC base, at least—he couldn't be sure he was getting any closer to the follows settlement.

If only this vehicle were a living creature, like a horse or a dog, it would sniff its way unerringly back to the place Kurtzberg had visited so many times before. Just like Joshua when he—

An ugly sound startled him. It was a human cry, right here in the vehicle with him. It was his own voice. It was his own cry. He bashed the steering wheel with his fists, butted the back of his head repeatedly against the seat. A brick wall would have been better.

He wiped his eyes and peered through the front window. In the distance, dimly, he could see something looming up from the tundra. Architecture of some sort. He'd been traveling a few minutes only, so it couldn't be the settlement yet. Unless, in his delirium, time had telescoped, so that he'd driven for hours in what seemed like seconds, or unless he'd fallen asleep at the wheel. But no. The looming thing was two huge spherical structures: the Big Brassiere. He was heading in the wrong direction.

"Christ!" It was his voice again. He'd slipped and forgotten to say "Crisis." He must calm down. God was in control.

He pressed a button on the navigation screen. It glowed brighter, as if delighted to be touched. The words CENTR POWER FAC manifested near the top, with an arrow that symbolized his vehicle pulsing underneath. He pushed some more buttons. No other destinations came up; instead, he was quoted various data about temperature, water level, oil, speed, fuel consumption. With a grunt of frustration, he wrenched the steering wheel ninety degrees, sending a flurry of damp soil flying. The Big Brassiere, the Centrifuge, the Mother, whatever the damn thing was called, receded into the darkness as he sped into unknown territory.

Within another few minutes, he saw the shapes and colors of the Oasan settlement. It wasn't possible, it just wasn't possible, it should be an hour yet before he got here, and yet . . . the blockish, uniform architecture, the flat roofs, the lack of pinnacles or poles of any sort, the amber glow . . . As he drove closer and closer, his vehicle's headlights illuminated lozenge-shaped bricks. Unmistakable. The poison must have deranged his sense of time.

He was approaching from an unfamiliar angle and couldn't get his bearings. Grainger's usual arrival point was the building with the white star and the illegible residue of

WEL COME

clinging to its outer wall like bird cack. But he was not with Grainger now. Never mind: his church was the true landmark. Set apart from the town, it would stand out in the bare prairie, hologrammed into life by the headlights.

He drove around the perimeter, looking for his church. He drove and drove. His high beam picked out nothing more substantial than pallid clumps of whiteflower. Eventually, he saw tire-tracks in the soil: his own vehicle's. He'd come full circle and there was no church. It was gone; it had been destroyed and every trace of it removed as if it had never existed. These people had rejected him, cast him off in one of those unfathomable flashes of antipathy that missionary history was so full of—cruel severances that came out of nowhere, revealing that all the intimacy you thought you'd forged was just an illusion, a church built on quicksand, a seed planted in windblown topsoil.

He stopped the vehicle and switched off its engine. He would walk into the settlement, lost and befuddled, and he would try to find someone he knew. He would call "Jesus Lover . . ."—no, that would be ridiculous. He would call . . . "ﬡﬢﬔﬕﬖﬡ." Yes, he would call "ﬡﬢﬔﬕﬖﬡ," he would call "ﬡﬢﬔﬡﬖ," he would call all the ﬖﬡﬔ names he could remember. And eventually someone—a Jesus Lover or more likely not a Jesus Lover— would be intrigued by his bellowing and come to him.

He opened the car's door and stumbled out into the humid night. There were no lights in the settlement, no signs of life. Unsteady on his feet, he lurched sideways, almost bashing his shoulder against the wall of the nearest building. He steadied himself against the polished bricks with his palm. As always, they felt warm and sort of alive. Not alive like an animal, but alive like a tree, as if each brick was a bulge of hardened sap.

He'd walked only a few meters when his hand plunged suddenly into empty space. A doorway. No string-of-beads curtain hanging in front of it, which was odd. Just a big rectangular hole in the building, with nothing visible inside but darkness. He ventured in, knowing that at the opposite end of the chamber there would be another door which would open out onto a network of laneways. He moved gingerly through the claustrophobic black space, shuffling one small step at a time in case he blundered face-first into an internal wall, or was apprehended by gloved hands, or tripped on some other obstacle. But he reached the far side without encountering anything; the room seemed to be completely empty. He found the back door—again, just a hole without a curtain—and emerged into the lane.

Even in daylight, all the ﬖﬡﬔ's lanes looked much the same; he'd never negotiated them without a guide. In the dark, they felt more like tunnels than pathways, and he advanced painfully slowly, hands outstretched, like a man newly blinded. The ᏚᏬᎠᎪᏃ might not have eyes, but they had something else that allowed them to move confidently through this maze.

He cleared his throat, willing himself to call out names in an alien language he imagined he'd learned quite well, but which he now realized he had only the feeblest grip on. Instead, he remembered the 23rd Psalm, his own paraphrase of it, carefully devised to remove consonants. He'd sweated blood over it and now, for some reason, it came to him.

"The Lord be he who care for me," he recited as he shuffled through the darkness. "I will need no more." This voice was the same one he used for preaching: not strident, but quite loud and with each word articulated clearly. The moisture in the atmosphere swallowed the sounds before they had a chance to carry very far. "He bid me lie in green land down. He lead me by river where no one can drown. He make my soul like new again. He lead me in the path of Good. He do all this, for he be God. Yea, though I walk through the long dark corridor of death, I will fear no evil, for you are with me. Your care wand make me feel no harm can come. You feed me even while unfriendly men look on in envy. You rub healing oil on my head. My cup runneth over. Good unfolding and comfort will keep me company, every day of my life. I will dwell in the home of the Lord forever."

"Hey, that's good!" cried an unfamiliar voice. "That's *good!*"

Peter whirled around in the dark, almost losing his balance. In spite of the fact that the words were friendly, he was adrenalized with instinctive, fight-or-flight fear. The presence of another male (for the voice was definitely male), a male of his own species, somewhere very nearby but invisible, felt as life-threatening as a gun-barrel to the temple or a knife in the side.

"I take my hat off to you! If I had a goddamn hat!" the stranger added. "You're a pro, what can I say, sheer class! *The Lord is my shepherd* without a fucking shepherd in sight. Only a couple of 't's and 's's in the whole damn thing!" Curses aside, the sincerity of the admiration was clear. "You wrote that for the ᏚᏬᎠᎪᏃ, right? Like, Open up for Jesus, this won't hurt. A banquet with all the bones taken out, a meal in a milkshake, thesaurus semolina. *Bravo!*"

Peter hesitated. A living shape had materialized from the gloom behind him. As far as he could make out, it was human, hairy and naked. "Tartaglione?"

"Got it in one! Put it there, palomino! *Come va?*" A bony hand grasped Peter's. A very bony hand. The fingers, though strong, were skeletal, pressing spoke-like phalanges into Peter's softer flesh.

"What are you doing here?" said Peter.

"Oh, you know," was the drawled reply. "Just hanging out, shootin' the breeze. Watching the grass not grow. Happy campering. What are *you* doing here?"

"I . . . I'm the minister," said Peter, divesting his hand from the stranger's. "The pastor for the ⴲⵓⴰⵙ . . . We built a church . . . It was right here . . ."

Tartaglione laughed, then coughed emphysemically. "Beg to disagree, *amigo*. Nobody here but us cockroaches. No gas, food, floozies or floorshows. *Nada*."

The word was released like a bat into the humid night, and disappeared. All of a sudden, a lightbulb went on in Peter's brain. He wasn't in C-2 at all: he was in the settlement that the ⴲⵓⴰⵙ had abandoned. There was nothing here but air and brick walls. And a naked madman who'd slipped through the net of human civilization.

"I got lost," Peter explained, feebly. "I'm sick. I think I've been poisoned. I . . . I think I may be dying."

"No shit?" said Tartaglione. "Then let's get drunk."

The linguist led him through the dark into still more dark, then through a doorway into a house where he was made to kneel and told to get comfy. There were cushions on the floor, large plump cushions that might have been cannibalized from a couch or armchair. They felt mildewy to the touch, like the decaying peel of orange or lemon. When Peter sat on them, they sighed.

"My humble abode," said Tartaglione. "*Après* the exodus, *moi*."

Peter offered a grunt of gratitude, and tried to breathe through his mouth rather than his nose. Oasan interiors usually smelled of nothing much except food and the honeydew air currents that continually flowed through the windows and lapped around the walls, but this room managed to reek of human uncleanness and alcoholic ferment. In its center stood a large object which he'd thought at first was a sleeping crib, but which he now identified as the source of the liquor stink. Maybe it *was* a sleeping crib, serving as an alcohol storage tub.

"Is there any light?" asked Peter.

"You bring a torch, *padre?*"

"No."

"Then there isn't any light."

Peter's eyes simply couldn't adjust to the darkness. He could see the whites—or rather yellows—of the other man's eyes, a bristle of facial hair, an impression of emaciated flesh and flaccid genitals. He wondered if Tartaglione had developed, over the months and years he'd lived in these ruins, a kind of night vision, like a cat.

"What's wrong? You choking on something?" asked Tartaglione.

Peter hugged himself to stop the noise coming from his own chest. "My . . . my cat died," he said.

"You brought a *cat* here?" the other man marveled. "USIC's allowing *pets* now?"

"No, it was . . . it happened at home."

Tartaglione patted Peter's knee. "Now, now. Be a good little camper, don't lose Brownie points. Don't use the H-word. The H-word is *verboten! È finito! Distrutto! Non esiste!*"

The linguist was making theatrical motions with his palms, shoving the word *home* back into its gopher-hole each time it popped up. Peter suddenly hated him, this poor crazy bastard, yes, he hated him. He closed his eyes tight and opened them again, and was bitterly disappointed that Tartaglione was still there, that the darkness and the alcohol stink were still there, when what *should* be there when he opened his eyes was the place he should never have left, his own space, his own stuff, Bea. He moaned in grief. "I miss my wife."

"None of that! None of that!" Tartaglione sprang up, waving his arms about. His bare feet thumped a mad rhythm on the floor, and he emitted a bizarre "*sh!-sh!-sh!-sh!*" as he danced. The effort of it triggered an extended burst of coughing. Peter imagined loose fragments of lung swirling in the air like nuptial confetti.

"Of course you miss your wife," muttered Tartaglione when he'd calmed down slightly. "You miss every damn thing. You could fill a book with all the things you miss. You miss dandelions, you miss bananas, you miss mountains and dragonflies and trains and roses and . . . and . . . fucking junk mail for Christ's sake, you miss the rust on the fire hydrants, the dogshit on the pavement, the sunsets, your dumbass uncle with the lousy taste in shirts and the yellow teeth. You want to throw your arms around the old sleazeball and say, 'Uncle, what a great shirt, love your aftershave, show me your porcelain frog collection, and then let's promenade down the old neighborhood, just you and me, whaddaya say?' You miss snow. You miss the sea, *non importa* if it's polluted, bring it on, oil spills, acid, condoms, broken bottles, who cares, it's still the sea, it's still the ocean. You dream . . . you dream of newly mown lawns, the way the grass smelled, you swear you'd give ten thousand bucks or one of your kidneys if you could have just one last whiff of that grass."

To emphasize his point, Tartaglione sniffed deeply, a stage sniff, a sniff so aggressive it sounded as if it might damage his head.

"Everyone at USIC is . . . concerned about you," said Peter carefully. "You could get transported home."

Tartaglione snorted. "*Lungi da me, satana! Quítate de delante de mí!* Haven't you read the USIC contract? Maybe you need help translating the lingo? Well, I'm your man. Dear highly skilled misfit: We hope you enjoy your stretch on Oasis. There's chicken tonight! Or something very like it. So settle in, don't count the days, take a long view. Every five years, or maybe sooner if you can prove you're batshit insane, you can have a trip back to the festering scumhole you came from. But we'd rather you didn't. What you wanna go back there for? What's the point? Your uncle and his goddamned frog collection are gonna be history soon. Everything's gonna be history soon. *History* will be history." He paced back and forth in front of Peter, his feet scuffling the dirty floor. "USIC concerned about me? Yeah, I'll bet. That fatso chink dude, forget his name, I can just see him lying awake at nights thinking, *I wonder if Tartaglione is OK. Is he happy? Is he getting enough vitamins? Do I hear a bell tolling, has a clod been washed away by the sea, is a piece of the continent gone, am I just a little fucking diminished here?* Yeah, I can feel the love. Who's on love duty today?"

Peter dipped out of consciousness for a second or two. The flesh of his brow was contracting tight against his skull, pushing in on the bone. He remembered once having a fever, some sort of forty-eight-hour flu, and lying helpless in bed while Bea was at work. Waking in the middle of the day half-deranged and parched with thirst, he was puzzled to feel a hand on the back of his head, lifting it from the pillow, and a glass of iced water raised to his lips. Much later, when he was better, he found out that Bea had traveled all the way home to give him that drink, and then all the way back to the hospital, in what was supposed to be her lunch break.

"I would have survived," he'd protested.

"I know," she said. "But I love you."

When Tartaglione spoke again, his tone was philosophical, almost apologetic. "No use crying over spilt milk, my friend. Let it go rancid and live for *mañana*. The unacknowledged USIC motto, wise words, wise words, worthy of being tattooed on every forehead." A pause. "Hell, this place ain't so bad. I mean this place I've got here: *casa mia*. It's more cheerful in daylight. And if I'd known you were coming, I'd've had a bath, you know. Maybe trimmed the old *barba*." He sighed. "I had everything here once. *Tutte le comodità moderne. Todo confort.* Torches, batteries, shaver for my pretty face, paper to wipe my ass on. Pens, too. Prescription glasses, magnification 3:5. The world was my mollusk."

"What happened?"

"Moisture," said Tartaglione. "Time. Wear and tear. Conspicuous absence of a multitude of people working round the clock to keep me supplied with goodies. But!" He rummaged about, and there was the clatter of plastic, followed by a glotch of submersion into the liquid-filled crib. "But before they vamoosed, the little fairies in the bathrobes did teach me one of their secrets. The most important secret of all, right? *Alchemy.* Turning boring old plants into booze."

There was another glotch. Tartaglione handed Peter a mug, took a slurp from his own, and continued raving.

"You know the most wacko thing about the USIC base? The one, single, most sinister thing? I'll tell you: No distillery. And no whorehouse."

"That's two things."

Tartaglione ignored him, fueled now. "I'm no genius, but I comprehend a few truths. I understand nouns and verbs, I understand the labial fricative,

I understand human nature. And you know what people immediately start looking for, five minutes after they arrive someplace new? You know what's on their minds? I'll tell you: How are they gonna get laid, and where are they gonna find some mind-altering substances. That's if they're normal. So what does USIC do, in its infinite wisdom? What does USIC do? It scours the entire world to dig up people who don't need those things. Needed them *once upon a time* maybe, but not anymore. Sure, they crack a few jokes about cocaine and pussy—you've met BG, I take it?"

"I've met BG."

"Three hundred pounds of bluff. That guy has killed off every natural need and desire known to mankind. All he wants is a job and a half-hour under the big yellow umbrella to flex his biceps. And the others, Mortellaro, Mooney, Hayes, Severin, I forget all their damn names now, but who cares, they're all the same. You think *I'm* weird? You think *I'm* crazy? Look at those zombies, man!"

"They're not zombies," said Peter quietly. "They're good, decent people. They're doing their best."

Tartaglione spluttered fermented whiteflower juice into the space between them. "Best? *Best*? Take your cheerleader pom-poms off, *padre*, and look at what USIC has got here. What's the score on the vibrancy meter? Two and a half out of ten? Two? Anybody offered to teach you the tango or sent you a love letter? And how's USIC's maternity wing going? Any pitter-patter of *piccoli piedi*?"

"My wife's pregnant," Peter heard himself say. "They wouldn't let her come."

"Of course not! Only zombies need apply!"

"They're not—"

"*Cáscaras*, empty vessels, every single one of them!" declared Tartaglione, rearing up with such righteous vehemence that he farted. "This whole project is . . . *nefasto*. You cannot create a thriving community, let alone a new civilization, by putting together a bunch of people who are no fucking trouble! *Scuzi*, pardon me mama, but it cannot be done. You want Paradise, you gotta build it on war, on blood, on envy and naked greed. The people who build it have got to be egomaniacs and lunatics, they've gotta want it so damn bad they'll trample you underfoot, they've got to be charismatic and charming and they've got to steal your wife from under your nose and then sting you for a loan of ten bucks. USIC thinks it can assemble a dream team, well yeah, it *is* a dream, and they need to wake up and smell their wet pajamas. USIC thinks it can sift through a thousand applicants and pick the *one* man and the *one* woman who'll get along with everybody, who'll do their job without being a pain in the ass, who won't throw tantrums or get depressed or freak out and spoil the whole damn thing. USIC is looking for people who can feel at home anywhere, even in a big fat nowhere like this, people who don't care, they're not fussed, no sweat, keep cool, hey ho, hey ho, it's off to work we go, who needs a home anyway, who cares if the house where you grew up is burning down, who cares if your old neighborhood is underwater, who cares if your folks are being slaughtered, who cares if a dozen scumbags are raping your daughter, everybody's gotta die sometime, right?"

Tartaglione was panting. His vocal cords were in no shape for such heavy use.

"You really believe the world is coming to an end?" said Peter.

"Jesus fucking Christ, *padre*, what kind of a Christian *are* you? Isn't this the whole fucking point for you? Isn't this what you've been waiting for for thousands of years?"

Peter leaned back, allowed his weary body to sink into the rotting cushions. "I haven't been alive that long."

"Oooo, was that a putdown? Did I detect a putdown? Is this a ruffled godboy I see before me?"

"Please . . . don't call me *godboy*."

"You one of those decaffeinated Christians, *padre*? The diabetic wafer? Doctrine-free, guilt-reduced, low in Last Judgment, 100 percent less Second Coming, no added Armageddon? Might contain small traces of crucified Jew?" Tartaglione's voice dripped with contempt. "Marty Kurtzberg—now *he* was a man of faith. Grace before meals, 'A Mighty Fortress Is Our God,' none of this *Krishna-has-wisdom-too* crapola, always wore a jacket and pressed pants and polished shoes. And if you scratched him deep enough, he'd tell you: These are the last days."

Peter swallowed hard on what tasted like bile. Even if he was dying himself, he didn't think these were the world's last days. God wouldn't let go of the planet he loved so easily. He'd given His only son to save it, after all. "I'm just trying . . . just trying to treat people the way Jesus might have treated them. That's Christianity for me."

"Well, that's just fine and dandy. *Molto ammirevole!* I take my hat off to you, if I had a hat. Come on, godboy, have some booze, it's good."

Peter nodded, closed his eyes. Tartaglione's rant about USIC was starting to sink in. "So . . . the reason why you guys are all here . . . USIC's mission . . . it's not trying to extract . . . it's not . . . uh . . . finding new sources of . . . uh . . ."

Tartaglione scoffed more lung fragments into the air. "All that is *over*, palomino! *Over!* We've got the trucks but no depot, *capisce?* We've got the ships but no harbor. We've got the hard-on and the jism but the woman is *dead*. Pretty soon, *all* the women will be dead. The earth has *had* it. We've mined all the mines, we've exploited all the exploits, we've eaten all the eats. *È finito!*"

"But what about here on Oasis? What's supposed to happen here?"

"Here? Didn't you get your Happy Pioneer T-shirt? We're *supposed* to be creating a nest, a nursery, a place where the whole shebang can start over again. You've heard of the Rapture? Are you a Rapture kind of godboy?"

Peter raised the beaker to his face again. He was struggling to remain awake. "Not really," he sighed. "I think it's based on a misreading of Scripture . . ."

"Well, this project here," declared Tartaglione, imperious in contempt, "is sorta like the Rapture by committee. Rapture Incorporated. The Department of Rapture. Worried about the state of the world? Your hometown's just been flattened by a hurricane? Your kids' school is full of gangsters and pushers? Your mama just died in her own *merda* while the nurses were busy divvying up the morphine? No gas for your car and the shops are looking kinda Zen? Lights have gone off and the toilet doesn't flush anymore? Future's looking distinctly *caca?* Hey, *non dispera!* There is a way out. Come to beautiful Oasis. No crime, no madness, no bad stuff of any kind, a brand new home, home on the range, no deer or antelope but hey, accentuate the positive, there never is heard a discouraging word, nobody rapes you or tries to reminisce about Paris in the springtime, no sense sniffing that old vomit, right? Cut the strings, blank the slate, let go of Auschwitz and the

Alamo and the . . . the fucking *Egyptians* for God's sake, who needs it, who cares, focus on tomorrow. Onward and upward. Come to beautiful Oasis. Everything's sustainable, everything works. Everything's laid out and ready. All it lacks is *you*."

"But . . . who is it *for*? Who's going to come?"

"Aha!" Tartaglione was in an ecstasy of derision by now. "That's the five-billion-ruble question, isn't it? Who's gonna come . . . Who's gonna come. *Muy interesante!* Can't have vipers in the nest, can we? Can't have crazies and parasites and saboteurs. Only nice, well-adjusted folks need apply. Except—get this—you'll need to pay your fare. I mean, there's a time for planting and a time for reaping, right? USIC can't invest forever; time to cash in. So who's gonna come? The poor schlub who works in the 7-Eleven? I don't think so. USIC's gonna have to take the filthy-rich folks— but not the assholes and the prima donnas, no no no, the nice ones with the salt-of-the-earth values. Multi-millionaires who give up their seat on the bus. Tycoons who are happy to hand-wash their T-shirts 'cause, you know, they wouldn't want to waste electricity. Yeah, I can see it now. Step right up, book early for fucking Raptureland."

Peter's brain was closing down, but as he began to drift toward oblivion he recalled the clean corridors of the USIC medical center, the surgical equipment still shrouded in plastic wrapping, the yellow-painted room littered with boxes marked NEO-NATAL.

"But when . . . when is this supposed to happen?"

"Any day now! Never! Who fucking knows?" yelled Tartaglione. "Soon as they build a baseball stadium? Soon as they've figured out how to make pistachio ice cream out of toenail clippings? Soon as they grow a daffodil? Soon as Los Angeles slides into the Pacific? Search me. Would *you* want to live here?"

Peter imagined himself sitting cross-legged near his church, with the Jesus Lovers gathered around him, all of them holding their woven Bible booklets open at a parable. The afternoon was going on and on indefinitely, everyone was lambent with sunlight, and Lover Five was bringing a food offering to the newest arrival in their community—Bea, wife of Father Peter, seated at his side. "I . . . it would depend . . ." he said. "It's a beautiful place."

The room fell silent. After a while, Tartaglione's breathing grew louder and more rhythmic, until Peter realized he was saying "Uh-huh. Uh-huh. Uh-huh," over and over. Then, in a voice thick with disdain, he added, "Beautiful. I see."

Peter was too tired to argue. He knew there were no rainforests here, no mountains, no waterfalls, no exquisitely sculpted gardens, no breathtaking cityscapes, Gothic cathedrals, medieval castles, flocks of geese, giraffes, snow leopards, whatever, all those animals whose names he couldn't recall, all those tourist destinations he'd seen other people so hungry to visit, all the attractions of the earthly life that he had, quite frankly, never lived. The glory of Prague to him was nothing more than a dim memory of a photograph; flamingos were just film footage; he'd been nowhere; he'd seen nothing; Oasis was the first place he'd ever allowed himself to bond with. The first place he'd ever loved.

"Yes, beautiful," he sighed.

"You are out of your mind, *padre*," said Tartaglione. "Deee-ranged. *Loco-loco-loco*. This place is beautiful like the grave, beautiful like maggots. The air is full of voices, have you noticed that? Worms in your ears, they burrow right in, they pretend to be just oxygen and moisture but they're more than that, they're more than that. Switch off the car engine, switch off your conversation, switch off Bing fucking Crosby, and what do you hear, instead of silence? The voices, man. They never let up, they're a liquid, a liquid language, going *whisper-whisper-whisper*, in your ear canals, down your throat, up your ass. Hey! Are you falling asleep? Don't die on me, *amigo*, it's a long night and I could use the company."

The pungent odor of Tartaglione's loneliness dispelled some of the fog in Peter's brain. He thought of a question he should have asked before, a question that would no doubt have occurred to Bea immediately. "Is Kurtzberg here?"

"What?" The linguist was jolted off course, yanked from the slipstream of his ranting.

"Kurtzberg. Is he living here too? With you?"

There was a full minute of silence. "We had a falling out," said the linguist at last. "You might say it was . . . a philosophical disagreement."

Peter couldn't speak anymore, but uttered a noise of incomprehension.

"It was about the ᗱᑕᗩᔕ," Tartaglione explained. "Those creepy, insipid, dickless, ass-licking little pastel-colored vermin." A slurp of the beaker, a glug of the gullet. "He loved them."

More time passed. The air whispered softly, making its endless reconnaissance of the boundaries and emptinesses in the room, testing the ceiling, prodding the joins of the walls, brushing the floor, measuring bodies, combing hair, licking skin. Two men breathed, one of them strenuously, one of them barely at all. It seemed that the linguist had said all he was going to say, and was now lost in his own stoic despair.

"Plus," he added, in the final moments before Peter lost consciousness, "I cannot stand a guy who won't have a drink with you."

24

THE TECHNIQUE OF

JESUS.

The night was supposed to last longer. Much, much longer. Darkness should have kept him captive for hundreds, maybe even thousands of years until the Resurrection came and God pulled all the dead from the ground.

That's what confused him, when he opened his eyes. He was supposed to be underneath the earth, or hidden under a blanket in an unlit house in an abandoned city, not even decomposed yet, just a lump of inert material that couldn't feel or see. There wasn't supposed to be light. Especially not such dazzling white light, brighter than the sky.

It was not the light of Afterlife; it was the light of a hospital. Yes, he remembered now. He had broken his ankles, running from the law, and he'd been taken to a hospital and pumped full of anesthetic so that mysterious figures in masks could mend his splintered bones. There would be no more running; he would have to take what was coming to him. A woman's face floated down over his own. The face of a beautiful woman. Bending over him as if he was a baby in a crib. On her bosom, a name tag that said Beatrice. She was a nurse. He liked her instinctively, as though he'd been waiting for her to turn up all his life. He might even marry her one day, if she said yes.

"Bea," he croaked.

"Try again," said the woman. Her face grew rounder, her eyes changed color, her neck shortened, her hair rearranged itself into a boyish cut.

"Grainger," he said.

"You got it," she said wearily.

"Where am I?" The light hurt his eyes. He turned his head aside, into a pale green cotton pillow.

"In the infirmary," said Grainger. "Whoa—keep that arm still, it's got an IV drip in it."

He did as he was told. A thin tube dangled against his cheek. "How did I get here?"

"I told you I'd always look out for you, didn't I?" said Grainger. Then, after a pause: "Which is more than you can say for God."

He let his tethered arm fall back onto the coverlet and smiled. "Maybe God is working through you."

"Yeah? Well, as a matter of fact there's medications for thoughts like that. Lurasidone. Asenapine. I can prescribe you some anytime you're ready."

Still squinting against the light, he craned his head round to look at the bag that fed his intravenous line. The liquid in it was transparent. Glucose or saline, not blood.

"The poison," he said. "What happened?"

"You weren't poisoned," said Grainger, with a tinge of exasperation in her voice. "You just got dehydrated, that's all. You didn't drink enough. You could have died."

He laughed, and the laughter morphed into sobs. He laid his fingers on his chest, roughly where the inky crucifix was or used to be. The fabric was sticky and cold. He'd poured Tartaglione's vile liquor down his chin and onto his breast, pretending to drink it. Here in the sterile air conditioning, its sweet stench of ferment was bad enough to choke the breath.

"Did you bring Tartaglione back?" he asked.

"Tartaglione?" Grainger's voice was augmented by muted exclamations of surprise from elsewhere in the room: they were not alone.

"You didn't see him?" said Peter.

"He was there?"

"Yes, he was there," said Peter. "That's where he lives. Out in the ruins. He's not a well man. He probably needs to go home."

"Home? Well, fancy that." Grainger sounded bitter. "Who would've thought it."

Moving out of his range of sight, she did something he couldn't identify, some emphatic or even violent physical action which caused a clattering noise.

"Are you all right, Grainger?" A male voice, half-sympathetic, half-cautioning. The doctor from New Zealand. Austin.

"Don't touch me," said Grainger. "I'm fine. Finefinefine."

Peter realized all of a sudden that the alcohol he could smell was not emanating solely from his own clothing. There was an additional tang in the air, a spirits tang, which might have been created by tearing open a few dozen disposable surgical wipes, but could just as easily have come from a few shots of whiskey. Whiskey consumed by Alex Grainger.

"Maybe Tartaglione is happy where he is." A female voice this time. Flores, the nurse. She spoke calmly, as though to a child, as though a cat had been sighted in a tree and a naïve youngster was insisting that somebody should climb up to rescue it.

"Oh, yeah, I'm sure he's happy as a clam," retorted Grainger, her sarcasm escalating so fast that Peter was no longer in any doubt she was disinhibited by booze. "Happy as the day is long. Hey, you like that?—'As the day is long.' That's a pun, right? Or maybe not a pun . . . Maybe irony? What would you call it, Peter?"

"Might be best to let our patient recover a bit more," suggested Austin.

Grainger ignored him. "Tartaglione was a real Italian, did any of you know that? Like, genuine. He grew up in Ontario, but he was born in . . . I forget the name of the place . . . he told me once . . ."

"Perhaps not relevant to our work here just now?" suggested Austin. Masculine as his voice was, it had taken on a slightly whiny edge. He wasn't used to dealing with unreasonable colleagues.

"Right, right," said Grainger. "None of us come from anywhere, I forgot, excuse me. We're the Foreign fucking Legion, like Tuska keeps saying. And anyway, who'd want to go home? Who'd want to go home when everything *there* is so fucked up and everything *here* is so fantastic? You'd have to be crazy, right?"

"Please, Grainger," warned Flores.

"Don't do this to yourself," said Austin.

Grainger started to weep.

"You're not human, you people. You're just not fucking human."

"There's no need for that," said Flores.

"What do *you* know about need?" cried Grainger, hysterical now. "Keep your fucking hands off me!"

"We're not touching you, we're not touching you," said Austin.

There was another crash of toppled equipment: a metal IV-stand, perhaps. "Where's my daddy?" Grainger whimpered, as she stumbled out. "I want my daddy!"

After the door slammed, the infirmary went quiet. Peter wasn't even sure if Austin was still around, but fancied he could hear Flores fussing about, beyond his field of vision. His neck was stiff and he had a pounding headache. The liquid in his IV bag drained unhurriedly into his vein. When it was all gone and the bag hung limp and wrinkled as a condom, he asked to be allowed to leave.

"Dr. Austin wanted to discuss something with you," said Flores, as she unhooked him. "I'm sure he'll be right back."

"Later, maybe," said Peter. "I really have to go now."

"It would be better if you didn't."

He flexed his fist. The puncture wound where the cannula had just been removed oozed bright blood. "Can I have a Band-Aid on this?"

"Of course," said Flores, rummaging inside a drawer. "Dr. Austin said he was sure you would be very . . . ah . . . anxious to have a confab with him. About another patient here."

"Who?" Peter was itching to get out; he must write to Bea as soon as possible. He should have written to her many hours ago, instead of driving off in a haze of melodrama.

"I couldn't say," said Flores, frowning her monkey frown. "If you'll just care to wait . . ."

"Sorry," said Peter. "I'll be back. I promise." He knew even as he uttered these words that they might be a lie, but they had the desired effect: Nurse Flores stepped backward, and he was out of there.

With nothing to show for his ordeal but a small ball of cotton wool taped to his wrist, he walked to his quarters, unsteady on his feet but stubbornly alive.

Various USIC employees passed him in the corridors, looking askance at his pitiful appearance. Only a few meters shy of his room, he met Werner.

"Hi," said Werner, holding two chubby fingers aloft as he passed by. It was a gesture that could have signified any number of things: a wave that was too lazy to employ the whole hand, a casual approximation of the peace symbol, an unwitting echo of a Christian benediction. More likely, it signified nothing except Werner's determination to get on with his engineering or hydraulics or whatever, without having to concern himself with desperate-looking weirdos.

"Well, bless you, *too*, pal," Peter felt like calling out to the disappearing Chinese. But that would be sarcasm. He must avoid that, it was a sin to have even considered it, a lapse, a disgrace. He must cling to his sincerity. It was all he had left. There must be no bile in his soul, no barb in his speech. To love without discrimination, to mean all creatures well, even a rabid dog like Tartaglione, even a waste of space like Werner: that was his sacred duty as a Christian, and his only salvation as a person. As he opened the door of his quarters, he counseled himself to expunge all dislike of Werner from his heart. Werner was a poor lamb, precious in the eyes of the Lord, a charmless creep who couldn't help being a charmless creep, a geeky orphan who'd grown into a specialized form of survivor. We are all specialized forms of survivor, Peter reminded himself. We lack what we fundamentally need and forge ahead regardless, hurriedly hiding our wounds, disguising our ineptitude, bluffing our way through our weaknesses. No one—especially not a pastor—should lose sight of that truth. Whatever he did, however low he sank, he must never stop believing all men were his brothers.

And all women.

And all ⲋⲣⲁⲋ.

Dear Bea, he wrote,

There is nothing I can say that would make what happened to Joshua feel like anything other than obscenely unfair. He was a wonderful, delightful creature and it hurts me so much to think of him dead and how he died. It's awful to be reminded in such a brutal way that Christians have no magic immunity to the evil actions of malicious people. Faith in Christ leads to amazing blessings and strokes of good fortune, as we've observed together many times, but the world remains a dangerous place and we remain—merely by being human—vulnerable to the horrors that humans can cause.

I'm angry too. Not at God, but at the sick bastards who tortured Joshua. I should love them, but I want to kill them, even though killing them wouldn't bring Joshua back. I need time to work through my gut feelings and I'm sure you do too. I'm not going to tell you to forgive these boys because I can't forgive them myself yet. Only Jesus was capable of that level of grace. All I will say is that I have caused great grief to others and I have been forgiven. I once robbed a house that had boxes of cancer drugs in the bedroom, piles of them. I know they were cancer drugs because I rummaged through them in case there was anything I could use. I stole a box of analgesics and left the rest scattered on the floor. In the years since, I've often thought about what effect that must have had on those people when they got home from the hospital or wherever they'd gone that day. I don't mean the analgesics—they could have replaced those pretty quickly, I expect. I mean the fact that they got robbed on top of everything else they were going through, that there was no mercy, no allowance made for their already impossible circumstances. The boys who tortured Joshua did that to us. What else can I say? I'm not Jesus.

But I am still your man. We've been through so much together. Not just as a Christian husband-and-wife team, but as two animals who trust each other. Whenever I think of the gulf that's come between us, I'm sick with sorrow. Please accept my love. In sermons sometimes, I've told people that what I was enchanted by, in that hospital ward when we first met, was the light of Christ that shone out of you. I believed that when I said it, but now I'm not so sure. Maybe I devalued you in order to score an evangelistic point. There is a light in you that's intrinsic to who you are, a marvelous spirit that would dwell in you even if you weren't a Christian, a spirit that will continue to make you special even if your rejection of God proves to be permanent. I love you and want you regardless of your religious faith. I miss you. Don't let go.

I'm sorry if I've given you the impression that I'm not interested in what's going on in the world—our world, that is. Please tell me more. Everything you can think of, anything that strikes you. There is no news here whatsoever—no newspapers, not even outdated ones, no access to any information about current affairs, no history books or indeed books of any sort, just puzzle books and glossy magazines about hobbies and professional pursuits. And even those are censored. Yes, there's an industrious little USIC censor vetting all the magazines and tearing out any pages they don't approve of!

I finally met Tartaglione, the linguist who went missing. He's a very addled individual, but he told me the truth about USIC's agenda. Contrary to our suspicions, they aren't here for imperialist or commercial reasons. They think the world is ending and they want to make a new start on Oasis. They're getting the place ready. For who, I don't know. Not for the likes of you, evidently.

He paused in his typing, re-read what he'd written, considered deleting everything after Don't let go. In the end he erased Not for the likes of you, evidently, added Love, Peter and pressed the button to transmit.

For the usual several minutes his words trembled on the screen, waiting to be released. Then, superimposed on the text like a burn from a branding iron, a terse warning manifested in livid letters: NOT APPROVED—SEEK ASSISTANCE.

He stood at Grainger's door and knocked.

"Grainger!" he yelled. "Grainger! Open up, it's me, Peter!" No reply.

Without even looking up and down the corridor to check if anyone was watching, he opened the door and barged into Grainger's quarters. He would drag her out of bed if she was asleep. Not violently, you understand. But she must help him.

The layout of her quarters was identical to his; her space equally Spartan. She wasn't in it. Her bed was made, more or less. A white shawl hung on the clothesline, hitched up to the ceiling. A constellation of water-drops glimmered on the inside of the shower cubicle. A half-empty bottle of bourbon, labeled simply BOURBON in red block-letters on a white sticker, and priced at $650, stood on a table. Also displayed on the table was a framed photograph of a craggy-faced middle-aged man wearing heavy winter clothes, cradling a shotgun. Behind him, under an ominous gray sky, the Grainger family farm was covered in snow.

Ten minutes later, he found Charlie Grainger's daughter in the pharmacy, a place where he ought not have been surprised to find her, since she was, after all, USIC's pharmacist. She was seated at a counter, dressed as usual, her hair neat and still a little damp. When he walked in, she was writing in an old-fashioned ring-binder, with a pencil clutched awkwardly in her short fingers. Honeycombs of modular shelving, mostly vacant but punctuated here and there with petite plastic bottles and cardboard boxes, towered over her. She was calm, but her eyelids were raw from crying.

"Hey, I wasn't serious about the anti-delusional medication," she joked as he approached. *Don't mention what I said in the infirmary*, her eyes pleaded.

"I need your help," he said.

"You're not going anywhere," she said. "At least not with me."

It was a moment before he realized she was referring to driving, to chauffeuring him somewhere that wasn't good for his health.

"I just tried to send a message to my wife," he said, "and it's been blocked. I've got to get through. Please."

She put down the pencil, closed the folder.

"Don't worry, Peter, I can fix it," she said. "Probably. Depends on how bad a boy you've been."

She stood up, and he noted once again that she wasn't very tall. Yet at this moment, he felt smaller still; he was the little boy who'd let his brand-new bicycle get stolen, he was the pitiful disgrace slumped on a vomit-stained sofa in the Salford Pentecost Powerhouse, he was the fumbling missionary who'd reached the end of his rope—and each of these Peters could only throw himself on the mercy of a long-suffering female, a mother who might reassure him that he was more valuable than any expensive gift, a wife who might reassure him that he could break a sacred promise and still be loved, a friend who might be able to pull him out of his latest crisis. When it came down to it, it was not Jesus but these women on whose mercy he threw himself, and who must decide if he'd finally gone too far.

His room, when they entered it together, was a mess. His knapsack, filthy from its trips to the field, lay in the middle of the floor, surrounded by loose balls of wool that had fallen off the chair. Loose pills were scattered across the table next to the upended medication bottle and Grainger's note about what to take if needed, which was odd as he couldn't remember opening the bottle. His bed was in a shameful state: the bedsheets were so tangled it looked as though he'd been wrestling in them.

Grainger ignored the chaos, sat in his chair and read the letter he'd written to Bea. Her face betrayed no emotion, although her lips twitched once or twice. Maybe she wasn't a strong reader, and was tempted to mouth the words? He stood at her side, and waited.

"I'll need your permission to change this," she said when she'd finished.

"Change it?"

"Remove a few . . . problematic statements. To get it past Springer."

"*Springer?*" Peter had assumed that whatever had blocked his message was automated, some sort of computer program which sifted language brainlessly. "You mean Springer has been reading all my letters?"

"It's his job," said Grainger. "One of his jobs. We multi-task here, as you may have noticed. There are several personnel who check the Shoots. I'm pretty sure right now it's Springer."

He stared down at her. There was no shame or guilt or defensiveness on her weary face. She was merely informing him of a detail from the USIC duty roster.

"You take it in *turns* to read my private letters?"

Only now did it appear to register on her that there might, in some people's universe, be anything odd about this arrangement. "Is that such a big deal?" she brazened. "Doesn't God read your thoughts?"

He opened his mouth to protest, but couldn't speak.

"Anyway," she continued, in a down-to-business tone. "You want this message sent. So let's do it." She scrolled through his words. "The stuff about USIC censoring the magazines has to go," she said, pecking at the keyboard with her stubby nails. Letter by letter, the words "And even those are censored," and the twenty after that, disappeared from the screen. "Ditto the stuff about the world ending." More pecks. She stared at the glowing text, evaluating her amendments. One or two more words caught her eye and she eliminated them. Her eyes were bloodshot and she seemed sad beyond her years. "No end of the world," she murmured, in a gently scolding tone. "Uh-*uh*."

Satisfied with what she'd done, she pressed the transmission button. The text trembled on the screen while, elsewhere in the compound, another pair of tired eyes examined it. Then it vanished.

"Another five thousand bucks down the hatch," said Grainger, with a shrug.

"Sorry?"

"Each of your Shoots costs about five thousand dollars to send," she said. "And each of your wife's also, of course, to receive." She wiped her face with her hands, breathing deeply, trying to suck much-needed energy from her own palms. "Another reason why the personnel here aren't communicating daily with a bunch of pals back home."

Peter tried to do a mental calculation. Math wasn't his strong suit, but he knew the number was appallingly big. "Nobody told me," he said.

"We were told not to tell you," she said. "No expense spared for the missionary man."

"But why?"

"USIC wanted you real bad," said Grainger. "You were, like, our first VIP."

"I never asked . . ."

"You didn't need to ask. My . . . guidelines were to give you anything you wanted. Within reason. Because, you know, before you came, things were getting kinda . . . strained."

"Things?" He couldn't imagine what things. A spiritual crisis amongst the USIC personnel?

"Our food supply got cut off for a while. No more whiteflower from our little friends." Grainger smirked sourly. "They come across so meek and mild, don't they? But they can be very determined when they want to be. We promised them a replacement for Kurtzberg, but they thought it was too slow in coming. I guess Ella Reinman was ploughing through a million priests and pastors, poking them to see what was inside, then flunking them. Next pastor please! What's your favorite fruit? How much would you miss Philadelphia? Frying ducklings alive—OK or not OK? What would it take to make you lose patience with my stupid questions and wring my scrawny neck?" Grainger's hands mimed the action, her thumbs crushing her interrogator's windpipe. "Meanwhile in Freaktown, our little friends couldn't wait. They flexed the only muscle they could flex, to make USIC hurry up and find you." Observing the bemusement on his face, she nodded, to signal that he must stop wasting energy on incredulity and just believe.

"How bad did it get?" said Peter. "I mean, did you starve?"

Grainger was annoyed by the question. "Of course we didn't starve. It just got . . . *expensive* for a while. More expensive than you wanna think about."

He tried to think about it and discovered she was right.

"The stand-off wouldn't have been such a big deal," she went on, "if only we could grow stuff ourselves. God knows we've tried. Wheat. Corn. Maize. Hemp. Every seed known to man has gone into this soil. But what comes up is not impressive. Vanity farming, you could call it. And of course we tried growing whiteflower too, but it was the same story. A few bulbs here, a few bulbs there. Like cultivating orchids. We just can't figure out how those guys get it to grow in large amounts. What the hell do they fertilize it with? Fairy dust, I guess."

She fell silent, still seated in front of the Shoot. She'd spoken in a dull, enervated tone, as though it was a stale subject, a humiliation too pathetic and tedious to revisit yet again. Gazing down at her face, he wondered how long it had been—how many years—since she had been truly, deeply happy.

"I want to thank you," he said, "for helping me. I was in . . . a bad state. I don't know what I would have done without you."

She didn't take her eyes off the screen. "Got somebody else to help you, I guess."

"I don't just mean the message. I mean, coming to find me. As you said, I could have died."

She sighed. "It actually takes a lot for someone to die. The human body is designed not to quit. But yeah, I was worried about you, driving off like that when you were sick."

"How did you find me?"

"That part wasn't difficult. All our vehicles have collars with bells on, if you get my drift. The tough part was getting you into my car, 'cause you weren't rousable. I had to wrap you in a blanket and drag you along the ground. And I'm not strong."

The vision of what she'd done for him flared up in his mind, even though he had no memory of it. He wished he had a memory of it. "Oh, Grainger . . ."

She stood up abruptly.

"You really love her, don't you?" she said. "Your wife."

"Yes. I really love her."

She nodded. "I thought so."

He wanted to embrace her, hesitated. She turned away.

"Write her as much as you want," she said. "Don't worry about the cost. USIC can afford it. And anyway, you saved our bacon. And our chicken, and our bread, and our custard, and our cinnamon, et cetera, et cetera, et cetera."

From behind, he laid his hands on her shoulders, aching to let her know how he felt. Without looking round, she took hold of his hands with her own, and pulled them hard against her chest, not as low as the bosom, but near the sternum, where her heart beat.

"And remember," she said. "When you mention USIC, keep it nice. No accusations, no end of the world."

I'll be back, he'd told Flores, just to shut her up, just to smooth his getaway, but now that he had a chance to think it over, a promise ought to be a promise. Grainger was gone now, the message to Bea was sent. He should find out what Dr. Austin had on his mind.

He showered, washed his hair, massaged his scabby scalp. The water swirling around his feet was brownish, gurgling down the plughole like tea. On his two admissions to the USIC infirmary he must have introduced more bacteria into their sterile environment than they'd encountered in all the years previous. It's a wonder they didn't dunk him in a vat of disinfectant the size of Tartaglione's booze bath before consenting to treat him.

Shower finished, he dried himself carefully. The cannula puncture had already healed up. Various scratches from earlier on were crusted over. The bite wound on his arm was doing nicely; the one on his leg stung a bit, and looked a bit swollen, but if it got worse a quick course of antibiotics would fix it. He replaced the bandages and dressed in jeans and T-shirt. His dishdasha was so rank from Tartaglione's hooch that he considered giving up on it, but he stuffed it in the washing machine instead. The CON-SERVE WATER—COULD THIS LOAD BE HAND-WASHED? placard was still in place, complete with its ARE YOU OFFERING, LADY? addendum. He half-expected the graffiti to have been erased by some routine intruder, some multi-tasking engineer or electrician assigned to inspect everybody's rooms for stuff that might offend the USIC ethos. Nothing would surprise him now.

"Good to see you," said Austin, appraising Peter's conventional attire with obvious approval. "You're looking much better."

"I'm sure I *smell* better," said Peter. "I'm sorry I stank up your surgery."

"Couldn't be helped," breezed the doctor. "Alcohol is evil stuff." That was as close as he was going to come to mentioning Grainger's unprofessional insobriety. "You're walking a bit stiffly," he observed, as the two of them moved from the doorway into the consulting room. "How are your injuries?"

"They're fine. I'm just not used to wearing clothes—these sorts of clothes—anymore."

Austin smiled insincerely, no doubt adjusting his professional assessment of how well Peter was doing. "Yes, there are days *I* quite fancy coming to work naked," he joked, "but the feeling passes."

Peter smiled in return. One of his flashes of pastoral instinct, like the one he'd had about Lover One's inconsolable sadness, came to him now: this doctor, this ruggedly good-looking New Zealand male, this man called Austin, had never had a sexual relationship with anyone.

"I want to thank you," said Austin, "for taking our conversation seriously."

"Conversation?"

"About the natives' health. About getting them to come to us so we can check them out, diagnose what they're dying of. Obviously you've been spreading the word." And he smiled again, to acknowledge the unintended evangelical meaning of the phrase. "At long last, one of them has."

Long last. Peter thought of the distance between the USIC base and the ⴽⵕⴰⵚ settlement, the time it took to drive there, the time it would take to walk. "Oh my . . . gosh," he said. "It's so *far.*"

"No, no," Austin reassured him. "Remember Conway? Your Good Samaritan? Apparently he wasn't satisfied with the signal strength of some doodad he installed at your church. So he went there again, and lo and behold—he came back with a passenger. A . . . friend of yours, I gather."

"Friend?"

Austin extended his hand, motioned toward the corridor. "Come with me. He's in intensive care."

The term stuck a cold spike into Peter's guts. He followed Austin out of the room, down the hallway a few steps, and into another room marked ICU.

Only one patient lay in the spotless twelve-bed facility. Tall IV drip stands, gleaming new and with transparent plastic sheaths still hugging their aluminum stems, stood sentinel by each empty bed. The lone patient wasn't hooked to a drip, nor was he attached to any other tentacles of medical technology. He sat erect against pillows, tucked up to the waist in pure white linen, his faceless, hairless kernel of head-flesh unhooded. In the great rectangle of mattress, designed to accommodate American bodies the size of BG's, he looked pathetically small. His robe and gloves had been replaced with a thin cotton hospital gown, pale gray-green like stale broccoli, the color Peter associated with Jesus Lover Twenty-Three, but that didn't mean he *was* Jesus Lover Twenty-Three, of course. With a shame so intense it was close to panic, Peter realized he had no way of knowing who this was. All he knew was that the ⴽⵕⴰⵚ's right hand was wrapped in a bulbous mitten of white gauze. In the left hand, he clutched a shabby toiletries bag—no, it wasn't a bag, it was . . . a Bible pamphlet, one of Peter's handsewn assemblages. The paper had been dampened and dried so many times it had the texture of leather; the loose strands of wool were yellow and pink.

Seeing Peter enter, the 𝑪𝑸𝑨𝑺 cocked his head to one side, as if puzzled by the minister's bizarrely unfamiliar raiment.

"God ble𝑪 our reunion, Father Pe𝑿er."

"Lover Five?"

"Ye𝑪."

Peter turned to Austin. "What's wrong with her? Why is she here?"

"She?" The doctor blinked. "Pardon me." He reached for a clipboard on which a single sheet was clamped, and, with a scrawl of a pen, he amended the patient's gender.

"Well, as you can see from the bandage," he continued, escorting Peter to Lover Five's bedside, "she's sustained a hand injury. A very serious hand injury, I must say." He motioned to the gauze mitten. "May I?" This last question was directed at the patient.

"Ye𝑪," she said. "𝑪how."

While the bandages were being unwrapped, Peter recalled the day of Lover Five's injury: the painting falling from the ceiling, the bruise on her hand, the fervid sympathy offered by her fellow 𝑪𝑸𝑨𝑺. And how, ever since then, she'd been protective of that hand, as if the memory of that injury refused to fade.

The white mitten dwindled in size until Austin removed the last of the gauze. A sweet, fermented smell was released into the room. Lover Five's hand was no longer a hand. The fingers had fused into a blueish-gray clump of rot. It looked like an apple that had sustained a bruise and then been left for weeks.

"Oh my God," Peter breathed.

"Do you speak his . . . do you speak her language?" said Austin. "Because I'm not sure how to get proper consent here. I mean, not that there's any alternative to amputation, but even explaining what a general anesthetic is . . ."

"Oh . . . my . . . God . . ."

Lover Five ignored the men's conversation, ignored the putrid mess on the end of her wrist. With her uninjured hand, she opened her Bible pamphlet, deftly using three fingers to flip to a particular page. In a clear voice unhampered (thanks to her pastor) by impossible consonants, she recited:

"The Lord give them power in their bed of pain, and make them whole again." And, from the same page of inspirational selections from *Psalms* and *Luke:* *"The people learned the good new way and followed him. He welcomed them and helped them know God, and healed all them who needed healing."*

She raised her head to fix her attention on Peter. The bulges on her face that resembled the knees of fetuses seemed to glow.

"I need healing," she said. "Or I die." Then, after a brief silence, in case there was any ambiguity that should be clarified: "I wish, please, to live."

"My God . . . my God . . ." Peter kept saying, ten meters down the hall, as Austin leaned against the edge of his consulting room desk, arms awkwardly folded. The doctor was tolerant of the pastor's emotional incontinence—he wouldn't dream of telling him that nothing was achieved by all this groaning and fist-clenching and agitated face-wiping. Even so, as the minutes ticked on, he became more keen to discuss the way forward.

"She'll have the best of care," he reassured Peter. "We have everything here. Not to blow my own horn, but I'm a pretty good surgeon. And Dr. Adkins is even better. Remember the great job he did on you? If it sets your mind at rest, he can do her as well. In fact, yes, I'll make sure he definitely does her."

"But don't you realize what this means?" cried Peter. *"Don't you fucking realize what this means?"*

The doctor flinched at the unexpected cursing from a man who was, as far as he'd been given to understand, a bona fide Christian minister.

"Well, I appreciate that you're upset," he remarked carefully. "But I don't think we should jump to any pessimistic conclusions."

Peter blinked tears from his eyes, allowing him to see the doctor's face in focus. The ragged scar on Austin's jaw was as conspicuous as ever, but now, rather than wondering how Austin got it, Peter was struck by the scar's essential nature: it was not a disfigurement, it was a miracle. All the scars ever suffered by anyone in the whole of human history were not suffering but triumph: triumph against decay, triumph against death. The wounds on Peter's arm and leg (healing still), the scabs on his ears (gone now), every trifling scratch and burn and rash and bruise, thousands of injuries over the years, right back to the ankle-bones he'd broken the week before he'd met Bea, his skinned knees when he'd fallen off his bike as a kid, the nappy rash he'd probably experienced as a baby . . . none of them had stopped him being here today. He and Austin were comrades in stupendous luck. The gouge in Austin's chin, which must have been a gory mess when it was first inflicted, had not reduced the entire head to a slimy lump; it magicked itself into fresh pink flesh.

Nothing shall hurt you, said Luke. *When thou walkest through the fire, thou shalt not be burned,* said Isaiah. *The Lord healeth all thy diseases,* said *Psalms.* There it was: there it was, plain as the scar on this smug doctor's face: the perpetual reprieve the Oasans called the Technique of Jesus.

2 5

SOME OF US HAVE WORK

TO DO.

Outside, the sky turned dark, even though it was day. Ominous cloud-masses had formed, dozens of them, almost perfectly circular, like giant moons of vapor. Peter stared at them through the window of his room. Lover One had once assured him that there were no storms on Oasis. It looked like that was about to change.

The giant globes of moisture, as they advanced, became at once more familiar and more alarming. They were swirls of rain, only rain, no different in their motion from the rain-swirls he'd witnessed many times before. But their relationship with the sky around them was not as subtle and freely shifting as usual; instead, it was as though each vast congregation of water-droplets was restrained by an inner gravitational pull, held together like a planet or some gaseous heavenly body. And the spheres were so dense that they had lost some of their transparency, casting an oppressive pall over what had been a bright morning.

There are rain clouds on the way, he thought of writing to Bea, and was hit with a double distress: the memory of the state Bea was in, and deep shame at how inadequate his letters to her were, how inadequate they'd been from the beginning. If he could have described what he'd experienced better, she might not have felt so separated from him. If only the tongue that God lent him when he was called upon to speak in public to strangers could have come to his aid when writing in private to his wife.

He sat at the Shoot and checked for a message. None.

The truth was as plain as a dull blank screen where words had once glowed: she saw no point in responding to him now. Or she was unable to respond—too busy, or too upset, or in trouble. Maybe he should write again regardless, not wait for an answer, just keep sending messages. The way *she* had done for him when he'd first got here, message after message which he'd left unanswered. He searched his mind for words that might give her hope, maybe something along the lines of "Hope is one of the strongest things in the universe. Empires can fall, civilizations can vanish into dust . . ." But no: the rhetoric of a sermon was one thing; his wife's grim reality was another. Civilizations did not vanish smoothly and easefully; empires did not set like suns: empires collapsed in chaos and violence. Real people got pushed around, beaten up, robbed, made destitute. Real lives went down the toilet. Bea was scared and hurt, and she didn't need his preaching.

Bea, I love you, he wrote. I;m so worried about you.

Was it right to spend five thousand dollars of USIC's money to send those nine impotent little words through space? With barely a moment's hesitation, he pressed the transmission button. The letters trembled on the screen for two, three, then four minutes, making Peter fear that his feelings had been judged, by some jaded shiftworker elsewhere in the building, to have failed a test, to have sinned against the USIC ethos, attempting to undermine the great mission. Staring at the screen, sweat forming on his brow, he belatedly noticed the typo—a semi-colon instead of an apostrophe. He lifted his hand to fix it, but the words evaporated.

APPROVED. TRANSMITTED, the screen said in a wink.

Thank God for that.

Outside the compound, a rumble of thunder.

Peter prayed.

In every Christian's life there comes a time when he or she needs to know the precise circumstances under which God is willing to heal the sick. Peter had reached that pass now. Until today, he'd muddled through with the same hodgepodge of faith, medicine and common sense that everyone else in his church back in England was likely to rely on: Drive carefully, take the pills as stated on the package, pour cold water on a scald, get the cyst removed by a surgeon, be mindful that a Christian diabetic needs insulin just as much as an atheist diabetic does, regard a heart attack as a warning, remember that all human beings must die, but remember too that God is merciful and may snatch your life back from the jaws of death if . . . if what? If what?

A few hundred meters from here, confined in a metal cot, lay Lover Five, so small and helpless in that big empty space labeled Intensive Care. Nothing that USIC's doctors had to offer could fix the rot in her flesh. Amputating her hand would be like cutting the rotten part out of an apple; it was just tidying up the fruit as it died.

But God . . . God could . . . God could what? God could cure cancer, that had been proven many times. An inoperable tumor could, through the power of prayer, miraculously shrink. Sentences of death could be commuted for years, and, although Peter disapproved of charlatan faith-healers, he had seen people wake from supposedly fatal comas, had seen hopelessly premature babies survive, had even seen a blind woman regain her sight. But why did God do it for some Christians and not for others? Such a basic question, too simpleminded for theologians to bother discussing at their synods. But what was the answer? To what extent did God feel bound to respect the laws of biology, letting calcifying bones crumble, poisoned livers succumb to cirrhosis, severed arteries gush blood? And if the laws of biology on Oasis were such that the ⳹ⲢⲀⳉ couldn't heal, that the mechanism for healing didn't even exist, was there any point in praying to God for help?

Dear God, please don't let Lover Five die.

It was such an infantile prayer, the sort of prayer a five-year-old might pray.

But maybe those were the best kind.

What with the thunder in the skies outside and the rumble of worry in his own head, it was difficult for him to recognize the knocking at his door for what it was. Eventually he opened up.

"How are you feeling?" said Grainger, dressed for going out.

Like hell, he almost said. "I'm very upset and worried about my friend."

"But physically?"

"Physically?"

"Are you up for going out with me?" Her voice was firm and dignified; she was wholly back to normal now. Her eyes were clear, no longer red-rimmed; she didn't smell of alcohol. In fact, she was beautiful, more beautiful than he'd given her credit for before. As well as her usual driving shawl, she wore a white tunic top with loose sleeves that barely reached past her elbows, exposing the network of scars on her pale forearms to public view. *Take me as I am*, was the message.

"We can't leave Tartaglione to rot," she said. "We've got to bring him back."

"He doesn't want to come back," said Peter. "He feels utter contempt for everybody here."

"He's just saying that," said Grainger, bristling with impatience. "I know him. We used to talk. He's a real interesting guy, very smart and charming. And sociable. He'll go insane out there."

A naked bogey-man from medieval depictions of the damned leapt around in Peter's memory. "He's insane already."

Grainger's eyes narrowed. "That's kinda ... judgmental, wouldn't you say?"

Peter looked away, too burdened with care to argue. Clumsily, he pretended to be distracted by the demands of unloading the washing machine.

"Anyway," said Grainger, "*I'll* talk to him, *you* don't have to talk to him. Just get him to come out of hiding. Whatever you did last time, do it again."

"Well," Peter recalled, "I was stumbling around in pitch darkness, delirious, convinced I was dying, loudly reciting a paraphrase of Psalm 23. If that's what it takes, I'm not sure I could . . . uh . . . replicate the conditions."

She put her hands on her hips, provocatively. "So does that mean you're not willing to give it a shot?"

And so they set off. Not in the delivery jeep Grainger preferred for her drug and food runs, but in the hearse-like station wagon Peter had commandeered, the one with the bed in the back. Grainger took a while to adjust to driving it, sniffing at its unfamiliar smells, fiddling with its unfamiliar controls, wriggling her buttocks on the unfamiliar shape of its seat. She was a creature of habit. All the USIC staff were creatures of habit, he realized now. There wasn't a reckless adventurer among them: Ella Reinman's vetting process made sure of that. Maybe he, Peter, was the closest thing to an adventurer they'd ever allowed to come here. Or maybe Tartaglione was the closest. And that's why he'd gone insane.

"I figure he's more likely to show," Grainger explained, "if the vehicle's the same. He probably saw you coming for ages."

"It was night."

"The vehicle would have lit itself up. He could've been watching it from a mile away."

Peter thought this was unlikely. He was more inclined to believe that Tartaglione had been watching the twinkles in his vat of moonshine, watching musty memories slowly decay inside his own skull.

"What if we don't find him?"

"We'll find him," said Grainger, focusing her eyes on the featureless landscape.

"But what if we don't?"

She smiled. "You gotta have faith." The heavens rumbled.

A few minutes later, Peter said, "May I check the Shoot?"

Grainger fumbled on the dashboard, not sure where the Shoot was located in this vehicle. A drawer slid out like a tongue, offering two repulsive objects that looked like large mummified slugs but which, at second glance, were moldy cigars. Another drawer revealed some sheets of printed paper that had turned rainbow colors and shriveled to a fragile tissue resembling autumn leaves. Evidently, the USIC personnel had made little or no use of Kurtzberg's hearse since his disappearance. Maybe they regarded it as cursed with bad luck, or maybe they'd made a conscious decision to leave it just as it was, in case the minister came back one day.

Grainger's fingers found the Shoot at last, and swiveled it over Peter's lap. He switched it on: everything looked and behaved as it should. He checked for messages from Bea. Nothing. Maybe this particular machine was not configured like the others. Maybe its promise of connection was an illusion. He checked again, reasoning that if Bea had sent a message, a few extra seconds could make all the difference between its not-yet-having-arrived and its arrival.

Nothing.

The sky continued to darken as they drove further. Not exactly black as sackcloth, but certainly ominous. Thunder boomed again.

"I've never seen it like this," he said.

Grainger glanced cursorily out the side window. "I have," she said. Then, sensing his skepticism, she added: "I've been here longer than you." She shut her eyes and breathed deep. "Too long."

"What happens?"

"Happens?"

"When it goes dark like this?"

She sighed. "It rains. It just rains. What do you expect? This place is one big anti-climax."

He opened his mouth to speak. To defend the awesome beauties of this planet, or else to make some comment about the USIC project, he would never know which, because as he opened his lips, a fork of lightning split the sky, the windows flared with a blinding flash, and the vehicle was struck from above as if by a colossal fist.

Shuddering from the bang, the car rolled to a standstill.

"Jee-*zus*!" cried Grainger. She was alive. They were both alive. And not just that: they were holding each other by the arm, squeezing tight. Animal instinct. Embarrassed, they unclasped.

No harm had come to them, not even a hair on their head was singed. The Shoot suspended over Peter's lap had gone blank, its screen reflecting his own bone-white face. On the dashboard in front of him, all the glowing words and symbols were gone. Grainger reached forward to prompt the ignition and was exasperated to find that the engine failed to revive.

"That's not supposed to happen," she said. Her eyes were a little wild;

she was possibly in shock. "Everything should still be working fine." She kept turning the ignition, to no avail. Fat raindrops began to splash against the windows.

"The lightning must have blown something," said Peter.

"Impossible," said Grainger. "No way."

"Grainger, it's amazing enough that we survived."

She was having none of it. "A car's the safest place to be in a thunderstorm," she insisted. "The metal shell acts as a Faraday cage." Observing the incomprehension on his face, she added: "Grade-school science."

"I must have been away from school that day," he said, as she examined, prodded and tickled controls and gauges that were clearly dead. The odor of fried circuitry began to seep into the cabin. The downpour clattered against the windows, which fogged up until Peter and Grainger were confined inside an opaque casket.

"I cannot *believe* this," said Grainger. "All of our vehicles are designed to take punishment. They're built like cars *used* to be, before people started to load them full of dumb-ass technology that breaks down all the damn time." She pulled the headscarf off. Her face was flushed, her neck wet with sweat.

"We need to think," said Peter gently, "about what to do."

She leaned her head back against the seat, stared up at the roof. The patter of the rain beat out a military rhythm, like soldiers from a long-past millennium walking into battle with their snare drums slung on their hips.

"We've only been driving for a few minutes," Grainger said. "The base may still be in sight." Reluctant to step outside the vehicle and get soaked, she twisted round in her seat and tried to look out the back window. There was nothing to see except fogged glass and the bed. She swung open the door, letting in a gleeful swarm of humid air, and hove herself into the rain. She stood next to the car for twenty seconds or more, her clothing trembling and flapping as it got pelted. Then she took her seat again and shut the door.

"No sign," she said. Her tunic was drenched, transparent. Peter could see the delineation of her bra, the points of her nipples. "And no sign of C-1, either. We must be exactly halfway." She stroked the steering wheel in frustration.

The rain passed over. The sky brightened up, casting pearly light on their bodies. Tendrils of air nudged under Grainger's sleeves, visibly lifting the sodden fabric, traveling underneath like swollen veins. They penetrated Peter's clothing, too, slipping inside his T-shirt, up his trouser-cuffs, tickling the hollows of his knees. They were especially keen to get past the tight ruck of denim around his genitals.

"Walking back would take us an hour," said Grainger. "Two hours, max."

"Have the tires left tracks in the dirt?"

She went out again to check. "Yes," she said, on her return. "Straight and clear." One last time she turned the ignition, casually and without looking at it, as if hoping to trick the engine into performing despite itself.

"Looks like Tartaglione made a deal with God," she said.

They packed carefully for the journey. Grainger filled a tote bag with first-aid provisions. Peter found a mildewed old briefcase of Kurtzberg's, removed a New Testament which had fused into a solid block, and replaced it with a couple of plastic two-liter bottles of water.

"I wish there was a shoulder-strap for this," he said, testing the briefcase in his grip. "These bottles are heavy."

"They'll be lighter as we drink them," said Grainger.

"It'll rain again, twice, before we're at the base," prophesied Peter.

"What good will that do us?"

"You just lift your head and open your mouth," he said. "That's how the ʆᏜᴀᏕ—the natives—do it."

"If you don't mind," said Grainger, "I'd rather not do it the way the natives do it."

The outside of the vehicle, they noted, was disfigured with scorch-marks. A web of damage tattooed the hubcabs, and all four tires had deflated. The vehicle had ceased to be a vehicle and begun its metamorphosis into something else.

Peter and Grainger followed the tire-tracks back toward the USIC compound. Grainger was a good walker, shorter-legged than her companion but with a brisk enough pace for him not to need to hobble his speed. They covered a decent distance in a short time, and despite the flatness of the land the vehicle grew rapidly smaller in retrospect and then vanished altogether. As they walked on, the tracks became more difficult to discern in the rain-smoothed soil; there was ambiguity between man-made and naturally occurring patterns. The sky's ominous pall evaporated and the sun shone bright and constant. Grainger took swigs from one of the water bottles; Peter was OK to wait. He was more hungry than thirsty. In fact, the gnaw of appetite distracted him as he walked.

The ground was not the best terrain for progress on foot, but they must have covered two miles at least in the first hour. In the second hour perhaps the same. The USIC base obstinately refused to manifest on the horizon. All traces of their outward journey were by now erased from the soil. They were, of course, hopelessly lost.

"If we retrace our steps to the car, USIC may send someone to check it out," suggested Peter, "eventually."

"Yeah," said Grainger. "Eventually. When we're dead."

They were both taken aback to hear the word spoken so prematurely. Even though the mistake they'd made hung obvious in the air, there was an etiquette of optimism to be observed.

"*You* came to fetch *me*," Peter reminded her.

She laughed out loud at his naïveté. "That was on my own initiative, it had nothing to do with USIC. Those guys wouldn't rescue their own mothers. I mean, literally. Why do you think they're here in the first place? They're cool, they might as well have SHIT HAPPENS tattooed on their foreheads."

"But they'll notice you're missing."

"Oh, I'm sure. Somebody will come to the pharmacy for a tube of wart-killer and I won't be there and they'll think, Hey, no sweat, a few warts ain't so bad. And when I don't turn up to test tomorrow's food, Hey, it's just a formality, we'll eat it anyway. Maybe mention it at the next meeting."

"I can't believe they'd be so unconcerned," said Peter, but his voice was weakened by uncertainty.

"I know these guys," said Grainger. "I know how they operate. They noticed Kurtzberg and Tartaglione were missing—after God knows how long. What did they do? Did they send vehicles out in all directions, driving day and night until they covered every inch of a fifty-mile radius? Forget it, baby. Chill out and read a magazine. Flex a bicep. The fucking world is falling apart and it still doesn't rate as an emergency. Do you really think they're gonna panic over us?"

"I would hope so," said Peter.

"Well, hope is a fine thing," she sighed.

They walked further, and began to tire.

"Maybe we should stop walking," said Peter.

"And do what instead?"

"Rest a while."

They sat on the earth and rested a while. Two cotton-wrapped, pink mammals marooned on a dark ocean of soil. Here and there, a few small clumps of whiteflower grew, sweating in the sunshine. Peter reached out to one near his foot, plucked off a fragment and put it in his mouth. It tasted bad. How strange that a substance which, when ingeniously processed, cooked and seasoned, could be delicious in so many ways, should be so unpleasant in its pure form.

"Enjoying that?" said Grainger.

"Not much," he said.

"I'll wait till we're back at the base," she said, lightly. "Good menu today. Chicken curry and ice cream." She smiled, willing him to forgive her earlier lapse of morale.

Not much refreshed, they walked on. And on. Grainger had drunk half a water bottle by now, and Peter drank his fill direct from the sky when, just as he'd foretold, another rain-shower drenched them.

"Hey!" called Grainger as he swayed erect and awkward, his head tilted back, Adam's apple bobbing, mouth wide open to the downpour. "You look like a turkey!"

Peter put on a grin, as Grainger's comment was clearly meant in fun, but he felt his grin falter as he realized that he'd forgotten what turkeys looked like. All his life he'd known, starting from the first day his parents had shown him a picture of one in a book. Now, in his brain's storehouse, where so many Bible passages lay spotlit ready for quoting, he searched for a picture to go with "turkey," and there was none to be found.

Grainger noticed. Noticed and was not pleased.

"You don't remember, do you?" she said, as they sat down together once more. "You've forgotten what a turkey looks like."

He confessed with a nod, caught out like a naughty child. Until now, only Bea had ever been able to guess what he was thinking.

"Mental blank," he said.

"That's what happens," said Grainger, solemn and intense. "That's what this place is about, that's how it works. It's like one huge dose of Propanolol, erasing everything we ever knew. You mustn't let them break you."

Her sudden vehemence discomfited him. "I . . . I'm probably just . . . absent-minded."

"That's what you've gotta watch," she said, hugging her knees, contemplating the empty tundra ahead of them. "Absence. The slow, insidious . . . *disposal* of everything. Listen: you wanna know what got discussed at the last USIC personnel meeting? Besides technical stuff and the bad smell in the loading bay behind H wing? I'll tell you: whether we really need all those pictures hanging in the hallways. They're just a dusting and cleaning problem, right? An old photo of a city on earth somewhere, way back when, with a bunch of guys eating lunch on a steel girder, it's cute but we've seen it a million times walking past it, it gets old, and anyway those guys are all dead, it's like being made to look at a bunch of dead people, so enough already. Blank walls: clean and simple: end of story."

Grainger raked her fingers through her clammy hair: an irritable gesture. "So . . . Peter . . . Let me remind you what a turkey is. It's a bird. It's got a kind of dangle of flesh hanging off of its beak, looks like a big trail of snot or . . . uh . . . a condom. Its head is red with little bumps on it, like lizard skin, and its head and neck are in an S-shape, and they go like this . . ." With her own head and neck she acted out the ungainly motion of the bird. "And then this scrawny, snake-like head and neck are attached to this oversized, fat, fluffy gray body." She looked Peter in the eyes. "Ring any bells?"

"Yes, you've . . . uh . . . brought it back to life for me."

Satisfied, she allowed herself to relax. "That's it. That's what we've got to do. Keep the memories alive." She arranged her body more comfortably on the ground, stretching out as if sunbathing, using the tote bag as a pillow. A brilliant-green insect settled on her shoulder and began to flex its hind-quarters. She seemed unaware of it. Peter considered brushing it away, but let it be.

A voice in his head said: *You are going to die here, in this wilderness. You will never see Beatrice again. This flat terrain, these sparse clumps of whiteflower, this alien sky, these insects waiting to lay eggs in your flesh, this woman at your side: they are the contents of your life in its final days and hours.* The voice spoke clearly, without accent or gender: he'd heard it many times before, and always been certain it was not his own. As a child, he'd thought it was the voice of conscience; as a Christian, he'd trusted it was the voice of God. Whatever it was, it had always told him exactly what he needed to be told.

"What's your earliest memory?" Grainger asked.

"I don't know," he said, after giving it thought. "My mum strapping me into a special plastic child seat at a Turkish restaurant, maybe. It's hard to know what's a real memory and what's something you construct afterward from old photos and family stories."

"Oh, don't be like that," she said, in the same tone she might have used if he'd declared that love was merely a meeting of sperm and ovum. "Tuska's big on that idea. No such thing as childhood memories, he says. We're just playing games with our neurons every day, tossing them around the hip-pocampus, constructing little fairy tales featuring characters named after people we used to live with. 'Your dad is just a flurry of molecular activity in your frontal lobe,' he'll tell you, grinning that smug grin of his. Asshole."

She held out her hand. Peter wasn't sure what she wanted him to do. Then he handed her the water bottle. She drank some. There wasn't much left.

"My dad," she continued, "used to smell of gunpowder. We lived on a farm, in Illinois. He was always shooting rabbits. They were just bugs to him, big furry bugs. I'd ride around on my bicycle, and there'd be dead rabbits everywhere. Then later he'd sweep me up in his arms and I'd smell the gunpowder on his shirt."

"A very . . . uh . . . mixed-emotion sort of memory," said Peter carefully.

"It's a *real* memory, that's the important thing. The farm was real, the dead rabbits were real, the smell on my father's shirt was gunpowder and not tobacco or paint or aftershave. I know, I was there." She spoke defiantly, as if doubt had been cast on whether she was there, as if there was a conspiracy among the USIC personnel to reinvent her as a city kid from Los Angeles, the daughter of a Ukrainian dentist, a German Chinese. Two more insects had settled on her, one on her hair, the other on her bosom. She paid them no mind.

"What happened to your farm?" asked Peter, for politeness' sake, when it became evident that the conversation had stalled.

"Get the *fuck* out of my face!" she exclaimed, clapping her hands to her eyes.

He jerked back, prepared to apologize profusely for whatever he'd said to enrage her, but she wasn't addressing him. She wasn't even addressing the insects. With a cry of disgust, she cast a glittering shred first from one eye, then the other. Her contact lenses.

"The damn *air*," she said. "It was trying to get under my contacts, lifting them up at the edges. Creeped me out." She blinked. One discarded hydrogel petal was stuck to her shoe, the other lay on the soil. "I shouldn't have done that; my eyesight is not good. You might end up leading me along. Where were we?"

With effort, Peter retrieved the thread of the narrative. "You were going to tell me what happened to the farm."

She rubbed her eyes, experimented with looking out of them. "We went broke," she said. "The farm got sold and we moved to Decatur. We were in Bethany before, we weren't that far out, but we got ourselves a maisonette in the city, right near the Sangamon River. Well, not like walking distance or anything. But a short drive."

"Uh-huh," said Peter. He realized, with a deep pang of melancholy, that he was not in the least interested. So much for being a people person . . . If he survived, if he got back to civilization, his career as a minister was over. The minutiae of human beings' lives—the places they'd lived, the names of their relatives, the names of the rivers they'd lived near, the mundane complexities of the jobs they'd done and the domestic squabbles they'd endured—had ceased to have any meaning for him.

"Decatur is kind of a boring place now," reflected Grainger. "But it's got some pretty amazing history. It used to be called the Soybean Capital of the World. You've heard of Abraham Lincoln?"

"Of course. Most famous of all American presidents."

She exhaled gratefully, as if they had struck a blow against ignorance together, as if they were the only two educated people in a colony of philistines. "Lincoln lived in Decatur, way back in the 1700s or whenever. He was a lawyer then. He became president later. There's a statue of him with his bare foot on a stump. I sat on that stump when I was a little girl. I didn't think it was disrespectful or anything; I was just tired."

"Uh-huh," said Peter. Insects were settling on him now, too. In a week or so—maybe in a few days—the two of them would be seedbeds. Maybe, when the time came for them to breathe their last, they should be lying in each other's arms.

"I loved what you said at the funeral," she said.

"The funeral?"

"Severin's funeral. You made him so real. And I didn't even like him."

Peter struggled to recall what he'd said about Severin; struggled to recall Severin at all. "I had no idea you were impressed."

"It was beautiful." She basked in the afterglow of his compassion for a few seconds. Then her brow wrinkled. "Too beautiful for those . . . dickwads, that's for sure. There was a meeting about it afterward, and everyone agreed you'd overstepped a line, and if there were any more deaths of USIC personnel in the future, it would be best to keep you out of it." The insects were venturing back now. A lustrous jade one settled directly on her forehead. She was oblivious. "I defended you," she said, staring up at the sky.

"Thank you."

Resting on one elbow, he gazed at her. Her bosom rose and fell with her breath, just two lumps of fatty tissue on a ribcage, two milkbags designed to feed children she would never have. Yet to him that bosom was intoxicatingly lovely, an aesthetic marvel, and the rhythmic swell of it made him desire her. Everything about her was miraculous: the downy hair behind her ear, the symmetry of her collarbones, her soft flushed lips, even the puckered scars on her arms. She wasn't his soul mate: he had no illusions about that. The intimacies he had once shared with Bea were impossible with her; she would quickly find him ridiculous, and he would find her too much trouble. In fact, like most men and women who had made love since the beginning of time, they had almost nothing in common. Except that they were male and female, thrown together by circumstances, and, for the moment at least, alive. He lifted his hand, held it in space, prepared to settle his palm, gently, on her breast.

"Tell me about your wife." Grainger's eyes were closed now. She was tired, torpid in the heat, and a little drunk on the liquor of reminiscence.

"She's turned against me," Peter said, withdrawing his hand. "We've grown apart." Although he intended merely to state facts, his words sounded peevish, craven, the clichéd complaining of the typical adulterer. He could do better than this. "She's been having a horrific time back home, everything is falling apart, all sorts of disasters, and she . . . she's lost her faith in God. Our cat Joshua got killed, tortured, and I think it pushed her over the edge. She's scared and lonely. I haven't been giving her the support she needs."

Grainger shifted the orientation of her body, for comfort. One arm cradled her head, the other draped across her chest. She didn't open her eyes. "You're not telling me about Bea," she said. "You're telling me what's going on between you. Tell me about her. What she looks like. The color of her eyes. Her childhood and stuff."

He lay down next to her, rested his head on his arms. "Her name is Beatrice. She's a few years older than me, thirty-six. She doesn't mind people knowing her age. She's the most . . . un-vain woman I've ever known. I don't mean in terms of appearance. She's beautiful and she dresses with style. But she doesn't care what other people think. She has pride in herself. Not a puffed-up pride, just . . . self-esteem. That's so rare. Incredibly rare. Most people are the walking wounded, you know. And Bea really ought to be, with the childhood she had. Her father was abusive, a total control freak. He burned everything she had several times, all her possessions, I mean everything, not just toys and books and special things, but everything. She remembers going to Tesco's, a supermarket in the industrial park that was open all night, with her mother. It was about two o'clock in the morning, Bea was maybe nine years old, and she was in her pajamas, she was barefoot and her feet were blue, because it was January and snowing and she'd had to walk from the car to the store. And her mother took her to the girlswear section and bought her underpants, socks, T-shirts, shoes, trousers, the lot. That happened more than once."

"Wow," said Grainger, without any perceptible awe. Peter guessed she was comparing Bea's formative sufferings to her own and judging them to be no big deal. That's what people, unless they were ﬗﬓﬗ, tended to do.

"What does she look like?" Grainger said. "Describe her to me."

"She has brown hair," said Peter. "Auburn." It was a struggle to conjure up a vision of Bea's hair as it really was; maybe he was just recalling mentioning its color in other conversations. "She's tall, almost as tall as me. Brown eyes, slim." These details were generic, unevocative; they would fit a million women. But what was he to do? Describe the mole under her left nipple? The precise shape of her navel? "She's very fit, she's a nurse. We met at the hospital where she worked. I'd broken my ankles jumping off a ledge."

"Ow. Were you trying to commit suicide?"

"No, I was trying to escape from the police. I was a drug addict then; I did a lot of burglaries. That day, my luck ran out. Or I should say, I got lucky."

Grainger grunted agreement. "She lost her job over you?"

"How did you know that?" He'd never shared this with her, he was pretty sure.

"Just a guess. Nurse gets involved with patient. Who's a drug addict. And a criminal. It doesn't look good. Did you ever go to jail?"

"Not really. Detention in police cells, a fortnight once when I was awaiting trial and nobody would bail me out, that was about it." Only now did it strike him that he'd been shown extraordinary leniency.

"Figures," said Grainger, in an odd, philosophical tone.

"Why does it figure?"

"You're a lucky guy, Peter. One of life's charmed creatures."

For some reason, this stung him. He wanted her to know he had suffered just as much as anyone.

"I was homeless for a few years. I got beaten up." He hoped he was speaking with quiet dignity, rather than whining, but he suspected not.

"All part of life's adventure, right?" said Grainger. There was no sarcasm in her voice, just a weary, tolerant sadness.

"What do you mean?"

She sighed. "Some people go through heavy stuff. They fight in wars. They're in jail. They start a business and it gets shut down by gangsters. They end up hustling their ass in a foreign country. It's one long list of setbacks and humiliations. But it doesn't touch them, not really. They're having an adventure. It's like: What's next? And then there's other people who are just trying to live quietly, they stay out of trouble, they're maybe ten years old, or fourteen, and one Friday morning at 9:35 something happens to them, something private, something that breaks their heart. Forever."

He lay silent, absorbing what she'd said.

"I felt that way," he said at last, "when Bea told me it was over."

It began to rain again. Without shelter, they had no choice but to lie where they were and get soaked. Grainger just closed her eyes. Peter watched her bra materializing again under her tunic, watched the contours of her breasts take shape. She hitched the sleeves off her arms, let the old injuries breathe. Each time he'd spent time with Grainger he'd wondered if a natural opportunity would arise to ask her about her self-harm. There would never be a better time than now. He tried to frame the question, but none of the obvious words—the *whys* and *whens*—would move from his brain to his tongue. He realized that he no longer wanted to know what caused those scars. Grainger's pain was in the past and there was no point revisiting it. Here, today, lying by his side, she was a woman with faint ridges on her arms: if he stroked her flesh gently, he would feel them. That was all.

When the shower had moved on and the sun was warming them again, Grainger said: "Did you get married in a church or an office?"

"A church."

"Was it a big, fancy wedding?"

"Not so much. No parents or family members on either side, for various reasons. A few people from Bea's own church, which became my church in the end." In truth, he remembered nothing much about the event, but he remembered the light beaming through the windows, the way a gray November afternoon had been unexpectedly transformed by a sunburst. "It was nice. I think everyone had a good time. And there was loads of alcohol and I didn't drink, I wasn't even tempted. Which was quite an achievement for me because, you know . . . I'm an alcoholic."

"Me too," she said.

"It never leaves you," he said.

She smiled. "Like God, huh? More loyal than God."

They lay quietly for a while. Two small insects of the same species found each other on Grainger's abdomen and started mating.

"I bet Ella Reinman is a secret lush," she said.

"Sorry?"

"A lush. American word for alcoholic. I thought you'd know that one."

"Never too late for vocabulary building," he said.

"She thinks she's so damn smart," bitched Grainger. "Thinks she can look right inside you and tell if you're ever gonna drink again. Well, she got it wrong with us, didn't she?"

Peter was silent. Nothing would be gained by telling her that the booze she'd smelled on him when she dragged him out of Tartaglione's den was all spillage. Let her think they'd fallen off the wagon together. Let her think he'd broken his sacred promise, let her think he'd lost his last shred of dignity. It was kinder that way.

"I was a different person when I did that interview," she said. "It was a million years ago. People change."

"Yes, people change."

The insects were finished, and flew off.

"Tell me about your wife's wedding dress," said Grainger.

"It was white," he replied. "It was exactly what you imagine a wedding dress to be, conventional, nothing unusual about it. Except that it was a huge symbolic statement. The whiteness of it. Bea had a terrible past, sexually. She was . . . let's just say she was used and abused. And she refused to be destroyed by it."

Grainger scratched at her arms. The repeated drenchings had activated an allergy in the scars. "Not so much of the symbolism. Tell me more about the dress."

He cast his mind back. He cast it across the galaxy, aiming for the bedroom of his home in England.

"It . . . it didn't have a huge flouncy train behind it," he said. "It was a proper dress, a dress to move around in. It had puff shoulders, not balloony, just elegant, and then it was tight on the arms, with a brocade kind of texture, right down to the wrists. There was brocade on the . . . uh . . . abdomen as well, and on the collar, but the bosom was smooth and silky. The skirt was ankle-length, it didn't touch the floor."

Grainger was nodding, humming. She was getting what she wanted.

"One of the amazing things about Bea," said Peter, "is that she wore that dress many times afterward. At home. Just for us."

"That's so romantic." There were tears in Grainger's eyes.

Peter felt suddenly disconsolate. The memory of Bea's bitter disappointment with him was more recent than these fond memories he was sharing with Grainger. "I suppose it's just a story I'm telling myself, like Tuska says," he said. "An old story. Life has moved on. Bea is a different person. You know, not long ago, I wrote to her about the dress, about how much I loved her in it, and she . . . she said I was just being sentimental, focusing on a memory of who she used to be, not who she is now."

Grainger shook her head. "That's bullshit," she said softly. Tenderly, even. "Take it from me, Peter, her heart swells up when you talk about that dress. She would be devastated if she thought you'd forgotten about that dress. Can't you see that? Everybody's sentimental, everybody. There's only about fifty people in the whole damn world who aren't sentimental. And they're all working here."

They both laughed. "We should try once more to get back," said Peter.

"OK," she said, and hauled herself to her feet. Her movements were stiffer than before. His too. They were carbon-based life forms, running low on fuel.

An hour or so later, with the USIC base still eluding them, they found a structure of a different kind. It had shimmered in their sights for the longest time, and while heading for it they discussed the possibility that it was a mirage. But it proved real enough: the skeletal remains of a large camping tent. The metal struts were intact, staking out the shape of a house, the kind of house a child would draw. The canvas hung in tatters.

Inside the tent, nothing. No provisions, no bedding, no implements. A square of ground, a blank panel for the imagination to fill.

Behind the tent, planted in the ground and only slightly tilted, a cross. A wooden one, of very modest scale, about knee-height. Where had the wood come from? Not from this world, that's for sure. It must have been transported, stashed in a ship along with the medicines and the engineering magazines and the raisins and the humans, billions of miles from its point of origin. Just two pine slats, never intended to be nailed together in this manner, two sturdy slices of tree varnished to resemble antique oak. Two nails were driven through the crux: one to join the two pieces of wood together, and another, crudely hammered and bent, to secure two small circlets of metal. Gold. Kurtzberg's wedding ring, and the wedding ring of the wife he'd lost in another galaxy long, long ago.

On the horizontal slat of the cross, the minister had carved a message, then painstakingly blackened each letter with the flame of a cigarette lighter or some similar tool. Peter expected a motto in Latin or an allusion to faith or Christ or the Afterlife.

FOR ALL THAT I'VE HAD AND SEEN, I AM TRULY THANKFUL, the inscription said.

They stood and looked at that cross for several minutes, while the ragged remains of the tent flapped in the breeze.

"I'm going home," announced Grainger, in a voice shaky with tears, "to find my dad."

Peter put his arm around her shoulders. This was the moment when he was called upon to say the right thing; nothing less than the right thing would do. As a man or as a minister of God, his challenge was the same: to reconcile them both to their fate. There would be no going home; there was no dad to be reunited with; they were lost and soon they would be dead. Lightning had struck them, and they had failed to understand its message.

"Grainger . . ." he began, his mind blank, trusting that inspiration would lend words to his tongue.

But before he could continue, the dull thrum which they'd both imagined was the wind agitating the canvas shreds of the tent grew suddenly louder, and an olive-green military jeep drove past them, slowed to a stop, and reversed.

A brown head with white eyes and white teeth poked out of the window.

"Are you guys finished here?" hollered BG, revving the engine. "'Cause some of us have work to do."

26

HE ONLY KNEW THAT THANKS WERE DUE.

All the way back, Peter could hear—only hear, not see—the weeping and the labored breathing and the outbursts of anxiety and anger, sometimes incoherent, sometimes lucid. He was in the front passenger seat next to BG, almost shoulder to shoulder with the big man, although his own shoulder looked emaciated in comparison with BG's bulge of meat and muscle. Invisible in the space behind them, Alexandra Grainger was going through hell.

BG drove in silence. His normally benign face was a grim mask, frozen under the sheen of sweat, as he concentrated, or pretended to concentrate, on the road ahead—the road that was no road at all. Only his eyes betrayed any stress.

"They'd better not try to stop me," Grainger was saying. "They can't keep me here. I don't care how much it costs. What are they gonna do? Sue me? Kill me? I've got to go home. They can keep my salary. Four years for free. That makes us even, right? They've got to let me go. My dad is still alive. I know he is. I feel it."

BG glanced up at the rear-view mirror. Maybe from his angle he could see more than Peter. All Peter could see was a narrow rectangle of black upholstery which, through the distorted veil of the air currents trapped in the cabin, appeared to be pulsing and throbbing.

"Four years as a pharmacist," Grainger ranted on, "handing out drugs to those creepy little freaks: What's that worth, BG? Worth a ride on a ship?"

BG grimaced. Crises of confidence were not what he was accustomed to dealing with. "Chill out, Grainger, is my advice to you," he said pensively. "The cost ain't an issue. I been back, Severin went back a couple times, a few other guys took a break too. Nobody slapped them with a bill. If you need to go, you need to go. No big deal."

"You really think so?" Her voice was tremulous, the voice of a farm girl from Illinois who was deeply ashamed to waste millions of dollars of someone else's money to indulge her own pain.

"Money don't mean shit," said BG. "We play this little game: ten bucks for a bar of chocolate, fifty bucks for a bottle of Pepsi, deducted from your salary, blah blah blah. It's just a Friday-night card game, Grainger, it's Monopoly, it's Go Fish, it's kids gambling for peanuts. The salary's a game too. Where we gonna spend this cash? We ain't goin' nowhere."

"But you *did* go home," said Grainger. "Not that long ago. Why?"

BG's mouth set hard. He clearly didn't want to discuss it. "Unfinished business."

"Family?"

BG shook his head. "Call it . . . loose ends. A guy in my line of work needs his mind clear. So I did some stuff and cleared it. Came back to the job a new man."

This silenced Grainger for a few seconds. Then she was anxious again. "But that's it, that's the whole point—you came back, you didn't quit. I've got to quit, you understand? I've got to leave and never come back. No way, never."

BG jutted out his chin. "Never say never, Grainger. Never say never. That's in the Bible somewhere, ain't that right, Peter?"

"I'm not sure," Peter mumbled. He knew perfectly well that the Bible said nothing of the sort.

"It's gotta be right there in Chapter One," affirmed BG. "God's advice to Moses and the whole crew: Seize the day! Get on top of it, people!"

Peter watched BG's right hand rise up from the steering wheel and form a triumphal fist in the air. Long ago, in a previous life, BG had no doubt stood among other dark-skinned creatures in his Nation of Islam brotherhood, all raising their fists likewise. Now, their slogans had mingled in BG's mind with a thousand windblown leaves from the Qur'an, the Bible, assorted self-help books, magazines and TV programs, combining into a mulch. A mulch from which his self-esteem grew healthy and strong.

The Bible stored inside Peter was pure and unadulterated, not a word of it confused with anything else. And yet, for the first time, he was ashamed of it. The holy book he'd spent so much of his life preaching from had one cruel flaw: it was not very good at offering encouragement or hope to those who weren't religious. *With God, nothing shall be impossible,* proclaimed Luke, and that message, which Peter had always thought was the most joyously positive reassurance you could wish for, now turned itself over like a dying insect, and became *Without God, everything shall be impossible.* What use was that to Grainger? What use was that to Bea? The way things had turned out, they might need to manage without a savior; they might need to forage and scrabble for whatever future they could get on their own. And the thing about the Bible was, once you asked for a future without faith, the Scriptures washed their hands of you. *Vanity, all is vanity.*

"What was it like, BG?" said Grainger. "Come on, tell me, what's happening back home?"

"*This* is my home now," BG cautioned her, tapping his chest with his fingers. Maybe, rather than referring to Oasis, the home he meant was his own body, wherever in space it might be located.

"OK, fine, fine," said Grainger, barely controlling her annoyance, "but tell me anyway, damn it. It's been so long since I left. There must have been big changes. Don't spare me, BG, skip the pep talks, give it to me straight. What's it like?"

BG hesitated, weighing up the wisdom of responding. "Same as always," he said.

"That's not true!" yelled Grainger, instantly hysterical. "Don't lie to me! Don't patronize me! I know everything's falling apart!"

Why not ask me? Peter thought. She was treating him as if he didn't exist.

"Everything's *always* been falling apart," BG stated calmly. There was no defensiveness in his tone: the facts were too self-evident for dispute. "Planet Earth got fucked up a loooong time ago, excuse my French."

"That's not what I *mean,*" whined Grainger. "I mean . . . What about your old neighborhood, where you grew up, your relatives, your house . . ."

BG squinted through the windscreen at the expanses of nothingness, then glanced down at the navigation gadget on his dashboard.

"Grainger, I got another wise old saying for you. Listen up: You can't go home again."

Thomas Wolfe, circa 1940, thought Peter helplessly.

"Yeah? Well, just watch me," said Grainger, belligerent in her fear. "Just fucking watch me."

BG was silent, obviously judging that Grainger was on too delicate a hair-trigger for more discussion. But the silence provoked her just as much. "You know what you are?" she wheezed, her voice ugly as if soaked in alcohol. "You're just a little boy. Running away from home. Big tough guy, but you can't face reality. All you can do is pretend it's not happening."

BG blinked slowly. He did not lose his temper. He had no temper left to lose. That was his tragedy, and his mark of dignity too.

"I faced all the reality I got to face, Grainger," he said, without raising his voice. "You don't know what I've done and what I have not done; you don't know where I came from and why I left; you don't know who I've hurt and who's hurt me; you ain't seen my scorecard and I ain't gonna show it to you. You want a juicy fact about my daddy? He died when he was the exact age I am now. A blood vessel in his heart got blocked up: bye-bye Billy Graham Senior. And all you need to know about me is, if I inherited that same blood vessel, and I die next week, well . . . I'm OK with it." BG changed gear, slowed the vehicle down. They were approaching the base. "In the meantime, Grainger, whenever you need a ride out of the desert, I'm your man."

She was quiet after that. The vehicle's wheels made the transition from earth to tarmac, giving the illusion of airborne cruising. BG parked in the shadow of the compound, right in front of the entrance nearest Grainger's quarters, then scooted round and opened the car door for her: a perfect gentleman.

"Thank you," she said. She had not acknowledged Peter's presence for the duration of the drive. Peter twisted round in his seat to catch a glimpse of her as she was maneuvering her stiff, weary body out of the car. BG's arm was offered like a metal rung; she took hold of it and pulled herself up. The door slammed shut, and Peter continued to watch through the fogged window: two white-clad USIC personnel shimmering in and out of recognizability like degraded video images. He wondered if they would walk into the building side by side, arm in arm, but as soon as Grainger was on her feet, she broke free and was gone.

"I figure it's the lightning," said BG when he returned to the car. "Can't be good for a person, being whammoed like that. Give her time, she'll get over it."

Peter nodded. He was unsure if he would get over it himself.

It was Dr. Adkins who found Peter outside the intensive care unit, on his knees. "Found" was the wrong word, perhaps: he almost tripped over him. Unfazed, the surgeon looked down at Peter's body, assessing in a couple of seconds whether any part of it was in urgent need of medical intervention.

"You OK?" he said.

"I'm trying to pray," said Peter.

"Oh . . . OK," said Adkins, glancing over Peter's shoulder to a place further down the corridor, as if to say, *Could you try it somewhere where people won't break their neck over you?*

"I've come to see Jesus Lover Five," said Peter, hauling himself off the floor. "You know about her?"

"Of course. She's my patient." The doctor smiled. "It's nice to have a real patient for a change. Instead of a five-minute wham-bam-thank-you-ma'am with someone who's got conjunctivitis or hit their thumb with a hammer."

Peter stared into the doctor's face, searching for evidence of empathy. "I got the impression Dr. Austin didn't really understand what's happening to Lover Five. I got the impression he's assuming you can make her better."

"We'll do what we can," said Adkins inscrutably.

"She's going to die," said Peter.

"Let's not go there yet."

Peter clenched one hand inside the other, and found that his strenuous attempts to pray had bruised the tender flesh between his knuckles. "These people don't heal, you understand that?" he said. "They *can't* heal. Our bodies . . . your body, my body . . . we're living inside a miracle. Forget religion, we're a miracle of nature. We can hit our thumb with a hammer, we can tear a hole in our skin, we can get burnt, broken, swollen up with pus, and a little while later, it's all fixed! Good as new! Unbelievable! Impossible! But true. That's the gift we're given. But the ᴌᴏᴀᵴ—the Oasans—they never received this amazing gift. They get one chance . . . just one chance . . . the body they're born with. They do their best to take care of it, but when it gets damaged, that's . . . that's it."

Dr. Adkins nodded. He was a kindly man, and not unintelligent. He laid a palm on Peter's shoulder.

"Let's take it day by day with this . . . lady. She'll lose her hand. That's obvious. Beyond that . . . We'll try our best to figure something out."

Peter's eyes stung with tears. He wanted so much to believe.

"Listen," said Adkins, "remember when I was patching you up, I told you that medicine is just carpentry, plumbing and sewing. Which doesn't apply in this lady's case, I appreciate that. But I forgot to mention: there's chemistry too. These people take painkillers, they take cortisone, they take lots of other medicines from us. They wouldn't take them, year after year, if nothing had any effect."

Peter nodded, or tried to; it was more of a facial tremor, a shiver of the chin. The cynicism he'd thought he'd banished forever was coursing through his system. *Placebo, all is placebo.* Swallow the pills and feel invigorated while the cells die inside you. Hallelujah, I can walk on these septic feet, the pain is gone, barely there, quite bearable, praise the Lord.

Adkins looked down at the palm that he'd laid on Peter's shoulder a minute ago, briefly appraised that palm as if there was a vial of magic serum nestling in it. "This . . . Lover Five of yours: she's our way in. We never had one of these people to study before. We'll learn a lot and we'll learn fast. Who knows, we may be able to save her. Or if we can't save *her*, we may be able to save her children." He paused. "They do have children, don't they?"

Peter's mind re-played the vision of the calf-like newborn, the cheering crowd, the dressing ceremony, the eerie beauty of little ᴀᴀᴧᴐᴌᴚ, clumsily dancing on his inaugural day of life, waving his tiny gloved hands.

"Yes, they do," he said.

"Well, there you go," said Adkins.

* * *

Lover Five, confined to bed in her brightly-lit chamber of care, looked just as small and alone as before. If only there could have been a USIC worker laid up with a broken leg in one of the other beds, or a few healthy ⲱⲣⲁⲋ sitting nearby, conversing with her in their native tongue, it would have been less awful. Awful for who, though? Peter knew it was for his own sake as well as for hers that he yearned for the pathos to be less sharp. In his career as a minister, he'd visited many hospital wards, but never, until now, to confront a person whose impending death he felt responsible for.

"God bleⲱ our reunion, Father Peⲭer," she said as he walked in. Since he'd last seen her, she'd gotten hold of a USIC bathtowel and deftly folded it around her head as an improvised hood. It lent her a more feminine appearance, like a hijab or a wig. She'd tucked the loose ends under the neckline of her hospital gown, and pulled the blankets up to her armpits. Her left hand was still naked; her right was snugly bound in its cotton sheath.

"Lover Five, I'm so, so sorry," he said, his voice already cracking.

"ⲱorry noⲭ neⲱeⲱary," she reassured him. The absolution cost her an absurd amount of effort to pronounce. Insult to injury.

"The painting that fell on your hand . . ." he said, lowering himself onto the edge of the bed near the meager hump of her knees. "If I hadn't asked for . . ."

With her free hand she did a surprising thing, a thing he'd never have imagined anyone of her kind doing: she silenced him by laying her fingers against his lips. It was the first time he had been touched by the naked flesh of an ⲱⲣⲁⲋ, unmediated by the soft fabric of gloves. Her fingertips were smooth and warm and smelled like fruit.

"Nothing fall if God have no plan for the falling."

Gently he enclosed her hand in his. "I shouldn't say this," he said, "but out of all your people . . . you're the one I care about the most."

"I know," she said, with barely a heartbeat's hesitation. "Buⲭ God have no favoriⲭⲱ. God care for all alike."

Her constant allusions to God poked a spear into his soul. He had big confessions to make, confessions about his faith, confessions about what he intended to do next. "Lover Five . . ." he began. "I . . . I don't want to lie to you. I . . ."

She nodded, slowly and emphatically, to signal that he need not complete the thought. "You feel . . . in lack of God. You feel you can be no Father any more." She turned aside, looked at the doorway through which he had come, the doorway that led to the outside world. Somewhere in that direction was the settlement where she'd first accepted Jesus into her heart, the settlement that now lay empty and abandoned. "Father Kurಶಒberg alಒo came ಶo thiಒ feeling," she said. "Father Kurಶಒberg became angry, ಒpoke in a loud voiಒe, ಒaid, I am no Father now. Find another Father."

Peter swallowed hard. The Bible booklet he'd sewn lay curled up on the blanket near his useless arse. Back in his quarters, there were so many balls of brightly colored wool still waiting to be used.

"You are . . ." said Lover Five, and paused to find the right word. ". . . man. Only man. God iಒ more big than you. You carry the word of God for a while, then the word become ಶoo heavy, heavy ಶo carry, and you muಒಶ reಒಶ." She laid her hand on his thigh. "I underಒಶand."

"My wife . . ." he began.

"I underಒಶand," she repeated. "God join you and your wife ಶogether. Now you are unjoined."

In a flash Peter recalled his wedding day, the light through the church windows, the cake, the knife, Bea's dress. Sentimental daydreams, as irreclaimably lost as a bug-eaten Scout uniform tossed in a bin and taken away by garbagemen. He forced himself to think instead of his own house as it was now, surrounded by filth and debris, the interior plunged into darkness, and, half-hidden in those haunted shadows, the shape of a woman he couldn't recognize. "It's not just that we're apart," he said. "Bea's in trouble. She needs help."

Lover Five nodded. Her bandaged hand screamed louder than any words of recrimination that there could be no trouble more serious than the trouble she was in. "ಒo," she confirmed, "you will fulfill the word of Jeಒuಒ Luke: you will leave the nineಶy-nine in the wilderneಒ, and look for the one who iಒ loಒಶ."

He felt his face redden as the parable found its mark. She must have learned it from Kurtzberg.

"I've talked to the doctors," he said wretchedly. "They're going to try their best, for you and for . . . the others. They won't be able to save your hand, but they might be able to save your life."

"I am happy," she said. "If **ᴄᴐ**aved."

He shifted uncomfortably on his perch at the edge of her bed. His left buttock was going numb and his back was getting sore. In a few minutes from now, he would be out of this room and his body would revert to normal, restoring normal blood circulation, pacifying disturbed neurological activity, soothing over-extended muscles, while she was left here to contemplate the rotting of her flesh.

"Is there anything I can do for you right now?" he said.

She thought for a few seconds. "**ᴄᴐ**ing," she said. "**ᴄᴐ**ing only with me."

"Sing what?"

"Our **ᴄᴐ**ong of welcome for Father Pe**ꙅ**er," she said. "You will go away, I know. Then I hope you will come back, in the **ᴄᴐ**wee**ꙅ** by and by. And when you come back, we will **ᴄᴐ**ing again the **ᴄᴐ**ame **ᴄᴐ**ong." Without further prelude, she began. "*Amaaa**ᴄᴐ**iiing graaa**ᴄᴐ**e . . .*"

He joined in at once. His voice, hoarse and muted in speech, found strength when called upon to sing. The acoustics in the intensive care unit were actually better than in his church, where the humid atmosphere and the throng of bodies always dampened the sound; here, in this chilly concrete cavity, with only empty beds, dormant machinery and metal IV stands for company, "Amazing Grace" reverberated rich and clear.

"Waaaas bliiiind," he chanted, "*but nooooow I seeeee . . .*"

The length of her breaths, even though she shortened them for his sake, made the song last a very long time. He was exhausted by the end.

"Thank you," said Lover Five. "You will go now. I will remain alway**ᴄᴐ** . . . your brother."

There was no message from Bea.

She was finished with him. She'd given up.

Or maybe . . . maybe she had committed suicide. The state of the world, the loss of Joshua, the loss of her faith, the rift in their marriage . . . these were terrible griefs to bear, and maybe she just hadn't been able to bear them. As a teenager, she'd been suicidal. He'd almost lost her then, without even knowing she was there to lose.

He opened a fresh page on the Shoot. He must trust that she was still alive, still able to receive his messages. The blank screen loomed so large: so much blankness to envelop whatever meaning he might attempt to put there. He thought of quoting or paraphrasing the bit in 2 *Corinthians* 5 about the house "not made with hands" that awaits us if our earthly home is destroyed. Sure, it was a Bible quote, but maybe it was relevant in a non-religious context, like BG tapping his own chest to indicate that home wasn't bricks and mortar, home could be anywhere.

A voice came to him and said, *Don't be stupid.*

I'm coming home, he wrote, and that was all.

Having promised that he would return, he was aware that he had no idea how to make it happen. He clicked on the green scarab icon, and the Shoot revealed the three paltry options on his menu: *Maintenance (repairs)*, *Admin* and *Graigner*. None of them seemed quite right. He clicked on *Admin* and wrote:

> I'm sorry, but I need to go home. As soon as possible. I don't know if
> I'll be able to come back sometime in the future. If so, it would need
> to be with my wife. I'm not trying to blackmail you, I'm just saying
> that's the only way I could do it. Please respond and confirm when I
> can go. Sincerely, Peter Leigh (Pastor).

He re-read what he had written, deleted everything from I don't know to the only way I could do it. Too many words, too much explanation. The essential message, the one which demanded action, was simpler than that.

He stood up, stretched. A sharp sting on his leg reminded him of the injury there. The wound was healing well, but the flesh was tight along the suture line. He would always have a scar, and it would occasionally hurt. There were limits to what the miraculous human organism could repair.

His dishdasha, hanging on the washing line, was dry now. The blurry marks of the ink crucifix had been almost obliterated, faded to the palest lilac. The hems were so badly frayed they looked as if they'd been deliberately manufactured that way, as a fluffy frill. "You don't think it's too girly, do you?" he recalled Bea saying, when they first took the garment out of its shrinkwrap. Not only did he recall the words, but also the sound of Bea's voice, the expression in her eyes, the light on the side of her nose: everything. And she'd said: "You can be naked underneath. If you want." She was his wife. He loved her. Surely somewhere in the universe, allowing for the laws of time and space and relativity, there must be a place where that could still be possible.

"Imagine you're in a tiny inflatable dinghy, lost at sea," Ella Reinman had suggested to him, during those endless interviews on the tenth floor of the swanky hotel. "Far in the distance, there's a ship; you can't tell whether it's moving toward you or away. You know that if you try to stand up and wave, the dinghy will capsize. But if you sit still, nobody will see you and you won't get rescued. What do you do?"

"Sit tight."

"Are you sure? What if the ship is definitely moving away?"

"I'd have to live with that."

"You'd just sit and watch it go?"

"I'd pray to God."

"What if there was no answer?"

"There's always an answer."

His calmness had impressed them. His refusal to embrace wild, impulsive gestures had helped him make the grade. It was the calmness of the homeless, the calmness of the ᕼᕐᐅᐸᣘ. Without knowing it, he'd always been an honorary alien.

Now, he was pacing his quarters in a frenzy, an animal trapped in a cage. He needed to be home. Get going, get going, get going. The needle in the vein, the woman saying *This will sting some*, then blackness. Yes! Come on! Every minute of delay was a torment. Pacing around, he almost tripped on a discarded shoe, seized hold of it, hurled it across the room. Maybe Grainger, in her quarters, was doing the same. Maybe they should go berserk together, share the bourbon. He really wanted a drink.

He checked the Shoot. Nothing. Who was supposed to read his message anyway? Some off-duty engineer or kitchenhand? What kind of a fucking system was this, where there was no one in charge, no one with an office you could barge into, no one you could grab by the shirt? He paced his quarters some more, breathing too heavily. The floor, the ceiling, the window, the furniture, the bed: it was all wrong, wrong, wrong. He thought of Tuska, delivering his Légion Étrangère spiel, all that stuff about the weaklings who'd gone crazy, climbing the walls, begging to "go *ho-ome.*" He could still taste Tuska's sarcasm. Smug bastard!

Eighteen minutes later, on his Shoot, there was an answer from Admin.

> Howdy. Forwarded your request to USIC hq. Typical response timelag is 24 hrs (even big shots got to sleep sometimes) but I predict they will say yes. Diplomacywise it might have been good to make some noises about coming back to finish your mission but hey its not my business to tell you how to win friends & influence people. I wasnt scheduled to do my next flight for another month but what the heck Ill make the best of it, maybe get some new tennis shoes, buy an ice cream, visit a steakhouse. Or a whorehouse! Just kidding. Im a fine upstanding pilgrim, you know me. Stand by and Ill give you the word when its time to go. Au reviore, Tuska

As soon as Peter finished reading these words, he leapt up, knocking his chair over, and jumped exultant into the air, clenching his fists like a sportsman granted victory against the odds. He would have yelled *Hallelujah*, too, if it hadn't been for the searing spasm that shot through his injured leg. Crying in pain, laughing in relief, he fell to the floor, curled up like a bug, or a thief who'd broken his ankles, or a husband who was clutching his wife's flesh rather than his own.

Thank you, he breathed, *thank you* . . . but who was he thanking? He didn't know. He only knew that thanks were due.

27

STAY WHERE YOU ARE.

His name was Peter Leigh, son of James Leigh and Kate Leigh (née Woolfolk), grandson of George and June. He was born in Horns Mill, Hertford, Hertfordshire. The names of his cats, in the order that he'd owned them, were Mokkie, Silky, Cleo, Sam, Titus and Joshua. When he returned home, he would have another cat, from an animal refuge, if such places still existed when he got back. As for his own child, he would call him, or her, whatever name Bea wanted. Or maybe Kate. They would discuss it when the time came. Maybe they'd wait until the baby was born, and see what its personality was. People were individuals from Day One.

He stood as straight as he could in his soul-destroying room in the USIC base and appraised himself in the mirror. He was a thirty-three-year-old English male, deeply tanned as if he'd been on a long holiday to Alicante or some such Mediterranean resort. But he did not look fit. His chin and collarbones were worryingly sharp, sculpted by inadequate diet. He was too thin for the dishdasha, although he looked even worse in Western clothes. There were a few small scars on his face, some of them dating from his alcoholic years, some more recent and delineated with neat crusts. His eyes were bloodshot and there was fear and grief in them. "You know what would sort you out?" a fellow dosser once said to him as they stood in the rain waiting for a homeless shelter to open. "A wife." When Peter asked him if he spoke from experience, the old wino only smiled and shook his grizzled head.

* * *

The USIC corridors that had once seemed like a maze were now familiar—too familiar. The familiarity of a prison. The framed posters hung in their appointed places, marking his progress through the base. As he walked toward the vehicle bay, the glazen images gazed sightlessly down at him: Rudolph Valentino, Rosie the Riveter, the dog in the basket with the ducks, the smiling picnickers by Renoir. Laurel and Hardy caught frozen, stoic, forever interrupted in their hopeless attempt to build a house. And those 1930s construction workers suspended high above New York . . . they would be suspended there eternally, never finishing their lunch, never falling off their girder, never growing old.

He pushed through the last door and was greeted by the smell of engine grease. For his farewell visit to the ᑕᕐᗅᐢ, he wanted to travel to C-2 himself, alone, not as a passenger in someone else's car. He cast his eyes over the vehicle bay in search of the person who was manning it today, hoping it might be someone he'd never met before, someone who knew nothing about him except that he was the VIP missionary man who should be given whatever he asked for, within reason. But the person bending into the engine of a jeep, canopied by the open hood, had a rump he recognized. It was Craig again.

"Hi," he said, knowing even as he opened his mouth that oratory would get him nowhere.

"Hi," she said, only half-acknowledging him as she continued to slather the engine innards with lubricant.

Their negotiation was short and sweet. He could hardly blame her for refusing to hand over a vehicle, given what happened last time. Maybe she'd been criticized by her fellow USIC personnel for allowing him—clearly off his head—to drive Kurtzberg's hearse into the night, only to need emergency rescue later, while the vehicle had to be schlepped back to base in a separate trip. Craig was all smiles and casual body language, but the subtext was: *You are a pain in the ass.*

"There's a drug and food exchange scheduled just a few hours from now," she said, as she wiped her hands on a rag. "Why not go along for the ride?"

"Because this is goodbye. I'm saying goodbye to the ᑕᕐᗅᐢ."

"Goodbye to the what?"

"The Oasans. The native people." *The freaks in Freaktown, you fat idiot,* he thought.

She chewed on this. "You need your own vehicle to say goodbye in?"

He hung his head in frustration. "If I'm shoulder to shoulder with USIC personnel, it might look like I was using you guys as . . . uh . . . bodyguards. Emotional bodyguards, if you see what I mean." Craig's direct yet unfocused stare told him that no, she didn't see. "It might look like I didn't want to face them on my own."

"OK," said Craig, idly scratching her snake tattoo. Seconds passed, making it obvious that her "OK" did not mean "In that case, I will give you a car"; it did not even mean "I understand why that might worry you"; it meant "So be it."

"Also," he said, "I'm not sure that Grainger will want to be going out to the settlement today."

"Won't be Grainger," said Craig breezily, and consulted a printed roster. "Grainger is off-duty for . . ." She flipped pages, scanning for the name. "The foreseeable," she summarized at last, and flipped back to today. "It'll be . . . Tuska and Flores."

Peter looked over her shoulder, at all the greased-up vehicles he could drive out of this place if only she wasn't in the way.

"Your choice," she grinned, and he understood that sometimes there is no choice at all.

"I see you standing on the shore of a huge lake," Bea had said, the last time he'd held her in his arms. "It's night and the sky is full of stars." And she had shared her vision of him preaching to a multitude of unseen creatures in fishing boats, bobbing on the sea. Perhaps they'd both known that it was a dream, that nothing like that would really happen. It was another sunny, torpid day on Oasis, and the natives were dozing in their cots, or making food for their foreign guests, or washing clothes, or spending time with their children, hoping that their flesh would survive unharmed until the sun set and they were cocooned in their cots again. Maybe they were praying.

Filling in time before the appointed hour for his ride, Peter considered what, if anything, to take with him to the settlement. A stack of half-finished booklets lay on the table, next to some balls of wool. He picked up the nearest, a paraphrase of *Revelation*, Chapter 21. He'd reduced the number of "s" sounds to four, and gotten rid of all the "t"s: that was probably as much as he could achieve.

And there I found a new heaven and a new earth, for the heaven and the earth from before were gone. And I heard a loud voice from heaven declaring, Behold, God will dwell with you, and you will be His very own people, and God will be your very own God. And there will be no more death, no more sorrow, no more pain. And God upon the throne said, Behold, I make everything new.

To avoid the need for explanations that might go nowhere, he'd omitted Jerusalem, the sea, the tabernacle, the apostle John, the bride and the husband, men, and a few other things. The God of this pamphlet no longer wiped tears from eyes, partly because those words were too difficult to pronounce, partly because, after all this time, it was still a mystery whether the ⲥⲣⲁⲥ had eyes or wept. Peter reconnected with how long he'd sweated to think of an alternative word for "true." All that labor, and for what? The only words he had to offer them now were "sorry" and "goodbye."

"Beautiful day," said Tuska, and it was. The atmosphere was putting on a show for them, as if in honor of a momentous occasion. Two huge columns of unfallen rain, one to the west and the other to the east, had drifted toward each other and were now mingling in their topmost reaches, forming a glistering arch in the sky. It was a long way off yet, miles probably, but it conjured the illusion that they were about to pass under a colossal portal made of nothing more substantial than water droplets.

"Gotta admit," said Tuska, "view-wise, that's a nine out of ten."

"Rear windows are shut, I hope?" said Flores. "Don't want those drugs to get rained on."

"Yes, they're shut," said Peter. Tuska and Flores, stationed in the front seats, had barely said a word to him since the jeep had left the compound. He felt like a child stashed in the back, allowed to come along for no better reason than that he couldn't be left unattended, and with nothing to do on the journey but hope that his parents didn't quarrel.

The hermetic seal of air conditioning that Grainger tried so diligently to maintain was not Tuska's style. He kept the front windows open as he drove, allowing the air free access to the vehicle's interior. The languid agitations of the atmosphere were joined by an artificial breeze from the speed of the vehicle.

"Where's Grainger?" asked Peter.

"Taking it easy," said Tuska, only his shoulder and driving arm visible to Peter.

"Drunk and incapable," said Flores, wholly hidden.

"She's been a pretty good pharmacist all these years," said Tuska.

"There are other pharmacists," Flores remarked.

"Well, let's see what Santa Claus brings, shall we?" said Tuska, and Flores shut up.

The brilliant arch in the sky had drawn no nearer, so Peter looked out the passenger window instead. The landscape, which he'd grown to love, was still austerely beautiful, but today he saw its simplicity through different eyes, and it disturbed him. He could imagine a farm girl like Grainger scanning the terrain's serene emptiness, searching in vain for wildlife, plant-life, or any kind of life, to remind her of her childhood habitat.

"Grainger needs to go home," he said, the words springing out of his mouth before he even knew he'd formed them.

"Yeah," said Tuska, "I think she does."

"Soon," said Peter, and recalled, for the first time in years, that *Soon* was the name of a Scripture pamphlet he and Bea had produced ages ago for the Jesus lovers of Arunachal Pradesh. In a flash, in his mind's eye, he saw his hands and Bea's moving near each other on the kitchen table: his hands folding the pamphlet in three, with the *Soon* letterhead facing out; Bea's hands slipping the paper into an envelope, sealing it, addressing it to some mountain-dwelling Adivasi with an unpronounceable name. Cardboard boxes full of *Soon* pamphlets had been sent overseas at six-monthly intervals, an absurd expense in the electronic age, but not everybody in the world had a computer and, besides, there was something special about holding Bible verses in your hand.

How long ago it was. His hand holding a pamphlet called *Soon*, reaching across the table to Bea's hand.

"I forwarded her request too," Tuska was saying. "My guess is you'll both go together." He yawned. "Two simultaneous bailouts from our little paradise! Do you guys know something I don't? On second thought, don't tell me."

"There's nothing wrong with this place," said Peter, staring out the window again. "I'm sorry to let everybody down."

"Some people can take it, some can't," said Tuska lightly. "Can't reuse an EPFCG."

"Sorry?"

"Explosively pumped flux compression generator."

Those words, which to Peter were as weird and incomprehensible as any arcane Scripture would be to his hosts, were the last spoken for a long while. The illusion that they were about to pass under a vast, twinkling archway faded gradually, as the two columns of water drifted apart and morphed into different, unsymmetrical shapes. Rain splattered against the windscreen and roof, its rhythm strange as ever, determined by physics beyond human understanding. Then the shower passed and the windscreen wipers squeaked annoyingly against clear glass before Tuska switched them off. The caramel façades of Freaktown were only a few hundred meters away now, and Peter could already make out a tiny figure standing in the appointed spot.

"When we arrive," he piped up from the back, "I just need a minute, two minutes alone with that person."

"OK," said Tuska, changing gear for the final stretch. "But no tongues."

Jesus Lover One was waiting in front of the building with the white star painted on it. When he caught sight of Peter, his body jerked in surprise, but he managed to compose himself in the few seconds that elapsed between the revelation and Peter's deposition from the jeep.

"You are alive," he said.

"I hope so," Peter said, and regretted it at once: the ⳍⳊⳆⳍ didn't do flippancy, and the quip only made it harder for Lover One to adjust to Peter's miraculous recovery from his mortal wounds.

"All the other𝕤 believe you are dead," said Lover One. "I believe you are alive. I alone have faith."

Peter struggled to think of the appropriate response to that. An affectionate embrace was out. "Thank you," he said.

Behind the bead curtains in the doorways of the buildings, shadowy figures had gathered. "𝕤𝕩 𝕓𝕤𝕒," called a voice. Peter knew enough of the language to know that this meant "The task is still asleep." Or, to paraphrase: *Get on with it.*

Lover One roused himself from his trance and accepted his official role. He turned toward the vehicle in anticipation of greeting the USIC envoy, the scarf-wearing woman Grainger who abhorred him and all his kind.

Nurse Flores stepped out of the vehicle. As she approached the Oasan, it was evident that there was not much difference between them in size. By chance, their garments—her uniform, his robes—were almost the same color.

Lover One was visibly thrown by these unexpected parities. He appraised Flores quite a few seconds longer than politeness allowed, but she stared right back.

"You and I," said the Lover One. "Never before now." And he reached forward and touched her gently on the wrist with his gloved fingertips.

"He means, Hi, I haven't met you before," explained Peter.

"Glad to meet you," said Flores. While that may have been an overstatement, she seemed quite free of Grainger's unease.

"You bring medi𝕤ine?" said Lover One.

"Of course," said Flores, and went to the rear of the vehicle to fetch it. Several other Oasans ventured out from hiding, then several more. That was unusual: two or three had been the maximum in Peter's experience.

Flores carried the box in her sinewy arms. It looked bigger and fuller than last time, perhaps because she was smaller than Grainger. Still, she wielded it without effort and handed it to one of the Oasans with smooth confidence.

"To whom shall I address the explanations?" she said.

"I understand more," said Jesus Lover One.

"To you, then," said Flores, in a friendly but businesslike manner.

The box, as always, was crammed with a mixture of branded and un-branded medicines. Flores extracted each little plastic bottle, cardboard packet and tube, held it aloft like an auction hammer while describing its function, and slotted it back into place.

"I'm not a pharmacist," she said. "But it's all written on the labels and the leaflets anyway. The main thing is for you to tell us what's working and not working. Pardon me saying so, but there's been too much mystery here. Let's take the mystery out of it, try more of a scientific approach. Think you can do that?"

Lover One was silent for a few seconds, just focusing on the creature standing head-to-head with him. "We are grateful for medicine," he said at last.

"That's nice," said Flores flatly. "But listen: this here is a packet of Su-mycin. It's an antibiotic. If you get an infection in your waterworks or your guts, it could fix you. But if you've taken a lot of Sumycin in the past, it might not work so well. You might be better taking this one here, Amoxicil-lin. These two packets of Amoxicillin are generics . . ."

"Name from where all other name come," said Jesus Lover One.

"That's right. Now, Amoxicillin is fine if you've never had it before, but if your body has become resistant to it, you're better with this purple one here, Augmentin, which has some extra stuff in it to overcome that resis-tance." Flores put the Augmentin back in the box and scratched her nose with a simian finger. "Listen, we could stand here all day talking about the pros and cons of each and every antibiotic in this box. But what we really need is to match up specific drugs with specific problems. For example, take you. Are you sick?"

"Thank God no," said Lover One.

"Well, bring out someone who *is* sick and let's talk."

There was a pause. "We are grateful for medicine," said Lover One. "We have food for you." The tone was neutral, and yet there was stubborn-ness, even threat in it.

"Great, thanks, we'll get around to that in a minute," said Flores, un-swayed. "But first, can I meet someone who thinks they need antibiotics? As I said, I'm not a pharmacist. I'm not a doctor. I would just prefer to get a little better acquainted with you folks."

As the two of them stood their ground, more Oasans ventured out from shelter. Peter realized that they must always have been there, in the past, whenever these handovers were done, but had lacked the courage to emerge into view. What was it about Flores? Her smell, perhaps? Peter turned to Tuska. Tuska winked.

"Obey the mighty Flores," he said wryly. "Or else."

Once it had become clear that the handover was going to take some time, Peter excused himself and began to walk across the tundra to his church. It was quite a windy day, and his dishdasha flapped around his ankles, but the breeze was useful in reducing the humidity, promoting the illusion of fresher oxygen. Inside his sandals his feet were already slippery with sweat. He looked down at them as he walked, and recalled the sensation of stepping into crisp snow with thick-soled boots on a raw January morning in Richmond Park with his newly divorced father smoking a cigarette nearby. No sooner had he glimpsed the image than it was gone.

Every now and then as he crossed the plain to the temple that he and his flock had built, he looked over his shoulder, in case Lover One was following. But Lover One was not following, and Peter's view of the tiny figures near the USIC vehicle grew indistinct through the blur of interlapping air currents.

When he reached his church, he extended his palms and swung open the doors, expecting to find the place empty. But no. There were fifty or sixty brightly colored souls gathered inside, already seated in the pews, as if by firm pre-arrangement. Not the full congregation, but a healthy turnout—especially considering they'd gathered to worship on their own, with no pastor. Quite a few of them had been working in the whiteflower fields on the day of his downfall, and had witnessed the piercing of his flesh, had watched the vermin's teeth mutilate him so badly that there could be no hope of survival, even with the Technique of Jesus. Maybe this gathering was a memorial service for Father Peșer, and here he was, gatecrashing it.

A murmur of wonder passed through the crowd. Then a swell of communal elation charged the air, taking up palpable space, pushing against the walls, threatening to lift the ceiling. If he'd wanted to, he could have done anything with them at this moment, taken them anywhere. They were his.

"God blesƨ our reunion, Father Peșer," they exclaimed, first one-by-one, then as a chorus. Each voice aggravated the grief in his chest a little more. Their faith had been buoyed up to the heavens, and he had come to let them down.

The doors thudded shut behind him, their well-oiled motion aided by the wind. Plentiful light beamed through the windows, illuminating the hooded heads of the Jesus Lovers so that they glowed like candle-flames in a votive rack. As he walked between the pews, the surreal montage of paintings on the ceiling hung heavy over him. Lover Twelve's bright pink Jesus walking hand in hand with a glistening gray Lazarus, Lover Fourteen's blue and yellow Nativity, Lover Twenty's Mary Magdalene spewing forth ectoplasmic devils, Lover Sixty-Three's Thomas the Doubter . . . and, of course, Lover Five's painting of the risen Christ and his women, secure in its place, fastened with extra care after the accident that had maimed her. The scarecrow in the loincloth, so different from the kindly *mensch* of Christian tradition, had suddenly become terrifying. The blaze of light where His head should be and the eye-shaped holes in His starfish hands, which Peter had once taken as evidence that God could not be confined to the iconography of one race, now struck him as proof of an unbreachable gulf.

He took his stand behind the pulpit. He noted that the ƨᘁɑƨ had tidied his bed, washed and dried and folded the linen, cleaned the boots that Lover Five had sewn for him, and placed a mislaid pencil on the pillow where it could be admired as a sacred relic by future generations. Now, blessed with his miraculous return, they sat in rapt attention, Bible booklets at their side, awaiting the call to sing the first hymn, which might, according to custom, be "In The Garden" or "For God Be The Glory." He cleared his throat. He trusted, against hope, that inspiration would come from somewhere, as it always had before.

"ᔕᓄᕆᗯᘢᒐᒿᕲᗯ," he said. "ᐱᔆᔆᕲᗝᒐ. ᔕᓄᕆᗯ ᗰᗃ ᔕᕆᗯᗰᏚt ᕕuᒥᕲ ᗰᗃᏚᒐᕲᔆ ᒐᕲᗯᔆᔆᗃᏚᒐᕲᗯ."

Some of the congregation made the shoulder-trembling motions he'd always interpreted as laughter. He hoped it *was* laughter, elicited by his clumsy pronunciation, but maybe he'd never really known what those motions meant after all.

"ᔕᓄᐱᔆᔆᕲᗝᒐ Ꮪtᕲ ᔕᔆᔆᓄᕆᗝ ᔕᓄᐱ Jesus ᐱᕲᗯᘢᒐᒿᗯᗰs," he continued. He could sense their bemusement at his strained and childish speech, so unnecessary when they were only too willing to listen to the holy language of James the King. But he wanted to address them, just once, in a way that they could fully understand. He owed them that much: their dignity at the expense of his own. "ᒿᗰᔆᔆ Jesus ᔕᏚt ᔕᕲᗝᔆ ᔕᓄ ᐱᓄ ᐱᕲᗝ."

He finished his exact tally of the worshippers, begun as a habitual reflex: fifty-two. He would never know how many more souls were concealed in the settlement, never know how far away he'd been from bringing the entire community to Christ. He only knew that he recognized each and every person here, and not just by the colors of their robes.

"Ꮯ ᐱᕲᗯᘢᒐᒿᗯᔆᔆ ᔕᕲᗯᗰᓄᕲ ᕕuᒥᕲ ᔕᕲ," he said, "ᕲᒐᒿᗯᗰᔆᔆ ᔕᕲᒐᕲᗯᗰᓄ the Book of Strange New Things." He extracted the King James Bible from his bag, and, instead of thumbing the gilt-edged pages to a selected passage for reading aloud, he stepped out from behind the pulpit and carried the book to the Jesus Lovers in the front pew. With fastidious gentleness—not because of reverence for the book, but because of concern for the fragile flesh before him—he handed it to Lover Seventeen, who cradled it in her lap.

He returned to the pulpit. "ᔕᕲ sᏚ Ꮯ ᔕᕲ," he said, "ᗰᓄ ᐱᔆᔆᕲ ᔕᔆᔆᔕᏚ God. ᔕᕲ God ᐱᗰᓄ ᔕᓄ ᐱᓄ ᐱᕲᗯᘢᒐᒿᗯᗰᔆᔆ ᗰᗃᏚ ᒿᗰᔆᔆ ᒐᕲᗃᏚᒐᕲ."

A thrill of consternation was passing through his flock. Heads tilted, hands agitated. Lover Fifteen uttered a cry.

"ᐱᕲᗯᔕᕲ ᒐᒐᓄᐱᔆᔆ ᒿᗰᔆᔆ ᗰ God ᗰᗃ ᐱᕲᗯᒐ Ꮪᒐᕲᕲ ᒿᗰᔆᔆ," he pressed on. "ᗰᓄ tᔕᕲ Ꮯ Ꮪᗰᓄ ᔕᕲ Ꮪᗰᕲ ᕲ ᔕᕲᗯᗰᓄ ᐱᔆᔆᕲᗝᒐ ᒿᗰᔆᔆ Jesus Lover Five . . ." His voice broke, and he had to grip the wings of his pulpit to keep himself from trembling. "Jesus Lover Five ⲋⲟⲢⲁⲋ ⲋⲟⲢ ⳤⲩⲋ‖ ⳤiⲢ ⲋⲟⲢⲁⲋ ⲋⲟⳤt ⳤⲟⲢⲟ. ⲗⲟⲋ ⲋⲟⲗⲟ ⲋⲟⲢⳤ ⲟⲋⲋⳤⲟ USIC." He took a deep, shuddering breath. ⲋⲟⳤtⳤⲋⳤ ⲋⳤⲟⲗⲃⳤⲢⳤⲟⲟⲗⳤⲋ ⳤ ⲋⲟⳤt ⲟurⲟ. ⲗⲟ ⲗⲟⲗ ⳤⲟⲢⲟ ⳤⲋⳤⲢⲟⲗ ⲋⲟⲗⲟ Bea. ⳤtⲢ ⲋⲟⲗⲟ ⲟss . . ."

And that was it: he could go no further: the word he needed, the most crucial word, was one he didn't know in the ⲋⲟⲢⲁⲋ language. He bowed his head, and took refuge, at the last, in his own foreign tongue.

". . . forgive."

He left the pulpit, picked up the canary-yellow boots, one in each hand, and walked stiffly down the aisle, toward the exit. For the first few seconds, which felt like minutes, he walked in silence, alone. Then the Jesus Lovers rose from their seats and gathered all around him, touching him tenderly on the shoulders, the back, the abdomen, the buttocks, the thighs, anywhere they could reach, while saying, in clear, unhampered voices, "Forgive."

"Forgive."

"Forgive."

"Forgive."

"Forgive."

"Forgive," each in their turn, until he blundered through the doors into the harsh sunlight.

On the way back to the settlement, as his flaccid, empty bag flapped against his waist, he looked around several times at his church silhouetted against the brilliant sky. No one had emerged from it but him. Belief was a place that people didn't leave until they absolutely must. The ⲋⲟⲢⲁⲋ had been keen to follow him to the kingdom of Heaven, but they weren't keen to follow him into the valley of doubt. He knew that one day—maybe very soon—they would have another pastor. They'd taken from him what they needed, and their search for salvation would go on when he was long gone. After all, their souls dreamt so ardently of a longer stay in the flesh, a longer spell of consciousness. It was natural: they were only human.

* * *

Back at the USIC jeep, things had moved on. Lover One was nowhere to be seen, the medicines had all been distributed, and the food was being loaded into the vehicle. More ꟼꙅꙇ than usual were involved, quite a crowd of them. Both Tuska and Flores were available to take hold of the tubs, sacks and tins brought out to them, but Peter noticed, even from a distance, that the ꟼꙅꙇ approached Flores first, and detoured to Tuska only when Flores already had her hands full. He figured it out at last: they liked her. Who would've thought it? They liked her.

"Let me carry that," said Tuska, as Flores took charge of a particularly heavy bag of whiteflower dough.

"I'm OK," said Flores. Her hair was plastered with sweat, emphasizing the smallness of her skull, and blue veins stood out on her temples. Her whole torso was sodden. She was having a grand time.

A little while later, when the three of them were seated in the vehicle and Tuska was driving away from C-2, she said:

"We're going to crack them, Joe."

"Crack them?" echoed Tuska.

"Find out what makes them tick," she explained.

"Yeah?" said Tuska, clearly not much interested in the prospect.

"Yes. And then, God willing, we'll fix them."

Peter was surprised to hear such words uttered by a USIC employee. But then, Flores's face appeared in the gap between the front seats, like a gargoyle head jutting out from a Gothic wall, seeking out the minister stashed in the back.

"Just a figure of speech, you understand," she said. "I really meant, with luck." Her face vanished again, but she wasn't done talking. "I guess you don't believe there's such a thing as luck, huh?"

Peter turned his face to stare out the window. At the speed Tuska was driving, the dark earth could be mistaken for tarmac, and the occasional outcrop of pale wildflower swept past in a blur like the painted white lines of a motorway. If he imagined hard enough, he might even see M25 road signs estimating the distance to London.

"I hope there is," he answered Flores, a little too late. He was pretty sure the word "luck" appeared nowhere in the Bible, but that didn't mean there was no such thing. Grainger had called him a lucky guy. And, with Bea at his side, for the best part of his life, he truly had been.

When he got back to his quarters, there was, finally, a message from Bea. It said,

> Peter, I love you. But please, don't come home. I beg you. Stay where you are.

2 8

AMEN.

"What I like about this place," said Moro, making brisk progress on her treadmill, "is that every day there's something a little bit different, but also it's the same."

She, BG and Peter were exercising in the gazebo. It was just another day on Oasis, another scheduled break in the task at hand, a few hours of R&R before work resumed on the great project. The canopy was shading them from the sun, but the light was so intense at this stage of the afternoon that it penetrated the canvas, casting a yellow tinge over their flesh.

Moro had worked up a big sweat already; the fabric of her shalwar was sculpted to her thighs as she paced, and her bare midriff glistened. She had announced three hundred steps as her goal and must be about halfway through by now, never letting the rhythm slacken. She swiveled her wrists on the treadmill's handlebars, as if revving the throttle grip of a motorcycle.

"You should try it with just your legs, no holding on," advised BG, resting between bouts of press-ups. "Better for your quads, your tibs, everything."

"I see it as exercise for my hands, too," said Moro. "People who lose a finger often let the hand get sloppy. I made a decision: not me."

Peter was lifting a sandbag on a pulley, or trying to. His arms had become quite strong and wiry from working in the whiteflower fields, but the muscles he'd toughened must be a different set from the ones he was straining now.

"Don't bust a gut on the lifting," advised BG. "The lowering's just as good. Do it slow. Slow as you can."

"It's still too heavy for me, I think," said Peter. "What's the bag filled with? Not sand, surely?" He couldn't imagine USIC approving the shipment of a sack of sand when, for the same cost-weight ratio, they could transport a sack of sugar or a person.

"Earth," said BG, gesturing at the bare acres around the exercise yard. He removed his singlet and wrung it out in his fists. An arc of puckered scars came to life near his left armpit, marring the smooth swell of his pectoral. He put his singlet back on.

"I don't suppose we could let some of the soil out?" said Peter.

"I don't suppose so, bro," said BG. His facial expression was unsmilingly serious, but he was amused. Human beings could be read quite easily once you got to know them a bit. It was all in the tone, the cadences, the twinkle in the eyes, so many subtle factors that defied scientific description but which you could, if you wished, build a lifelong friendship on.

Peter tried to lift the sandbag again. This time, he barely raised it above knee-level before his biceps began to hurt.

"Part of your problem there," said BG, coming over, "is you need more of a balanced approach." He unhooked the sandbag from the pulley, hoisted it without much effort to his chest, then cradled it in one arm. "Most important muscle is your brain. You gotta plan what you're gonna do, warm up to it. Find an exercise that pushes you to the limit but not beyond it. With this sandbag, I suggest a straight carry."

"Sorry?"

BG stood close to Peter, transferred the sack from his own arms into Peter's, carefully as if it was a sleeping baby.

"Just hug it to your chest," he said. "Wrap your arms around it and walk. From one end of the gazebo to the other, and again, and again, as many times as you can until you can't do it no more. Then lower it to the ground nice and easy."

Peter did as he was told. BG watched. So did Moro, who had finished her three hundred steps and was drinking from a bottle of pale green liquid, possibly rainwater, possibly a small fortune's-worth of carbonated soft drink from a faraway multinational corporation. Peter hurried past them with the sack in his arms, back and forth, back and forth. He performed reasonably well with the carrying part, but when he reached his limit, the lowering part was clumsy.

"I need more practice," he said, panting.

"Well," sighed BG, "you ain't gonna get it, are you?" It was the first time he'd alluded to Peter's imminent departure.

"I might," said Peter, sitting down on a low wooden pedestal whose purpose he couldn't guess. "Nothing to stop me carrying a sandbag when I'm back home. Actually, I might have to, if there's a flood. There's been a lot of flooding lately."

"They need to put more thought into their sorry-ass water management systems," BG remarked.

Moro stood up and smoothed her clothing. Her exercise break was over and duty called. "Maybe you should do what you have to and then come straight back," she said.

"Not without my wife," said Peter.

"Well, maybe she can come too."

"USIC decided she couldn't, apparently."

Moro shrugged, and a flash of defiance animated her normally passionless face. "USIC schmusic. What's USIC anyway? *We're* USIC. Us, here. Maybe it's time the eligibility tests got loosened up a little."

"Yeah, they're tough," agreed BG, in a wistful tone, half-proud of himself for having made the grade, half-rueful for all the potential brothers and sisters who hadn't made it. "Eye of a goddamn needle. That's in the Bible, ain't it?"

Almost as a reflex, Peter girded himself to craft a diplomatic answer, then realized he didn't have to. "Yes, BG, it is. *Matthew*, chapter 19, verse 24."

"I'll remember that," said BG, then grinned broadly, to signal that he knew very well he wouldn't.

"Husband and wife team," said Moro, stowing the bottle in her tote bag. "I think that would be kind of romantic." She spoke in a wistful tone, as though romance was something exotic and strange that might be observed in a tribe of monkeys or snow geese, not in anyone she'd ever known.

Peter closed his eyes. Bea's final message, and his reply, were imprinted there, as clear as any verse of Scripture:

Peter, I love you, she'd written. But please, don't come home. I beg you. Stay where you are. It's safer and I want you safe.

This is the last message I'll be able to send you, I'm not going to be able to stay in this house. I will be living with other people, strangers. I don't know where exactly. We'll be moving around. I can't explain, just take it from me that it's best. Nothing here is as it was when you left. Things can change so fast. It's irresponsible for me to bring a baby into this rotten world but the alternative is killing it and I just don't have the courage to do that. I expect things will end badly anyway, and it will be much kinder on you not to be here to see it. If you love me, don't make me watch you suffer.

It's funny, all those years ago when we first met, people warned me what a hardened, devious exploiter you were, always manipulating people to fall for you, but I know you're just an innocent little kid at heart. This planet's too cruel for you now. I'll take comfort from thinking of you in a safe place, with some chance of a happy life.

Beatrice

To which he had replied, without pause for doubt or deliberation, just this:

Safe or unsafe, happy or unhappy, my place is by your side. Don't give up. I will find you.

"You take care of yourself, OK?" said BG. "You're goin' to a baaaaad place. Stay strong. Keep focused. You promise me that?"

Peter smiled. "I promise."

He and the big man shook hands, formally and decorously, like diplomats. No bear hugs, no high fives. BG knew how to tailor the gesture to the occasion. He turned and walked away, with Moro at his side.

Peter watched their bodies dwindle and disappear into the ugly exterior of the USIC base. Then he took a seat on a swing, holding the chains loosely, and wept a while. Not big sobs, not even aloud, nothing that Lover

Five might have called a very long song. Just tears on his cheeks, which got licked up by the atmosphere before they could fall to the earth.

Eventually he walked back to the sandbag and kneeled down next to it. Without much difficulty, he dragged it up his thighs onto his lap. Next, wrapping his arms around it, he hauled it to his chest. It was heavier than Bea, he supposed, although it was hard to be sure. Lifting a person was easier somehow. It shouldn't be, because both of you were subject to gravity; there was no escaping that. Yet he'd tried lifting an unconscious body and he'd lifted Bea and there was a difference. And a baby . . . a baby would be lighter still, much lighter.

He sat holding the sandbag until his knees were hurting and arms were sore. When he finally let it slip to the ground, he couldn't guess how long Grainger had been standing near him, watching.

"I thought you were angry with me," he said.

"So you ran away?" she said.

"I just wanted to give you space," he said.

She laughed. "I have all the space I can handle."

He checked her appearance, unobtrusively he hoped. She looked sober, dressed as normal, ready for work.

"You're going home too, right?"

"Right," she said.

"We'll be together," he said.

The reassurance cut no ice with her. "We'll be in the same ship but we won't be aware of it."

"We'll wake up together at the other end," he said.

She looked away. They were heading for different destinations, and both knew it.

"Is there . . ." he began, then got stuck for a few seconds. "Is there a part of you that's sorry to leave?"

She shrugged. "They'll get another pharmacist; they'll get another minister. Everyone's replaceable."

"Yes. And irreplaceable, too."

The sound of an engine revving distracted them. Not far off, a vehicle had pulled away from the base and was now driving in the general direction of the Big Brassiere. It was the black station wagon, the one Kurtzberg had always used. Mechanics had fixed it, proving that if you were a car, you could be struck by lightning, pronounced dead and yet be brought back to life. Not exactly good as new, but saved from the scrap heap by the grace of experts. The rear of the wagon was crammed with pipes of some sort, which stuck out some distance from the hatch and were secured with rope. The bed must have been ditched. Evidently, now that the USIC personnel knew for certain that the pastor was dead, they no longer felt constrained to keep his car as he liked it, permanently parked in a bay earmarked PASTER, but to put it to general use instead. Waste not, want not. And hey, Kurtzberg had even handled his own funeral, instead of causing headaches by dying at the base. What a guy.

"Are you still praying for my dad?" said Grainger.

"I'm having trouble praying for anyone right now," he said, gently removing a bright-green insect from his sleeve and launching it into the air. "But tell me . . . How are you going to find him?"

"I'll figure it out," she said. "I just need to be back. Then I'll know what to do."

"Are there relatives who could help?"

"Maybe," she said, in tone that suggested that maybe, in equal likelihood, a Tibetan football team, a herd of talking buffalo or a host of angels might pitch in to assist.

"You never married," he confirmed.

"How do you know that?"

"Still called 'Grainger.'"

"A lot of women don't change their name when they get married," Grainger said. The opportunity to spar with him seemed to cheer her up.

"My wife changed hers," he said. "Beatrice Leigh. Bea Leigh." He smirked, embarrassed. "Sounds ridiculous, I know. But she hated her father."

Grainger shook her head. "Nobody hates their father. Not deep down. You can't. He made you."

"Let's not go there," said Peter. "We'll end up talking about religion."

Kurtzberg's hearse was a dot on the horizon now. A sparkling constellation of rain hung right above it.

"What are you gonna call your kid?" asked Grainger.

"I don't know," he said. "It's all. . . . It's hard for me to conceive of yet. It's a bit scary. They say it changes you forever. I mean, not that I don't want to be changed, but . . . You can see what's happening to the world, you can see where things are heading. The decision to put a child in danger like that, to expose an innocent child to God knows—goodness knows . . ." He faltered and fell silent.

Grainger appeared not to have been listening. She hopped onto the treadmill and swayed her hips like a dancer, keeping her feet still, to see if the thing would move. She jerked her pelvis. The treadmill advanced maybe a couple of centimeters. "Your kid will be brand new to the planet," she said. "Your kid won't be thinking about all the things we've lost, the places that went to hell, the people who died. All that stuff will be pre-historic like the dinosaurs. Stuff that happened before time began. Only tomorrow will matter. Only today." She smiled. "Like, what's for breakfast?"

He laughed.

"Are you packed?" he said.

"Sure. I didn't come with much. Leaving the same way."

"I'm packed too." It had been a three-minute job; there was scarcely anything in his luggage now. Passport. Keys to a house that might, by the time he got there, have a different lock. Some pencil stubs. The bright yellow boots sewn by Lover Five, each stitch of which had been executed with infinite care so as not to risk injuring her hands. A pair of trousers that fell off his hips, a few T-shirts that would hang so loose on him that he'd look like a refugee decked out in charity hand-me-downs. Anything else? He didn't think so. The other clothes he'd brought with him were ruined by mildew or sacrificed as rags during the construction of his church. He knew that when he got home it would be cold, and he'd not be able to ponce about in a dishdasha with nothing underneath, but that was a problem for another day.

The weirdest absence from his rucksack was his Bible. He'd owned that Bible since his conversion, it had counseled, inspired and comforted him for so many years, he must have thumbed its pages thousands of times. The weave of the linen-enriched paper probably contained so many cells from his fingertips that a new Peter could be grown from the DNA. "Before you came," Jesus Lover Seventeen once said, "we were all alone and weak. Now,

ℬogether, we are 𝔰𝔱rong." He hoped that she and her fellow Jesus Lovers would derive some strength from his cherished King James, their very own Book of Strange New Things.

It was all committed to memory, anyway. The parts that were important, the parts he might need. Even now, he was pretty sure he could recite the gospel of Matthew, all twenty-eight chapters of it, except for the Ezekias-begat-Joatham stuff at the very start. He thought of Bea, reading to him from Chapter 6 in the bedroom of her tiny flat when they were first together, her voice soft and fervent as she spoke of the heavenly sanctuary where precious things were safe from harm: "For where your treasure is, there will your heart be also." He thought of Matthew's last words, and the meaning they could have for two people who loved each other:

I am with you always, even unto the end of the world. Amen.

ACKNOWLEDGMENTS

A far-flung coterie of people read portions of this book during its composition and offered valuable feedback. I would like to thank Francis Bickmore, Jamie Byng, Jo Dingley, Viktor Janiš, Mary Ellen Kappler, David Kappler-Burch, Lorraine McCann, Paul Owens, Ann Patty, Angela Richardson, Anya Serota, Iris Tupholme and Zachary Wagman. My wife Eva was, as always, my closest and most insightful advisor and collaborator.

The final drafts were finished under difficult circumstances in Lucinda's attic and in the basement of the Primrose Hill Book Shop, made available for me day & night by Jessica and Marek. My thanks to them.

I would like also to express my appreciation for the team of writers, pencilers and inkers who worked at Marvel Comics during the 1960s and 1970s, giving me such enjoyment as a child and ever since. All the surnames in *The Book of Strange New Things* are based on theirs, sometimes slightly altered or disguised, sometimes not. My choice of which names to use was governed by narrative concerns and does not reflect my esteem of the comics creators homaged & not homaged. No similarity is intended between the attributes of the Marvel Bullpen and the attributes of the characters in this novel, except for some obvious allusions to that pioneer of new universes, Jakob Kurtzberg (Jack Kirby).

ABOUT THE AUTHOR

MICHEL FABER is the internationally bestselling and critically acclaimed author of *The Crimson Petal and the White*, *Under the Skin*—shortlisted for the Whitbread First Novel Award—and several other books. Faber has won many short story awards and his writing has appeared in *Granta* and *The O. Henry Prize Stories*, among others. He lives in Scotland.

Surprised	Upbeat	Festive	Exhilarated	Ecstatic
Hyper	Cheerful	Motivated	Inspired	Elated
Energized	Lively	Excited	Optimistic	Enthusiastic
Pleased	Focused	Happy	Proud	Thrilled
Pleasant	Joyful	Hopeful	Playful	Blissful
At Ease	Easygoing	Content	Loving	Fulfilled
Calm	Secure	Satisfied	Grateful	Touched
Relaxed	Chill	Restful	Blessed	Balanced
Mellow	Thoughtful	Peaceful	Comfortable	Carefree
Sleepy	Complacent	Tranquil	Cozy	Serene

HIGH ENERGY

LOW ENERGY

PERMISSION
TO FEEL

PERMISSION TO FEEL

UNLOCKING THE POWER OF EMOTIONS TO HELP OUR KIDS, OURSELVES, AND OUR SOCIETY THRIVE

Marc Brackett, Ph.D.

DIRECTOR, YALE CENTER FOR EMOTIONAL INTELLIGENCE

PROFESSOR, YALE CHILD STUDY CENTER

CELADON
BOOKS

NEW YORK

PERMISSION TO FEEL. Copyright © 2019 by Marc Brackett. All rights reserved. Printed in the United States of America. For information, address Celadon Books, a Division of Macmillan Publishers, 120 Broadway, New York, NY 10271.

www.celadonbooks.com

Endpapers by Jerry Todd

ISBN 978-1-250-21284-9 (hardcover)
ISBN 978-1-250-21282-5 (ebook)

Our books may be purchased in bulk for promotional, educational, or business use. Please contact your local bookseller or the Macmillan Corporate and Premium Sales Department at 1-800-221-7945, extension 5442, or by email at MacmillanSpecialMarkets@macmillan.com.

First Edition: September 2019

10 9 8 7 6 5

For Uncle Marvin
And Mom and Dad

Contents

PERMISSION
TO FEEL

Prologue

OKAY, LET'S GET THE easy questions out of the way first: What's up with that title? Since when does anybody need permission to feel?

True, we all have feelings more or less continuously, every waking moment—even in our dreams—without ever asking or getting anybody's approval. To stop feeling would be like to stop thinking. Or breathing. Impossible. Our emotions are a big part—maybe the biggest part—of what makes us human.

And yet we go through life trying hard to pretend otherwise. Our true feelings can be messy, inconvenient, confusing, even addictive. They leave us vulnerable, exposed, naked to the world. They make us do things we wish we hadn't done. It's no wonder our emotions scare us sometimes—they seem so out of our control. Too often we do our best to deny them or hide them—even from ourselves. Our attitudes about them get passed along to our children, who learn by taking their cues from us, their parents and teachers—their role models. Our kids receive the message loud and clear, so that before long, they, too, have learned to suppress even the most urgent messages from deep inside their beings. Just as we learned to do.

You haven't even begun reading this book yet, but I'll bet you already know what I'm talking about.

So, we deny ourselves—and one another—the permission to feel. We suck it up, squash it down, act out. We avoid the difficult conversation with our colleague; we explode at a loved one; and we helplessly go through an entire bag of cookies and have no idea why. When we deny ourselves the permission to feel, a long list of unwanted outcomes ensues. We lose the ability to even identify what we're feeling—it's like, without noticing, we go a little numb inside. When that happens, we're unable to understand why we're experiencing an emotion or what's happening in our lives that's causing it. Because of that we're unable to name it, so we can't express it, either, in terms the people around us would understand. And when we can't recognize, understand, or put into words what we feel, it's impossible for us to do anything about it: to master our feelings—not to deny them but to accept them all, even embrace them—and learn to make our emotions work for us, not against us.

I spend every minute of my working life dealing with these issues. Through academic research and plenty of real-life experience, especially in the world of education, I've seen the terrible cost of our inability to deal in healthy ways with our emotional lives.

Here's some evidence:

- In 2017, about 8 percent of adolescents aged twelve to seventeen and 25 percent of young adults aged eighteen to twenty-five were current users of illicit drugs.
- The number of incidents of bullying and harassment in U.S. K–12 schools reported to the Anti-Defamation League doubled each year between 2015 and 2017.
- According to a 2014 Gallup poll, 46 percent of teachers report high daily stress during the school year. That's tied with nurses for the highest rate among all occupational groups.

- A 2018 Gallup poll revealed that over 50 percent of employees are unengaged at work; 13 percent of those are "miserable."
- From 2016–2017, more than one in three students across 196 U.S. college campuses reported diagnosed mental health conditions. Some campuses have reported a 30 percent increase in mental health problems per year.
- According to the 2019 World Happiness Report, negative feelings, including worry, sadness, and anger, have been rising around the world, up by 27 percent from 2010 to 2018.
- Anxiety disorders are the most common mental illness in the U.S., affecting 25 percent of children between thirteen and eighteen years old.
- Depression is the leading cause of disability worldwide.
- Worldwide mental health problems could cost the global economy up to $16 trillion by 2030. These include direct costs of health care and medicines or other therapies and indirect costs such as loss of productivity.

We seem to prefer spending more money and effort on dealing with the results of our emotional problems rather than trying to prevent them.

I have a personal interest in the bad things that happen when we deny ourselves permission to feel. Meaning I've been there, but thanks to someone who cared, I made it out alive. We'll talk about that too.

Only a few naturally insightful among us can claim to have the skills discussed in this book without consciously pursuing them. I had to learn them. And these *are* skills. All personality types—loud or quiet, imaginative or practical, neurotic or happy-go-lucky—will find them accessible and even life-changing. These are clear, simple, and tested skills that can be acquired by anyone of almost any age.

Recently, I was training administrators in one of the country's most challenging school districts. I was warned, "They'll eat you alive." At lunch on the first day, I was standing in the buffet line next to a principal, and to make small talk, I asked him, "So, what do you think about the session so far?" He looked me in the eye, then looked down at the food and said, "The desserts look pretty good." I realized at that moment what I was up against. I'm used to resistance, but his attitude hit hard. I decided at that moment that he was going to be my project. His superintendent was fully on board, but it was clear that we would succeed in this district only if principals, like this guy, were also believers.

At the end of a couple of days of intensive teaching, I ran into him again. "The other day, when we met, you weren't so sure this course was going to work for you," I said. "I'm curious. Now that you've spent two days learning about emotions and how to integrate emotion skills into your school, what do you think?"

"Well, I'll tell you," he said, pausing to collect his thoughts. "I realize now that I didn't know what I didn't know. The language of feelings was foreign to me."

That was encouraging, I thought. Then he went on.

"So, thank you for giving me the permission to feel."

Let's begin there.

PART ONE

PERMISSION TO FEEL

1

Permission to Feel

How are you feeling?

Given the subject of this book, it's a reasonable question. I may ask it more than once before we're through. In theory, given that it's something we're asked so often in one form or another, that should make it the easiest question ever, instead of the hardest—depending on how honest we're going to be when we answer.

I'm speaking now not only as a psychologist and director of a center devoted to emotional well-being but also as a fellow human. To be perfectly honest, I wish someone had asked me that question when I was a kid—asked it and really, truly, wanted to know the answer and had the courage to do something about what I would have revealed.

I was not a happy child.

I felt scared, angry, hopeless. Bullied. Isolated. And I suffered.

Boy, did I suffer.

When I was in middle school, you only had to look at me to see that something was seriously wrong. I was a poor student in school, mostly

Cs and Ds. My eating was so messed up that I went from severely thin to overweight. I had no real friends.

My parents loved me and cared for me—I knew that. But they had their own miseries. Mom was anxious and depressed and had a drinking problem. Dad was raging, scary, and disappointed in a son who wasn't as tough as he was. But they had at least one thing in common: no clue about how to deal with feelings—neither their own nor mine.

I would spend hours alone in my room, crying or anguishing over the bullying I silently endured at school. But my main response to life was rage. I would talk back to my mother, yell, scream. "Who do you think you are to talk to me like that?" she would holler back. "Wait till your father gets home!" When he did, my mother would tell him how I had mistreated her, and then he would storm into my room, shouting, "If I have to tell you one more time to stop speaking to your mother that way, I'm going to lose it!" Sometimes he'd spare me the lecture and just start hitting.

Then my mother would jump in, and the two of them would battle over how he was handling the situation. Finally, he would give up, and my mother would come into my room and say, "Marc, I saved you *this* time . . ."

I wondered: What did she think she had saved me from?

Without meaning to, they taught me a powerful lesson. Keep my feelings to myself. Definitely do not allow my parents to see them. That would just make a bad scene worse.

This was around the time they learned my most terrible secret— that a neighbor, a friend of the family, had been sexually abusing me. When my parents finally found out, my father grabbed a bat from the basement and nearly killed the man. My mother almost had a nervous breakdown. The police came and arrested the neighbor, and soon the whole neighborhood knew. It turned out my abuser had been violating dozens of other children as well.

You'd think everyone would be glad that I had come forward and exposed this horror. But you'd be wrong. I became an instant pariah.

Every adult warned their kids to stay away from me. The bullying got even worse.

Suddenly, the source of my constant emotional meltdowns was clear to my parents. My bad grades. My bulimia. My social isolation. My despair. My rage.

My parents did what many people do under similar pressures.

They freaked out.

That's not entirely accurate—they knew enough to send me to a therapist. They were too overwhelmed by their own problems, just trying to survive, to be able to deal with anybody else's emotional life. They either missed or ignored all the signals I was sending, which doesn't really come as a surprise. Maybe they felt safer not asking too many questions about my life at school or in our neighborhood. Maybe they were afraid of what they'd find out—afraid that once they knew, they'd have to do something about it.

Perhaps if their parents had asked them the right questions, and taught them how to deal with their feelings and what to do when problems arose, my life back then might have been different. Maybe my parents would have been able to see the pain I was in and know how to help me.

Never happened.

Some of this may sound familiar to you. In my line of work, I meet a lot of people who spent their childhoods as I did. Unseen, unacknowledged, bad feelings buried deep inside. No two stories are identical. People tell me how they were physically abused. Or ignored and silenced. Or made to suffer emotional abuse. Or smothered by parents who lived vicariously through them. Or neglected by parents who were alcoholics or addicts. It's our responses that are the same.

Sometimes the tales aren't nearly so dramatic—just people who grew up in homes where everyday emotional issues were ignored because no one had ever learned how to talk about them or take actions to address them. Your life didn't have to be tragic for you to feel as though your emotional life didn't matter to anyone but you.

Here's how I responded: I became numb to how I felt. I was under emotional lockdown. Survival mode.

And then a miracle took place.

Its name was Marvin. Uncle Marvin, actually.

He was my mother's brother, a schoolteacher by day and a bandleader at night and on the weekends. Our family would travel from New Jersey up to the resorts in the Catskill Mountains to see our family celebrity perform. Uncle Marvin was truly an outlier—unique among all my relatives and every other adult I knew. He was like the Robin Williams character in *Dead Poets Society*.

In his day job, even back then in the 1970s, Uncle Marvin was trying to create a curriculum that would encourage students to express how they felt. He believed it was the missing link in their education— that *emotion skills* would improve their learning and their lives. I would help Uncle Marvin by typing his notes as he read them aloud. I encountered terms such as "despair," "alienation," "commitment," and "elation" and recognized myself in many of them.

One summer afternoon, while we were sitting in our backyard together, he asked if he could give me an IQ test. Turns out that I was smarter than my dismal report cards suggested. I also think he suspected that I had a lot of turmoil going on deep inside having to do with school and being abused. It led Uncle Marvin to ask me a question I had rarely, if ever, heard coming from an adult or anyone else:

"Marc," he said, "how are you feeling?"

With those words, the dam inside me broke, and out came the torrent. Every horrible thing I was experiencing at the time, and every feeling I had in response, all came tumbling out in a rush.

That one little question was all it took to change my life. It wasn't just what he said, it was the way he said it. Truly wanting to hear the answer. Not judging me for what I felt. He just listened, openly and with empathy, to what I was expressing. He didn't try to interpret me or explain me.

I really let loose that day.

"I have no real friends, I suck at sports, I'm fat, and the kids at school all hate me," I wailed, sobbing.

Uncle Marvin just listened. He heard me out. My uncle was the first person who had ever chosen not to focus on my outward behavior—snarky, withdrawn, defiant, definitely unpleasant to be around—and instead sensed that something else was going on, something significant that no one, not even I, had acknowledged.

Uncle Marvin gave me permission to feel.

Given all that, it's no surprise that for the past twenty-five years I've been researching and writing about emotions and running around the world talking to people about their feelings. It's become my passion and my life's work. I'm a professor in the Yale Child Study Center and founding director of the Yale Center for Emotional Intelligence. At the center, I lead a team of scientists and practitioners who conduct research on emotions and emotion skills and develop approaches to teach people of all ages—from preschoolers to CEOs—the skills that can help them thrive. Our center's goal is to use the power of emotions to create a healthier and more equitable, innovative, and compassionate society.

Each year I give dozens of talks to educators, schoolchildren, parents, business executives, entrepreneurs, political leaders, scientists, medical practitioners, and every other kind of person you can imagine, all over the world. My message for everyone is the same: that if we can learn to identify, express, and harness our feelings, even the most challenging ones, we can use those emotions to help us create positive, satisfying lives.

Whenever I speak to a group, I start by asking people to spend a few minutes thinking about how they're feeling right in the moment. Then I call on them to share. Their answers reveal a lot—not necessarily about their emotions but about our difficulty in discussing our emotional lives. What I find is that we don't even have the vocabulary to describe our feelings in useful detail—three-quarters of the people have a hard time coming up with a "feeling" word. When the words do come, they don't usually tell us very much. People fumble around a bit, hem and haw, and then use the most commonplace terms we all rely on—*I feel fine, good, okay . . .*

It makes you wonder: Do I even know how I'm feeling? Have I given myself permission to ask? Have I ever really asked my partner, my child, my colleague? Today, when nearly every question can be handled instantly by Siri, or Google, or Alexa, we're losing the habit of pausing to look inward, or to one another, for answers. But even Siri doesn't know everything. And Google can't tell you why your son or daughter is feeling hopeless or excited, or why your significant other feels not so significant lately, or why you can't shake that chronic low-level anxiety that plagues you.

It makes perfect sense that we're uncomfortable and awkward when expressing our emotional lives. This is true even when we're experiencing positive feelings. But it's especially so when they're unpleasant— sad, resentful, scared, rejected. Those all connect us to our weaknesses, and who wants to show those off? The instinct to protect ourselves by hiding our vulnerability is natural. Even animals in the wild do it. It's self-preservation, pure and simple.

And yet we all ask this question or something like it countless times a day, and we're called on to answer it just as often:

How are you? How are you doing? How are you feeling?

We ask it so reflexively that we scarcely hear ourselves. And we answer in the same spirit:

Great, thanks, how are you? Everything's fine! Busy!

Without pausing for even a second to think before we reply.

It's one of the great paradoxes of the human condition—we ask some variation of the question "How are you feeling?" over and over, which would lead one to assume that we attach some importance to it. And yet we never expect or desire—or provide—an honest answer.

Imagine what would happen if next time an acquaintance (or the barista at Starbucks) says, "Hi, how are you?" you were to stop and take the next five minutes to give a detailed—unedited—response. Really bare your soul. I guarantee it would be a long time before that particular person inquired again.

There's something meaningful going on in there—in that huge disconnect between our willingness to ask how we feel and our reluctance to respond thoughtfully. We now know that, aside maybe from physical health, our emotional state is one of the most important aspects of our lives. It rules everything else. Its influence is pervasive. Yet it is also the thing we steer around most carefully. Our inner lives are uncharted territory even to us, a risky place to explore.

Our lives are saturated with emotions—sadness, disappointment, anxiety, irritation, enthusiasm, and even tranquility. Sometimes—often—those feelings are inconvenient. They get in the way of our busy lives, or at least that's what we tell ourselves. So we do our best to ignore them. It's everywhere, from the stiff upper lip of our country's Puritan founders to the tough-it-out ethos of schoolyards and playgrounds. We all believe that our feelings are important and deserve to be addressed respectfully and fully. But we also think of emotions as being disruptive and unproductive—at work, at home, and everywhere else. Until the 1980s, most psychologists viewed emotions as extraneous noise, useless static. Our feelings slow us down and get in the way of achieving our goals. We've all heard the message: Get over it. Stop focusing on yourself (as though such a thing were possible!). Don't be so sensitive. Time to move on.

The irony, though, is that when we ignore our feelings, or suppress them, they only become stronger. The really powerful emotions build up inside us, like a dark force that inevitably poisons everything we do, whether we like it or not. Hurt feelings don't vanish on their own. They don't heal themselves. If we don't express our emotions, they pile up like a debt that will eventually come due.

And I'm not talking only about the times we're feeling something unpleasant. We may also fail to understand exactly how we feel when things are going great. We're content just to enjoy the emotions and not probe too deeply. It's a mistake, of course. If we're going to make positive choices in the future, we need to know what will bring us happiness—and why.

Proof of our inability to deal constructively with our emotional lives is all around us. In 2015, in collaboration with the Robert Wood Johnson Foundation and Born This Way Foundation (founded by Lady Gaga and her mother, Cynthia Germanotta), we conducted a large-scale survey of twenty-two thousand teenagers from across the United States and asked them to describe how they feel while in school. Three-quarters of the words they used were negative, with "tired," "bored," and "stressed" topping the list. This wasn't surprising given that around 30 percent of elementary and middle school students now experience adjustment problems severe enough to require regular counseling. In economically disadvantaged schools, this runs as high as 60 percent.

American youths now rank in the bottom quarter among developed nations in well-being and life satisfaction, according to a report by UNICEF. Research shows that our youths have stress levels that surpass those of adults. Our teenagers are now world leaders in violence, binge drinking, marijuana use, and obesity. More than half of college students experience overwhelming anxiety, and a third report intense depression. And over the last two decades, there has been a 28 percent increase in our suicide rate.

How clearly will kids think when they are feeling tired, bored, and stressed? How well do they absorb new information when they are anxious? Do they take their studies seriously? Do they feel inclined to express their curiosity and pursue learning?

Here's a story that tells me a lot about the emotional atmosphere in schools.

The superintendent of a major metropolitan district was out making classroom visits. As she walked the halls with the principal, she saw a little girl headed to a classroom and greeted her, attempting to start up a conversation.

The girl refused to acknowledge her.

"She wouldn't say hello to me," the superintendent told me. After a moment of mutual confusion, the little girl put her head down and continued on her way. Apparently, students had been told they could walk only on the white line painted down the middle of the corridors. "Stepping over to talk to me would mean breaking the rules," said the superintendent.

We'll never know how that conversation might have gone. The natural instinct of both student and educator to engage with each other was squelched by the school's demand for order above all else.

What can happen in a single exchange? A moment of small talk in a hallway? Probably very little. Although if you are like me, you have some memories from early childhood that stand out from the fog of years, that have endured over time for no other reason than that a grown-up made space in his or her life, for a moment, for you. A small thing like that, if it is heartfelt, can reverberate.

It's not only students who feel oppressed. What about their teachers? In 2017, in collaboration with the New Teacher Center, we surveyed more than five thousand educators and found that they spend nearly 70 percent of their workdays feeling "frustrated," "overwhelmed," and "stressed." This conforms with Gallup data showing that nearly half of U.S. teachers report high stress on a daily basis. A frightening snapshot of our educational system, wouldn't you agree?

How effective are our educators when they feel just as frustrated, overwhelmed, and stressed as the kids? Will they give 100 percent to their lessons? Do they snap at students unintentionally, or ignore their needs, because they are emotionally exhausted? Are they leaving work feeling burned out, dreading tomorrow's return to the classroom?

If we don't understand emotions and find strategies to deal with them, they will take over our lives, as they did for me as a child. Fear and anxiety made it impossible for me to try to deal with my problems. I was paralyzed. The science now proves why. If there had been someone to teach me the skills—if there had been someone to even tell me there *were* such skills—I might have felt more in control of my situation. Instead, all I could do was endure it.

During presentations, I'll often make the observation that many children today are in serious crisis mode. Usually this will prompt someone to ask a question that's really more of an opinion: "Don't you think these kids lack the toughness and moral fiber that people had generations ago?"

My response to this has matured over the years. Once, a statement like that would really rile me. It sounded like somebody looking for a reason to feel superior and blame the victims. Now I think it's irresponsible.

Let's suppose that children today *do* lack the emotional strength we, or some other generation, had in abundance. Let's assume that in the past kids were just as challenged—maybe more—but they were able to buckle down and deal with it.

So what?

Would that mean we abdicate responsibility for doing our best to help today's kids? If they do require a little help, isn't it our job to give it to them, without judging? And if they need so much support, how did they end up that way? Did it have anything to do with how we raised them?

There was a time, not so long ago, that children did have a serious need that was not being met. Our national response was instructive. In 1945, while World War II was still raging, a general (and former teacher) named Lewis B. Hershey testified before Congress that almost half of all army draftees were turned away for reasons owing to poor nutrition. He was in a good position to know: Hershey was in charge of the Selective Service System. He saw the underfed and malnourished young American men and realized their unfitness for war.

Congress did not issue a proclamation condemning the fecklessness of the younger generation. It passed a bipartisan bill: the National School Lunch Act.

In other words, we fed our kids.

. . .

It's time to feed our kids again.

At the Yale Center for Emotional Intelligence, that's all we think about: how we can help people to identify their emotions, understand the influence of their feelings on all aspects of their lives, and develop the skills to make sure they use their emotions in healthy, productive ways.

Once, after a talk to mental health professionals at a major hospital, the head of child psychiatry approached me. He said, "Marc, great job. But, you know, according to our data we're going to need another eight thousand child psychiatrists to deal with the problems these kids will be having."

I was stunned.

"You misunderstood me. I want to put you all out of business," I said half-jokingly.

He was thinking that all those troubled children would need professional interventions in order to deal with their lives. I was saying that we need to remake education so that it includes emotion skills—so that professional interventions become less necessary.

It's been nearly thirty years since the idea of emotional intelligence was introduced by my mentors, Peter Salovey, professor of psychology and current president of Yale University, and Jack Mayer, professor of psychology at the University of New Hampshire. It's been a quarter century since Daniel Goleman published his bestselling book *Emotional Intelligence*, which popularized the concept. And yet we're still grappling with the most basic questions, such as "How are you feeling?"

Feelings are a form of information. They're like news reports from inside our psyches, sending messages about what's going on inside the unique person that is each of us in response to whatever internal or external events we're experiencing. We need to access that information and then figure out what it's telling us. That way we can make the most informed decisions.

That's a major challenge. It's not as though every emotion comes with a label telling us precisely what prompted it, and why, and what can be done to resolve it. Our thinking and behavior absolutely change in response to what we're feeling. But we don't always know why or how best to address our emotions. For parents, this might be a familiar scenario: we see a child who's clearly suffering, and the reason isn't apparent. Ask simply, "What's wrong?" and the answer will almost never reveal the source of the anguish. Maybe the child doesn't even know what's wrong.

Here's an example: Anger can sometimes seem unprovoked or inexplicable, but in almost every case it's a response to what we perceive as unfair treatment. We've suffered an injustice of some kind, big or small, and it makes us mad. Someone cut in front of you in line—and you're irritated. You were up for a promotion at work, but it went to the boss's niece—and you're outraged. But it's the same basic dynamic at work.

Most of us don't enjoy dealing with anger, whether it's our own or someone else's. When a parent or teacher is faced with what might appear to be an angry child, often the first impulse is to threaten discipline—if you don't stop yelling, or speaking rudely, or stamping your feet, you'll go sit in the corner, or I'll send you to your room, or you'll lose your privileges!

When it's an adult who's angry, our response isn't much different. We immediately pull back. We stop listening sympathetically. We feel under attack, which makes it nearly impossible for us to deal with the information the person is conveying. But that anger was an important message. If we can try to mollify the injustice that sparked it, the anger will go away, because it's outlived its usefulness. If not, it will fester, even if it seems to subside.

Thankfully, there's a science to understanding emotion. It's not just a matter of intuition, opinion, or gut instinct. We are not born with an innate talent for recognizing what we or anyone else is feeling and why. We all have to learn it. *I* had to learn it.

As with any science, there's a process of discovery, a method of investigation. After three decades of research and practical experience, we at the Yale Center have identified the talents needed to become what we've termed an "emotion scientist."

Here are the five skills we've identified. We need to

- recognize our own emotions and those of others, not just in the things we think, feel, and say but in facial expressions, body language, vocal tones, and other nonverbal signals.
- understand those feelings and determine their source—what experiences actually caused them—and then see how they've influenced our behaviors.
- label emotions with a nuanced vocabulary.
- express our feelings in accordance with cultural norms and social contexts in a way that tries to inform and invites empathy from the listener.
- regulate emotions, rather than let them regulate us, by finding practical strategies for dealing with what we and others feel.

The rest of this book is devoted to teaching those skills and how to use them.

In the late 1990s, Uncle Marvin and I set out together to bring these skills to schools. We failed. We were prepared to deliver classroom instruction only to children. But some teachers were resistant. "Teaching kids about anxiety makes me nervous," one said. "I'm not opening that Pandora's box of talking about how these kids feel," said another. If the teachers didn't believe in the importance of these emotion skills, they'd never be effective at instructing their students. So Marvin and I, along with new colleagues at Yale, went back to the drawing board. We saw that we would never reach children until we first enlisted teachers who understood the importance of emotion skills. And soon after that we realized that only if there was commitment at the very top, at the school board, superintendent, and principal levels, could entire school systems be transformed.

Then it became clear that the skills must be even more widely shared. We adults *all* need to understand how our emotions influence us and everyone around us, not just schoolchildren. We need to develop the skills and be positive role models. Educators and parents have to demonstrate the ability to identify, discuss, and regulate their own emotions before they can teach the skills to others. Our classroom research shows that where there is an emotionally skilled teacher present, students disrupt less, focus more, and perform better academically. Our studies show that where there is an emotionally skilled principal, there are teachers who are less stressed and more satisfied. And where there is an emotionally skilled parent, there are children who have a greater ability to identify and regulate their emotions.

Once our children grow into emotionally skilled adults, the entire culture will change—for the better. But learning the skills and improving the way we respond to our feelings doesn't mean we'll suddenly become happy all the time. Perpetual happiness can't be our goal—it's just not how real life works. We need the ability to experience and express all emotions, to down- or up-regulate both pleasant and unpleasant emotions in order to achieve greater well-being, make the most informed decisions, build and maintain meaningful relationships, and realize our potential.

But that starts with all of us. If you're a parent, ask yourself this: What are the qualities you most want your children to possess as they grow into adults? Is it math skills, scientific knowledge, athletic ability? Or is it confidence, kindness, a sense of purpose, the wisdom to build healthy, lasting relationships? When we consult with corporations, they tell us they're searching for employees who persevere with a task, who take personal responsibility for their work, who can get along with others and function as members of a team. Not technical abilities or specialized knowledge—they're looking first for emotional attributes. A colleague from the RAND Corporation told me that technology advances so rapidly today that companies don't hire workers for their current skills—firms are looking for people who are flexible, who can present new ideas, inspire cooperation in groups, manage and lead teams, and so on.

We may acquire some of those skills by osmosis—by watching and emulating others who possess them. But for the most part they must be taught. And they are best learned in communities. Emotion skills are both personal and mutual. They can be used privately, but their best application is throughout a community, so that a network emerges to reinforce its own influence. I have seen this happen—these skills are being deployed in thousands of schools all over the world, with dramatic results. The children benefit, naturally: there is less bullying and emotional distress, better attendance, fewer suspensions, and greater academic achievement. But we have also seen that schools where these skills are taught have teachers with lower levels of stress and burnout, fewer intentions to leave the profession, greater job satisfaction, and more engaging classrooms.

We all want our lives, and the lives of the people we love, to be free of hardship and troubling events.

We can never make that happen.

We all want our lives to be filled with healthy relationships, compassion, and a sense of purpose.

That we can make happen.

Uncle Marvin showed me how. It starts with the permission to feel, the first step of the process.

2

Emotions Are Information

So, HOW *ARE* YOU FEELING?

It's not a trick question. But it's more complicated than it sounds. We're always feeling something, usually more than one thing at a time. Our emotions are a continuous flow, not an occasional event. Inside each of us there's a river—placid and contained sometimes, but raging and overflowing its banks at others. There's a lot to navigate.

Picture yourself at the moment you awaken. Even then, as you slowly regain consciousness, you're feeling something. Perhaps you're desperate for another hour of rest. Or you feel supercharged and ready to vault out of bed. On a bad day, maybe it's dread at the thought of your commute or what you'll have to face at work in a few hours. It might be raining, which could dampen your mood even more. Or you could be feeling completely joyous and full of energy thanks to whatever it is you're going to do later. Maybe it's the great relief upon remembering that today is Saturday. Or the anticipation of a day that will be filled with creativity and excitement. Ten minutes from now, your emotional state might be completely different, depending on what you saw on the morning news, what your significant other told you about your plans for tonight, or what you just noticed about the shingles on the roof. Our emotional lives are a roller coaster, climbing high one moment and plunging the next.

Imagine how it must be for children. The same constant flow of feelings, running the gamut from crushingly negative to euphorically positive—from the moment they wake up in the morning, through the entire school day, to the moment they fall asleep. Except that children haven't learned yet how to manage their emotions—how to suppress and compartmentalize whatever's inconvenient at the moment, how to channel useful feelings for maximum benefit. They experience everything so intensely—boredom, frustration, anxiety, worry, excitement, elation. And they sit for hours in a classroom, expected to pay attention to every word spoken by a teacher who's probably under similar emotional pressures. Children's brains are less developed than ours, their defenses less robust, and yet the rivers of emotion that course through kids often are more powerful than the ones we experience. It's a wonder anybody learns anything.

So—a lot to contend with, second by second. We can't spend every minute focused on our emotions. We wouldn't have the time or attention to do much else. However, we can't go through life ignoring what we feel or minimizing its meaning. All emotions are an important source of information about what's going on inside us. Our multiple senses bring us news from our bodies, our minds, and the outside world, and then our brains process and analyze it and formulate our experience. We call that a *feeling*.

We humans have a long history of disregarding our feelings, however. It goes back millennia, even before the Stoic philosophers of ancient Greece argued that emotions were erratic, idiosyncratic sources of information. Reason and cognition were viewed as higher powers within us; once, the idea of "emotional intelligence" would have seemed inconceivable, a contradiction in terms. A great deal of Western literature, philosophy, and religion ever since has taught us that emotions are a kind of internal interference that gets in the way of sound judgment and rational thought. It's no coincidence that we still like to think of intelligence and emotion as coming from two completely separate parts of our bodies—one from the head, the other from the heart. Which of the two have we been taught to trust most?

Scientists didn't like emotions because, unlike intelligence, they can't be measured with standardized tests. IQ relies primarily on "cold" cognitive processes such as remembering a strand of digits or historical facts, while emotional intelligence relies on "hot" social-emotional-cognitive processes that are often highly charged, relationship driven, and focused on evaluating, predicting, and coping with feelings and behaviors—our own and other people's.

That's why the study of intelligence, formalized around 1900, continued the tradition of disregarding emotions. Throughout most of the twentieth century, psychologists and philosophers still debated whether emotions were associated in any way with logical thought and intelligent behavior. It's no wonder that the identification of an emotional intelligence occurred late compared with that of other kinds.

Then, in 1990, psychologists Peter Salovey and John Mayer introduced the first formal theory of emotional intelligence to the scientific literature. They defined it as "the ability to monitor one's own and others' feelings and emotions, to discriminate among them and to use this information to guide one's thinking and actions."

At Yale I interviewed Salovey, who said, "I started studying human emotions in a lab in college in the late 1970s. At that time, there wasn't much interest in emotions in psychology. The cognitive revolution was in full force and people viewed emotions as 'noise.' The idea was that we had emotions, but they didn't predict anything important. I just couldn't believe that was true, so I got very motivated to study emotions to show they mattered in a positive way. I wanted to show that we had an emotion system for a reason. We had an emotion system that helped us get through life."

Emotional intelligence was a synthesis of three burgeoning areas of scientific research, which demonstrated that emotions, when used wisely, supported reasoning and complex problem solving.

First was the rediscovery of Charles Darwin's functional view of emotion. Back in the nineteenth century, he pioneered the idea that emotions signal valuable information and energize adaptive behavior central to survival. Fear finally got its due as being very useful indeed, especially in our species' early, threat-dense environments. Nothing like a good scare to get you up and fleeing a hungry saber-toothed cat.

Next came how emotions and moods play an essential role in thought processes, judgment, and behavior. Social scientists using clever experiments, and brain scientists who studied different brain regions, began to discover ways that emotions interact with cognition and behavior. Research showed that emotions give purpose, priority, and focus to our thinking. They tell us what to do with the knowledge that our senses deliver. They motivate us to act.

Psychologists proposed the idea of a "cognitive loop" that connects mood to judgment. For example, when a person is in a good mood, they're more likely to have positive thoughts and memories, which in turn keep the person thinking about positive things (the loop). In a classic study, psychologist Gordon Bower at Stanford University used hypnosis to make subjects feel happy or sad. Then they had to complete three tasks: recall lists of words, write entries in a diary, and remember experiences from childhood. Subjects who were made to feel sad recalled more negative memories and negative words and remembered more unpleasant events for their diaries. Likewise, the participants who were made to feel happy recalled happier memories and words and more positive events. Another study, by the late Alice Isen, a professor at Cornell University, and colleagues, showed some participants a comedy film and others no film at all and then tested them all for creative thinking. Results indicated a clear increase in creativity for those who saw the film—the ones in a "positive affect condition"—compared with the people in the other group. It's a natural bias—we all perceive and retrieve "mood-congruent" information most easily. It's just one of many ways that our emotions influence our thinking.

The third area of scientific inquiry was a search for "alternative" intelligences, to include a broad array of mental abilities rather than a single mental ability: IQ. There was increasing frustration among researchers with the inability of IQ tests to explain important life outcomes among individuals. Howard Gardner, a professor from Harvard University, proposed a theory of multiple intelligences that advised educators and scientists to place a greater emphasis on abilities beyond verbal and mathematical skills, such as intrapersonal (the awareness of one's own strengths and weaknesses) and interpersonal (the ability to communicate effectively and empathize with others) skills. Other researchers, including Robert Sternberg, a psychologist now at Cornell University, proposed a theory of "successful intelligence" and urged scientists and educators to consider creative and practical abilities. Nancy Cantor and John Kihlstrom, psychologists at Stanford University, built upon research in the 1920s by Edward Thorndike, pushing for a greater focus on "social intelligence"—the ability to accumulate knowledge about the social world, understand people, and act wisely in social relations.

By the late 1990s, emotional intelligence finally had achieved parity with the other forms of intelligence. Neuroscientists, psychologists, and intelligence researchers came to agree that emotion and cognition work hand in hand to perform sophisticated information processing. Research began to emerge that demonstrated there were individual differences in people's ability to reason with and about emotion. For example, research showed a wide range of skill in the abilities to perceive emotions accurately in facial expressions and regulate emotions.

Everything in this book is based on the past five decades of research into the roles—plural—that emotions play in our lives. At their highest level, from an evolutionary perspective, emotions have an extremely practical purpose: They ensure our survival. They make us smarter. If we didn't need them, they wouldn't exist.

I've championed five areas where our feelings matter most—the aspects of our everyday lives that are most influenced by our emotions. First, our emotional state determines where we direct our attention, what we remember, and what we learn. Second is decision making: when we're in the grip of any strong emotion—such as anger or sadness, but also elation or joy—we perceive the world differently, and the choices we make at that moment are influenced, for better or for worse. Third is our social relations. What we feel—and how we interpret other people's feelings—sends signals to approach or avoid, to affiliate with someone or distance ourselves, to reward or punish. Fourth is the influence of emotions on our health. Positive and negative emotions cause different physiological reactions within our bodies and brains, releasing powerful chemicals that, in turn, affect our physical and mental well-being. And the fifth has to do with creativity, effectiveness, and performance. In order to achieve big goals, get good grades, and thrive in our collaborations at work, we have to use our emotions as though they were tools. Which, of course, they are—or can be.

EMOTIONS AND ATTENTION, MEMORY, AND LEARNING

All learning has an emotional base.—PLATO

Let's start there, by examining how our emotions affect our attention and our memory, which together determine our ability to learn.

Think about it: emotions determine what you care about in the moment. If we're bored to tears or daydreaming about the coming weekend, we're not likely to absorb what we are reading on this page right now. If we're fearful, the source of that fear occupies all our thoughts.

If the house is on fire, we have but one goal: *Get me out of here!* If we're faced with sudden physical danger—whether we're out hiking and come face-to-face with a growling bear or we're strolling in the city at night and are stopped by an armed stranger—we've pretty much stopped thinking of anything else. Nature has wired our brains this way, and it's a good thing: any distraction in that moment could prove fatal.

Fear of intangible harm—of embarrassment, of shame, of looking foolish or inadequate in any way—works in a similar way. We may experience it as anxiety or worry instead of terror. The emotion may seem vain and irrational even to ourselves. Doesn't matter. As we've seen, feelings are highly impervious to cold logic. When we anticipate an unfavorable outcome under any circumstances, we're inhibited from thinking about much else. Perhaps our attention should be elsewhere, but we're helpless to redirect our minds at that moment.

Strong, negative emotions (fear, anger, anxiety, hopelessness) tend to narrow our minds—it's as though our peripheral vision has been cut off because we're so focused on the peril that's front and center. There's actually a physiological side to this phenomenon. When these negative feelings are present, our brains respond by secreting cortisol, the stress hormone. This inhibits the prefrontal cortex from effectively processing information, so even at a neurocognitive level our ability to focus and learn is impaired. To be sure, moderate levels of stress—feeling challenged—can enhance our focus. It's chronic stress that's toxic and makes it biologically challenging to learning. It's why I was a C student in middle school. I was too overwhelmed by family problems and bullying to be mentally present in class. When I was forty years old, I went to my hometown to visit the middle school I attended. Two unforgettable things happened. First, the moment I walked in I had a visceral reaction: I felt the fear and shame all over again. I immediately regressed to the fragile thirteen-year-old boy. Second, the only things I could remember were related to my bullying experiences. I couldn't remember most teachers' names or recall any subject matter I had learned.

It's not only negative feelings that can impair our mental capacity.

Let's say a high school student is in the grip of the typical hormonal hurricane that besets most teenagers. Romantic fantasies are fun to indulge, and world history can't be expected to compete. It's a wonder that adolescents manage to learn anything when you recall all the intoxicating daydreams that fill our heads at that age. Younger children are no less obsessed, but they're imagining the fun they'll have playing once the school day is through or going to Disney World for spring break. Joy and exuberance are as powerful as any other emotion when it comes to our ability to direct our thoughts where we want them to go. Instead of stimulating the production of cortisol, positive emotions are generally associated with the excretion of serotonin, dopamine, and other "feel-good" neurochemicals that exert their influence on thinking and behavior.

What research now shows is that different emotions serve different purposes for learning. If we need to engage our critical faculties—if, for instance, we have to edit a letter we've written and want to seek out flaws and correct any mistakes—a negative frame of mind might serve us better than its opposite. Pessimism can make it easier for us to anticipate things that could go wrong and then take the proper actions to prevent them. Guilt acts as a moral compass. Anxiety keeps us trying to improve things that a more generous mood might be willing to accept. Even anger is a great motivator—unlike resignation, it drives us to act and perhaps to fix what made us angry in the first place. If we're furious watching someone being mistreated, we're likely to step up and seek redress.

Imagine feeling smiley and bubbly, giddy with excitement, as you complete your final draft of a job application. It's possible, but it's a healthy fear, not joy, that can make us triple-check our punctuation and sentence structure. Negative emotions have a constructive function: they help narrow and focus our attention. It's sadness, not happiness, that can help us work through a difficult problem. It's excitement that stimulates lots of ideas. But too much enthusiasm won't bring needed consensus to a group—it will disperse the energy necessary for reasoning through the problem at hand, whether mathematical or interpersonal.

We're currently experiencing what seems like a crisis in education. Our students are tired, bored, and stressed. Their teachers are frustrated, pressured, and overwhelmed. Chronic disengagement and absenteeism are at record highs. How have we responded? By attempting to control student behavior even more than we already do. Or by introducing new math and literacy programs or instituting tougher learning standards. None of these solutions address the fact that how students feel is what gives meaning to what they are learning. The research is clear: emotions determine whether academic content will be processed deeply and remembered. Linking emotion to learning ensures that students find classroom instruction relevant. It's what supports students in discovering their purpose and passion, it's what drives their persistence.

Whenever we notice that we're suddenly having difficulty paying attention, or focusing, or remembering, we should ask ourselves: What emotion information is there, just beneath the surface of our thoughts? And what if anything can we do to regain a handle on our minds?

EMOTIONS AND DECISION MAKING

Affect is not just necessary for wisdom; it's also irrevocably woven into the fabric of every decision.
—ANTONIO DAMASIO, NEUROSCIENTIST,
UNIVERSITY OF SOUTHERN CALIFORNIA

Have you ever made a bad decision? You went with your gut, and when it turned out wrong you slapped your forehead and said, "Well, *that* was a dumb thing to do! What were you thinking?" It was a mental lapse or maybe just poor reasoning. In hindsight, it's plain to see what you failed to take into account. Let's just hope you learned a lesson.

A sensible thing to wish for—but what was the lesson?

We believe that our ability to reason and think rationally is our highest mental power, above our unruly emotional side. This is but a trick our brains play on us—in fact, our emotions exert a huge, though mostly unconscious, influence over how our minds function. This fact is especially evident when it comes to the decision-making process.

There are the obvious instances where emotion alone determines our actions. If we fear flying, we'll drive despite the increased danger. When we're overcome by passion, we might skip our usual measures to prevent unwanted pregnancy or sexually transmitted infections.

But emotion's influence extends far beyond that. Most decisions are attempts at predicting future outcomes: We ought to buy this house. I'm not going to take that job. Pasta is a great choice. In every case, we consider all the options and choose the one that seems most likely to result in a favorable outcome. In theory, at least.

In reality, our emotions largely determine our actions. If we're feeling something positive—confidence, optimism, contentment—we'll come to one conclusion about what we ought to do. If our emotions are negative—anxiety, anger, sadness—our decision may be quite different, even though we're working with the same set of facts.

The resulting patterns are fairly predictable. As discussed earlier in this chapter, anxiety narrows our attention and improves our focus on details. It makes us anticipate what could go wrong. That may not seem like a feeling we'd welcome, but it's a good frame of mind when we're performing tasks involving numbers, such as finances, for instance. If we're deciding whether to make an investment or a major purchase, a sunny mood might lead us to minimize the risks and do something we'll regret later. Negative emotions make us weigh facts carefully and err on the side of caution.

Positive emotions, on the other hand, fill us with the sense that life is going our way. If we're feeling strong, exuberant, energetic, we're more likely to base our decisions on heuristics—our gut instinct at that moment—than on careful reasoning. That's a useful outlook if we're planning a birthday party or when someone is in need of moral support, but maybe not so helpful when we're filing our tax return.

Emotion's true role in our decision making has been measured abundantly in experiments. Researchers will induce a mood in their subjects—by having them read or watch something happy or sad, for example—and then ask them to make decisions. In one study, subjects were seated in rooms that were either comfortable or uncomfortable and then asked about their satisfaction with their lives. The comfortable-room group reported being more satisfied. In a separate study, when subjects were made to feel sad, they perceived a mountain to be steeper than it actually was. And in a study on medical school admissions, it was found that applicants were more likely to be admitted on sunny days than when it rained (yes, admissions officers' decisions were biased by the weather!).

In an experiment we conducted at Yale, teachers were divided into two groups. One was told to remember and write about positive classroom experiences, and the other was assigned to recall a negative memory. Then all were asked to grade the same middle school essay. The positive-mood group marked the essay a full grade higher than the negative-mood group. When we asked the teachers if they believed their moods affected how they evaluated the papers, 87 percent said no. Judgments that entail a greater degree of subjectivity, such as grading a creative essay, are generally at a heightened risk of emotional bias compared with judgments that are more objective, such as grading a math test.

And our feelings can linger long past the moment that inspires them—influencing subsequent behavior without us knowing—it's known as "the incidental mood bias." So, for instance, if you argue with your kids over breakfast and are still angry while driving to work, you might drive more aggressively than usual and make risky decisions. When we recall happy moments from our past, we're likely to make deci-

sions based in optimism and confidence. If we're remembering negative things, we'll feel skeptical and pessimistic, and we'll decide things
differently.

Anger's influence isn't what you might expect: researchers found
that when people are angry, they tend to believe that individuals are
at fault when things go wrong. When we're sad, we're more likely to
blame external circumstances. Interestingly, anger makes people more
optimistic than does sadness, possibly because angry people feel in
greater control of their lives.

We make decisions continually, all day long, and most of them
are small. We can't deliberate over each one, so we rely on our brains
to make snap judgments. These issues come up all the time in contemporary research into how our brains operate. There's the "thinking
fast and thinking slow" concept, where our brains are believed to work
on two separate but overlapping tracks, one that immediately responds
without any or much deliberation and the other that takes its time and
weighs the information first. When we use our brains for familiar or
relatively simple functions, we come to quick responses, while novel
situations or complex problems cause us to cogitate. These quick decisions are particularly susceptible to our moods and unconscious biases,
especially when additional information is unavailable. We decide often
with minimal conscious thinking.

None of this is to say that emotion inherently clouds our judgment.
In fact, with greater emotional awareness, just the opposite may be
true: our feelings can serve as another form of information, telling us
important things about how we're responding to any given situation.
When we are faced with a decision, anxiety may tell us one thing, enthusiasm something completely different. Knowing this, we can take
our emotional state into account before choosing a course of action. Is
it our negative mood that's making us suspicious, or do we have a genuine reason to worry? Is our confidence a result of our exuberant mood,
or is this truly the perfect decision?

EMOTION AND RELATIONSHIPS

No one cares how much you know, until
they know how much you care.
—THEODORE ROOSEVELT

Here's an experiment you can conduct using yourself as the guinea pig: Go through the list of everyone you encounter in the course of your daily life. Everybody—from your significant other and immediate family members to every co-worker, from the top to the bottom, every relative, friend, and acquaintance, the cashier at the supermarket, your doctor, your barber, the desk clerk at your gym, on and on. Just every human being whose path crosses yours, whether for hours on end or just five minutes.

Okay, now go through the list and ask yourself for your instant, top-of-the-head answer to this question: How do I feel when I encounter each and every one of them? How much do I look forward to my interactions with them all, individually? Do I smile at the thought of seeing this one or that? Does it leave me emotionally neutral? Or does something inside me tense up a little at the prospect? It doesn't have to be outright antipathy, just that little edge of anxiety knowing that this person and I will be face-to-face at some point.

What word would you use to describe the feeling you associate with each one? Is it anxiety? Joy? Confidence? Inadequacy? Boredom? Affection? Irritation? Those all make us more or less attractive to one another. Do you look forward to working alongside the colleague who's perpetually mad at the world?

Normally, this emotion isn't something we ever put into words or even think much about. It's like an instinctive reaction that comes from somewhere deeper than labels can easily express. Almost animalistic. When I see this person, something inside me leaps with joy. Or crashes in dejection. Or something in between.

Experiment over. Now perhaps you have a clearer notion of how our strongest emotional reactions dictate the nature of all our relationships.

In seminars I conduct with teachers, I'll sometimes ask them to list their students and consider the feeling that each name automatically prompts. Is it love, dislike, trust, joy, fear, disgust? Next I'll say, Be honest and think about how that emotion causes you to act toward each of those children. I've had people break down crying during this exercise. They instantly recognize how differently they treat each child depending solely on their perception of how he or she makes them feel. It has little to do with how the child performs in class, or the child's needs, or anything they can name. It's just a strong, almost visceral reaction that usually has to do with something about the teacher, not the student. These are mostly good teachers who do their best to treat each student equally and want to establish a positive, nurturing relationship with them all. But in the real world, despite all our best intentions, it doesn't work that way. For some reason, teachers can barely make eye contact with one child or give her or him focused attention, while they eagerly look forward to interacting with other students and seek them out during classroom activities.

Outside the classroom, we all operate in the same way. Human relations are infinitely complex because we ourselves are, but the basic dynamic is rather simple: approach or avoid. We tell people to come closer or we tell them to back off. People communicate the same thing to us. So much of what happens between human beings is a result of how we communicate our emotions. And it all depends on something deep inside us, perhaps hidden from our own view: our emotional state.

Relationships are the most important aspects of our lives. There's plentiful scientific research showing the enormous influence they have on our well-being—people with robust social networks enjoy better mental and physical health and even live longer, while unfavorable outcomes are associated with a lack of connections to other people. The purpose of relationships can be seen in all societies, even among animals: being surrounded by allies is a form of protection that can mean the difference between life and death. Our need to attach ourselves to others isn't solely sentimental, even if it sometimes seems that way today.

Throughout this book, we will discuss all the ways we communicate our feelings about whomever we're dealing with at any given moment—the subtle, lightning-fast facial expressions, body language, vocal inflections, touch, and everything else in our arsenal of signals.

When we're expressing positive emotions authentically— contentment, compassion, joy—we do so in a way that draws in other people, whether it's your best friend or the supermarket cashier. They can read our signals clearly and may respond in kind, but that depends on *their* emotional state. People feeling emotions such as sorrow, shame, or anxiety often wish to discourage social interactions, and those signals are also being communicated. Those people might benefit most from engagement with others, but too often it's unlikely to happen. This is a particularly serious problem in our schools, which often reprimand children when they express a negative emotion rather than see it as a cry for help. These are the kids who are neglected, ignored, or suspended for misbehavior, when they should be given empathy, extra attention, and opportunities to build skills and meaningful relationships. Research shows that having just one caring adult can make the difference between whether a child will thrive or not.

We all have multitudes of relationships—with our children and parents and significant others, but also with the plumber, the driver in the next lane, our softball teammates, our boss or colleague, and the woman who holds the door open for us at the mall. And all these connections operate on the same basic principle: Our mood at any given moment is expressed in the signals we send out. If we're feeling joyful and open and expansive, it will make us confident and accepting of others. If we're feeling down on ourselves, it will color how we relate to other people—or if we connect at all. We tell people what we want from them by the messages we send, whether warm and hoping for a response in kind, or off-putting, when all we want is distance. This is the challenge for many people on the autism spectrum: they have difficulty reading the cues and coming up with a fitting response, and they have difficulty sending cues that other people understand. As a result, they struggle building and maintaining relationships.

We also express emotions in order to get what we want from the people in our lives. If we make a show of anger, we may not earn much empathy, but we instill fear in others and maybe remove any obstacles that were in our way. If, on the other hand, we need cooperation and understanding, we know what emotion message to send that will get the response we desire.

People feeling compassion see greater common humanity with strangers. They punish others less, are more generous and cooperative, and are willing to sacrifice for others. Research shows that high-powered individuals tend to be less responsive to the emotions of people around them. In one study, these individuals responded with less compassion than people with less power when listening to someone describe suffering. Does this phenomenon explain anything about our political and business leaders?

Sometimes the emotions we feel send signals that elicit the opposite of the response we want and need. Picture a typical child: if he's troubled or anxious, he may wish that his parent or teacher would reach out and offer comfort. But when those adults sense that child's emotional state, especially when he's "acting out," they may respond in just the opposite way, because of their own emotional response to the signals of a negative mood. This dynamic rules much of human interaction—when we need emotional support most is when we're least likely to receive it.

I remember being in seventh-grade math class, where two students would regularly write all over a jacket I wore each day. I'm certain I wore that jacket as a form of protection. My fear and despair had to show in my face, body, and chronic disengagement. But the teacher didn't intervene. What was his mindset? Stay away—this kid's a wimp who needs to toughen up? Was he too preoccupied with his own issues to pay attention to mine? Perhaps he was just at a loss about what to do. Either way, I suffered socially, emotionally, and academically.

There was a great moment in the film *Broadcast News* where a character asks, "Wouldn't this be a great world if insecurity and desperation made us more attractive? If 'needy' was a turn-on?" Unfortunately, we humans don't work that way (yet).

EMOTIONS AND HEALTH

Emotional sickness is avoiding reality at any cost.
Emotional health is facing reality at any cost.
—M. SCOTT PECK

You lie awake at three A.M., staring at the ceiling, anxious about some serious problem. Impossible to sleep. We've all been there. You're too pressured and distracted to even think about working out, and besides, you have too much else on your plate, so you skip the gym, even though you know it makes you feel good to go. Can't be helped. Meals are erratic. Instead of thinking about dinner and planning to shop and cook, you grab a pizza on the way home from work. It's been happening a lot lately. And after that's done, you need to decompress, so it's a pint of ice cream in front of the TV for an hour. Until it's finally time for bed and another three A.M. staring at the ceiling. . . .

For a moment, forget about your emotional health—imagine what you're doing to your physical health.

When considering the influence of emotion on our well-being, we must first remember that our brains—where most of our feelings originate—are as much a part of our bodies as any other organ, fed by the same flow of blood, oxygen, and nutrients. Our emotions are linked to physiological reactions in our brains, releasing hormones and other powerful chemicals that, in turn, affect our physical health, which has an impact on our emotional state. It's all connected.

That's why physical sickness can be caused by a mind under emotional stress. But there's also the opposite phenomenon: physical wellness that's fostered by positive feelings. Both kinds underscore the importance of managing our emotional lives.

Even our *mindset* about stress can influence health outcomes, from weight loss to insomnia. In one study, Alia Crum, an assistant professor at Stanford University, randomly assigned three hundred employees at a finance company to watch two different three-minute videos about stress. Half of the participants watched a video that reinforced the negative aspects of stress; the others watched a similar video, but the messaging reinforced the positive side. After four weeks, the employees were surveyed: the "stress is bad" group experienced more negative health symptoms than those in the "stress is good" group.

Inside our brains, hormones and other neurochemicals are being turned on and off depending on what we're feeling at any given moment. The hypothalamic-pituitary-adrenal (HPA) axis, located in the midbrain, is one of the major neuroendocrine systems that controls how we respond to stress and also regulates emotions and moods. The HPA axis is where certain hormones, such as adrenaline and cortisol, originate. Researchers studying this region of the brain have found that early-life exposure to mild, everyday stressors enhances our future ability to regulate emotions and confers lifelong resilience. But exposure to extreme or prolonged stress does just the opposite—it induces hyperactivity in the HPA axis and lifelong susceptibility to stress.

The difference between good stress and bad stress mainly has to do with duration and intensity. For instance, having to prepare a compelling presentation for a client is a form of stress, but the good kind. It's caused by the challenge of achieving a desired goal and lasts only a short time. The ending of a game, or a major event such as a wedding day, affects us similarly. Stress inducing but happy. These events prompt the momentary release of stress hormones, but then it ends. Research at the Stanford University School of Medicine found that short bouts of stress can boost immunity and raise levels of cancer-fighting molecules—and the effect lasts for weeks after the stressful situation ends.

We have evolved to handle short-term stress—hormones are released, allowing us to respond successfully to the crisis, and then turn off at the tap. That's not what happens at some workplaces, where we may be forced to endure eight hours daily with a boss who makes life a living hell, or at schools where students may dread the bullies on the bus ride home. Many of us spend hours and entire days under emotional duress, until it becomes a chronic condition. Our brains are bathed in a constant flow of stress hormones, for which evolution has definitely not prepared us. We don't suffer only emotionally in those instances—our physical health is affected too.

"Stress leaves you in a fight-or-flight state in which your body turns off long-term building and repair projects," said Robert Sapolsky, a professor at Stanford University, in his book *Behave*. "Memory and accuracy are impaired. You tire more easily, you can become depressed and reproduction gets downgraded."

There's ample scientific evidence of the long-term harm caused by childhood emotional trauma, such as bullying. Children may experience compromised immunity to disease, digestive tract pain and upset, headaches, poor sleep, inability to concentrate, and depression. These effects can persist into adulthood, creating physical and mental health problems long after the bullying is in the past.

Feeling "down"—pessimism, apathy, depression—is linked to low levels of serotonin and dopamine, the so-called feel-good neurotransmitters. Serotonin plays a role in pain perception, which may be why people experiencing negative emotions report more severe symptoms of illness, and nearly half of patients with depression also suffer aches and pains.

Negative emotional states—anxiety, anger, sadness, stress—are closely associated with unhealthy behaviors, such as poor diet, smoking, excessive drinking, physical inactivity, and social isolation, many of which we found in a recent study with more than five thousand teachers from across the United States. Those are the same lifestyle factors that contribute to our most feared and widespread illnesses: heart disease, cancer, type 2 diabetes, addiction, dementia. These conditions in turn have a devastating impact on our emotional lives, and the feedback loop turns into a downward spiral for our health, mental and physical. Ultimately, they deepen our feelings of hopelessness and despair that we will ever manage to improve our moods or our health. Interestingly, we found that a positive workplace climate acted as a buffer for the deleterious effects of negative emotions on health outcomes for teachers.

There's a great deal of medical research linking hostility and anger to heart disease. Men reporting the highest levels of anger were over two and a half times more likely to suffer cardiac events such as heart attack than other men. Negative emotions have been associated with hypertension, increased heart rate, constriction of peripheral blood vessels, unhealthy blood lipids, and decreased immune system function.

Not only does an angry outburst cause a spike in blood pressure, but every time we recall what made us so mad, our blood pressure rises again. According to one study, a thirty-minute argument with your significant other can slow your body's ability to heal by at least a day. And if you argue regularly, that delay is doubled. Even subtle forms of anger, such as impatience, irritability, and grouchiness, may damage health.

We can see the influence of our emotions on our physical health in less dire ways too. The stress associated with knowing you have to deliver a speech can double the severity of allergy symptoms for two days. Feeling sad makes symptoms of illness seem more severe and cause greater discomfort. In one study, people who scored low on positive emotions were three times as likely to become sick after exposure to a virus than those who scored higher. When the latter group did get sick, their symptoms were less severe.

But our emotions can also prompt the release of beneficial neuro-chemicals and hormones. Crying is soothing because it carries stress hormones out of our bodies. Feelings of gratitude increase oxygen levels in our tissues, speed healing, and boost our immune system. Being in love was found to raise the level of nerve growth factor, a hormone-like substance that restores the nervous system and improves memory. The effect lasts for about a year, according to researchers. In one study, laughter caused by watching a comedy film increased the flow of beta-endorphins, which enhance our mood, and stimulated growth hormones, which repair our cells. Even the anticipation of laughter was found to lower the levels of cortisol and adrenaline. Laughter may also reduce the risk of heart attack. Feeling good, therefore, may encourage healthy behaviors, which in turn can promote greater emotional well-being and physical health.

In the wake of the September 11, 2001, attacks, U.S. college students were tested, and those who experienced the most positive emotions—gratitude, love, and so forth—were less likely to develop depressive symptoms later on. This suggests that after a crisis, people who have more positive feelings may be more resilient than those who experience fewer positive emotions.

We'll never eradicate negative emotions from our lives or those of our kids. Nor should we. But we need to attend to the play of positive and negative emotions, which is out of balance for too many of us. As we reported earlier, our research at Yale revealed that high school students, teachers, and business professionals experience negative emotions up to 70 percent of the time they are in school or at work. Their feelings aren't the only thing at stake—so is their health. What will it take to switch the ratio of negative-to-positive emotions? What's your ratio?

EMOTIONS AND CREATIVITY

*Rational thoughts never drive people's
creativity the way emotions do.*
—NEIL DEGRASSE TYSON

Many of us need to feel creative in order to feel alive, engaged, and fully involved in life and whatever it throws at us. Otherwise we're just treading water. But what do we mean by creativity?

There's the obvious answer—artistic work such as painting, music, literature, and the professions that demand (and reward) creativity, such as architecture, science, design, and engineering, among others.

But creativity is much more universal than that. It's an important element of every human life. Whenever we make a decision or face a challenge, we have an opportunity to be creative—to respond to the moment in a way that doesn't just repeat what's always been done before (and perhaps always failed before too). Daily, each of us has many chances to be creative, to act in new and thoughtful ways. It's what makes life an adventure.

But there can be something scary about creativity too. It represents a break with the status quo and a step into the unknown. Creative decisions, even in the smallest matters, are a way of saying we think we have a better idea. And then comes the feedback—from others, but even from ourselves: What if your new way doesn't work out so well? What if you've made things worse (at least in somebody's eyes, though maybe not yours)? What makes you think you're so creative anyway? You can see that our creative impulses and our emotions are closely intertwined.

Many of us believe that personality and intelligence alone drive our ability to be creative. Or that creativity is an all-or-nothing gift, rather than a set of skills that can be improved with practice. True, some personality traits such as "openness to experience" are reliably related to it, but traits alone don't account for everything. And research confirms that creativity is only modestly associated with IQ (meaning you don't have to be a genius to be creative!).

This is where our emotional lives extend even beyond the personal. Creativity is the lifeblood of our culture and our economy. In a poll, fifteen hundred corporate CEOs said that an employee's creativity was the single best indicator of future success. Without innovation, societies stagnate and die.

Creativity also includes two other factors: performance and effectiveness. Creativity can't exist only in the abstract, in our minds and nowhere else. That's just having a rich imagination! The creative process needs to be followed by concrete action. Once we devise new strategies, we must have the confidence to put them to use. Effective performance is as much a part of creativity as the initial, animating idea.

But whether we take advantage of all the possibilities every time is a different matter. Safe to say, at times we all *feel* less creative than we'd like to be. That's because our creativity is so closely tied to our emotional state—even though the connection may not be so obvious.

Again and again, in working with educators, families, and children, we wind up discussing the ubiquitous problems of stress and frustration— the despair of feeling as though we lack the power to make meaningful changes for the better. It's hard to imagine a worse feeling. For a child, it can be devastating—children have little control over their lives under the best of conditions. We all go through tough times, but most of us believe that if we persevere, we can find solutions. That's another form of creativity: everyday creativity, the ability to keep discovering new answers when the old ones no longer work. What must life be like for the children and adults who can't hope even for that?

We can see how it plays out in schools. Kyung Hee Kim, a professor at the School of Education at the College of William & Mary, made extensive studies of creativity among schoolchildren and found that it has been in decline for the past two decades. Her conclusions are based on results from the Torrance Tests of Creative Thinking (TTCT), which measure creativity, defined as the ability to respond to situations in ways that are novel and original. For example, people could be asked for all the possible uses for a paper clip or the consequences of people becoming invisible at will. She examined normative data for the TTCT through time, from kindergarten to senior year of high school, and writes, "Children have become less emotionally expressive, less energetic, less talkative and verbally expressive, less humorous, less imaginative, less unconventional, less lively and passionate, less perceptive, less apt to connect seemingly irrelevant things, less synthesizing, and less likely to see things from a different angle." Who or what could we blame except parents and an educational system that often squash original thinking and penalize students for using their imagination? Our students get the message rather quickly from our obsession with kindergarten "readiness," to society's detriment. Interestingly, when the developer of the creativity test, Dr. E. Paul Torrance, administered it to students and then tracked them years into the future, he found that scores on his famous creativity tests were a better predictor of adult creative achievements than IQ.

When discussing creative thinking, psychologists often use the terms *convergent* and *divergent* thinking. The former operates when searching for only one correct solution to a problem or only one proper answer to a question and tries to arrive at it by mostly straight-ahead, linear thinking. The divergent approach moves in all directions—it assumes there are many possible solutions and tries to consider each, especially the most creative, unusual ones.

The impulse to create seems to come naturally to the human brain. However, we must be encouraged to express it. In schools, it's hard to be creative when convergent thinking—the ability to remember facts and perform well on standardized tests—is most highly rewarded. To engage children and prepare them for the workforce, they must be given more opportunities and encouragement to be creative. For that to happen, schools need to restructure learning so that it promotes unconventional thinking and fresh approaches to problem solving across content areas, not just in the arts. For example, more and more schools are incorporating project-based learning and design thinking—a five-stage process for solving complex problems that includes (1) defining a problem; (2) understanding the human needs involved; (3) reframing the problem in human-centric ways; (4) generating a multitude of ideas; and (5) a hands-on approach in prototyping and testing.

Research shows that divergent thinking results in feelings of joy, pride, and satisfaction. A study across five countries with four different languages found that working on creative tasks leads to an increase in positive emotions and autonomy. Another study showed that creative behavior on a given day leads to more positive emotions and a sense of flourishing the next day. As with so much about our emotional lives, there's a feedback loop at work: feeling good encourages us to act creatively, which makes us feel even better.

But happiness is not the single key to creativity. In fact, modest levels of stress have been found in some cases to significantly improve creative performance compared with no stress at all. Even emotions such as anger and distress can serve as motivation for creative thinking and enhance creativity. Take the high school students in Parkland, Florida. They have channeled their anger about the horrific school shooting to build a persuasive campaign around gun reform. The role of sympathy in creative thinking has also been explored. College students were induced to feel sympathy through a slide show of distressed elderly adults, then asked to generate ideas and design a floor plan for an office reception area to make it more welcoming to the elderly. Compared with the control group, the "sympathy" participants showed greater originality in thinking. One explanation is that sympathy is a reaction to other people's suffering and therefore produces intrinsic motivation to generate solutions that reduce their distress.

Creativity is especially important in the face of adversity—when we're disappointed because plan A didn't work out; when we tried hard and still received negative feedback; when someone stands in the way of our progress or even tries to prevent it. We first have to manage our hurt or anger—not deny it but accept it and then put it to good use, as a motivational force. That's where our creativity can come to our rescue and allow us to achieve our goal despite obstacles.

According to my colleague at Yale, Zorana Ivcevic Pringle, a creativity researcher, "Emotions are both the spark that fires the engine of creativity and the fuel that keeps the fire burning when other people try to douse it, or the kindling runs low." Emotions rule the whole creative process, from motivating creative work to idea generation to persisting toward the actualization of our own ideas. It's the challenge that keeps us striving.

Now do you see how complex that simple question "How do you feel?" really can be? That emotional roller coaster is no small matter—it has an enormous influence over the most important areas of our lives. Religious leaders, poets, and playwrights have known this for centuries; over the past few decades, the scientists have begun to catch up. Now we know better than the ancients (and not so ancients) the degree to which emotions guide everything else. That's the first step toward accepting who we truly are. What, then, is the next step?

3

How to Become an Emotion Scientist

How ARE YOU FEELING right now? Can you be sure?

That may seem like a ridiculous question—of course we all know exactly what we're feeling. It may be the only thing about which we can be certain.

So if it's all so completely, effortlessly self-evident, why would we need a science of emotion and emotional intelligence? We speak of emotion skills, but doesn't that mean there is something to be learned—or not? Indeed it does: it's a safe bet that no one in the history of the human race has ever known precisely what she or he is feeling, in all its complexity and contradiction and chaos, at all times. Our neurons are firing hundreds of times a second, and lots of what goes on up there is pure, roiling emotion.

Scientists refer to intelligences as hot or cold, hot being the emotional one and cold, of course, the rational one.

But they don't take turns operating. If I'm computing what I owe in taxes, I'm using cold intelligence, though my reasoning powers will absolutely be affected if five minutes ago I noticed a weird lump on my dog's neck or I had an argument with my next-door neighbor. We have one brain made up of several regions, each with its own functions, and sometimes they pull us in different directions.

Given all that, how could anyone *but* a scientist make sense of it? That's why we all must strive to become emotion scientists.

You could be brilliant, with an IQ that Einstein would envy, but if you're unable to recognize your emotions and see how they're affecting your behavior, all that cognitive firepower won't do you as much good as you might imagine. A gifted child who doesn't have the permission to feel, along with the vocabulary to express those feelings and the ability to understand them, won't be able to manage complicated emotions around friendships and academics, limiting his or her potential.

As we saw in the previous chapter, our most important mental functions have an emotional aspect, even if they seem to be purely in the realm of "cognition." And those factors determine significant real-life outcomes—our relationships, our performance, our decision making, even our physical health. Our feelings encourage us to treat the people we care about with love and respect or disregard their needs and wishes; help us focus our thinking or distract us; fill us with enthusiasm and energy or deplete our will; open us up to the outside world or wall us off from it. Feelings motivate us to do things that improve our lives and those of the people around us, but they can also adversely influence our actions—without us even realizing it. In fact, that's when we're most vulnerable to emotion's impact: when we fail to detect it.

When we are making a decision, there are two kinds of emotions: *integral* and *incidental*. Integral emotions are directly caused by the action at hand—we're fearful while climbing a tricky mountain path; we're joyful as we're falling in love. All completely understandable and connected to the moment. Incidental emotions have nothing to do with what's going on—as we described earlier, we had an argument with our kids, and our lingering feelings of frustration and anger influence how we drive to work or interact with colleagues at the office. These are the emotions that infiltrate our thinking without us being aware.

Only by becoming emotion scientists will we learn the skills to use our emotions wisely. Not suppress them or ignore them—in fact, just the opposite. We'll no longer be controlled by feelings we may not even perceive. We'll also be able to help the people we interact with—loved ones, colleagues—manage theirs.

Knowing what emotions tell us is the first, necessary part of the process. For example, anxiety is a signal that we feel something important is beyond our control. Fear or uneasiness can make us risk-averse. That can be a positive thing—it may steer us away from taking foolish chances. But if we're too risk-averse, or give up in the face of obstacles too easily, we'll never try anything, thereby guaranteeing failure. That's why we need to understand our emotions, be aware of how they influence our actions, and have strategies to regulate them.

Becoming an emotion scientist will help us to recognize the physical symptoms that sometimes accompany strong feelings. Suddenly I'm feverish and my heart is racing; or I'm feeling a queasy ache in my stomach. All real sensations, sometimes emotional rather than physiological, sometimes not. Lisa Feldman Barrett, a professor at Northeastern University, recently shared with me that when our "body budget" is running low and we feel distressed, our brains search around for things that might be wrong in our lives to make sense of the distress. When these symptoms present themselves, we don't always pause to ask: Is there an emotion behind this, and what can I do about it? Or am I just dehydrated or hungry or tired and need to drink or eat something or just go to bed?

An emotion scientist has the ability to pause even at the most stressful moments and ask: What am I reacting to? We can learn to identify and understand all our feelings, integral and incidental, and then respond in helpful, proportionate ways—once we acquire emotion skills. But what exactly are they?

In 1990, Peter Salovey and John Mayer published a landmark paper, "Emotional Intelligence," in a little-known journal (after it was rejected by multiple top-tier publications). That article has since served as the academic foundation for most research into emotional intelligence. In it, they asserted that the majority of life tasks are influenced by emotion. We all have emotion skills, the authors wrote, but to varying degrees. And we can all increase our emotional intelligence, which Salovey and Mayer defined as

> the ability to perceive accurately, appraise, and express emotion; the ability to access and/or generate feelings when they facilitate thought; the ability to understand emotion and emotional knowledge; and the ability to regulate emotions to promote emotional and intellectual growth.

That's a fine textbook definition. We should all possess those skills. But it's hard to infer what emotional intelligence looks like in practice from that definition alone. There are individual differences in how we process information of every type. Some of us are naturally better at math than others, while some of us excel at language-based tasks. But we all learn and improve in those areas. Similarly, some of us are more fluent and intuitive than others when it comes to emotional matters. But we can all learn and improve here too.

In my seminars, I often ask people to describe an emotionally intelligent person. Try it yourself now: What are the skills?

Some people say *empathy*, which allows us to relate to what others are feeling. Empathy is about having a shared emotional experience. If you feel shame from childhood experiences, and I've also experienced shame, then we can feel empathy for each other. Empathy often is enriched with emotion skills. Empathy can help you connect with someone, but it won't necessarily help you to support a person in managing his or her difficult emotion or stop you from getting lost in someone else's shoes. That's where emotion skills come into play.

Neither is what we commonly think of as *emotional stability*. We tend to view a calm, poised demeanor as a sign of superior emotional wisdom. It denotes inner peace and harmony. People who are serene and "together" may possess great emotion skills, but the same may be true of those who are conspicuously neurotic. In fact, sometimes—out of pure necessity—people who are high in neuroticism also demonstrate great emotion skills. They need them in order to regulate their own tumultuous inner lives. But neither stability nor neuroticism equals emotional intelligence.

Grit, which Angela Duckworth, a professor at the University of Pennsylvania, defines as "perseverance and passion for long-term goals," has become a popular psychological construct in recent years. Research shows that grit is associated with many important outcomes from academic achievement to income. But grit isn't an emotion skill. There are plenty of gritty people who struggle with regulating their emotions. Grit and emotional intelligence are not in competition with each other but rather work hand in hand to support people in achieving their goals. Here's how: On the path to success, gritty people (like myself) often fail to achieve certain goals; we get frustrated, disappointed, or overwhelmed and receive negative feedback. Therefore, having a repertoire of emotion-regulation strategies can help gritty people to overcome difficult emotions and obstacles that arise on the journey toward achieving long-term goals. And as we know, the right amount of persistence may lead to success, but too much can be counterproductive. I've had my share of students who, emboldened by the belief in the power of grit, go so far overboard that they undermine their own best efforts owing to their lack of social awareness.

Resilience also is mentioned as an emotion skill. According to the American Psychological Association, it is "the process of adapting well in the face of adversity, trauma, tragedy, threats or significant sources of stress—such as family and relationship problems, serious health problems or workplace and financial stressors." Research by Tom Boyce from the University of California–San Francisco and colleagues has revealed biological markers that differentiate how "sensitive" children (referred to as "orchids") respond to environmental changes compared with how "resilient" children (who they call "dandelions") react. Dandelion children may thrive in most any condition, whereas orchid children tend to be more fearful and overwhelmed in uncertain social situations. Whether an orchid or a dandelion child does better or worse likely has to do with how families, teachers, and peers support their emotional development. If neglected, orchid children promptly wither—but if they are raised in supportive conditions, they not only survive but flourish compared with dandelion children. Emotion skills are likely the antecedent to building resilience.

Finally, emotion skills are not a constellation of traits, such as confidence or charisma or popularity. It doesn't mean having a "good" personality, whatever that is. It isn't kindness or warmth or high self-esteem. It isn't optimism. Those may all be desirable qualities that make us appealing to the rest of the world. We may aspire to any or all of the above. But they're not emotion skills.

So, what are they? First, emotion skills must be acquired. Nobody is born with them all in place and ready to work. Emotion skills amplify our strengths and help us through challenges. If I'm an extrovert and need to shine, then I must learn to read my environment, so I can see when I overwhelm others and tone myself down. If I'm an introvert, my tendency to be quiet and subdued might underwhelm people at home, school, or the workplace, so I will need to amp myself up at times, so the world can see my enthusiasm.

Over the years, I've run into some strange ideas about emotional intelligence and its purposes. Once, during a seminar I led at a major tech company, a top executive took issue with the idea that he had anything to learn. "I want you to teach the people who work for me to learn how to deal with *my* emotions," he said.

At a conference for intellectually gifted individuals, where I was a presenter, people were wearing name tags with colored dots. When I asked my host what the colors meant, she said that green indicated "I'm comfortable with receiving a hug," yellow meant "Ask before hugging," and red proclaimed "Stay away!" That was the first (and only) conference I've attended where people publicly announced their comfort levels around emotion and physical contact. It also was my first "on-the-scene learning" experience that supported the empirical research I had done, which demonstrated the small correlation between emotional intelligence and IQ.

Another time, at a demanding medical school, a senior professor made little effort to hide his skepticism. When I asked if there were any questions, he stood up and said, "What happened to academia? We are training future Nobel laureates here, not nice people." As if the two qualities couldn't coexist within one person. There were so many prejudices, weaknesses, and contradictions encoded into that statement, it would have taken many hours of discussion (and probably a lot of therapy) to untangle it all. The plainest, shortest response I had was, "Well, you *could* be training a lot *more* Nobel laureates if . . ." (I later asked the chair of the department, "Is this really happening?" He whispered, "Why do you think I brought you in?")

To some observers, emotional intelligence or emotion skills signify something fuzzy and touchy-feely, like a retreat from reality. This is especially so in the business world. In fact, just the opposite is true. These are mental skills like any others—they enable us to think smarter, more creatively, and to get better results from ourselves and the people around us. There's nothing squishy about that. Emotional intelligence doesn't allow feelings to get in the way—it does just the opposite. It restores balance to our thought processes; it prevents emotions from having undue influence over our actions; and it helps us to realize that we might be feeling a certain way for a reason.

For more than twenty years, our team has synthesized research in psychology, education, and neuroscience in order to teach the emotion skills necessary for children and adults to thrive. These abilities represent the principal aspects of emotion knowledge, competencies, and processes found in the psychological literature on emotional development and intelligence. Based on that, we've developed an approach for making emotion skills an integral part of education for leaders, managers, teachers, students, and families. It's being used all over the world, in school systems, in corporations, and in other institutions.

Throughout the rest of this book, we'll explore those skills in detail. Here, I'll provide a brief introduction. They're known by an acronym—RULER.

The first skill: Recognizing the occurrence of an emotion—by noticing a change in one's own thoughts, energy, or body or in someone else's facial expression, body language, or voice. That's the first clue that something important is happening.

The second skill: Understanding, which means that we know the cause of emotions and see how they influence our thoughts and decisions. This helps us make better predictions about our own and others' behavior.

The third skill: Labeling, which refers to making connections between an emotional experience and the precise terms to describe it. People with a more mature "feelings vocabulary" can differentiate among related emotions such as pleased, happy, elated, and ecstatic. Labeling emotions accurately increases self-awareness and helps us to communicate emotions effectively, reducing misunderstanding in social interactions.

The fourth skill: Expressing, which means knowing how and when to display our emotions, depending on the setting, the people we're with, and the larger context. People who are skilled in this area understand that unspoken rules for emotional expression, also called "display rules," often direct the best way to express what they feel and modify their behaviors accordingly.

The fifth skill: Regulating, which involves monitoring, tempering, and modifying emotional reactions in helpful ways, in order to reach personal and professional goals. This doesn't mean ignoring inconvenient emotions—rather, it's learning to accept and deal with them. People with this skill employ strategies to manage their own emotions and help others with theirs.

In the RULER framework, the first three skills—Recognizing, Understanding, and Labeling—help us to accurately identify and decode what we and others are feeling. Then, the two remaining skills—

Expressing and Regulating—tell us how we can manage those emotions to achieve desired outcomes—our ultimate goal.

Research on general intelligence, or IQ, dates back to the early 1900s. Part of the reason the concept of emotional intelligence lags behind that of IQ is that there are reliable, scientifically proven tests to measure the latter. A licensed psychologist will charge a couple thousand dollars to administer a standardized three-hour examination that produces a defining number: your intelligence quotient. IQ has been with us for more than a century. No such comprehensive evaluation exists—yet—for emotional intelligence. Without a precise measure, we find it easy to dismiss it as a subjective, imprecise notion.

Daily life requires emotion skills at every turn yet provides little reliable feedback on how well we're doing or if we're improving. Few institutions of learning devote any time to teaching or assessing emotion skills. We're still in the beginning stages of unpacking emotion science, including how best to measure and teach the skills. Think about it: How much formal instruction, at home or at school, did you receive in the five key emotion areas described above? If you're like most of us, not much.

Yet I am comfortable making the case that emotional intelligence is as important as IQ. We know for a fact that no matter how smart you are, your emotions will have an influence—positive or negative—on your rational thought processes. That's important.

We've already explained the five key emotion skills, so let's try an experiment: a simple self-test you can take to measure your own. You'll have to score yourself from 1 (very unskilled) to 5 (very skilled) on five statements that neatly sum up what it takes to be an emotion scientist:

- I am able to accurately recognize my own and others' emotions.
- I am aware of the causes and consequences of my own and others' feelings.

- I have a refined emotion vocabulary.
- I am skilled at expressing the full range of emotions.
- I am skilled at managing my own emotions and at helping others manage theirs.

Okay, what was your score? A 25 is perfect and a 5 is the worst you can do.

How confident are you in the significance of your score? Let's admit the fatal flaw in this test: none of us is completely unbiased when it comes to estimating our own mental skills, emotional or otherwise. In a study we conducted of college students, we asked how they thought they would perform on the standardized emotional intelligence assessment compared with their roommates and all other undergraduates at the university. Nearly 80 percent of the students believed they would perform above the fiftieth percentile. So clearly we're inclined to overstate our emotion skills. Perhaps unsurprising, male students' estimates of their scores were significantly higher than those of the women, despite the fact that the men did worse than the women when they took a performance-based test.

It's possible to go online and find many similar self-tests that purport to quickly and accurately measure emotional intelligence. Like the one we just took, these are mostly superficial and misleading, often measuring personality traits rather than emotion skills and reflecting the universal desire to feel superior to our fellow human beings when it comes to the wisdom of the heart.

In the corporate world, emotional intelligence is regularly assessed using a "360-degree" format for the purposes of promotion or executive coaching. In this case, a person's score is based on his or her own self-report *in addition* to evaluations provided by peers, subordinates, and supervisors. These assessments are mostly concerned with self-control, trustworthiness, conscientiousness, adaptability, teamwork ability, the ability to influence others, and inspirational leadership—all potentially important aspects of being a good leader and manager. The general consensus among researchers is that these tools measure perceived traits, competencies, and aspects of one's reputation, but not emotion skills.

For the reasons stated above, there is a general agreement in psychology that performance tests (as opposed to self-report scales) are the gold standard, because they measure actual capacity for mental tasks. In regard to emotional intelligence, Salovey and Mayer, along with David Caruso, cofounder of Emotional Intelligence Skills Group, developed a performance test. It endeavors to measure how well people perform tasks and solve emotion-laden problems. The test has been an important tool for research purposes, but even the most sophisticated test can't predict how someone would respond in real-life situations where emotion skills are required. The real test of emotion skills isn't while reading on the beach; it's when someone kicks sand in your face! Currently, our team is working with Professor Sigal Barsade at the Wharton School, University of Pennsylvania, to build a suite of dynamic performance tests of emotional intelligence to capture emotion skills in real time.

There's another reason why defining emotional intelligence is so elusive: the lack of clear terminology. Most of us use words such as "emotion" and "feeling" more or less interchangeably, with a general understanding of what they mean. But there are some subtle and important distinctions too. Let's go through the glossary.

An *emotion*—happy, sad, angry—arises from an appraisal of an internal or external stimulus. By appraisal I mean an interpretation of what is happening in the world or my mind through the lens of my present goals or concerns. We hear, see, feel (through touch), taste, or smell something that alerts us to a shift in the environment. We are provoked by a memory or sensation, or an event, something someone says or does, or something we witness or experience. I think about someone who treated me unfairly or someone actually treats me unfairly, and I feel angry.

Emotions are mostly short-lived (have you ever felt surprised for an hour?). They usually include a physiological reaction, such as a blush, chills, or an increased heart rate, and a release of neurochemicals to prepare you for action. They are often expressed automatically in our facial expressions, body language, and other nonverbal cues. Emotions also are accompanied by a subjective experience in our conscious minds. When we feel happy we have positive thoughts. Being upset turns us into pessimists. Finally, emotions mobilize us into action—to approach or avoid, fight or flee.

The classical view of emotions was that they were evolutionary adaptations and that people across all cultures experienced and displayed the same basic emotions in the same ways. For example: We developed the feeling of fear because it was advantageous to our survival, and we all express it in the same way because it is part of our biological nature.

Today, our understanding has become more nuanced. Recent research emphasizes that emotions are fully intertwined not only with our biology but also with our individual life experiences and culture. We don't all fear the same things, and we don't all express joy in the same ways. When schoolchildren in the United States are asked to draw a happy face, it sports a huge smile. When Asian children are given the same task, the smiles are smaller. This doesn't mean they are less happy than their American counterparts, only that perhaps they experience and express their happiness differently. As we mature, our emotional repertoire becomes more precise (one hopes). Preschoolers have one word for angry: mad. Older children in schools where we work learn to make fine distinctions, using concepts such as annoyed, aggravated, irritated, livid, and enraged.

A *feeling* is our internal response to an emotion. I'm angry about something that's happening between us, it's caused me to give up hope, and I can't keep going this way. That's a feeling. It's nuanced, subtle, multidimensional. When you ask someone how they're feeling, the answer is sometimes an emotion, such as happy, sad, afraid, angry. But they may also say they're feeling supported, connected, valued, respected, and appreciated. These words do not refer to emotions per se but are motivational and relationship states that are steeped in emotion. Technically, an athlete doesn't *feel* motivated to run a marathon; it's the athlete's current and anticipated feelings of joy and pride that motivate him or her to run each day in order to participate in the marathon.

We often have more than one emotion at the same time. I'm excited about my new job, and I'm anxious over whether I can handle it. I'm angry at how you're treating me, and I feel superior because I've never treated you so badly. Here's one I know all too well: The airline lost my luggage, and I'm simultaneously angry over their carelessness, worried because my medicine was in there, embarrassed because I'll have to attend a meeting dressed in what I wore on the plane, and discouraged because I know they'll never find my suitcase before my trip is over.

We can even have emotions about emotions. We call them *meta-emotions*. I could be afraid of public speaking and embarrassed about being afraid. Or I'm being bullied so I feel victimized, and I'm ashamed of myself for allowing that to happen.

A *mood* is more diffuse and less intense than an emotion or a feeling but longer lasting. Most typically, we don't quite know why we're feeling the way we are during a mood, but we are very certain when feeling an emotion. Moods also can be the aftermath of an emotion. Have you ever been annoyed at someone, couldn't stop thinking about it, and ended up in a bad mood? Often, it doesn't feel as though anything caused it—it's just a state of being, but one that's completely tied in with our emotional responses to life. "Mood disorder" is a common term nowadays, describing a psychiatric condition such as depression, bipolarity, or anxiety disorder. These all impair everyday functioning—they're at the extreme of how mood affects our lives.

In addition to emotions, feelings, and moods, there are emotion-related *personality traits*. This feels like who we are, at our core—our predisposition to feel, think, and act in a particular way. We're optimists or pessimists, we're take-charge types or fatalists, we're introverts or extroverts, we're calm or hyper. To be sure, personality traits can change over time, but when they do, it happens gradually. This means we need patience with kids who are growing into themselves. But for the most part, traits are the constants, which can have influence over how we feel but should not be confused with feelings. People who are more optimistic tend to experience greater positive emotions, but they also can overestimate other people's positive emotions.

All of these distinctions matter more to research psychologists and social scientists than to anyone else. For our purposes, we'll use the words *emotions* and *feelings* to mean more or less the same thing. But we'll all better understand our emotional lives if we have the vocabulary to express every nuance of what we feel.

On the road to becoming emotion scientists, we need to avoid the temptation to act as emotion judges.

In both cases, we're attempting to recognize emotions and their source and then to foresee how they might be influencing our thoughts and actions. But an emotion scientist seeks to understand without making value judgments or rendering opinions about whether feelings are justified or not, beneficial or not, or reflecting an objective reality. An emotion scientist comes equipped only with questions and a desire to listen and learn.

An emotion judge, on the other hand, is seeking something else. An emotion judge attempts to evaluate feelings (even his or her own— we're not immune to harsh self-judgment) and deem them good or bad, useful or harmful, grounded in reality or a figment of the imagination. An emotion judge wants the power to validate feelings or negate them—to pass judgment.

Their reasons are understandable. A parent, for instance, has a lot on the line when it comes to a child's emotional life. Any negative feelings that are expressed—anxiety, rage, shame—can be seen as a reflection of the child's upbringing. If an employee feels browbeaten, if a loved one feels despair, if you yourself feel worthless, there's a temptation to deflect responsibility and assign guilt. This is why it's easier to sentence an angry child to a time-out than it is to listen to his or her feelings and explore what's lurking behind them. Where emotion scientists operate with open minds and good intentions, emotion judges are afraid of hearing something dreadful. They come prepared to deny, defend, and blame.

Carol Dweck, a professor at Stanford University and author of the bestselling book *Mindset,* has shown in decades of research how our beliefs about skills determine our success or failure at developing them. Here's what that means: When we believe that emotion skills can be taught, we have greater faith in their ability to change outcomes for the better. If we think that our emotional makeup is more or less fixed and unchangeable, we're less likely to invest much time or effort in developing our own skills or teaching them to others. Emotion scientists share the mindset that says education is possible. To an emotion judge, all that remains is to deem someone's emotional state helpful or harmful, positive or negative, good or bad, without a hope for growth and improvement.

In our judicial system, judges play a valuable and necessary role. In our emotional lives, it's just the opposite.

Having a high degree of emotional intelligence, and possessing what I've described as the five necessary emotion skills, makes all our lives better. Sounds obvious, I realize, but if we need evidence, there's plenty of science to back it up.

The work of researchers Jeremy Yip, an assistant professor at Georgetown University, and Stéphane Côté, a professor at the Rotman School of Management, University of Toronto, demonstrated the concept at the heart of this: Individuals with more developed emotion skills were better able to correctly identify the events that caused their emotions and, therefore, were able to screen out the influence of incidental emotions on their decisions.

We base most of life's decisions on how we think our actions will make us feel. But without emotion skills, research shows that we are notoriously bad at predicting what will make us happy. Many of us have spent time chasing the wrong goals or refusing to engage in activities that actually might make us feel better. We eat sugar to lift a depressed mood when exercise likely will do a better job; we engage with social media to feel connected when we know it amplifies anxiety.

Back when John Kerry ran for president against George W. Bush, we surveyed Yale students to see how angry they would be if their candidate lost. After the election, we tested Kerry voters and found that they had grossly overestimated how mad they would be. In a second study conducted at Duke University, we asked students to predict their feelings about an upcoming basketball game against the school's archrival, University of North Carolina. They were told to imagine how excited they would be if Duke won. They were also asked to predict how they would feel if Duke lost. The day after the game—which UNC won—the students were called and asked to report their levels of excitement. Again, participants overestimated how they would feel. However, in both studies, students who had higher emotional intelligence scores were better at anticipating their emotions. Emotionally intelligent individuals had an intuitive understanding of one of the central conclusions of happiness research: Well-being depends less on objective events than on how those events are perceived, dealt with, and shared with others. Because emotionally skilled people are more likely to recognize this core concept, they are likely to have an advantage in their decision making.

These are critical skills at all ages. Will our children be able to resist the temptation of hurting a friend or alcohol and drug abuse? Will they know how to use their creativity to push beyond boredom and not surrender to it? Will they understand how emotional upsets may lead them to consider poor decisions on social media, then adjust their thinking accordingly? Teaching them emotion skills will help, and there's research to prove it. Young school-age children with more developed emotion skills have fewer conduct problems, are better adjusted, and perform better academically than children with less developed skills.

We're all familiar—firsthand—with the dramatic emotion sensitivities and emotional dysregulations that come with adolescence. They can undermine the success of even the smartest, hardest-working students. But emotional intelligence makes a big difference. The ability of young people to thrive even when feelings (positive *or* negative) threaten to overwhelm their intentions is associated with more developed emotion skills.

Among adolescents, higher emotional intelligence is associated with less depression and anxiety and may be a protective factor against suicidal behavior. Those who are higher in emotional intelligence also are rated both by themselves and by their teachers as being easier to get along with than students with less developed skills. There is also data suggesting that emotional intelligence is related to higher SAT scores, greater creativity, and better grades among high school and college students. In one study, emotional intelligence was a predictor of academic success above grit, a well-known predictor of achievement.

The benefits don't go away once we reach adulthood. Individuals who score higher on emotional intelligence tests tend to report better relationships with friends, parents, and romantic partners. Makes sense. They're more likely to accurately interpret nonverbal cues, understand someone else's feelings, and know which strategies could support another person to feel something more or less.

Research has also linked emotional intelligence to important health and workplace outcomes, including less anxiety, depression, stress, and burnout and greater performance and leadership ability. Individuals with higher emotional intelligence scores also tend to perform better particularly in service-oriented jobs and those involving contact with customers. Think about the reasons you return to the same coffee shop or restaurant. Might it be more about how the barista makes you feel than it is about the coffee or the food?

In two studies, emotion skills correlated with leadership emergence, which is defined as the extent to which someone not in an official position exerts influence over his or her colleagues. Other studies have shown promising associations between emotional intelligence and "transformational" leadership—the kind where leaders motivate and inspire their subordinates to work toward a common vision.

When you have emotion skills, you are perceived by peers to be more sensitive; you have better relationships with colleagues and romantic partners; and you are seen as more confident and secure.

A number of researchers have examined whether emotion skills can be learned in brief interventions. One study found that athletes randomly assigned to participate in ten three-hour workshops had significantly higher emotional intelligence scores post-test than before and had significantly higher scores than their peers in the control group. A second study found similar results among business school students. Participants assigned to a sixteen-hour, not-for-credit course in emotional intelligence showed a significant gain in overall emotional intelligence, while the pre- and post-test scores of their peers in an attention control (that is, business etiquette) course showed no significant change. In our own research we found that classrooms that implemented RULER (the name of our center's systemic, evidence-based approach to social and emotional learning) with the greatest fidelity had students with more developed emotion skills after ten months compared with classrooms that implemented RULER with less fidelity.

Having emotion skills—giving yourself and those around you the permission to feel—doesn't mean you become a doormat or you roll over and agree with everything everyone else says or does. People higher in emotional intelligence are just as likely to push back when attacked—but they will have an easier time dealing with the emotions in a confrontation and will be more skillful at finding a peaceful solution.

None of this means that the emotionally wise person is perfect. You're tired, you're angry, you're worried about something, and so naturally you may not pause to think before you react. You have to give yourself permission to feel even that. You're going to fly off the handle. You're a work in progress. If you mishandled it today, and you have sufficient emotion skills to recognize that, you may do better tomorrow.

It's not always easy to reckon with our own and others' emotional lives. But when kids and adults are given the permission to feel all emotions, and learn how to manage them, it opens doors to collaboration, relationship building, improved decision making and performance, and greater well-being. Almost all the essential ingredients for success arise from emotion skills.

When I give talks, I share the research on emotional intelligence and then ask people about the importance of developing the skills. Naturally, everyone agrees that they are essential. But we keep putting off their acquisition. Students will tell me, *As soon as I get through high school and these tests . . . As soon as I get accepted into graduate school . . .* And then, too soon, they're adults. They are the future doctors, teachers, flight attendants, lawyers, and everyone else who tells us they feel "stressed" most of their waking hours. This isn't how life is supposed to be. But it's how life typically is when we're raised in families, taught in schools, and work in institutions that ignore the importance of emotions.

By failing to address the most significant element of what makes us human, we are choking off the fire of passion and purpose, stunting and distorting the growth and maturity of entire generations, and burning out the adults who are there to help them grow. Emotion skills are the missing link in a child's ability to grow up to be a successful adult. It's up to us to launch the revolution in which the permission to feel drives our success in ways we have yet to imagine.

Again, the necessary skills:

The first step is to recognize what we're feeling.

The second step is to understand what we've discovered—what we're feeling and why.

The next step is to properly label our emotions, meaning not just to call ourselves "happy" or "sad" but to dig deeper and identify the nuances and intricacies of what we feel.

The fourth step is to express our feelings, to ourselves first and then, when right, to others.

The final step is to regulate—as we've said, not to suppress or ignore our emotions but to use them wisely to achieve desired goals.

In the next section, we'll take those steps one by one.

PART TWO

THE RULER SKILLS

4

R: Recognizing Emotion

HERE, AGAIN, IS THE key question: How are you feeling?

This time, before you answer, stop and *don't* think. Just sense it. *Feel* it. It might help to take a slow, deep breath.

My guess is that if you can turn off your analytic mind for a moment, you will get a clear—*visceral*—sense of your underlying emotional state. You know what I'm talking about, even if you don't always put it into words. I mean your basic, fundamental state, right now:

I feel great.

I'm fine.

I feel bleh.

I'm stressed.

You don't even have to use words to articulate it—yet. That will come later. But we can't get there without first being here.

We need to pause—to physically stop whatever we're doing, check in with the state of our minds and bodies, and ask ourselves: At this exact moment, what is my emotional state? Am I feeling up or down? Pleasant or unpleasant? Would I like to approach the world or steer clear? Next, let's check for physical clues. Am I energized or depleted? Is my heart racing, am I clenching my fists, is there a knot in my stomach, or am I feeling balanced, cool, and at ease?

The first of the RULER skills we need to acquire in order to become emotion scientists is Recognition. That's what we're learning in this chapter: simply how to recognize emotions in ourselves and others with accuracy.

As we've seen, asking people to find the words for what they're feeling doesn't always produce the desired result. Over the past decade, I've asked hundreds of thousands of adults—from educators to parents to physicians to CEOs—why it's so hard for them to describe how they're feeling. This is what I hear:

"We never stop to ask ourselves that question."

"We were never taught a comprehensive emotion vocabulary."

"We're used to saying fine or okay, automatically."

"It's not always safe to share how you really feel."

"Nobody actually *cares* how you feel."

"We've been taught to not discuss our feelings."

"If we acknowledge how we feel, we'll have to own it and *do* something about it."

"Emotions are unnatural."

"I don't want to be judged."

"There's no time!"

"I have ten feelings."

"There is too much social pressure to risk being honest."

"If I shared how I felt, no one would want to be around me."

"I feel as if I grew up in the witness protection program. We were told to never share anything."

You can see what we're up against. But until we can recognize our own emotions, we can't learn the skills necessary for regulating them. To recognize our emotions is to acknowledge that we're all feeling beings and we're experiencing emotions every instant of our lives.

And Recognition doesn't apply only to our own feelings—we need to be able to recognize them in other people too. That's a bit more challenging because you can't constantly ask someone, "Hi, what's your basic, underlying emotional state right now?" (Trust me, try it once and see.) But unless we're mind readers, we can go only by appearances, which are not always accurate indicators, or by our intuition, which works best with people we know well but not with the rest of the world.

Recognition is especially critical because most of our communication is nonverbal. This includes everything from facial expressions to body language to vocal tones—not the words but simply the way we say them. Words can lie or hide the truth. Physical gestures rarely do. That underscores the importance of the first R in RULER—it requires us to recognize a person's general emotion or mood before attempting to get at the details of exactly what he or she is feeling and why. It points us in the right direction.

Here's what can happen when we don't recognize something as basic as another person's emotional state. An engaged, friendly child becomes increasingly hostile. A teenager who was once bright and bubbly becomes lethargic and barely functional. An adult who used to radiate well-being now suffers from crippling anxiety. And in the worst-case scenarios, people become mysteriously depressed and are now gone, by their own hand. After the fact, we often find the same thing: a bullied, abused, or alienated adult or child who was ignored but would have benefited from outside intervention. We look at one another and ask, "How did everybody miss the signals?" As a child, I was secure in the knowledge that I was loved by my parents. However, I went to school every day and played after school on our street where I was being abused and bullied for many years. How did this go unnoticed? All the obvious signs were there. But loving me was not synonymous with *seeing* me.

There are times when we express our negative feelings in behavior that is itself destructive, off-putting, unbearable. At moments like these, we practically defy the people in our lives to reach out and engage with us or try to help. Other times we alienate ourselves, avoid being with friends, and withdraw from social activities. At these moments, we send signals that we just want to be alone or that everything is okay, when it's not. In my childhood, I was a textbook example of self-defeating outbursts and calculated seclusion. But these are the times when we need to try hardest to break through the displays of rage or self-alienation. This is when we must remember that our behavior sometimes sends the exact opposite message of what we really need. Our actions scream, "Get away!" or, "I'm fine!" while our emotions beg for attention.

The first step toward fully engaging with our own and someone else's emotions—even before we know the specifics of what's causing those feelings—is developing the skill of Recognition.

There's a tool that can help.

The Mood Meter was built based on what is called "the circumplex model of emotion," as developed by James Russell, a professor at Boston College. He said that human emotions have two core properties or dimensions—energy and pleasantness. Russell had the insight to intersect these dimensions to create a single graph that could represent all feelings. The horizontal axis represents the degree of pleasantness, from very unpleasant to very pleasant. The vertical axis represents the degree of energy, from very low to very high.

Those two forces alone tell us a great deal about our emotional lives at any given moment. Even when we are not aware of how we are feeling, our emotion system is continuously monitoring our surroundings for changes that may be relevant to our goals, values, and well-being.

As a tool to help people recognize emotions, the Mood Meter was first used in *The Emotionally Intelligent Manager,* a 2004 book by David Caruso and Peter Salovey. Later, Caruso and I built on that and developed it into the centerpiece of RULER, our evidence-based approach to social and emotional learning that currently is in more than two thousand schools and districts in the United States and in other countries, including Australia, China, England, Italy, Mexico, and Spain.

The Mood Meter is designed to chart every feeling a human being can experience and project it onto a graph similar to the one Russell proposed. It allows us to chart our observations about pleasantness and energy in order to understand key information about emotions at a glance. Using the tool, we can readily visualize hundreds of emotions, from rage to serenity, ecstasy to despair, their co-occurrences, and everything in between.

As you can see in the figure above (and on the endpapers), the Mood Meter is a square divided evenly by the horizontal axis (pleasantness) and vertical axis (energy) into four quadrants. At the far left end of the horizontal axis is the extreme of unpleasantness, which we represent with a −5; at the far right end is its opposite—very pleasant, at +5. Likewise, at the top of the vertical axis is high energy and at the bottom is the opposite. We measure everything on both axes by a number—at dead center of the graph we would be neutral on both pleasantness and energy, which is scored as 0.

We gave each quadrant a different color, chosen to reflect its emotional state.

The top right quadrant is yellow. That's where we experience high levels of pleasantness *and* energy. If you're in the yellow, you're feeling happy, excited, optimistic. Your posture is likely erect, your eyes likely sparkling. You feel energized and ready to take on the world.

The top left is red. This is the quadrant for low pleasantness but high energy. Here you may be angry, anxious, frustrated, or scared, but also passionate, assertive, competitive. Your body might feel tense, your breath is likely shallow, and your heart might be pumping fast. You might have furrowed or raised eyebrows depending on whether you're feeling angry or afraid. You're preparing to fight or flee; maybe you're psyching yourself up to win a race; or you might be preparing to valiantly defend someone who needs your help. No matter what, in this quadrant, you are in the grip of something strong.

The bottom right is green, for high pleasantness but low energy. Here you're peaceful, contented, serene—and mellow. Your body likely feels at ease, you're breathing slowly. You have a gentle smile and feel safe and secure.

And the bottom left is blue, indicating low pleasantness *and* energy— which could be anything from sadness to apathy to outright depression, but also empathy and concern. Your gaze might be down, you might have a frown on your face, and your body posture likely is slumped. You feel like retreating or disappearing or have the desire to comfort someone who has experienced a misfortune.

In the coming chapters, we'll get into the intricacies of the Mood Meter as we discuss each emotion and its exact position. For now, we'll concern ourselves with the four quadrants only.

Maybe a few examples will help.

It's a Saturday morning in spring, the weather is gorgeous, and I'm sitting in a garden surrounded by flowers and budding trees. Okay, you don't need a PhD to know that I'm pretty high on the pleasant-ness scale—deep into the green quadrant if it's a sleepy Saturday morning. If I were just as happy but feeling supercharged, I'd be up in the yellow.

Or, I arrive at the airport for a work trip, and as I'm checking in I sud-denly realize I don't have my laptop. Did I leave it at home? Did I leave it in the car? No time to go back and find it. Right now, I'm at the highest intensity for sure and also in the quadrant of extreme unpleasantness—deep in the red zone. Once I glumly accept that it's a lost cause and I'm probably not going to have the laptop for my presentation, I may slip over into the blue—low on pleasantness *and* energy.

Recognition is the key first step toward understanding anyone's—our own or someone else's—present emotional state. Unfortunately, it's not foolproof. There are many ways to misunderstand what's right before our eyes and ears. This is why the four other skills that we'll discuss in the following chapters are so important.

A few stories to explain what I mean:

I have a relative who never has a nice word for anyone. (I have to be careful here—I don't want to make him too recognizable!) He's the most negative person I've ever known, with a huge chip on his shoul-der. If he weren't family, none of us would put up with him.

It's my habit at family gatherings to bring along facial expression recognition materials that research psychologists use in experiments. These are photos of people displaying typical emotions, scientifically designed to be as universal as possible. You're supposed to look at the face and identify what the person is feeling. I make it into a kind of parlor game, but I always learn something along the way.

I showed my relative a photo of a person expressing fear.

"All right," I said, "tell me what you think she's feeling."

"Looks like anger to me," he said.

"But do you see how her eyes are wide open?" I asked him. "And her mouth is slightly open and turned down? Doesn't that look more like fear, or even like angst?"

"Maybe it's fear to you," he said, "but it's anger to me." Which made perfect sense—through his eyes, *everything* looks like anger.

Once, at a dinner with friends and colleagues, I tried something else I'll do from time to time at gatherings. I went around the table and asked people where they believe they live, emotionally speaking.

"I think I'm kind of bubbly and happy," one woman said.

"Really?" another friend replied. "I'm surprised to hear that. I don't see you that way at all."

I moved on to someone else, who said he feels as though he comes across as calm and relaxed.

"Well, *I* always thought you were kind of anxious," the same friend told him.

It went on that way for a while.

After dinner, I took this friend aside and pointed out that in every case, she shared a more negative view of people than they had of themselves. She was mortified and shocked—it didn't occur to her that her view of anyone was particularly sour. But it surely was.

A final story, one that took place when I was still a graduate student. A friend had just experienced something truly disturbing, and she was telling me all about it, weeping as she spoke. Just then, another student—one who was notoriously self-involved—came breezing by, stopped, and said, "You'll never believe what my boyfriend and I did over the weekend!"

My friend and I looked up, stunned. We had never seen somebody misread all the cues so badly.

Sometimes even I am prone to misinterpretation, even though I've devoted significant time to studying this. I had a graduate student who developed a strange habit—when she had to turn in a paper, she would come into my office, toss it on my desk, and then run out without saying a word.

Finally, I asked her about this, and she told me that when I was reading her work a look of disgust would come over my face. She couldn't bear watching, she said, which was why she would flee. I was shocked—I had absolutely no problem with her work. Part of this student's reaction may have been her own insecurity about her writing. But the truth is that I have no idea what signals I may have been sending while I was concentrating on grading papers. Either way, she was responding to something, and it was getting in the way of our working relationship.

We've all sometimes misunderstood other people's emotions when we based our assumptions only on unspoken signals. But often, that's the only evidence we have.

In my work, I come up against this all the time. When I conduct seminars for educators, I'll often ask the room how skilled they are at recognizing students' emotions. Everyone says, "Well, this is what we do all day, every day."

"Great," I say. "I'm going to express an emotion, and all of you will write down what feeling you detect." Then I turn my back on the room, assume a facial expression, and turn around again.

"Okay," I'll ask after a few moments, "what do you think I was feeling?"

One person will say I was angry. Another says I looked calm. To a third, I seemed disapproving. One thinks I was flirting with her. Someone else says she couldn't tell what I was feeling.

Actually, I tell them, I was trying to express contentment. That leads to the discussion of who (if anyone) was right. I know what I was trying to display, but does that mean I know how I was coming across? Observers are often certain they know how I feel. I recall one participant who said, "Marc, I don't think you're even aware of what you were really displaying." It's possible I'm no more of an expert on my own emotional expressions than anyone else. But the fact is that we are making these automatic judgments about how people feel all day long—and we're often wrong. Think about the implications. How often are you misread? How often are you misreading those around you? Do you even know?

Of course, if I display a very conspicuous emotion, such as surprise—eyes popped open wide, mouth agape—everyone gets it right. But how often do we get surprised in a day?

Given all that, it's easy to see why emotion science must rely so heavily on verbal communication—knowing which questions to ask other people and how to listen and process the answers. We also have to articulate what we're feeling, especially the subtleties that distinguish one emotion from another that's close but not quite the same. Otherwise we'll never reach our ultimate goal: understanding, communicating, and regulating our emotions effectively so that they become a help and not a hindrance.

"The human face—in repose and in movement, at the moment of death as in life, in silence and in speech, when seen or sensed from within, in actuality or as represented in art or recorded by the camera—is a commanding, complicated, and at times confusing source of information," rhapsodized Paul Ekman, the legendary psychologist who is known as the greatest human lie detector and was the inspiration for the TV series *Lie to Me*.

Imagine trying to keep track of every possible facial expression of emotion! Many of those are so-called microexpressions, the kind that briefly flicker across one's features, so quickly they're barely visible. Could any of us, even Dr. Ekman, track so much emotional activity day in and day out?

Still, we have all spent our entire lives, from before we can remember, studying facial expressions for their emotional content. It's the basis for all human relationships, starting with mother and newborn. We do it instinctively, as a matter of survival, because the better we are at reading facial expressions, the more we'll know about the intentions of the people around us. We've all evolved to become emotion scientists. But we still need to learn the skills.

A century before Ekman, in 1872, Charles Darwin published his third major work, *The Expression of the Emotions in Man and Animals*. In it, he wrote that animals and humans both express their emotions physically, and there are some universals of expression among people—raised eyebrows denoting surprise, for example—as well as great diversity in emotion expression.

Ekman and other psychologists ran a series of cross-cultural studies in the 1970s, making the case that all human faces express six "basic emotions" in much the same way:

Happiness
Sadness
Anger
Fear
Surprise
Disgust

Sounds about right. But then the literature goes on to say that we all display these emotions in more or less the same fashion, and that's where it gets a little murky. We academics all make ample use of those materials depicting prototypical facial expressions of different emotions that I bring to family gatherings. But we know it's a stretch to say that everybody everywhere manifests these emotions in exactly the same way.

Certainly there's something universal about those six. From childhood on, we're all capable of making the faces associated with those emotions. We don't require lessons—we inherently understand them. More recent research by Dacher Keltner, a professor at the University of California–Berkeley, and his colleagues suggests that as many as twenty-two emotions are recognized in the face at above-chance levels (that is, above 50/50) across different cultures.

We also rely on sound for hints of someone's emotional state. Tone of voice can send an unmistakable message—when we're angry or sad or frightened, we may sound alike no matter what language we speak. In one study, college students from ten different countries and villagers in remote Bhutan were all tested to see if they could match the spontane-ous sounds we make when inspired by various emotions—amusement, awe, contempt, relief, sympathy, triumph, sixteen in all—with stories that elicited the same feeling. They found "very strong recognition" in all eleven cultures. In another study, subjects were extremely proficient at distinguishing fake laughter from real.

In a series of clever studies, researchers showed that emotions also can be detected in touch. Two participants, one assigned to be the en-coder and the other the decoder, were asked to work together. The de-coder was instructed to sit at a table separated by a curtain. The encoder was given a list of emotions and asked to communicate thirteen dif-ferent ones on the decoder's arm, using any form of touch that lasted a second or two. Of the so-called basic or universal emotions, anger, fear, and disgust were reliably decoded. Pro-social emotions, those that help us build and maintain relationships, such as love, gratitude, and sympathy, also were easily detected. Self-focused emotions such as em-barrassment, pride, and envy were not detected, as might be predicted. Given their communicative function, it makes sense that we are better able to recognize social emotions than self-focused ones through touch.

As we discussed earlier, the primary emotional message we inter-pret from reading people's emotions, strangers or intimates alike, is to either approach or avoid—or freeze to some extent, as with surprise. We welcome people into our circle, or we warn them to keep their distance. If I'm a teacher or a parent, the approach-or-avoid dynamic is what tells our children whether they are valued or dismissed, loved or just tolerated. We send the same signals to our fellow adults too.

Accurately reading nonverbal cues—facial expressions, vocal tones, body language—makes social interaction possible. It tells us how (or even if) to start a conversation, whether a person is paying attention or not, if we're dealing with someone we'd rather avoid or who truly needs to engage with us right now. An expression as simple as a smile can sig-nify emotions and intentions ranging from joy, interest, and romantic attraction to disapproval, deference, and even aggression. Interestingly, a sincere smile tends to last for a few seconds, whereas a polite or disingenuous smile tends to last for just a quarter second.

Psychologists are fond of testing how we register and analyze the nonverbal cues of emotion. They typically show subjects photos of faces displaying all the usual expressions—smiling, frowning, eyes popped wide open or narrowed, lips parted and teeth showing or mouths clamped shut. But the cues are fairly obvious—there's a big difference in my face if I just hit the lottery or broke my toe. If I show you a face with furrowed eyebrows, piercing eyes, and pressed lips, you don't have to be a genius to see anger. Still, they don't reflect real life—how often do we see full-blown anger in a business meeting? In real time, the emotions we're attempting to read in others are a good deal more subtle, ambiguous, fleeting, and mixed.

However, for all those universals in reading emotional states, there are complex differences, too, depending on a variety of factors.

Cultural influences matter. We are more accurate at reading emotions of people from our own cultural background. In addition, people from different cultures tend to attribute varied meanings to facial expressions. In one study, Japanese and American participants were shown images of people displaying a happy expression. The Japanese rated the person's inner experience and outward expression at the same level of happiness. The Americans thought that the external display was more intense than the person's actual inner experience.

There are also differences due to personality. People who are agreeable, one of the "big five" personality traits, tend to perceive people who are displaying angry or hostile facial expressions as being friendlier than they really are. There are even differences based on relationship quality. A colleague I've worked with for fifteen years is reliably better than anyone else at identifying when I am bored. Finally, there are differences based on context or setting. Our interpretation of someone's gritted teeth and clenched fist will be different if they are at a political rally or in a brawl at a bar. In one study, people's ratings of a facial expression meant to depict disgust ranged from 91 percent when a person was holding a soiled article to only 11 percent when the person had clenched fists. In the real world, all those neat categories of emotion no longer work so well at interpreting others' inner lives.

Our perception of emotion is easily swayed by the opinions of others. In a classic study, a person posing as a visiting professor gave a lecture to university students. Before the speaker appeared, half of the students received information that he was a rather warm person. The other half of the students were told that he was cold. The second group of students perceived the lecturer to be more irritable than those who were told he was a nice guy.

There are also other prejudices—gender stereotypes and racial implicit bias (both attitudes that affect our actions and decisions in an unconscious manner)—that influence how we read emotions. We are more likely to detect anger in men's expressions of emotion but sadness in women's. U.S. participants are more likely to perceive anger in the emotional expressions of African Americans. Chinese participants' scores on a pro-Chinese/anti-white implicit bias test correlate with their ratings of the intensity of white subjects' angry, fearful, and sad facial expressions.

No wonder we're all so prone to being misinterpreted and to misunderstanding the emotional states of others. We make fatal miscalculations—judging by his stone-faced expression when I said hello to my boss this morning, he's clearly disappointed with the report I turned in yesterday. How was I to know that he had just come from a tough meeting with *his* boss? The term psychologists use for this phenomenon is "attribution bias," meaning we observe someone's cues or behavior and wrongly attribute them to our own emotional state.

We saw how my relative responded to the photo I showed him. His own emotional state overpowered his ability to objectively look at someone else and see what they feel. In my relative's case there's an even more precise term: "hostile attribution bias," since his own anger causes him to see that same emotion everywhere, even where it may not exist. Back in the eighteenth century, the poet Alexander Pope said it well: "All looks yellow to the jaundiced eye." If you go through life angry, you will see anger everywhere you look. The same is true of other emotions—even positive ones.

It's human nature to pay more attention to negative emotional information than positive. Starting in childhood, it's how we rely on the reactions of other people to measure the danger in any given situation. This is the reason kids study their parents' faces before trying anything potentially risky—they're searching for a clue as to how risky it might really be.

Still, some of us are more prone than others to sensing negative emotions. When looking at faces with neutral expressions, depressed people are more likely to read them as sad than happy; those with anxiety disorders tend to see fear; people who grew up in homes where parents argued frequently see anger; irritable children see hostility or fear. Brain scientists have even identified where in the brain this bias might reside—in the perigenual anterior cingulate cortex (the pgACC for short).

Here's a question I get often: Are we actually getting worse at reading one another's emotions? There's evidence that says we are. The more time we spend communicating through electronic screens, the less face-to-face (or even voice-to-ear) time we spend and the less practice we get at reading the nonverbal cues. In one study, sixth graders who went five days without glancing at a smartphone or other digital screen were better at reading emotions than their peers from the same school who continued to spend hours each day looking at their phones, tablets, computers, and so on.

And that's not the only obstacle modern life poses. At a seminar I taught in Los Angeles, a principal stood up and said she was concerned that students today could have extra difficulty decoding facial expressions owing to the popularity—especially in her hometown—of Botox. Which makes perfect sense, because how could you tell how Mom and Dad feel if their foreheads, eyebrows, and corners of their eyes and mouths have been chemically paralyzed?

. . .

The recognition skill improves only with practice. And because it relies on nonverbal information, we have to be sensitive to the sensations and nuances of emotions, our own and those of other people. If you overthink it, you're doing it wrong. At this point in the process, we're not looking to nail down the precise emotion, just the general area where it exists—the quadrant of the Mood Meter. Are we feeling up or down? Pleasant or unpleasant? It's the kind of question you can ask yourself every hour on the hour and get a different answer. You can try the same thing with the people in your life—whether it's your spouse, your boss, your kids, or the desk clerk at the library. There's no penalty for exploring and quite a bit of potential benefit from developing this skill. In any event, it's the first necessary step.

However, as we've seen, we can't rely solely on that visceral sense to tell us everything we need to know. For that, we must go deeper. We also have to allow for the possibility that we can be wrong. As we've seen, there are many ways to misunderstand and misinterpret nonverbal communication. It's okay to misidentify once in a while. That's what the following steps are for—to correct our paths and bring us closer to understanding. Because in order to know an emotion, our own or someone else's, we need to know what's behind it—its causes. For that, we need the U—as in Understanding emotion.

5

U: Understanding Emotion

LET'S START THIS CHAPTER with a slightly different question: How am *I* feeling?

Or, more precisely, how *was* I feeling?

When I was thirteen, and the victim of daily bullying in school, my dad pushed me to do martial arts—to toughen me up. He was a strong guy from the Bronx and only ever wanted the same for me. (Now, I've had a fifth-degree black belt in Hapkido, a Korean martial art, for a long time and it still has not made me a tough guy.)

I wasn't even athletic back then, but I was determined to make my dad happy, so I tried. Before long, I was gearing up to qualify for my yellow belt. I practiced every day for three months and then literally begged my martial arts instructor to let me take the test early.

The big day finally came. I had to perform a series of kicks, punches, blocks, and self-defense moves. I was so nervous I didn't even want my mom in the studio, so she waited in the car.

And then I failed the test.

I left the studio, opened the car door, got in, and started screaming,

"I hate you! I'm never going back to Hapkido again! I'm a loser! You should never have let me go! You knew I'd never be good at it! And I'm not going to school tomorrow either!" Total freak-out.

Okay, how am I feeling?

When I role-play this story during presentations and ask people what they think, their most common answers are anger, disappointment, embarrassment, humiliation. Certainly those are all fair assumptions based on my behavior, but really, they're just guessing. All my listeners have to go on is their intuition and my howls of hurt. They're committing one of a couple of possible attribution biases: either they're inferring how I'm feeling based solely on my behavior—or they're labeling my emotions based on how they believe *they'd* feel in that situation. We can't really call these people emotion scientists at this point. They don't know enough to say what I was feeling or why, and they haven't done anything to find out. We adults want to believe that the emotional lives of children are less complex and messy than our own, but it's not so. Indeed, sometimes the opposite is true.

Now, put yourself in my mother's place. She's in the car, waiting, praying that I'll pass the test for the sake of my self-esteem if nothing else. She's watching the studio door, trying to read my body language as I emerge.

And then she gets an earful. If she had any intention of finding out why I was overcome by so many horrible emotions, that good impulse was drowned out by my fury. My outrage triggered hers, and she yelled right back, "Stop screaming at me! How dare you talk to me this way! Stop it this instant! Wait until I tell your father how you're treating me!"

Not exactly what I needed at that moment. But it's what I was accustomed to getting from my parents. It's not that they didn't want to do better. They just had no idea how. The way they treated me was probably the way they were treated when they were children. Pain isn't pretty. And so the refusal to acknowledge unhappy childhood emotion, or the inability to deal with it, gets handed down from one generation to the next.

What exactly was needed at that moment? Well, you could say "understanding" and you'd be right. But what exactly are we trying to understand? And how do we go about it?

Of all the five RULER skills required to be an emotion scientist, this is one of the most challenging to acquire. In the previous chapter, we learned about the importance of being able to discern our own feelings and to read, at a glance or soon thereafter, someone else's overall emotional state. And with that, we took the important first step toward emotional well-being.

Now, the real work begins.

Here is where we have to decide whether we even wish to understand what might have caused our own or the other person's feelings. This is certainly true of our own feelings—there are plenty of times when it's easiest to take whatever emotion we're experiencing and hide it in an airtight compartment, to be dealt with at a more convenient time (maybe). This is also the moment of truth when we're faced with exploring someone else's feelings. It's like opening Pandora's box: we don't know what will emerge, or how it will affect us, or—most critically—what we'll be expected to do about it.

All this drama is triggered by a single word: *Why?* Why this feeling? Why now? Understanding emotions begins when we start to answer that question—why do you or I feel this way? What is the underlying reason for this feeling? What's causing it? It's rarely a simple matter. There may be a complex web of events and memories, of one emotion provoking another. Usually, asking one question will lead to more questions, a succession of follow-ups that can go deep. Like peeling the layers of an onion. No wonder it's scary: once we start asking, there's no turning back.

Understanding emotions is a journey. Possibly an adventure. When it's finished, we may find ourselves someplace new, someplace unexpected, somewhere, perhaps, we had no intention of going. And yet there we are, wiser than before—maybe wiser than we wished to be. But there's no other way forward.

If we're faced with the emotions of someone close to us—a loved one, a valued colleague, a good friend—the stakes are even higher, because now there's a distinct possibility that we are somehow complicit. That something we've said or done (or failed to do) is the reason for the difficult feelings that confront us. Here's where we take a deep breath before we start digging. This, I can imagine now, is how my parents must have felt during the worst days of my childhood: *What if this is our fault?*

The core skill of Understanding is the search for the underlying *theme* or possible cause that fuels the emotion. We're not asking questions and listening to answers just to provide a sympathetic ear. As we listen, we're looking for a meaning that goes deeper than the words being said.

"I hate school and I'm never going back!" That's important information, but only if we know what to do with it. What's the cause? Is this child afraid of something related to school? Possibly. There are times we hate what we fear. What causes fear? Its underlying theme is danger, threat. So perhaps in this instance hate equals danger, in which case we know the direction our next questions should take.

Now when we ask, "What's happening at school that makes you hate it so much?" we know what to listen for: a potential source of danger. A difficult teacher? An impending bad report card? A schoolyard bully? We suspect it's there somewhere, and we gently investigate until we find it. This is how a scientist operates—with a theory that will be either proved or disproved by further investigation. Maybe it's not fear that's fueling the emotion. Perhaps it's disappointment, or shame. In every case, there's one or a couple of needs or emotional states underlying our feelings, and that's what Understanding helps us to find.

We also need to keep in mind what psychologists refer to as "appraisal theory." Many emotions—both positive and negative—have universal, underlying themes, but their individual causes vary from person to person. All day, each of us rapidly, and even unconsciously, evaluates situations or experiences, and these evaluations lead to different emotions. But what makes me feel excited about public speaking might make you feel terrified. What strikes fear or anxiety into the heart of one person may scarcely register in another. But what matters is the person's experience—that's what we're trying to identify, so we can address it. That's another part of the emotion scientist's skill set— the ability to put aside one's own appraisals so we can comprehend and empathize with those of other people.

Acquiring the Understanding skill is not always such an easy process. Typically, the need to understand an emotion increases with its intensity—the stronger the feeling, the higher the stakes. This is true for us all but especially for children, who don't have the vocabulary, prefrontal cortical circuitry, or presence of mind to make their innermost feelings clear. When a child says, "I hate you!"—as most probably do, sooner or later—we recoil. There are few things more dispiriting a parent can hear. But *hate* in all likelihood isn't really the issue. Those words are fueled by something impossible (in the moment) to articulate. It's the listener's job to remain calm and try to hear the words that aren't being said—yet.

Now, with all that in mind, let's go back to the four quadrants of the Mood Meter and start there. Within each quadrant, there exists a wide range of individual emotions. Knowing these can help us direct our questions.

Yellow, as we've said, is where the high-pleasantness, high-energy feelings are located. These are the emotions of joy, surprise, and excitement, among many others. What's causing them? Something positive and possibly unexpected has happened and we're celebrating inside. We've made significant steps toward an important goal. We're anticipating an event or an experience that will make us happy.

The red quadrant denotes unpleasant emotions that are high in energy. It's red for a reason: this is where anger, fear, and anxiety all are situated. Because these are in some ways similar, it's easy to confuse them. That's a mistake when we're trying to determine what feelings are dictating someone's actions. Red also is where passion lives. Emotions in this quadrant generally make us hyperalert, owing to our perception of opposition. It's the fight-or-flight response that raises our heart rate, respiration, and blood pressure. When angry, we're focused on someone or something external treating us unfairly, unjustly—our attention is pointing outward, hypervigilant, assertive. When fearful, we're alert to impending danger. When we're passionate, our desire is to convince others that our views are correct.

Blue is the space where pleasantness and energy are both low, meaning we might be somewhere on the sadness-depression continuum. Our thinking is narrowly focused and pessimistic. We're looking inward and focused on failure, loss, or whatever else might be causing these feelings.

Green is the space where our pleasantness is high and energy is low. It's the place on the Mood Meter where we generally feel calm or content. Our body and mind are at ease and we feel complete. Our thoughts are focused on ways to appreciate the present moment. Our need to solve problems or fix things is at a minimum.

Now that we know our quadrant, our emotional space, we're ready to zero in on specifics.

These are some of the questions we can ask when we're trying to understand our own feelings:

- What just happened? What was I doing before this happened?
- What might have caused my feelings or reaction?
- What happened this morning, or last night, that might be involved in this?
- What has happened before with this person that might be connected? (In the event that your emotion has to do with a relationship.)
- What memories do I have about this situation or place?

When we're acting as an emotion scientist with someone else, we can ask the other person:

- What might have happened to cause this feeling?
- What usually makes you feel this way?
- What's going on that you're feeling this way?
- What were you doing just before you started feeling this way? Who were you with?
- What do you need right now? What can I do to support you?

As a teaching exercise, we'll sometimes have children read a story, then ask them:

- What does this character feel?
- Why does he or she feel that way? What do you think might have caused this character to feel this way?
- What about what happened to the character helps you to understand his or her feelings?
- If the same thing happened to you, what do you think you would feel?

We can better understand emotions and their linked causes and ramifications by considering them in pairs and groupings. We can develop pattern recognition to help us know what questions to ask as we search for the truth. For example:

Shame, guilt, and embarrassment

Shame is a judgment, but from the outside—from our perception that other people believe we broke a moral or ethical rule or some shared convention. We believe we are diminished in their eyes. A great deal of bullying's damage to the victim, and resulting isolation, comes from this more than any physical suffering.

Guilt is a judgment we make of ourselves when we feel remorse or responsibility for something we did, usually something that feels wrong.

Embarrassment is when we've been caught violating some social norm, such as how to dress for an occasion, or which fork to use, or how to behave in a certain situation. We all have had plenty of such moments and go far out of our way to avoid them.

These three all seem closely related in our emotional lives, but researchers have found that they have unique psychological causes and cognitive-behavioral consequences, which should remind us to distinguish among them when we're searching for the reasons we feel them.

Jealousy and envy

Often, we use the words *jealousy* and *envy* to mean the same thing, but they're different emotions. Jealousy is a form of fear—fear of losing someone important to you, especially to someone else. We've all witnessed (and sometimes even experienced) romantic or sexual jealousy that is coupled with anger or even rage. It's a combustible combination. Children can be jealous of a sibling or classmate when they perceive their parent or teacher spending more time with the other child. They are jealous because they feel threatened and fear the loss of their relationship with the adult or that they're being cheated out of valuable relationship time.

Envy, on the other hand, has to do with wanting something that someone else has. Again, it could be a person or a thing, a position, even a reputation. Envy is caused by our coveting something that's not ours. Envy could lead us to focus our efforts and work harder to attain something desired. In that case, it may be a force for good. But it can also be the opposite—it can lead to resentment and even to aggression toward the person who has what we desire.

Joy and contentment

In most dictionaries the definitions of joy and contentment are nearly identical—"states of being happy and satisfied." But are they *really* the same? On the Mood Meter, we tend to place joy in the yellow quadrant—high pleasantness and energy—whereas contentment is in the green quadrant—high pleasantness but low energy. We do this for a reason: both the subjective experience and core appraisals that cause these emotions are different. Joy *feels* energetic and contentment *feels* calm, and joy is *caused by* a sense of getting what one wants and contentment is *caused by* a sense of completeness (not wanting or needing anything).

For most of us in the West, joy is something we strive for (think the pursuit of happiness). Contentment, however, is more a state of psychological balance, not something we actively pursue—we feel contentment when we cherish the present moment. Research has highlighted the ways in which *happiness* facilitates creativity and social bonds. But what kind of happiness are we referring to? Paradoxical to what we've been taught, the constant pursuit of happiness can be self-defeating. Accumulating research shows that the more we value happiness, the more likely we are to feel disappointed. Thus, although happiness is often seen as highly desirable, we need to distinguish between the different kinds of happiness. Not all of its forms are beneficial for all purposes in life and in every situation.

Stress and pressure

Stress can be deceptive because it's become such a catchall term for children and adults alike. An interlude I had with a student is a perfect example. Here's an email (removing all identifying information) she sent me at nine P.M. on a Sunday before the midterm exam:

Hey professor!
I don't know you well enough to know how you feel about these kinds of things, but I was wondering if I could take a makeup exam without a dean's excuse. I was playing in a tournament all weekend, waking up at 6:30 every morning (if you want verification you can go to the website) and I thought I could study each evening

but my parents came with my sister and I've gone out to eat with them and had a banquet with the team one night. Anyway, now I can start studying but I'm *so fucking tired and stressed* and I would like to sleep but I have the exam tomorrow. I understand if you say no, please let me know *asap* however so I know if I can sleep right now or not.

Entitlement and disrespect are triggers for me. So I did what any good professor would do: I didn't respond. Better that than writing something I'd later regret. Truth is, I did reply, but not until after the exam the following day.

She didn't show up for the exam.

When she returned to class, I approached her and said, "I'm not sure about that email. . . ."

She said, "But you're such a fun professor!"

I said, "Fun is one thing, but your email was really *off.*"

A week later, she came to me and said, "I've really thought a lot about what happened, and want to apologize."

I thanked her.

"And I'd really like to work for you," she said.

Surprised, I asked her, "What are you interested in?"

"I'm not really sure," she said, "but when I decide what I'd like to do in your center, I'll let you know."

Again, I was triggered. Who *is* this entitled . . . ?

In that moment, I decided to make her my emotional intelligence project. I asked her to come see me during office hours.

Once there, I said, "First you sent that email about not taking the exam. Then you gave me an attitude in class. Then you said you'd *let me know* what you're interested in when you figure it out. Tell me something: What's going on?"

She said she was under "tremendous stress." Like every other college student, I thought.

"What's *really* going on?" I asked.

She told me that her grandmother had just passed away, that her mother has a fear of dying, that her mother texts her ten times per day and wants her to go home every weekend, or she wants to come to campus to visit her.

That sounded like something more than typical college student stress.

Stress is a response to too many demands and not enough resources—managing both family/work responsibilities and financial burdens—to meet them. Pressure is a situation in which you perceive that something at stake is dependent on the outcome of your performance like performing in front of a group or acing an interview.

In the end, my student really needed support dealing with the *pressure* her mother was putting on her. She had misattributed that pressure as stress about other stuff, such as sports, school, my exam, and so on. It was easier to blame those things than to address the real source of emotional tension in her life—her parent.

But I wouldn't have learned any of that had I been turned off by her attitude, which came across as pure arrogance. I had to probe and keep probing. The questions we ask to understand someone's feelings are necessary to encourage answers that go beyond a simple yes or no, or "I feel angry," or "I feel sad," and so on. We're emotion scientists, remember. We're trying to uncover the deepest of feelings.

But we're not just verbalizing questions—we're also sending unspoken messages as we make our inquiries. I'm talking about the nonverbal cues we display, the facial expressions, body language, and vocal tone that say we're genuinely interested in the answers, that we care about the feelings of the person to whom we're talking and are willing to give this conversation the time and attention it deserves. If I ask about your feelings but I'm glancing at my phone or at the clock on the wall, or if I'm leaning away from you with my arms crossed and my eyes narrowed, the message is clear: I don't really want to know. I'm just waiting for you to say something—*anything*—so I can cut this talk short and do something else.

I may even be sending *this* destructive message: I already know what you're going to say, and I definitely am going to push back. That's not the attitude of an emotion scientist. It's how an emotion judge approaches the situation: just waiting to hear enough to blame you for your feelings and shut this conversation down.

You may remember the story I told earlier about my uncle Marvin and how he got me to open up. He didn't have any trick questions or techniques. His sincere interest in me and how I felt and his obvious desire to help me were all it took. It's impossible to fake.

Understanding is where the science of emotion really becomes a pursuit—almost a detective story. If my mother or father had asked me that day of my Hapkido test, "Marc, what's wrong?" I guarantee that my reply would have been something like "I hate you! Leave me alone!"

An unmistakable expression of rage, but not much else useful there. Clearly, I was expressing an inability or unwillingness to discuss at that moment what was really going on. Why that might have been was anybody's guess. Even I would have been hard-pressed to explain my feelings. So how could my parents know?

This is how the investigation behind Understanding often goes. We're not catching someone at their best moment. It may be a time of terrible suffering and shame. It would be hard to expect lucid, cool-headed analysis from anyone, especially from a child who doesn't yet have a developed emotion vocabulary or the ability to articulate complex feelings while still experiencing them. Every parent has been through this and knows exactly what I'm talking about.

The situation gets worse when adults misinterpret emotional information—say, humiliation rather than malice—and act only on the most conspicuous evidence. Recognizing that something is wrong is only the first step. The skill of Recognition is most valuable for the information it supplies to help us begin to understand what is really happening underneath.

An emotional outburst signals that something is going on, but it doesn't tell us *what*. We need to grant the permission to feel, and then ask the right questions, if we wish to know what's behind that outburst.

Put yourself in the place of a second-grade teacher. Two of your students, Ian and Leila, are working together on a science project. It sits, nearly finished, on Leila's desk.

All of a sudden, Ian jumps up from his seat, takes a swing at Leila's desk, shouts in her face, "I hate you!" and stomps out of the classroom. Their project flies across the room.

Leila picks up the ruined project and starts crying.

You're not going to have an easy time calming either child down and asking the questions necessary to figure out what just happened and why. So all you can do is guess. How must poor Leila be feeling? Ian was belligerent, even violent—what brought that on? It seems clear who was the aggressor and who was the victim.

If you were their teacher, the first thing you might do is help Ian calm down and then ask him to apologize. Nothing Leila did could excuse his outburst. And you'd be right—if your main goal was to teach them both a lesson in social skills and what is acceptable versus unacceptable classroom behavior. This is the kind of sudden explosion that happens in classrooms all the time, just as it happens in homes, among siblings. Our first impulse is to restore order so we can go on with our lives.

This is a critical moment in our attempts to understand emotions. It's easy to get this part wrong. We focus on behavior rather than on what might have caused it. It's like treating the symptom and not the disease. As a result, the best we manage to do is modify behavior—by force. And this distracts us from the underlying causes.

Had we been able to restrain our impulse to control and punish, what might we have done differently in that classroom? Certainly behavior such as Ian's has to be addressed. But rather than cast one child as the wrongdoer and the other as the innocent victim, we might have withheld judgment and talked to them separately, asking a few simple questions: What happened? How are you feeling? And: Why do you feel that way?

Had their teacher done that, and then pursued the answers through as many follow-up questions as it took, she might have learned something interesting.

Ten minutes before Ian's explosion, the children were playing at recess. In front of all the other kids, Leila announced that Ian wets the bed. Even worse, she revealed that the source of her information was the boy's little sister.

To some, that still might not make a difference—Ian was in the wrong no matter how humiliated he felt. But punishing him or making him apologize did nothing about what caused the incident. If we had gotten to the root of Ian's anger, we might have helped him find another way to respond to similar provocations in the future. And if there was a reason Leila did what she did, we'd try to deal with that too.

Understanding requires the use of our storytelling ability, perspective-taking skills, and pattern seeking to piece together the concatenation of feelings and events that led to the current situation. It begins with being an emotion scientist, not a judge. If you aren't asking questions, you haven't acquired the skill yet. If you aren't listening to the answers, you aren't *using* the skill. The emotion scientist has a genuine desire to understand and acknowledges that all emotions are information. Until we understand the *causes* of emotion, we'll never really be able to help ourselves, our kids, or our colleagues.

Had either my mother or father been able to cope with my tantrums and reach out to me, maybe with a hug or some show of affection and acceptance, who knows how those scenes might have ended? If my mother had said something like "Okay, Marc, I can tell you don't want to talk about Hapkido now, how about if we stop for ice cream on the way home and then watch TV?" perhaps we would have found the space to explore what had happened. Maybe at bedtime, a few gently probing questions might have elicited some honest answers, enough to begin understanding what went wrong and why. But, as I said, it was not to be.

Now, through the lens of the emotion scientist, let's go back to the martial arts test and the aftermath. In the absence of any explanation from that raging child, let's imagine four possible versions of what happened.

In scenario number one, the test itself was legitimate and not to blame. All the blocks, punches, and so on that I was required to perform were understood. But my blocks were not strong enough. The sensei said, "Sorry, Marc, it's clear you put in a lot of effort, but your blocks need work. Another couple of weeks and I think you'll get that yellow belt."

Sounds possible. My emotion: most likely disappointment, and completely understandable.

In scenario two, the sensei comes up to me just before the test and says, "Marc, you've been practicing all this time with your friend Mike, but I can't let you do the test with him." Instead, he says, I'll be taking it with a senior student, one of the toughest in the class.

Also plausible. To me, this would have been completely unfair—he should have told me before so I could have prepared. No surprise that I'm angry. I'm also anxious about what the sensei might decide to do if I come back for the retest.

In scenario three, the sensei throws in a few surprise items, all of which are beyond my skills, and I fail. Could also be true. Again, I'm angry over the injustice of his decision.

In scenario four, I fail the test fair and square, but that's just where the problem begins. In the locker room afterward, while I'm changing back into my clothes, one of my tormentors from school comes up to me and says, "You loser, we knew you'd fail! Wait till tomorrow morning on the bus, we'll see how your yellow belt moves help you then."

Of course, how could my mother know which, if any, of those had been the case? She couldn't, unless she began the arduous process of asking the right questions, listening to the answers without judging them, without challenging them, and instead letting them sink in. And then asking more questions.

My tantrum made that unlikely.

Do you see the value of being an emotion scientist in a situation like this? Each emotion has what psychologist Richard Lazarus termed a "core relational theme"—a meaning. The only way to get at the meaning of an emotion is to learn the *why*—how someone perceived the situational factors that produced it. Behavior alone is a clue to the riddle, not an answer.

Let's look again at the four scenarios of my martial arts disaster and search for the underlying themes.

In scenario one, the core meaning of the experience was "unmet expectations." The result was disappointment.

Scenario two's core meaning was "uncertainty"—hence, anxiety.

Scenario three's core meaning was "unfairness"—thus, anger.

Scenario four's core meaning was "impending danger"—hence, fear—and "diminished self-worth"—hence, shame.

Knowing the core relational themes provides critical information about how to understand the emotion. It also helps us figure out how to label, express, and manage what we feel. Think about it: Would the strategies you would use to support your child vary depending on the emotion she or he was feeling? Most likely yes.

Had you known your child was disappointed, you might have helped practice the moves that needed work for the next time.

Had you detected the anxiety, you could have suggested strategies to calm your child's nerves, like a breathing or visualization exercise.

If your child was angry because of unfair treatment, you could have approached the teacher to see if anything could be done differently.

If your child was afraid of being physically beaten the next day, an immediate action was needed—a talk with the principal or bus monitor.

If your child had felt shame, it's possible that professional counseling was needed.

My truth that day was a scenario four. Does knowing this change anything? You might say no. It was unacceptable for me to behave as

I did. I won't disagree. But I can't regulate my reactions until I know what I feel. And it will be hard to do that if the adults who are raising me don't model the skills first or ask the right questions.

Can you imagine how much miscommunication is caused by the inability to see behavior as simply a signal for emotions? This is why we have to be emotion scientists and not emotion judges.

As I started by saying, Understanding is in some ways the most challenging skill to acquire. It calls on all our powers of analysis to honestly and correctly answer that powerful three-letter question: *Why?* Once we ask it, of our own reasons for feeling something or of someone else's, we begin a line of inquiry that can go on for some time. What caused this emotion? Once we find an answer, the next question instantly arises: Why, of all the possible reactions, *that* particular one? At some point we need to feel as though we've answered that original *Why?* But if we stop short, we may never understand our emotions. Sometimes, granted, it takes real bravery to follow the investigation to the end. That's when our skills make us scientists. And paired with genuine motivation, this skill empowers us to be better friends, family members, students, colleagues, and partners.

Now that we've learned how to understand an emotion, we're ready to move on to the next step: labeling it.

6

L: Labeling Emotion

"HOW ARE YOU FEELING TODAY?"

That's how I began a talk I recently gave before a group of business-people in Napa Valley. At a winery, of course.

Like most of my audiences, nearly all the participants had trouble finding more than a word or two to describe their emotions. As usual, "fine" and "good" were the most popular answers. I tried to dig deeper. There was no deeper. A few broke all the way through to "curious" and "intrigued."

Instead of pressing for reasons why they had such difficulty describing their feelings, I took this group in a different direction.

"Given your expertise," I said, "I'm curious: How do you describe the red wines you're representing?"

Suddenly, these emotional illiterates sounded like poets.

"Rich spice and mineral accents."

"Smoky roasted meat and floral blackberry aromas."

"Bold, supple flavors of apricot and licorice."

"Pepper and cigar box notes."

"Tannins that are big but polished."

"Well-structured, sinewy finish."

"Balanced and driven, with a long finish that lets the fruit echo."

"Dense tannins with a mouth-coating impression."

"Approachable, but built for the cellar."

Can you imagine being so eloquent about fermented grape juice but so limited in describing your inner life?

In recent years there's been discussion of a "vocabulary gap" between rich and poor families. Children growing up in higher-income environments are exposed to more words than their poorer counterparts, and this gap may help account for future educational performance, earning power, even intelligence.

That gap fades when it comes to the words we use to describe our feelings. There, ignorance is egalitarian. There are hundreds of words we could use to describe our feelings, but most of us use one or two: "fine" or "busy."

The question at the core of this book—"How are you feeling?"— doesn't get very far if we don't have any useful answers. Without a proper vocabulary, we can't label our emotions, and if we can't label them, we can't properly consider them or put them into perspective. This isn't just rhetoric. We know from neuroscience and brain-imaging research that there is real, tangible truth to the proposition that "if you can name it, you can tame it." Labeling an emotion is itself a form of regulation. We'll dive more deeply into this science later.

The Recognition chapter was about determining our overall emotional state and locating it on one of the four colored quadrants—red, blue, yellow, or green. The chapter on Understanding was devoted to a single word: *Why?* We talked about the skill of discovering what causes our feelings. Labeling is where we take those two skills to the next level. Here's where we zero in on exactly the emotions we're experiencing, to the point where we can name them precisely.

Are you in the red? Sorry to hear, but now we can determine exactly *where* in the red you are. Are you enraged or merely frustrated?

Frightened or simply concerned? Or, if you're in the green, are you secure or complacent? Blissful or content?

Quite a difference in those emotions, each with its own cause and requiring its own course of action. This is why the Mood Meter is such an important tool: we start with a quadrant, visualized as a basic color, and then narrow the search for a particular shade. This isn't just a device to help us visualize emotions—it's how we discover and label which emotions we're truly experiencing.

In the arc formed by the RULER process, L—Labeling—is the pivot point, the hinge. It connects Recognition and Understanding with Expression and Regulation, which is where we take the actions necessary to draw strength from our emotion lives. Without Labeling, our feelings remain inchoate. Once we name them, we begin to possess their power.

The Labeling skill exists in that space between our understanding of what we feel and our ability to describe it accurately to ourselves and others. When we use the same few emotion words over and over, we revert to that near-mute teenage state of being. Do we really *not* want to know our true feelings? Do we really *not* want other people to understand how we feel? Is this how our fear of vulnerability manifests itself? If you ask me how I feel and I say, "Fine," it spares me having to tell my tale of weakness and woe. "Fine" becomes our polite way of saying, "Please don't ask me how I feel." If I say "Fine" often enough, and you say it often enough, anything more descriptive will seem unnatural—even alarming. But our feelings shouldn't alarm us.

Often, instead of accurately naming our emotions, we'll use figures of speech. I'm on top of the world. You're burned up. He's happy as a clam. I'm down in the dumps. She's blue. All highly evocative, of course. But still, they allow us to evade having to confront, plainly and exactly, what we feel. These inventive metaphors may be descriptive on the written page, but they often create distance between our feelings and our words.

Labeling our emotions with precise words does four main things:

- It legitimizes and organizes our experiences. When we attach a word to a feeling, it gives emotion substance and creates a mental model of the word, which means it can be compared with other feelings we have and also with other people's feelings.
- It helps others to meet our needs. Once we are able to communicate, with specificity, what we're feeling, the people in our lives can look beyond our behaviors to understand their causes. Now, empathy is more available.
- Similarly, it helps us to meet the needs of others. Once we know how someone is feeling, it's easier for us to support them.
- Finally, it connects us to the rest of the world. Our emotions become a form of communication, a way to share the experience of being alive. There's a body of research showing the health benefits of social connectivity, and this is where it begins—in being able to identify with one another. The terminology of emotion allows us to read one another's lives, almost as we would in a novel. The words give us each a story to tell.

That's the power of Labeling.

There are, it is said, around two thousand words in the English language that broadly refer to emotion. That's a lot of possibilities, which makes sense considering the variety of emotions and feelings we all experience in the course of a day.

But then there's the question of how many of those words we actually use. And that's where our attitudes toward emotion begin to peek through our language. To put it bluntly, our emotion vocabulary is woefully insufficient.

For the most part, the emotions that require the most attention, the ones that tend to preoccupy us, are the negative ones—the variations on anger, fear, sadness, and shame. Studies show that feeling words are about 50 percent negative, 30 percent positive, and 20 percent neutral. But even this doesn't mean we're good at describing our negative emotions. We don't like to dwell on unpleasant feelings. We just want them to go away—preferably on their own, without any engagement on our part. Whether they're our own negative emotions or someone else's, they're painful to deal with.

One possible explanation for the preponderance of words defining negative emotions is that our brains process positive and negative feelings differently. We tend to give our positive emotions superficial attention only; we see no need to modulate them, just cross our fingers and hope they last. We don't expend much mental energy analyzing why we feel so good.

But we experience negative emotions more deeply—they slow our processing down because they indicate a problem. Out of necessity we devote more words to their description. Back when my uncle Marvin was building what he called his "Feeling Words Curriculum," he would talk about things such as alienation, deprivation, and other dark feelings, and educators freaked out—they were scared by the idea that children might actually experience such things. But kids *do* have negative feelings frequently, he insisted, and we can either discuss them or ignore them. He didn't get very far with that argument in the 1970s and 1980s, but he was right then and right now.

It's instructive to witness how our understanding of emotion progresses as our brains develop, starting right after birth. Researchers have found that infants are unable to perceive distinct emotions by facial expressions—but they *can* differentiate between pleasant, unpleasant, and neutral expressions. Two-year-olds who know only the most basic emotion words *sad* and *happy* can't tell the difference between negative facial expressions—they perceive all unpleasant faces as "sad." Three- and four-year-olds begin to grasp the terms *anger* and *fear* and learn to tell one negative expression from another. There's ample research showing that children who can accurately label their feelings enjoy more positive social interactions than kids who cannot, who experience more learning and behavioral problems.

This isn't simply theorizing or conjecture. Matthew Lieberman and his colleagues at UCLA conducted experiments to see if using words to describe feelings (which they refer to as "affective labeling") would moderate distressing emotional experiences—actually ease the pain.

In one study, subjects were shown photos displaying negative emotions. The participants who were asked to label the facial expressions reported less distress than those subjects who simply saw the photos but weren't asked to comment. In another, participants who were identified as having extreme fear of spiders—arachnophobia—were placed in a room with a caged spider. Some subjects used emotion words to describe their feelings in that situation, while others used emotion-neutral words to simply state the facts.

The result? Members of the first group were able to take more steps closer to the cage than the other participants. Additionally, greater use of words such as "anxiety" and "fear" during exposure to the spider was associated with reductions in those emotions. Before the experiments were begun, participants stated that they didn't believe Labeling would be an effective emotion regulation strategy. But they were wrong. Lieberman referred to this as "incidental emotion regulation," because the subjects were not aware that Labeling had reduced the unpleasantness.

Other research has shown that affective labeling is linked to lower activation of the amygdala, the brain region that's activated when we feel negative emotions, and higher activation in the right ventrolateral prefrontal cortex (RVLPFC), which supports emotion regulation. And just as our brains make use of neural pathways to connect one region to another, our emotions travel on pathways too. If we're disposed to anger, then certain kinds of stimuli will routinely trigger it, and anger becomes our immediate, go-to response. But if we are able to define multiple shades of that low-pleasantness, high-energy emotion—such as annoyed, disgusted, irritated, frustrated, and so on—then we can modulate our responses and in doing so stop ourselves before we hit full-blown rage at every provocation. Every possible term becomes a moment to pause for self-reflection: Am I feeling it *this* strongly or perhaps something not quite so extreme?

The term *granularity* provides a useful way of thinking about how we label our emotions. All it means is that we define what we feel as precisely and narrowly as words allow—down to the grains—rather than settle for the generalized terms we tend to lean on. Psychologist Lisa Feldman Barrett wrote, in *The New York Times,* that what she calls *emotional granularity* is the "adaptive value of putting feelings into words with a high degree of complexity"—complexity that mirrors our inner lives. In her experiments, participants who were deemed *granular* were better able to differentiate their emotional experiences. Subjects who were low in granularity—called *clumpers*—were less skilled at differentiating emotions (e.g., angry, worried, frustrated). When the two groups were compared, she reported, granular individuals were less likely to freak out or abuse alcohol when under stress and more likely to find positive meaning in negative experiences. They also were better at emotion regulation—moderating their responses in order to achieve desired outcomes. The clumpers, on the other hand, scored worse on those counts, tending to be physically and psychologically ill at a higher rate than the granular crowd.

There's even a term for people who have the slimmest vocabulary to describe emotions: *alexithymia* (the term also refers to the difficulty in recognizing and expressing emotions). One study examining the brains of alexithymic people found that they had less gray matter than non-alexithymic people in areas of their anterior cingulate cortex that are associated with language processing.

It's hard to overstate the connection between the emotions we feel and the words we use to describe them. The Sapir-Whorf hypothesis, named for a pair of linguists, maintains that the language we speak determines our worldview and even how our minds work. This hearkens back to a nineteenth-century idea that language expresses the spirit of a culture. Those beliefs have fallen somewhat out of favor, but scholars are still studying the ways in which language influences thought and the way we experience the world.

The Inuit of Alaska and Canada have dozens of words for snow, or so the popular belief holds. The rest of us make do with just a few. The implication seems clear: the importance of a subject is demonstrated by the number of words available to describe it.

There are emotion words in other languages that don't exist in English. Does this mean that the feelings themselves don't arise among the English-speaking population? Possibly not—it seems unlikely that we're unable to experience certain emotions just because we don't have a single word for them. But the fact that those terms don't appear in our vocabulary must be indicative of something. Anna Wierzbicka, a Polish linguist, contends that we rely too heavily on the English language, which might actually keep us from attaining greater self-awareness.

One word that gets a lot of attention in psychology textbooks describes the feeling of happiness or satisfaction caused by someone else's misfortune, or what is known in German as *schadenfreude*. There are supposedly words with similar meaning in Dutch, Arabic, Hebrew, Czech and Finnish, but no such term in English. Does this mean we're less likely to enjoy seeing someone suffer or that those other nationalities are more malicious than we Anglophones? Maybe it just means they are more comfortable owning up to such a nasty sensation.

That's not the only emotion word that appears in other languages but not in English. Here are a few more:

Litost is a Czech word meaning, according to the novelist Milan Kundera, "a state of torment created by the sudden sight of one's own misery."

Iktsuarpok is the Inuit word that describes the anticipation you feel when you're so impatient for a guest's arrival at your home that you keep going outside to check.

Hygge is the fabled Danish sensation experienced while sitting around a fire in winter surrounded by friends.

Kvell is the Yiddish word that describes the feeling of overwhelming love and pride you get when you see what your child can do.

And *ya'arburnee* is Arabic for "May you bury me"—meaning, the hope that you will die before a loved one because you couldn't stand to live without him or her.

Is there any significance to these differences? In all likelihood, the existence of these terms is in some way a reflection of their cultural patrimony. The words we use are dependent on our values.

On the other hand, there's no word for *emotion* in Tibetan, Tahitian, Bimin-Kuskusmin, Chewong, or Samoan. Presumably, people who speak those languages still have feelings.

But is there really a connection between what we're capable of feeling and what we're able to express? You might think not—even if we never named one of our feelings, we all experience the same set of emotions, don't we? Can our ability to feel be influenced by our vocabulary?

To some degree, it can. If we can acknowledge only the basics that every child knows—*I'm mad, I'm happy, I'm scared, I'm sad*—we're missing a lot of information.

The number of English words and associations for "shame" is no match when compared with the Chinese. In Mandarin, there were more than one hundred different shame-related terms and phrases found in one research article.

In that same spirit, we have to assume that there's a connection between the size of our emotion vocabulary and the importance of emotions in our lives. The more words we can use to describe what we feel, the better able we'll be to understand ourselves and to make ourselves understood to others. And if our counterparts, too, have robust emotion vocabularies, it will be much easier for us to understand them—not just to empathize but also to help them, when needed, to regulate and modulate the feelings they experience.

This, as you can imagine, is of huge importance when dealing with children. Their emotional lives are often a mystery to us precisely because they haven't yet learned to process and express what they feel.

The more words that children can use, the better able we'll be to support them. When we use a wide variety of terms to describe emotions, our children learn the words, but they also absorb the lesson that describing their feelings is a natural, positive thing to do.

Attaching the correct label to the emotion is critical because once we've labeled a feeling, we've also begun figuring out what to do about it. If we assume incorrectly that our child is feeling anxious, we'll fail to address the actual emotion—perhaps embarrassment, maybe fear, both of which can look a lot like anxiety from the outside. Imprecise Labeling can lead us astray as we search for ways to resolve negative emotions.

And that's why emotion vocabulary—Labeling—matters so much.

So it's plain to see the advantages of acquiring (and using) a robust emotion vocabulary. But we haven't yet discussed how we acquire this skill.

One way is simply by using the Mood Meter, which is like a map of emotions. If we refer to it often enough, we may begin to adopt some of the terms as our own. The Mood Meter attempts to cover all the bases of each emotion category: In the upper left red quadrant, it goes from *peeved* to *enraged*, from *uneasy* to *panicked*. The green reaches from *at ease* to *serene*, from *calm* to *balanced*. The blue goes from *down* to *despair* and *lonely* to *alienated*. And the yellow moves from *joyful* to *ecstatic* and *hopeful* to *optimistic*. The full Mood Meter with one hundred words appears on the endpapers. In collaboration with HopeLab, we've also developed an app (www.moodmeterapp.com) so you can track your emotions over time.

In RULER, we teach children emotion concepts using our Feeling Words Curriculum with a goal that by middle school every child will learn a minimum of eighty-four terms that describe, specifically, things they feel. It teaches them the words, and by doing so it also emphasizes the value of acknowledging and accepting the full range of emotions. That lesson is as important as the vocabulary itself.

When we use a general, undefined term to describe how we feel—"lousy," "fine," "mad"—we make it challenging for anyone to help us. It could require a lot of investigation to figure out that "lousy" actually means "I'm *disappointed* because my presentation was not well received and I thought I aced it" or "I'm *afraid* to tell my colleagues that my presentation was not well received because they'll blame me for not being prepared." The more skilled we become at labeling what we feel and describing why, the more likely we are to get the empathy or help we need. The ability to accurately label our feelings cuts the rest of the world a break.

The trick in Labeling is to make sure we've hit on the correct word. If we go too far afield here, we may find ourselves addressing a problem that doesn't exist and ignoring one that does. When we become emotion scientists, we find quite a few of these potential near misses that can lead us astray if we're not attentive.

A challenge with labeling emotions that's common today, in both our classrooms and our workplaces, is the one centered on what everyone simply calls "stress." When we probe with our questions, we usually uncover at least four possible—separate—emotions: anxiety, fear, pressure, and stress. At first they seem almost interchangeable, but in fact they are distinct feelings, each with its own source.

Anxiety, as we learned earlier, is worry about future uncertainty and our inability to control what will happen to us.

Fear is the palpable sense of a danger that lies just ahead and will eventually strike at us.

Pressure is the force from the outside that tells us something important is at stake, and whether we succeed or fail will depend on how we perform.

And, finally, stress is what we feel when we're facing too many demands from all of the above and fear we may not be up to it.

All interconnected feelings, certainly, but distinctly different. Each has its own underlying theme and cause, and we must first untangle them if we're to understand them and eventually figure out what to do about them. Some of the causes are internal, others are intrusions from the outside world.

It's also entirely possible that stress is masking a completely different emotion. I asked a couple hundred students at Yale about their "stress" and learned that it was mostly related to envy. Envy? They would see fellow students getting an A without studying, securing great job offers because of their parents' connections, and so on. I wonder how many college counseling offices are helping kids manage their envy as opposed to offering "stress reduction"?

About ten years ago I suffered with acid reflux and anxiety and blamed it on my neuroses. I lived in a constant low-level dread of the immediate future, and when I went to my doctor he said, "Welcome to Yale." Then he said, "Take some Prilosec and I'll prescribe you some Ativan to alleviate the stress." I wasn't expecting that and left determined to figure out the problem on my own. Was I really stressed or anxious, or was I feeling something else instead?

Finally, I realized that I felt "stressed" because I was taking on too many tasks—more than anyone could easily complete. Stress wasn't the root of my problem—I was overwhelmed. I had too much on my plate. When I cut back a little on my work obligations, scheduled exercise and downtime, my stress levels subsided considerably. I couldn't have come up with that fix if I hadn't been able to analyze exactly what I was feeling, and that began with naming it.

In chapter 5 we discussed jealousy and envy, which are often confused. They're not interchangeable terms, and if we treat them the same, we're going off course. Recall, jealousy is a relationship-driven emotion. It has to do with feeling threatened that you will lose the attention of someone important to you. This could be any relationship—one kid feels like Mom or Dad is spending more time with a sibling, or two work colleagues are at odds because the boss favors one over the other, or it could also be the typical romantic triangle. Envy, on the other hand, has to do with coveting something that someone else possesses. Could be an object but could also be a relationship, an attitude, someone's skill or talent, a frame of mind. If we can't tell any two emotions apart, how are we going to address them and resolve them?

Often, I'll ask audiences to define the difference between anger and disappointment. I'm always surprised to see that people have such a hard time with that one. Most of them say they can't really put the difference into words, which speaks volumes about our difficulty with the vocabulary of emotion. But, as we've said before, anger is usually a response to unfair treatment or an injustice. Disappointment is about an unmet expectation. The strategies we might use to deal with our own or another's disappointment likely would be different from those we'd use for ire.

One of our RULER trainers was having dinner at home with his family when one of his sons began acting out. The boy's mother asked him, "Why are you so angry?" The boy's older brother, who was in a classroom where RULER is implemented, said, "Mom, I don't think Jeremy is angry, I think he's disappointed. He was hoping to go outside to play, but now that it's raining, he can't." Both parents' jaws dropped. They were both extremely conversant in the RULER system but were startled—pleasantly so—to see it in action at their dinner table.

Another common mistake is waiting so long to identify our feelings that they become daunting. We skip over *irritated* or *nervous* or *apprehensive* and, left unattended, they turn into *livid* or *panicked*. We ignore *apathetic* or *drained* until they metastasize into *hopeless* or *depressed* and we're forced to deal with them. We also tend to talk exclusively about our negative emotions, but why not explore our feelings of serenity or cheerfulness? If we never acknowledge those emotions, we may go through life with the sense that we never really experience them. Also, if we devote time and thought to our positive moments, we may discover ways to extend them.

Giving kids awareness of what *peeved* or *irritated* feels like and what thoughts they are having around those feelings is a strategy in itself for preventing outbursts and outbreaks of violence at the extreme ends. If they can recognize a difficult internal state while it's still manageable, kids can get support before they are overwhelmed and unable to regulate. Labeling short-circuits the kinds of spirals that end in tears or tantrums.

A teacher we were coaching in New York City who worked in a school for children with emotional challenges demonstrated this problem. When we first interviewed her, she reported that her students' emotions came out mainly in the extreme—like the enraged kids who threw a desk, or beat up a fellow student, or broke down hysterically crying in class; or the children who were silent but despondent and seriously depressed. Her strategies for dealing with all these situations was to call in the intervention team. But she felt unable to do anything before matters reached the breaking point. As a result, she was routinely the object of their outbursts, even their violence. She went years without reporting the welts and bruises she suffered from blows she received almost daily— because she didn't want her kids to be expelled or go to prison.

Then we introduced the Mood Meter to her school. For the first time, it gave those children a way to become aware of what they were feeling before they erupted into violence and other extreme behaviors. Once they had *irritated* and *frustrated* and *annoyed* in their vocabulary, they were able to acknowledge what was going on before it zoomed all the way to *enraged*. They could explain to their teacher what they were feeling and ask for help while that was still a possibility.

"After a year of using the Mood Meter," she told us, "I had no more welts. The need for intervention decreased. Kids could tell the difference between a little bit of anger and a lot. When they felt a little bit of anger, they could raise their hand and I or the assistant teacher would support them with a strategy to shift before it got out of control. With practice, many students internalized the strategies and used them independently both in class and outside of school."

Bit by bit, the kids took control of their own emotional destinies, without ignoring or silencing what was going on inside. Research shows that a large percentage of children with language impairment exhibit emotional and behavioral problems. But, as we've discussed, when you can name and understand a specific emotion, your brain circuits and nervous system will calm you down. Language skills facilitate executive control and metacognitive processing. Thus, the simple act of acknowledgment creates a shift, and change becomes possible.

I have witnessed the immense power of Labeling firsthand in my own family, not with a child per se but with my dad. When he was seventy-eight, I got an email from his wife, Jane:

"Hi Marc, I wanted to make you aware that I am having problems with Dad. His rages seem more frequent and so is his verbal abuse. I am at the end of my rope. I think he needs medication or maybe a therapist. He, of course, thinks his rages are justified and I am sure he will be extremely mad if he knows I told you. Right now, he gets really mad when I babysit my grandson. I don't do it often, but I love to watch him. I am thankful that I am healthy enough to take care of him once in a while. I don't know what your father's problem is, but I never know when he will explode. I am worn down living this way. I thought maybe you could help. Thank you."

I immediately called my brothers. Of course, our initial conversation brought us all back to our stormy childhood.

We decided to take a road trip to chat with our dad. We had to do this carefully because Jane was afraid of how our dad would respond. We didn't want our visit to backfire on her. We took him out for coffee and brought up Jane's email. Like good emotion scientists, we investigated and looked for cues. I said, "Dad, what's going on with you and Jane? She's really upset about how you are treating her."

"I can't take it anymore," he said.

"What can't you take anymore?" I asked, and then trotted out all the emotion scientist questions, carefully crafting them so as not to offend.

"What's going on?"

"Tell me more."

"What's making you angry?"

"What is Jane doing?"

"When do you get these feelings?"

Here's what he said:

"Her daughter is using her, dropping off her grandson for hours on end. She's spending *so* much time taking care of her grandson. I didn't expect my retirement was going to be spent like this."

I had a hunch, based on the emotion themes coming out of my father's mouth, that he wasn't so much angry as he was jealous of the grandson who was getting all his wife's attention.

To be sure, he resented her children, too, for how much they were relying on her. But the core theme was that he felt threatened by the grandson because Jane seemed to prefer to be with him, leaving my dad alone.

So I said, "Dad, it seems like you might be jealous of Jane's grandson."

He looked at me as if I were nuts.

Then I said, "Well, it seems like you want to spend more time with Jane, and you're not happy with the fact that she's spending so much time with her grandson. That's jealousy."

"Are you telling me I'm jealous?" he said.

"No," I said, "*you're* telling me you're jealous."

At that point, my dad started crying. He suddenly realized what he was actually feeling. He felt threatened by a little kid.

Now we had an opening to make a change. We had created a space to help my father manage his feelings.

That day transformed the lives of my dad and his wife. About a month later, Jane called and said, "Marc, I have no idea what you did that day, but whatever it was, it worked. Thank you. He's *different*!"

When you can understand and name your emotions, something magical happens. The mere fact of acknowledgment creates the ability to shift. When we don't have the words for our feelings, we're not just lacking descriptive flourish. We're lacking *authorship* of our own lives.

After the challenges of U—Understanding emotions—Labeling should feel like a break. We all know plenty of words that describe emotions, feelings, and moods. Even if we don't normally use them in connection with our own lives, we read them and hear them all around us. A great deal of life is defined by words such as *ecstatic, anxious, furious, content, dubious, hopeful, acquiescent.* Any thesaurus or dictionary can handle that part of this skill. Our job then becomes just to begin affixing those commonplace terms to what we're feeling inside. When we settle for the six or seven words that we all rely on, we're short-changing ourselves—it's like taking a vow of emotional poverty when riches await. Ask yourself now: How am I feeling? And try coming up with as many words—more thoughtful and precise ones than you usually deploy. That's how this skill improves. Without it, we remain unknown to ourselves or anyone else, which brings us to our next step: expressing emotion.

7

E: Expressing Emotion

RATHER THAN ASK HOW you're feeling (again!), I'll just say I hope you're feeling brave.

The three previous chapters required us to learn valuable emotion skills. Recognizing our own feelings and those of other people. Understanding the causes and consequences. Labeling those emotions precisely.

Those steps have something important in common: they're about the inner experience of emotions. Digging deep into feelings isn't always easy, but there's not much external risk involved.

With this chapter, that changes. With Expression, we reveal ourselves. Now we'll have to decide: *Can I share this?*

And if the answer is yes, then how much exactly do we share, and when, and where, and with whom? Do I let my mom/dad, colleague, friend, significant other, child, know what I'm really feeling and why? It can be terrifying—as it was for me to share what was happening in my childhood. The abuse, the bullying. Before we express our emotions, we can't help but wonder: Will I be heard? Accepted? Judged? Will I get the support I need? Will I get disowned? Am *I* even ready to own these feelings?

E can be the scariest of the five letters, because here's where we take what we've discovered in RUL—the intimate things we've learned about ourselves—and begin to do something about them.

This could be a sensitive moment, depending on what we have to express and to whom we're about to express it. On the one hand, it's important to be honest and forthcoming. On the other, we need to take the possible consequences of our honesty into account. In a sense, expressing emotions is like a transaction between people. You express, and I react. In that back-and-forth, we may come to understand each other and be better off for it. But the opposite could also be true—your emotions might provoke something negative in me, something I'm not prepared to deal with or control. In which case, honest expression has the potential to distance us or make both our lives significantly worse, at least in the short run. We need the sensitivity to balance one thing with another.

Looking back, I realize that the inability to express emotion was at the center of all my childhood trauma. Had I been able to tell my parents the horrible things I was feeling—fear, anxiety, shame—then they would have discovered the source of all those destructive emotions. They would have heard about the sexual abuse I endured in secret and the bullies who victimized me every day at school. It isn't only feelings that we hide—it's what is causing them.

Today, this comes up often regarding the women, men, and children who have been sexually abused or harassed and yet never uttered a word or called out their abusers. It's no secret why—many believed their feelings of shame and guilt would be even more unbearable once they were out in the open. Others might not share because they don't think anyone would believe them or because of fear of retaliation. The inability to express those emotions is like a continuous pain that lingers on. In a way, the silence is as damaging as the assault itself.

In my childhood, the causes of my emotional pain were overwhelming to me, but they were mostly things my parents or teachers could have helped me to manage. I might have been spared a world of torment—if only I had felt free to say what I was feeling.

Instead, I tortured myself with questions: How will they react if I tell them? What will they think of me? Will they be angry or disappointed in me? What will they do in response—blame me, ignore me, shame me? For whatever reasons, I didn't have permission to feel at home or at school, so my emotions remained bottled up inside, leading to self-doubt, low self-worth, extreme loneliness.

And when my feelings did boil over—as they always do—they often came out as fury I was unable to articulate. My behavior only made things worse. I knew of no other way to express myself.

In elementary school, those pent-up feelings turned into physical pain—I began suffering with a mysterious gastrointestinal ailment that defied all attempts to diagnose it. That's because there likely *was* no physiological cause of my illness. It was the result of emotional suffering that had no other way out. The pain *was* my form of expression. And in middle school my unexpressed emotions turned into self-hatred and an eating disorder.

I've been describing the negative emotions that plagued me as a child. And it's true that feelings such as shame, jealousy, anxiety, and so on are the hardest ones to express. But we also have trouble making our positive feelings known to others. Perhaps we don't want to sound as though we're bragging or gloating. Maybe it's because happiness doesn't require empathy from other people—it's its own reward in that sense. But it's equally important to know how to label all our positive emotions and make them known to the people who are closest to us. It's part of what keeps us close.

During those times when we suffer in silence, we make it impossible for anyone to truly know us, understand us, empathize with us, or—the big one—help us. When we suppress those feelings, we send a message to everyone in our path: I'm fine even when I'm not. Stay back. Keep your distance. Don't ask why, because I don't want to tell you what's going on.

But when we express our emotions, we're saying:

Here's what I feel and why.

Here's what I want to happen next.

Here's what I need from you right now.

It's probably as intimate as we'll ever be.

In public settings, I'll frequently ask educators, "How many of you are in the yellow or green quadrant?" Nearly everyone will raise a hand. Then I tell them that in our confidential surveys, people report being in the red or blue quadrant roughly 60 to 70 percent of the time. Mostly positive feelings when I ask in public, mainly negative when we pose the question privately.

You can't really fault people for this. We all do it. It's human nature. Who wants to look like the emotional oddball—the sad, anxious, depressed, angry one in a crowd of people claiming to be upbeat and optimistic? We have a natural bias in favor of displaying positive emotions, especially in the United States, which translates into a pressure on all of us to seem happy no matter what. Which, as it turns out, often backfires and makes us *less* happy.

It's the lie we all tell, meaning it can't be much of a lie, since we're not fooling anybody. But that doesn't stop us.

At a recent talk I gave to more than five hundred business managers and community leaders, after I asked how they were feeling, I said, "Who's willing to share?"

Only two people raised their hands. Instead of trying to coax more, I asked everyone to choose a partner and discuss *why* they thought no one wanted to open up.

"Does anybody *really* want to know how we feel?" asked one.

"Why would we talk about it?" another said. "When you're a woman, talking about your feelings only makes you seem weak."

I go through this same drill with practically every group I meet. I'm forever trying to find reasons we're so reluctant to share how we feel. I'm always learning new ones.

One student told me, "My school is like a prison. Our school rules dictate how we *should* feel, so why would I bother expressing how I really feel?"

A student who was a witness in the Parkland, Florida, shootings said, "I want to share how I feel with my mom, but she's under so much stress I don't want to bother her."

A parent said, "I would never share that I was bullied with my son, he'll think I'm not tough enough to raise him."

Someone I interviewed who works in a tech company said, "In my office, it's not safe to share, people will just gossip."

One high school girl said, "After we lost my brother, my dad shut down and we never talked about my sister's suicide. It just wasn't an option."

A teacher once told me, "I don't share because I'm afraid that once I open up, I'll never be able to close the floodgate."

A high school boy said, "Every time I try to have a conversation, it gets brushed off. My dad says things like 'Don't worry about it. It'll be fine.' What he doesn't know is that I'm *not* fine."

A burned-out teacher recently told me, "If I shared how I felt to all my students, none of them would want to come to class. They'd have no respect for me."

A lawyer in her fifties told me, "I've lived long enough with my husband without sharing, who knows what would happen to our relationship if I start now?"

A lesbian in high school said, "My parents' background makes it really difficult for me to be open. They just don't understand. I can't talk about the girls I want to date. They'll disown me."

Chances are if I were to ask you the same question, your answer would sound a lot like these. We all experience the same emotions, yet we all hide them from one another. It's weird.

Emotional suppression is a major force in schools, and it's not just the students who are discouraged from showing their feelings. An old adage that circulates among teachers tells us, "Don't smile until Christmas," meaning that educators should start out acting like strict, uninviting taskmasters to maintain tight control over their classrooms.

But is that how educators can best demonstrate their standards and expectations? Is smiling—or making any sort of kind, genuine gesture, even telling jokes—going to hinder the educational process? Though it is the responsibility of teachers to maintain sufficient control and set expectations for student performance and behavior, our classrooms are not meant to be *ruled*. Teachers are guides, not dictators. The research is clear: the best way to engage students is to develop relationships, not prevent them, and the currency of relationships is emotional expression.

We've all heard the saying "Children should be seen and not heard." It hearkens back to a time when people actually believed such nonsense. As a society, we've moved beyond that, thankfully. But it's easy to detect the vestiges of that outlook. We tend not to appreciate excessive emotional expression even from children.

"My teacher said I'm not allowed to cry in class," a colleague's six-year-old son told her one day. "She said I have to be a big boy and feel happy at school." This is a result of the idea that happiness is the only acceptable feeling in public, and if we're not happy at all times, we've failed. We're sending our kids this message when they're at their most impressionable. What about the child who is just temperamentally subdued? Or one who is experiencing sadness or struggling at home? That poor kid may have no place else to be emotionally honest.

Because of their still developing vocabularies and powers of communication, we need to listen extra closely to our children if we're interested in knowing what they feel and why. We need to make sure they understand that we welcome hearing what happens in their lives—the good and the bad, the happy and the sad, the successes and the failures.

As infants, before we acquire the language to express emotions, we are helpless to hide them. We're pure emotion, though our feelings may be elemental and our needs limited to a very few practical ones. Researchers have identified the following in the newborn's supply of emotional expressions:

- Interest
- Enjoyment
- Surprise
- Sadness/distress
- Anger
- Discomfort/pain
- Fear
- Disgust

Wordlessly, babies get their messages across loud and clear, as any parent can attest. Infant emotions are focused on the basics of survival—the need for food, sleep, physical comfort, and security. This underscores the primary purpose of emotional expression: it keeps us alive. From a Darwinian perspective, demanding attention to our feelings is a necessity, not a choice.

As we develop and acquire language, our emotional needs become more complex, and so does how we make them known. But paradoxically, as we acquire the power to express our emotions, we also develop the ability (and the desire) to hide them—to obfuscate, to deceive, to deny. It's a trade-off—the more sophisticated we become in our ability to say what we feel, the more control we exert over ourselves. Out of shame? For self-protection? Or do we sense that the people around us wish, for their own reasons, that we should keep at least some of our feelings to ourselves?

As we've said before, it's scary to hear other people express their feelings, because we may have to accept some hard truths about ourselves. And in response, we may feel obliged to take some action—even to change, which is usually the last thing we want to do.

Years ago, I was excited to have my two older brothers come to hear me speak. They're convinced I make a living by sitting around in coffee shops thinking (they are partially right). It was a large presentation to a couple thousand people in a New York hotel auditorium. They sat up front. I kept an eye on them and noticed the look of pleasure and pride on their faces during the first fifteen minutes of the talk. Their facial expressions said: Wow, that's my brother up there!

Then I began telling the audience about the bullying I endured as a child, the anger and anxiety I witnessed in my parents, the "strategies" they used to regulate their own emotions, such as my mother's secret Styrofoam cup filled with Dewar's scotch. I also talked about their more memorable child-rearing tools. Suddenly, my brothers weren't looking so pleased or proud.

After the talk ended, I caught up with them heading toward the exit and asked, "Hey, what did you think?"

"Don't walk out with us," one brother said.

"I can't believe how much you shared about yourself," the other one said. "People are going to think you're *weak*."

I was surprised, but not shocked. They grew up in the same house I did, under the same rules. I knew where they were coming from. I didn't tell them this, but I remember thinking: You guys would both benefit from doing a little more talking about your emotions.

I'm reminded of the old tune "Smile," the lyrics of which convey some real truths about the way we think of emotions, especially the unhappy ones. The song tells us to smile when our hearts are aching and breaking. The clear message is that we should hide our negative feelings—not just hide them but wear a mask to tell the world the exact opposite of the truth. Strangely, there is something utterly heartrending about that sentiment. We are moved by the thought of masking our negative emotions behind a "show of gladness." At some level we find it oddly ennobling when someone hides their unhappiness.

But why?

It's an implicit acknowledgment that, as human beings, our impulse is to sometimes do as the song says and *hide every trace of sadness*—to cover up the emotions we associate with vulnerability and loss and show the world that we're unaffected, at least on the surface.

So how do we square these two sides of ourselves? Is it possible for us to pursue emotional health by expressing the things we feel—*all* the things we feel—without feeling too exposed for comfort?

Picture it: Today is the day you finally worked up the courage to express what you truly feel, fearlessly and with no attempt to hide it, deny it, or couch it in terms meant to comfort others. Maybe for the first time in your adult life, you spoke your heart with utter honesty.

And it felt fantastic—like a cleansing, like a purge. At first, it was scary to vent so completely, with no regard for how it would be received, but you did it. Congratulations.

And as you finished, you looked around to see your spouse packing his or her bags, your kids cowering in the corner, and the dog hiding under the bed—and then your boss calls to say you're fired.

And you wonder, was there a better way of handling this?

We need to clear up a misunderstanding that may have been building in your mind: that permission to feel means license to let it all hang out, to whine, yell, act on every emotional impulse, and behave as though we have no control over what we feel, so we should just go for it and freak out. Some people think of this kind of venting as being authentic. But habitual, unhealthy methods of expression—yelling, gossiping, verbal or physical aggression, among many others—almost always creates havoc in our lives.

Psychologists and social workers use the term *emotional labor* to describe the effort required to manage the way we express our feelings. The sociologist Arlie Hochschild first defined it as creating "a publicly visible facial and bodily display within the workplace" and studied how people in certain professions—nurses, kindergarten teachers, police officers, flight attendants, and any jobs involving customer contact—frequently are required to put on false fronts. Of course, a similar disconnect happens in nonwork settings too—at home, with family and friends, even among the people with whom we are most intimate.

It may not sound like labor in the usual sense, but managing how and when we express emotions does require sustained effort, and it wears us down, especially when there's a big contrast between what we express and what we actually feel. After a while, it begins to feel natural to suppress our true feelings and a little scary to let them show. Research shows that this so-called surface acting leads to burnout, lower job satisfaction, and even increased anxiety and depression.

It should come as no surprise that something as untamed and unpredictable as our emotional selves requires a complex set of regulations governing expression. So we have what are known as "display rules"—the unwritten but widely agreed-upon guidelines for how, where, when, and in whose presence we may express our feelings. As with any unwritten rules, there's quite a bit of nuance and variation, depending in this case on many factors, including culture, gender, race, age, social status, and power—specifically, the power differential.

We all have different expectations and personal rules about how to express our emotions. Many of these rules are fine as long as they don't interfere with our ability to live healthy lives. But a whole lot of these rules are related to stigma, which only holds us back or can even backfire. My father's rule that prevented him from talking to me about his own childhood victimization may have had an internal logic—but it came out in real life as shame and aggression.

Over the years, I've noticed that people have varying levels of comfort expressing their emotions, depending on where they are and whom they're around. Some of us also are unaware when we are actually expressing certain emotions—we think we're masking our true feeling or showing a poker face, but our microexpressions, which can include that subtle fake smile, quick eye roll, or flirtatious gaze into someone's eyes, reveal something very different might be going on underneath.

Expression is generally a co-skill. It's kind of like tennis—you can't really do it alone. If the listener doesn't do her or his part, it's unlikely that anything useful will come of it. How many of us have been on the brink of some seriously emotional moment, and we've looked up to see our loved one checking their email, or posting something on Instagram, or looking out the window, possibly dreaming of escape. This likely is someone who either doesn't care, is addicted to technology, or is fearful that you'll say something they'd rather not hear.

We're all expert at sending the unmistakable signals of indifference. It's in our defensive body language, our lack of eye contact, the subtle vocal inflections, the silences that last just a little too long. At the same time, we all know how much it hurts to have someone refuse to pay attention.

And so a key skill involved in Expression is listening. Not just hearing. We must be conspicuously open, patient, and sympathetic to whatever's being said. No crossed arms. No restless moving around. No looking away. This is also where the difference between the emotion scientist and the emotion judge comes into play. By our responses to what we're hearing—by our words, body language, facial expressions, and eye contact—we send the message *I'm here for you. I'm not judging. I want to understand you and help you.*

Aside from all the personal restrictions we put on ourselves and one another, there are plenty of societal rules for who may and may not express which emotions. These regulations are far from simple and often stem from stereotypes that are themselves damaging. In times of social upheaval, as we are experiencing today, the norms are shifting and evolving. As we've seen, inequality, injustice, and unfairness are generally met with anger—that's how we humans are built. And anger is, in turn, often met with fear. Taken altogether, it makes for a potent mix of discontent and discord, which sounds a lot like the world as it exists today.

In truth, many of the controversies that dominate the news today have their roots in differences in how we experience and express our feelings.

For instance, gender is a major force in determining emotional expression. According to research, women tend to express themselves more overall, particularly positive emotions, and also internalize negative ones such as sadness and anxiety more than men do. Men, on the other hand, tend to express higher levels of aggression and anger than women. But when subjects' physiological signs of emotional excitement, such as blood pressure and cortisol release, are measured, men score higher—indicating that they likely feel as much as women do but keep more pent up inside.

Women make it easier to tell what they're feeling because they're freer with facial expressions, gestures, and vocal tones. Researchers say that while women smile more often than men, that gender divide doesn't begin to appear until children are in middle school. Women have always been expected to smile, which is now part of the ongoing realignment of relations between the sexes—women have begun to reject strangers' exhortations that they smile and instead see these encounters as a form of harassment. Their anger is understandable—the constant pressure to always appear happy is a requirement that doesn't exist for the men who are doing all the urging.

Both genders cry, but women are more apt to do so in the company of family or friends, while men tend to do it alone. Women also report higher empathy than men, which may account, in part, for those tears.

Race is another strong influence.

Minorities report fears that emotional displays will fall into traps set by old stereotypes and trigger a backlash. So African American mothers, in a survey, said that they counsel their sons and daughters to temper their expressions of anger, lest they be judged more harshly than whites. Anger is the usual response to feelings of injustice and unfairness, while fear is the reaction to the imminent possibility of harm. That dynamic can be seen as an unspoken acknowledgment by whites of how unfairly African Americans have been treated. But on the emotional plane, the group most entitled to anger feels least able to express it, while whites enjoy what's known as "anger privilege"—the right to display anger without the worry of being penalized for it.

Another factor in emotion suppression: children who grow up in high-crime neighborhoods are taught to display toughness and unemotionality, regardless of what they're feeling inside. This may serve a short-term purpose—it's a form of self-preservation—but in the long run it can create one more barrier to self-knowledge.

Gender, race, culture, and class together make a potent combination to suppress the expression of certain emotions.

During the 2018 U.S. Open final, Serena Williams was penalized for calling the umpire "a thief" when he took a point from her for smashing her tennis racket. In the past, male players have yelled, screamed, and called umpires names and have not been penalized in a game. That was just the latest example of how male and female anger are perceived differently. This gender gap comes in many forms, and we've heard them all debated in recent years. When men are forceful, they're strong and assertive; when women are, they're called bossy and controlling. When a man raises his voice, everyone snaps to attention; when a woman does, she's dismissed as shrill or hysterical.

Society tells us that when a woman expresses her intense negative emotions publicly, she's lost control and should be penalized. When a man does the same, it's normal male behavior and does not merit punishment. Widely held beliefs, sometimes outside our awareness, align with gender stereotypes and influence how we express our own emotions as well as how we perceive those of others.

If we notice increasingly intense anger expressed by women, African Americans, and other historically disadvantaged groups, we can take that as a positive sign—an indication that we live in a more just society than before. Even if the price of social justice is more anger than ever—at least for some time.

Power inequality is a strong influence.

The workplace is a perfect arena for studying how the power differential decides who may and may not express emotion freely. The chairman of the board and the CEO are invulnerable, so they enjoy relative freedom to display their feelings without fear of overstepping boundaries. They can express certain negative emotions—anger, frustration, irritation—without paying any price. Indeed, making those feelings known may strike fear into subordinates' hearts and bring about desired results.

But employees further down the totem pole might quickly be out of a job for displaying the same emotions. For those workers, expressions of happiness, optimism, and high energy are safer bets. Meanwhile, the boss might be unwise to express sadness, fear, or anxiety, feelings a junior employee can probably get away with. So the sword cuts both ways.

We take it for granted that in a relationship, the person with more power has greater latitude in expressing emotions. Parents get away with displays they'd never tolerate in their children. In the classroom, the teacher is the boss and the children are the bossed, a dynamic that carries over into the workplace, whether we want it to or not. When we are made to deal with police officers, we recognize the wisdom in emotional restraint, no matter what the officer says or (within limits) does. Right at this moment, we have a chief executive who seems to be absolutely unbridled when it comes to emotional expressiveness, while those around him walk on eggshells, doing their best not to provoke his wrath. Many of the worst injustices in contemporary life revolve around the inability of the powerless to express their fear and outrage at inhumane treatment by abusers. So when we discuss whether or not emotions should be expressed, it's not a trivial matter. Sometimes, it's literally life or death.

Culture is another strong influence.

On a global level, display rules become even more of an issue than they are at home. They dictate which emotional expressions are considered appropriate in any given culture, including how we interact. In the United States, where individuality is prized, the custom is to establish eye contact and deal with people in a direct, face-to-face way. When I first traveled to Korea to study martial arts, I was told never to look the master in the eye and to bow in his presence. I may have overdone it—I avoided looking into his face so assiduously that he finally asked me if anything was wrong.

Wallace Friesen conducted some of the original research on the expression of emotion across cultures. In one study, he showed stress-inducing films and neutral films to American and Japanese participants and compared their facial expressions while they watched the films. When the participants in each culture watched the films alone, they both showed virtually the same facial responses. However, when an older, male scientist was present while the participants watched the stress-inducing film, Japanese participants masked negative emotional expressions with smiles more than American participants.

Recent research by Jeanne Tsai, a professor at Stanford University, and her colleagues has revealed that cultures are more likely to express the specific emotions they value. In one study, top-ranked U.S. government officials, executives, and university leaders used more excited-looking smiles than leaders in China. The display of high-arousal positive emotions is often viewed as a violation of social rules in China where there is an emphasis on cohesiveness among individuals and a prioritization of the group over the self. Other research has shown that competitors from more collectivist cultures tend to express more intense shame displays (head drops, postural constrictions) upon losing, which is consistent with the more pronounced emphasis on modesty and not standing out in collectivist cultures.

Consider another way emotional expression varies. Perhaps you have been on a trip and noticed differences in how strangers interact when passing on the street, how friends express affection, or how children show their deference toward adults. Years ago, I traveled to Croatia with my graduate school classmate Zorana, who was born and raised there. One morning I took a walk and noticed that my normal smiles and waves good morning to people on the street were not being reciprocated. After a few unreturned greetings, I even realized that people were pausing to stare at me.

When I returned to the hotel, I asked Zorana what was up. She said that in Croatia people do not generally say "hi" to strangers on the street. But when they do, it means they want to engage you in conversation. So, here I was thinking, Why are people so unfriendly here? while they were thinking, Who is this weirdo who waves and then keeps walking? This was another lesson on how being an emotion judge and not an emotion scientist leads to major misunderstandings.

Cultural differences don't exist just on a global scale. The rules are different in New Haven, Connecticut, than seventy miles away in New York City. On Wall Street, the top guys bond with big grins and bone-crushing handshakes. Here in the genteel Ivy League, many maintain their emotional—and physical—coolness at all times.

Permission to feel can sometimes mean expressing an emotion we *don't* necessarily feel—it's not being dishonest but rather finding a way of communicating that takes other considerations into account.

A few times in my career I've walked out onto a stage to do a presentation in front of thousands of educators while feeling totally despondent. In one case, I had just gotten the news that Uncle Marvin died. I had a few alternatives: I could have canceled my talk; I could have taken the stage and shared my sad news with the group; I could have put on a smile and a stiff upper lip and pretended nothing had happened. These are the kinds of choices we all are forced to consider throughout the day without thinking much about them. For whatever reason, you feel awful. Are you going to unload on everyone you meet? Go into temporary denial and carry on? These strategies are obvious, accessible, and second nature after a while.

In the case of my presentation after Uncle Marvin's death, I had another option: Find a way to perform well, serve the people in the audience who had come to be inspired, and still express and honor the emotions I was feeling. Without mentioning that Marvin had died, I started by dedicating my talk to Uncle Marvin and thought about how elated he would be that our work was reaching ever more people.

I knew that after the talk was over, I would have support from my family and the chance to feel my grief. Which is exactly what happened.

Expression doesn't affect just our emotional lives—there's abundant research into the physical and mental benefits of expressing emotions. And we should keep in mind that expression need not be only of the spoken, face-to-face variety. Sometimes, sharing with other people is too difficult. In those cases, it may be better to express it in writing. Many of us have had the experience of writing something in a journal or letter that seemed impossible to say in conversation.

According to Professor James Pennebaker, of the University of Texas–Austin, keeping secrets can actually make people ill. But when we transform our feelings and thoughts into language, his research has found, our health often improves.

Expressing emotions benefits us in these specific ways:

- Significant drops in physician visits
- Increases in immune function
- Lower blood pressure
- Long-term improvement in mood
- Reduction in stress
- Higher grades for college students
- Less absenteeism at work

In one study, Pennebaker divided fifty students into two groups and asked one group to write essays about emotionally significant issues and the other group to write about superficial matters for four consecutive days. When tested months afterward, the first group showed improvements in immune system function and fewer trips to the university's student health center. And even though members of that first group said they felt distress when writing about sensitive subjects, three months later they reported being happier than the other group. Pennebaker concluded that suppressing traumatic experiences is debilitating, while confiding them to someone else, or writing them down, can bring relief.

More good reasons for expressing how we feel.

Now that we've learned something about Expression, I'm wondering: What emotions do you show the most, at home and at work? Are they what you are really feeling or only the ones you feel you're allowed to display? How would your spouse or partner, colleague or boss, or kids rate your expression skills?

Are you comfortable expressing the emotions in each quadrant: yellow, red, blue, and green? What rules have you created about what you'll express to whom? How much emotional labor are you putting in each day? Is it affecting your performance at work, your relationships, your overall well-being?

These are tough questions to answer, I realize. But they're the ones we need to ask ourselves regularly.

What can we do when the fear of stigma chokes off our ability to express? First: Give ourselves and others permission to feel. Accept and acknowledge that there's no shame in expressing our emotions. We don't need to fix or hide what we feel. Expression enhances our lives in many ways, not all of them obvious. It propels us forward, in this case to the final step—Regulation.

8

R: Regulating Emotion

OKAY, SAME OLD QUESTION: How are you feeling? But now I'd also like to know what (if anything) you're going to do about it.

Imagine it's Friday afternoon and you're away from the office at a conference you're required to attend. It's been a long week and you'd give anything to be home, unwinding, or even back at work. Instead, you're stuck in a windowless meeting room, supposedly paying attention, but here's what's going through your head: *I can't believe I have to sit here for three hours and listen to these people talk while I pretend to listen.*

You're irritated. You're distracted. You're tired. Perfectly understandable.

I describe this scenario when I speak before groups and then ask participants to share the strategies they'd use to deal with their feelings. Here's what they say:

"I'll leave my feelings at the door."

"I'm going to sit up front with good posture."

"I'll drink a lot of coffee."

"I'll focus on you and not let anything distract me."

"I'll take good notes."

"I'm just going to stay positive."

"I'm going to get up and stretch or move around once in a while."

"I'll doodle."

"I'm just going to push through it."

"I'll have a cigarette in the parking lot."

Over the last couple of years, these answers have become quite fashionable:

"I'm going to breathe and be present."

"I'm going to be mindful."

"I'll pray for the best."

And here are a few of my personal favorites:

"I can always leave."

"I'm going to stare at the clock."

"It's up to *you* to keep me engaged!"

"I'm giving you five minutes to keep my attention, otherwise I'm going back on Facebook."

"What kind of question is this? I came to hear a talk by a Yale professor. All you're doing is asking us how we manage our feelings. Do your lecture and I'll listen." (You can't make this stuff up!)

But then I ask my audience: Are these strategies really going to help you? Are they so good that you'd teach them to your kids to help them get through similar situations?

Imagine that instead of adults at a work conference, you're one of a bunch of fifth graders filled with all the typical urges and anxieties that children experience. It's Friday afternoon and you're in social studies. Maybe you stayed up late last night working on your science project that was due today, and you're exhausted. Maybe you bombed on a math quiz this morning and you're afraid you're going to flunk and get grounded. Maybe at breakfast today your father told you that he and your mother are getting a divorce, adding, "You'll probably be getting a new stepfather real soon." (That's a real-life one I heard.)

Okay, now let's revisit those adult strategies to see how well they'll work here.

Would you advise children to walk around the classroom at their leisure? To ignore the teacher and go on Instagram? Leave their feelings at the door? Stare at the clock? Challenge the teacher to justify today's lesson?

Are you laughing yet? Will you ever be able to imagine a weary eleven-year-old dragging herself to the coffeepot at the back of the classroom? Or a student who says, "I'm giving myself permission to go back on Snapchat because this lesson is *boring*." And how might the rest of the class respond to a dozen students randomly popping up out of their seats to stretch and walk around the class?

Emotion regulation is at the top of the RULER hierarchy. It's likely the most complex of the five skills and the most challenging. It's nearly impossible to imagine what life would be like without the power to regulate our emotions. You've been doing it since you were born—and you've done it, to some degree or other, every minute of your waking life.

Except that if you're like most of us, you haven't been very good at it. You've been doing it in haphazard, ad hoc, inconsistent ways. Sometimes your attempts to manage your emotions even have done more harm than good. Have you ever just lost your temper and yelled at someone? You almost certainly haven't been doing it consciously, in the most mindful ways, at the appropriate moments, with a positive outcome as your goal.

Every emotional response is a unique experience. What triggers an unpleasant emotion today may not even register tomorrow. Today you're waiting in line at Starbucks for what seems like an eternity, and all you want to do is leap over the counter, grab your coffee out of the barista's hands, and split. Tomorrow, same Starbucks, but your emotional state is serene, so you happily gaze around the place and people-watch while you wait.

This underscores the importance of the first three emotion skills we learned—we need to know what we're feeling and why before we can anticipate which emotion regulation strategies we might require in the next five minutes.

All of which explains why it's so important that we fully understand and master this, our final skill—Regulation.

Up until now, all the RULER skills have been essentially thoughts and words. Now comes the hard part: putting all that wisdom you gathered from the first four RULER skills into action. This is the nuts-and-bolts chapter, where the real work gets done. It's also where the rewards lie.

Stanford University psychology professor James Gross, an authority on emotion regulation, defines it as "the process by which individuals influence which emotions they have, when they have them, and how they experience and express these emotions."

Our center is especially interested in how people develop constructive strategies that promote personal growth, foster and maintain positive relationships, and lead to both greater well-being and goal attainment.

Of all the skills, this is the one with the most moving parts. In a way, that makes it both the easiest and the hardest one to tackle—the number of specific strategies for Regulation is nearly limitless, depending on the situation and the emotions involved. The strategies that work for you today might not work for you tomorrow. And the strategies that work for you might not work for your partner or child.

As I said earlier, our emotions flow in a continuous stream, like a river, and to keep up with that we're constantly regulating them. It's how we maintain our balance and keep from being swept away by one strong feeling or another. We all know people who seem particularly unskilled at regulating their emotions. They're easily knocked off course by their feelings, and routinely overreact in unhelpful ways. Or, at the other extreme, they suppress their emotional responses so much that they seem cold and numb. They don't permit themselves to feel at all, which is just as harmful as reacting in excess.

We start regulating early. Babies suck their thumbs because it provides emotional comfort. Distressed infants will turn their faces away from the source of their displeasure, another rudimentary form of Regulation. So you see, you've been doing it all your life. You just didn't know it was a skill. I never even heard the term *emotion regulation* until I was in graduate school!

The initial goal of Regulation is to manage our own emotional responses, but then this skill makes a leap into even greater complexity: co-regulation. Every human interaction we've ever had, from infancy onward, has involved co-regulation. It's impossible to be in the company of another being and not be influenced by her or his emotional state, and vice versa.

Originally, co-regulation was a term used to describe the back-and-forth between a caregiver and infant to support a baby's stress regulation. Beginning in the earliest days of life, an infant's socioemotional circuitry is molded by adults. A caregiver who reliably provides physical and verbal comfort and reassures the infant teaches it that emotional distress is manageable. A caregiver who does not provide such support teaches the infant that he or she may be at the mercy of their emotions. In this way, co-regulation is the precursor to healthy self-regulation.

In adult relationships, co-regulation can be intentional, as when we speak soothingly to someone who's upset or try to inspire someone into action. You're joyous, or furious, or bored, and I automatically read the signals and my mood is altered. We're all constantly affecting each other's emotional state.

Sometimes we can use this skill to keep colleagues motivated and striving toward a common goal. In 2015, our center collaborated with Born This Way Foundation to host the Emotion Revolution Summit at Yale. The goal was to build awareness of the critical role emotions play in young people's lives. We wanted to bring together youths from around the country for a summit to share their ideas with educators, academics, and policy makers.

Our first order of business was simply to figure out what we wanted to do at the conference. That was the fun part, and Regulation played a big part. During those early brainstorming meetings, we played upbeat, lively music to inspire dynamic, ambitious thinking. As a result, the energy flowed and everybody was psyched and we had a lot of fun coming up with a long list of possibilities. Nothing got shot down, no matter how far out or impractical. The sky was the limit.

Once we had those ideas, it was time to get practical. We needed to begin winnowing the list and agree on how it all would get done and who would be doing what. For these meetings, we again used music to regulate the team's mood—except now it was gentle and reflective, conducive to building consensus about what we had dreamed up in those previous sessions. We went from the yellow quadrant—positive and energized—to the green—still positive, but now calm and rational.

Then we needed a third set of meetings, to sort out the nuts-and-bolts phase. In these sessions, we turned off the music. We sat quietly and addressed all of the details in a businesslike way and came up with timetables, budgets, contingency plans. We decided who would manage the research, who would oversee publicity, who would arrange for security and insurance. We went from the green to light blue in order to narrow our focus and engage in deductive reasoning. By the end of those sessions we had a workable, realistic plan for going forward.

Before the big conference began, we had one more decision to make: What was the feeling we hoped our audience members would take away? We wanted them to end up in the red quadrant—aware of the injustices in the status quo and motivated, even passionate, about making changes. Not merely enthusiastic, but a little angry, because anger is how we respond to unfairness. To manage that, we had to deliver closing remarks about our findings and the path forward in a way that activated our listeners. I didn't want the public officials to walk out saying, "Wow, that conference was a great experience!" I wanted them to realize that there was an emergency they needed to address. I wanted them energized with a sense of mission when they got back to work.

Now it's time to treat Regulation as a practical—necessary—skill we can master.

So far, we've been describing the RULER method as a fairly orderly procession from one step to the next, from Recognition to Understanding and so on. But human minds and emotions aren't so neatly organized, and we don't process information one piece at a time. Often, we regulate before we're even fully conscious of what we're feeling. Someone is rude to you at work, and your brain instantly jolts you from peaceful green into the fiery red quadrant of angry activation, ready to defend your dignity. Without thinking, you take a deep breath and get some distance. That's Regulation (specifically, implicit or automatic Regulation).

Emotion regulation can be as simple as this: You can't stand your neighbor? Avoid her. Your parents are coming to visit and you don't want them to see some of your more outré artwork? Hide it until they leave. You're tired? Splash some water on your face.

Emotion regulation is not about *not* feeling. Neither is it exerting tight control over what we feel. And it's not about banishing negative emotions and feeling only positive ones. Rather, emotion regulation starts with giving ourselves and others the permission to own our feelings—all of them.

Years ago, I visited a classroom in a high-poverty area of New York. A boy named George who was in the fourth grade shared that he was in the blue quadrant, and with good reasons: his pet hamster had been killed by a rat that morning. Later, I learned he lived in temporary housing, and his life was full of anxiety and uncertainty.

The teacher asked the class, "What can we do to support George today?" and the answers came back quickly. One student said, "Can I give you a hug?" Another said, "George, I'm here for you anytime today if you want to talk." The shift in George's facial expression was instant. He came to class distraught but was comforted by his peers in a way that let him know he was cared for. He wasn't being urged to shift out of the blue quadrant; rather, he was given support and affection so he could be comfortable where he was. George was no longer alone in his misery but now in the company of peers and a teacher who wanted to hear him and understand his needs. Too often we look for strategies that will shift people out of negative emotion spaces, but that's not always possible. During difficult times, sometimes we just need to be there for one another.

For the remainder of this chapter, we'll dive deeply into five broad categories of emotion regulation. Within each category, the number of specific strategies is virtually infinite, each one determined by the moment, context, and emotion, by our age, personality, and culture, by whatever came before and whatever we wish to happen next.

The first category is a strategy that literally keeps us alive: breathing. Specifically, *mindful breathing* helps us to calm the body and mind so we can be fully present and less reactive or overwhelmed by what's happening around us.

The second category we'll call *forward-looking strategies*. This simply means that we anticipate something will cause an unwanted emotion and either steer clear of it or modify our physical environment.

The third category is *attention-shifting strategies*. This takes many forms, but all are based on the same principle—that we can temper the impact of an emotion by diverting our attention away from its source. It can be as simple as turning on the TV, walking away from a stressful encounter, or repeating a positive phrase to ourselves.

The fourth we'll call *cognitive-reframing strategies*. We first analyze whatever's triggering an emotional experience and then find a new way of seeing it—essentially, transforming our perception of reality as a way of mastering it.

Finally, I'll introduce the *Meta-Moment,* a tool which helps us to act as our best selves would, as opposed to reacting (and overreacting) to emotional situations.

Mindful breathing

I'd like you to take two minutes to pause, get comfortable, and breathe naturally. If it will help, you can time yourself. Begin now.

How'd it go? Did you even do it? Or did you just keep reading? If you did try it, how did it feel? Did you get impatient, anxious, bored? Did your mind wander? Maybe it was the first time you've taken a minute for yourself all day, and you feel calm or centered. Allowing our minds to be idle is a major challenge for many of us given our busy lives. And it's especially hard when we're faced with strong emotions such as anxiety, anger, and even excitement.

Our brain responds to intense emotions by activating the sympathetic nervous system: our heart rate goes up, stress hormones and/or endorphins are released depending on the emotion, and (when pressured) we prepare to flee or freeze.

Mindful breathing helps us to hit the brake on the activation of our stress response system by decreasing our heart rate. Breathing through the nose is helpful because mouth breathing tends to be faster and shallower (think of a panting dog), which can reactivate the stress response system. And when we count our breaths or repeat a calming phrase while breathing, we regain balance and control because the area of the brain in charge shifts from the brain stem to the motor cortex. Breathing also helps us to reset the autonomic nervous system by activating the parasympathetic nervous system and inhibiting the sympathetic (excitatory) one.

When we breathe mindfully, we don't have to sit in a fancy yoga posture or use any special techniques. But it is important to have good posture whether sitting or standing. Mindful breathing can be practiced anywhere: at home, school, work, or even while trying to fall asleep.

It's best to build a practice of mindful breathing in small steps over time. Start by taking a few minutes a couple of times a week to sit and breathe mindfully. Over time you can build up to a five-, ten-, or even fifteen-minute practice each day. That way, when you are in the situation where you'll need to deactivate, you'll be prepared.

Do your best to

o remove distractions such as your cell phone.
o get comfortable.
o close your eyes or lower your eyelids.
o be aware of your posture and body. You can place your hand on a spot where you feel the breath, but it's not necessary.
o breathe naturally.
  • You can count to 10: inhale 1/exhale 1, inhale 2/exhale 2, and so on until you get to 10. Then repeat.
  • Or you can breathe while repeating a phrase. I learned my favorite more than twenty years ago from Thich Nhat Hanh, a leader in the mindfulness community. It's simple: On the inhale you say "in" and on the exhale you say "out." Then "deep/slow," "calm/ease," "smile/release." Repeat. This particular one helps me at night when my mind is racing and I have a hard time falling asleep.
  • bring your attention back to your breath if you notice your mind wandering.

If you are like me and get easily distracted during the practice, you might start thinking: I can't do this. It's hopeless. Try to be an emotion scientist, not a judge about it. Even have a little self-compassion and try it again. You're exercising a new muscle. Once you're comfortable with these two basic exercises, you can try others, but it's not necessary. I've stuck with the basic ones for years.

Today, dozens of experiments demonstrate the benefits of mindful breathing on our emotional, social, and cognitive functioning. Over time, not only do we deactivate more quickly, but our ability to focus and to be present grows stronger. Research suggests that just fifteen minutes of this practice daily can positively affect our attunement to family and friends, emotional reactivity, attention, memory, immune function, hypertension, asthma, autonomic nervous system imbalances, and mental health.

Forward-looking strategies

The following strategies require enough self-awareness for us to know what exactly will set us off, or bring us joy, and why. We consider how we will feel in an upcoming situation and devise a plan ahead of time to alter the emotional impact. This skill depends on R, U, and L—Recognition, Understanding, and Labeling.

For instance, you have an aunt who always manages to infuriate you over Thanksgiving dinner. Rather than grit your teeth through another tense holiday, you decide in advance to sit at the opposite end of the table. Problem solved!

Or there's a subordinate at the office who's been after you for a one-on-one meeting, but there's a problem: he makes you nervous and you know it will be an extremely awkward session. You've been stalling him, but that only makes things worse, as your dread keeps growing. There's probably some good reason behind your aversion, but you can address that another day. Right now, a good regulation strategy would be to turn your one-on-one meeting into a group session with other employees on your team. The instant that solution occurs to you, you feel better.

This strategy requires some self-knowledge, but if we can predict which situations or encounters will provoke an emotional reaction, we can take measures to prevent them from happening.

When it's impossible to avert the future completely, we can still anticipate it and change it. Your annual job review is coming up, which always fills you with fear and insecurity for a week before it happens and outright dread as it finally takes place. But if you try to imagine every possible scenario—all the criticisms of your performance that your boss might bring up and all the calm, well-reasoned responses you will make in response—you might not be your usual stammering, defensive self when the time comes.

Likewise, avoidance is a strategy. It doesn't sound like an advisable one, but it can be useful under certain circumstances. I won't go to a certain restaurant because they have amazing fries and I can't resist them. So I stay away and save myself a lot of anguish. No great loss. You're in a store and the cashier is rude, but it's not as though you and he are likely to interact in the future, so there's no long-term need to do anything about it. Just never go near the place again or look for a different cashier.

However, if you realize that there have been other instances, at work or at home with your spouse or children, where you've just walked away from rudeness because you felt incapable of facing it down, and every time it happens you feel belittled and humiliated or enraged, maybe there's something else going on—like an inability to have a difficult conversation or stand up for yourself and deal with unpleasantness. Perhaps you need to find a long-term strategy better than avoidance.

There's another aspect of forward-looking strategies worth mastering. It involves pleasure only. Let's say you're having a hellish week at work, and you already know that Friday will be the absolute capper. You're dreading it, but if you schedule a date for Friday night or make plans to go to the beach as soon as you leave the office, you suddenly have something great waiting for you at the end of the tunnel. Or if you have a root canal appointment looming, you can plan to do something you love right afterward and give yourself a treat to look forward to. As a rule, doing something you enjoy is a very effective strategy for regulating negative emotions.

Attention-shifting strategies

These take many forms, but all are based on the same principle—that we can temper the impact of an emotion by diverting our attention from it. It can be as simple as looking away from a stressful encounter or as reflective as delivering a self-talk as though we were speaking to a friend who was under duress, telling them to visualize being on a beautiful beach.

Bored waiting in a cashier line, so you check your Instagram feed? That's distraction. Pretty common today. Not terribly useful. You could have devoted those moments to thinking about a new business idea you had or planning your vacation. Still, it beats standing there and steaming.

Or your credit card payment is due tomorrow and your checking account balance is low, so you ease the angst by vowing to change your spending habits and start saving. If it makes you feel better, fine. It's a good way to avert moments like this in the future. But diverting your attention won't pay the bill that's staring you in the face.

A nervous wreck until you get back the results from a blood test, so you binge-watch Netflix? Better than suffering. So frustrated over your inability to lose weight that only ice cream will ease the pain? Could help you through the next fifteen minutes, but maybe not the perfect strategy going forward for achieving that particular goal.

The list of potential distractions is infinite. Everything from day-dreaming to drugs. Food—snacking—is a great short-term strategy, not unlike other recreational mood enhancers for its ability to provide physical comfort that overrides mental anxiety. It's that surge of sugar in the bloodstream that prompts the rush of pleasure to the brain. If you depend on junk food as a regulation strategy just occasionally, you're like the rest of us. If it's three times a day, you may have some emotional *and* physical issues to deal with.

It's possible to distract ourselves to such a degree that we avoid deal-ing with anything difficult—even when our lives would be improved by facing reality and doing something about it. What we commonly call "denial" is just an extreme form of distraction—akin to burying our heads in the sand during a crisis.

Still, it's emotion regulation.

Procrastination is a popular way of creating some emotional distance using time rather than space. If a situation is causing you stress, just decide you'll deal with it next week, or next month, or at some indefinite point in the future. Poof, it's gone. Politicians and public officials love this one—in their world it's known as "kicking the can down the road," and it allows them to avoid dealing with painful deficits, deadlines, and other challenges. Procrastination must be effective, otherwise we wouldn't make such abundant use of it. But like other cheap, easy fixes, it's got plenty of potential to harm and not much to help.

"Self-talk" is something we all do at one time or another—it's simply expressing our thoughts silently as though we're speaking to ourselves out loud. The best part about self-talk is that it's effortless, since we all talk to ourselves from time to time. Many of us aren't particularly nice about it—think of when you've called yourself an idiot if something goes wrong. Positive self-talk just requires us to be kind and empathic when we do it. The challenge, as we've learned, at least in Western cultures, is that our inborn negativity bias contributes to our negative self-talk, not to mention all of the negative talk we've picked up from our parents and peers. We can't just drop it—we need to replace it. Harsh self-criticism activates the sympathetic nervous system (fight/flight) and elevates stress hormones. Self-compassion, on the other hand, triggers the mammalian caregiving system and hormones of affiliation and love such as oxytocin.

Researchers Ethan Kross at the University of Michigan and Jason Moser at Michigan State University have studied how our brains respond to self-talk. In particular, they compared what happens when we address ourselves in the third person rather than the first, meaning that I'd start by saying, "Marc . . . ," as though I were speaking to someone other than myself. It may not seem like much of a difference, but it turns out to be significant.

In one experiment, subjects were shown neutral and disturbing images or asked to recall negative moments from their own lives. By monitoring their emotional brain activity, the researchers found that the subjects' distress decreased rapidly—within one second—when they performed self-talk in the third person compared with the first person.

Why would that make a difference? Jason Moser wrote, "Essentially, we think referring to yourself in the third person leads people to think about themselves more similarly to how they think about others, and you can see evidence for this in the brain. That helps people gain a tiny bit of psychological distance from their experiences, which can often be useful for regulating emotions." Essentially, third-person self-talk is a way of being empathetic to ourselves.

I find myself making use of self-talk to regulate my own moods all the time. I have found it very useful to have go-to phrases for different purposes. When I start catastrophizing, I say, "Marc, you are making this up." When I'm overwhelmed before bed, I say, "Marc, you know this feeling is impermanent. Go to bed. You'll be fine in the morning."

Sometimes, self-talk is more elaborate. I give seminars before groups all around the world. Most of the time, I'm energetic and enthusiastic about my mission and the people who want to learn about it. Sometimes, though, it's the third talk I've given in the past two days, and it's coming at the end of a long work session, and all I really want to do is lie down in my hotel room and watch HBO. Instead, I've got to get up and perform for the next three hours.

Here's what I tell myself:

"Marc, you're about to talk with one hundred school superintendents. They oversee tens of thousands of teachers, each of whom is in front of classrooms all day long, educating hundreds of thousands of children. And you now have the opportunity to share something that could have a profound effect on the lives of those kids. What happens tonight in that room will help those children to learn better and succeed not only in school but in *life*."

"Wow!" I reply. "How lucky am I to be in this position?" And with that I'm psyched and ready to go.

Cognitive-reframing strategies

"There is nothing either good or bad, but thinking makes it so," says Hamlet. That idea is the basis for our fourth, most sophisticated, intellectually engaged method of emotion regulation—*cognitive-reframing strategies*, better known in the research literature as *reappraisal*.

In a sense, this can be seen as an offshoot of cognitive behavioral therapy, in which people are encouraged to seek alternate ways of viewing their difficulties as a path to coming into balance with them.

For our purposes, we use reappraisal as a way to reimagine or reframe whatever is triggering an emotional experience and then react instead to that new interpretation.

Here's an example. You come down to breakfast, say good morning to your partner, and are met with a surly look instead of the usual warm greeting. If your first reaction is that you did nothing to deserve such rudeness, you may hold a grudge all day (or at least until dinner). You may even respond in kind, which will only perpetuate the foul mood in the air.

Instead, you could pause and consider alternate reasons for what just happened. Maybe she's anxious about something she's afraid to talk to you about? Perhaps he's furious about a work interaction that had nothing to do with you but has left him humiliated and hurt? Those possibilities might remind you that she or he is never this rude under normal circumstances, and suddenly you're feeling empathetic and wondering how you can help. And in that fashion, your emotional response has been regulated, to the benefit of all.

The basic principles of reframing are that we consciously choose to view a situation in a way that generates the least negative emotion in us or we attempt to take the perspective of the person who is activating you and assume the best intention. For example, if a clerk is rude and dismissive, we could think, This guy is being a jerk to me, or, He obviously has a real problem with women, or, Maybe he thinks I don't have enough money to shop here—all of which would make you at least indirectly responsible for his behavior. With reframing, we might think instead, This guy must *really* hate his job, or, I wonder if he's just gotten bad news—both of which might turn your bruised ego into feelings of compassion or even curiosity.

The goal of reframing isn't only to regulate bruised feelings. You could be a teacher on your first day at a new school and the faculty meeting leaves you crestfallen—the teachers all seem so inexperienced and ill prepared. Instead of despairing, you could view this as a chance to mentor younger colleagues and have an impact on the entire school and come away excited instead of depressed.

Here's an example from an experiment conducted with employees at a large financial institution. Over the course of a week, one group of workers was shown videos about the harmful effects of stress—bad for health, detrimental to job performance, an obstacle to learning and growth. A second group of workers saw videos containing the opposite message—that stress is actually good for our health, inspiring better job performance as well as learning and growth.

Participants who watched the three-minute "stress is positive" videos three times a week had a significant reduction in negative health symptoms and an increase in work performance compared with those who watched the "stress is negative" videos. Other studies show that people who endorse the stress-is-enhancing mindset have a stronger desire to receive feedback.

Research done at Harvard found similar results. Students who were asked to think of pretest anxiety as being beneficial performed better on exams than a control group. In another experiment, reframing anxiety as excitement was found to improve negotiating and public-speaking skills.

Studies conducted using functional fMRI measures of brain activation found that reappraisal significantly dampens activity in the amygdala, an area of our brain that becomes activated when we experience strong emotions, and instead activates the lateral temporal cortical areas of the brain, which help us to modulate our emotional responses.

As is true of all regulation strategies, reframing has the potential to harm as well as help.

Imagine: You're at a party when your spouse shares something that embarrasses you. You're about to blow your top and storm out of the room, but instead you resist the urge, take a series of mindful breaths, and reconsider what just happened.

"He didn't *mean* to humiliate me," you tell yourself. That might help—at least now you believe he didn't intentionally hold you up to ridicule.

"He had a couple drinks too many," you reason. That could also lessen the sting. Now the martinis are at fault.

"I'm being hypersensitive, it wasn't such a big deal," you decide. And that's possible—maybe you're just tired and feeling more fragile than usual. Perhaps you're the only one in the room who thinks what he said was inappropriate.

Reframing the incident calmed you down and prevented an ugly scene, so we can consider this a successful regulation of a very strong emotion.

Or not.

Same scenario. You conduct the same self-talk to help you handle the situation without melting down. Until you recall that it's the third time something like this has happened in the past two months. And deep down you believe that maybe his intentions weren't so pure and he took some satisfaction from everyone having a laugh at your expense. And he's been having a few too many drinks a little too often lately. Now you realize that you weren't being hypersensitive—any normal person would have been outraged by what he said in the middle of a crowded party.

Which means that reframing has been allowing you to live in denial or disavowal about something unspoken and unhealthy that's going on between the two of you. He's attacking you in a passive-aggressive way, and for some reason you're allowing it. You haven't called him on it, and you haven't even admitted to yourself how bad it makes you feel. Your reluctance is understandable—once you face your feelings, you'll have to do something about them. It may not be easy. But until you do, and start dealing with them instead of regulating them out of existence, things won't get any better.

And that's how it can sometimes go with cognitive reappraisal, a very intelligent and helpful—and persuasive—strategy for emotion regulation.

When it comes to reappraisal, we need to ask ourselves: Am I doing this simply to justify avoiding a difficult, sensitive problem? Am I doing this because I know that addressing the issue is going to lead to a long, tortured, anguished conversation? In that case, reappraisal may be a useful short-term solution—you're on your way to a party, not the ideal moment for an ugly face-off. But it's also a poor long-term strategy, because ducking the issue now will only ensure that it will reemerge later on.

This is why we must make the effort to be an emotion scientist—we need to check in with ourselves regularly, to evaluate our feelings honestly, without judging ourselves for having them. Every time we believe we've successfully employed a strategy to regulate our feelings, we have to ask: That may have worked (for now), but what did it accomplish (for the long run)?

The Meta-Moment

Here we are, finally, at the pinnacle of emotion regulation, the most complex and also the most potentially rewarding of the RULER skills. But there's a catch.

As we all know, our best attempts at calm, thoughtful reflection work only when we feel in control of our emotions. If you're raging with resentment or crushed by disappointment, it's unlikely that you're capable of the extended reasoning required to see a situation in a new light. In that scenario, you'd first need to bring down your emotional temperature, to lower your activation and give yourself the space required for rational thought. Maybe you take a few deep breaths, a few steps back, a walk around the block.

Then, maybe you're ready for the Meta-Moment.

A decade ago, Robin Stern, psychoanalyst and associate director of our center, and I were wondering why, as a society, so many people are addicted to strategies that derail them from achieving their goals. Robin had worked with hundreds of patients who were unsuccessful even after learning strategies, and I observed schoolchildren and educators who didn't employ the strategies they were learning, even when they knew they were helpful.

Many of us were exposed to destructive strategies starting early in life—negative talk, screaming, blaming, and so on. Those responses require little cognitive control but are often effective at getting rid of negative feelings and providing (temporary) gratification. In the moment, we fail to realize that these strategies also can ruin our relationships. They fail to take in long-term consequences and derail us from achieving our goals.

We needed to suggest something—a tool—that would help people find beneficial strategies on their own.

So we developed a tool we call the Meta-Moment. In simplest terms, it's a pause. The Meta-Moment involves hitting the brakes and stepping out of time. We call it *meta* because it's a moment about a moment. We often associate it with counting, as in "one, two, three," or even one to ten, depending on the severity of the emotion we're struggling to manage. Taking one or more deep breaths may also be a part of it. Anything to give ourselves a little room to maneuver and deactivate.

This is where we stop the action and say, "Am I hearing this correctly?" Or even, "I need to pause and take a deep breath right now so I don't blow my top, break down sobbing, or react in some other way I will probably regret." Looking at the encounter dispassionately may help us go beyond our first impulse and find a better response. As the author and consultant Justin Bariso wrote, "Pausing helps you refrain from making a permanent decision based on a temporary emotion."

Instinctively, we sense that this will help, and biology proves us right. Pausing and taking a deep breath activates the parasympathetic nervous system, which reduces the release of cortisol, a major stress hormone, and naturally lowers our emotional temperature.

Pausing also gives us the chance to quickly ask a few questions that might be useful, such as "How have I handled situations like this in the past?" Or "What would my *best self* do right now?" That ideal, hypothetical person comprises attributes we would use to describe our best selves from our own perspective and from the perspective of others—how we'd like to be seen and experienced. For some people it's a set of adjectives such as compassionate, intelligent, or conscientious; for others it can be an image or an object. A good friend who is principal of a middle school has a Smurf on her desk that reminds her to be her best self.

Visualizing our best self redirects our attention away from the "trigger" and toward our values. This helps us to choose a helpful regulation strategy such as positive self-talk or reappraisal and then respond accordingly.

A couple of years ago, I had a student who raised his hand in class and said, "I have a question that I don't think *even you'll know* how to answer." To say that I was activated is an understatement; arrogance is a trigger for me. I wanted to reply: I might not know the answer, but remember I grade your papers. I would have thrown in a few expletives too. Instead, I reached down into my "professor of emotional intelligence" self and said, "How about if I get questions from some of the other students now and we can chat after class?" There, I politely informed him that his question could have been worded more diplomatically.

More recently, I was giving a presentation to a large group when someone challenged me on a point I was making. She didn't just ask a question or offer a dissenting opinion. She came at me with the intention of putting me down. "A lot of us in the room would not necessarily agree with that model," she said. My first impulse was to fire right back and embarrass her in front of her colleagues with a comment like "A lot of us, meaning you and your thirty personalities." But I didn't allow myself that petty pleasure. Instead, I took myself out of the moment, visualized my best self as "the feelings master," and paused as though I were formulating a reply. In that small window of time I calmed myself, then made a comment without belittling her and moved on. "I'd love to connect with you later to hear your thoughts," I said. Nobody in that room knew how close I came to losing it. Truth is, a couple of years prior, I likely would have crumbled.

The Meta-Moment is not just for down-regulating unpleasant emotions. Sometimes our best selves help us to stand up for what's right. Once, during a speech, a colleague bullied me in an unusual way—he joked about the fact that I was bullied as a child. I hate to admit it, but my first impulse was to run onstage and deliver a flying dropkick to his head. I regressed to feeling like that middle schooler being pushed around in the locker room. But I took a Meta-Moment and waited until after the presentation, when I went up to him and said, "I have no idea what motivated you to say those words, but it wasn't cool and you can't ever do it again."

I count these as victories for the Meta-Moment.

How skilled are you at taking a Meta-Moment? What adjectives characterize your best self? What are your go-to strategies when you are triggered or caught off guard? Do you ignore your feelings, act out, or meet them head-on?

When your boss criticizes your work and you feel disappointed, devastated, or resentful, how successful are you at taking a Meta-Moment, then saying to yourself something like "Feedback is a gift, there is always something I can learn."

When your daughter won't do her homework, do you argue, threaten, plead, grimace in disgust, explode in rage . . . or do you take a deep breath, evoke your best self, think about the most effective strategy with this particular child, and calmly take action?

Here are the steps to take so you can begin practicing the Meta-Moment.

1. *Sense the shift:* You are activated, caught off guard, or have an impulse to say or do something that you might regret. There is a shift in your thinking or physiology or both.
2. *Stop or pause!* Create the space before you respond. Step back and breathe. Breathe again.
3. *See your best self.* You imagine your best self. You think of adjectives or even an image that helps your *best self* appear in vivid detail. You might also think about your reputation: how do you want to be seen, talked about, and experienced? What would you do if someone you respect were watching?
4. *Strategize* and *act.* You reach into your RULER tool kit (for instance, positive self-talk or reframing) and choose the path that will support you in closing the gap between your "triggered" self and your emerging best self. (Always the last step.)

There are a few, final aspects of Regulation we need to consider. Because emotion regulation requires brainpower—moving from automatic and unhelpful to deliberate and helpful strategies is hard work!—it depends on seemingly unrelated factors such as diet, exercise, and sleep. When we eat poorly, our minds don't function properly. Too much sugar or refined grain causes our blood glucose to spike and then plummet, which affects cognitive functioning and self-control, especially around healthy eating. Easy solution: Make sure you have some healthy snacks in your desk at work or set a reminder on your phone to ensure you nibble every three hours or so.

Too little physical activity has a negative effect on our mental capacity and moods. In one study, subjects were exposed to a stressor, and then half of the participants did aerobic exercise while the others did not. The exercisers reported feeling significantly less negative than the other group. Even anxiety and depression can be reduced by exercise. Accumulating research is showing how a regular yoga practice might be beneficial for both our mental and physical health.

Poor quality or insufficient sleep has similar effects on our emotions—when we're tired, our defenses are down and our ability to function mentally is low. Sleep serves a restorative function. When we don't get enough, or we get too much, we show more symptoms of anxiety and depression, greater fatigue, and hostility. Inadequate sleep is associated with reduced connections between brain regions responsible for cognitive control and behavior and the use of effective emotion regulation strategies.

There are two more measures we can take to safeguard our overall well-being. The first is by doing things we love. Spend time with family and friends, pursue passions and pastimes, get in touch with your spiritual side, immerse yourself in nature, read a good book, watch a funny movie. We build up cognitive reserves that way, which will help us when emotional turmoil inevitably strikes. We are hardwired to seek social contact and support—people who lack it are prone to anxiety, depression, and cardiovascular disease.

The second measure is to practice mindful breathing, which is perhaps the ultimate prevention strategy. As we've learned, daily practice enhances our ability to be present, accept feelings as they come and go, and not be overly reactive or overwhelmed by them.

Just take everything we know about how to maintain good physical and mental health and apply it to your emotional fitness. It's all connected.

With that, we've completed our education in the final RULER skill. But we're not quite finished yet.

Learning the five RULER skills and how and why they work is essential. But it's just the beginning of your education. Now comes the part where you put them all to good use.

It's not so simple, learning five interrelated skills all at once. Think of what it was like to learn any skill you now possess. For example, it took me four years of daily practice to get a black belt and another ten years to obtain a fifth-degree black belt. Like learning a martial art, developing emotion skills takes time. It takes work. It takes practice. It takes openness to feedback. It takes refinement.

Owing to the emotional nature of these particular skills, you may find that you're better at some than at others. It's certainly that way for me. I know that I'm often better at R, U, and L than I am at E or R. I suppose that means I'm better at the thinking parts of RULER than I am at putting them into action. Recently, after a long, exhausting day of delayed flights, missed connections, and other irritations, I felt that I was on the verge of a meltdown. Then I asked myself, If a college professor with a doctorate in psychology has difficulty regulating emotions, what must it be like for a nine-year-old child or an adult under genuinely challenging pressures who have had little to no training in emotion skills? That calmed me down in a hurry. It also reminded me how much work needs to be done to ensure every child gets an emotion education.

I think Mike Tyson had it right when he said, "Everybody has a plan until they get punched in the mouth." What's true in the boxing ring is true everywhere else—it's easy to say that from now on we'll master all our emotional responses, until our significant other or cranky child or unreasonable boss triggers us with a word or a look, and suddenly all the RULER training goes out the window.

So, along with permission to feel, we must also give ourselves permission to fail. When that happens, we can only try again—take a deep breath or two, envision our best selves, and start over at the first R. At such moments, we also need the courage to apologize and to forgive ourselves as we'd forgive others. Courage can even mean seeking professional help when all else fails.

We'll never stop having to work at being our best selves. But the payoff is worth it: better health, decision making, relationships, better everything.

Of course, all the emotion mastery in the world won't help much if everyone else is still playing by the bad old rules of engagement. As Uncle Marvin and I discovered decades ago, it's not enough to teach these skills to schoolchildren. Their teachers must also become emotion scientists. And their parents too. And everyone else with any influence over their lives, including employers and work colleagues. Which is what the next section is all about.

PART THREE

APPLYING EMOTION SKILLS FOR OPTIMUM WELL-BEING AND SUCCESS

9

Emotions at Home

A WOMAN APPROACHED ME after a seminar I did for parents and caregivers. She whispered, "Can we talk privately? I am really worried about my son."

"Sure," I said, "tell me the problem."

"I am afraid he has no emotional intelligence," she said. "He's throwing things and is just too aggressive. He's different from my oldest son, who is gregarious and highly skilled. I am really worried. My husband and I are a mess. Should we bring him to a psychologist?"

I made some suggestions for how she could support her child in learning how to regulate emotions, but she said, "We can't use any of those strategies."

"Why not?" I asked.

"Because he's only eleven months old."

I stood there speechless. The first thing that came to mind to say was, "Yes, I think you should call a psychologist—for *you*." Instead, I took a breath and gently suggested that maybe she was being overly worried about her son's emotional intelligence and could wait a little while longer before seeking professional help.

We all arrive in this world programmed differently where emotions are concerned. Each of us has a different threshold for being provoked, activated, aroused, startled. Some of us experience feelings more intensely than others. We recover from emotional reactions at different speeds. But these individual differences don't determine whether we will develop emotion skills. Research shows that even highly reactive kids who are raised in nurturing families can turn out just fine.

Of course we're all concerned about the emotional lives of our children. We know what's at stake—virtually everything. As we've seen already, their physical and mental well-being, their ability to learn in school, their future success at work and in families of their own, all depend on it. There's no greater measure of how we did as parents than the success of our kids in this regard. Few influences can match those of family and home.

But *which* home?

There's the home where we grew up, where our emotional lives were formed. We're not born with emotion knowledge; we mostly respond to stimuli—we're hungry, we're cold, we're uncomfortable for one reason or another, and so we react. Nature provides that response to make sure we get the attention we need to survive infancy. Everything beyond that is learned in the nest.

Along the way, as we learn what we need to be an adult and to sustain a home or family, we take in the emotional experiences, like the air we breathe. We carry those emotional patterns forward with us—the good and the bad—often replicating them. And in our new home, the cycle repeats—built on the emotional foundations of the one where we started out.

Many of us go through life trying our hardest to avoid precisely that fate. We strive to be anything *but* our parents. And then, inevitably, comes the moment when we hear ourselves say, "Where did that come from?" Suddenly we realize we've been carrying our parents around inside us all our lives.

When there are two adults building a family, there are even more emotional inheritances in that home. And even if there are no children present—or you live alone—that past is always somewhere inside of you.

Given this, what steps can we take to create healthy home environments, places where our children and loved ones will feel supported, valued, treasured, understood, *heard*? Homes filled with patience and acceptance and humor and joy?

Few parents today would argue with the idea that their children will do best if they're well loved. That wasn't always so. Early in the twentieth century, the fields of child psychology and development were divided over how best to raise children, especially on the merits of strictness or leniency, discipline or tenderness. The president of the American Psychological Association, John B. Watson, warned in 1915 that too much love and comforting was dangerous for children and that their lives would be spoiled by cuddling.

Today, nothing could sound more misguided or damaging. Current scientific research on attachment of children to parents, on the power of feeling seen and felt, and on the benefits of comfort all show one thing: Children do best with demonstrative love and caring.

But parents seem ambivalent when it comes to their children's emotional lives. I routinely encounter RULER-resistant parents who think I'm advocating for everybody sitting in a circle on the living room floor and *discussing their feelings* ad nauseam. They see our work as overindulging their children instead of preparing them for real life.

What those parents miss is that a focus on emotion skills is about real, practical *skills*.

Permission to feel doesn't mean obsessing over every time somebody is mean to us or ignores us. It's really just the opposite—teaching the ability to get through those moments, to learn from them, and to continue to function normally. Emotion skills are a bulwark against the epidemic of anger, bullying, disengagement, anxiety, and dread in this country, especially among young people. They clear away the most persistent drags on our creativity, relationships, decisions, and health.

Permission to feel *strengthens*. It's not always easy to face the truth about who we are and to reckon with our own and our children's emotional lives. But it is a whole lot better than the alternative: denial, overreacting, and so on. You teach your children to express their emotions by skillfully expressing yours. Conversely, if you are reluctant to express your feelings, or do so only sparingly, in as few words as possible, then that's what your children will learn to do when they grow up. This is why we adults need to be open to learning and practicing strategies in our own emotional lives before we can support our kids.

Researchers have found many ways that parents' own emotions affect their children's:

Beliefs about feelings. Family researchers such as John Gottman and developmental psychologists such as Amy Halberstadt have shown that parents who value emotions tend to be aware of their children's feelings and are able to act like coaches. They don't respond with threats of discipline when their kids express anger or sadness—instead, they see strong feelings as a central part of healthy development. Parents who view emotions as harmful or disruptive are the ones who command their children to "suck it up" and see their kids' emotional expressions as manipulative. Those are the same parents who mask their own emotions and send implicit messages that feelings are unimportant.

Even when we do acknowledge others' emotions, we have to be careful about *how* we do so. Boys and girls often receive different messages about emotions from parents. And these gender differences tend to increase with age: Nancy Eisenberg, a professor of developmental psychology at Arizona State University, reported that there are few gender differences in preschool children, but by second grade larger disparities emerge. For example:

- Mothers speak more to daughters about feelings and display a wider range of feelings to daughters than to sons.
- Fathers discourage boys from expressing emotional vulnerability and use tougher language with sons than they do with daughters.
- When parents tell stories to their preschool children, they use more emotion words with daughters than with sons.
- Mothers smile more and are more expressive to infant and toddler girls than boys and talk more about sadness with daughters and more about anger with sons.

Emotion vocabulary. Most of us are unaware of how important vocabulary is to emotion skills. As we've seen, using many different words implies valuable distinctions—that we're not always simply angry but are sometimes annoyed, irritated, frustrated, disgusted, aggravated, and so on. If we can't discern the difference, it suggests that we can't understand it either. It's the difference between a rich emotional life and an impoverished one. Your child will inherit the one you provide.

In one study, researchers found that mothers who used more sophisticated language when talking about feelings had children who were better at regulating their own emotions. The authors wrote, "The ability to talk about one's own affective state has its most obvious importance for regulating affect in its power to enlist others as sources of aid or comfort." What that means, essentially, is that if mothers and fathers use many words to describe emotions rather than just a few basic ones, their children will be better able to express their feelings to others. They'll also be more empathic.

Co-regulation. Researchers use the term *co-regulation* to refer to how we affect one another's feelings, moving another's feelings up or down by our own actions. In the parent-child dyad, the child is an active participant in his or her own regulation, but the parent is the source of the strategy.

At the most basic level, it includes a caregiver's warmth, responsiveness, and sensitivity, as well as methods for buffering a child against stress and creating routines to promote a sense of security. For young children it might include offering strategies such as distraction: "You sound upset. Are you angry because he took your toy? Let's play with this toy together instead."

Another way involves scaffolding children's self-regulation of emotion using prompts: "What happened? How are you feeling? How do you want to feel?" The adult may act as a partner to support problem solving—"Why don't you let him play with your toy? After two minutes, I'll make sure he gives it back"—and reappraisal: "Perhaps he thought it was his own toy and not yours. I see he has a very similar one behind him."

And yet another strategy is metacognitive prompting, which emphasizes empowering children to generate and/or choose from alternative emotion regulation strategies: "Is there another way to think about what happened? What could you do instead? What's worked before when you've felt this way?"

I'm an obsessive eavesdropper on families in public. For me, it's research. Sometimes I find skilled parents who nurture their children's developing emotion skills. But not always.

This happened one morning while I was eating breakfast in a hotel restaurant:

"You're going to calm down right *now*," the father said to his daughter, who looked to be about three years old. "Thank you for ruining our day." I couldn't tell what prompted his outburst.

He then picked up the menu, ordered breakfast, and turned to his phone, as did the little girl's mother. For thirty minutes, that man never once looked up at his daughter or his wife. As they rose to leave, he turned at last to his daughter and said, "You're not going to behave that way again, are you?"

It wasn't a question.

"If you continue to behave like this, you aren't going swimming for the rest of the vacation."

The child began to sob. Do you think she cried because she couldn't go swimming? If you asked that three-year-old child how she was feeling—if she had adult language—you'd probably hear that she felt ignored, stifled, worthless in her father's eyes.

This father lacked the ability to recognize, understand, and label his daughter's feelings, and it broke my heart. As the family left the restaurant, I wondered: Was this a typical morning for them? Does this little girl believe she has the permission to feel? What is the implicit message her dad is sending her about her character? What learning will she carry forward into her future? How would a RULER-ized father manage the situation?

On a train once, I watched a mother and her son, who looked to be about seven. I first noticed them when I heard her say to the boy, "Remember, *train behavior.*" When I looked up I saw that she was staring at her cell phone and he was standing next to the seat. Two minutes later, he was wandering down the aisle. "I need you to *sit,*" she said. He did, and she went back to her phone. A few minutes later he was up again, walking around, until she noticed and said, *"Remember your train behavior!"* This little comedy kept playing out, and I was riveted. Finally, when he jumped up again, she screamed, *"Sit! And look at me when I'm talking to you!"* This was accompanied by a finger pointing to the seat next to hers and a piercing glare into his eyes.

I remember thinking, I have to put up with an hour of this? I wondered what would happen if I went over to her and said, "Excuse me, ma'am, but I am the director of the Yale Center for Emotional Intelligence, and I'd like to give you a little advice about how to handle this situation better."

What I really wanted to do was go to her son and whisper, "Quick, run away now while you can!"

Sometimes parents avoid dealing with their child's feelings by turning to technology as a way of removing themselves from the stress of the moment. According to research, this only increases the child's misery and inspires even more bad behavior . . . which parents then use as an excuse to isolate themselves even further. Children feel unimportant when parents use electronic devices during meals or conversations. Toddlers express more distress particularly when their mothers use their phones. And parents who are engrossed in their devices while at restaurants respond most harshly when their children want attention.

What about children's use of technology? According to a 2018 report by the Pew Research Center, 45 percent of teenagers are online "almost constantly" and U.S. high school seniors spend about six hours a day texting, on social media sites, or surfing the Internet. Research conducted by Jean Twenge, a professor at San Diego State University, shows that more hours of screen time are associated with lower well-being in children and adolescents; that higher users show less curiosity, self-control, and emotional stability; and that twice as many high versus low users of screens are diagnosed with anxiety or depression.

Okay, now it's time to examine how we were raised and search our memories for clues about the family we carry in our heads.

Take a moment and think back to the home you grew up in. Consider how it felt to be in your home, your relationship with your mom, dad, or caregiver. With that in mind, what's one word you would use to describe the emotional climate of your childhood home?

Here's a summary of thousands of responses from people across the globe. They fall into three categories: about 70 percent of the terms were negative, 20 percent were positive, and 10 percent were neutral.

The top negative responses: stuck, heavy, toxic, suppressed, inconvenient, stunted, avoidant, blind, intense, and unsupportive.

The top positive answers: supportive, loving, caring, nurturing, and accepting.

The top neutral words: unaware, selective, clueless, even, and neutral.

When I asked my brother this question, he immediately wrote back, "Ashtrays, hangers, and belts!" I knew exactly what he meant.

Ask yourself these questions: What did you learn about emotions growing up? What did you witness? Which feelings did your parents easily express, and which were never displayed? How did your parents handle your emotions, especially the difficult ones such as anger, fear, sadness? Were they emotion scientists, trying to figure out what you were feeling and why, as a way of helping you to deal with it? Or were they judges, blaming or finding fault with you for how you felt? Did you feel free to say what you felt? Did your parents' behavior encourage you to express, or did they send an implicit message to suppress your emotions?

Another way to think about this is to consider any defining moments—key points in your childhood that influenced who you are today. They can be memories of people or events that stand out as having a positive or negative effect on your development. Maybe these took place at home, or school, or the playground. What are some of your key defining moments?

Really think about this—try to remember what it was like in your home, at your school, with your family and friends. What were the positives that make you smile to recall? What were the painful or stressful moments, perhaps ones you've spent your life trying hard to forget? They matter just like the happy ones—no more but no less. Now, see what connections, if any, you can make between those moments, good and bad, and the adult you are today and the emotional life of your family.

Given our natural bias to remember negative events better than positive ones, I often think back to the bullying and abuse I suffered in elementary and middle school. One of my strongest memories of my childhood was when my parents made me run around the block on Christmas Eve before they would let me open presents. (Somehow, they believed that was an effective strategy to help me to lose weight.) But

I also had other, happy experiences, such as studying martial arts and earning my black belt, my girlfriend and best friend from high school, spending time with Uncle Marvin. Those were great times that brought me joy. Ultimately, it was both the positive and the negative experiences that led me to dedicate my life to helping others find the permission to feel and to express what they're feeling without shame or fear.

Once we've acknowledged the power of the past in our current emotional lives, we're ready to begin dealing with the present. RULER shows us how: First we recognize what we're feeling, so that we may understand why. Only then can we see *how* our feelings drive us to act—meaning what triggers us. We can regulate our emotional responses only if we can anticipate what will set us off.

When I ask parents to name their triggers, I get quick answers. Nobody has to think long before compiling this list:

"I'm triggered every day at seven forty A.M., when the war over getting my child up and dressed and out of the house on time begins."

"When I have to repeat the same thing over and over."

"When I've gone to all the trouble of cooking dinner and they refuse to eat."

"That snotty tone of voice no matter what I ask."

"Her bedroom is a pigsty."

"The never-ending arguing and fighting."

"Any time I'm reminded that we've raised two spoiled, entitled brats."

If you're a parent or caregiver, what are your triggers? What can you add to this list?

Once we air out that list of grievances, I ask parents how they typically respond to being triggered. These answers don't come so quickly. It takes a certain amount of honesty and bravery to confess how fierce and disproportionate our reactions can be:

"I scream at my daughter—*scream*. At the top of my lungs."

"I threaten."

"I'll take things away."

"I give the silent treatment."

"I've guilted them into doing what I wanted them to do."

"I blame my wife for not controlling them."

"I've bribed them to behave."

One mother told this story: Her high school son's sleepaway camp didn't work out one summer, so he returned home. "And he was slowly driving me out of my mind. He was a slob. He made the house a mess. He refused to look for work. So, he was always there. It got to the point where I couldn't even look at him, I was so irritated and frustrated. When I got to the breaking point I would lock myself in the bathroom. After about a month of that, my husband asked me if I had a urinary tract infection."

Do any of these reactions look familiar to you? What are your automatic, go-to strategies when you are triggered? When we feel threatened by our kids, our compassion switch turns off.

When I tell audiences how extreme reactions, over the course of time, can actually alter the brain structure of their children, the room goes quiet. Everyone is silently totaling up the times they lost their temper and went crazy on their kids, sizing up how much permanent damage they did to those impressionable young minds. The mood turns serious. Parents are mortified and filled with regret.

"It's pretty scary to think that all the yelling and screaming I've been doing for the past six years has damaged my kids' brains forever," one mother said, speaking for everyone in the room.

"Well," I tell them, "you don't have to worry too much, because a child's brain is still plastic, meaning that the structure is always changing. The minute you start regulating your emotions better, their brains will change to reflect that."

There's a sigh of relief all across the room.

"*However*," I say. "This doesn't get you off the hook. It doesn't mean you can keep yelling and screaming and punishing and stressing everybody out. It just means that if you can start regulating your emotions now, and help your children to regulate theirs, then there's hope."

"Triggered" is a telling word choice to describe the way we react to our emotions. We say it as though there's something outside us pulling a trigger—your child talked back in a rude tone, or stomped her foot, and that's what triggered your anger. But the trigger is inside us, not out there. We have to take responsibility for our actions rather than shift the blame elsewhere. It may not have felt like a choice, but it surely was—we decide how we'll respond to life's provocations. Don't want to explode in rage every time that kid is disrespectful? Come up with a better way to respond. Clearly, the old way—matching nastiness for nastiness—wasn't working.

So, what does work? This brings us back to the final R of RULER—Regulation, of our own emotional responses and those of our children too. The first step of Regulation, the single most powerful force in our arsenal, is the Meta-Moment. The pause for a breath (or two) when we're about to react in a way we'd really rather avoid.

Pausing to breathe when challenged is an ancient technique for mastering our responses to life. But that's just where the emotion regulation process begins. A breath can deactivate a strong reaction and buy us a second or two to think. But the full Meta-Moment is key.

Okay, so we've inhaled and exhaled deeply and hit the pause button. We covered this in chapter 8. Now what?

Something we call your *best self.*

By that we mean the ideal parent, the one who is kind, loving, patient, nurturing, calm, fair, reasonable, supportive, and encouraging. The same parent who never acts irrationally out of anger or frustration, who is never sarcastic, seething, withering, dictatorial, or scary.

Sounds like most parents, right? I wish. Never going to happen. We're all far too human and fallible for that. But the best self is like a golden ideal we can hold in our heads. We may not be that best self all of the time. We may not even get very close most of the time. But it's important to know *that* person well. It's the one you aspire to be. If during the Meta-Moment we ask ourselves, *How would my best self respond?*, we will at the very least know how we'd like to behave at this critical juncture. And maybe we'll get close this time and even closer the next.

If we try hard enough, we can begin to embody the emotional attributes most parents say they wish to possess, for the sake of their loved ones and themselves. I often ask audiences to complete the following sentence:

I promise to work toward being a parent who is . . .

Here are the most common answers:

- Passionate
- Encouraging
- Inspiring
- Compassionate
- Patient
- Engaged
- Supportive
- Kind
- Understanding
- Loving
- Responsible

It's a pretty good start. What other words would you add to the list?

Here's another way of approaching the ideal of your best self. In the world—at your workplace, in your community, wherever you are known—you have a reputation. If you're like most people, you take it seriously and do your best to maintain it.

We each have a reputation at home too. The "community" there may be quite a bit smaller than how we usually mean that word. But it still fits the definition. In this community, you have a reputation for being kind or patient or understanding or forgiving, or the opposite of those qualities, or somewhere in between. You're known for being quick or slow to anger, easy or hard to talk to, honest and sincere or snarky and sarcastic. You're famous for keeping your promises or forgetting them, for being generous or selfish. You earned your reputation at home the same way you did everywhere else—by your actions.

So, what's your reputation at home? And what did you do (or fail to do) to deserve it?

Remember, your children have been studying you closely since they were newborns. They've read every vocal inflection, facial microexpression, every gesture and touch and body language clue. They sense the vibe that says more than your words ever could.

Thinking about our reputation makes us behave in ways that cause people to admire and respect us. We're willing to be a little bit better than we might otherwise, all for the sake of reputation. Doesn't your family deserve the same effort you give to the rest of the world? You might think about your response to this question: How do you want your children to talk about you when they're older and looking back?

Another way to effectively regulate our emotions is to remind ourselves in advance when they're likely to require regulation. For many of us, reentering home at the end of the day is a potential flash point. At work, we're on our best behavior, which often means sublimating our natural emotional responses and pretending to be the person who is always calm, competent, and in control. It's hard keeping such a tight leash on our emotions. When that day is done, we experience an automatic release. It's palpable, like a big exhale. We can finally be ourselves.

So here you are, headed home at last. Drained. Harried. Possibly hungry. You reach for the doorknob, turn it, and enter into . . . peace and serenity. Calm and tranquility. The loving, nourishing embrace of your family. A release from all your cares and woes.

Well, maybe that's how it goes at your house. If it does, may I congratulate you on being such a shining exception to the rule.

If that's not your typical experience, you may need to find some kind of reminder—something to warn you, maybe just before you walk in the door, that you need to remain cool for the sake of your family, no matter how severely you may be tested. That doorknob, then, becomes an important part of your emotional life. It's the object that reminds you it's time to regulate your emotions, no matter what you encounter on the other side of that door.

Anything can be your personal reminder. I have a friend whose evening commute takes her past the Golden Gate Bridge. She's made that her signpost—every day when she sees it, she knows it's time to begin lowering her emotional temperature. Another acquaintance lives in Manhattan and uses the Statue of Liberty as his talisman. When he sees it on the way home, he automatically starts to power down and prepare for the place where he'll need all his best qualities.

But all these strategies will work only after we've taken that Meta-Moment. It has to become almost second nature. How long will it take for that to happen? More than a day or two? More than a week or a month? If you try hard and apply yourself and hit the pause button as you formulate your response to whatever just triggered you, maybe in six months it will begin to feel like a habit. It's unrealistic to think the Meta-Moment is going to become automatic overnight. I spend most of my life researching and teaching and discussing emotion skills and the Meta-Moment as a tool of the emotionally intelligent person. Yet after a long day of work, when I get home tired and hungry and brain-dead, even *my* skills sometimes go out the window.

There's another tool we can try that usually succeeds in groups where emotion skills are valued: a *charter*. This is a written document or pact that details how everybody in your home wishes to feel. It also includes a list of commitments that everyone in the family will make to one another to create the best possible home environment. Depending on the age of the children, they may need help with the writing part. But even young kids know the right words to use.

The charter is created by asking three questions. The first is: *How do we want to feel as a family?* This question can be asked over an evening meal or, perhaps, over the weekend when there is some downtime. Some of the words we've seen come up frequently among families are loving, respectful, included, safe, happy, calm, grateful, and playful.

The second question is: *What can we do to experience these feelings as often as possible?* You can get highly specific with responses to this question, such as deciding how you'll set the proper mood when it's time to do homework, or at bedtime, or when dinner is served. Some families make a commitment to saying "I love you" each night before bed.

The third question, which gets answered after the charter has been "lived" for a while, is: *What can we do when we are not living the charter?* Again, it's helpful to get specific. For example, if one family member says something that makes another member feel disrespected, what's the best way to express the feeling and settle whatever dispute might have caused it? Many charters include statements like "We will listen carefully without judgment to the person who feels like the charter has been broken."

Simply allowing everyone to help create a charter is empowering. It gives everyone in the home a sense of agency over their emotional environment. In most households, that alone would be a big step forward.

A charter can benefit parents by accommodating their needs too. After a certain hour, adults want to enjoy peace and quiet and no conflicts or excess noise—so the charter requires everyone to respect those wishes. It's a way of reminding children that their parents are human, too, with the same emotional needs as anyone else. In the long run, that's an important lesson for kids to learn, but too many parents try to shield them from that reality. As an unintended result, children have a hard time acknowledging adults' feelings, let alone respecting them.

Putting our emotional needs in writing has a way of making them real for ourselves and everyone else. It acts as a reminder for those times when we feel overwhelmed. It serves like a contract—a formal agreement drafted in a moment of calm consideration, to help you during moments when you are anything but calm and considerate. You may feel a little self-conscious posting a charter on your refrigerator door or hanging it on a wall. But if you try it, you might find that it works.

I'm reminded of an interview I did with a dad at a RULER workshop. "I reamed my six-year-old son, David," he said. "He walked into the kitchen and started bugging me for batteries for his gaming console while I was in the middle of another bickering match with my wife. I was already pissed and David's 'Dad-Dad-Dad-Dad-Dad-Dad' just sent me over the edge. I exploded and sent him to his room. In fact, I half chased him out of the kitchen and up the stairs."

Next morning, while the kids were getting ready for school, the man saw a note next to David's bed, but the handwriting belonged to his son Jason, who was ten. "It was puzzling," the dad said, "so I picked it up and read it. It was a script, showing David how to manage his feelings. *Take three deep breaths. Daddy was just in a really bad mood. He will feel better tomorrow after he rests.*

"It was a wake-up call like nothing I'd ever had in my life," the man said. "My older son, Jason, was learning in school how to handle emotions, and my wife and I realized we'd not only been terrible role models, but we'd been subjecting both our kids to a lot of unnecessary hurt. When I asked Jason how he thought we should have handled it, he said, 'You know, Dad, at school we have a charter to tell us how we all want to feel. Maybe we should have one for home too.'"

Sometimes, during sessions with parents, I'll drag up a difficult moment from my own childhood—when I failed the test for my yellow belt in Hapkido and I took it out on my parents. We turn this into role-play.

Imagine I'm your adolescent son, and I arrive home after failing my martial arts test. I walk into the kitchen yelling and screaming, "I *hate* you. . . . I *hate* Hapkido. . . . I never should have tried taking that test, you knew I wasn't ready but you made me do it. . . . I'm never going back. And I'm not going to school tomorrow *either*!"

Also imagine I'm likely not getting you at a very patient and understanding moment. You worked all day, then had your hour-long commute home. You're beat, you have the beginning of a headache, you're hungry, and now this. You know I need your help to get through this moment. You want to be the parent who is there for your kids when they feel down and defeated.

But instead my bad behavior triggers yours. You ignore what I'm saying, zero in on how I'm saying it, and start yelling right back. It's a reflex action—like a counterpunch. Here are some of the role-play responses parents offer up:

"You are not allowed to talk to me that way!"

"You need to calm down and lower your voice and stop crying over nothing!"

"You're not going to be a quitter. I paid for those lessons and you're going to take them."

"Don't tell me you're not going to school tomorrow, because you *are*! You'll do as you're told!"

Some parents go to the other extreme to sound conciliatory but still trying their hardest not to engage with this child's disappointment and shame.

"You'll be okay, honey. Those teachers don't know what they're doing."

"You know Mom loves you always, no matter what."

"Look, calm down now and I'll take you to the mall after dinner, we'll get you something fun."

"You don't have to go back if you really don't want to."

And here are some of my favorite responses:

"We'll go buy you a yellow belt this weekend. We don't need to wait for your sensei to give it to you."

"How about if we find you a sexy Hapkido coach?"

"Let's go shopping for some new clothes."

After we stop laughing, we go through what highly skilled parents might say:

"It's understandable. I get it and it stinks. How about we take a walk and talk about it?"

"Just stop a second and take a deep breath. I know how upset you are."

"Let me give you a hug."

"It seems like you need some space to calm down. Do you want to go up to your room for a few minutes and we can talk during dinner?"

After the role-play is over, I ask parents about how they felt when that hypothetical child unloaded on them. Here's what they say:

"Like a bomb just went off."

"Like I need my own time-out."

"Desperate and scared."

"I ask myself, '*Why* did I want to be a parent?'"

And this becomes the *a-ha* moment of the exercise: adults come to the seminar to learn strategies for helping their kids regulate their emotions—and then realize that for that to happen, parents first have to regulate their own.

We can boil the entire process of bringing emotional intelligence into your family down to these four steps.

- Step 1: *Set yourself up for success.* Build your family charter! Consider the words on the charter each day. Those adjectives should always be somewhere in your mind. Remember, you have to take the Meta-Moment and be your best self before you can help a child to regulate. You are the role model. Your facial expressions, vocal tones, and body language matter.
- Step 2: *Explore.* Be the emotion scientist—the learner, not the knower—and listen to understand, not to build your own argument. Remember that behavior is the symptom, it's not the emotion. Validate, show unconditional love and support, help to deactivate if necessary. Don't attribute emotions to your child. Allow them to express their feelings. Listen for themes and help them to label.
- Step 3: *Strategize.* Once you know what your child is feeling and have a sense of the situation, you can support with a short-term

strategy: self-talk, reappraisal, a hug, and just being present. The strategy you might want your child to use might not be the strategy that works best for you. And strategies often bomb at first, so your child needs your support to build this muscle. And have long-term strategies ready—from helping your child to problem-solve to seeking professional counseling.

• Step 4: *Follow up*. Emotion regulation is a lifelong journey. History often repeats itself. Kids need regular check-ins and continuous support. Consider: What are the conditions we can create for our children to support their healthy emotional development? How might my best self support my child? And have compassion for yourself and your child. It doesn't mean letting yourself or your child off the hook. It means you approach setbacks in a more constructive way, learning from them instead of beating yourself up.

Here's a good example of that process from my own life. I have a niece, Esme, who was adopted from Guatemala as a baby by my cousin Ellyn, who has red hair and fair skin. I consider Esme my niece because Ellyn is more like my sister than a cousin. When Esme was in kindergarten in upstate New York, one of her classmates said to her, "Eww, you're a different color than your mother!"

Esme was devastated.

Ellyn called me and said, "She was teased about her skin color. Now she's crying and upset that she looks different from me and the rest of her family and all the kids in her school. She doesn't want to go back to school, she says. She's scared. I knew this was going to happen at some point, but I didn't think it would be in kindergarten. I'm losing it and about to get into my jeep and drive over to this kid's house."

Okay, so the first needed step here had nothing to do with Esme— her mother, Ellyn, had to take a Meta-Moment so she could model a healthy response for her daughter. Because that's how it works—our kids watch us intensely and examine everything we do for clues about how they should behave in similar situations.

Ellyn was triggered, understandably. She was like a mother tiger protecting her cub. But if she freaked out, Esme would get the message that even her mom couldn't handle the situation calmly. If Esme was ever going to find a way to navigate this incident or others like it, Ellyn had to show the way.

I wasn't surprised at what had happened. Research shows that about one-third of American kids are bullied at some point, and appearance is the top reason. Children can be cruel when it comes to looking different.

Still, it hurt to know that my five-year-old niece was being attacked for the color of her skin. Given my own childhood struggles with bullying and the anxiety and fear that followed, I had to help her and her mother.

We all owe it to one another to stop bullying when we encounter it. It's not just a matter of a child being mistreated—peer victimization actually changes the biology of the brain. It disrupts the development of the stress regulation system and related neurocircuitry, leading to a host of problems, from physical and mental illness to difficulties with social relationships and academic challenges. And these effects persist well into adulthood, contributing to problems with employment, relationships, and overall quality of life. Bullying isn't just something that happens in playgrounds or on school buses. Its effects never completely go away.

Meanwhile, most of us will face moments like Esme's at some point during our lives. According to someone, we're too fat or too skinny, our nose is too big, we're too dark, not smart enough, not tough enough. These comments devastate us and stick with us long afterward. The lingering self-hate and self-doubt are lacerating.

When a child hears sentiments like that over and over, soon the voice is coming not from the outside but from inside. She's internalized that negative view of herself. When she feels shame, fear, self-loathing, she'll need help to regulate those emotions—a caring adult to help prevent any negative views of herself from holding her back in life.

If Esme had been able to react like an adult, she would have instantly realized she might have been dealing with a racist family, and she might have said something like "Yeah, my mother and I are different colors, so what? Plenty of families have members who are different colors. But why do you care?"

Instead, those vicious words found their mark. We did our best to support Esme's regulation of her hurt feelings. Ellyn's response wasn't textbook perfect. There was no charter in place to guide her. But she did everything else right. She asked Esme the right questions and listened to her answers, like a good emotion scientist. She helped her daughter strategize future responses she could use if anyone tried to shame her again. She reminded Esme that her family was diverse. We all coached her on go-to phrases she could say to herself when she felt uncomfortable. We reached out to her teacher and school principal. Our goal was to lay the groundwork that would support Esme for years to come. Our immediate intervention was not a quick fix, but the beginning of a journey.

Esme carried that wound for a long time, and it wasn't the last time she was made to feel inferior because she was different. But given the careful attention her mom gave to supporting her healthy emotional development, Esme's now a highly resilient and academically successful high school student.

Often, when we're under psychological assault, our default position is surrender—we accept that this negative view of us must be true, and we adopt it as our own. Children do not have the inner strength or knowledge about people and their motivations to be able to say, "Who are you to define me? What gives you the right? Why do you need to belittle me? I reject you and your judgment of me—I know who I am." They need our unconditional adult support.

. . .

As I've said before, the permission to feel begins with the question that Uncle Marvin had the courage to ask me: "How are you feeling?" Likewise, its denial begins with the failure to ask it.

When our children don't have the permission to feel—they still will. But those feelings will go on in the dark, and the pathways between those feelings and their visible manifestations and behaviors will become almost totally obscure. Not only will our children suffer—we'll also have no idea why. (I doubt that scenario sounds unfamiliar.) However, when we support our children to be their full, feeling selves, we'll see how deeply and enduringly they can flourish. And it starts with us as their role models.

10

Emotions at School:
From Preschool to College

DURING SEMINARS FOR EDUCATORS I'll usually ask, "How many of your students receive a comprehensive emotion education from pre-K through high school?"

They all look at me as if I'm from another planet.

Then I'll ask, "How much did *you* learn about emotions in your own schooling?"

I get back a similar look, one that says, You *really* have to ask?

And when I ask what they learned during teacher training about the role of emotions and emotion skills in education, here's what they say:

"I learned how to teach my subject."

"I learned how to make a lesson plan."

"We discussed how to establish an orderly classroom."

"We read a chapter on bullying prevention."

Later, when I speak with those teachers one-on-one and ask how they infuse emotions into the classroom, here's the typical answer:

"Honestly, I make it up as I go."

Unfortunately, that approach is not working very well. If it were, all of our schools would be thriving havens of positivity filled with emotionally healthy teachers and students. Many are not.

The teaching profession is known for being highly rewarding *and* extremely taxing. The pressures of high-stakes testing, large class sizes, supporting a diverse range of learners in their classrooms who have complex needs, inadequate wages, and administrators who are not always supportive contribute to high attrition rates—40 percent of teachers leave the profession within five years, and in some communities the rate is as high as 30 percent annually.

In a survey we distributed to more than five thousand teachers, we found that 70 percent of the emotions they reported feeling each day were negative—mainly "frustrated," "overwhelmed," and "stressed." This is especially troubling because teachers who experience more negative emotions are also more likely to have sleep problems, anxiety, and depression, be overweight and burned out, and have greater intentions to leave the profession.

Those negative emotions also have serious ramifications for students: teachers who are stressed offer less information and praise, are less accepting of student ideas, and interact less frequently with students. If we want children to flourish, we have to begin taking care of our teachers.

As mentioned previously, when we asked twenty-two thousand high school students across the United States, "How do you feel each day in school?," 77 percent of their responses were negative. The three most frequent answers were "tired," "stressed," and "bored." Among all students, LGBTQ students reported the greatest anxiety and depression and the least positive feelings such as acceptance and psychological safety. LGBTQ youths in the United States experience greater rates of bullying, lower academic achievement, and higher dropout rates than their non-LGBTQ peers.

Many of the high school students we surveyed reported feeling that their schools gave little thought to creating an atmosphere where students can actively participate in their education, where they're expected and encouraged to think about a lesson and find meaning in it. One study in Connecticut discovered that thirty-nine thousand students were either disengaged or entirely disconnected from school. It's no wonder that by high school so many students are tuned out.

And as much attention as bullying gets, it continues to go on unabated. Students who are bullied report feeling fear and hopelessness while in school. You'd hope that schools would know how to deal with these extremes of emotional distress, since they happen under the eyes of teachers and administrators. But on the contrary, most teachers report feeling unprepared to deal with classroom bullying. Teachers also miss most incidents of bullying because of where and how it occurs, are unlikely to interfere in disputes between students, and when not trained in emotion skills often base their disciplinary strategies on what they themselves experienced in their childhood at home. The result: A lot of children go unprotected from bullying, as I did. They go through the school day feeling so afraid and ashamed that they can't fully focus in class or develop academically or socially. Even the bullies are ill-served—they tend to have emotional or psychological problems of their own, which go unaddressed and unmediated without appropriate teacher training. And schools are known to overreact to challenging behavior by confusing normal conflicts with bullying or relying on harsh interventions, especially with preschool children and African American boys.

One in five American children is experiencing a mental health issue such as depression or anxiety, and over half of all seventeen-year-olds report having either experienced trauma directly, ranging from neglect to abuse, or witnessed it at least once as a child. By failing to recognize trauma's effects on learning, educators risk compounding the trauma and jeopardizing students' prospects in school. For many children, school might be the only place any of these issues are recognized and addressed.

So even before the doors open, we know there are challenges to creating an atmosphere where all children will feel ready for learning.

It's true—we can't change every child's home environment. But research shows that the presence of a caring adult allows a child to manage stress more effectively. Yet in a study of two thousand teachers, only about 50 percent said they have strong individual relationships with their students. In the same study, two thousand students also were surveyed and only 34 percent reported having such relationships.

Traditionally, feelings and behavior mattered to teachers primarily when students failed to sit still, be quiet, pay attention, and remember what they were taught. Although misbehavior was addressed—disciplined and punished, for the most part—the underlying causes, which are nearly always emotional, were left untouched.

Consider the fact that classroom corporal punishment is still allowed in nineteen states, and suspensions and expulsions, disproportionately applied to black students, have continued to rise. Problems are exacerbated when instructors and staff misunderstand students' emotions and behavior or are unaware of their own biases. And when teachers are not given the support they need and are asking for, there's little reason to hope for improvement.

"From a Nation at Risk to a Nation at Hope" is the title of a January 2019 report from the Aspen Institute's National Commission on Social, Emotional, & Academic Development. It's worth quoting here. It reads:

> The promotion of social, emotional, and academic learning is not a shifting educational fad; it is the substance of education itself. It is not a distraction from the 'real work' of math and English instruction; it is how instruction can succeed. It brings together a traditionally conservative emphasis on local control and on the character of all students, and a historically progressive emphasis on the creative and challenging art of teaching and the social and emotional needs of all students, especially those who have experienced the greatest challenges.

All true. Yet when I talk with administrators, principals, and teachers about the role of schools in providing students with a social and emotional education, here's what I hear:

"We don't have the time or training to deal with the social and emotional challenges my students are facing. They're too complex."

"I don't want our school to spend time teaching about emotions, because that will take away from AP classes and affect whether our students qualify to get into the top universities."

"I'm here to teach. Leave these issues to parents, the ones who *should* be dealing with emotions."

Their fears of what might happen if there's an emotional aspect to education are unfounded. In fact, students are grateful to learn that their teachers are human beings with feelings too.

David Brooks, the *New York Times* columnist, wrote that once, when he was teaching a college course, he announced to his class that he had to cancel office hours to deal with some unspecified "personal issues." Ten or fifteen students emailed him to say he was in their thoughts and prayers. For the rest of the term, he wrote:

"The tenor of that seminar was different. We were closer. That one tiny whiff of vulnerability meant that I wasn't aloof Professor Brooks, I was just another schmo trying to get through life. That unplanned moment illustrated for me the connection between emotional relationships and learning."

He continued:

"A key job of a school is to give students new things to love—an exciting field of study, new friends. It reminded us that what teachers really teach is themselves—their contagious passion for their subjects and students. It reminded us that children learn from people they love, and that love in this context means willing the good of another, and offering active care for the whole person."

Emotion as a part of the learning experience doesn't simply mean that students and teachers will bare their souls and grapple with difficult emotional issues. It also means that students will engage more fully with what they're learning.

Related to this, in two studies we conducted with fifth and sixth graders, we found that when the classroom climate was rated as warm and supportive by outside observers, children reported feeling more connected to their teacher, there were fewer conduct problems, and students' grades were higher.

A colleague, Mary Helen Immordino-Yang, neuroscientist at the University of Southern California, reminded me of a self-evident principle we often forget: Children learn what they care about. They're no different from adults in that regard. We can try to force them to absorb a lesson, but we're not going to accomplish much. Some kids may be able to commit facts to memory and regurgitate them on demand, but that's not the same thing as learning.

Earlier I discussed how brain scientists have found that depending on our emotional state, our chemical and hormonal profiles change dramatically and our brains function differently. The three most important aspects of learning—attention, focus, and memory—are all controlled by our emotions, not by cognition. Immordino-Yang's research shows that when students feel deeply engaged and connected in the learning process, and when what they learn is relevant and meaningful to their own lives, there is activation in the same brain systems (for instance, the medulla) that keep us alive.

Students have no problem addressing emotion skills in the classroom. In fact, they love it. I recently watched a room of fifth graders practice putting RULER skills to use. I told them about the day when I was around their age and failed my karate test and how shattered and dejected I felt. Then I asked them to come up with some emotion regulation strategies they might have suggested had they been my friends that day.

"I would tell you jokes," one student said.

"Okay, that's interesting," I said. "It might lift my mood, at least. What else?"

"I would say let's go get ice cream," said another.

"That would definitely improve my mood," I said, "but what would happen if we did that every time I was disappointed or sad?"

"We'd get sick or fat!"

"Very possible," I said. "What else could you do?"

"I would say keep trying . . . because you miss one hundred percent of the shots you don't take," said another student, quoting the hockey legend Wayne Gretzky.

"I've never heard that line, but I really like it," I said. "That might help me feel better, but what if I'm feeling more hopeless than sad? Like I never will pass the test."

"I'd want to know which moves you messed up," said another student, "and I'd help you practice them."

I wasn't looking for a right answer—I just wanted them to run through all the possible emotion regulation strategies they could imagine.

Meanwhile, their teachers were witnessing this in disbelief. Later, they told me how insecure they were about their ability to teach emotion skills until they realized how much those skills resemble science, math, or any other academic subject. The goal isn't to tell children what to feel or what specific strategy to use to regulate—it's to turn them into caring citizens who are emotion scientists, with tools for gathering important information and putting what they discover to good use.

At the end of the class I said to the students, "Thank you for letting me into your classroom. Does anyone have questions or final thoughts?"

One student said, "I really liked the lesson because *I* was involved."

A boy named Kevin raised his hand, which his teacher told me he never does.

"What would you like to share?" I asked him.

"Sir," he said, "I just wanted you to know that you remind me of myself."

The teacher couldn't believe it. I was deeply moved. Later that afternoon, I learned that Kevin lived across the street from school, alone with his alcoholic mother. He didn't like going home, I was told, because most of the time no one else was there. You can just imagine the emotional issues Kevin brings into the classroom. Is there even a chance that his academic performance is not affected?

I've mentioned my uncle Marvin before and made clear, I hope, what a huge influence and inspiration he's been for me. His presence is in everything I do in my work, but especially when it comes to the role of emotions in the classroom.

Uncle Marvin was a middle school teacher in upstate New York for two decades. He had unusual success with the kids who passed through his sixth-grade classroom. Back then, there were no controlled experiments to confirm his observations, but many of the students he kept track of made it through high school and college without becoming derailed, even in the face of major obstacles.

Marvin had figured out instinctively that something was often missing in a child's journey toward success—the ability to embrace and use emotions wisely. He knew that if we grew up acquiring emotion skills, they would make us better learners, decision makers, friends, parents, and partners, better able to maintain our health and well-being, deal with life's ups and downs, and achieve our dreams.

I knew firsthand, from a young age, that his ideas worked, because they made it possible for me to navigate the extreme bullying and loneliness in my early life. Without him, I would never have made it through middle and high school.

Fast-forward ten or so years. I graduated from college with a major in psychology but was teaching martial arts and working in sales, uncertain about my professional path. That's when I came across the landmark book *Emotional Intelligence* by Daniel Goleman, published in 1995. There was a chapter about the burgeoning field of social and emotional learning (SEL), a term used to describe school-based programs to teach emotional intelligence. A light bulb clicked on. SEL was exactly what Uncle Marvin had been teaching in his classroom way back in the 1970s.

I called my uncle immediately, and within a few weeks we had begun to write a curriculum for middle school students. Together, we were going to marry his decades of experience as an educator with the new psychology of emotional intelligence and transform the schoolhouse.

Goleman's book also introduced me to two researchers, Peter Salovey at Yale University and Jack Mayer at the University of New Hampshire. They were the psychologists who had written the seminal 1990 article on emotional intelligence that formulated the concept itself. I contacted each of them, and they agreed to meet me. At lunch with Salovey, I shared my enthusiasm about writing and testing the curriculum Uncle Marvin and I were creating.

"What's your theoretical model?" he asked me. I had no clue what he was talking about. I had been out of college for a couple of years and had no formal background in social science research.

That year, I got rejected from Yale's doctoral program and accepted at the University of New Hampshire's. Marvin and I continued to work on our curriculum throughout my graduate school years and even more once I eventually got to Yale to work with Salovey as a postdoctoral researcher.

There, I met Edward Zigler, a renowned child psychologist who was known as the father of the federal Head Start program. He was one of the few psychologists at Yale who had a background in public school education. I explained what Uncle Marvin and I were trying to do.

"What's your logic model?" he asked me. Again, I was stumped. I had no idea what he was asking. I thought I had learned my lesson from Salovey and read up on all the theories of emotion in graduate school. But now I had my second wake-up call. I needed to show *why* and *how* RULER would lead to better outcomes for kids and adults.

By 2004, our middle school curriculum was finally finished and ready to be tested. My uncle and I were off like the Wright brothers, trying to make a difference in the world. Marvin flew up from his home in Florida, and together we started recruiting schools and training educators. We had some small successes here and there, but for the most part, here's what we heard:

"Teaching kids about anxiety makes me anxious."

"I'll teach words like happiness and excitement, but I'm not opening the Pandora's box to anything else like despair and despondent."

At one school meeting, a principal said, "You're going to turn the boys into homosexuals." An experienced teacher then said, "My job is not to talk to you *or* my students about feelings," and stormed out. "Does anyone have *another* perspective?" I asked the room. After everyone finished laughing, a young male teacher shouted, "Sir, I was actually a student in this school, and she was *my* teacher. I really wish she would have stayed for this."

At another seminar, a teacher came up to me during a break and said, "Nothing you could say today could help. I'm emotionally bankrupt!" I couldn't stop thinking about what his students must experience in class. Will they develop curiosity and passion? Will they be engaged? Will they even learn?

To be clear, Uncle Marvin and I had some successes, but implementation of our curriculum was uneven at best. The message became more and more apparent: educators were mostly uncomfortable talking about emotions—their own *or* those of their students.

And the leaders set the tone of the school or district. They can make or break any program.

A group of teachers took me aside at an early RULER training and said, "We love this, but our principal has already told us we can't start RULER until after the state tests." I remember thinking: It's August, and the state tests aren't until March. We're all wasting our time.

The CEO of one network of schools said to me, "I want my students to learn facts, not feelings. In my schools, there is no place for feelings. Just teach them to sit still during tests." Ironically, while leaving that school, I overheard a kindergarten teacher yelling at a five-year-old, "Zip it! Go to your seat! We're not friends anymore!"

I left there in shock, wondering, How safe can that child feel in this school? How inspired? How much will that child actually learn today?

In the end, Uncle Marvin and I failed. We were too narrow in our approach. We failed because we focused solely on the students. The missing piece was educators' own emotion skills. In hindsight, it makes perfect sense.

Over time, we learned, as with everything for children, it takes a village. If children are to develop emotion skills, *all* the adults around them need these skills too.

Several years ago, I created an award in honor of my uncle, to recognize educators who exhibit outstanding teaching practices on emotional intelligence. One of Uncle Marvin's former students heard about it and sent me a letter to forward to him. Here, with permission, is what she wrote:

Dear Mr. Maurer,

I am sending this note with the hope that you are well and enjoying the important work that you continue to do with your nephew in the realm of empowering students and teachers.

The class I had with you in 6th grade was, to this day, one of the most meaningful educational experiences I have ever had. Your kindness and ability to personalize learning has inspired me throughout my life in countless ways.

I currently teach second grade in NY and am working on a degree in Educational Administration. I am driven by my desire to fix a broken education system. My focus is on the continuous inequities in standardized testing and the lack of acknowledgment of children's social and emotional needs in the classroom. Unfortunately, we have to justify wanting to teach in a way that allows children to discover who they are as people and learners, and show how powerful it can be when a child's feelings and needs are honored and celebrated. (No easy task, as you know.)

I have two beautiful boys, Jonathon, 11, and Henry, 9. They are both sensitive and kind. As Jonathon begins his middle school adventure in September, I reflect fondly on my experience in your classroom, and only hope that my son can make a similar connection to a teacher that will empower him and teach him the way you taught me.

Quite a tribute to Uncle Marvin and what he tried to accomplish. Compare that with the letter I received from the head psychologist of a network of schools—the same network whose CEO said he wanted students to focus on facts, not feelings. Here, with permission, is the letter:

Hi Marc-

I think that the major roadblock to the successful rollout of RULER and our other SEL initiatives is the lack of training and understanding of child development, social-emotional health, and appropriate expectations and needs of students by the people that are making the decisions. Very few people at the top have any training in these areas.

I was told just yesterday by a principal that nobody in our network cares about a child's confidence, emotional well-being, mental health, integrity, overall success as a person (characteristics I brought up specifically)—they only care about test scores. That is what they are judged on, and that is the message that they are sending to our kids. The focus is punitive ("effort" academy during recess and after school for children who don't have high scores or who make errors like not underlining the evidence or finishing in the time limit) with the expectation that teachers should use "a punishment so severe" that the children never engage in those behaviors again. My questions about this approach were met with a comment about whether or not this is the right place for me since that is the direction the network is moving.

That's what we're up against.

. . .

Thankfully, many educators have begun to recognize what's missing. According to a 2018 survey by McGraw-Hill Education, an overwhelming majority of administrators, teachers, and parents believe that SEL is just as important as academic learning. But at the same time, 65 percent of teachers said they need more time than they currently have to teach emotion skills. The most effective educators recognize that social, emotional, and academic learning are intertwined. Yet there is a disconnect between what we expect teachers to know about SEL and the offerings of teacher training programs in colleges and universities. Few teacher preparation programs fully integrate SEL into the curriculum.

So what exactly does a school that prioritizes SEL look like? That's been the big question in educational circles over the past two decades or so, ever since we realized that many kids and schools were struggling with problems such as violence, drugs, inadequate learning, and teacher attrition.

Here's a definition: It's a school where "children and adults understand and manage emotions, set and achieve positive goals, feel and show empathy for others, establish and maintain positive relationships, and make responsible decisions."

That definition comes from a group called the Collaborative for Academic, Social, and Emotional Learning (CASEL), which was formed in 1994 with the goal of "establishing high-quality, evidence-based social and emotional learning as an essential part of preschool through high school education." SEL recognizes that three intertwined factors—cognition, behavior, and emotion—must all be considered in order to create emotionally healthy environments where learning can take place. According to CASEL, when that happens, children are able to "build self- and social-awareness skills, learn to manage their own emotions and behavior (and those of others), make responsible decisions, and build positive relationships."

Since the inception of CASEL, numerous approaches and programs have emerged with the goal of creating an equitable education system for all children irrespective of race, ethnicity, gender, sexual orientation, language disability, family background, family income, citizenship, or tribal status. Not all have succeeded. Some attempted only to teach children self-esteem, thinking that would be enough. It turns out that giving kids unmerited praise backfires and can even decrease intrinsic motivation. Other programs have focused on teaching scripts like "I feel . . ." statements, where teachers and children are told to declare their emotions using sentences beginning with those two words. But these statements alone don't guarantee everyone will develop emotion skills or that SEL will be embraced as a consistent part of teaching and learning.

The best SEL approaches are systemic, not piecemeal

SEL has to have buy-in from the top and the bottom. If the principal is less than completely committed, teachers will get the message, and students will be shortchanged by half-hearted efforts. Leaders need to make room for ongoing professional development—all the adults in the school must learn the skills so they can be role models for kids. Teachers at each grade level need to understand social, emotional, and cognitive development and be steeped in culturally responsive pedagogy. Teachers have to recognize that they're the students' primary role models during the school day. Not just when the subject is SEL—all the time. And students must have a voice in how SEL is implemented; if it's not relevant and meaningful to their particular circumstances, it will fail.

Research shows that teachers with more developed emotion skills report less burnout and greater job satisfaction; they also experience more positive emotions while teaching and receive more support from the principals with whom they work. The presence of emotionally intelligent leaders also makes a difference. When school leaders have emotion skills, the teachers in their buildings report feeling more inspired, less frustrated and burned out, and more satisfied with their job. In turn, teachers' relationships with their students are warmer; their class-rooms are better organized and managed and more supportive; and they use more practices that cultivate creativity, choice, and autonomy. And when children have better relationships with their teachers, they are more engaged and committed to school, adjust better socially, and are willing to take on more challenges and persist in the face of dif-ficulty. They also disrupt less, focus more, and perform better academi-cally.

SEL can't be addressed only in a ten-minute morning meeting or every Thursday, fourth period. It can't be isolated in occasional assem-blies for students or in workshops for teachers. SEL has to be an ev-eryday thing—it has to become part of the school's DNA. There needs to be a common language among all stakeholders. SEL has to be in-tegrated into leadership, instruction, faculty meetings, family engage-ment, hiring procedures, and policies.

In regard to classroom instruction, students watch their teachers closely, paying attention to each facial expression, every gesture, the rise and fall of their voices. They're constantly picking up information on how teachers feel about the topic, about teaching, about them as students. That emotional subtext exists in every lesson ever taught—whether the teacher intends it or not.

If students are going to learn, they need to feel the teacher's emo-tional investment. History can be boring or it can be exhilarating. Geometry can be confusing or awe-inspiring. Foreign languages can shut students down or open doors to exciting new worlds. The subjects themselves don't change, the emotion the teacher infuses into the les-son does.

At the best RULER schools, every adult walks the walk—not just teachers, principals, and guidance counselors but also security per-sonnel, cafeteria workers, janitors, and bus drivers. There's a school in Seattle where the attendance officer has a huge Mood Meter on the wall behind her desk. The kids often race into school late and flustered. When they enter her office, she slows them down, and they plot their feelings. That alone has a way of calming students' nerves. Together they explore different strategies to help them prepare emotionally to enter the classroom. In some schools, there are even Mood Meters on the buses, and as kids board, they check in and consider whether that's a helpful emotional space for beginning the school day.

Even the building has to be part of the effort. I'm thinking of the schools I've visited where, right inside the entrance, the vision and mission statements make it clear that SEL is part of the education, and there is a huge Mood Meter with feeling words in multiple languages. Inside classrooms, there are student creations reflecting a strong commitment to the diverse backgrounds of students, including self-portraits surrounded by adjectives representing their best-self attributes.

Classroom seating arrangements also have an influence. How creative or inspired would you feel if you spent all day sitting and staring at the back of a colleague's head? Typical school architecture sends an emotionally rigid message of its own. Schools need to allow for some flexibility and acknowledge the human need for connection with our peers.

Beyond the classroom, we've collaborated with organizations such as Playworks, which helps schools to figure out how to integrate SEL into recess with games and sports. And we've worked with the Boys & Girls Clubs of America to expand opportunities for SEL skill building to after-school time. I often think about how scared and unsafe I felt on the playground during recess and in my after-school program and what would have been different if the adults in these spaces were emotion scientists.

Comprehensiveness also means SEL goes home. When I was a kid, conversations with my parents about school went something like this:

"How was school?"

"Fine."

End of discussion.

But in schools that engage families, conversations go more like this one, which was shared with me by a parent:

"Hey, Mom, I just learned a new word, *alienation,* because we are studying the civil rights movement. We had to think about what makes us feel alienated. I thought about the time I wasn't chosen to be on the baseball team. It was the worst feeling to be left out and not know why. What makes you feel alienated, Mom?"

"Actually, honey, it's a really good question. I feel that way a lot of the time at work. I'm the only female officer in my precinct, and so I don't get invited to do a lot of things with the other officers."

That mother told me that she hadn't really thought about how isolated she felt at work until her son started her talking. Not only did it help them bond, but it was a big moment for her personally. As a result, she decided to talk to her lieutenant about it.

The best SEL efforts are proactive, not reactive

Being proactive means we don't wait for problems to arise and then deal with them—we adopt measures to prevent them.

Not many kindergartners will raise their hands and say, "Excuse me, I don't feel emotionally supported in this classroom." Most high schoolers won't go to the principal to complain, "I feel anxious and fearful during most of my classes, and I need some strategies to deal with that." Our schools have to take the initiative. They have to make it clear to every student that emotion skills are an integral part of their education.

How does that work? In practical terms, at some point during the first couple weeks of school, a teacher might say, "Everyone, we all know that emotions matter, so let's talk about the feelings that we all want to experience as students in this classroom." That opens up the discussion for building their *Emotional Intelligence Charter.* The point of the exercise is to have students describe how they want to feel, including how they'll help one another feel those emotions, to give them control over their classroom environment. In some schools this means a shift in mindset, from following rules to creating an emotionally safe space of their own. It's an act of hope, a switch from a passive to an active voice.

Younger children say they wish they felt happier, safer, calmer. Older students have more nuanced needs: they want to feel empowered, respected, motivated, supported, trusted.

In every grade, students love it—being asked for their input is something of a novelty. All day long, year after year, their emotions are bottled up, and suddenly here comes a teacher wondering what they're feeling, how they want to feel, and what they'll do to get there.

Leaders, teachers, and staff go through the same process. Typically, they'll say they wish to feel more valued, appreciated, inspired, connected, and supported. Many of their desired emotions are the same ones named by students. It makes me wonder: Is there something missing in the school environment as it's been constructed over the course of decades and centuries—something both students *and* teachers need?

The information that is gathered is then turned into a visual display— often a large, creative poster—which everyone signs. Once that's complete, and routines are formed, adults and kids are more willing to share feelings and speak up when they feel the need.

Here's an example. "We were playing at recess and another girl— she was new—came over and tried to join in," said Callie, an eight-year-old from Seattle. "We didn't really want her to play with us, but then we thought about our classroom charter and how all of us agreed that everyone should feel *included*. If we didn't let her play with us, then we'd be breaking the charter, and she would feel bad. If the same thing happened to us, we would feel left out and lonely. So, we made room for her to join. We had a lot more in common with her than we thought."

The most effective approaches integrate SEL into the curriculum and provide skill building across *all* grade levels to reach *all* children

Of course, how SEL is taught and learned depends on age, but there is no age at which it is too early or too late to start. And when students come to school having lived through multiple traumatic events or from homeless shelters or temporary housing, as one in ten New York City public school students do, they often require additional support from a school psychologist, social worker, or counselor.

SEL needs to be culturally responsive. For example, in New York City there are more than 160 different languages spoken by students and their families. Programs that are developed within a Western culture may not address cultural subgroups adequately and might even alienate students from different backgrounds, because how people express and regulate emotions varies greatly across cultures.

The most comprehensive SEL interventions focus on developing social and emotional skills through classroom topics, conversations, and activities that relate to students' interests, needs, relationships, and lives—in and out of school. For example, in one RULER classroom I visited in Tulsa, a book about the Holocaust, *The Boy in the Striped Pajamas,* was used to teach emotion skills. Students tracked and analyzed different characters' emotions throughout the story, providing evidence from the text for the possible causes and consequences of the emotions and their impact on each character's decision making and relationships. Students also made connections to their own lives and their larger community.

Development matters too. The way our brains process emotions and emotion skills is inextricably linked to our social and cognitive development. For example, five-year-olds might learn about sadness and pride, fifth graders about hopelessness and elation, and middle schoolers about jealousy and envy.

In secondary school, SEL needs to match the unique developmental needs of adolescents, who want more autonomy as they explore topics such as identity, relationships, and decision making. At a Los Angeles middle school, students created a Mood Meter journal to track their feelings at the end of each class for two weeks and then analyzed the data, including the causes and consequences of their feelings. The goal was to look for patterns of emotions related to time of day, day of week, and subject area in school. Students also monitored their sleep, exercise, and eating habits to help them make greater inferences from their own data. Then they considered helpful emotion regulation strategies and made other recommendations for how they could perform at their best. The project culminated in a personal plan to enhance student well-being. It also was a great example for how SEL can be integrated seamlessly with English-language arts, math, science, or health classes—and the real world.

At the heart of our high school approach is helping students answer three big questions. The first is: Who am I? Here, students explore their personality traits and motivation, among other competencies. The second question is: What do I want out of my high school career? Here, students explore their goals for their relationships, academics, and extracurricular activities. The third question is: What do I need to achieve my goals and support my well-being?

Students continue to learn strategies to build empathy and for managing interpersonal conflict. Jorge and Ali were close friends at a Chicago high school. As with other fifteen-year-old males, their joking often became physical. On the way to soccer practice, Ali was texting a new girlfriend. Jorge tried to see, but Ali wanted his privacy. He raised the phone high over his head, shouting, "Dude, cut it out! You're worse than my little brother."

Jorge forced Ali's arm down, grabbed the phone, and dashed through the locker room door, taunting Ali to catch him. Ali's backpack got caught on the door handle, and while he struggled to free himself, Jorge decided to rub it in by throwing a dirty sneaker at him.

Immediately, Ali tore himself out of his backpack, leaving it swinging from the doorknob. He ran toward Jorge in a rage that stunned everyone in the locker room. The coaches had to pull Ali off Jorge as he was about to punch him in the face.

The boys were brought to the administration office.

"Guys, I know you're good friends," the assistant principal said upon entering the office, "and you know we have tools for dealing with this. Ali, you sit here outside of the office, and Jorge, take that empty chair in the waiting area. Let's take some calming breaths and then I'm going to ask you to complete these 'Emotionally Intelligent Blueprints,' and I'll come back for you in about five minutes."

The lists of prompts on the blueprint required each boy to say how the other might have felt, the possible cause of the feelings, and how each of them expressed and regulated their emotions. The act of taking each other's perspectives helped Jorge and Ali move from the red quadrant to the green, so they could begin to think clearly.

When they were finished, the assistant principal brought them back together and said, "Okay, let's hear what each of you wrote. And remember, no interruptions or judgment."

Ali explained that in Iraq, where he was born, throwing a shoe at someone was the worst possible insult you could hurl. As he spoke, Jorge realized his mistake. "I'm really sorry. I truly didn't know. I won't do it again. I promise," he said.

Ali and Jorge collaborated on strategies they could use in the future to manage their feelings more effectively. As a follow-up, the boys worked together on a class presentation comparing Middle Eastern and Spanish cultures, making it a restorative practice for them and the class.

In addition to classroom content, we've collaborated with Facebook to build inspirED, a free resource center to elevate student voices and empower high school students in creating positive changes in their schools and communities. Students follow a four-step process, with resources and tools to support each phase: (1) Assessing their school climate with a variety of measures; (2) Brainstorming passion projects to serve their school communities; (3) Committing to and completing a plan; and (4) Debriefing their successes and impact.

The best SEL approaches pay attention to outcomes

Monitoring the progress and impact of SEL is an integral part of implementation. Is it working? Are people delivering the lessons? Are expected outcomes improving?

Over the last decade, evidence has accumulated for RULER's positive impact on students' emotional intelligence skills, social problem-solving ability, work habits, and grades; on classroom and school climate, including fewer instances of bullying; and on teacher stress, burnout, and instructional support for students. Two meta-analyses have also demonstrated that a systematic process integrating SEL is the common element among schools that report improved relationships between teachers and students, a decrease in emotional challenges and problematic behavior, and an increase in academic success. The benefit can even be measured in dollars and cents. In 2015, a benefit-cost analysis of six SEL interventions in American schools found that the ratio was about eleven to one. A benefit-cost analysis compares the monetary cost of an investment (implementing an SEL program) with the monetary value of its outcomes (for example, education attainment). This means that, on average, for every dollar invested in SEL, there is a return of eleven dollars, a substantial economic return.

The difference between schools that embed SEL and those that don't can be endlessly studied. But there's one example that never ceases to move me.

A boy named Jordan had transferred into a RULER school from an elementary school where he was horrifically bullied. As part of a RULER lesson, he was assigned to write a poem about the word *isolated*, using it in the context of his feelings—almost like a letter to the bullies who once tormented him. He wrote the poem but was afraid to share it—he feared he'd be bullied all over again. His teacher, who was trained in RULER, asked him if she could share the poem with her colleagues. Reluctantly, he agreed and got compliments, which gave him the courage to read his poem aloud to his fellow students.

Here, with his permission, is his poem:

You're ugly
I know
I have been told this

You're silly
I know
I have realized this
You look like an alien
I know this has been pointed out to me
You have big eyes
I know I have looked in the mirror
You can't be a pilot
You're not smart enough
It is possible. I have considered this
With every insult you invent it's strange but it's true
You point out my many failings
And help me to improve
As you highlight my many weaknesses you also highlight my strengths
My openness leads to my kind personality
My silliness brings laughter to the world
My resemblance to movie aliens only highlights my intelligence
My big eyes portray my feelings and widen my view
I may not make it as a pilot, but I could be
You see, every insult you invent gives me a view into your mind
And although I have many problems, I feel sorry for you
Why oh, why do I feel sorry for you?
Because your mind cannot break free
The wall of insults you build limits your mind and feelings
So soon if you don't stop, you'll turn inhuman
And have the biggest problem of all
Loneliness
Think about it

Within seconds of Jordan reciting the last line, his classmates shot straight out of their seats, teary eyed and clapping—a standing ovation he never expected.

"We can't believe this happened to you," one told him. "It's not like that here." Once he realized that his new school was a safe haven, Jordan blossomed.

In fact, when I visited the school a year later, I ran into him in the cafeteria. He told me excitedly, "I'm doing a lot of writing, and I think I want to be a poet." When I nodded, he came back with a large stack of papers and a broad grin. Before he turned away, he said confidently, "Look for me on the bookshelves."

Had Jordan been in a school that wasn't devoted to SEL, perhaps he would have found a sensitive teacher who would recognize what he needed after his previous horrible experience. But, perhaps not—in which case he'd likely go the rest of his life without ever confronting what had happened to him or knowing that he could and should feel safe and a worthy contributor to society. If we truly believe in the mission of SEL, Jordan's poem is a testament that key outcomes go far beyond test scores and must include how students feel in school.

And how do all the issues we see in schools play out once our kids get to college? Pretty much how you'd expect.

According to a report by the Center for Collegiate Mental Health, between 2009 and 2015, the number of students who visited campus counseling centers increased by more than 30 percent. Anxiety and depression are the top reasons students seek out counseling.

In 2018, the World Health Organization released findings from a study of nearly fourteen thousand students from nineteen colleges in eight countries. More than one in three students reported symptoms consistent with at least one mental health disorder, mostly depression, anxiety, and substance abuse. The 2018 Healthy Minds Study found that 23 percent of college students are taking psychiatric medication, up from 18 percent in 2016. In another survey, 87 percent of college students said they "felt overwhelmed," and 63 percent said they "felt very lonely."

In my own nonclinical research, especially at Ivy League institutions,

I've found that at the beginning of a semester, college students experience a healthy mix of pleasant and unpleasant emotions—excitement and anxiety, happiness and exhaustion, pride and fear. But by midterms, they mostly feel stressed, overwhelmed, and frustrated. When I probe for the reasons, they say things like "I don't believe you can be successful without being stressed," or "I must persevere at all costs," or "I have to look out for number one." Their strategies for managing these emotions—sleep deprivation, excessive video-gaming, poor eating habits, drug and alcohol consumption—are not helping. Recently, I asked students to share how they hoped to feel at college. The top answer was "loved." When I asked why, they said, "I feel manufactured," "I feel like an impostor," "I don't know who I am." I was floored.

Our traditional approach has been to address students' mental health issues after the fact. They are diagnosed with anxiety or depression or say they are thinking about suicide. Then they are offered medication or therapy. But colleges, like primary and secondary schools, need to take a preventive approach. How will there ever be enough resources to provide counseling for all of the college students who need it?

But integrating SEL into higher education is a challenge. Unlike the K–12 setting, where it's easier to take a systemic approach, the college or trade school structure presents bigger obstacles for teaching SEL skills, given the sheer size of student populations and the distant nature of relationships between faculty, college counselors, and students.

As a result of how higher education is structured, piecemeal approaches abound: some colleges have created "relaxation stations" that include massage chairs and beanbags, while others offer yoga and mindfulness classes. But a more systemic approach is absent.

I've found that students often arrive at college with interesting mindsets about SEL training. For example, I've taught a university course called Emotional Intelligence for nearly a decade. It's classified as an academic course, but my goal is to teach students evidence-based practices to support their well-being and to help them develop the "soft" skills employers are asking for. But I get serious pushback from many students. In my class here is what I've heard:

"I didn't need these skills to get into Yale."

"Now you want me to put emotion regulation on my already long to-do list?"

"I took this class to learn about the science of emotional intelligence, not to practice breathing exercises!"

At that point I needed a Meta-Moment to stop myself from saying, "You might not have needed them to get in, but you'll need them to get out." Instead, I explained how only 42 percent of top employers believe new graduates are adequately prepared for the workforce, especially with respect to social and emotional skills. One survey, "The Class of 2030 and Life-Ready Learning"—conducted in collaboration with Microsoft and McKinsey & Company's Education Practice—suggests that 30 to 40 percent of today's jobs will require social and emotional competencies. I also explain that among college students there is a "restriction of range" of IQ scores, which means that IQ no longer has much predictive value. In other words, it's not a high IQ that gets you places. It's the social and emotional skills that give today's college students the competitive edge.

If university students are to achieve the benefits of SEL, they must be convinced that learning and practicing the skills makes a difference. At Yale, my colleague Emma Seppälä, author of *The Happiness Track,* and I have piloted a few SEL interventions. In our first study with more than two hundred undergraduates, students reported less stress and burnout, higher self-compassion and acceptance of their emotions, and greater school engagement after a six-week intervention. In a pilot study conducted by a graduate student in public health, sixty-seven students were divided into two groups. One group (the intervention group) was asked to track their moods, using our Mood Meter app, up to six times per day, for four weeks. The other group (the control group) did "business as usual" (until after the study, when they got the same access to the Mood Meter app). The intervention group also attended a weekly two-hour class focused on developing emotional intelligence skills, practicing self-care, and goal setting. Compared with the students in the control group, those in the intervention group had significant reductions in depression, stress, and anxiety and a significant increase in self-rated mindfulness (for instance, feeling more present). This year, we are launching our first ever randomized controlled trial to test the effectiveness of our approach.

What's most telling from the study were student anecdotes:

"I learned that being vulnerable opens up wonderful opportunities for friendships and deeper connections. I learned that sometimes you have to be as gentle with yourself as you are with others, and be as understanding with others as we are sometimes of ourselves."

"I wish this class could continue as long as possible because I fear that this peace that I feel will drift away, but I must have hope that I will take the lessons with me always."

"Calm, serenity, focus, and overall happiness are all within my reach, so long as I interiorize the wisdom gathered in this workshop."

"This class gave me a sense of waking up from a long dream. I had this feeling of not actually being alive or 'here' for many years, and now I feel that I am out of my slumber. If I had to describe the way I saw my life in colors, before it would be a pale gray, and now it would be a bright white. Almost as if I had a new blank canvas to put vibrant colors on, this workshop taught me that one can improve and detoxify oneself through putting attention and awareness on one of the most basic principles of living."

What I hear in all this is a cautionary tale: We're not doing these kids justice in supporting their emotional development. So by the time they're young adults in college, they're suffering from the absence of an education in emotions.

Whether it's cyberbullying or guns, pressure to do drugs or to be thin, helicopter parents or neglectful ones, learning differences or identity struggles, our kids' brains are overwhelmed with emotion, cutting off pathways to higher reason and learning . . . unless they know how to handle all of the emotions that come along with these situations. And when kids are on a hamster wheel of achievement—test scores, volunteering, tutoring, advanced placement classes—it puts SEL at the bottom of the list.

SEL is the universal life jacket, keeping students afloat and open to learning. Only when children learn in psychologically safe environments that nurture their emotion skills can they can move from helplessness to resilience, from anxiety to action, from scattered to centered, from isolated to connected.

But, as my colleague Dena Simmons, assistant director of our center, has espoused, SEL must be grounded in a larger context of equity and justice efforts to ensure *all* children, especially the most marginalized, have the opportunity to thrive and take greater control over the direction of their lives. With SEL, we can raise youths who are academically strong as well as kind, compassionate, resilient, and successful, all at the same time. We can raise kids who are able to collaborate, follow through, and bounce back after failing. With SEL, we can model and teach that confidence, vulnerability, passion, and achievement are inextricably linked.

Over the years, our center has moved from working with individual schools and districts to building citywide and statewide approaches. In New York City, we have trained and coached nearly every superintendent. At present RULER has been integrated into about a quarter of the seventeen hundred public schools. In Connecticut, with generous support from the Dalio Foundation, Hartford Foundation for Public Giving, Seedlings Foundation, and Tauck Family Foundation, among others, and in collaboration with policy makers and organizations such as the Connecticut Association of Public School Superintendents and Connecticut Association of Boards of Education, we have launched an initiative, "Making Connecticut the First Emotionally Intelligent [Education] State!" Our goal is to bring the principles and practices of SEL into every school and after-school program in the state, to ensure that all five hundred thousand–plus students, eighty-five thousand educators and staff, and families benefit from an education in emotion skills.

Until SEL permeates the entire school village and community leaders become a vocal, energized force for SEL, it won't occupy its proper place. This is the tough lesson Uncle Marvin and I learned: only when everyone demonstrates that SEL matters will politicians, school boards, and administrators pay attention and make the necessary effort. That commitment filters into the classroom, the cafeteria, the gymnasium, the playground, the school bus, to the principals and teachers and aides and guidance counselors, to parents, and, ultimately, to the benefit of all.

When we unlock the wisdom of emotions, we can raise heathy kids who will both achieve their dreams and make the world a better place.

11

Emotions at Work

It's easy to see why the workplace might be an emotionally challenging environment.

After all, we spend half our waking hours there, surrounded by people we didn't choose to hang around with and who don't necessarily share our habits, our values, or our tastes. And yet we need to get along with them, and find a way to cooperate and collaborate, or risk being unhappy—and possibly unsuccessful—adults. The very means by which we support ourselves and our families is dependent on how we perform in this arena. And unlike at school, in the workplace there's no graduating—we're in this for the long haul, as in decades. We'll enter in our youth and exit, most of us, on the cusp of old age.

No wonder the emotional stakes are so high.

We think of work as being driven by skill sets and information, by brainpower and experience, and by the hunger for achievement and accomplishment. All those things are in the mix, of course. But emotions are *the* most powerful force inside the workplace—as they are in every human endeavor. They influence everything from leadership effectiveness to building and maintaining complex relationships, from innovation to customer relations. In chapter 2 we discussed how our cognitive abilities—what we focus on, where we devote our efforts, what we remember, how we make decisions, our levels of creativity and engagement—all depend on our emotional state. And as we've seen in chapters 4 through 8, our ability to use those emotions wisely—to recognize, understand, label, express, and regulate them effectively—often determines the quality of our relationships, health, and performance.

So let's start by thinking about the moment you wake up. Are you glad at the thought of getting out of bed and off to your job, or do you want to pull the covers over your head and hide? Picture the handful of co-workers with whom you come into contact most often. Do you smile at the thought of these encounters or groan inside? In the office or shop or factory, do the hours fly by as you immerse yourself in the challenges and pleasures of your job, or are you watching the clock and praying for a fire drill? Those are all unmistakable signs of your emotional state while at work, which will have a major impact on how you feel and behave even when you're not working.

Now ask yourself: How accurate are you at identifying your own and others' emotions while at work? What feelings do you experience most often each day? Are you aware of what causes you—and your colleagues—to be in the yellow, red, blue, and green? What are the unwritten rules in your workplace to guide how emotions are expressed? Which expressions are acceptable? Frowned upon? How much emotional labor is required to meet your work demands? How skilled are you at regulating your own emotions and supporting others in regulating theirs?

A woman I know was in the habit of arriving early at the office and starting work while the place was silent and empty. She loved the solitude and accomplished a lot in a short amount of time, but once her colleagues punched in, it was a different story. When she was forced to interact with her co-workers, she got more and more drained, and the hours began to drag. Often, after work, her husband would suggest dinner out, but most nights all she wanted to do was go home and decompress alone, with a book and a glass of wine.

After going through our training, she realized what was happening: she would start work in the yellow quadrant, energized and positive, but gradually move into the green and then, by the end of the day, into the blue—low energy and negative. That emotional shift was taking its toll on her marriage and her home life. It was time to begin regulating her feelings throughout the day, to employ the strategies necessary to avoid ending each day in the blue. That way she would have enough cognitive resources to devote to her job *and* maintain a healthy relationship with her husband.

That just underscores how much our work lives and our emotional lives intersect and commingle. It doesn't matter if you're the CEO of General Motors or you work at a car wash, your emotional needs—to belong and feel seen and heard—are the same. And just because you're twenty-five and brilliant and just got hired at Goldman Sachs or Facebook doesn't mean you excel at emotional intelligence or will be able to function optimally at home *or* in the workplace.

Today especially, when so many jobs require the ability to communicate, our emotion skills determine how we'll perform. If we can't recognize and understand our own feelings, label them, and then express and regulate them successfully, we'll struggle. Many of us are interacting with other people—colleagues, customers, counterparts at other firms—and if we can't empathize with them, and use that information to co-regulate *their* emotions, we won't be effective. If we can't find grounds for friendly collaboration, it will be almost impossible for most of us to do our jobs well.

On the surface, all our workplace interactions are about work—we're in a planning meeting, we're exchanging information about a new project, we're sharing research on a joint venture, negotiating a contract, exploring a partnership. But those interactions take place within relationships often forged in nonwork moments: a bit of small talk on the elevator, or swapping restaurant advice, or sharing some office gossip, and so on. A workplace is a community like any other. The professional friendships born of personal moments make our work easier and more pleasant or the opposite.

Your new colleague is a joy to be around and has made your job more enjoyable than you thought possible? Wonderful. Your boss is a manipulative bully who likes making your day difficult? Not so good. These are typical workplace minidramas, and like it or not, you're involved—emotionally. You'll have to take the bad with the good and deal with it. Developing emotional intelligence will help. And creating an emotionally intelligent ecosystem will yield even greater benefits.

Everything that happens at work is, at heart, an emotional moment. "I deserve a promotion" means I think I'm worth more to you than you realize (and if I don't get that new title, I'll feel unappreciated and look for another job). The tenor of our face-to-face encounters, the location of my office, how you greet me on the elevator—these all are expressions of how you feel about me, which will determine how I feel about you.

"Businesslike" is a total misnomer—beneath the veneer of our corporate mission, business is anything *but* businesslike.

Research shows that our emotions and moods transfer from one person to another and from one person to an entire team—both consciously and unconsciously. It's called "emotional contagion," and its study dates back to the 1890s. Someone smiles and you smile back, or someone frowns and your expression changes, and suddenly you feel happy or sad without knowing why. Sigal Barsade, a professor at the Wharton School, University of Pennsylvania, conducted the first study to test whether emotion contagion occurred in groups and whether it subsequently predicted people's behavior in the group. Study participants were randomly assigned to four different groups, each representing one quadrant in the Mood Meter. A trained confederate, acting as a participant, was assigned to each group to elicit the appropriate feeling. Participants were told they were playing a manager who was responsible for negotiating a bonus for an employee. Each group also knew they had a fixed pot of money and needed to consider what was best for both the employee and the company. Results showed not only that the confederate elicited the emotional contagion but that it also influenced subsequent behavior. Specifically, participants in the yellow and green quadrants reported less conflict, greater cooperation, and better individual performance, and they even allocated money more evenly compared with the participants in the red and blue quadrants.

As we develop emotion skills, hopefully we become more aware of how we are actively creating emotional contagion and understand its impact on others. We also need to ask ourselves: Am I generating the best emotion to achieve the best outcomes for our group?

Recently I interviewed my colleague David Caruso on the role of emotions in effective leadership. It's critical, he said, to match the emotion to the task at hand. He talked about a product development meeting he attended where the manager was energetic and positive. His mood was infectious and useful during the brainstorming part of the meeting. But later, when the group turned its attention to detailed product plans and market data, that same enthusiasm wasn't so helpful. The high-energy, confident vibe that encouraged creative new ideas resulted in a launch schedule that was overly optimistic and riddled with hasty mistakes. This was a case of an emotion not facilitating the kind of problem solving required. After realizing what had gone wrong, the team leader changed the emotional tone of the room but did it in a way that was barely detectable: she used the tone of her voice and the cadence of her speech to lower the energy level and provided examples of the importance of getting details right. This allowed the product manager to slow his thinking, become more reflective, and check his assumptions. Emotions, Caruso said, flow throughout organizations. Leaders must understand the role of those emotions in influencing how people decide, think, and work toward their goals.

The organization itself must also enable individuals to influence emotions. "Having the skills is one thing," Jochen Menges, a leadership scholar at the Universities of Cambridge and Zurich, shared with me recently. "But it's another to be able to apply the skills at work." According to his research, emotionally intelligent workplaces are distinguished by how people *behave* at work, and that behavior is heavily influenced by *structure*—the way people are organized, meaning hierarchies—and by *culture*—what people believe is appropriate. If the people in charge are not drawing on their emotional intelligence in how they convey themselves and manage others, who will?

But if emotional intelligence is so necessary in the workplace, how are we supposed to acquire it? In school, emotion skills can be integrated into the subjects already being taught. After all, education is school's sole purpose. It's trickier to develop new emotion skills in the workplace. When exactly would that training happen? During our coffee breaks? Over lunch? A yearly retreat? We're not at work to learn—we're there to *do*. Businesses have invested millions into "emotional intelligence training and development programs." But I've yet to see a *comprehensive* program in an organization that helps employees improve their emotional intelligence in a way that builds lasting habits. That's one reason I cofounded Oji Life Lab, which offers emotional intelligence training to businesses. In a carefully designed sequence of bite-size learning steps, learners develop emotion skills through a wide range of thought-provoking activities including fast-paced videos, an interactive Mood Meter, personal reflections, and engaging exercises. The program even includes live video discussions with a trained coach, in both group and one-on-one settings. By exploring emotion skills over time, people retain more and develop habits that become automatic.

Even when modern organizational thinking attempts to introduce these skills into the workplace, employers often resent it for taking time and focus away from the bottom line. Many managers still don't get it—that the bottom line depends on a workforce that's motivated, energized, and committed to a common goal.

I recently spent some time consulting at a company where the relationship between two key executives was causing a serious problem. Both were skilled and good at their jobs. But one was by nature anxious, and she took every reaction and feedback to heart. The other was a loud, outspoken man who always said whatever came to mind, without stopping to think how it would be received. You can see how that combination might clash, and it did. Neither of them had the emotion skills to recognize what was going on and attempt to control the situation by talking it out and regulating their reactions to each other. Every interaction was tense and not as productive as it should have been.

That left it to their supervisor to try to mediate these very different temperaments. Not exactly how the boss wanted to spend her time, but if she didn't help those two regulate their emotions, the work in their department would have suffered.

These interactions play out constantly in business situations. Think about what happens when you sense that a co-worker is in a foul mood. It immediately changes the office vibe. No one wants to get too close. Communication falters. There's a nervous pall over everything that saps the psychic energy from the place.

Or there's a supervisor who dampens all enthusiasm and crushes all creativity. In meetings, he greets every dissenting opinion with a piercing glare and a grimace. His subordinates figure, why bother trying? Soon, they go from discouraged to disengaged. They're spending time on Facebook instead of developing new ideas. Before long, they're online looking for new jobs.

Business schools devote semester-long case studies to significant business flameouts. But do they ask whether a lack of emotional intelligence and related skills had anything to do with them? It's important for them to do so, given all of the research on the impact of poor emotion skills on how employees feel and operate. To be sure, some business schools, including the Yale School of Management and the University of Zurich's Graduate School of Business, have begun investing in developing students' emotional intelligence. But none are accustomed to factoring emotional intelligence into their thinking about students' success and failure, and no wonder—there are no numbers to rely on, no charts or graphs to provide reliable answers (yet).

When you look into the research on the inner life of workers, the results are cause for worry.

With support from the Faas Foundation, which funds efforts to create healthy, safe, and fair workplaces, a team at our center, led by senior research scientist Zorana Ivcevic Pringle, has conducted numerous studies on the role of emotions in the workplace. In one study we surveyed one thousand people and in another fifteen thousand people. Both studies had a demographically representative sample from across the United States.

Among the many questions in the studies, we asked these two: How are you feeling at work? What are your experiences like at work? Participants provided their answers to these questions *in their own words* in addition to completing surveys.

Here's what we found:

- About 50 percent of workers used the words *stressed, frustrated,* or *overwhelmed* to describe their feelings at work.
- About a third of workers indicated that they felt happy or proud less than 50 percent of the time they are at work.
- Many of the things they shared that caused them to feel unpleasant emotions were related to other people—colleagues not taking their jobs seriously, administrators lacking good decision-making skills, co-workers slacking off, and people lacking empathy/listening skills.

We also asked subjects for three words to describe what they would most like to feel at work. "Happy" was the number one choice. That came as no surprise—in all my work with various groups, whenever

I ask how people would like to feel, the first word out of everyone's mouth is "happy." It's like the default choice, the one that we blurt without much thought.

But it was the number two and three choices that were most revealing. After *happy*, respondents said they wanted to feel *excited, joyful, appreciated, supported, fulfilled, respected, inspired, accomplished*. The word *valued* was another top choice, and women were about twice as likely as men to use it. That list indicates what's most lacking in the typical workplace.

Other research supports our findings:

- According to a 2018 Gallup survey based on a random sample of 30,628 full- and part-time U.S. employees, over half are "not engaged" at work—while another 13 percent say they have miserable work experiences. The estimated cost to businesses is $450 billion a year in lost productivity.
- In the nonprofit sector, 45 percent of young employees insist that their next job will *not* be in the nonprofit sector, citing burnout as one of the main reasons.
- Thirty-five percent of employees surveyed say they routinely miss three to five workdays a month owing to job stress.
- Forty-five percent of physicians say they feel burned out. Recently, I asked a large group of medical residents to consider a typical day and how they felt throughout it. Then I asked them to summarize the experience in one word. Seventy percent of the residents shared terms such as *meh, bored, polarized, overwhelmed, stressed,* and *pensive*. Only 30 percent used words such as *content* or *calm*.
- According to a Stanford University study, more than 120,000 deaths annually may be attributable to workplace stress, which accounts for up to $190 billion in health care costs. The stressors include a lack of health insurance, work-family conflicts, and inequitable treatment.

Recent research shows that when it comes to burnout and engagement, it's not either/or—it can be both. Julia Moeller, formerly a researcher in our center who is now an assistant professor at the University of Leipzig, led a study that focused on the burnout rate of the best, most capable workers. Those employees suffer burnout precisely because of their high levels of engagement; they are so committed to their jobs, and so good at them, that they wind up with more responsibilities than they can handle—and rather than turn down assignments, they continue to accept them until they are completely overwhelmed. In a related *Harvard Business Review* article by Moeller and Emma Seppälä, who leads our center's college student well-being work, they described a woman whose task it was to organize an ambitious conference for her company, and she did a great job, except that

> in the last weeks prior to the event . . . her stress levels attained such high levels that she suffered from severe burnout symptoms, which included feeling physically and emotionally exhausted, depressed, and suffering sleep problems. She was instructed to take time off work. She never attended the conference and needed a long recovery before she reached her earlier performance and well-being levels. Her burnout symptoms had resulted from the long-term stress and the depletion of her resources over time.

Meanwhile, as that Gallup poll found, half of all workers feel just the opposite—unengaged. Clearly, there's a precise emotional balance that must be struck—employees must be sufficiently engaged to do a good job, but not to such an excess that it causes burnout.

Part of avoiding burnout is encouraging workers to speak up when feeling pressured or unfairly burdened. But that doesn't happen in isolation—the freedom to express yourself, positive or negative, has to be a part of the everyday experience. When I teach in Yale's Executive Education program, I'll often ask: "Are you comfortable expressing your authentic emotions at work?"

"No!" most reply without hesitation.

"I think it is dependent on whom you are speaking with or whom you are negotiating with in a meeting," said one audience member.

"I might say something to a team member or a colleague that I would most certainly *not* say to the CEO," said another. "Like, I would never say, 'Jeremy, you really embarrassed me in that meeting, let me tell you why.'"

They were both saying the same thing: that at work they'd rarely, if ever, express how they felt to the people who could do something about it.

Owing to my role as the director of a center, I know firsthand the impact of suppressing emotions in the workplace.

Do you know the one thing that keeps me up at night? How my employees feel. That should haunt the sleep of every CEO, supervisor, manager, and boss in the world. It's the prime determinant of virtually everything that will happen in an organization—good and bad. If we're an emotionally intelligent workplace, most challenges (though not all) are manageable; if we're not, everything is a struggle.

Before we hire someone at the center, I know that they have the experience, talents, and brains necessary to do the job. But I have little to no idea whether they possess emotion skills. Will they know how to get along with their new co-workers and collaborate, without rivalries or competitiveness getting in the way? Can they adapt to a new environment and contribute but not disrupt? Will they be able to empathize with clients and understand how to interact in a way that serves their needs as well as those of the organization? If not, we're doomed to fail. If the people make the place, as Benjamin Schneider of the University of Maryland once wrote in a famous essay, then surely an organization would be much better off if the employees had emotion skills.

As a company grows, it becomes even more vulnerable to the lack of emotion skills. Here's an example. Years ago, I hired someone as a supervisor, and this person decided it would help if he shielded me from any work-related complaints that his team might have had. Perhaps he thought he was doing me a favor. Maybe to some misguided executives this might have seemed like a good thing. But it was a disaster. For a variety of reasons, my colleagues had become progressively more dissatisfied in their jobs, but no one was letting me know. Things went on that way for a while until this supervisor left, at which point employees felt free to come forward and express to me the feelings they had been forbidden to share. We had become an emotionally dysfunctional workplace, and it showed in the work itself. It took over a year for the place to return to normal. If an institution that bills itself as a center for emotional intelligence can be afflicted by poor emotion skills, it can happen anywhere.

The lesson for me was that I needed to make myself more vulnerable by expressing my own feelings more often and to more of my colleagues. Only if I did that first would they feel safe expressing themselves to me. I had to learn to operate with less authority and more humanity.

Another example from my own workplace: Years ago, I had an employee who consistently looked uninterested and apathetic. She was difficult to read, but she got the job done. So I did my best to accept that and regulate my emotions when I was around her. Then we had a meeting with a school superintendent, and this employee sat there looking conspicuously bored. I was seething the entire time. It was so bad that after the meeting ended, the superintendent said to me, "What's up with that woman?" I had to assure him that we were interested in working with him. It shows how one person's emotional state and lack of skills—even a subordinate's—can infect an entire workplace.

It took me weeks to figure out how to speak about it with that employee. I didn't have the language or an opening to discuss with the employee how she seemed to the rest of us. But once I did, I learned that she was suffering with depression and in need of help. In that situation, it was tempting to be an emotion judge—*What's wrong with this woman, is she rude or something?*—instead of an emotion scientist who genuinely wanted to know what was going on. Back then, we still hadn't come up with a charter for the center, one similar to the family and school ones described in the previous chapters. Today, when there is a disagreement or something feels off, the charter acts as our guide for how to identify and address even uncomfortable feelings.

As Jack Welch, General Electric's legendary management guru, said, "No doubt emotional intelligence is more rare than book smarts, but my experience says it is actually more important in the making of a leader. You just can't ignore it."

Emotional intelligence has attracted considerable attention among organizational behavior scholars. Stéphane Côté, a professor at the Rotman School of Management, University of Toronto, has summarized a couple of decades of research that demonstrates that emotional intelligence, measured as a set of skills, correlates with a wide range of important workplace outcomes, including the following:

- Creativity and innovation
- Organizational commitment
- Job satisfaction
- Customer service ratings
- Managerial performance
- Social support from team members
- Leadership emergence—the extent to which someone not in an official leadership position exerts influence over colleagues
- Transformational leadership, including greater motivation and inspiration
- Job performance, particularly in jobs requiring more emotional labor
- Merit pay

It's important to note that emotionally intelligent managers and leaders need not always be "nice" bosses. Often they need to use emotion skills to perform difficult, delicate tasks. Emotional intelligence in the workplace doesn't merely mean providing comfort and sympathy; sometimes it requires the ability to deliver difficult feedback to help people build greater self-awareness and skills. We may even need the ability to have challenging conversations about sensitive subjects that will cause hurt feelings. That requires emotion skills too. Emotion skills help us to foster successful workplaces and to correct them when things go awry, as they inevitably will.

Recently, our team developed a measure to assess supervisors' emotionally intelligent behavior to examine whether supervisor skills were predictive of employees' feelings and behavior at work. Survey questions included "My supervisor understands how their decisions and behaviors affect how others feel at work" and "My supervisor is good at helping others feel better when they are disappointed or upset." Prior research has found that employees tend to agree in their reports of supervisor behavior.

Here's what we found: Inspiration, respect, and happiness are about 50 percent higher, and frustration, anger, and stress are 30 to 40 percent lower when there is a supervisor with strong emotion skills. We also found that employee engagement, feelings of purpose and meaning in work, and creativity and innovation are significantly higher and that burnout, unethical behavior, and fear of speaking up when there's a problem or when we think there's a better way to do something are all significantly lower when there is a manager with strong emotion skills. Another noteworthy finding: Employees who are afraid to speak up or feel forced to do something unethical are significantly more likely to miss work and have greater intentions of leaving their job, not to mention the toll it takes on their mental health.

Turnover is the one thing most intelligent businesspeople truly dread. It's a huge drain on any organization. Having consulted with many firms, I can guarantee that if there's higher than normal turnover, it's usually because somewhere there's a bad boss. As the saying goes, "People don't leave jobs, they leave bad bosses." While many business leaders would say that a bad boss is one who doesn't deliver results and a good boss is one who exceeds expectations, I would add that a bad boss is one who is low in emotional intelligence, while a good boss is high in it. We all use the term *corporate culture* as shorthand for the DNA of a company. A big part of that is its emotional state, which begins with the emotional intelligence of the people in charge. And for leaders with high emotional intelligence to be successful, they also need to be placed in organizations with a workplace culture that allows these leaders to use their emotional intelligence.

If you're one of those bosses who thinks emotional issues are nonsense and have no place in the office or at the plant or in the store, I can practically guarantee that you're having trouble keeping good employees. If you can't deal in a healthy way with your own emotions, you probably won't be able to deal with anyone else's.

Having said all that, I must add that there are plenty of successful businesspeople with spectacularly bad emotion skills. Not to speak ill of the dead, but Steve Jobs was a notoriously difficult person to deal with, and it's hard to knock him as an executive. Corporate America is replete with bullies and megalomaniacs occupying the corner offices. They are successful if the only measure of success is making money.

So perhaps you *can* bully your way to the top of a thriving business, but you're going to be lonely up there. And if you look around and think your employees are functioning well, you're blind to the fact that they could be operating at an even higher level had you bothered to pay attention to the emotional state of your workplace. Imagine what Steve Jobs could have inspired in his employees had he possessed some emotional intelligence. Perhaps Apple wouldn't be suffering from the lack of innovation and creativity it has experienced in the years since his death.

When I do seminars for business leaders, I show them the data and I say, "Look here, employees say they feel inspired about twenty-five percent of the time when they have supervisors with low emotional intelligence and seventy-five percent of the time under managers with high emotional intelligence. So what does this tell us?" That's a huge difference. Think of productivity and all the creative ideas that will exist in the emotionally intelligent workplace, and now ask yourself why they don't exist in those other companies.

As I've worked in the corporate world, what I've learned is that creating change in these environments is a daunting task—no different from the obstacles Uncle Marvin and I faced when trying to bring change to schools. The kids were always open to it. The adults, not so much. At work, it's the employees who are most likely to embrace the idea of better emotion skills, while their supervisors are skeptical.

There have been times when I was hired to run seminars at workplaces and heard comments like this, from the big boss who did all the hiring: "Oh, no, *I'm* not going through the training. I want you to teach the people who report to me how to deal with their emotions to become better workers. I don't think I need to change anything—I've already proven I'm successful." Another time a hedge fund executive said to me, "Do you really think we're going to sit around a table and share our feelings?" (Later, talking to someone else at his firm, I heard that he once told her, "It doesn't matter how *you* feel—your job is to represent *me*.")

Research shows that high-power individuals tend to be less responsive to the emotions of people around them. In one study, these individuals responded with lower compassion than people with less power when listening to someone describe suffering.

I talked recently with a woman who's running a major nonprofit. She's brilliant. The chairman of the board is a famous guy. She hates her job for one reason—the way he makes her feel. "He's such a big personality that I'm always second-guessing myself," she said. "I always wonder if maybe he's right and I'm wrong about things, just because he expresses his opinions with such force, where I always have my doubts. He says things like 'Why are you so sensitive?' I go home every night depressed and anxious. I've been an executive and I've run big companies for over a decade, but this is driving me crazy, to the point where I might have to quit."

Over the years I've heard from many people in business who feel this way. They're hired to do a job, but they're being undermined and hampered by a superior who thinks that's a good way to maintain control. Of course, it's not—it simply damages the entire organization.

Had this woman taken a Meta-Moment to calm her anxiety and collect her thoughts, she might have realized that this guy was intentionally messing with her and then devised a strategy for dealing with that. She could have sat him down and expressed her feelings, which may or may not have been productive. At the very least she would know soon enough whether there was any hope for improvement.

If she wasn't willing to do that, my advice was to enlist support from the rest of the board and find a way to get the chairman to back off. And if the board wouldn't support her, she needed to find a better job, because this situation was never going to change.

Fortunately for everyone involved, she finally found strategies to help her regulate her feelings of anger and anxiety and had the difficult conversation with the chairman, expressing what she felt and why. She also went to the board and said that structural changes would have to be made if they wanted her to stay. The chairman relented and has changed the way he treats her, and the board took her suggestions, so she is still there—a much happier, and more effective, executive.

In a 2014 research article titled "What's Love Got to Do with It?," the authors, Sigal Barsade from the Wharton School, University of Pennsylvania, and Olivia O'Neill from George Mason University, showed data supporting that particular emotion's power to transform the workplace. They put forth the idea that "feelings of affection, compassion, caring, and tenderness for others" are beneficial even among work colleagues, creating what they call "a culture of companionate love."

At companies where that type of culture is weak, they write,

expressions of affection, caring, compassion, or tenderness among employees are minimal or non-existent, showing both low intensity and low crystallization. Employees in cultures low in companionate love show indifference or even callousness toward each other, do not offer or expect the emotions that companionate love comprises when things are going well, and do not allow room to deal with distress in the workplace when things are not going well.

Once, in the context of corporate cultures, notions like that would have seemed absurdly touchy-feely. Today, however, respected companies such as Southwest Airlines, Pepsi, Whole Foods, Zappos, and a long list of others espouse those values and even enumerate *love* and *caring*—using those words—in their stated management principles. A study led by Andrew Knight, a professor at Washington University in St. Louis, which surveyed more than twenty-four thousand employees from 161 firms, showed that businesses in which positive emotions prevail have significantly lower levels of employee exhaustion and fewer sick days. Another study found that amplifying positive emotions at work reduced employee burnout and absenteeism and increased commitment, but suppressing negative emotions did just the opposite and decreased customer satisfaction.

Other research shows similar results—that customer outcomes such as the intention to return to and recommend a store to a friend are greater when employees display more positive emotions. But it has to be genuine. If employees are faking the good feelings without actually feeling them, the impact on the customer is lost.

The evidence is clear: businesses that wish to remain relevant and competitive in the workplace can't ignore the power of emotions. In our work at Oji Life Lab, we hear from many people about the benefits of the emotion skills explored throughout this book. Professionals who were once anxious at work now use regulation strategies to find relief. One doctor shared that before he had learned the RULER skills it hadn't occurred to him that he had agency over shifting his emotional states. He shared, "Mindful breathing and reappraisal have drastically shifted my ability to be present and work collaboratively with my colleagues, especially when there is tension in the operating room."

According to Susan David, author of *Emotional Agility*, business leaders throughout the world are starting to realize that by attending to emotions, they can improve both their employees' well-being *and* their organizations' success. And the students now developing emotional intelligence in schools will soon join the workforce and select their future employers in part based on how it will feel to work for them.

In the workplace, we often face a trade-off—it's either a job doing something we enjoy, in an environment that feels supportive and creative, or it's one where the emotional satisfactions are few (or nonexistent) but the money is too good to turn down. There are entire professions that count on the willingness of intelligent, educated people to endure high levels of stress and exhaustion in exchange for the big payday. At some point, most of them discover, no matter how much they were paid, it wasn't worth the toll it took.

So when we're being considered for a job, among our main concerns—beyond the usual inquiries about salary, working conditions, room to advance—we should wonder about the emotional atmosphere where we'll be spending so much time and energy. We might even just come right out and ask, "Honestly, how does it make *you* feel to work here?" Beyond possibly startling the interviewer—though maybe in a good way—we're sure to get some interesting, useful replies.

The message for employers and managers in all this is unmistakable. In today's workplace, top employees will gravitate toward firms that acknowledge emotion's power to foster positive, productive environments. They'll quit bad jobs, leaving behind co-workers who may be no less miserable but who are—for whatever reasons—unwilling or unable to find employment elsewhere. That thought alone should encourage companies to take emotion skills seriously.

Creating an Emotion Revolution

At the end of my seminars, I often ask people to imagine a world where all leaders, teachers, and children are taught emotion skills—where colleges and universities, teacher preparation programs, medical and law schools, sports teams, police departments, corporations, and so on are trained to value emotional intelligence. What would be different if everyone was taught to be an emotion scientist? Here's what kids, parents, teachers, and business professionals have said over the years:

- Everyone would listen more and judge less.
- Fewer kids would be living in poverty.
- There would be less stigma and racism.
- Emotional intelligence would be as important to education as math, literacy, and science.
- All emotions would be appreciated, especially the negative ones.
- There would be less self-deception.
- Feelings would be seen as strengths, not weaknesses.
- More people would be their authentic, best selves.

- Schools would be places where students spend time reflecting on their purpose and passion and developing the skills they need to make their dreams come true.
- People would leave their workplace thinking, I can't wait to return tomorrow.
- We'd see less self-destruction and greater self-compassion.
- There would be less bullying, a greater sense of belonging, and more harmonious relationships.
- Depression and anxiety rates would be dramatically reduced.
- Families and schools would work together to support kids' healthy development.

My personal favorite was one third grader's answer. He said, "There would be world peace!" That's the promise of giving children the permission to feel.

With emotion skills, we will create a more inclusive, compassionate, and innovative world. The science is there to show why this is the missing link in well-being and success. Keeping emotion skills separate from our lives at home, in school, and at work harms us all. We need to launch an emotion revolution in which the permission to feel moves us in ways we have yet to imagine.

When the friendship between passion and reason can freely exist, it will mean greater equity as emotion skills level the playing field for all children, regardless of race, class, or gender. For adults in the workplace, it will mean that collaboration functions seamlessly; no one will ever have to use words such as "synergy," "team building," or "creating a leadership pipeline" again, because emotion skills will turn these concepts into reflexes.

Developing emotion skills isn't about attending a workshop, going on a retreat, or adopting a "program." It's a way of life. It's about recognizing that how people feel and what we do with our feelings determines, to a large extent, the quality of our lives.

A commitment to developing emotion skills means providing extra resources to neighborhoods and communities in need, reducing, at last, wide swaths of harm. Communicating through the lens of emotion skills no longer leaves room for toxic masculinity, feminine objectification, and prejudice of all sorts. It means rolling back policies that create widespread inequality, rethinking violence-saturated media, and revising harmful approaches to discipline, punishment, and bullying. And it means policy makers must join families and educators in tending to the "gardens" in which our children grow.

When I share stories about my childhood, people often say, "But you made it somehow, even with all of the pain. If it weren't for your pain, you might not be doing what you are doing today."

It's possible, I reply. Maybe even probable.

"But I was fortunate," I say. And then I ask a few questions.

How many kids will have parents who recognize their inability to help their child and seek therapy for him? How many will have an uncle who happens to be a pioneer in thinking about the importance of emotional intelligence and can provide unconditional love and support? How many will study the martial arts? How many will dedicate their lives to emotion science? My hunch is not many. If we just hope for the best, many children will fall by the wayside.

Emotion skills are the key to unlocking the potential inside each one of us. And in the process of developing these skills, we each, heart by heart, mind by mind, create a culture and society unlike anything we've experienced thus far—and very much like the one we might dare to imagine.

It's not easy to change a whole society. But we have to try.

Our future—and our children's future—depends on it.

References

Prologue

Adkins, A. (2016, January 13). Employee engagement in U.S. stagnant in 2015. Gallup Inc. Retrieved from https://news.gallup.com/poll/188144/employee -engagement-stagnant-2015.aspx

Anti-Defamation League. (2017). ADL Audit: U.S. anti-Semitic incidents surged in 2016–17. Retrieved from www.adl.org/sites/default/files/documents/Anti -Semitic%20Audit%20Print_vf2.pdf

Gallup Inc. & Healthways Inc. (2014). Gallup-Healthways Well-being Index. Retrieved from https://wellbeingindex.sharecare.com/

Helliwell, J., Layard, R., & Sachs, J. (2019). *World Happiness Report 2019*. New York: Sustainable Development Solutions Network.

Kelland, K. (2018, October 9). Mental health crisis could cost the world $16 trillion by 2030. Reuters. Retrieved from www.reuters.com/article/us-health -mental-global/mental-health-crisis-could-cost-the-world-16-trillion-by-2030 -idUSKCN1MJ2QN

Lipson, S. K., Lattie, E. G., & Eisenberg, D. (2018). Increased rates of mental health service utilization by US college students: 10-year population-level trends (2007–2017). *Psychiatric Services, 70*(1), 60–63. doi.org/10.1176/appi.ps.201800332

Substance Abuse and Mental Health Services Administration. (2018). *Key substance use and mental health indicators in the United States: Results from the 2017 National Survey on Drug Use and Health* (HHS Publication No. SMA 18-5068, NSDUH Series H-53). Rockville, MD: Center for Behavioral Health Statistics and

Quality, Substance Abuse and Mental Health Services. Retrieved from www
.samhsa.gov/data/

1. Permission to Feel

American Psychological Association. (2018). *Stress in America: Generation Z*. Stress
in America Survey. Retrieved from www.apa.org/news/press/releases/stress/2018
/stress-gen-z.pdf

Centers for Disease Control and Prevention. (2018, June 7). Suicide rates rising
across the U.S. [Press release]. Retrieved from www.cdc.gov/media/releases/2018
/p0607-suicide-prevention.html

Floman, J. L., Brackett, M. A., Schmitt, L., & Baron, W. (2018, May). School climate, teacher affect, and teacher well-being: Direct and indirect effects. Presented
at the Association for Psychological Science Convention in San Francisco, CA.

Gallup Inc. (2014). State of America's schools: The path to winning again in education. Retrieved from www.gallup.com/services/178709/state-america-schools
-report.aspx

Goleman, D. (1997). *Emotional Intelligence: Why It Can Matter More Than IQ*. New
York: Bantam Books.

Lipson, S. K., Lattie, E. G., & Eisenberg, D. (2018). Increased rates of mental health
service utilization by US college students: 10-year population-level trends (2007–
2017). *Psychiatric Services, 70*(1), 60–63. doi.org/10.1176/appi.ps.201800332

Moeller, J., Ivcevic, Z., Brackett, M. A., & White, A. E. (2018). Mixed emotions:
Network analyses of intra-individual co-occurrences within and across situations.
Emotion, 18(8), 1106–1121. doi.org/10.1037/emo0000419

Moeller, J., Brackett, M., Ivcevic, Z., & White, A. (under review). High school students' feelings: Discoveries from a large national survey and an experience sampling study. *Learning and Instruction*.

Salovey, P., & Mayer, J. D. (1990). Emotional intelligence. *Imagination, Cognition
and Personality, 9*(3), 185–211. doi.org/10.2190/DUGG-P24E-52WK-6CDG

Steinberg, L. (2014). *Age of Opportunity: Lessons from the New Science of Adolescence*.
New York: Houghton Mifflin Harcourt.

UNICEF. (2013). Child well-being in rich countries: A comparative overview, innocenti
report card 11. Florence: UNICEF Office of Research. Retrieved from www
.unicef-irc.org/publications/pdf/rc11_eng.pdf

2. Emotions Are Information

Aldao, A., Nolen-Hoeksema, S., & Schweizer, S. (2010). Emotion-regulation strategies across psychopathology: A meta-analytic review. *Clinical Psychology Review,
30*(2), 217–237. doi:10.1016/j.cpr.2009.11.004

Amabile, T. M., Barsade, S. G., Mueller, J. S., & Staw, B. M. (2005). Affect and creativity at work. *Administrative Science Quarterly, 50*(3), 367–403. doi.org/10.2189/asqu.2005.50.3.367

Anderson, N., De Dreu, C. K., & Nijstad, B. A. (2004). The routinization of innovation research: A constructively critical review of the state-of-the-science. *Journal of Organizational Behavior, 25*(2), 147–173.

Appleton, A. A., Holdsworth, E., Ryan, M., & Tracy, M. (2017). Measuring childhood adversity in life course cardiovascular research: A systematic review. *Psychosomatic Medicine, 79*(4), 434–440.

Aristotle. (1984). *The Complete Works of Aristotle: The Revised Oxford Translation.* J. Barnes (Ed.). Princeton, NJ: Princeton University Press.

Aschbacher, K., O'Donovan, A., Wolkowitz, O. M., Dhabhar, F. S., Su, Y., & Epel, E. (2013). Good stress, bad stress and oxidative stress: Insights from anticipatory cortisol reactivity. *Psychoneuroendocrinology, 38*(9), 1698–1708.

Baas, M., De Dreu, C. K., & Nijstad, B. A. (2008). A meta-analysis of 25 years of mood-creativity research: Hedonic tone, activation, or regulatory focus? *Psychological Bulletin, 134*(6), 779–806. doi.org/10.1037/a0012815

Bal, E., Harden, E., Lamb, D., Van Hecke, A. V., Denver, J. W., & Porges, S. W. (2010). Emotion recognition in children with autism spectrum disorders: Relations to eye gaze and autonomic state. *Journal of Autism and Developmental Disorders, 40*(3), 358–370.

Barrett, L. F. (2017). *How Emotions Are Made: The Secret Life of the Brain.* Boston: Houghton Mifflin Harcourt.

Barrett, L. F., Mesquita, B., Ochsner, K. N., & Gross, J. J. (2007). The experience of emotion. *Annual Review of Psychology, 58,* 373–403. doi.org/10.1146/annurev.psych.58.110405.085709

Barsade, S. G., & Gibson, D. E. (2007). Why does affect matter in organizations? *Academy of Management Perspectives, 21*(1), 36–59. doi.org/10.5465/amp.2007.24286163

Batson, C. D. (2011). *Altruism in Humans.* Oxford: Oxford University Press.

Bennett, M. P., & Lengacher, C. (2008). Humor and laughter may influence health: III. Laughter and health outcomes. *Evidence-Based Complementary and Alternative Medicine, 5*(1), 37–40.

Berna, C., Leknes, S., Holmes, E. A., Edwards, R. R., Goodwin, G. M., & Tracey, I. (2010). Induction of depressed mood disrupts emotion regulation neurocircuitry and enhances pain unpleasantness. *Biological Psychiatry, 67*(11), 1083–1090.

Berridge, K. C. (2007). The debate over dopamine's role in reward: The case for incentive salience. *Psychopharmacology, 191*(3), 391–431. doi.org/10.1007/s00213-006-0578-x

Blair, C., & Raver, C. C. (2016). Poverty, stress, and brain development: New directions for prevention and intervention. *Academic Pediatrics, 16*(3), S30–S36. doi.org/10.1016/j.acap.2016.01.010

Bodenhausen, G. V., Sheppard, L. A., & Kramer, G. P. (1994). Negative affect and social judgment: The differential impact of anger and sadness. *European Journal of Social Psychology, 24*(1), 45–62.

Boekaerts, M. (2010). The crucial role of motivation and emotion in classroom learning. In H. Dumont, D. Istance, & F. Benavides (Eds.), *The Nature of Learning: Using Research to Inspire Practice* (pp. 91–111). Paris: OECD.

Bower, G. H. (1981). Mood and memory. *American Psychologist, 36*(2), 129–148. doi.org/10.1037/0003-066X.36.2.129

Bower, G. H. (1992). How might emotions affect learning. In S. Christianson (Ed.), *The Handbook of Emotion and Memory: Research and Theory* (pp. 3–31). Oxford: Psychology Press.

Bower, G. H., & Forgas, J. P. (2001). Mood and social memory. In J. P. Forgas (Ed.), *The Handbook of Affect and Social Cognition* (pp. 95–120). Mahwah, NJ: Erlbaum.

Bowers, T. (2004). Stress, teaching and teacher health. *Education 3–13: International Journal of Primary, Elementary and Early Years Education, 32*, 73–80. doi.org/10.1080/03004270485200361

Brackett, M. A., Floman, J. L., Ashton-James, C., Cherkasskiy, L., & Salovey, P. (2013). The influence of teacher emotion on grading practices: A preliminary look at the evaluation of student writing. *Teachers and Teaching, 19*(6), 634–646.

Brackett, M. A., Rivers, S. E., & Salovey, P. (2011). Emotional intelligence: Implications for personal, social, academic, and workplace success. *Social and Personality Psychology Compass, 5*(1), 88–103. doi.org/10.1111/j.1751-9004.2010.00334.x

Bradley, M. M., & Lang, P. J. (2000). Emotion and motivation. In J. T. Cacioppo, L. G. Tassinary, & G. G. Berntson (Eds.), *Handbook of Psychophysiology* (pp. 602–642). Cambridge: Cambridge University Press.

Brooks, J. L. (Producer & Director). (1987). *Broadcast News.* [Film]. USA: Twentieth Century Fox.

Burgdorf, J., & Panksepp, J. (2006). The neurobiology of positive emotions. *Neuroscience & Biobehavioral Reviews, 30*(2), 173–187. doi.org/10.1016/j.neubiorev.2005.06.001

Cantor, N., & Kihlstrom, J. F. (2000). Social intelligence. In R. J. Sternberg & S. B. Kaufman (Eds.), *Handbook of Intelligence* (pp. 359–379). Cambridge: Cambridge University Press.

Chida, Y., & Steptoe, A. (2009). The association of anger and hostility with future coronary heart disease: A meta-analytic review of prospective evidence. *Journal of the American College of Cardiology, 53*(11), 936–946.

Christianson, S. A. (2014). *The Handbook of Emotion and Memory: Research and Theory.* Oxford: Psychology Press.

Cohen, T. R., Panter, A. T., & Turan, N. (2012). Guilt proneness and moral character. *Current Directions in Psychological Science, 21*(5), 355–359. doi.org/10.1177/0963721412454874

Cosmides, L., & Tooby, J. (2000). Evolutionary psychology and the emotions. In M. Lewis & J. M. Haviland-Jones (Eds.), *Handbook of Emotions* (pp. 91–115). New York: Guilford Publications.

Côté, S., & Miners, C. T. (2006). Emotional intelligence, cognitive intelligence, and job performance. *Administrative Science Quarterly, 51*(1), 1–28. doi.org/10.2189/asqu.51.1.1

Cozolino, L. (2014). *The Neuroscience of Human Relationships: Attachment and the Developing Social Brain.* New York: W. W. Norton & Company.

Crum, A. J., Akinola, M., Martin, A., & Fath, S. (2017). The role of stress mindset in shaping cognitive, emotional, and physiological responses to challenging and threatening stress. *Anxiety, Stress, & Coping, 30*(4), 379–395.

Crum, A. J., Salovey, P., & Achor, S. (2013). Rethinking stress: The role of mindsets in determining the stress response. *Journal of Personality and Social Psychology, 104*(4), 716–733.

Damasio, A. R. (1995). *Descartes' Error.* New York: Random House.

Darr, W., & Johns, G. (2008). Work strain, health and absenteeism: A meta-analysis. *Journal of Occupational Health Psychology, 13*, 293–318. doi.org/10.1037/a0012639

Darwin, C. (1872/1998). *The Expression of the Emotions in Man and Animals.* Oxford: Oxford University Press.

Dave, N. D., Xiang, L., Rehm, K. E., & Marshall, G. D. (2011). Stress and allergic diseases. *Immunology and Allergy Clinics, 31*(1), 55–68.

Davidson, R. J., & Begley, S. (2012). *The Emotional Life of Your Brain: How its unique patterns affect the way you think, feel, and live—and how you can change them.* London: Penguin.

Deci, E. L., & Ryan, R. M. (2008). Self-determination theory: A macrotheory of human motivation, development, and health. *Canadian Psychology/Psychologie Canadienne, 49*(3), 182–185.

DeLongis, A., Folkman, S., & Lazarus, R. S. (1988). The impact of daily stress on health and mood: Psychological and social resources as mediators. *Journal of Personality and Social Psychology, 54*(3), 486–495.

Denson, T. F., Spanovic, M., & Miller, N. (2009). Cognitive appraisals and emotions predict cortisol and immune responses: A meta-analysis of acute laboratory social stressors and emotion inductions. *Psychological Bulletin, 135*(6), 823–853.

DeSteno, D., Gross, J. J., & Kubzansky, L. (2013). Affective science and health: The

importance of emotion and emotion regulation. *Health Psychology, 32*(5), 474. doi
.org/10.1037/a0030259

Dhabhar, F. S. (2014). Effects of stress on immune function: The good, the bad, and
the beautiful. *Immunologic Research, 58*(2–3), 193–210.

Dunbar, R. I. (1998). The social brain hypothesis. *Evolutionary Anthropology: Issues,
News, and Reviews, 6*(5), 178–190.

Durlak, J. A., Weissberg, R. P., Dymnicki, A. B., Taylor, R. D., & Schellinger, K. B.
(2011). The impact of enhancing students' social and emotional learning: A meta-
analysis of school-based universal interventions. *Child Development, 82*(1), 405–
432. doi.org/10.1111/j.1467-8624.2010.01564.x

Ekman, P. (1992). An argument for basic emotions. *Cognition & Emotion, 6*(3–4),
169–200. doi.org/10.1080/02699939208411068

Ekman, P. E., & Davidson, R. J. (1994). *The Nature of Emotion: Fundamental Questions.* Oxford: Oxford University Press.

Elzinga, B. M., & Roelofs, K. (2005). Cortisol-induced impairments of working
memory require acute sympathetic activation. *Behavioral Neuroscience, 119*(1),
98–103. doi.org/10.1037/0735-7044.119.1.98

Emanuele, E., Politi, P., Bianchi, M., Minoretti, P., Bertona, M., & Geroldi, D.
(2006). Raised plasma nerve growth factor levels associated with early-stage romantic love. *Psychoneuroendocrinology, 31*(3), 288–294.

Epel, E., Prather, A. A., Puterman, E., & Tomiyama, A. J. (2016). Eat, drink, and be
sedentary: A review of health behaviors' effects on emotions and affective states,
and implications for interventions. In L. F. Barrett, M. Lewis, & J. M. Haviland-
Jones (Eds.), *Handbook of Emotions* (pp. 685–706). New York: Guilford Publications.

Fischer, A. H. & Manstead, A. S. R. (2016). Social functions or emotion and emotion
regulation. In L. F. Barrett, M. Lewis, & J. M. Haviland-Jones (Eds.), *Handbook
of Emotions* (pp. 424–439). New York: Guilford Publications.

Floman, J. L., Brackett, M.A., Schmitt, L., & Baron, W. (2018, May). School climate, teacher affect, and teacher well-being: Direct and indirect effects. Presented
at the Association for Psychological Science Convention in San Francisco, CA.

Forgas, J. P. (1998). On being happy and mistaken: Mood effects on the fundamental
attribution error. *Journal of Personality and Social Psychology, 75*(2), 318–331.

Forgas, J. P. (2011). Can negative affect eliminate the power of first impressions? Affective influences on primacy and recency effects in impression formation. *Journal
of Experimental Social Psychology, 47*(2), 425–429.

Forgas, J. P. (2013). Don't worry, be sad! On the cognitive, motivational, and interpersonal benefits of negative mood. *Current Directions in Psychological Science,
22*(3), 225–232.

Forgas, J. P. (2014). On the regulatory functions of mood: Affective influences on memory, judgments and behavior. In J. P. Forgas & E. Harmon-Jones (Eds.), *Motivation and its Regulation: The Control Within,* (pp. 169–192). New York: Psychology Press.

Forgas, J. P., & East, R. (2008). On being happy and gullible: Mood effects on skepticism and the detection of deception. *Journal of Experimental Social Psychology, 44*(5), 1362–1367.

Forgas, J. P., & George, J. M. (2001). Affective influences on judgments and behavior in organizations: An information processing perspective. *Organizational Behavior and Human Decision Processes, 86*(1), 3–34. doi.org/10.1006/obhd.2001.2971

Fowler, J. H., & Christakis, N. A. (2008). Dynamic spread of happiness in a large social network: Longitudinal analysis over 20 years in the Framingham Heart Study. *BMJ, 337,* a2338.

Fredrickson, B. L. (1998). What good are positive emotions? *Review of General Psychology, 2*(3), 300–319.

Fredrickson, B. L. (2013). Positive emotions broaden and build. In P. Devine & A. Plant (Eds.), *Advances in Experimental Social Psychology* (vol. 47, pp. 1–53). Cambridge, MA: Academic Press.

Fredrickson, B. L., & Branigan, C. (2005). Positive emotions broaden the scope of attention and thought-action repertoires. *Cognition & Emotion, 19*(3), 313–332. doi.org/10.1080/02699930441000238

Fredrickson, B. L., Tugade, M. M., Waugh, C. E., & Larkin, G. R. (2003). What good are positive emotions in crisis? A prospective study of resilience and emotions following the terrorist attacks on the United States on September 11th, 2001. *Journal of Personality and Social Psychology, 84*(2), 365–376.

Frevert, U. (2016). The history of emotions. In L. F. Barrett, M. Lewis, & J. M. Haviland-Jones (Eds.), *Handbook of Emotions* (pp. 49–65). New York: Guilford Publications.

Gardner, H. (1992). *Multiple intelligences* (vol. 5, p. 56). Minnesota Center for Arts Education.

Goetz, J. L., Keltner, D., & Simon-Thomas, E. (2010). Compassion: An evolutionary analysis and empirical review. *Psychological Bulletin, 136*(3), 351–374.

Goetzmann, W. N., Kim, D., Kumar, A., & Wang, Q. (2014). Weather-induced mood, institutional investors, and stock returns. *Review of Financial Studies, 28*(1), 73–111.

Goleman, D. (1995). *Emotional Intelligence: Why It Can Matter More Than IQ.* New York: Bantam Books.

Greenberg, M. T., Brown, J. L., & Abenavoli, R. M. (2016, September). *Teacher stress and health: Effects on teachers, students, and schools.* Edna Bennett Pierce Prevention

Research Center, Pennsylvania State University. Retrieved from www.rwjf.org/en /library/research/2016/07/teacher-stress-and-health.html

Gross, J. J. (2002). Emotion regulation: Affective, cognitive, and social consequences. *Psychophysiology, 39*(3), 281–291. doi.org/10.1017/S0048577201393198

Guhn, M., Schonert-Reichl, K. A., Gadermann, A. M., Hymel, S., & Hertzman, C. (2013). A population study of victimization, relationships, and well-being in middle childhood. *Journal of Happiness Studies, 14*(5), 1529–1541.

Guilford, J. P. (1967). *The Nature of Human Intelligence.* New York: McGraw-Hill.

Haidt, J. (2001). The emotional dog and its rational tail: A social intuitionist approach to moral judgment. *Psychological Review, 108*(4), 814–834. doi.org/10.1017 /CBO9780511814273.055

Haidt, J. (2012). *The Righteous Mind: Why Good People Are Divided by Politics and Religion.* New York: Vintage.

Hajcak, G., Jackson, F., Ferri, J., & Weinberg, A. (2016). Emotion and attention. In L. F. Barrett, M. Lewis, & J. M. Haviland-Jones (Eds.), *Handbook of Emotions* (pp. 595–612). New York: Guilford Publications.

Hargreaves, A. (1998). The emotional practice of teaching. *Teaching and Teacher Education, 14*(8), 835–854. doi.org/10.1016/S0742-051X(98)00025-0

Hascher, T. (2010). Learning and emotion: Perspectives for theory and research. *European Educational Research Journal, 9*(1), 13–28. doi.org/10.2304/eerj.2010.9 .1.13

Hawkley, L. C., & Cacioppo, J. T. (2010). Loneliness matters: A theoretical and empirical review of consequences and mechanisms. *Annals of Behavioral Medicine, 40*(2), 218–227.

Hirshleifer, D., & Shumway, T. (2003). Good day sunshine: Stock returns and the weather. *Journal of Finance, 58*(3), 1009–1032.

Huntsinger, J. R. (2013). Does emotion directly tune the scope of attention? *Current Directions in Psychological Science, 22*(4), 265–270. doi.org/10.1177 /0963721413480364

Huntsinger, J. R., Isbell, L. M., & Clore, G. L. (2014). The affective control of thought: Malleable, not fixed. *Psychological Review, 121*(4), 600–618. doi.org/10 .1037/a0037669

Hutcherson, C. A., & Gross, J. J. (2011). The moral emotions: A social-functionalist account of anger, disgust, and contempt. *Journal of Personality and Social Psychology, 100*(4), 719–737. doi.org/10.1037/a0022408

IBM. (2010, May 18). IBM 2010 global CEO study: Creativity selected as most crucial factor for future success. Retrieved from www-03.ibm.com/press/us/en /pressrelease/31670.wss

Innes-Ker, Å., & Niedenthal, P. M. (2002). Emotion concepts and emotional states in social judgment and categorization. *Journal of Personality and Social Psychology,* *83*(4), 804–816.

Isbell, L. M., & Lair, E. C. (2013). Moods, emotions, and evaluations as information. In D. Carlston (Ed.), *Handbook of Social Cognition* (pp. 435–462). Oxford: Oxford University Press.

Isen, A. M. (1999). On the relationship between affect and creative problem solving. In S. W. Russ (Ed.), *Affect, Creative Experience, and Psychological Adjustment* (pp. 3–17). Oxfordshire, UK: Taylor & Francis.

Isen, A. M., Daubman, K. A., & Nowicki, G. P. (1987). Positive affect facilitates creative problem solving. *Journal of Personality and Social Psychology, 52*(6), 1122–1131. doi.org/10.1037//0022-3514.52.6.1122

Isen, A. M., Niedenthal, P. M., & Cantor, N. (1992). An influence of positive affect on social categorization. *Motivation and Emotion, 16*(1), 65–78.

Ivcevic, Z., Bazhydai, M., Hoffmann, J., & Brackett, M. A. (2017). Creativity in the domain of emotions. In J. C. Kaufman, V. P. Glaveanu, & J. Baer (Eds.), *Cambridge Handbook of Creativity Across Different Domains* (Pp. 525–549). Cambridge: Cambridge University Press.

Ivcevic, Z., Brackett, M. A., & Mayer, J. D. (2007). Emotional intelligence and emotional creativity. *Journal of Personality, 75*(2), 199–236.

John, A., Glendenning, A. C., Marchant, A., Montgomery, P., Stewart, A., Wood, S., . . . Hawton, K. (2018). Self-harm, suicidal behaviours, and cyberbullying in children and young people: Systematic review. *Journal of Medical Internet Research, 20*(4), e129.

Kabat-Zinn, J. (1990). *Full Catastrophe Living: Using the wisdom of your body and mind to face stress, pain, and illness.* New York: Delta.

Kahneman, D., (2011). *Thinking, Fast and Slow.* New York: Farrar, Straus and Giroux.

Keltner, D. (2019). Toward a consensual taxonomy of emotions. *Cognition and Emotion, 33*(1), 1–6. doi.org/10.1080/02699931.2019.1574397

Keltner, D., & Gross, J. J. (1999). Functional accounts of emotions. *Cognition and Emotion, 13*(5), 467–480. doi.org/10.1080/026999399379140

Keltner, D., & Haidt, J. (1999). Social functions of emotions at four levels of analysis. *Cognition and Emotion, 13*(5), 505–521. doi.org/10.1080/026999399379168

Keltner, D., & Kring, A. M. (1998). Emotion, social function, and psychopathology. *Review of General Psychology, 2*(3), 320–342.

Keltner, D., Ellsworth, P. C., & Edwards, K. (1993). Beyond simple pessimism: Effects of sadness and anger on social perception. *Journal of Personality and Social Psychology, 64*(5), 740–752.

Kemp, A. H., Gray, M. A., Silberstein, R. B., Armstrong, S. M., & Nathan, P. J. (2004). Augmentation of serotonin enhances pleasant and suppresses unpleasant cortical electrophysiological responses to visual emotional stimuli in humans. *Neuroimage, 22*(3), 1084–1096. doi.org/10.1016/j.neuroimage.2004.03.022

Kensinger, E. A. & Schacter, D. L. (2016). Memory and emotion. In L. F. Barrett, M. Lewis, & J. M. Haviland-Jones (Eds.), *Handbook of Emotions* (pp. 564–578). New York: Guilford Publications.

Kiecolt-Glaser, J. K., McGuire, L., Robles, T. F., & Glaser, R. (2002). Emotions, morbidity, and mortality: New perspectives from psychoneuroimmunology. *Annual Review of Psychology, 53*(1), 83–107.

Kim, K. H., Cramond, B., & VanTassel-Baska, J. (2010). The relationship between creativity and intelligence. In J. C. Kaufman, & R. J. Sternberg (Eds.), *The Cambridge Handbook of Creativity* (pp. 395–412). New York: Cambridge University Press.

Kubzansky, L. D., & Kawachi, I. (2000). Going to the heart of the matter: Do negative emotions cause coronary heart disease? *Journal of Psychosomatic Research, 48*(4–5), 323–337. doi.org/10.1016/S0022-3999(99)00091-4

Kubzansky, L. D., Huffman, J. C., Boehm, J. K., Hernandez, R., Kim, E. S., Koga, H. K., . . . Labarthe, D. R. (2018). Positive psychological well-being and cardiovascular disease: JACC health promotion series. *Journal of the American College of Cardiology, 72*(12), 1382–1396. doi.org/10.1016/j.jacc.2018.07.042

LeDoux, J. (1997). The emotional brain: The mysterious underpinnings of emotional life. *World and I, 12,* 281–285.

Lempert, K. M. & Phelps, E. A. (2016). Affect in economic decision making. In L. F. Barrett, M. Lewis, & J. M. Haviland-Jones (Eds.), *Handbook of Emotions* (pp. 98–112). New York: Guilford Publications.

Lerner, J. S., Li, Y., Valdesolo, P., & Kassam, K. S. (2015). Emotion and decision making. *Annual Review of Psychology, 66,* 799–823. doi.org/10.1146/annurev-psych-010213-115043

Lerner, J. S., Small, D. A., & Loewenstein, G. (2004). Heart strings and purse strings: Carryover effects of emotions on economic decisions. *Psychological Science, 15*(5), 337–341.

Lewis, M. (2016). The emergence of human emotions. In L. F. Barrett, M. Lewis, & J. M. Haviland-Jones (Eds.), *Handbook of Emotions* (pp. 272–292). New York: Guilford Publications.

Lopes, P. N., Salovey, P., Côté, S., Beers, M., & Petty, R. E. (2005). Emotion regulation abilities and the quality of social interaction. *Emotion, 5*(1), 113–118. doi.org/10.1037/1528-3542.5.1.113

Lumley, M. A., Cohen, J. L., Borszcz, G. S., Cano, A., Radcliffe, A. M., Porter, L. S., . . . Keefe, F. J. (2011). Pain and emotion: A biopsychosocial review of recent research. *Journal of Clinical Psychology, 67*(9), 942–968.

Lupien, S. J., McEwen, B. S., Gunnar, M. R., & Heim, C. (2009). Effects of stress throughout the lifespan on the brain, behaviour and cognition. *Nature Reviews Neuroscience, 10,* 434–445. doi.org/10.1038/nrn2639

Lyubomirsky, S., & Lepper, H. S. (1999). A measure of subjective happiness: Preliminary reliability and construct validation. *Social Indicators Research, 46*(2), 137–155. doi.org/10.1023/A:1006824100041

Lyubomirsky, S., King, L., & Diener, E. (2005). The benefits of frequent positive affect: Does happiness lead to success? *Psychological Bulletin, 131*(6), 803–855. doi.org/10.1037/0033-2909.131.6.803

Mackintosh, N., & Mackintosh, N. J. (2011). *IQ and Human Intelligence.* Oxford: Oxford University Press.

Martin, R. A., & Ford, T. (2018). *The Psychology of Humor: An Integrative Approach.* Cambridge, MA: Academic Press.

Mayer, J. D., Caruso, D. R., & Salovey, P. (2016). The ability model of emotional intelligence: Principles and updates. *Emotion Review, 8*(4), 290–300. doi.org/10.1177/1754073916639667

Mayer, J. D., Gaschke, Y. N., Braverman, D. L., & Evans, T. W. (1992). Mood-congruent judgment is a general effect. *Journal of Personality and Social Psychology, 63*(1), 119–132. doi.org/10.1037/0022-3514.63.1.119

Mayer, J. D., McCormick, L. J., & Strong, S. E. (1995). Mood-congruent memory and natural mood: New evidence. *Personality and Social Psychology Bulletin, 21*(7), 736–46. doi.org/10.1177/0146167295217008

Mayer, J. D., Salovey, P., & Caruso, D. R. (2008). Emotional intelligence: New ability or eclectic traits? *American Psychologist, 63*(6), 503–517. doi.org/10.1037/0003-066X.63.6.503

McCrae, R. R. (1987). Creativity, divergent thinking, and openness to experience. *Journal of Personality and Social Psychology, 52*(6), 1258–1265. doi.org/10.1037/0022–3514.52.6.1258

McCraty, R., & Childre, D. (2004). The grateful heart: The psychophysiology of appreciation. In R. A. Emmons & M. E. McCullough (Eds.), *The Psychology of Gratitude* (p. 230). Oxford: Oxford University Press.

McEwen, B. S., Bowles, N. P., Gray, J. D., Hill, M. N., Hunter, R. G., Karatsoreos, I. N., & Nasca, C. (2015). Mechanisms of stress in the brain. *Nature Neuroscience, 18*(10), 1353–1363. doi.org/10.1038/nn.4086

McGonigal, K. (2016). *The Upside of Stress: Why stress is good for you, and how to get good at it.* London, England: Penguin.

McIntyre, T., McIntyre, S., & Francis, D. (2017). *Educator Stress.* New York: Springer.

Moeller, J., Ivcevic, Z., Brackett, M. A., & White, A. E. (2018). Mixed emotions: Network analyses of intra-individual co-occurrences within and across situations. *Emotion, 18*(8), 1106–1121.

Moore, S. E., Norman, R. E., Suetani, S., Thomas, H. J., Sly, P. D., & Scott, J. G. (2017). Consequences of bullying victimization in childhood and adolescence: A systematic review and meta-analysis. *World Journal of Psychiatry, 7*(1), 60–76.

Niedenthal, P. M., Mermillod, M., Maringer, M., & Hess, U. (2010). The simulation of smiles (SIMS) model: Embodied simulation and the meaning of facial expression. *Behavioral and Brain Sciences, 33*(6), 417–433.

Nowak, M. A. (2006). Five rules for the evolution of cooperation. *Science, 314*(5805), 1560–1563.

Nusbaum, E. C., & Silvia, P. J. (2011). Are intelligence and creativity really so different? Fluid intelligence, executive processes, and strategy use in divergent thinking. *Intelligence, 39*(1), 36–45.

Oatley, K., Keltner, D., & Jenkins, J. M. (2018). *Understanding Emotions.* Hoboken, NJ: Blackwell Publishing.

Öhman, A., Flykt, A., & Esteves, F. (2001). Emotion drives attention: Detecting the snake in the grass. *Journal of Experimental Psychology: General, 130*(3), 466–478. doi:10.1037/AXJ96-3445.130.3.466

Oveis, C., Horberg, E. J., & Keltner, D. (2010). Compassion, pride, and social intuitions of self-other similarity. *Journal of Personality and Social Psychology, 98*(4), 618–630.

Panksepp, J. (2009). Brain emotional systems and qualities of mental life: From animal models of affect to implications for psychotherapeutics. In D. Fosha, D. J. Siegel, & M. F. Solomon (Eds.), *The Healing Power of Emotion: Affective Neuroscience, Development & Clinical Practice* (pp. 1–26). New York: W. W. Norton & Company.

Pekrun, R., & Linnenbrink-Garcia, L. (2012). Academic emotions and student engagement. In S. Christenson & A. Reschly, & C. Wylie (Eds.), *Handbook of Research on Student Engagement* (pp. 259–282). Boston, MA: Springer.

Phelps, E. A. (2004). Human emotion and memory: Interactions of the amygdala and hippocampal complex. *Current Opinion in Neurobiology, 14*(2), 198–202. doi .org/10.1016/j.conb.2004.03.015

Psychologies. (2011, August 24). The link between emotions and health. Retrieved from www.psychologies.co.uk/self/the-link-between-emotions-and-health.html

Raven, J. C., & Court, J. H. (1998). *Raven's Progressive Matrices and Vocabulary Scales.* Oxford: Oxford Pyschologists Press.

Redelmeier, D. A., & Baxter, S. D. (2009). Rainy weather and medical school admission interviews. *Canadian Medical Association Journal, 181*(12), 933.

Redwine, L., Henry, B. L., Pung, M. A., Wilson, K., Chinh, K., Knight, B., . . . Mills, P. J. (2016). A pilot randomized study of a gratitude journaling intervention on HRV and inflammatory biomarkers in Stage B heart failure patients. *Psychosomatic Medicine, 78*(6), 667–676.

Rook, K. S. (2001). Emotional health and positive versus negative social exchanges: A daily diary analysis. *Applied Developmental Science, 5*(2), 86–97.

Roorda, D. L., Koomen, H. M., Spilt, J. L., & Oort, F. J. (2011). The influence of affective teacher–student relationships on students' school engagement and achievement: A meta-analytic approach. *Review of Educational Research, 81*(4), 493–529. doi.org/10.3102/0034654311421793

Roseman, I. J. (2013). Appraisal in the emotion system: Coherence in strategies for coping. *Emotion Review, 5*(2), 141–149. doi.org/10.1177/1754073912469591

Salim, S., Asghar, M., Chugh, G., Taneja, M., Xia, Z., & Saha, K. (2010). Oxidative stress: A potential recipe for anxiety, hypertension and insulin resistance. *Brain Research, 1359*, 178–185.

Salovey, P., & Mayer, J. D. (1990). Emotional intelligence. *Imagination, Cognition and Personality, 9*(3), 185–211. doi.org/10.2190/DUGG-P24E-52WK-6CDG

Salovey, P., Rothman, A. J., Detweiler, J. B., & Steward, W. T. (2000). Emotional states and physical health. *American Psychologist, 55*(1), 110–121.

Sands, M., Ngo, N., & Isaacowitz, D. M. (2016). The interplay of motivation and emotion: View from adulthood and old age. In L. F. Barrett, M. Lewis, & J. M. Haviland-Jones (Eds.), *Handbook of Emotions* (pp. 336–349). New York: Guilford Publications.

Sapolsky, R. M. (2015). Stress and the brain: Individual variability and the inverted-U. *Nature Neuroscience, 18*(10), 1344–1346.

Sbarra, D. A., & Coan, J. A. (2018). Relationships and health: The critical role of affective science. *Emotion Review, 10*(1), 40–54. doi.org/10.1177/1754073917696584

Scarantino, A. (2016). The philosophy of emotions and its impact on affective science. In L. F. Barrett, M. Lewis, & J. M. Haviland-Jones (Eds.), *Handbook of Emotions* (pp. 3–48). New York: Guilford Publications.

Schmeichel, B. J., & Inzlicht, M. (2013). Incidental and integral effects of emotions on self-control. In M. D. Robinson, E. R. Watkins, & E. Harmon-Jones (Eds.), *Handbook of Cognition and Emotion* (pp. 272–290). New York: Guilford Publications.

Schonert-Reichl, K. A., Guhn, M., Gadermann, A. M., Hymel, S., Sweiss, L., & Hertzman, C. (2013). Development and validation of the Middle Years Development Instrument (MDI): Assessing children's well-being and assets across multiple contexts. *Social Indicators Research, 114*(2), 345–369.

Schupp, H. T., Flaisch, T., Stockburger, J., & Junghöfer, M. (2006). Emotion and attention: Event-related brain potential studies. *Progress in Brain Research, 156*, 31–51. doi.org/10.1016/S0079-6123(06)56002-9

Schutz, P. A., Pekrun, R., & Phye, G. D. (2007). *Emotion in education* (vol. 10). P. A. Schutz & R. Pekrun (Eds.). San Diego, CA: Academic Press.

Schwarz, N., & Clore, G. L. (1983). Mood, misattribution, and judgments of well-being: Informative and directive functions of affective states. *Journal of Personality and Social Psychology, 45*(3), 513–523. doi.org/10.1037/0022-3514.45.3.513

Schwarz, N., & Clore, G. L. (2003). Mood as information: 20 years later. *Psychological Inquiry, 14*(3–4), 296–303. doi.org/10.1080/1047840X.2003.9682896

Schwarz, N., & Clore, G. L. (2007). Feelings and phenomenal experiences. In A. W. Kruglanski & E. T. Higgins (Eds.), *Social Psychology: Handbook of Basic Principles* (pp. 385–407). New York: Guilford Press.

Selye, H. (2013). *Stress in Health and Disease.* Waltham, MA: Butterworth-Heinemann.

Selye, H., Memedovic, S., Grisham, J. R., Denson, T. F., & Moulds, M. L. (2010). The effects of trait reappraisal and suppression on anger and blood pressure in response to provocation. *Journal of Research in Personality, 44*(4), 540–543.

Sharma, S. (2016). Life events stress, emotional vital signs and hypertension. In A. K. Dalal & G. Misra (Eds.), *New Directions in Health Psychology* (pp. 389–408). New Delhi, India: Sage Publications.

Shields, G. S., Sazma, M. A., & Yonelinas, A. P. (2016). The effects of acute stress on core executive functions: A meta-analysis and comparison with cortisol. *Neuroscience & Biobehavioral Reviews, 68,* 651–668. doi.org/10.1016/j.neubiorev.2016.06.038

Shiota, M. N., Campos, B., Oveis, C., Hertenstein, M. J., Simon-Thomas, E., & Keltner, D. (2017). Beyond happiness: Building a science of discrete positive emotions. *American Psychologist, 72*(7), 617–643. doi.org/10.1037/a0040456

Shonkoff, J., Levitt, P., Bunge, S., Cameron, J., Duncan, G., Fisher, P., & Nox, N. (2015). Supportive relationships and active skill-building strengthen the foundations of resilience: Working paper 13. Cambridge, UK: National Scientific Council on the Developing Child.

Silvia, P. J., & Beaty, R. E. (2012). Making creative metaphors: The importance of fluid intelligence for creative thought. *Intelligence, 40*(4), 343–351.

Silvia, P. J., Martin, C., & Nusbaum, E. C. (2009). A snapshot of creativity: Evaluating a quick and simple method for assessing divergent thinking. *Thinking Skills and Creativity, 4*(2), 79–85. doi.org/10.1016/j.tsc.2009.06.005

Sinclair, R. C., & Mark, M. M. (1992). The influence of mood state on judgment and action: Effects on persuasion, categorization, social justice, person perception, and judgmental accuracy. In L. L. Martin & A. Tesser (Eds.), *The Construction of Social Judgments* (pp. 165–193). Hillsdale, NJ: Lawrence Erlbaum Associates, Inc.

Singer, J. A., & Salovey, P. (2010). *Remembered Self: Emotion and Memory in Personality.* New York: Simon & Schuster.

Stefanucci, J. K., Gagnon, K. T., & Lessard, D. A. (2011). Follow your heart: Emotion adaptively influences perception. *Social and Personality Psychology Compass, 5*(6), 296–308.

Steinberg, L. (2005). Cognitive and affective development in adolescence. *Trends in Cognitive Sciences, 9*(2), 69–74. doi.org/10.1016/j.tics.2004.12.005

Sternberg, R. J. (1999). The theory of successful intelligence. *Review of General Psychology, 3*(4), 292–316. doi.org/10.1037/1089-2680.3.4.292

Sy, T., & Côté, S. (2004). Emotional intelligence: A key ability to succeed in the matrix organization. *Journal of Management Development, 23*(5), 437–455. doi.org/10.1108/02621710410537056

Tamir, M., Mitchell, C., & Gross, J. J. (2008). Hedonic and instrumental motives in anger regulation. *Psychological Science, 19*(4), 324–328.

Tan, H. B., & Forgas, J. P. (2010). When happiness makes us selfish, but sadness makes us fair: Affective influences on interpersonal strategies in the dictator game. *Journal of Experimental Social Psychology, 46*(3), 571–576.

Tangney, J. P., Stuewig, J., & Mashek, D. J. (2007). Moral emotions and moral behavior. *Annual Review of Psychology, 58*, 345–372. doi.org/10.1146/annurev.psych.56.091103.070145

Tarullo, A. R., & Gunnar, M. R. (2006). Child maltreatment and the developing HPA axis. *Hormones and Behavior, 50*(4), 632–639.

Thorndike, E. L. (1920). Intelligence and its uses. *Harper's Magazine, 140*, 227–235.

Torrance, E. P. (1988). The nature of creativity as manifest in its testing. In R. J. Sternberg (Ed.), *The Nature of Creativity: Contemporary Psychological Perspectives* (pp. 43–75). Cambridge: Cambridge University Press.

Tversky, A., & Kahneman, D. (1974). Judgment under uncertainty: Heuristics and biases. *Science, 185*(4157), 1124–1131.

Van Kleef, G. A., Anastasopoulou, C., & Nijstad, B. A. (2010). Can expressions of anger enhance creativity? A test of the emotions as social information (EASI) model. *Journal of Experimental Social Psychology, 46*(6), 1042–1048.

Van Kleef, G. A., Oveis, C., Van Der Löwe, I., LuoKogan, A., Goetz, J., & Keltner, D. (2008). Power, distress, and compassion: Turning a blind eye to the suffering of others. *Psychological Science, 19*(12), 1315–1322.

Vingerhoets, A. J., & Bylsma, L. M. (2016). The riddle of human emotional crying: A challenge for emotion researchers. *Emotion Review, 8*(3), 207–217.

Waber, D. P., De Moor, C., Forbes, P. W., Almli, C. R., Botteron, K. N., Leonard, G., . . . Brain Development Cooperative Group. (2007). The NIH MRI study of normal brain development: Performance of a population based sample of healthy children aged 6 to 18 years on a neuropsychological battery. *Journal of the International Neuropsychological Society, 13*(5), 729–746. doi.org/10.1017/S1355617707070841

Wechsler, D. (1955). *Manual for the Wechsler Adult Intelligence Scale.* Oxford: Psychological Corp.

Weng, H. Y., Fox, A. S., Hessenthaler, H. C., Stodola, D. E., & Davidson, R. J. (2015). The role of compassion in altruistic helping and punishment behavior. *PLoS One, 10*(12), e0143794.

Wolke, D., Copeland, W. E., Angold, A., & Costello, E. J. (2013). Impact of bullying in childhood on adult health, wealth, crime, and social outcomes. *Psychological Science, 24*(10), 1958–1970.

Woodman, T., Davis, P. A., Hardy, L., Callow, N., Glasscock, I., & Yuill-Proctor, J. (2009). Emotions and sport performance: An exploration of happiness, hope, and anger. *Journal of Sport and Exercise Psychology, 31*(2), 169–188.

World Health Organization. (2017, May 17). Cardiovascular diseases (CVDs). Retrieved from www.who.int/news-room/fact-sheets/detail/cardiovascular-diseases -(cvds)

World Health Organization. (2017, December 12). Dementia. Retrieved from www .who.int/news-room/fact-sheets/detail/dementia

World Health Organization. (2018, October 30). Diabetes. Retrieved from www .who.int/news-room/fact-sheets/detail/diabetes

World Health Organization. (2018, September 12). Cancer. Retrieved from www .who.int/news-room/fact-sheets/detail/cancer

Wright, B. L., & Loving, T. J. (2011). Health implications of conflict in close relationships. *Social and Personality Psychology Compass, 5*(8), 552–562.

Yang, H., & Yang, S. (2016). Sympathy fuels creativity: The beneficial effects of sympathy on originality. *Thinking Skills and Creativity, 21*, 132–143.

Yiend, J. (2010). The effects of emotion on attention: A review of attentional processing of emotional information. *Cognition and Emotion, 24*(1), 3–47. doi.org/10.1080 /02699930903205698

Yip, J. A., & Côté, S. (2013). The emotionally intelligent decision maker: Emotion-understanding ability reduces the effect of incidental anxiety on risk taking. *Psychological Science, 24*(1), 48–55. doi.org/10.1177/0956797612450031

Yip, J. A., Stein, D. H., Côté, S., & Carney, D. R. (2019). Follow your gut? Emotional intelligence moderates the association between physiologically measured somatic markers and risk-taking. *Emotion.* Advance online publication. doi.org/10.1037 /emo0000561

Zadra, J. R., & Clore, G. L. (2011). Emotion and perception: The role of affective information. *Wiley Interdisciplinary Reviews: Cognitive Science, 2*(6), 676–685.

Zelazo, P. D., & Müller, U. (2002). Executive function in typical and atypical development. In U. Goswami (Ed.), *Blackwell Handbook of Childhood Cognitive Development* (pp. 445–469). Hoboken, NJ: Blackwell Publishers.

Zeman, J., Cassano, M., Perry-Parrish, C., & Stegall, S. (2006). Emotion regulation in children and adolescents. *Journal of Developmental & Behavioral Pediatrics*, 27(2), 155–168. doi.org/10.1097/00004703-200604000-00014

Zimmermann, P., & Iwanski, A. (2014). Emotion regulation from early adolescence to emerging adulthood and middle adulthood: Age differences, gender differences, and emotion-specific developmental variations. *International Journal of Behavioral Development*, 38(2), 182–194. doi.org/10.1177/0165025413515405

3. How to Become an Emotion Scientist

American Psychological Association. (2002). *The road to resilience*. Retrieved from www.apa.org/helpcenter/road-resilience

Boyce, T. W. (2019). *The Orchid and the Dandelion: Why Some Children Struggle and How All Can Thrive*. New York: Alfred A. Knopf.

Brackett, M. A., Mayer, J. D., & Warner, R. M. (2004). Emotional intelligence and its relation to everyday behaviour. *Personality and Individual Differences*, 36(6), 1387–1402. doi.org/10.1016/S0191-8869(03)00236-8

Brackett, M. A., & Rivers, S. E. (2014). Transforming students' lives with social and emotional learning. In R. Pekrun & L. Linnenbrink-Garcia (Eds.), *International Handbook of Emotions in Education* (pp. 368–388). New York: Routledge.

Brackett, M. A., Rivers, S. E., Bertoli, M. C., & Salovey, P. (2016). Emotional intelligence. In L. F. Barrett, M. Lewis, & J. M. Haviland-Jones (Eds.), *Handbook of Emotions* (pp. 513–531). New York: Guilford Publications.

Brackett, M. A., Rivers, S. E., Shiffman, S., Lerner, N., & Salovey, P. (2006). Relating emotional abilities to social functioning: A comparison of self-report and performance measures of emotional intelligence. *Journal of Personality and Social Psychology*, 91(4), 780–795. doi.org/10.1037/0022-3514.91.4.780

Brackett, M. A., & Salovey, P. (2004). Measuring emotional intelligence with the Mayer-Salovey-Caruso Emotional Intelligence Test (MSCEIT). In G. Geher (Ed.), *Measuring Emotional Intelligence: Common Ground and Controversy* (pp. 179–94). Happauge, NY: Nova Science Publishers, Inc.

Côté, S., Lopes, P. N., Salovey, P., & Miners, C. T. (2010). Emotional intelligence and leadership emergence in small groups. *Leadership Quarterly*, 21(3), 496–508. doi.org/10.1016/j.leaqua.2010.03.012

Crombie, D., Lombard, C., & Noakes, T. (2011). Increasing emotional intelligence in cricketers: An intervention study. *International Journal of Sports Science & Coaching*, 6(1), 69–86. doi.org/10.1260/1747-9541.6.1.69

Damasio, A. (2018). *The Strange Order of Things: Life, Feeling, and the Making of Cultures*. New York: Vintage Books.

Duckworth, A. (2016). *Grit: The Power of Passion and Perseverance*. New York: Scribner.

Dunn, E. W., Brackett, M. A., Ashton-James, C., Schneiderman, E., & Salovey, P. (2007). On emotionally intelligent time travel: Individual differences in affective forecasting ability. *Personality and Social Psychology Bulletin, 33*(1), 85–93. doi.org /10.1177/0146167206294201

Dweck, C. (2006). *Mindset: The New Psychology of Success.* New York: Ballantine Books.

Fernandez-Berrocal, P., Alcaide, R., Extremera, N., & Pizarro, D. (2006). The role of emotional intelligence in anxiety and depression among adolescents. *Individual Differences Research, 4*(1), 16–27. Retrieved from http://emotional.intelligence .uma.es/documentos/pdf60among_adolescents.pdf

Ivcevic, Z., & Brackett, M. (2014). Predicting school success: Comparing conscientiousness, grit, and emotion regulation ability. *Journal of Research in Personality, 52,* 29–36. doi.org/10.1016/j.jrp.2014.06.005

Ivcevic, Z., Brackett, M. A., & Mayer, J. D. (2007). Emotional intelligence and emotional creativity. *Journal of Personality, 75*(2), 199–236. doi.org/10.1111/j.1467 -6494.2007.00437.x

Kumar, S. (2014). Establishing linkages between emotional intelligence and transformational leadership. *Industrial Psychiatry Journal, 23*(1), 1–3. doi.org/10.4103 /0972-6748.144934

Martins, A., Ramalho, N., & Morin, E. (2010). A comprehensive meta-analysis of the relationship between emotional intelligence and health. *Personality and Individual Differences, 49*(6), 554–564. doi.org/10.1016/j.paid.2010.05.029

Miao, C., Humphrey, R. H., & Qian, S. (2017). A meta-analysis of emotional intelligence and work attitudes. *Journal of Occupational and Organizational Psychology, 90*(2), 177–202. doi.org/10.1111/joop.12167

Reuben, E., Sapienza, P., & Zingales, L. (2009). *Can we teach emotional intelligence.* (Unpublished manuscript.) New York: Columbia Business School, Columbia University.

Rivers, S. E., Brackett, M. A., Reyes, M. R., Mayer, J. D., Caruso, D. R., & Salovey, P. (2012). Measuring emotional intelligence in early adolescence with the MS-CEIT-YV: Psychometric properties and relationship with academic performance and psychosocial functioning. *Journal of Psychoeducational Assessment, 30*(4), 344–366. doi.org/10.1177/0734282912449443

Salovey, P., & Mayer, J. D. (1990). Emotional intelligence. *Imagination, Cognition and Personality, 9*(3), 185–211. doi.org/10.2190/DUGG-P24E-52WK-6CDG

Schutte, N. S., Malouff, J. M., Bobik, C., Coston, T. D., Greeson, C., Jedlicka, C., . . . Wendorf, G. (2001). Emotional intelligence and interpersonal relations. *Journal of Social Psychology, 141*(4), 523–536. doi.org/10.1080/00224540109600569

Sharot, T. (2011). The optimism bias. *Current Biology, 21*(23), R941–R945. doi.org/10 .1016/j.cub.2011.10.030

Tsai, J. L., Louie, J. Y., Chen, E. E., & Uchida, Y. (2007). Learning what feelings to desire: Socialization of ideal affect through children's storybooks. *Personality and Social Psychology Bulletin, 33*(1), 17–30. doi.org/10.1177/0146167206292749

Yip, J. A., & Côté, S. (2013). The emotionally intelligent decision maker: Emotion-understanding ability reduces the effect of incidental anxiety on risk taking. *Psychological Science, 24*(1), 48–55. doi.org/10.1177/0956797612450031

Zhang, H.-H., & Wang, H. (2011). A meta-analysis of the relationship between individual emotional intelligence and workplace performance. *Acta Psychologica Sinica, 43*(2), 188–202. Retrieved from http://en.cnki.com.cn/Article_en /CJFDTOTAL-XLXB201102009.htm

4. R: Recognizing Emotion

Ackerman, J. M., Shapiro, J. R., Neuberg, S. L., Kenrick, D. T., Becker, D. V., Griskevicius, V., . . . Schaller, M. (2006). They all look the same to me (unless they're angry) from out-group homogeneity to out-group heterogeneity. *Psychological Science, 17*(10), 836–840.

Adams Jr., R. B., Hess, U., & Kleck, R. E. (2015). The intersection of gender-related facial appearance and facial displays of emotion. *Emotion Review, 7*(1), 5–13.

Ambady, N., & Weisbuch, M. (2010). Nonverbal behavior. In S. T. Riske, D. T. Gilbert, & G. Lindzey (Eds.), *Handbook of Social Psychology* (vol. 5, pp. 464–497). Hoboken, NJ: John Wiley & Sons.

Aviezer, H., Hassin, R. R., Ryan, J., Grady, C., Susskind, J., Anderson, A., . . . Bentin, S. (2008). Angry, disgusted, or afraid? Studies on the malleability of emotion perception. *Psychological Science, 19*(7), 724–732.

Bar-Haim, Y., Lamy, D., Pergamin, L., Bakermans-Kranenburg, M. J., & Van Ijzendoorn, M. H. (2007). Threat-related attentional bias in anxious and nonanxious individuals: a meta-analytic study. *Psychological Bulletin, 133*(1), 1–24.

Barrett, L. F. (2017). *How Emotions Are Made: The Secret Life of the Brain.* Boston, MA: Houghton Mifflin Harcourt.

Barrett, L. F., Mesquita, B., & Gendron, M. (2011). Context in emotion perception. *Current Directions in Psychological Science, 20*(5), 286–290.

Baumeister, R. F., Bratslavsky, E., Finkenauer, C., & Vohs, K. D. (2001). Bad is stronger than good. *Review of General Psychology, 5*(4), 323–370.

Becker, M. W., & Leinenger, M. (2011). Attentional selection is biased toward mood-congruent stimuli. *Emotion, 11*(5), 1248–1254.

Brackett, M. A., Patti, J., Stern, R., Rivers, S. E., Elbertson, N. A., Chisholm, C., &

Salovey, P. (2009). A sustainable, skill-based approach to building emotionally literate schools. In M. Hughes, H. L. Thompson, & J. B. Terrell (Eds.), *Handbook for Developing Emotional and Social Intelligence: Best Practices, Case Studies, and Strategies* (pp. 329–358). San Francisco, CA: Pfeiffer/John Wiley & Sons.

Brackett, M. A., & Rivers, S. E. (2014). Transforming students' lives with social and emotional learning. In R. Pekrun & L. Linnenbrink-Garcia (Eds.), *International Handbook of Emotions in Education* (pp. 368–388). New York: Routledge.

Bryant, G. A., Fessler, D. M., Fusaroli, R., Clint, E., Amir, D., Chávez, B., . . . Fux, M. (2018). The perception of spontaneous and volitional laughter across 21 societies. *Psychological Science, 29*(9), 1515–1525.

Caruso, D. R., & Salovey, P. (2004). *The Emotionally Intelligent Manager: How to Develop and Use the Four Key Emotional Skills of Leadership.* Hoboken, NJ: John Wiley & Sons.

Clark, M. S., Von Culin, K. R., Clark-Polner, E., & Lemay Jr., E. P. (2017). Accuracy and projection in perceptions of partners' recent emotional experiences: Both minds matter. *Emotion, 17*(2), 196–207.

Clore, G. L., & Huntsinger, J. R. (2007). How emotions inform judgment and regulate thought. *Trends in Cognitive Sciences, 11*(9), 393–399.

Cohen, D., & Gunz, A. (2002). As seen by the other . . . : Perspectives on the self in the memories and emotional perceptions of Easterners and Westerners. *Psychological Science, 13*(1), 55–59.

Cordaro, D. T., Keltner, D., Tshering, S., Wangchuk, D., & Flynn, L. M. (2016). The voice conveys emotion in ten globalized cultures and one remote village in Bhutan. *Emotion, 16*(1), 117–128.

Cordaro, D. T., Sun, R., Keltner, D., Kamble, S., Huddar, N., & McNeil, G. (2018). Universals and cultural variations in 22 emotional expressions across five cultures. *Emotion, 18*(1), 75–93.

Dalili, M. N., Penton-Voak, I. S., Harmer, C. J., & Munafo, M. R. (2015). Meta-analysis of emotion recognition deficits in major depressive disorder. *Psychological Medicine, 45*(6), 1135–1144.

Darwin, C., & Prodger, P. (1872/1998). *The Expression of the Emotions in Man and Animals.* Oxford: Oxford University Press.

Demenescu, L. R., Kortekaas, R., den Boer, J. A., & Aleman, A. (2010). Impaired attribution of emotion to facial expressions in anxiety and major depression. *PloS One, 5*(12), e15058.

Ekman, P. (1992). An argument for basic emotions. *Cognition & Emotion, 6*(3–4), 169–200.

Ekman, P., & Friesen, W. V. (1971). Constants across cultures in the face and emotion. *Journal of Personality and Social Psychology, 17*(2), 124–129.

Ekman, P., Friesen, W. V., & Ellsworth, P. (1972). *Emotion in the Human Face: Guidelines for Research and an Integration of Findings*. New York: Pergamon.

Elfenbein, H. A., & Ambady, N. (2003). Universals and cultural differences in recognizing emotions. *Current Directions in Psychological Science, 12*(5), 159–164.

Forgas, J. P., & Bower, G. H. (2001). Mood effects on person-perception judgments. In W. G. Parrott (Ed.), *Emotions in Social Psychology: Essential Readings* (pp. 204–215). Philadelphia: Psychology Press.

Füstös, J., Gramann, K., Herbert, B. M., & Pollatos, O. (2012). On the embodiment of emotion regulation: Interoceptive awareness facilitates reappraisal. *Social Cognitive and Affective Neuroscience, 8*(8), 911–917.

Gendron, M., Roberson, D., van der Vyver, J. M., & Barrett, L. F. (2014). Perceptions of emotion from facial expressions are not culturally universal: Evidence from a remote culture. *Emotion, 14*(2), 251–262.

Gilovich, T., Medvec, V. H., & Savitsky, K. (2000). The spotlight effect in social judgment: An egocentric bias in estimates of the salience of one's own actions and appearance. *Journal of Personality and Social Psychology, 78*(2), 211–222.

Hertenstein, M. J., Holmes, R., McCullough, M., & Keltner, D. (2009). The communication of emotion via touch. *Emotion, 9*(4), 566–573.

Hertenstein, M. J., Keltner, D., App, B., Bulleit, B. A., & Jaskolka, A. R. (2006). Touch communicates distinct emotions. *Emotion, 6*(3), 528–533.

Hess, U., Adams Jr, R. B., & Kleck, R. E. (2004). Facial appearance, gender, and emotion expression. *Emotion, 4*(4), 378–388.

Hess, U., Adams, R. B., Grammer, K., & Kleck, R. E. (2009). Face gender and emotion expression: Are angry women more like men? *Journal of Vision, 9*(12), article 19.

Isbell, L. M., & Lair, E. C. (2013). Moods, emotions, and evaluations as information. In D. Carlston (Ed.), *The Oxford Handbook of Social Cognition* (pp. 435–462). New York: Oxford University Press.

Ito, T., Yokokawa, K., Yahata, N., Isato, A., Suhara, T., & Yamada, M. (2017). Neural basis of negativity bias in the perception of ambiguous facial expression. *Scientific Reports, 7*(1), 420.

Izard, C. E., Woodburn, E. M., Finlon, K. J., Krauthamer-Ewing, E. S., Grossman, S. R., & Seidenfeld, A. (2011). Emotion knowledge, emotion utilization, and emotion regulation. *Emotion Review, 3*(1), 44–52.

Joseph, D. L., & Newman, D. A. (2010). Emotional intelligence: An integrative meta-analysis and cascading model. *Journal of Applied Psychology, 95*(1), 54–78.

Knapp, M. L., Hall, J. A., & Horgan, T. G. (2013). *Nonverbal Communication in Human Interaction*. Boston, MA: Cengage Learning.

Knyazev, G. G., Bocharov, A. V., Slobodskaya, H. R., & Ryabichenko, T. I. (2008).

Personality-linked biases in perception of emotional facial expressions. *Personality and Individual Differences, 44*(5), 1093–1104.

Krumhuber, E., & Kappas, A. (2005). Moving smiles: The role of dynamic components for the perception of the genuineness of smiles. *Journal of Nonverbal Behavior, 29*(1), 3–24.

Lewis, M. D. (2005). Bridging emotion theory and neurobiology through dynamic systems modeling. *Behavioral and Brain Sciences, 28*(2), 169–194.

Matsumoto, D. (1999). American-Japanese cultural differences in judgements of expression intensity and subjective experience. *Cognition & Emotion, 13*(2), 201–218.

Matsumoto, D., & Ekman, P. (1989). American-Japanese cultural differences in intensity ratings of facial expressions of emotion. *Motivation and Emotion, 13*(2), 143–157.

Mesquita, B., De Leersnyder, J., & Boiger, M. (2016). The cultural psychology of emotions. In L. F. Barrett, M. Lewis, & J. M. Haviland-Jones (Eds.), *Handbook of Emotions* (pp. 393–-411). New York: Guilford Publications.

Nathanson, L., Rivers, S. E., Flynn, L. M., & Brackett, M. A. (2016). Creating emotionally intelligent schools with RULER. *Emotion Review, 8*(4), 305–310.

Pope, A. (1903). *Essay on criticism.* London: JM Dent.

Roseman, I. J. (2013). Appraisal in the emotion system: Coherence in strategies for coping. *Emotion Review, 5*(2), 141–149.

Rosenthal, R. (2003). Covert communication in laboratories, classrooms, and the truly real world. *Current Directions in Psychological Science, 12*(5), 151–154.

Rozin, P., & Royzman, E. B. (2001). Negativity bias, negativity dominance, and contagion. *Personality and Social Psychology Review, 5*(4), 296–320.

Russell, J. A. (1980). A circumplex model of affect. *Journal of Personality and Social Psychology, 39*(6), 1161–1178.

Schönenberg, M., & Jusyte, A. (2014). Investigation of the hostile attribution bias toward ambiguous facial cues in antisocial violent offenders. *European Archives of Psychiatry and Clinical Neuroscience, 264*(1), 61–69.

Wang, Q., Chen, G., Wang, Z., Hu, C. S., Hu, X., & Fu, G. (2014). Implicit racial attitudes influence perceived emotional intensity on other-race faces. *PloS One, 9*(8), e105946.

Weiss, B., Dodge, K. A., Bates, J. E., & Pettit, G. S. (1992). Some consequences of early harsh discipline: Child aggression and a maladaptive social information processing style. *Child Development, 63*(6), 1321–1335.

Widmeyer, W. N., & Loy, J. W. (1988). When you're hot, you're hot! Warm-cold effects in first impressions of persons and teaching effectiveness. *Journal of Educational Psychology, 80*(1), 118–121.

5. U: Understanding Emotion

Bowers, M. E., & Yehuda, R. (2016). Intergenerational transmission of stress in humans. *Neuropsychopharmacology, 41*(1), 232–244.

Brackett, M. A., Patti, J., Stern, R., Rivers, S. E., Elbertson, N. A., Chisholm, C., & Salovey, P. (2009). A sustainable, skill-based approach to building emotionally literate schools. In M. Hughes, H. L. Thompson, & J. B. Terrell (Eds.), *Handbook for Developing Emotional and Social Intelligence: Best Practices, Case Studies, and Strategies* (pp. 329–358). San Francisco, CA: Pfeiffer/John Wiley & Sons.

Brackett, M. A., & Rivers, S. E. (2014). Transforming students' lives with social and emotional learning. In R. Pekrun & L. Linnenbrink-Garcia (Eds.), *International Handbook of Emotions in Education* (pp. 368–388). New York: Routledge.

Campos, B., Shiota, M. N., Keltner, D., Gonzaga, G. C., & Goetz, J. L. (2013). What is shared, what is different? Core relational themes and expressive displays of eight positive emotions. *Cognition & Emotion, 27*(1), 37–52.

Clore, G. L. & Schiller, A. J. (2016). New light on the affect-cognition connection. In L. F. Barrett, M. Lewis, & J. M. Haviland-Jones (Eds.), *Handbook of Emotions* (pp. 532–546). New York: Guilford Publications.

Cordaro, D. T., Brackett, M., Glass, L., & Anderson, C. L. (2016). Contentment: Perceived completeness across cultures and traditions. *Review of General Psychology, 20*(3), 221–235.

Dekel, R., & Goldblatt, H. (2008). Is there intergenerational transmission of trauma? The case of combat veterans' children. *American Journal of Orthopsychiatry, 78*(3), 281–289.

Fredrickson, B. L. (2013). Positive emotions broaden and build. In P. Devine & A. Plant (Eds.), *Advances in Experimental Social Psychology* (vol. 47, pp. 1–53). Cambridge, MA: Academic Press.

Genzel, B., Rarick, J. R. D., & Morris, P. A. (2016). Stress and emotion: Embodied, in context, and across the lifespan. In L. F. Barrett, M. Lewis, & J. M. Haviland-Jones (Eds.), *Handbook of Emotions* (pp. 707–735). New York: Guilford Publications.

Kelley, H. H., & Michela, J. L. (1980). Attribution theory and research. *Annual Review of Psychology, 31*(1), 457–501.

Lazarus, R. S. (1991). Progress on a cognitive-motivational-relational theory of emotion. *American Psychologist, 46*(8), 819–834.

Lewis, M. (2016). Self-conscious emotions: Embarrassment, pride, shame, guilt, and hubris. In L. F. Barrett, M. Lewis, & J. M. Haviland-Jones (Eds.), *Handbook of Emotions* (pp. 792–814). New York: Guilford Publications.

Lupien, S. J., McEwen, B. S., Gunnar, M. R., & Heim, C. (2009). Effects of stress throughout the lifespan on the brain, behaviour and cognition. *Nature Reviews Neuroscience, 10*, 434–445.

Mendes, W. B. (2016). Emotion and the autonomic nervous system. In L. F. Barrett, M. Lewis, & J. M. Haviland-Jones (Eds.), *Handbook of Emotions* (pp. 166–181). New York: Guilford Publications.

Moeller, J., Ivcevic, Z., Brackett, M. A., & White, A. E. (2018). Mixed emotions: Network analyses of intra-individual co-occurrences within and across situations. *Emotion, 18*(8), 1106–1121.

Moors, A., Ellsworth, P. C., Scherer, K. R., & Frijda, N. H. (2013). Appraisal theories of emotion: State of the art and future development. *Emotion Review, 5*(2), 119–124.

Nathanson, L., Rivers, S. E., Flynn, L. M., & Brackett, M. A. (2016). Creating emotionally intelligent schools with RULER. *Emotion Review, 8*(4), 305–310.

Parrott, W. G., & Smith, R. H. (1993). Distinguishing the experiences of envy and jealousy. *Journal of Personality and Social Psychology, 64*(6), 906–920.

Roseman, I. J. (1991). Appraisal determinants of discrete emotions. *Cognition & Emotion, 5*(3), 161–200.

Roseman, I. J. (2013). Appraisal in the emotion system: Coherence in strategies for coping. *Emotion Review, 5*(2), 141–149.

Russell, J. A. (1980). A circumplex model of affect. *Journal of Personality and Social Psychology, 39*(6), 1161–1178.

Salovey, P. (Ed.). (1991). *The Psychology of Jealousy and Envy.* New York: Guilford Press.

Scherer, K. R., Schorr, A., & Johnstone, T. (Eds.). (2001). *Appraisal Processes in Emotion: Theory, Methods, Research.* New York: Oxford University Press.

Shields, G. S., Sazma, M. A., & Yonelinas, A. P. (2016). The effects of acute stress on core executive functions: A meta-analysis and comparison with cortisol. *Neuroscience & Biobehavioral Reviews, 68*, 651–668.

Steinberg, L. (2005). Cognitive and affective development in adolescence. *Trends in Cognitive Sciences, 9*(2), 69–74.

Tracy, J. L., & Robins, R. W. (2006). Appraisal antecedents of shame and guilt: Support for a theoretical model. *Personality and Social Psychology Bulletin, 32*(10), 1339–1351.

Weiner, B. (1985). An attributional theory of achievement motivation and emotion. *Psychological Review, 92*(4), 548–573.

Weisinger, H., & Pawliw-Fry, J. P. (2015). *Performing Under Pressure: The Science of Doing Your Best When it Matters Most.* New York: Crown Publishing.

Zeman, J., Cassano, M., Perry-Parrish, C., & Stegall, S. (2006). Emotion regulation in children and adolescents. *Journal of Developmental & Behavioral Pediatrics, 27*(2), 155–168.

Zimmermann, P., & Iwanski, A. (2014). Emotion regulation from early adolescence to emerging adulthood and middle adulthood: Age differences, gender differences, and emotion-specific developmental variations. *International Journal of Behavioral Development, 38*(2), 182–194.

6. L: Labeling Emotion

Barrett, L. F. (2006). Solving the emotion paradox: Categorization and the experience of emotion. *Personality and Social Psychology Review, 10*(1), 20–46.

Barrett, L. F. (2017). *How Emotions Are Made: The Secret Life of the Brain.* Boston: Houghton Mifflin Harcourt.

Barrett, L. F. (2017). The theory of constructed emotion: An active inference account of interoception and categorization. *Social Cognitive and Affective Neuroscience, 12*(1), 1–23.

Barrett, L. F., Gross, J., Christensen, T. C., & Benvenuto, M. (2001). Knowing what you're feeling and knowing what to do about it: Mapping the relation between emotion differentiation and emotion regulation. *Cognition and Emotion, 15*(6), 713–724.

Baumeister, R. F., Bratslavsky, E., Finkenauer, C., & Vohs, K. D. (2001). Bad is stronger than good. *Review of General Psychology, 5*(4), 323–370.

Bird, G., & Cook, R. (2013). Mixed emotions: The contribution of alexithymia to the emotional symptoms of autism. *Translational Psychiatry, 3*(7), e285.

Camras, L. A., Fatani, S. S., Fraumeni, B. R., & Shuster, M. M. (2016). The development of facial expressions: Current perspectives on infant emotions. In L. F. Barrett, M. Lewis, & J. M. Haviland-Jones (Eds.), *Handbook of Emotions* (pp. 255–271). New York: Guilford Publications.

Cosmides, L., & Tooby, J. (2000). Evolutionary psychology and the emotions. In M. Lewis & J. M. Haviland-Jones (Eds.), *Handbook of Emotions* (pp. 91–115). New York: Guilford Publications.

Creswell, J. D., Way, B. M., Eisenberger, N. I., & Lieberman, M. D. (2007). Neural correlates of dispositional mindfulness during affect labeling. *Psychosomatic Medicine, 69*(6), 560–565.

Demaree, H. A., Everhart, D. E., Youngstrom, E. A., & Harrison, D. W. (2005). Brain lateralization of emotional processing: Historical roots and a future incorporating "dominance." *Behavioral and Cognitive Neuroscience Reviews, 4*(1), 3–20.

Durkin, K., & Conti-Ramsden, G. (2010). Young people with specific language impairment: A review of social and emotional functioning in adolescence. *Child Language Teaching and Therapy, 26*(2), 105–121.

Durlak, J. A., Weissberg, R. P., Dymnicki, A. B., Taylor, R. D., & Schellinger, K. B. (2011). The impact of enhancing students' social and emotional learning: A meta-analysis of school-based universal interventions. *Child Development, 82*(1), 405–432.

Eisenberg, N., Sadovsky, A., & Spinrad, T. L. (2005). Associations of emotion-related regulation with language skills, emotion knowledge, and academic outcomes. *New Directions for Child and Adolescent Development, 2005*(109), 109–118.

Elert, E. (2013, January 4). 21 emotions for which there are no English words [infographic]. *Popular Science.* Retrieved from www.popsci.com/science/article/2013 -01/emotions-which-there-are-no-english-words-infographic

Harris, P. L., de Rosnay, M., & Pons, F. (2016). Understanding emotion. In L. F. Barrett, M. Lewis, & J. M. Haviland-Jones (Eds.), *Handbook of Emotions* (pp. 293–306). New York: Guilford Publications.

Hart, B., & Risley, T. R. (1995). *Meaningful Differences in the Everyday Experience of Young American Children.* Baltimore, MD: Paul H. Brookes Publishing.

Hussein, B. A. S. (2012). The Sapir-Whorf hypothesis today. *Theory and Practice in Language Studies, 2*(3), 642–646.

Izard, C. E., Woodburn, E. M., Finlon, K. J., Krauthamer-Ewing, E. S., Grossman, S. R., & Seidenfeld, A. (2011). Emotion knowledge, emotion utilization, and emotion regulation. *Emotion Review, 3*(1), 44–52.

Izard, C., Fine, S., Schultz, D., Mostow, A., Ackerman, B., & Youngstrom, E. (2001). Emotion knowledge as a predictor of social behavior and academic competence in children at risk. *Psychological Science, 12*(1), 18–23.

Kashdan, T. B., Barrett, L. F., & McKnight, P. E. (2015). Unpacking emotion differentiation: Transforming unpleasant experience by perceiving distinctions in negativity. *Current Directions in Psychological Science, 24*(1), 10–16.

Kircanski, K., Lieberman, M. D., & Craske, M. G. (2012). Feelings into words: Contributions of language to exposure therapy. *Psychological Science, 23*(10), 1086–1091.

Larsen, J. K., Brand, N., Bermond, B., & Hijman, R. (2003). Cognitive and emotional characteristics of alexithymia: A review of neurobiological studies. *Journal of Psychosomatic Research, 54*(6), 533–541.

Lewis, M. (2016). The emergence of human emotions. In L. F. Barrett, M. Lewis, & J. M. Haviland-Jones (Eds.), *Handbook of Emotions* (pp. 272–292). New York: Guilford Publications.

Li, J., Wang, L., & Fischer, K. (2004). The organisation of Chinese shame concepts? *Cognition and Emotion, 18*(6), 767–797.

Lieberman, M. D., Eisenberger, N. I., Crockett, M. J., Tom, S. M., Pfeifer, J. H., & Way, B. M. (2007). Putting feelings into words. *Psychological Science, 18*(5), 421–428.

Lieberman, M. D., Inagaki, T. K., Tabibnia, G., & Crockett, M. J. (2011). Subjective responses to emotional stimuli during labeling, reappraisal, and distraction. *Emotion, 11*(3), 468–480.

Lindquist, K. A., Gendron, M., & Satpute, A. B. (2016). Language and emotion: Putting words into feelings and feelings into words. In L. F. Barrett, M. Lewis, & J. M. Haviland-Jones (Eds.), *Handbook of Emotions* (pp. 579–594). New York: Guilford Publications.

Mohammad, S. M., & Turney, P. D. (2010, June). Emotions evoked by common words and phrases: Using mechanical turk to create an emotion lexicon. In Proceedings of the NAACL HLT 2010 workshop on computational approaches to analysis and generation of emotion in text (pp. 26–34). Stroudsburg, PA: Association for Computational Linguistics.

Pennebaker, J. W. (1993). Putting stress into words: Health, linguistic, and therapeutic implications. *Behaviour Research and Therapy, 31*(6), 539–548.

Pennebaker, J. W. (2018). Expressive writing in psychological science. *Perspectives on Psychological Science, 13*(2), 226–229.

Robson, D. (2017, January 26). The "untranslatable" emotions you never knew you had. BBC. Retrieved from www.bbc.com/future/story/20170126-the-untranslatable-emotions-you-never-knew-you-had

Rozin, P., & Royzman, E. B. (2001). Negativity bias, negativity dominance, and contagion. *Personality and Social Psychology Review, 5*(4), 296–320.

Schrauf, R. W., & Sanchez, J. (2004). The preponderance of negative emotion words in the emotion lexicon: A cross-generational and cross-linguistic study. *Journal of Multilingual and Multicultural Development, 25*(2–3), 266–284.

Sperry, D. E., Sperry, L. L., & Miller, P. J. (in press). Reexamining the verbal environments of children from different Socioeconomic backgrounds. *Child Development.*

St. Clair, M. C., Pickles, A., Durkin, K., & Conti-Ramsden, G. (2011). A longitudinal study of behavioral, emotional and social difficulties in individuals with a history of specific language impairment (SLI). *Journal of Communication Disorders, 44*(2), 186–199.

Taylor, G. J., & Bagby, R. M. (2000). An overview of the alexithymia construct. In R. Bar-On & J. D. A. Parker (Eds.), *The Handbook of Emotional Intelligence: Theory, Development, Assessment, and Application at Home, School, and in the Workplace* (pp. 40–67). San Francisco, CA: Jossey-Bass.

Toivonen, R., Kivelä, M., Saramäki, J., Viinikainen, M., Vanhatalo, M., & Sams, M. (2012). Networks of emotion concepts. *PLoS One, 7*(1), e28883.

Torre, J. B., & Lieberman, M. D. (2018). Putting feelings into words: Affect labeling as implicit emotion regulation. *Emotion Review, 10*(2), 116–124.

Torrisi, S. J., Lieberman, M. D., Bookheimer, S. Y., & Altshuler, L. L. (2013).

Advancing understanding of affect labeling with dynamic causal modeling. *NeuroImage, 82*, 481–488.

Tugade, M. M., Fredrickson, B. L., & Feldman Barrett, L. (2004). Psychological resilience and positive emotional granularity: Examining the benefits of positive emotions on coping and health. *Journal of Personality, 72*(6), 1161–1190.

Weisleder, A., & Fernald, A. (2013). Talking to children matters: Early language experience strengthens processing and builds vocabulary. *Psychological Science, 24*(11), 2143–2152.

Widen, S. C. (2016). The development of children's concepts of emotion. In L. F. Barrett, M. Lewis, & J. M. Haviland-Jones (Eds.), *Handbook of Emotions* (pp. 307–318). New York: Guilford Publications.

Wierzbicka, A. (2006). *English: Meaning and Culture.* New York: Oxford University Press.

Yew, S. G. K., & O'Kearney, R. (2013). Emotional and behavioural outcomes later in childhood and adolescence for children with specific language impairments: Meta-analyses of controlled prospective studies. *Journal of Child Psychology and Psychiatry, 54*(5), 516–524.

7. E: Expressing Emotion

Barrett, L. F. (2017). *How Emotions Are Made: The Secret Life of the Brain.* Boston: Houghton Mifflin Harcourt.

Barrett, L. F., Lewis, M., & Haviland-Jones, J. M. (Eds.). (2016). *Handbook of Emotions.* New York: Guilford Publications.

Brody, L. R. (1993). On understanding gender differences in the expression of emotion. In S. L. Ablon, D. P. Brown, E. J. Khantzian, & J. E. Mack (Eds.), *Human Feelings: Explorations in Affect Development and Meaning* (pp. 87–121). Hillsdale, NJ: Analytic Press, Inc.

Brody, L. R. (2000). The socialization of gender differences in emotional expression: Display rules, infant temperament, and differentiation. *Gender and Emotion: Social Psychological Perspectives, 2,* 24–47. doi.org/10.1017/CBO9780511628191.003

Buck, R. (1977). Nonverbal communication of affect in preschool children: Relationships with personality and skin conductance. *Journal of Personality and Social Psychology, 35*(4), 225–236.

Buck, R. (1984). *The Communication of Emotion.* New York: Guilford Press.

Chaplin, T. M., & Aldao, A. (2013). Gender differences in emotion expression in children: A meta-analytic review. *Psychological Bulletin, 139*(4), 735–765.

Chaplin, T. M., Hong, K., Bergquist, K., & Sinha, R. (2008). Gender differences in response to emotional stress: an assessment across subjective, behavioral, and physiological domains and relations to alcohol craving. *Alcoholism: Clinical and Experimental Research, 32*(7), 1242–1250.

Danner, D. D., Snowdon, D. A., & Friesen, W. V. (2001). Positive emotions in early life and longevity: Findings from the nun study. *Journal of Personality and Social Psychology, 80*(5), 804–813.

Darwin, C., & Prodger, P. (1998). *The Expression of the Emotions in Man and Animals.* Oxford: Oxford University Press.

Domagalski, T. A., & Steelman, L. A. (2007). The impact of gender and organizational status on workplace anger expression. *Management Communication Quarterly, 20*(3), 297–315.

Ekman, P. (2009). Lie catching and microexpressions. In C. Martin (Ed.), *The Philosophy of Deception* (pp. 118–137). Oxford: Oxford University Press.

Finkenauer, C., & Rimé, B. (1998). Keeping emotional memories secret: Health and subjective well-being when emotions are not shared. *Journal of Health Psychology, 3*(1), 47–58.

Friesen, W. V. (1972). *Cultural differences in facial expressions in a social situation: An experimental test of the concept of display rules* (Unpublished doctoral dissertation). University of California–San Francisco, San Francisco, CA.

Grandey, A. A. (2015). Smiling for a wage: What emotional labor teaches us about emotion regulation. *Psychological Inquiry, 26*(1), 54–60.

Grandey, A., Foo, S. C., Groth, M., & Goodwin, R. E. (2012). Free to be you and me: A climate of authenticity alleviates burnout from emotional labor. *Journal of Occupational Health Psychology, 17*(1), 1–14.

Gross, J. J., & John, O. P. (1997). Revealing feelings: Facets of emotional expressivity in self-reports, peer ratings, and behavior. *Journal of Personality and Social Psychology, 72*(2), 435–448.

Hagenauer, G., & Volet, S. E. (2014). "I don't hide my feelings, even though I try to": Insight into teacher educator emotion display. *Australian Educational Researcher, 41*(3), 261–281.

Hall, J. A., Carter, J. D., & Horgan, T. G. (2000). Gender differences in nonverbal communication of emotion. In A. H. Fischer (Ed.), *Studies in Emotion and Social Interaction. Second series. Gender and Emotion: Social Psychological Perspectives* (pp. 97–117). New York: Cambridge University Press. doi.org/10.1017 /CBO9780511628191.006

Hall, J. A., & Schmid Mast, M. (2008). Are women always more interpersonally sensitive than men? Impact of goals and content domain. *Personality and Social Psychology Bulletin, 34*(1), 144–155.

Harker, L., & Keltner, D. (2001). Expressions of positive emotion in women's college yearbook pictures and their relationship to personality and life outcomes across adulthood. *Journal of Personality and Social Psychology, 80*(1), 112–124.

Hertenstein, M. J., Hansel, C. A., Butts, A. M., & Hile, S. N. (2009). Smile intensity in photographs predicts divorce later in life. *Motivation and Emotion, 33*(2), 99–105.

Hochschild, A. R. (2012). *The Managed Heart: Commercialization of Human Feeling.* Oakland, CA: University of California Press.

Johnston, V. S. (1999). *Why We Feel: The Science of Human Emotions.* New York: Perseus Publishing.

Kirschbaum, C., Kudielka, B. M., Gaab, J., Schommer, N. C., & Hellhammer, D. H. (1999). Impact of gender, menstrual cycle phase, and oral contraceptives on the activity of the hypothalamus-pituitary-adrenal axis. *Psychosomatic Medicine, 61*(2), 154–162.

Kotchemidova, C. (2005). From good cheer to "drive-by smiling": A social history of cheerfulness. *Journal of Social History, 39*(1), 5–37.

Kring, A. M., & Gordon, A. H. (1998). Sex differences in emotion: Expression, experience, and physiology. *Journal of Personality and Social Psychology, 74*(3), 686–703.

LaFrance, M., Hecht, M. A., & Paluck, E. L. (2003). The contingent smile: A meta-analysis of sex differences in smiling. *Psychological Bulletin, 129*(2), 305–334.

Lease, S. H. (2018). Assertive behavior: A double-edged sword for women at work? *Clinical Psychology: Science and Practice, 25*(1), e12226.

Leitenberg, H., Greenwald, E., & Cado, S. (1992). A retrospective study of long-term methods of coping with having been sexually abused during childhood. *Child Abuse & Neglect, 16*(3), 399–407.

Levenson, R. W., Carstensen, L. L., & Gottman, J. M. (1994). Influence of age and gender on affect, physiology, and their interrelations: A study of long-term marriages. *Journal of Personality and Social Psychology, 67*(1), 56–68.

Machiavelli, N. (2008). *The Prince.* Indianapolis, IL: Hackett Publishing.

Matsumoto, D. (1990). Cultural similarities and differences in display rules. *Motivation and Emotion, 14*(3), 195–214.

Nelson, J. A., Leerkes, E. M., O'Brien, M., Calkins, S. D., & Marcovitch, S. (2012). African American and European American mothers' beliefs about negative emotions and emotion socialization practices. *Parenting, 12*(1), 22–41.

Oatley, K., Keltner, D., & Jenkins, J. M. (2006). *Understanding Emotions.* Hoboken, NJ: Blackwell Publishing.

Pennebaker, J. W. (1995). *Emotion, Disclosure, & Health.* Washington, DC: American Psychological Association.

Pennebaker, J. W. (1997). Writing about emotional experiences as a therapeutic process. *Psychological Science, 8*(3), 162–166.

Pennebaker, J. W., Kiecolt-Glaser, J. K., & Glaser, R. (1988). Disclosure of traumas and immune function: Health implications for psychotherapy. *Journal of Consulting and Clinical Psychology, 56*(2), 239–245.

Randolph, S. M., Koblinsky, S. A., & Roberts, D. D. (1996). Studying the role of family and school in the development of African American preschoolers in violent neighborhoods. *Journal of Negro Education*, 282–294.

Roorda, D. L., Koomen, H. M., Spilt, J. L., & Oort, F. J. (2011). The influence of affective teacher–student relationships on students' school engagement and achievement: A meta-analytic approach. *Review of Educational Research, 81*(4), 493–529.

Sheldon, K. M., Titova, L., Gordeeva, T. O., Osin, E. N., Lyubomirsky, S., & Bogomaz, S. (2017). Russians inhibit the expression of happiness to strangers: Testing a display rule model. *Journal of Cross-Cultural Psychology, 48*(5), 718–733.

Tracy, J. L., & Matsumoto, D. (2008). The spontaneous expression of pride and shame: Evidence for biologically innate nonverbal displays. *Proceedings of the National Academy of Sciences, 105*(33), 11655–11660.

Tronick, E. Z. (1989). Emotions and emotional communication in infants. *American Psychologist, 44*(2), 112–119.

Tsai, J. L., Ang, J. Y. Z., Blevins, E., Goernandt, J., Fung, H. H., Jiang, D., . . . Haddouk, L. (2016). Leaders' smiles reflect cultural differences in ideal affect. *Emotion, 16*(2), 183–195.

Uono, S., & Hietanen, J. K. (2015). Eye contact perception in the West and East: A cross-cultural study. *Plos One, 10*(2), e0118094.

Waldstein, D. (2018, September 8). Serena Williams accuses official of sexism in U.S. Open loss to Naomi Osaka. *New York Times*. Retrieved from www.nytimes.com /2018/09/08/sports/serena-williams-vs-naomi-osaka-us-open.html

Wallbott, H. G. (1998). Bodily expression of emotion. *European Journal of Social Psychology, 28*(6), 879–896.

Walsh, K., Fortier, M. A., & DiLillo, D. (2010). Adult coping with childhood sexual abuse: A theoretical and empirical review. *Aggression and Violent Behavior, 15*(1), 1–13.

8. R: Regulating Emotion

Alderman, L. (2016, November 9). Breathe. Exhale. Repeat: The benefits of controlled breathing. *New York Times*. Retrieved from www.nytimes.com/2016 /11/09/well/mind/breathe-exhale-repeat-the-benefits-of-controlled-breathing .html

Alvaro, P. K., Roberts, R. M., & Harris, J. K. (2013). A systematic review assessing bidirectionality between sleep disturbances, anxiety, and depression. *Sleep, 36*(7), 1059–1068.

Astin, J. A. (1997). Stress reduction through mindfulness meditation. *Psychotherapy and Psychosomatics, 66*(2), 97–106.

Bariola, E., Gullone, E., & Hughes, E. K. (2011). Child and adolescent emotion regulation: The role of parental emotion regulation and expression. *Clinical Child and Family Psychology Review, 14*(2), 198.

Bariso, J. (2018, February 28). 13 signs of high emotional intelligence. *Inc.* Retrieved from www.inc.com/justin-bariso/13-things-emotionally-intelligent-people-do .html

Barrett, L. F., Gross, J., Christensen, T. C., & Benvenuto, M. (2001). Knowing what you're feeling and knowing what to do about it: Mapping the relation between emotion differentiation and emotion regulation. *Cognition & Emotion, 15*(6), 713–724.

Beilharz, J., Maniam, J., & Morris, M. (2015). Diet-induced cognitive deficits: The role of fat and sugar, potential mechanisms and nutritional interventions. *Nutrients, 7*(8), 6719–6738.

Black, D. S., & Slavich, G. M. (2016). Mindfulness meditation and the immune system: A systematic review of randomized controlled trials. *Annals of the New York Academy of Sciences, 1373*(1), 13–24.

Brooks, A. W. (2014). Get excited: Reappraising pre-performance anxiety as excitement. *Journal of Experimental Psychology: General, 143*(3), 1144–1158.

Brown, K. W., & Ryan, R. M. (2003). The benefits of being present: Mindfulness and its role in psychological well-being. *Journal of Personality and Social Psychology, 84*(4), 822–848.

Burg, J. M., & Michalak, J. (2011). The healthy quality of mindful breathing: Associations with rumination and depression. *Cognitive Therapy and Research, 35*(2), 179–185.

Butler, E. A., & Randall, A. K. (2013). Emotional coregulation in close relationships. *Emotion Review, 5*(2), 202–210.

Cho, H., Ryu, S., Noh, J., & Lee, J. (2016). The effectiveness of daily mindful breathing practices on test anxiety of students. *PloS One, 11*(10), e0164822.

Cohen, S. (2004). Social relationships and health. *American Psychologist, 59*(8), 676.

Consolo, K., Fusner, S., & Staib, S. (2008). Effects of diaphragmatic breathing on stress levels of nursing students. *Teaching and Learning in Nursing, 3*(2), 67–71.

Crum, A. (2011). Evaluating a mindset training program to unleash the enhancing nature of stress. In *Academy of Management Proceedings* (vol. 2011, no. 1, pp. 1–6). Briarcliff Manor, NY: Academy of Management.

Crum, A. J., Akinola, M., Martin, A., & Fath, S. (2017). The role of stress mindset in shaping cognitive, emotional, and physiological responses to challenging and threatening stress. *Anxiety, Stress, & Coping, 30*(4), 379–395.

Crum, A., & Lyddy, C. (2014). De-stressing stress: The power of mindsets and the art of stressing mindfully. In A. Ie, C. Ngnoumen, & E. J. Langer (Eds.), *The Wiley Blackwell Handbook of Mindfulness* (vol. 1, pp. 948–963). Malden, MA: John Wiley & Sons.

Crum, A. J., Salovey, P., & Achor, S. (2013). Rethinking stress: The role of mindsets in determining the stress response. *Journal of Personality and Social Psychology, 104*(4), 716–733.

Deslandes, A., Moraes, H., Ferreira, C., Veiga, H., Silveira, H., Mouta, R., . . . Laks, J. (2009). Exercise and mental health: Many reasons to move. *Neuropsychobiology, 59*(4), 191–198.

Dobson, K. S., & Dozois, D. J. (Eds.). (2019). *Handbook of Cognitive-Behavioral Therapies.* New York: Guilford Publications.

Drabant, E. M., McRae, K., Manuck, S. B., Hariri, A. R., & Gross, J. J. (2009). Individual differences in typical reappraisal use predict amygdala and prefrontal responses. *Biological Psychiatry, 65*(5), 367–373.

Evans, C. A., & Porter, C. L. (2009). The emergence of mother–infant co-regulation during the first year: Links to infants' developmental status and attachment. *Infant Behavior and Development, 32*(2), 147–158.

Feldman, G., Greeson, J., & Senville, J. (2010). Differential effects of mindful breathing, progressive muscle relaxation, and loving-kindness meditation on decentering and negative reactions to repetitive thoughts. *Behaviour Research and Therapy, 48*(10), 1002–1011.

Gross, J. J. (1998). Antecedent- and response-focused emotion regulation: Divergent consequences for experience, expression, and physiology. *Journal of Personality and Social Psychology, 74*(1), 224–237.

Gross, J. J. (1998). The emerging field of emotion regulation: An integrative review. *Review of General Psychology, 2*(3), 271–299.

Gross, J. J. (2001). Emotion regulation in adulthood: Timing is everything. *Current Directions in Psychological Science, 10*(6), 214–219.

Grossman, P., Niemann, L., Schmidt, S., & Walach, H. (2004). Mindfulness-based stress reduction and health benefits: A meta-analysis. *Journal of Psychosomatic Research, 57*(1), 35–43.

Herrero, J. L., Khuvis, S., Yeagle, E., Cerf, M., & Mehta, A. D. (2017). Breathing above the brainstem: Volitional control and attentional modulation in humans. *Journal of Neurophysiology, 119*(1), 145–159.

Hofmann, S. G., Heering, S., Sawyer, A. T., & Asnaani, A. (2009). How to handle anxiety: The effects of reappraisal, acceptance, and suppression strategies on anxious arousal. *Behaviour Research and Therapy, 47*(5), 389–394.

Hülsheger, U. R., Alberts, H. J., Feinholdt, A., & Lang, J. W. (2013). Benefits of mindfulness at work: The role of mindfulness in emotion regulation, emotional exhaustion, and job satisfaction. *Journal of Applied Psychology, 98*(2), 310–325.

Jamieson, J. P., Crum, A. J., Goyer, J. P., Marotta, M. E., & Akinola, M. (2018). Optimizing stress responses with reappraisal and mindset interventions: An integrated model. *Anxiety, Stress, & Coping, 31*(3), 245–261.

Jamieson, J. P., Mendes, W. B., Blackstock, E., & Schmader, T. (2010). Turning the knots in your stomach into bows: Reappraising arousal improves performance on the GRE. *Journal of Experimental Social Psychology, 46*(1), 208–212.

Johnson, D. R. (2009). Emotional attention set-shifting and its relationship to anxiety and emotion regulation. *Emotion, 9*(5), 681–690.

Kingston, J., Chadwick, P., Meron, D., & Skinner, T. C. (2007). A pilot randomized control trial investigating the effect of mindfulness practice on pain tolerance, psychological well-being, and physiological activity. *Journal of Psychosomatic Research, 62*(3), 297–300.

Kross, E., & Ayduk, O. (2017). Self-distancing: Theory, research, and current directions. In J. Olsen (Ed.), *Advances in Experimental Social Psychology* (vol. 55, pp. 81–136). Cambridge, MA: Academic Press.

Kross, E., Bruehlman-Senecal, E., Park, J., Burson, A., Dougherty, A., Shablack, H., . . . Ayduk, O. (2014). Self-talk as a regulatory mechanism: How you do it matters. *Journal of Personality and Social Psychology, 106*(2), 304–324.

LeDoux, J. (1998). *The Emotional Brain: The Mysterious Underpinnings of Emotional Life.* New York: Simon & Schuster.

Levenson, R. W. (2014). The autonomic nervous system and emotion. *Emotion Review, 6*(2), 100–112.

Ma, X., Yue, Z. Q., Gong, Z. Q., Zhang, H., Duan, N. Y., Shi, Y. T., . . . Li, Y. F. (2017). The effect of diaphragmatic breathing on attention, negative affect and stress in healthy adults. *Frontiers in Psychology, 8*, 874.

Mangelsdorf, S. C., Shapiro, J. R., & Marzolf, D. (1995). Developmental and temperamental differences in emotion regulation in infancy. *Child Development, 66*(6), 1817–1828.

Mauss, I. B., Troy, A. S., & LeBourgeois, M. K. (2013). Poorer sleep quality is associated with lower emotion-regulation ability in a laboratory paradigm. *Cognition & Emotion, 27*(3), 567–576.

McRae, K., Ciesielski, B., & Gross, J. J. (2012). Unpacking cognitive reappraisal: Goals, tactics, and outcomes. *Emotion, 12*(2), 250–255.

McRae, K., Jacobs, S. E., Ray, R. D., John, O. P., & Gross, J. J. (2012). Individual differences in reappraisal ability: Links to reappraisal frequency, well-being, and cognitive control. *Journal of Research in Personality, 46*(1), 2–7.

Minkel, J. D., McNealy, K., Gianaros, P. J., Drabant, E. M., Gross, J. J., Manuck, S. B., & Hariri, A. R. (2012). Sleep quality and neural circuit function supporting emotion regulation. *Biology of Mood & Anxiety Disorders, 2*(1), 22.

Morris, A. S., Silk, J. S., Steinberg, L., Myers, S. S., & Robinson, L. R. (2007). The role of the family context in the development of emotion regulation. *Social Development, 16*(2), 361–388.

Moser, J. S., Dougherty, A., Mattson, W. I., Katz, B., Moran, T. P., Guevarra, D., . . . Kross, E. (2017). Third-person self-talk facilitates emotion regulation without engaging cognitive control: Converging evidence from ERP and fMRI. *Scientific Reports, 7*(1), 4519.

Ochsner, K. N., & Gross, J. J. (2008). Cognitive emotion regulation: Insights from social cognitive and affective neuroscience. *Current Directions in Psychological Science, 17*(2), 153–158.

Parkinson, B., & Totterdell, P. (1999). Classifying affect-regulation strategies. *Cognition & Emotion, 13*(3), 277–303.

Pbert, L., Madison, J. M., Druker, S., Olendzki, N., Magner, R., Reed, G., . . . Carmody, J. (2012). Effect of mindfulness training on asthma quality of life and lung function: A randomized controlled trial. *Thorax, 67*(9), 769–776.

Petruzzello, S. J., Landers, D. M., Hatfield, B. D., Kubitz, K. A., & Salazar, W. (1991). A meta-analysis on the anxiety-reducing effects of acute and chronic exercise. *Sports Medicine, 11*(3), 143–182.

Porter, C. L. (2003). Coregulation in mother-infant dyads: Links to infants' cardiac vagal tone. *Psychological Reports, 92*(1), 307–319.

Shakespeare, W., & Hibbard, G. R. (1994). *Hamlet.* Oxford: Oxford University Press.

Spencer, S. J., Korosi, A., Layé, S., Shukitt-Hale, B., & Barrientos, R. M. (2017). Food for thought: How nutrition impacts cognition and emotion. *npj Science of Food, 1*(1), 7.

Steel, P. (2007). The nature of procrastination: A meta-analytic and theoretical review of quintessential self-regulatory failure. *Psychological Bulletin, 133*(1), 65–94.

Ströhle, A. (2009). Physical activity, exercise, depression and anxiety disorders. *Journal of Neural Transmission, 116*(6), 777–784.

Tsuno, N., Besset, A., & Ritchie, K. (2005). Sleep and depression. *Journal of Clinical Psychiatry, 66*(10), 1254–1269.

Umberson, D., & Karas Montez, J. (2010). Social relationships and health: A flashpoint for health policy. *Journal of Health and Social Behavior, 51*(Suppl), S54–S66.

Wehner, M. (2017, July 27). Talking to yourself isn't crazy, it's a stress relief. *New*

York Post. Retrieved from https://nypost.com/2017/07/27/talking-to-yourself-isnt
-crazy-its-stress-relief/

Wielgosz, J., Schuyler, B. S., Lutz, A., & Davidson, R. J. (2016). Long-term mindfulness
training is associated with reliable differences in resting respiration rate. *Scientific
Reports, 6,* 27533.

9. Emotions at Home

AVG Technologies. (2015, June 24). Kids competing with mobile phones for parents'
attention [Web log message]. Retrieved from https://now.avg.com/digital-diaries
-kids-competing-with-mobile-phones-for-parents-attention

Baumeister, R. F., Bratslavsky, E., Finkenauer, C., & Vohs, K. D. (2001). Bad is stronger than good. *Review of General Psychology, 5*(4), 323–370. doi:10.1037//1089-
2680.5.4.323

Bigelow, K. M., & Morris, E. K. (2001). John B. Watson's advice on child rearing:
Some historical context. *Behavioral Development Bulletin, 10*(1), 26–30. http://
dx.doi.org/10.1037/h0100479

Bowlby, J. (1988). *A Secure Base: Parent-Child Attachment and Healthy Human Development.* New York: Basic Books.

Boyce, T. W. (2019). *The Orchid and the Dandelion: Why Some Children Struggle and
How All Can Thrive.* New York: Alfred A. Knopf.

Cacioppo, J. T., & Gardner, W. L. (1999). Emotion. *Annual Review of Psychology,
50*(1), 191–214. doi:10.1146/annurev.psych.50.1.191

Chaplin, T. M., & Aldao, A. (2013). Gender differences in emotion expression
in children: A meta-analytic review. *Psychological Bulletin, 139*(4), 735–765.
doi:10.1037/a0030737

DeClaire, J., & Gottman, J. (1997). *The Heart of Parenting: How to Raise an Emotionally Intelligent Child.* New York: Simon & Schuster.

Denham, S. A., Cook, M., & Zoller, D. (1992). "Baby looks *very* sad": Implications
of conversations about feelings between mother and preschooler. *British Journal
of Developmental Psychology, 10*(3), 301–315. doi.org/10.1111/j.2044-835X.1992
.tb00579.x

Fogel, A. (1993). *Developing Through Relationships.* Chicago, IL: University of Chicago
Press.

Hooven, C., Gottman, J. M., & Katz, L. F. (1995). Parental meta-emotion structure
predicts family and child outcomes. *Cognition & Emotion, 9*(2–3), 229–264. doi
.org/10.1080/02699939508409010

Johnson, D. J. (2017). Parents' perceptions of smartphone use and parenting practices.
(Master's thesis). University of Nevada, Las Vegas. Available from Digital Schol-
arship@UNLV database. (No. 3141)

McDaniel, B. T., & Radesky, J. S. (2018). Technoference: Longitudinal associations between parent technology use, parenting stress, and child behavior problems. *Pediatric Research, 84*(2), 210–218. doi.org/10.1038/s41390-018-0052-6

Moore, S. D., Brody, L. R., & Dierberger, A. E. (2009). Mindfulness and experiential avoidance as predictors and outcomes of the narrative emotional disclosure task. *Journal of Clinical Psychology, 65*(9), 971–988. doi.org/10.1002/jclp.20600

Myruski, S., Gulyayeva, O., Birk, S., Pérez-Edgar, K., Buss, K. A., & Dennis-Tiwary, T. A. (2018). Digital disruption? Maternal mobile device use is related to infant social-emotional functioning. *Developmental Science, 21*(4), e12610. doi.org/10.1111/desc.12610

Ouellet-Morin, I., Odgers, C. L., Danese, A., Bowes, L., Shakoor, S., Papadopoulos, A. S., . . . Arseneault, L. (2011). Blunted cortisol responses to stress signal social and behavioral problems among maltreated/bullied 12-year-old children. *Biological Psychiatry, 70*(11), 1016–1023. doi.org/10.1016/j.biopsych.2011.06.017

Pew Research Center. (2018). *Teens, social media & technology 2018.* Retrieved from www.pewinternet.org/2018/05/31/teens-social-media-technology-2018/

Radesky, J. S., Kistin, C. J., Zuckerman, B., Nitzberg, K., Gross, J., Kaplan-Sanoff, M., . . . Silverstein, M. (2014). Patterns of mobile device use by caregivers and children during meals in fast food restaurants. *Pediatrics, 133*(4), e843–e849. Retrieved from https://pediatrics.aappublications.org/content/pediatrics/133/4/e843.full.pdf

Reed, J., Hirsh-Pasek, K., & Golinkoff, R. M. (2017). Learning on hold: Cell phones sidetrack parent-child interactions. *Developmental Psychology, 53*(8), 1428–1436. doi.org/10.1037/dev0000292

Rozin, P., & Royzman, E. B. (2001). Negativity bias, negativity dominance, and contagion. *Personality and Social Psychology Review, 5*(4), 296–320. doi.org/10.1207/S15327957PSPR0504_2

Steiner-Adair, C., & Barker, T. H. (2013). *The Big Disconnect: Protecting Childhood and Family Relationships in the Digital Age.* New York: Harper Business.

Stelter, R. L., & Halberstadt, A. G. (2011). The interplay between parental beliefs about children's emotions and parental stress impacts children's attachment security. *Infant and Child Development, 20*(3), 272–287. doi.org/10.1002/icd.693

Teicher, M. H., Samson, J. A., Sheu, Y. S., Polcari, A., & McGreenery, C. E. (2010). Hurtful words: Association of exposure to peer verbal abuse with elevated psychiatric symptom scores and corpus callosum abnormalities. *American Journal of Psychiatry, 167*(12), 1464–1471. doi.org/10.1176/appi.ajp.2010.10010030

Twenge, J. M., & Campbell, W. K. (2018). Associations between screen time and lower psychological well-being among children and adolescents: Evidence from a population-based study. *Preventive Medicine Reports, 12,* 271–283. doi.org/10 .1016/j.pmedr.2018.10.003

U.S. Department of Education, National Center for Education Statistics. (2015). Student reports of bullying and cyber-bullying: Results from the 2013 School Crime Supplement to the National Crime Victimization Survey (NCES No. 2015–056). Retrieved from https://nces.ed.gov/pubs2015/2015056.pdf

Vaillancourt, T., Hymel, S., & McDougall, P. (2013). The biological underpinnings of peer victimization: Understanding why and how the effects of bullying can last a lifetime. *Theory into Practice, 52*(4), 241–248. doi.org/10.1080/00405841.2013 .829726

10. Emotions at School: From Preschool to College

Anxiety and Depression Association of America. Facts & statistics. Retrieved from https://adaa.org/about-adaa/press-room/facts-statistics

Aspen Institute National Commission on Social, Emotional, and Academic Development. (2019). From a nation at risk to a nation at hope. Retrieved from http://nationathope.org/wp-content/uploads/2018_aspen_final-report_full _webversion.pdf

Belfield, C., Bowden, A. B., Klapp, A., Levin, H., Shand, R., & Zander, S. (2015). The economic value of social and emotional learning. *Journal of Benefit-Cost Analysis, 6*(3), 508–544. doi.org/10.1017/bca.2015.55

Bell, C. C., & Jenkins, E. J. (1993). Community violence and children on Chicago's southside. *Psychiatry, 56*(1), 46–54. doi.org/10.1080/00332747.1993.11024620

Belsky, J., & de Haan, M. (2011). Annual research review: Parenting and children's brain development: The end of the beginning. *Journal of Child Psychology and Psychiatry, 52*(4), 409–428. doi.org/10.1111/j.1469-7610.2010.02281.x

Boyne, J. (2006). *The Boy in the Striped Pajamas.* Oxford: David Fickling Books.

Brackett, M. A., Elbertson, N. A., & Rivers, S. E. (2016). Applying theory to the development of approaches to SEL. In J. A. Durlak, C. E. Domitrovich, R. P. Weissberg, & T. P. Gullotta (Eds.), *Handbook of Social and Emotional Learning: Research and Practice* (pp. 20–32). New York: Guilford Press.

Brackett, M. A., Reyes, M. R., Rivers, S. E., Elbertson, N. A., & Salovey, P. (2011). Classroom emotional climate, teacher affiliation, and student conduct. *Journal of Classroom Interaction,* 27–36. Retrieved from www.jstor.org/stable/23870549

Brackett, M. A., Rivers, S. E., Reyes, M. R., & Salovey, P. (2012). Enhancing academic performance and social and emotional competence with the RULER feeling words curriculum. *Learning and Individual Differences, 22,* 218–224. doi.org /10.1016/j.lindif.2010.10.002

Bradley, C., Floman, J. L., Brackett, M. A., & Patti, J. (2019). Burnout and teacher well-being: The moderating role of perceived principal emotional intelligence. (Unpublished data.) Yale University, New Haven, CT.

Brooks, D. (2019, January 17). Students learn from people they love. *New York Times.* Retrieved from www.nytimes.com/2019/01/17/opinion/learning-emotion -education.html

Castillo, R., Fernández-Berrocal, P., & Brackett, M. A. (2013). Enhancing teacher effectiveness in Spain: A pilot study of the RULER approach to social and emotional learning. *Journal of Education and Training Studies, 1*(2), 263–272. doi.org /10.11114/jets.v1i2.203

Center for Collegiate Mental Health. (2016). *2015 annual report* (Publication No. STA 15-108). Retrieved from https://sites.psu.edu/ccmh/files/2017/10/2015 _CCMH_Report_1-18-2015-yq3vik.pdf

Collaborative for Academic, Social, and Emotional Learning. (2015). Effective social and emotional learning programs. Retrieved from http://secondaryguide.casel .org/casel-secondary-guide.pdf

Divecha, D. & Brackett, M. A. (in press). Rethinking school-based bullying prevention through the lens of social and emotional learning: A bioecological perspective. *International Journal of Bullying Prevention.*

Durlak, J. A., Weissberg, R. P., Dymnicki, A. B., Taylor, R. D., & Schellinger, K. B. (2011). The impact of enhancing students' social and emotional learning: A meta-analysis of school-based universal interventions. *Child Development, 82*(1), 405–432. doi.org/10.1111/j.1467-8624.2010.01564.x

Gershoff, E. T., & Font, S. A. (2016). Corporal punishment in US public schools: Prevalence, disparities in use, and status in state and federal policy. *Social Policy Report, 30,* 1–37.

Gladden, R. M., Vivolo-Kantor, A. M., Hamburger, M. E., & Lumpkin, C. D. (2014). Bullying surveillance among youths: Uniform definitions for public health and recommended data elements, version 1.0. National Center for Injury Prevention and Control, Centers for Disease Control and Prevention, and U.S. Department of Education. Retrieved from www.cdc.gov/violenceprevention/pdf /bullying-definitions-final-a.pdf

Goleman, D. (1995). *Emotional Intelligence: Why It Can Matter More Than IQ.* New York: Bantam Books.

Greenberg, M. T., Brown, J. L., & Abenavoli, R. M. (2016, September). *Teacher stress and health: Effects on teachers, students, and schools.* Edna Bennett Pierce Prevention Research Center, Pennsylvania State University. Retrieved from www.rwjf.org/en /library/research/2016/07/teacher-stress-and-health.html

Holzapfel, B. (2018, January 20). Class of 2030: What do today's kindergartners need to be life-ready? [Web log message]. Retrieved from https://educationblog .microsoft.com/en-us/2018/01/class-of-2030-predicting-student-skills/

Immordino-Yang, M. H. (2015). *Emotions, Learning, and the Brain: Exploring the Educational Implications of Affective Neuroscience.* (Norton series on the social neuroscience of education). New York: W. W. Norton & Company.

Lipson, S. K., Lattie, E. G., & Eisenberg, D. (2018). Increased rates of mental health service utilization by US college students: 10-year population-level trends (2007–2017). *Psychiatric Services, 70*(1), 60–63. doi.org/10.1176/appi.ps.201800332

Loveless, T. (2017). 2017 Brown center report on American education: Race and school suspensions. Retrieved from www.brookings.edu/research/2017-brown -center-report-part-iii-race-and-school-suspensions/

McGraw-Hill Education. (2018). 2018 social and emotional learning report. Retrieved from www.mheducation.com/prek-12/explore/sel-survey.html

Microsoft Education. (2018). The class of 2030 and life-ready learning. Retrieved from https://education.minecraft.net/wp-content/uploads/13679_EDU_Thought _Leadership_Summary_revisions_5.10.18.pdf

Moeller, J., Ivcevic, Z., Brackett, M. A., & White, A. E. (2018). Mixed emotions: Network analyses of intra-individual co-occurrences within and across situations. *Emotion, 18*(8), 1106–1121. doi.org/10.1037/emo0000419

Murphey, D., Bandy, T., Schmitz, H., & Moore, K. (2013). Caring adults: Important for positive child well-being. *Child Trends.* Retrieved from www.childtrends.org /wp-content/uploads/2013/12/2013-54CaringAdults.pdf

Nathanson, L., Rivers, S. E., Flynn, L. M., & Brackett, M. A. (2016). Creating emotionally intelligent schools with RULER. *Emotion Review, 8*(4), 305–310. doi.org /10.1177/1754073916650495

New York State Education Department, New York City Department of Education. (2016). Memorandum of understanding. Retrieved from www.nysed.gov/common /nysed/files/DOE_MOU_FINAL.pdf

Parthenon-EY Education Practice, Ernst & Young LLP. (2016, September). Untapped potential: Engaging all Connecticut youth. Retrieved from http://cdn.ey.com /parthenon/pdf/perspectives/Parthenon-EY_Untapped-Potential_Dalio-Report _final_092016_web.pdf

Reyes, M. R., Brackett, M. A., Rivers, S. E., White, M., & Salovey, P. (2012). Classroom emotional climate, student engagement, and academic achievement. *Journal of Educational Psychology, 104*(3), 700–712. doi.org/10.1037/a0027268

Rivers, S. E., Brackett, M. A., Reyes, M. R., Elbertson, N. A., & Salovey, P. (2013). Improving the social and emotional climate of classrooms: A clustered randomized controlled trial testing the RULER Approach. *Prevention Science: The Official*

Journal of the Society for Prevention Research, 14, 77–87. doi.org/10.1007/s11121-012-0305-2

Salovey, P., & Mayer, J. D. (1990). Emotional intelligence. *Imagination, Cognition and Personality, 9*(3), 185–211. doi.org/10.2190/DUGG-P24E-52WK-6CDG

Simmons, D. N., Brackett, M.A., & Adler, N. (2018, June). Applying an equity lens to social, emotional, and academic development. Edna Bennett Pierce Prevention Research Center, Pennsylvania State University. Retrieved from www.rwjf.org/en/library/research/2018/06/applying-an-equity-lens-to-social-emotional-and-academic-development.html

Sperduto, C., Kershaw, T., Brackett, M. A., & Monin, J. (in preparation). An app-based, emotional intelligence intervention for wellbeing in university students. Yale School of Medicine, Child Study Center, Yale University, New Haven, CT.

Taylor, R. D., Oberle, E., Durlak, J. A., & Weissberg, R. P. (2017). Promoting positive youth development through school-based social and emotional learning interventions: A meta-analysis of follow-up effects. *Child Development, 88*(4), 1156–1171. doi.org/10.1111/cdev.12864

White, A. E., Moeller, J., Ivcevic, Z., Brackett, M. A., & Stern, R. (2018). LGBTQ adolescents' positive and negative emotions and experiences in US high schools. *Sex Roles, 79*(9–10), 594–608. doi.org/10.1007/s11199-017-0885-1

11. Emotions at Work

Barsade, S. G. (2002). The ripple effect: Emotional contagion and its influence on group behavior. *Administrative Science Quarterly, 47*(4), 644–675.

Barsade, S. G., Brief, A. P., & Spataro, S. E. (2003). The affective revolution in organizational behavior: The emergence of a paradigm. *Organizational Behavior: The State of the Science, 2,* 3–52.

Barsade, S. G., & Gibson, D. E. (2007). Why does affect matter in organizations? *Academy of Management Perspectives, 21*(1), 36–59.

Barsade, S. G., & O'Neill, O. A. (2014). What's love got to do with it? A longitudinal study of the culture of companionate love and employee and client outcomes in a long-term care setting. *Administrative Science Quarterly, 59*(4), 551–598.

Caruso, D. R., & Salovey, P. (2004). *The Emotionally Intelligent Manager: How to Develop and Use the Four Key Emotional Skills of Leadership.* Hoboken, NJ: John Wiley & Sons.

Côté, S. (2014). Emotional intelligence in organizations. *Annual Review of Organizational Psychology and Organizational Behavior, 1*(1), 459–488.

Côté, S., Lopes, P. N., Salovey, P., & Miners, C. T. (2010). Emotional intelligence and leadership emergence in small groups. *Leadership Quarterly, 21*(3), 496–508.

David, S. (2016). *Emotional Agility.* New York: Penguin Group.

Grandey, A. A. (2003). When "the show must go on": Surface acting and deep acting as determinants of emotional exhaustion and peer-rated service delivery. *Academy of Management Journal, 46*(1), 86–96.

Harter, J. (2018, August 26). Employee engagement on the rise in the U.S. *Gallup News.* Retrieved from https://news.gallup.com/poll/241649/employee-engagement-rise.aspx

Hatfield, E., Cacioppo, J. T., & Rapson, R. L. (1993). Emotional contagion. *Current Directions in Psychological Science, 2*(3), 96–100.

Hennig-Thurau, T., Groth, M., Paul, M., & Gremler, D. D. (2006). Are all smiles created equal? How emotional contagion and emotional labor affect service relationships. *Journal of Marketing, 70*(3), 58–73.

Ivcevic, Z., Moeller, J., Menges, J., & Brackett, M. A. (under review). Supervisor emotionally intelligent behavior and employee creativity. *Journal of Creative Behavior.*

Knight, A. P., Menges, J. I., & Bruch, H. (2018). Organizational affective tone: A meso perspective on the origins and effects of consistent affect in organizations. *Academy of Management Journal, 61*(1), 191–219.

LaPalme, M. L., Rojas, F., Pertuzé, J. A., & Espinoza, P. Surface acting can be good . . . or bad: The influence of expressing inauthentic emotions on burnout, absenteeism, commitment, and patient complaints. (Manuscript submitted for publication).

Mayer, J. D., Roberts, R. D., & Barsade, S. G. (2008). Human abilities: Emotional intelligence. *Annual Review of Psychology, 59,* 507–536.

Menges, J. I. (2012). Organizational emotional intelligence: Theoretical foundations and practical implications. In C. E. J. Härtel, W. J. Zerbe, & N. M. Ashkanasy (Eds.), *Research on Emotions in Organizations* (vol. 8, pp. 355–373). Bingley, UK: Emerald.

Menges, J. I., & Bruch, H. (2009). Organizational emotional intelligence and performance: An empirical study. In C. E. J. Härtel, W. J. Zerbe, & N. M. Ashkanasy (Eds.), *Research on Emotions in Organizations* (vol. 5, pp. 181–209). Bingley, UK: Emerald.

Moeller, J., Ivcevic, Z., White, A. E., Menges, J. I., & Brackett, M. A. (2018). Highly engaged but burned out: Intra-individual profiles in the US workforce. *Career Development International, 23*(1), 86–105.

Rosete, D., & Ciarrochi, J. (2005). Emotional intelligence and its relationship to workplace performance outcomes of leadership effectiveness. *Leadership & Organization Development Journal, 26*(5), 388–399.

Schoenewolf, G. (1990). Emotional contagion: Behavioral induction in individuals and groups. *Modern Psychoanalysis, 15*(1), 49–61.

Seppälä, E. & Moeller, J. (2018, January 2). 1 in 5 employees is highly engaged and at risk of burnout. *Harvard Business Review.* Retrieved from https://hbr.org/2018/02/1-in-5-highly-engaged-employees-is-at-risk-of-burnout

Taylor, C., Ivcevic, Z., Moeller, J., & Brackett, M. A. (under review). Gender and creativity at work. *Creativity and Innovation Management.*

Acknowledgments

I have immense gratitude for the countless people and organizations that have contributed to my personal and professional growth and to the contents in this book.

I would first like to thank my wonderful agent, Richard Pine, and the team at Inkwell Management, especially Eliza Rothstein, William Callahan, and Lyndsey Blessing, for all their guidance and care through every stage of the publishing process. I also thank Amy Hertz who, early on, was instrumental in helping me shape the structure of this book. I'm grateful for Bill Tonelli, who supported me throughout the writing of this book, and especially for helping me make my own and others' academic research accessible for a broad audience.

I cannot say thank you enough times to the dedicated and talented people at Celadon Books, my publisher, who have been far more encouraging than I had imagined possible, including: Jamie Raab, my editor and publisher, and the entire team: Deb Futter, Rachel Chou, Ryan Doherty, Anne Twomey, Christie Mykityshyn, Heather Graham, Jaime Noven, Randi Kramer, Alexis Neuville, Cecily Van Buren-Freedman, and Clay Smith. Their suggestions, support, and especially all of their excitement about my ideas have made my dream of writing this book a reality.

Over the last twenty-five years, I have had the unique privilege of working with talented educators in thousands of schools across the United States and in other countries. I learned something from each person and school with whom I've interacted, particularly those schools and districts that participated in my research or shared their stories with me. I send a special shout-out to Valley Stream District 24 on Long Island and Ed Fale and Bruce Alster, who partnered with our team to do RULER's very first study over fifteen years ago. A second shout-out goes to the Roman Catholic Diocese of Brooklyn and Queens, and especially their former district administrator, Michael Pizzingrillo, who was instrumental in our first randomized controlled trial of RULER. I extend deep gratitude to the NYC Department of Education with special thank-yous to Dolores Esposito, Carmen Fariña, LeShawn Robinson, Richard Carranza, Brooke Jackson, Dawn DeCosta, and David Adams. I am eternally grateful to Bonnie Brown, who brought RULER into NYC's special education District 75, helping us reach thousands of children with emotional challenges and those on the autism spectrum.

Other schools to whom I'm indebted include our early adopters and partners: New Line Learning, especially Chris Gerry and Clare Collins; Girton Grammar, especially Paul Flanagan, Les Evans, and Matthew Maruff; Brewster Academy, especially Mike Cooper and Allie Cooper; the Shipley School, especially Steven Piltch; Horace Mann, especially Deena Neuwirth and Tom Kelly; Prospect Sierra, especially Katherine Dinh and Heather Rogers; Seattle Public Schools, especially Helen Walsh and Bryan Manzo; Highline Public Schools, especially Susan Enfield, Laurie Morrison, and Kimberly Kinzer; Fairfax County Public Schools, especially MaryAnn Panarelli, Dede Bailor, and Jeanne Veraska; Aidan Montessori, especially Kathy Minardi; Bridgeport Public Schools, especially Fran Rabinowitz for her vision; Technológico de Monterrey, especially Paulino Bernot Silis and Rafael

Abrego Hinojosa; Academy District 20 in Colorado Springs, especially Susan Field, Maureen Lang, and Clark Maxon; the King David School, especially David Opat; Hamden Public Schools, especially Valerie Larose; Joel Barlow High School, and in particular, Gina-Marie Pin and Chris Poulos; and Coquitlam District No. 43, especially Tamara Banks.

I also want to thank key partners who have helped us scale RULER across the United States, including the Willows Community School, notably Lisa Rosenstein, Susan Sleeper, and Christina Kim, and Putnam North West BOCES in New York, especially Renee Gargano and Joan Thompson. In our journey to make Connecticut the first emotionally intelligent state, I want to acknowledge our biggest champions: Dianna Wentzel, commissioner of education; Fran Rabinowitz, executive director of the Connecticut Association of Public School Superintendents; Bob Rader, executive director of the Connecticut Association of Boards of Education; and Steven Hernandez, executive director of the Connecticut Commission on Women, Children, and Seniors. We wouldn't have reached a fraction of the children and educators in Connecticut and New York without their passion and dedication.

Our center's research and approach to SEL, RULER, was made possible with the support from these generous organizations: Anthony and Jeanne Pritzker Family Foundation, Arnow Family Foundation, Chan Zuckerberg Initiative (Brooke Stafford-Brizard, Gaby López, and Priscilla Chan), Corbett Family Foundation, Dalio Foundation (Barbara Dalio, Andrew Ferguson, Kevin Ashley), Dancing Tides Foundation, Einhorn Family Charitable Trust (Jennifer Hoos Rothberg and Itai Dinour), Faas Foundation (Andy Faas and Patrick Mundt), Facebook (Arturo Bejar and Jamie Lockwood), La Fundacíon Botín (Íñigo Sáenz and Fátima Sánchez), Graustein Memorial Fund, Greater Houston Community Foundation, Hartford Foundation (Richard Sussman), Hauptman Family Foundation, Institute for Education Science, Institute for Social Policy Studies at Yale, Lurie Family Foundation, The Meeting House (Paula Resnick), Novo Foundation (Jennifer Buffet), Oxman Family Foundation, Partners of '63 (Charley Ellis and

Jim Schattinger), Phillipe Costeletos Family, Pure Edge (Chi Kim), Robert Wood Johnson (Jennifer Ng'andu and Tracy Costigan), Seedlings Foundation (Karen Pritzker and Kathy Higgins), Simms/Mann Foundation, Susan Crowne Exchange (Susan Crowne and Haviland Rummel), Tauck Family Foundation (Mirellise Vazquez), Wallace Foundation (Gigi Antoni and Katherine Lewandoski), Wend Ventures (Nora Flood), William T. Grant Foundation, World Wrestling Entertainment, Inc., and Yale China Fund for Emotional Intelligence (Neil Shen and Leon Meng).

I also extend my deepest appreciation to many others who have contributed to this book, including Daniel Goleman, who helped me find my mentors, Peter Salovey and Jack Mayer; Richard and Susan Reiner; Mark Sparvell (Microsoft); Denise Daniels (Moodsters); Barbara Winston and Stephanie Winston Wolkoff (UN Women for Peace Association); Jeannie Francolini (Flawless Foundation); Ginny Deering and Bridget Durkan Laird (Wings); Bill Jackson (Great Schools); Crystal Brown (Boys and Girls Clubs of America); Leslie Udwin (Think Equal); Roger Weissberg, Karen Niemi, and Tim Shriver (CASEL); Wendy Baron and Ellen Moir (New Teacher Center); Christopher Rim (Command Education); and HopeLab, especially Fred Dillan, Brian Rodriquez, and Shane Brentham for their support in building and maintaining our Mood Meter App.

I want to thank those who shared their time and intellect in providing feedback to this manuscript: Dacher Keltner, Deb and Hugh Jackman, Diane Archer, Harriet Seittler, James Gross, Janet Patti, Jeff Clifford, Jochen Menges, Karen Niemi, Kathy Higgins, Jamie Lockwood, Roger Weissberg, Scott Levy, Sigal Barsade, Tara Westover, Tim Shriver, Jennifer Allen, and Zorana Ivcevic.

My research and thinking throughout the years have been influenced by countless other researchers and practitioners, including: Angela Duckworth, Carol Dweck, Dan Siegel, Erica Frydenberg, Kim Schonert-Reichl, Lisa Feldman Barrett, Mark Greenberg, Maurice Elias, Miriam Miller, Pam Cantor, Patricia Lester, Richard Durlak, Roger Weissberg,

Stephanie Jones, Tim Shriver, Shauna Tominey, and Sharon Shapses. I also thank my mentors and friends from the martial arts, who no doubt contributed to my views. And, I send special thank-yous to Doc Krawiec, Bob Bross, Mike Wollmershauser, Grand Master Im Hyun Soo, and my friend and martial arts partner for over thirty years, Michael D'Aloia. For the last fifteen years, I've also had two incredible yoga teachers I want to thank for their contributions to my mindset: Peg Olivera and Lori Bonazzoli. And, I owe my physical and mental health to Damian Paglia's relentless efforts.

I extend my gratitude to my partners at Oji Life Lab, including Matt Kursh, Andrea Hoban, and Camilla Mize, all of whom gave great feedback on this manuscript; to Diana Divecha and Robin Stern, who were with me every step of the way, reading multiple versions of each chapter; and James Floman, Nikki Elbertson, and Kathryn Lee, whose extensive feedback and editorial guidance enhanced this book. I want to give a special thank-you to Christina Bradley, who helped me gather the resources for this book and worked with me on the bibliography.

My colleagues, students, and research team over the last twenty years have made my career a complete joy. This work benefited enormously from Jack Mayer, Peter Salovey, and David Caruso. Each of these individuals has been an incredible mentor and colleague. Robin Stern and Janet Patti also have a special place in my heart for supporting my journey. Charley Ellis has been a tremendous mentor to me and I'm forever grateful for his guidance and support.

At Yale, I have many people to thank, including Linda Mayes, Kim Goff Crews, James Comer, Edward Zigler, and Heidi Brooks. At the Yale Center for Emotional Intelligence, we have been blessed with hundreds of talented individuals. I am especially grateful to Susan Rivers and Robin Stern, who were my co-founders. Susan and I conducted most of the original research on RULER while Robin and I worked together with David Caruso on the original RULER training materials. Their wisdom is spread throughout this book. Our current senior leadership team, which includes Scott Levy, Dena Simmons, and Robin Stern, provided tremendous support during the writing of this book. And Michelle Lugo, my executive assistant and daily partner, provided her unconditional support every step of the way in writing this book. Michelle—I would not have been able to write this book without you!

I also have tremendous gratitude for the dedication and creativity of our center directors, Danica Kelly, Christina Cipriano, Andrés Richner, Nikki Elbertson, and James Hagen, and our project directors and lead researchers, including Craig Bailey, Jessica Hoffmann, Zorana Ivcevic, James Floman, Jennifer Allen, Kathryn Lee, Charlene Voyce, and Emma Seppälä. All of these talented people lead teams of program and research managers, all of whom have contributed to my thinking—and have made our center what it is today. I also want to acknowledge Laura Artusio and Ruth Gualdo Castillo, who direct our work in Italy and Spain, respectively.

Above all, I thank my family for their love and encouragement. My parents, William and Diane Brackett; my brother, Steven Nadler, and my sister-in-law, Leticia Fraga Nadler, and their children, Benjamin and Sofia; my brother, David Nadler; my cousin Ellyn Solis and her daughter, Esme; and my cousins Richard and Lisa Maurer and their children, Jared, Jacob, and Megan. I also hold enormous gratitude for my mother-in-law, Irene; my aunt, Sandra Price; and Jane Brackett. Words cannot express my deepest gratitude to my partner of twenty-five years and husband of nine years, Horacio Marquínez. His love and commitment to me and my work goes beyond any expectation of a life partner.

This book is about personal growth and transformation through unlocking the wisdom of emotions. Writing it has given me greater insight into my own emotional life and inspired me to further develop my own emotion skills, and I hope it has done the same for you. So, last but not least, I thank you, the reader, for allowing me and this book to guide you through that journey.

CELADON
BOOKS
NEW YORK

Founded in 2017, Celadon Books, a division of
Macmillan Publishers, publishes a highly curated list
of twenty to twenty-five new titles a year. The list of
both fiction and nonfiction is eclectic and focuses
on publishing commercial and literary books and
discovering and nurturing talent.

Enraged	Panicked	Stressed	Jittery	Shocked
Livid	Furious	Frustrated	Tense	Stunned
Fuming	Frightened	Angry	Nervous	Restless
Anxious	Apprehensive	Worried	Irritated	Annoyed
Repulsed	Troubled	Concerned	Uneasy	Peeved
Disgusted	Glum	Disappointed	Down	Apathetic
Pessimistic	Morose	Discouraged	Sad	Bored
Alienated	Miserable	Lonely	Disheartened	Tired
Despondent	Depressed	Sullen	Exhausted	Fatigued
Despairing	Hopeless	Desolate	Spent	Drained